THE AVERY-

To John + Teresa

with
fond regards
and
much love,

Thomas .

The Avery-Stripes

THOMAS KENNEDY

ROBIN CLARK LIMITED

First published in 2014 by Robin Clark Limited
A member of the Namara Group
27 Goodge Street, London W1T 2LD

A catalogue record for this book
is available from the British Library

ISBN   978 0 7043 7374 7

Typeset by Antony Gray
Printed and bound in Great Britain by
T J International Ltd, Padstow, Cornwall

For George

Contents

Acknowledgements

I am very grateful to Milton Grundy whose generosity enabled me to concentrate on writing *The Avery-Stripes* for nearly as long as it took, also to Mark Studer for the extra help I required to see it through to the end.

I would like to express my deep gratitude to David Elliott for believing in the book from the start and for pushing it ever forward, and Barbara Elliott for her enthusiasm for the fictional family and her wise suggestions.

Thank you to Amanda Bayliss for her unwavering excited interest in the story, and to Dominic Barber for putting a roof over my head and a place to write when my home was full of builders. And I thank my parents: my mother for nurturing my imagination, and my father for cultivating my appreciation of the English language. I treasure both gifts and their combination is invaluable to me.

The Avery-Stripes

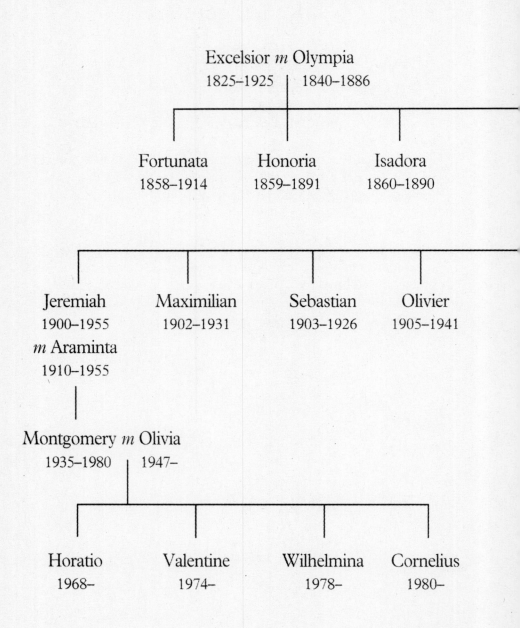

Excelsior *m* Olympia
1825–1925 | 1840–1886

Fortunata   Honoria   Isadora
1858–1914   1859–1891   1860–1890

Jeremiah   Maximilian   Sebastian   Olivier
1900–1955   1902–1931   1903–1926   1905–1941
m Araminta
1910–1955

Montgomery *m* Olivia
1935–1980 | 1947–

Horatio   Valentine   Wilhelmina   Cornelius
1968–   1974–   1978–   1980–

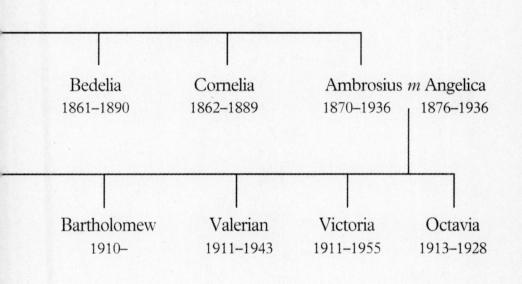

Bedelia
1861–1890

Cornelia
1862–1889

Ambrosius *m* Angelica
1870–1936   1876–1936

Bartholomew
1910–

Valerian
1911–1943

Victoria
1911–1955

Octavia
1913–1928

CHAPTER 1

Savoury-Tripe

BECAUSE IT WAS UNSUITABLE WEATHER FOR venturing out to the tree house, little Corny, resplendent in his highly coloured Native American war bonnet, was crouched beneath the Steinway grand. He had gathered around him the three Dalmatians – Monopoly, Calamity and Temerity – and was muttering in their ears. In all of his fifteen years, muttering to the dogs was the closest he had ever come to talking. It had been a great relief to his family when, three years ago, Corny first muttered because up until then, they had resigned themselves to the idea that he was entirely mute.

Corny was hatching a plan. He was not exactly sure what this plan was, or even of its aim, but he knew it had something to do with Great Uncle Bartholomew who was dozing comfortably in his worn-out leather wing chair in front of the fireplace, and snoring surprisingly softly for a man of his rotundness and age. There was marmalade from breakfast on his cravat and crumbs from his elevenses scattered over his generous stomach. The evidence of these past meals suddenly made Corny's tummy ache with hunger.

He wondered when Gretchen might next give him some food. He had no idea of the time; he tried very hard to concentrate on the ugly ormolu clock which sat majestically between two rhinoceros horns and amidst a crowd of long expired stiffies on the mantelshelf. He struggled to remember the meaning of the big hand and the little and battled with his brain to make sense of the roman numerals, but to no avail.

Corny knew his intellectual limitations and, with a silent sigh, surrendered himself to this lack. It then came to him that this clock may even be the one that the others had said did not give the right time. Frustrated, he thumped his fists on his head and bare knees until suddenly the clock chimed a quarter and filled him with such bliss that for a flash he quite forgot why he wanted to know the time in the first place. That was until he glimpsed a bowl of juicy grapes. Oh, how he would dearly love to eat those grapes! It did not have to be the entire bunch. Just a few would do, he told himself. He decided that he would, though it would not be easy as the grapes belonged to Remarkable, and the bird was not one to readily part with his food. Still, as luck would have it, Remarkable was asleep, sat on his perch – a ball of black feathers, head turned with his long sunset-coloured bill resting on his back, and his tail feathers folded over.

Corny resolved that he would risk it and carefully he crept towards the grapes. His hunger grew with every inch that he got closer. He hardly dared to breathe for fear of waking Remarkable. It seemed to take an eternity to get there but finally within reach of the bowl, he stretched out his arm. His hand hovered just above the grapes and then came a dreadfully deep croaking noise which sounded like mocking laughter.

Corny looked to Remarkable and saw the terrible toucan had flipped back his tail feathers and, with his bill still on his back, was staring with one large cobalt blue eye back down at him. Corny hurriedly turned around and scurried back to safety, under the piano, where he hid behind the three dogs, feeling very sorry for himself and thinking how mean the bird was.

Unbeknownst to Corny, his elder brother Valentine had all this while been sitting upon the chesterfield on the other side of the drawing room quietly piecing together a large puzzle of the *Scalinata di Spagna*.

Valentine had pieced together this puzzle many times and always the pink azaleas flummoxed him.

'Such a glorious pink though!' he thought to himself as he pulled the great Indian quilt closer to his asthenic frame, for he was only in his pyjamas and it was unseasonably chill for June. Nevertheless, Valentine was loathe to don anything other than pyjamas – predominantly striped, in honour of the family name.

'Gosh! I simply do love pyjamas! Don't you?' he would exclaim, 'Cool in the summertime, cosy in the winter . . . pyjamas are glorious! Don't you think?', which of course was a rhetorical question. Valentine would be unlikely to care a snap of his fingers what another's opinion may or may not be, especially when the opinion was in anyway related to himself.

Valentine was used to Corny's peculiarities but seeing him rush for refuge and hearing the dogs' consolatory licking, a sound that Valentine could not abide, his interest was aroused.

'Whatever can the matter be, Corny?' he called out as he pushed back his inky fringe from his verdant eyes.

Corny was startled to hear Valentine's mezzo-soprano voice. He peeked between the shoulders of Calamity and Monopoly, and upon seeing him across the room, all of his troubles evaporated. Valentine may not be big like Harry, but he was still someone capable of many things that Corny was not. He squeezed out from behind the dogs, scampered over and looked imploringly at him with his large china blue eyes. Valentine laughed at Corny's silly expression and at the funny angle of his war bonnet before lifting it to tousle the bright yellow mop of hair and replaced it perfectly.

As if remembering something very important, Valentine opened his monogrammed silver cigarette case, took one out and lit it with the table-lighter in the design of a scarab beetle. He then looked with dismay at the strategically placed champagne bucket catching the rain penetrating the house through the conservatory that adjoined the drawing room. He tutted, and said, 'Gosh! Cats and dogs, Corny! Small wonder you're bored!'

He turned to Corny once more only to see that he had put an azalea piece of jigsaw between his lips.

'Just the very bit!' Valentine exclaimed, removed the piece from Corny's mouth, and put it in its proper place in the puzzle, 'Glorious! Clever Corny! Anyway, you're beastfully bored, are you?'

Corny shook his head, clutched his tummy and winced theatrically.

'Gosh! Yes, I'm rather famished too but look what I have here,' and from within the folds of the Indian quilt, Valentine produced a box of violet creams.

Corny looked at him and the box in astonishment and clapped his hands in delight.

'Shush!' said Valentine, as he removed two violet creams and popped one of them in his mouth, and dropped the other into Corny's cupped palms.

Corny beheld the chocolate as if it were a ruby of the same size and then promptly made it vanish. Biting into it, his eyes were aglow with the purest pleasure.

Presently, there was a mighty bang from the hall, so loud that Remarkable, waking with a squawk, almost toppled from his perch but managed to regain his composure fast enough to save any serious injury to his dignity and suffer nothing worse than a few ruffled feathers. The three dogs leapt to their feet and looked confusedly at each other, and poor Corny virtually jumped out of his skin causing the violet cream to jam in his throat and slowly he was turning blue. Valentine, who had no more than gasped, gave him a hefty whack on the back, collected the horrid little lump of chocolaty mess in his hand and deposited it in the wastepaper basket.

Further commotion came from the hall, it was as if a small typhoon had been let in through the front door, only typhoons were not liable to such language.

'Not a happy Willy!' said Valentine wryly as he once more straightened Corny's war bonnet. The door to the drawing room burst open and in marched a rainsoaked Willy, her jodhpurs and boots drenched and muddied, riding hat in one hand, crop clenched in the fist of the other. Abruptly she brought her stout body to a halt, dripped rainwater onto the Axminster and glared at her brothers.

'I'm as cross as Hades!' she wailed.

'Gosh! Really not?' said Valentine. 'Anyway, you are a beast . . . such noise, enough to wake the dead!'

Corny pulled on Valentine's sleeve, and with an outstretched arm, pointed at their still sleeping great uncle.

'Gosh! Gubsy's not dead, Corny.'

'Never mind noise! Do you know what Agatha Strap said to me?' Willy growled.

'Certainly I don't know what Agatha Strap said to you. I don't even know who Agatha Strap is, do I?'

'Agatha Strap is the most poisonous, odious and wretched girl in all creation and she goes to gymkhana too!'

'Oh, yes, that Agatha Strap . . . no, I don't, but, well, what? What did she say to get my little sister as cross as Hades?'

'Savoury tripe!' howled Willy.

'Savoury tripe?' questioned Valentine. 'Why would she say that?'

Corny looked equally as bewildered.

'Oh you fool! Anyway she didn't say it, she sang it!'

'Sang it?'

Willy stepped closer, screwed her eyes and through gritted teeth, recited:

> 'Willy Avery-Stripe,
> Silly savoury tripe,
> Truly a guttersnipe,
> Willy Savoury-Tripe!'

Shaking as if a volcano on the verge, Willy opened her eyes, red with rage, glowered at Valentine and Corny and with great ferocity, she erupted, repeating, 'SAVOURY-TRIPE!'

Valentine suppressed the urge to laugh outright at the thought of what

instant fury such a chant would provoke in Willy. He feared for silly
Agatha Strap.

Yet, Willy was no more vainglorious than the rest of the Avery-Stripes
when it came to family, especially concerning its and their individual
names, the beginnings and importance of which the children's mother
had drummed into them from an early age.

They all knew the family legend by heart and Valentine remembered
that when still very young, he had to repeat after his mother daily: 'The
first Avery-Stripe on record dates back to 1825. His name was Excelsior
and he amassed himself a sizeable fortune exporting Peruvian guano.

['Yuck, Mummy!'; 'Shush, darling'.]

'A true Victorian gentleman, Excelsior served the British Empire by
supplying England with this much needed and highly valued commodity.

['Hurrah!'; 'Shush!']

'Having made his great fortune, he took himself a young wife, name of
Olympia and together they had six issues, of which only the youngest,
Ambrosius, was of the male gender.

['Ooh!'; 'Valentine!']

'The noble couple were rueful that only one of their progenies would be
able to continue the family name but to each of them they gave a four-
syllable Christian name, just as they had. Thus began the Avery-Stripe
tradition that our family continue to the present.

[Deep intake of breath]

'Excelsior begat Ambrosius, Ambrosius begat Jeremiah, Jeremiah begat
Montgomery and Montgomery begat Horatio, and myself, Valentino and
our younger siblings; Wilhelmina and Cornelius. We four have the honour
of being Avery-Stripes because we are the great-great-grandchildren of
Excelsior Avery-Stripe!'

[Whew!]

If the recitation proved to be satisfactory, Valentine would receive a
treat as a reward and if it had been poor he would have to repeat it, word
for word, after his mother. Although quite capable of performing the task
after only a few weeks, he would invariably feign difficulty purely to listen
to his mother's diction and he endeavoured to replicate her intonation to
perfection.

Willy's explosion caused Excelsior's elderly grandson, Bartholomew, to
wake with a start.

'Of all the effrontery! The impudence and insolence! Mock my family name in my own home will you! Intolerable! How dare you!' bellowed Gubsy at the three siblings across the room, the generous jowls of his old pit bull face quavering as he did so and he scrutinised them confoundedly.

Remarkable, with as gainly a swoop as he could muster, settled himself upon his master's shoulder and proceeded to nuzzle his great bill against Gubsy's neck and purr contentedly.

'Kik-kik-kik-kik,' Gubsy replied, as he stroked the bird's head with his forefinger.

'Oh Gubsy! It's us! You old silly!' Willy burst with joy as she flung her hat and crop to the floor and hurled herself over her great uncle's girth in a zealous embrace.

'So it is, so it is,' realised Gubsy as he surveyed the room and patted her on the back. 'Why, you're soaked to the skin my girl, you must have a change of clothes immediately.'

'No, Gubsy! I couldn't possibly leave where I am right now for a single moment. I'm as comfy as can be!' she gushed.

'Tut!' exasperated Valentine, shaking his head. Corny rolled his eyes.

'Sweet girl,' chuckled Gubsy, 'then you must stay with me always, just you and I.'

'How heavenly!' cried Willy.

'And we shall light the fire and be deliciously cosy and toast crumpets and marshmallows and . . . '

'Hot buttered toast!' interrupted Willy.

'Yes, hot buttered toast and . . . '

'Oh, how scrummy!' Willy squealed, almost girlishly, squeezing the great belly tighter.

'Devilishly scrummy!' agreed Gubsy 'and . . . hot cocoa.'

Willy squealed once again.

This is beyond anyone's endurance thought Valentine, and promptly sang out 'And savoury tripe!' causing Corny to kick his legs with delight and beam at him admiringly.

This rude ejaculation propelled the pair out of their snug fantasy with a jolt.

'Who said that?' boomed Gubsy, jowls a-wobbling. 'I demand to know this instant!'

Remarkable hopped from the quaking shoulder back to the safety of his perch. Corny clamped his hand over his mouth and shook with hilarity.

Willy rose and looked hatefully at Valentine, who looked the perfect picture of blamelessness.

'Agatha Strap, Gubsy,' she murmured, eyes now downcast. ' "Girl from gymkhana", said it.'

'Intolerable!' Gubsy boomed, and tightened his grip upon his cocobolo cane, 'Slander the family name! The audacity! The nerve! Why, when I was a boy, if a fellow expressed such disrespect to the family I'd have to show him what's what or I'd have been answerable to father's cane or grandfather's whip and been made to feel a very sorry chap indeed! I hope you young 'uns honour the family's name with the same reverence?'

'Yes, Gubsy,' chorused Valentine and Willy in unison. Corny, who had overcome his outburst, nodded fervently.

'And jolly glad I am to hear it!' growled Gubsy, gnashing his false teeth; a reliable indicator that he would soon work himself up into a fearful wax unless adequately mollified in sufficient time.

Accordingly, Valentine piped up, 'So, what did you do Willy? How did you go about defending the family name and righting this libellous lout?'

All eyes on her, Willy, already severely reprimanded by Mses Broach and Peeble for her retaliatory response to Agatha Strap's taunts, and told that her presence would not be required at gymkhana until further notice, was reluctant to answer, therefore, she scowled hard at the crack in the ceiling and wished that she were anywhere else.

'Plip-plop.' dripped the rain in the champagne bucket.

'Tick-tock.' clicked the innards of the ormolu clock.

'Gnash-gnash.' ground the false teeth in Gubsy's jaw.

'Tut.' smacked the tongue on Valentine's palate.

Willy sensed the tension mounting until she could bear it no longer.

'Oh botheration!' she expelled. 'Alright, I shall tell you how I defended the family name but I am quite certain that not a single one of you will think me to be a lady!'

'Stop dilly-dallying and out with it girl if you value your skin, for I promise you I shall certainly think the worse of you if you do not!' remonstrated Gubsy.

Tentatively, Willy began: 'On and on Strap went; "Savoury-Tripe! Savoury-Tripe!" getting some of the other girls in on it too, not so loudly that old Broach and Peeble could hear, but they made jolly well certain that I could. Made me foul up some of the jumps too.

'Well, I waited until the end, when all we girls were leaving the stables and I went up to Strap and I told her, "You're a nasty piece of work and need a thorough lesson in respecting your superiors." "Superiors?" Strap guffawed – she actually guffawed! So, I told her "yes, superior, in every way!" So she says "You are a funny fatty, Savoury-Tripe!" and she laughed in my face and turned to follow the others into the house. Seeing her prance off, I thought it's now or never, so I grabbed her, muffled her shrieks and dragged her kicking and screaming back into the stables, closed the door and threw her to the floor.'

Now, with more bravado, Willy went on: 'She tried to get up but in a thrice I was on her. I straddled her chest, pinning her arms under my knees. "Call me names! Laugh in my face! Insult my family will you! I'm going to teach you a lesson you shan't forget!" I told her, as she wriggled and squealed like a little piggy on the block. Too much noise I told myself, so do you know how I shut her up?'

Valentine shrugged, Corny stared and Gubsy gnashed.

'I gathered up great handfuls of hay and straw and horse mess and muck from the floor and, holding Strap's nose, I crammed it all in her filthy mouth!'

Her captive audience could scarcely believe their ears but knowing Willy as they did, it only took a moment to realise that what she said was true because she was a terrible liar.

'Gosh! Willy, you absolute brute!' admonished Valentine. and he pulled Corny close.

'She *is* a ruffian, Corny, don't you think?' but Corny could do nothing but look at Willy as if awestruck.

Rather put out by Valentine's discouraging response and not noticing Corny's, Willy turned to Gubsy with some trepidation. He was as silent as Corny, staring into space and grasping the armrests of his chair. He shuddered quite violently, his face became aubergine and his eyes looked ablaze. Willy reached out to touch him but she retracted when his head rolled back and he exploded not with brimstone but with roars of laughter like an exultant Vulcan. Low squawks of unease came from Remarkable and the dogs crept behind the chesterfield. Valentine was in a quandary as to whether or no he should do something and decided upon not.

Only Corny seemed to share the joke, and shook with inaudible laughter and kicked his legs spasmodically, though this was quite patently a nervous reaction.

Regaining his composure somewhat, Gubsy, face now crimson and streaked with tears, beamed at Willy and boomed, 'Come here and give me a hug, you wonderful girl!'

Willy rushed into his arms with overwhelming relief. 'Oh, Gubsy! You scared me, I thought you might be cross!' she howled.

Swabbing the snot from the nose of a now slightly less spastic Corny, Valentine confided in him, 'I thought the old bully was going to kick the bucket, didn't you?'

'Me? Cross! With you? Never!' said Gubsy, as he wiped away his tears with the backs of his liver-spotted hands. 'You defended the family name and disciplined the blackguard. You've done well. I'm tickled pink! My grandfather would've been very proud; you're a chip off the old block and no mistake!'

Willy glowed with pride for a moment and then she remembered: 'But Gubsy, old Broach and Peeble, they came looking for us when the girls noticed we were missing. They caught me astride Strap and old Peeble screamed at old Broach, "Get Willy off!" so old Broach pulled me off and took me outside and really gave me quite a hard time and I am not to go back to gymkhana again until they say!'

'They did, eh? Well to blazes with the lot of 'em! One can't be doing mixing with cads of that kidney. Jolly good riddance I say!'

'Oh, I do so love you, Gubsy!' squealed Willy, 'I just knew you would understand! Anyway, gymkhana is quite boring actually and really quite beastly on one's bottom too, all that cantering, trotting and jumping. I think I'd far rather do something else more fun instead!'

The mollified Gubsy smiled down at his sweet girl, stroking her mousey hair as she pressed her podgy cheek against his belly.

'Sweet little girl' he rumbled and she all but purred.

Viewing his two generously sized relations in such a pose, Valentine felt a mild sensation of queasiness come over him.

Fortunately, it was then that the ormolu clock chimed what it believed to be four o'clock and nobody was in any position to disagree. That is, nobody but the woman of a somewhat handsome yet homely countenance that appeared in the doorway.

'Ah! Gretchen, I do believe that I am quite ready for tea,' said Valentine, loftily.

'Time for tea-time is not yet, Master Valentine,' she replied, matter of factly, in her voice of some Continental kind. Though having been housekeeper to Gubsy for nigh on twenty years, and the youngest generation of Avery-Stripes powerless to recall a time before her, the family had never felt able, or in some cases never felt the desire, to inquire of Gretchen from whence she came.

It is possible that Gubsy once knew and had since forgotten but neither he nor the others ever raised the question. Gretchen enjoyed having this air of mystery about her and took great pleasure in keeping the family in the dark. She forever varied her costume that would always indicate a specific nation, and would cause further confusion with an accessory denoting an entirely different land. She intentionally made her accent versatile but constantly maintained an elusively international lilt.

Today Gretchen considered a kilt becoming and had complimented it with a beret and clogs.

'Your boots, Miss Willy, are diskustink!' she said, 'And you have made all of the beautiful floor in the hall that poor Kretchen has spent all mornink washink and cleanink a mess with all the mud! I come home and what I find but mud is all over the place! Diskraceful!'

'Sorry, Gretchen.'

'Just a pot of tea is all that I ask,' said Valentine.

'And you are makink Mr Bartholmoo so very damp, you must stand up now!'

'It's quite alright, Gretchen, Willy is keeping me company,' said Gubsy.

'And Remarkable, he is loose! You must keep chain on!' Gretchen said, as she fastened the loop at the end of the chain to a resentful Remarkable's ankle.

'There are no open windows, Gretchen, Remarkable cannot fly away!' argued Valentine, 'And if I am not very much mistaken, I do believe that we would all very much appreciate a pot of tea, if you would be so kind.'

Corny tugged on Valentine's sleeve and winced. 'And Corny is famished, so if you wouldn't mind bringing something to keep him from fading away altogether!'

Gretchen looked Valentine square in the eye and snorted disparagingly. 'Gosh! What?'

Shaking her head, she said, 'You are very lazy younk man. When I leave this mornink, you are sleeping where you are now. You have not moved. You have not seen the letter I have put on table for you.' With that, she left the room and the dogs scurried behind her, for they too were hungry.

Valentine searched the table. He looked under the jigsaw puzzle lid, in between the newspapers and magazines and under the ashtray, but could find no letter.

'Gosh! Could she not just tell me where it is?'

'Where what is?' Gubsy demanded to know.

'A letter for me but I think she is making it up!'

'Gretchen wouldn't make something silly like that up,' reasoned Willy.

'Wouldn't she? She says I'm lazy and she has conjured up a communication just to make me search high and low and get fatigued!'

'What's that Corny's sitting on?' pointed Willy.

Corny jumped up from the chesterfield and revealed that he had indeed been sitting upon a communication addressed to Valentino Avery-Stripe. Astonished to see it, Corny snatched it up and handed it over with a flourish.

'Thank you. Gosh, it's very warm and crumpled and it's from mummy and she sent it from Paris!'

'Who's it from? Speak up boy! Can't make out your sissy tones!' blustered Gubsy.

'Missive from mummy! It is from Olivia!' sung Valentine.

'Blasted woman!' Gubsy blared, and deciding it would be a good time for another forty winks, he spread *The Times* over his head.

'Open it, read it!' said Willy, as Corny clambered closer to get a better view. Both were eager to hear what their mother had written as they had neither seen nor heard from her in months.

'Gosh! I can't very well open it without a paper knife, now can I?' said Valentine, who did not want to risk damaging the red wax seal. It bore their family crest of a Peruvian Booby stood upon a chevron and around the edge, in letters so small they were barely legible, the family motto, *Nil Desperandum*.

'Use your fingers!' suggested Willy.

'Paper cuts!' said Valentine and he fanned out his digits.

'Use this then if your fingers are so delicate.'

From her pocket Willy pulled out a penknife and offered it to Valentine, who accepted it with a moue and a tut.

'This feels savagely wrong,' he complained as he ceremoniously sliced the envelope, 'Especially when somewhere we have that beautiful ivory paper knife. The one with the lovely little elephants. Where is it I wonder?'

Presently, he unfolded a single sheet. 'Gosh! Hotel Ritz and, oh . . . ,' holding it to his nose and inhaling, he exclaimed, 'Gosh! Glorious mummy! 19 by Chanel!'

'And Bottom by Corny!' joked Willy, causing Corny to blush. 'Just read it!'

Valentine cleared his throat and, in perfect imitation of Olivia, he announced: *'Torture here darling. Coming home. Have Gretchen rescue me from Waterloo, 3p.m., Friday 7th, if Horatio not home. Love, Mummy. XXX.'*

'That is *all* she said?'

23

'Gosh! Regard!'

Willy peered, scowled, and said, 'I hate her!'

'Elegant hand though, don't you think?'

'Not a mention of me, or of Corny!' Willy wailed, whereupon she stormed out of the room and served each baluster a mighty whack with her crop as she stomped up the stairwell.

Corny moved Valentine's arm into a position so he too could regard the communication. The corners of his mouth turned down and he furrowed his brow.

'Gosh, but look Corny, three big Xs! That's three big kisses. A kiss for me, a kiss for Willy and the last kiss for you because the last kiss is always the most special!'

Corny thought hard about this for a space and then, convinced that what Valentine said was so, he beamed stupendously.

As if on cue, Gretchen returned, wheeling in the squeaky tea wagon, which not only carried a pot of tea but also a stack of sandwiches and other savouries, and a delicious looking homemade Battenberg.

'Only tea for two?' she queried.

'Gosh, Gretchen! You glorious trump!' said Valentine, 'Verily, Gubsy is dozing and Willy's in a stew, so, yes, just tea for two!'

Corny ran over, hugged her and started to examine the treats upon the wagon, trying to decide what to have first – which was a serious undertaking.

'I think you like to have this first?' said Gretchen, 'I think perhaps it is one of Pernickety's.'

Corny adored Scotch eggs, and Pernickety was his favourite of their hens, so he needed no more persuasion.

As Gretchen poured his tea, Valentine noticed the *plip-plopping* had stopped.

'Gosh! I do believe I see the sun radiating! Perhaps Corny and the dogs should be let out.'

'I will ket wellinkton boots,' said Gretchen.

Wearing his war bonnet and wellingtons, Corny ran out into the garden with his third Scotch egg.

'Look!' said Gretchen pointing up at the sky, 'Rainbow!'

Upon seeing the multicoloured arc, Corny jumped and danced with wild abandon on the striped lawn as the Dalmatians rollicked about him.

Watching him from indoors, Valentine laughed and sipped his tea.

'Mummy homeward bound too!' he thought to himself. 'What fun!' and he placed his teacup back into its saucer with a civilised *clink*.

CHAPTER 2

Nil Desperandum

As the train departed from the Gare du Nord, Olivia Avery-Stripe settled her svelte physique into the expanse of her business class seat, and exhaled a deep sigh of relief. She was not at all sorry to be leaving Paris. Though she had a pleasant enough stay she would not miss the French and their tongue. She was grateful that when next her feet touched solid ground that it would be upon good and decent English soil.

Naturally, she would mention to her friends – of which there were few, for she was not fond of many people – that she had spent a week in Paris, on her way home from Monaco, so that they could trill 'How lovely,'. However, as far as Olivia was concerned, 'Visiting Paris is like an evening at the opera or ballet; that is, though a charming experience, it is let down by the unsavoury sorts there.'

Yet despite her abhorrence of the French, Olivia would admit the one area in which they excelled was fashion and her vertebrae tickled as she considered the countless items of fresh couture crammed into her cases.

She was aware that many would deem her fresh chattels ill-gotten if they had any notion of how she had gained them, but she believed that the end, no matter how questionable, justified the means. For to silence a room upon entering and to feel all eyes on her, in either envy or desire was, to her, the very height of felicity.

She may not have been very popular, but one thing that she did possess that no one could help but admire, even if in most cases somewhat reluctantly, was her unparalleled sense of style. She had a knack, no matter what or where, of always presenting herself perfectly. This was not just regarding her wardrobe. It was everything about her. There was not one aspect to her appearance and demeanour that she did not plan with pinpoint precision. One might, quite understandably, consider that the product of Olivia's fastidiousness was something altogether quite bogus, but in her defence she would argue that as this meticulousness was innate, one would be hard pushed to find such a natural lady as she.

Olivia wanted a drink and no sooner had she become conscious of this desire than the steward entered the carriage with his trolley. She watched as he served the other passengers and slowly made his way toward her.

His face displayed a splattering of pimples that one associates with adolescence, but Olivia estimated him to be of an age somewhere between Harry's and Valentine's.

Olivia noticed that griminess of the steward's white shirt as he enquired if she would care for a beverage. Immediately, she grimaced over the fact that he had been so unrefined as to substitute the word *drink* with *beverage* and in an incisive tone she informed him that she would have a gin and tonic, thank you.

She saw the smile vanish from his face as he responded with a 'Certainly madam,' and then she turned to suffer the view of the passing French countryside.

The making of the drink complete the steward asked, 'Will there be anything else madam?'

Olivia deigned to face him again: 'No, thank you, I expect the one drink perfectly sufficient providing it's satisfactorily proficiently made.'

The steward thanked her and pushed the trolley further down the aisle.

'What a depressing young man,' Olivia thought to herself. 'Such a shame he cannot find something better to do with his life,' whereupon she raised the drink to her carmine lips, sipped, and felt very glad to see the last of Europe hurtle past.

'What possible future can there be in serving *beverages* upon a train?' she wondered, 'And what of promotion? What comes next?'

She contemplated the hierarchy and, unable to regard ticket stamping as progress, she concluded that after being a train steward one must surely be elevated to the position of train driver.

'But who ever would want to be a train driver?' she asked herself. She knew that to drive a train was just the job that many small boys dream of having when they grow up, but then they grew up and wanted something better for themselves.

'Why, not even Cornelius wants to be a train driver!'

For, though she was aware that, technically, Corny was no longer a small boy, he was what she referred to as 'a little bit special'. To which she would invariably add, 'but we don't talk about that, darling.'

Irritated, Olivia realised that she had unwittingly turned her attention to a matter that made her feel very uncomfortable. It was not so much the matter of Corny, although that too made her feel ill at ease, especially when he would not respond to her and simply stood there staring as if she were a stranger. The matter was the children's father, her late husband and great grandson of Excelsior, Montgomery Avery-Stripe.

Olivia and Monty had been married for only thirteen years when he met his untimely demise. Harry, Valentine and Willy were aged twelve, six, and twenty months respectively, with Corny on his way, when Monty put a bullet through his brain.

It was an accident, of course. He had gone out with some of the men from the village to shoot rabbit. It was something that they did on a regular basis in an effort to control the local population and reduce crop damage. According to the inquest, Monty had fallen into a blackberry bush and in his efforts to free himself, his gun went off in the least favourable direction, thus reducing the local population, albeit the wrong species, by one.

In years to come, Olivia, in an effort to throw a sheet over his fatal cack-handedness, would say that she could quite believe it. 'Monty was liable to get in a filthy rage if his patience was tried, and to find oneself tangled in bramble would certainly be tremendously trying.'

What was more, 'Monty was always loathe to load his gun at the very last as one ought.'

She remembered their last night together; he had climbed into their vast and ancient Jacobean four-poster and for hours he had stroked her gravidity with his large hands calloused from his outdoor pursuits and kissed it all over, a hundred times then two hundred then three. He marvelled each time he felt Corny quicken and whispered to him what a 'jammy little dodger' he was to be joining such a fine and noble family.

When at last Monty looked up at her, it was with a look she would not forget, his harebell blue eyes were wide open and beaming at her with utter adoration, his grin was stupid, cheeks ruddier than ever and his golden hair in a dreadful mess. Olivia had reached out to him; he took her hand and manoeuvred his stalwart body on a level with hers. He pulled her into an ursine embrace and passionately he kissed her. She luxuriated in the open air reek of him and revelled in the reassurance the sheer size of him gave her, as he tried not to put too much of his weight on her.

Withdrawing his lips from hers, Monty looked at Olivia with a passion that she found grating.

'Darling?' she asked tersely, 'Darling, what is it?' Irritated, she stroked the lapel of his turquoise pyjama jacket.

Taking her hand in his, Monty kissed each finger, turned it over to kiss the palm, and travelled the length of her slender arm with yet more kisses. His usual tone was sonorous but on this occasion he spoke softly, 'My

27

dearest sweetest Olivia. My own darling, love of my life, thank you, a thousand times, thank you. I love you, I love you.'

Olivia was not sure how to receive his cloying conduct, for it was most unlike him. The Monty she knew was bullish and proud, he was rugged and robust, one to strut, rut and boast, not to bill and coo. He never had any reason to bill and coo as some men do; if he wanted it he would just take it, whether or no she liked it, and she did. What she did not like, however, was his present performance. He was mooning over her as if he were some lovesick poet. Moreover, dawn was drawing ever nearer and she was growing weary. Therefore, it was with a quelling look that she reiterated, 'Darling. Whatever is it?'

'You are with me, Olivia, aren't you?' his eyes penetrating hers.

'Don't be silly, darling. Of course I am. I am right here next to you. Larger than life . . . ', indicating her gestation with a nod. 'I couldn't move even if I desired to!'

'I am in earnest, Olivia. Are you with me?'

'Why, yes. I am . . . but whatever do you mean, darling? Oh, I am so very tired!'

'I am sorry, Olivia, I know that you are tired but this won't take long. I just need to know; are you with me? Do you want what I want? For the family I mean.'

'Oh, that!' she said, trying to hide her exasperation. 'Yes, darling you know I do. Aren't I about to give you your fourth? That is what you want isn't it? And that's what I'm giving you. Certainly, I am with you.'

'Cornelius is *our* fourth. He is mine *and* yours.'

'Yes, yes. Mine and yours but first and foremost he is an Avery-Stripe.'

'As are you, Olivia. You are my wife, Mrs Avery-Stripe. You are one of us. You do feel that, don't you? You must feel that. Tell me that you do.'

'Absolutely, darling!'

'Why, without you there would be no new Avery-Stripes, all of the others are dead and buried. All that is left of us now is Uncle Bartholomew, you and me and the children. *Our* children, Olivia. Together, you and I are rebuilding the family, and we will make it great again. Will we not?'

'Yes, Monty, we will make it great again.'

Olivia was now so tired that it was with supreme effort that she managed to keep her lids open.

'Do you swear it?' he growled.

'Oh, Monty! For goodness sake! Please do let me sleep!'

He sat up and raised her by her shoulders, his strong hands gripping her tightly, her négligee making a ripping sound.

'Ouch! Let me go this instant!' she pummelled her fists pathetically on his barrel chest. 'You brute! Unhand me now!'

'You must swear it, Olivia.'

'Oh! Ridiculous!' she spat as she struggled, in vain.

'You must!' he roared.

'Very well, I swear it! Now release me!'

Monty relinquished his hold. 'Thank you, I needed to hear it. I am sorry if I hurt you.'

'Yes, darling, you did hurt me!' She rubbed her sore shoulders and fingered the broken strap of her négligee with dismay: 'Oh, Monty! Chinese silk!'

'Cornelius is not hurt?'

'Cornelius is fine. Only I am certain that he is just as tired as I am!' and she nestled her head on her pillow. 'Now, turn off the light, I simply must sleep.'

Monty complied and in the twilight he pulled her close, enveloped her in his thick arms and buried his face in her hair.

'Good night, Mrs Avery-Stripe.' he whispered hoarsely, stretching his hand over her middle, 'Good night, Cornelius.'

'Good night, you bully!' Olivia murmured and, feeling exquisitely warm and safe, she at last fell asleep.

The following morning Olivia woke to find she was alone in the giant bed but this was normal as Monty was habitually up and out at the crack. Choosing not to fret about her damaged négligee, she put on her kimono and went down to breakfast.

For the past six months, she had a constant craving for kedgeree and nothing else could sate her deep hunger in quite the same way. She had just indulged herself to a second helping when she heard a tinkling of a bell which indicated that someone had come to call.

'Whoever could that be at such an hour?' she wondered and paying it no more heed she decided to leave it to the help. Moments later the help informed Olivia that a police officer was at the door asking for the lady of the house.

Much peeved, for her attire was by no means appropriate, Olivia went to meet the uncivilised officer, and in far too an irascible mood to honour the family's custom of receiving visitors of a formal variety in the library, she insisted that he tell her of the matter without ceremony. Therefore, standing at the open front door, the transparently awkward police officer imparted the regrettable news.

In the silence that followed, she heard the ormolu clock chime a quarter and fast felt her breakfast eager to reappear, so it was with a cat-like reflex that she made novel use of an umbrella stand that had been fashioned out of a genuine African elephant's foot.

Her memory of the following fortnight would forever remain misty. She knew only that she had felt despondent, and was advised to get as much rest as possible for the sake of the unborn baby. She retained no recollection of how, when or who told the children or of their immediate reactions and was thankful that she had a wet-nurse and nanny under their employ.

Uncle Bartholomew arranged the obsequies. They buried Montgomery at the family plot in Highgate Cemetery where he joined sixteen previous Avery-Stripes. One thing she could remember was thinking how joyous this family reunion would be for him. As they lowered the handsome black-walnut coffin into the ground, she imagined him meeting many of his ancestors for the first time and his awe at meeting Excelsior.

After that, her memory again drew blank. She could not recollect the wake or the details of his bequests. It was as if there were a barrier between herself and all else. She would not allow outside reality to penetrate her psyche before she was ready and she had no idea how long that would take, for her feelings of grief and shock seemed to her insurmountable. However, a far more formidable sense of guilt dwarfed these feelings and she felt this behemoth grow larger by the day as it consumed her very existence with its insatiable fury.

Repeatedly, she would recall her last hours with Monty; his uncharacteristic neediness and her cold response. She realised now that he had been reaching out to her for reassurance and all he had received was flippancy and that had pushed him to brutishness. Certainly, she had been tired, but if she had been more attentive, as she believed it a wife's duty to be, then maybe now she would not be full of such self-reproach.

It was true that he was excessively proud of his once magnificent family despite how meagre it had become, but she had loved him for that too.

From the very first, he had entertained her for hours with tales of his relations and of their history and traditions and she had relished the attention he lavished on her with them. For him to ask her to become Mrs

Avery-Stripe was the greatest compliment he could ever have paid and that she had ever received. She had accepted his proposal almost at once, hesitating for the sole reason that to give immediate consent would appear just too eager, and the subsequent thirteen years proved to be the most agreeable of her life thus far. He had taken her from nothing and placed her upon a pedestal, but once firmly established in her elevated position she became fiercely proud.

As her pride grew, Monty matched it by becoming increasingly bombastic, almost as if it were a battle of wills. She now believed that the significant difference between them was that whilst she had always felt his love shining through, with her basking in it like a conceited cat, she had never shown him much in return. For this reason, she felt riddled with remorse. She could feel her shame coursing through her veins like a poison and, for a while, her world turned black.

It was with the nativity of baby Cornelius that hope of atonement appeared upon Olivia's horizon. The birth, just thirteen days after Monty's departure, had been four weeks earlier than predicted and then one evening, after an anxious fortnight of Corny inhabiting an incubator, the doctors let Olivia take him home. She was scared to be handling something so miniscule and fragile and when scrutinising him in the Jaguar, she knew that he would always be a reminder of her loss of Monty. Once home, it was with relief that she handed him over to the buxom wet-nurse, Mrs Bovinus, who, though she already had Willy sucking on one teat, was delighted to have another on the other.

Crisp Nanny Cook brought the two boys in to have a look and to welcome home their mother, who felt rather uneasy at the prospect, for she had never had much contact with her sons without the presence of Monty providing a buffer.

'Hello, Horatio,' Olivia said as she proffered her cheek to Harry, who was all good looks, gangly limbs and in the process of puberty.

Harry kissed her.

'Hullo, Mummy,' he croaked in his breaking voice, and upon seeing Mrs Bovinus tending to his siblings with her generous bosoms, he blushed but managed to say, 'Hello, Cornelius. Welcome home!' and quickly he averted his gaze.

Dressed as a white rabbit and waving about an open yellow umbrella, Valentine hopped about the room and sang, 'I love mummy! Her hair is the colour of Marmite! I love Marmite! It is the colour of mummy's hair!'

and looked momentarily piqued when his performance was not met with the round of applause that his daddy would have given him.

Olivia looked at him in perplexity, and said 'Hello, darling,' whilst she wondered to herself, 'Is this child quite natural?'

'Come and see your new little brother,' said Nanny Cook, taking Valentine by the hand.

Valentine looked with astonishment and announced, 'Gosh! Nursie is being very greedy with two of them at both the same time, isn't she?' He looked to his elder brother to see if he was in accord, and asked, 'Why are you red, Harry?'

Harry's response was a flush of beetroot.

Mrs Bovinus chuckled.

Nanny Cook came to Harry's rescue: 'Little Cornelius and Wilhelmina are having a lovely time, and drinking lots of lovely milk, Valentino.'

'It doesn't look a very lovely thing to be doing,' he said, with a tut, 'does it, Mummy?'

Olivia grimaced.

'Don't you think Cornelius lovely?' Nanny Cook asked, encouragingly.

Valentine focused his attention on Corny for the first time and, with a gasp, he exclaimed, 'He is like a little peach!' and he stroked Corny's head with less care than Nanny Cook thought safe.

She snatched his arm away, and cautioned, 'Careful now, he is very delicate.'

'He's mine! I will look after him!' shouted Valentine, defiantly, upsetting Willy, who spat out the teat and reached for Olivia.

'Mamma! Mamma!' Willy wailed.

Olivia sidestepped her daughter's little pink hands and let Nanny Cook intervene, as the handling of one baby was enough for one day and Willy was slick with milk.

'Shall I take Valentino and Wilhelmina up to the nursery, Mrs Avery-Stripe?' she asked.

Olivia waved her hand dismissively, 'If you would.'

Nanny Cook bundled wailing Willy into her arms and led Valentine by the hand who, as if suddenly remembering his manners, turned around at the door and exclaimed, 'It has been lovely seeing you, mummy, I so do hope I shall again soon!'

'Goodnight, Valentino,' she responded, thankful for both his grasp of basic etiquette and his exit.

The departure had an uncomfortable effect on those left in the room.

Apart from the suckling Corny they each had their own reason to feel awkward. Harry felt awkward because half of Mrs Bovinus' chest was exposed and unattended. Mrs Bovinus felt awkward because she was a little bit scared of haughty Mrs Avery-Stripe and Olivia felt awkward because she did not know what to say to Harry.

She had always found it impossible to interact with very young children. It was a mystery to her how anybody could decipher from a baby's cries precisely what it desired. Then, when the babies grew a little older and able to talk and walk of their own accord, they were liable to say or do anything and they made an excessive amount of mess and noise.

However, Harry was aged twelve. He was, as far as Olivia was concerned, on the verge of young adulthood and she imagined that since he was now a full-time boarder, she would connect with him on a slightly more sophisticated level than she had hitherto.

Officially, he had become the man of the house the day his father died, but Olivia saw with dismay that even though his height was far above average for a boy of his age, and he was exceedingly good-looking, it would be a long time yet before he was a man and able to fill Monty's shoes.

Mindful of this, Olivia felt too defeated to rack her brains for something to say and was about to make her excuses and leave when Harry opened his mouth and said, 'Well, I ought to *wet*ire for the night, mummy, I've to be up ve*wy* early for *wo*-ing with the *wiv*erclub.' and he padded out of the room.

Astounded at herself for having forgotten her own son's speech impediment, Olivia was stunned into silence and she watched him depart with no external signal that she had heard him. Harry's rhotacism was no revelation. She had merely forgotten about it and assumed either he had grown out of it or Monty had fixed it.

'Really,' she told herself, 'it's no big thing, but surely he is too advanced in years for there to be any likelihood of his growing out of it now and where ever would one go to get it fixed, that is, if such a thing can be fixed. It would not matter under any other circumstance but he *is* the eldest, making him Monty's successor and as such, expected to perform the role sufficiently and what hope has he of that when he cannot even say his full name without sounding like a nincompoop?'

Sensing her strength rapidly dwindle, Olivia informed Mrs Bovinus that she also intended to retire and that she would have Nanny Cook relieve her of Corny.

'T'aint no trouble t'all, M'am. Why's n'oft'n I gets such a quiet'n res'ful one as this 'ere Master Cornelius!'

Olivia peered first at the wet-nurse then at Corny and frowned, 'Yes, I must say, he *is* mercifully quiet. Goodnight, Mrs Bovinus.' And she fled from the room.

Olivia lay on the Jacobean four-poster. Not in the centre of it, but on the side that had always been hers. It was so desolate without Monty. They had created each of their children in this bed and she reflected that each of them had been so for him. He was never to meet their youngest but he had at least known he was imminent. He had even chosen the name.

Corny's homecoming would have been reason for great celebration for Monty but, without him, that too had felt empty. It had all been for him and his dream of rebuilding his family back to some semblance of its former glory.

'What had it all amounted to?' she asked herself. It seemed so pointless and there she was, alone with four progenies. The possibility of eventually finding a new father for them flickered through her mind, after all, she was still young and she still had a better figure than most women did; it would not be so difficult to obtain a second husband she reasoned.

She then considered that if she remarried, she would no longer be Mrs Avery-Stripe and it was with this that it struck her that to no longer be Mrs Avery-Stripe would be to lose Monty altogether. Worse still, their children would be under the charge of someone not of their kin. The very notion of this filled her with unmitigated revulsion.

In a flash, the revelation hit her that she had always shared his ambition as strongly as if it were her very own and now that he had gone it was up to her to fulfil it and she resolved that she would! There would be no need of a new husband; just to think of it made her flesh creep. No, she alone would stand at the helm, her children were his children and his children deserved veneration. If she maintained the family's standards and encouraged, no, *insisted*, that each of his children do the same and raised them to accept nothing but the best and go fourth and multiply, then she would prove her love of Monty!

With that thought, Olivia sat bolt upright, climbed out of the four-poster, wrapped on her kimono, stepped out on to the moonlit balcony and there, standing amongst the potted bamboo and spider plants, she clenched her fists, faced the cosmos in its entirety and avowed: 'He will be in no doubt of my love for him. I shall honour him and his memory, his dream, our ambition and his family's name, spirit and heritage; for *I* am Mrs Montgomery Avery-Stripe and Avery-Stripes *never* despair!'

Retrospectively, Olivia could almost laugh at how naïve her promise to the universe had been. Oh, she had given it her best shot, still was in fact, but she knew now that one should not bandy words such as honour about if one has not got the funds to back it up.

In that matter too, she had been unwise. Monty had always taken care of money, or at least she thought he had, but he had made some unwise investments and within a year of his death, there was no option but to let the help go, even Nanny Cook.

Then, all the struggling and frugality in the world could not have saved her from having to sell the house and by the time Corny was able to walk, it was to be in the sanctuary of Uncle Bartholomew's home in a leafy west London garden suburb. Initially, the arrangement was to be temporary, but the children loved him and Gretchen took them in hand admirably.

Besides, a considerable amount of capital had remained after the sale and she would need as much capital as she was able, in order to raise the children adequately. There was no point in buying a house when they already had a perfectly decent roof over their heads. There were more important things, such as the children's schooling. True, Harry was the only one to be sent to one of any real worth but Harry was the immediate heir.

Admittedly, she had not spent an inordinate amount of time considering where best to put the others, but anyway, Valentine transpired never to take any interest in his lessons unless one of his fellow students happened to be a plebeian Adonis. Willy would not be carrying on the family name in any case, and Corny – well, Corny had alternative requirements. Nevertheless, she had gone to great pains to educate each of them in the family history and their importance, and they were knowledgeable of the family's expectations. A fraction of the reason of her returning home was to remind them all of that, particularly the two eldest.

Olivia observed the view from the train window and was pleased to see the hills of England's garden rolling by. Her eyes moistened in grateful relief, for it was her firm belief that no other country makes the colour green as splendidly as the English one does. It was good to be back in God's own country, she told herself. She had had some jolly times whilst away but she sensed that the Monaco lot were starting to tire of her and, knowing it best to always leave people wanting more, she said her farewells, but not before having a cocktail party upon someone's yacht to mark the occasion. The remembrance of which swiftly brought to her attention the fact that she had drained every drop of her gin.

It was just as well she had filled Monty's old hip flask with whisky, and she fished it out from the depths of her black crocodile Birkin. When she was quite certain that nobody was looking, she replenished her cup and as she did so she read the family maxim engraved on the flask. The words were of comfort to her, as was holding the object that used to appear so small when held by Monty.

Something that gave her an even greater sense of comfort however, was the contents of the small velvet drawstring pouch that she had retrieved alongside the flask and that she now clutched in her other hand. Without a doubt, it provided her with infinitely more reassurance and was well worth the sordid scrape in la Rue du Chat-Qui-Peche. Olivia felt a strong sense of satisfaction over what she had achieved and took a less than genteel sip of her drink before she settled back to await the arrival of Waterloo.

CHAPTER 3

Excelsior Incarnate

Since having received the communication from Paris, Valentine had decided to use his somewhat askew knowledge on the subject to educate Corny on all things French. He began with simple things such as frog's legs and l'éscargot and then moved on to meatier matters.

'Gosh! Just imagine being there with the revolting peasants! A front row seat with Madame Defarge knitting and cackling away. Pauvre Marie Antoinette! All of her fineries not being a jot of use when that razor sharp blade whizzed down and slashed off her petite tête!'

He drew his index finger across his throat and made a guttural slicing sound: 'Glorious! N'est pas?'

Corny clasped his neck and shuddered with relish.

Valentine then told of the 'tragic shaved heads of the Madames et Mademoiselles accused of "la collaboration horizontale".'

'As if being shorn of their lovely locks was not punishment enough, the tragic unfortunates were then paraded on lorries through the main rues! Worse yet, sometimes they were stripped, tarred and stamped with swastikas! All for having fallen for the wrong person!

'Everybody knows, though I wouldn't say this within earshot of Gubsy, that many of those golden boys had no choice but to submit to the criminal commands of the Fuhrer. I really can't say that I would not have ended up with a hairless head had I been about in 1944, for the Teutonic race has always seemed to me not an altogether physically unattractive one, the chaps, I mean.'

Scandalised by his confession and mindful that Corny might not be entirely enchanted to hear of his penchant for strapping blond boys heedless of their creed, Valentine thought it best to move swiftly on to something of a frothier nature. So it was that he began to tell of the Folies Bergeres and the magnificent Josephine Baker, of the Moulin Rouge and Henri de Toulouse-Lautrec.

He located high upon the bookcase an immense book of famous works of art of the twentieth century and presented it to Corny for him to see the artist's colourful paintings of the high kicking can-can girls. It was immediately evident that this part of his 'education Francaise' would be of greatest interest to Corny, as he eyed the plates with much enthusiasm. This filled Valentine to the brim with inspiration and in what he considered a fair transaction with Willy, said that he would handle the inevitable telephone conversation with Mses Broach and Peeble and the quite possible one from Mrs Strap, in return for her skills as a pianist.

Reluctant as she was, Willy was aware that Valentine knew he had her over a barrel; the last thing she wanted was for their mother to hear of yet another instance of her unladylike performances. Valentine also pointed out to her that threatening him with a Chinese burn would do little to help her cause.

If one were to look at Willy's sausage fingers one would never have guessed that she was capable of producing anything other than a monstrous din on a piano, but as it was, she played like an angel. This was the result of many years of tedious lessons as an alternative to the ballet classes that all of the nice girls attended but to which Willy adamantly refused to go. The score that Valentine required her to apply her angelic pianism to was that of Jacques Offenbach's *Orphée aux Enfers, Galop Infernal*.

Valentine had dug up the score during an excavation of the cellar, which was something he enjoyed doing on a regular basis, often unearthing interesting artefacts amongst the debris of long forgotten paraphernalia of his ancestors, which had travelled from house to house only to end up in a subterranean scrapheap.

Quite soon, Willy was able to play the piece unaided and though it was not something to which she would easily confess, she soon found that she rather enjoyed it. Valentine had also discovered a once handsome beaver-fur topper with which to crown her, and a pair of dusty old bridesmaid's dresses for him and Corny to wear as they danced and kicked about the drawing room.

Willy tickled the ivories with increasing velocity and volume, and cheered, 'Bravo! Encore!' as Valentine whooped and cried out, 'Plus rapide et plus haut mes belles filles!' Corny made strange sounds of excited exertion and cascaded with sweat.

The three dogs regarded them with confusion and barked loudly in consternation, but Remarkable enjoyed the commotion and ducked up and down on his perch. Skilfully, he caught in his beak each of the grapes that the dancing boys threw across the room at him from under their high kicked legs, which caused the brothers and sister to hoot and holler in exaltation and to stamp on the Axminster with unrestrained ferocity.

To the gradual annoyance of Gubsy, this boisterousness became a ritual that the siblings would perform every morning directly after his elevenses. Largely, he bore it with hardy stoicism and took refuge in his bedroom. There the noise was less of a bother, and he could peruse *The Times* and contemplate its crossword at his leisure.

Gretchen stated that it was 'Riddy-koo-lars!' that he should hide away in his own home, but Gubsy paid her no attention. The children were the direct descendants of his eldest brother and only nephew, not to mention his grandfather, and now only he was there to act as a paternal figure for them and to indulge them from time to time.

'Lord knows they get scant amount of anything from their own blasted mother!' he said to himself, and the thought of Olivia forced him to sound a roar that could just as likely have come from the head of the African lion on his floor, had it not been a rug for nigh on seven decades.

Despite his heroic tolerance of the racket, the morning came when he reached the end of his tether, but this had not so much to do with the noise as it had with the fact that this particular morning was on the day that Olivia was due to return.

To make matters worse he could not find his reading spectacles and without them, *The Times* would be nothing better than a blur, and with no clue as to where they might be, he blustered in on the children, gnashed his false teeth, roared profanities and thrashed his menacing cocobolo cane in all directions.

Lost in their tomfoolery, the children were barely aware of him or of the very near misses from his cane that would have met its mark had they not been so spry with glee, or he so blind with fury. Even Remarkable had his dexterity to thank for not being sent flying across the room without the aid of his wings.

Jowls juddering and fairly frothing at the mouth, Gubsy shook his once expert boxing fists for he realised he would receive no help from the rapscallions and retreated into the hall, but not before upending Valentine's latest puzzle of Delacroix's *Liberty Leading the People*, sending pieces of carnage, cleavage and *tricolore* all over the place. This upset of jigsaw also escaped their notice, even, somewhat miraculously, Valentine's and they continued to dance and play as if a trio of intoxicated mariners on twenty-four hour's leave of absence.

In fact, there was another member of the party, invisible to the naked eye, in the form of a little green fairy that they had located in the grotesque globe drinks' cabinet. Over the past few days, they had become very well acquainted with her because Valentine had decreed that absinthe would simply be in keeping with things, and it certainly helped make the mornings even jollier.

Gubsy roared with rage at having found himself somehow forced out of his own drawing room by the ne'er-do-wells and propelled into the hall as if he were of no account at all.

'How can this be?' he demanded to know. It was unfathomable to him that it had come to this. It did not seem all that long ago when he was fighting off the Huns virtually single-handedly, as he liked to tell it. However, the reality of it was that the dirtiest he got his hands during the last show was with a difficult fountain pen when signing official documents from the safety of his desk. This was not a part of his history that he cared to divulge, as two of his brothers, Olivier and Valerian, had lost their lives fighting for King and Country.

Gubsy bellowed for Gretchen until his throat became hoarse, and he realised that she had gone to the allotment and then on to collect Olivia from the station.

He began to search the drawers of the old Victorian hall-tree on the off chance that his spectacles might be there. This imposing piece of furniture had been in the family long before Gubsy's time and it used to stand in the entrance hall of Excelsior's place of residence.

Gubsy could remember with clarity watching his ancient grandfather admiring, with satisfaction, his reflection in the inlaid looking glass of the hall-tree, for he had been a fine-looking and vain man, and then how he had swooped down to serve him a smack for being a sneak. This vicious assault had sent the boy Bartholomew screaming down the seemingly never-ending corridors and through the myriad of chambers of his attacker's gothic pile – Ballestas, its namesake being the Peruvian islands that provided the avian excrement that made the fortune with which Excelsior built the pile.

'By Jove, Ballestas was a handsome building,' Gubsy would say, when too much brandy made him maudlin. 'A genuine castle, built by my very own grandfather. Every room led onto yet more rooms and every one of them a wonder and full of treasures from every nation under the sun, each of them bought or shot by Avery-Stripes. By Jove, I miss Ballestas!'

At which point all would hope that he would pass out before becoming too morose and start blubbing and blaming his need for a drink or two on the loss of the British Empire.

Strictly adhering to the traditional laws of lineage, Excelsior bequeathed

Ballestas to his only son Ambrosius, who then left it to his eldest son Jeremiah, but that is as far as it went. Because of World War II, Jeremiah sold the building and land not long after inheriting it and, in Ballestas' place, there now stood a retail park.

Ballestas scattered to the wind; much was put up for auction, the rest divided between the few remaining Avery-Stripes and when each of these passed away, their share ended up in Gubsy's possession. It amazed him to consider how much of Ballestas had squashed into his comparatively humble Queen Anne Revival detached that he had christened Chinchero in accordance with the Peruvian theme.

It made him feel proud that he had managed to keep hold of as much as he had, and he did not care in the least that it gave his house the air of a mausoleum so long as it was all kept within the family. However, it occasionally angered him beyond measure that he felt duped into taking onboard all of Olivia's belongings, including the children, when it had been presented to him as a temporary arrangement that was only necessary due to emergency. More than anything else in the world Gubsy deplored looking a fool, and that was precisely how he believed Olivia perceived him.

Having no luck in locating his spectacles in the drawers, Gubsy decided to investigate the pockets of the coats hung up on the hall-tree. The humiliation of having to do so was deeply vexing and he proceeded to bark profanities in an attempt to placate his anger and to drown out the din from the drawing room. As he vented, he withdrew from pockets all manner of things: from apple cores and soiled handkerchiefs to seashells and homemade catapults, and tossed each of these, and many more inexplicable items, over his shoulder.

He had a hunch that his hunt was to furnish him with everything save that that he desired, and he thought he would be happy to settle for some earplugs as the music was once again building to a crescendo. He cursed at his reflection in the hall-tree's looking glass and it was then that he saw someone familiar standing behind him. He turned and, though he had recognised the person's reflection, the shock of seeing him face to face, knocked him off his feet. His large backside crashed to the seat of the hall-tree and he stared up in fear and astonishment at the ghost of his grandfather.

'You have come!' sobbed Gubsy, and he raised his arms in submission, ready to be spirited away, whether his destination be Heaven or Hell. He surmised that it must be the former, as the apparition seemed to be in the very pink of health.

Excelsior was a tall and handsome young man again, clothed in brilliant white, and wearing sandals. Clearly, he was an angel and not a devil. He descended upon Gubsy and engulfed him in a warm embrace. Meekly, Gubsy surrendered and felt the weight lift from his earthly form. He believed that he could already hear Saint Gabriel out-trumpeting Offenbach's infernal racket and almost see Saint Peter at the Pearly Gates of Perpetual Paradise.

Therefore, it came as quite a surprise to hear the angel say, 'Hullo, Gubsy! How are you?'

In a flash, Gubsy lost sight of Saint Peter, the Pearly Gates vanished and the trumpeting came to an abrupt halt as reality crowded in on him.

'What the deuce!' he exclaimed, as he thrust the impostor away with all of his might. 'Who the blazes are you?'

'Gubsy! Don't you *we*cognise me? It's Ha*ww*y! You know, Ho*w*atio!' said Harry, as he straightened himself up to his full impressive height, 'Are you al*w*ight?' Harry was worried that during his five months in the Himalayas senile dementia may have started to affect his great uncle. Not that there was a history of it in the family, but then very few Avery-Stripes had lived long enough for senility to have become a possibility.

Scrutinising him for a space, Gubsy saw that it was so; Harry was indeed who he claimed to be, and this pleased Gubsy very much.

'So it is, so it is! Well, I'll be! Welcome! Welcome home! Help me up, there's a good fellow.' Harry took Gubsy's proffered hand and hoisted him. ' 'pon my soul! D'you know I could've sworn that you were my own grandfather?'

'You thought I was *gw*eat-*gw*eat-*gw*andfather Excelsior?' laughed Harry. 'Silly old fool, aren't I?'

'*We*ally not, Gubsy. It must be the beard. I didn't have one when I left, but there wasn't always *fw*esh water some of the places I went and, well, I just thought I'd give a beard a go and see how it looked. What do you think?'

'Yes, that's it. Just like grandfather's.' Gubsy admired the short boxed beard. 'Very striking, you cut quite a dash with it, I must say.'

Though pleased at having inherited Excelsior's good looks, Harry was a bashful boy at heart, and his modesty made him digress.

'Is there a party going on in there?' he asked, nodding toward the drawing room.

'Of sorts. Those scoundrel young'uns have been driving me doolally! Do go in and have a look at the hullabaloo!'

Harry turned the knob and pushed the door open to see what mischief his siblings were making. The scene that greeted him made him laugh and he strode into the room.

'Hullo, ev*w*ybody!' he shouted over the noise.

The dogs rushed over to welcome him. They jumped up and pulled him to his knees and his happy face received a thorough drenching from their eager tongues.

'Hullo, dogs!' said Harry, pulling them close.

The sudden absence of barking alerted the scoundrels to their brother's return, the music stopped and Corny was next in line to hurl himself at Harry.

'Hullo, *w*ascal!' laughed Harry, and he stood up again in order to hold his little brother, who was a good foot shorter than he was, upside down by the ankles, which was something that they had always done.

Corny enjoyed this colossally and thrashed his arms about excitedly, looking quite a picture as the bridesmaid's dress eventually turned itself almost completely inside out on his wriggling body.

'Why on earth are you two wea-*w*ing d*w*esses?' Harry asked.

'We are dancers at the Moulin Rouge,' explained Valentine, as if it was obvious. He had collapsed in a louche heap upon the chesterfield and was puffing away on one of Gubsy's Montecristo No.4's.

'And I am Toulouse Lautrec,' slurred Willy from the piano, elbows planted on the keys, and topper positioned on her head at a rakish angle, 'but with ordinary legs.' And to prove it, she shuffled her feet.

'But what have you come as?' queried Valentine, 'You look to be positively evangelical with that beard!'

Harry rubbed his beard with his palm, and said, 'Gubsy thought I was Excelsior come back from the dead! He got a d*w*eadful shock.' Jovially, he cuffed their great uncle on the shoulder.

The drawing room filled with honks of hilarity.

'You old funny Gubsy!' exclaimed Willy, as she tried to embrace his full circumference.

Much flustered, Gubsy gnashed and snatched the topper from her head and the Montecristo from Valentine's hand.

'*My* grandfather's hat! And *my* cigar!' he boomed, and landed in his wing chair with a *harrumph*.

Too insouciant to care, Valentine procured a cigarette from his silver case and lit it. As he did so, he viewed both Harry and the large portrait of his great-great grandfather that hung above the mantelshelf. He had to admit that, what with the beard and the effects that the Indian sun had had on Harry's complexion, the resemblance was quite uncanny.

The painting was clearly dated 1856, but the signature appeared as if purposefully smudged to render it illegible, however whoever the artist was they undoubtedly possessed an intense rapport with, or at least aimed to ingratiate Excelsior Avery-Stripe pictured standing tall, proud, and akimbo, before vermillion brocade. His burnished-copper hair looked luxuriously thick and his skin was ruddy and tan from his years in South America. He was devilishly handsome and leered out from the canvas with his rich brown eyes and, together with his cocked brow and the cruel curl of his conceited smile, one felt quite vulnerable to his, probably debauched, desires.

Excelsior's fitted tailcoat exaggerated his shoulders and puffed up his chest as well as suppressing his waist, and the tight sleeves accentuated the power of his upper arms. A ruby-headed gold pin pierced his sumptuously knotted cravat that was pillar-box red, as was his elaborately embroidered waistcoat, adorned with a gold pocket watch and chain. As if not satisfied with such a modest display of bibelots, and perhaps also to display his humour, he had, sat upon his broad shoulder, his garishly coloured Panther chameleon from the island of Nosy Be, situated to the northwest of Madagascar.

This foot-long lizard, for at the time of the painting it had not yet fully grown, was Excelsior's most beloved possession and, in the painting, its elastic tongue, easily another twelve inches, is theatrically protracted with the slimy suction cup at its end claiming the life of a incongruous dragonfly.

Ridiculous, being the chameleon's name, still resided with the family in the form of a rather sinister base for the ornamental lamp sat upon Gubsy's bedside table, yet because the taxidermist clamped the powerful jaws shut, the indecent tongue cannot be seen.

'Absolute spit, you are, Harry,' declared Gubsy, gesticulating his Montecristo in the direction of the portrait. 'I hadn't noticed before but now with your beard it is quite obvious, though somehow you are very different. You do not have grandfather's self-assuredness.'

'Gosh, Gubsy! I am quite certain you are understating it.' remonstrated Valentine, 'I believe that what Excelsior possessed was a case of self-aggrandisement.'

'I wonder then, who might have inherited that, young man!' Gubsy replied sharply.

Valentine tutted and thought that the retort had caused Willy to chuckle rather unnecessarily.

'Shush, Willy, do be quiet!' he snapped, 'I might not hear the telephone if *someone* might happen to call wishing to talk to mummy.'

Harry asked where mummy was and their realisation that the time of her arrival was imminent sent them into a hive of activity.

Gretchen had already given Chinchero a thorough tidying the previous day but had neglected the drawing room and delegated that responsibility to the children as they had persisted in using it like a playground.

Back into the jigsaw box went the scattered French Revolution, most of it anyway. Up onto the bookcase went the twentieth century's most famous works of art and down into the cellar went the bridesmaid's dresses and beaver topper. Offenbach's score maintained its position on the piano's music rack, but Willy told Valentine that she did not think she would be playing it again anytime soon, at least not under the influence of absinthe.

She shut the bottle back in the globe drinks' cabinet and said, 'It's easy to see why it's called a green fairy because that's just the colour I feel about the gills.'

'Poor you!' said Valentine, 'I feel quite glorious though I am most upset not to have seen a single hallucination, not even a little one! Unlike Gubsy who managed to hallucinate the incarnation of Excelsior, perhaps he's been helping himself when we've all been sound asleep!'

The idea of Gubsy tiptoeing about in his nightshirt and slippers, clandestinely imbibing before slipping back into his bed and hiccoughing, struck Willy as inordinately funny and she soon felt very much cheered up, even if did hurt her head to laugh.

Eventually the room was restored to some semblance of order, though not too strictly, as not one of them wished to rush about with a vacuum cleaner or look silly with a feather duster and did not even know exactly where Gretchen housed such things. Harry had taken his gigantic backpack and funny walking poles up to his bedroom, showered and changed into some of his clothes that Gretchen had kept protected for him. It was nice to put on a laundered shirt, but he was rather dismayed that she had ironed sharp creases in all of his jeans.

Corny's hair was still wet from his deep bubble bath, and neatly combed.

He was very proud to have removed all of the knots without the use of a pair of scissors again, and he had been encouraged by Valentine to wear a vintage children's sailor suit found in the cellar.

Valentine wore a new pair of Tricolore striped pyjamas that he had purchased especially for the occasion and he reeked of the violet scent with which he liked to spray, liberally, about his person.

Having vigorously scrubbed her face with a cold flannel, Willy was florid and looked stiflingly hot in her corduroys and chunky guernsey.

Gubsy, however, said he would not subject himself to any form of exertion for someone who has decided to put in an appearance purely because Paris is torture.

'She can jolly well take me as I am!' he said, 'And Chinchero!'

He decided he would ignore Olivia by being asleep when she returned and he unfolded *The Times* over his head.

Thus, the five Avery-Stripes of various shapes and sizes were dotted about the drawing room. The children sat and listened to the ticking of the ormolu clock and waited.

They had made a rough guess that it would be about four that Olivia would be at the door, but four came and went and so did five. By this time they had all become somewhat fidgety and with the exception of Corny, who had climbed up into the tree house to keep lookout, they started to play a game of scrabble.

Valentine quickly decided that the game was slowing down rather than speeding up time and chose to remedy this by amusing himself with fictitious words, and his insistence that they were genuine resulted in the necessity of the tombstone-sized dictionary. Eventually weary of words they abandoned the scrabble-board and decided that it would be a good idea to play dominoes. They did not mean Chicken-foot or Matador but rather to stand in line the tiles of several boxes, in elaborate curves and angles, tunnelling under footstools, bypassing piano legs, climbing stacked encyclopaedias and circumnavigating sleeping great uncles. Unfortunately, the thrill of it lay primarily in the preparation because mere seconds after tapping the maiden tile they all felt a sad sense of anti-climax.

It was at twenty to seven when they had just finished carpeting the drawing room floor with perfectly neat rows of playing cards, that a particularly excited Corny came bounding in from the garden and broke their game of Concentration. A moment later, they heard the peal of the front doorbell. Mummy was home.

*

Olivia was gratified that Gretchen had come to collect her in Monty's old Jaguar because having been subject to a lengthy, and what she considered disrespectful questioning at the customs desk, she wanted nothing more than to get home as swiftly as was possible. Nevertheless, it was most disagreeable to sit amongst carrier bags and cardboard boxes of fruit and vegetables and to suffer the canine aroma.

Olivia's agitation furthered when, due to a burst water pipe, they had to make a complex detour that involved much congestion of traffic and this, combined with her rude interrogation, was what had caused the delay.

Home at last, Olivia climbed out from the fruit and vegetables, crunched her heels across the gravel drive, then clicked them up the garden path to the front door and gave the bell pull a harsh tug. Much scuffling and whispering came from within Chinchero and she heard the chain jangle onto the latch. The door opened a crack and she pretended not to notice the big blue eye that popped out at her.

'*Ugh!* Already Corny is staring at me!' she thought with irritation.

Laden with shopping bags, suitcases and a hefty trunk, Gretchen lumbered up behind her and called out the words Corny was waiting to hear: 'Open says-me!'

The door shut, the chain released and the door reopened, this time fully and Corny stood gaping unabashedly at Olivia who because of her lengthy holidays seemed to him close to being a perfect stranger. She took the plunge, stepped over the threshold and looked back at him but all she could see was the memory of Monty. She steeled herself, pecked Corny on the cheek and asked if he did not think a gentleman would welcome her with more chivalry. Evidently, he did not and much to her chagrin, he continued to stare.

Valentine arrived on the scene, with Willy lurking behind, and more than made up for the chivalry that Corny lacked. Clasping Olivia's hands in his he sang out in an unrestrained French accent: 'Bonjour! Bonjour! Bienvenue, mummy! Comment mérveilleux pour vous voir! Avez-vous aime Paris? L'etait un bon voyage?'

Olivia grimaced and begged him to converse only in English.

'Gosh! Yes, mummy, of course, that is, after all, what we are; English through and through. Look, here's Willy! Say hello, Willy!'

'Hullo, mummy,' seemed to be the most gruelling words that one might ask Willy to say, but somehow she managed. Unlike Corny, she did not cast Olivia even the slightest glance and busied herself by helping Gretchen with the cases.

'Hello, darling. You're looking . . . wholesome,' Olivia replied and failed to hide, behind her crocodile smile, the mortification of her daughter's acute disregard for feminine apparel.

Valentine interrupted, 'Come and see what a surprise we have for you! And you, Gretchen! Close your eyes, mummy!'

He led Olivia into the drawing room which they had succeeded in tidying for the second time that day, and positioned her upon the chesterfield. She dared not think what sight might be waiting to meet her once she opened her eyes. The last time they had played this game she discovered that her wedding dress fitted Valentine exactly and now he informed her that on the count of three she was to open her eyes for a handsome shock.

'One . . . two . . . and . . . three!'

Olivia braced herself, feared the worst, hoped for the best, and opened her eyes only to see that Harry had returned from the Himalayas with a beard.

'A beard!' she exclaimed.

'It makes him look like Excelsior, don't you think?'

'Yes. A little. Perhaps.'

Harry smiled awkwardly and bowed to give her a kiss.

'Hullo, mummy. How was Pa*w*is?'

'At last! A person possessed of the wit to ask!'

Valentine tutted and made a moue in an outward display of sympathy whilst he thought of the people from ancient Philistia.

'Well, then, how was it?'

'I'm too tired to say.'

Willy was no longer able to resist looking at her mother so she safely stationed herself behind the mound of slumbering Gubsy and compensated for her earlier lack of regard by glaring. Corny was under the piano and still had not desisted in his staring.

Feeling both pairs of eyes boring into her, Olivia shifted uncomfortably and asked if Valentine would be a wonder and fix her a gin and tonic. Valentine tutted and Gretchen took the opportunity to give Harry a big kiss to welcome him home.

'Hullo, G*w*etchen! Thanks so much for keeping my *w*oom clean and all my clothes too.'

'Is no problem, Master Harry. Somethink I like to do. But I think it make you smell of moth's balls. Is not kood.'

'*W*eally? I hadn't noticed. I *w*eally app*w*eciate it. Thank you.'

'You such a kood boy. Always, you have been kood. Never any troubles from you. I am klad you are home akain! But why you no tell us you were coming?'

'So*ww*y, G*w*etchen, I only booked the flight on Tuesday. Spur of the moment sort of thing and low on funds.' Harry sheepishly said.

Olivia involuntarily bore her teeth like a rabid beast for a flash.

'I hope my *w*eturn hasn't *cw*eated any p*w*oblems,' Harry added.

Gretchen ignored Harry's silly concern, placed her large capable hands on his cheeks and stroked his beard. 'I like this beard. Is nice!'

'Mummy doesn't seem to like it ve*w*y much,' said Harry pitifully, and made puppy eyes.

'Why you no like, Mrs Olivia?' Gretchen demanded. 'Is very nice. Is lookink kood. Is right for a man.' To emphasise her point, she stroked with more vigour and Harry enjoyed it.

Swirling the ice in her gin and tonic, Olivia had watched the pair of them with amused disdain and though they were both well over six foot and she sitting down, it was still no problem for her to address them in a condescending tone: 'It's not that I don't like it. It's just that I'm not used to it but I daresay that given time the beard will grow on me.'

Valentine fell into fits of laughter. Olivia realised how idiotic she had just sounded and looked daggers at him. The noise woke Gubsy. He lifted *The Times*, and upon spying Olivia across the room, he cursed, replaced it and proceeded to gnash.

Olivia swiftly finished her drink, placed the glass on the table and glancing at the tiny Tiffany timepiece on her wrist, she rose, and said, 'I really must rest, I am extremely exhausted.'

'But, Mrs Olivia, first you must eat. I am goink to kitchen to cook somethink now. Is late so nothink fancy-smancy but I cook somethink for you.'

'I couldn't eat a thing right now, Gretchen. I must lie down before I fall down. But it is just a nap as I wish to have a very serious talk with the two of you later,' and she pointed at her two eldest children before disappearing from the room.

'Gosh! How tenterhooking!' exclaimed Valentine, and Harry felt so too.

Ascending the stairwell, Olivia examined the curious series of fresh scars Willy's crop had made in the oak balustrades, and then upon reaching the landing between the ground floor and first, she studied one of the many ancestral portraits that hung there. This painting, positioned beneath the shaggy head of a bison, was not quite as large as that of Excelsior and Ridiculous but the subject herself was by no means small. Excelsior's wife, Olympia certainly was a lady of olympic proportion and with no record of any previous Avery-Stripes, one could say that the family's fleshy gene originated with her.

She had a kind and beautiful face but the idea of carrying all of that round and pink excess flesh made Olivia feel nauseous, for the arms alone looked like sides of pork. She reflected that there was an overall porcine aspect to the poor woman and Olivia did consider her poor because despite her obvious wealth it required little intellect to deduce that married life with Excelsior would have been one of continuous torment.

The again plausibly intentionally obliterated artist presents enormous Olympia as Excelsior's vision of a Greek deity, playing a gigantic gold harp atop a mountain, presumably Olympus, in 1870. Naturally, the background is blue sky, snowy cumulus clouds and golden sunrays. The rays highlight the blonde tresses piled high upon Olympia's head and tumbling down her broad shoulders, and she is looking out at the viewer with petrified blue eyes. A white muslin dress so sheer and revealing of her Rubenesque figure makes one feel certain that during her existence the painting would not have left the confines of the bedroom. One could almost sense her discomfiture for despite her effort to appear wanton, she clasps the harp between her colossal thighs and close to her magnificent chest so desperately, as if to suggest that her letting go would result in her falling from the Heavens into the world of mere mortals with a thunderous crash.

Olivia, however, had not stopped to gaze upon the piggy face and feel pity or compassion, but to inspect the right hand frozen forever in mid-pluck, more specifically the third digit and what was on it; and just as she knew it would be, there it was, Olympia's 'Starfish'.

Excelsior and Olympia had tried many times to produce a male heir. They were very happy to have five healthy females; Fortunata, Honoria, Isadora, Bedelia and Cornelia, but it was not until their twelfth year of matrimony, when he was aged forty-five and she twenty-nine, that they were at last blessed with the son that he demanded.

Excelsior was so ecstatic with the nativity of baby Ambrosius that he went as far as to remove the mourning band he wore in commemoration of his beloved Ridiculous, who due to very old age, for he had lived almost twice as long as any healthy chameleon might hope to, had passed away and recently returned from the very best taxidermist. Not only this but Excelsior stopped regarding Olympia as merely a pleasantly pliable and somewhat imbecilic, plump young popsy eager to breed his seed and help him succeed in society. He found that he had fallen in love with her all over again, after a fashion, and thus on her thirtieth birthday, her first birthday after the arrival of Ambrosius, he presented her with the finest ring that money could buy.

It consisted of five briolette gems; a blood red ruby from India, a Colombian emerald, a Brazilian topaz, a sapphire from Burma and a Madagascan amethyst. They were set on a palladium band – with '*Nil Desperandum*' engraved on the inside – and formed the shape of a starfish.

Excelsior explained to his sweet silly wife that these five precious stones represented their five daughters who were equally as precious, if not more so. Around each of these stones were twenty small South African diamonds and he told her that these one hundred little twinklers were to show that he would love her for centuries. But the *pièce de résistance* of this rainbow-coloured cluster, sat in the centre of the five stones, was the pea-sized asscher diamond also from Africa. Excelsior said to Olympia that this dazzling whopper was, of course, Ambrosius.

Monty loved to tell Olivia this story. He was very sorry that he would not ever see her wear the ring or be able to bequeath it to one of their offspring because Olympia had given it to her favourite daughter, Fortunata, who then passed it down to her daughter. Monty considered this a heinous crime, as it should have remained with the Avery-Stripes proper and he had never been able to regard the portrait of his great-grandmother without exhibiting indecent outrage.

Olivia wished that he could join her now as she checked that she was quite alone and removed from her crocodile Birkin the small velvet drawstring pouch, loosened the string and fished out Olympia's Starfish. It was a little slack on her finger but that was of no consequence, Olivia felt like the cat that got the cream and she gave the precious ring a tender kiss, and thought of her darling Monty as she made her way to their four-poster.

Gubsy, and the four most recent additions to the Avery-Stripe dynasty, sat around the gingham clothed table in Gretchen's kitchen as she clattered and clanked numerous pots and pans of assorted sizes on the racing-green Aga.

Gretchen was exceedingly proud of her domain and it was by far and away the most productive room in the house. When not busying herself picking up or dusting down after the family, Gretchen would, more likely than not, be found baking, basting, roasting, toasting, chopping, stirring, whisking, beating or kneading in her kitchen. She cleaned as she went, for she liked to keep the place 'spick and spam'. The ship she ran was tight with no room for disorder, everything had its place and there were lots of everything. The larder was always full, the kettle always hot and there were plenty of homemade biscuits in the tin if hungry between meals. The only drawback was that no one could enter without Gretchen's permission. Harry was happy that this evening they were all welcome because after hours of sitting on an aeroplane, followed by hours of waiting for his mother, he was desperately hungry despite his dread of the serious talk.

'What's for sups, Gwetchen? I'm wavishing!'

Ever since adolescence Harry had muddled the words 'ravenous' and 'famished' and with anyone else the mistake might seem affected but with Harry it was transparently unintentional.

Potato masher in hand, Gretchen turned and grinned at him. He was most definitely ravishing but she grasped his meaning and was pleased to reveal that she was preparing one of his favourite suppers: 'Bankers and mash and spotty dick!'

Everyone made sounds of a highly appreciate nature, licked their lips and Gretchen's cup of happiness was filled to the brim as she continued to mash the potatoes with gusto.

With her gingham napkin tucked into the neck hole of her guernsey and wielding her cutlery, Willy, feeling a little left out, asked Harry and Valentine if they had any idea what it was that their mummy wanted to talk to them about.

'Gosh! Not an inkling!'

'Weally don't know, but it makes me feel wather wowwied.'

Willy narrowed her eyes and said, 'It sounded important. I wonder what it is and why only you two.'

'Well, she did say that is was *très sérieux*, but you know mummy, I am certain it's nothing of the sort. My personal fear though, *sérieux* or no, the tone in which she communicated persuades me to deduce it's bound to be something *painfully* trying, don't you think, Corny?' Corny responded with a roll of his eyes. 'So I shouldn't feel too sorry not to be privy.'

Patently not appeased, Willy flared her nostrils and girned.

Gretchen set the mountain of mustard and nutmeg mash and the pile of Gloucester Old Spot sausages on the table and saw that what Valentine had said had amplified Harry's anxiety. She heaped generous dollops of potato onto his plate, and said to him, 'Do not be worryink. Is all beink okay. Your mudder, she is full of hot airs and kraces but you not have to be worryink, always with her it is just talkink.'

Next to have his plate dolloped on was Gubsy who, starting with a gnash, added, 'Your mother's conduct is beyond the pale. Been here for less than two hours and already upsetting everybody and turning the house topsy-turvy! There's enough luggage in the hall to start a new colony! In Chinchero! Coming and going as she pleases and when it suits her, without a by your leave or care in the world! She is under the impression that this is an hotel! A free hotel and she is not even blood . . . '

'She's only an Avery-Stripe by marriage!' interjected Willy.

'I will not have it I tell you!' continued Gubsy, banging his dessert spoon on the table. 'Devil woman! She is the absolute limit! She makes my blood boil!'

Having served everyone and seen to it that the gravy boat made the full circuit, Gretchen took her seat and patted the back of his hand: 'Mr Bartholmoo, you must take thinks easy, you must be calm and eat. Is all beink okay. Maybe she is not stay so lonk but her beink here is kood for children. Is kood for them to see her. For them we must be toleratink.'

Gubsy expelled expletives, thrust a sausage in his mouth and devoured it angrily.

Sitting at the far end of the table, Corny used his fork to demolish the castle and moat he had sculpted in his mash. He raised his head guiltily and was shocked to see, through the gap in the door, his mummy standing in the unlit dining room – the virtual stranger was eavesdropping! His cutlery clattered loudly on his crockery when he dropped it, the room silenced and all attention was on him as the colour drained from his face.

'What is matter, Master Corny?'

'What's *wong, wascal*?'

'You look like a rabbit in headlights!'

Not one of them received a response. As if in a trance, Corny stared straight ahead and they all turned to follow its direction.

Sensing her cue, Olivia cleared her throat genteelly and nonchalantly entered the kitchen, her heels clicking on the flagstones.

Gretchen's chair scraped as she stood and offered it to Olivia.

'You like a plate, Mrs Olivia? Is plenty more food for you.'

'It's a funny thing, Gretchen, I couldn't manage a morsel. I find myself with a complete loss of appetite, so thank you but no.'

'Some toast? With honey? You like this. I make it for you.'

'Thank you. Gretchen. But no.'

'Did you have a good *west*, mummy?' enquired Harry.

'Yes, thank you, darling. It is always nice being back in one's own bed after having been away for a spell. I lay awake for hours some nights, wishing I was back home under my own roof.'

Miraculously, the noise that came from Gubsy was relatively tame and, fortunately, sounded like a mild release of wind.

'Sit down, mummy. I shan't speak French!' said Valentine.

'No thank you, Valentino. I have come to tell you and Horatio to join me in the dining room after supper and then we can have our much needed little talk.'

'What is this talk about, mummy?' asked Willy.

'Nothing that concerns you, darling. What a lovely looking little sausage you have there, darling, I think I might manage that one.' She picked up the sausage from Willy's plate and bit off one end with a quick snap of her teeth. 'I'll be waiting in the dining room, boys,' she said as she wagged the severed sausage at them, 'but please don't hurry; I am not going anywhere.'

She clicked across the flagstones back to the dining room and closed the door behind her.

Corny and the drinking glasses jumped when Gubsy thumped his fist on the table and Gretchen reached for both their hands. Willy's mouth had frozen into a small letter 'o' and Valentine tutted.

Putting his elbows on the table, Harry covered his face with his tanned hands and from behind them he said, 'It's enough to put you off your *gwub*!'

CHAPTER 4

The Ordains of Olivia

But for the glow that emanated from the candles in the gondola-shaped chandelier, the dining room was dark, yet the highly polished black lacquered dining table reflected the candlelight and illuminated Olivia's face to a startling degree. Whilst it hollowed out the sockets of her eyes, it lent an appearance of alabaster to her flawless skin that her tightly knotted chignon seemed to pull taut over her high forehead and razor-sharp cheekbones. Her lips were a thin horizontal slash of scarlet, and upon the arrival of Harry and Valentine, they stretched to form a smile that mirrored the toothy end of the curved six-foot crocodile mounted on the blood red wall above the vitrine of osteological articles behind her.

When the boys had taken their seats opposite, Olivia sucked two lungfuls of smoke from her cigarette, and eyed Harry with intent, as a cat might a canary. Lavender clouds escaped from her nostrils and, together with the tendrils of smoke from the cigarette, they climbed the rays of light up to the glittering gondola.

Caught in her gaze, Harry was visibly awkward, and just as Olivia opened her mouth to talk Valentine intercepted: 'How about fixing us some drinks, Harry? That would be nice, wouldn't it, mummy?'

Olivia raised her brows and drew in her cheeks, 'Very well. We shall drink but we must also talk. I'll have a gin and tonic, Horatio.'

'And I'd love a Grasshopper, Harry.'

'A Gwasshopper?'

'Yes, you know; crème de menthe, crème de cacao, milk and cream, lots of ice, all shook up, poured into a martini glass and garnished with a sprig of mint or grated nutmeg. I prefer the grated nutmeg, but whatever's easiest for you is fine by me.'

Harry looked defeated and Olivia narrowed her eyes at Valentine.

'Never heard of it, Valentine and I weally can't make something like that now. It's too fussy. You'll have to fix one yourself.' said Harry, as he poured Olivia a double gin.

'Gosh! He is slow on the uptake!' thought Valentine, 'I'm simply stalling mummy for him, but that said why can't anyone ever fix me a simple Grasshopper? Making it oneself extracts all the gloriousness from it.'

'I think you'll find that Valentine is procrastinating, darling.' said Olivia, frostily.

'Pwo-cwas-tinating?'

'I'm not, mummy, and I suppose a small sherry shall suffice, Harry.'

'One she-*wee* coming up!' said Harry, as he handed an increasingly impatient Olivia her drink.

'No, wait! Better make it a brandy, I think,' said Valentine, 'Yes, a brandy . . . On second thought . . . vodka, a White Russian. No, too complicated . . . just a Moscow Mule then . . . look, condensation on mummy's glass! She needs a coaster or it might damage the table. I *do* love this table . . . Actually, perhaps a whisky . . . Yes, yes. Whisky . . . Double . . . Neat . . . Just a little ice . . . well, not too little . . . and Scottish not American . . . whisky, I mean.'

Harry flurried about the sideboard, pouring from bottles, then pouring what he had just poured back into the bottles, searching for coasters, clinking the glasses until the right sort was found, and cracking the correct amount of ice.

Valentine could sense that Olivia was growing ever more irritated and realised that he could not hold her at bay forever. He wondered what it would take to push her that tiny inch too far.

Having fixed the drink, Harry put it on a coaster before Valentine who looked at it for a flash and said, 'Gosh! I dislike this glass, can you change it?'

Olivia's hand whizzed through the air with an audible *whoosh* and her palm slapped down hard on the lacquered table with an ear-splitting *whack*, which froze Harry and caused Valentine to feign shock and suppress a smile.

'Enough stupidity!' snarled Olivia, 'We have a critical issue to discuss!'

Harry had only just become alert to Valentine's ploy to stall their mother and realised the jig was up. He sat back down and resigned himself to what he was certain to come. 'What se*wious* matter, mummy?'

'Yes!' said Valentine, 'That's what I'd like to know!'

Olivia regained her poise, and patting her chignon back in place, she viewed her two eldest, inhaled and said, 'Well, you've already touched the issue, Horatio, when you said why you had to come home; due to lack of funds. That is part of the matter; money, and the lack of it.'

Harry emitted a doleful groan and he slumped in his chair as his long limbs went limp, whilst Valentine felt his rib-cage ache due to the imminent agony of being bored.

'This lack of money,' Olivia went on, 'presents many problems. It is one of the reasons why I too have had to return home instead of remaining with my friends abroad and trying to enjoy myself a little whilst bearing the life that the hand of fate has seen fit to deal me. The day after tomorrow I shall be a widow of exactly sixteen years and I can assure you the life of a widow is not an easy one but I endeavour to endure it.

'However, this is virtually impossible when the family faces the very serious prospect of penury, and at my age I should not be worried about such things. Therefore, I call upon the two of you, my two eldest, sons of Monty and heirs to the noble name of Avery-Stripe, to step up to the mark and remedy the situation before we find ourselves destitute. Further, I hasten to add, and with no small amount of regret, that the situation of finding ourselves financially challenged is but the mere tip of the berg.

'As your mother, I feel that it is my duty to remind you of the standing of our family, of its expectations of you, of what it means to be an Avery-Stripe and of the responsibilities entailed. You have certain requirements to fulfil. I know it can seem an intimidating undertaking for the onus to fall upon your young shoulders but I would also like to remind you of the family maxim, *Nil Desperandum*. In addition, you must remember all of your many admirable ancestors and of the heritage that they built for you so that you could hold your heads high and face the world and look it in the eye and say, "I am an Avery-Stripe! Who, pray tell, are you?" for you still bear the name despite it having lost some of its lustre, but here too is a matter that requires your immediate and devoted attention; to rebuild the past glory of the family as your father so greatly desired. He and I privileged you with the very best beginnings. It is now up to you to rise up and do what you know you must. The time has come for you to honour your father and our name, and before either of you start to question whether or no this is a task you are obliged to perform then let me put it to you in very firm and clear words the importance of *noblesse oblige*!'

Whilst giving her oration, Olivia had risen and journeyed a considerable distance, traversing the length of her side of the dining table. She had lost herself in her words and had forgotten she was addressing no more than two, for mentally she had been standing in a room crowded with a great number of people hanging on her every syllable.

'Did you compose that on the train?' asked Valentine in a disparaging tone.

'Of course not!' snapped Olivia. 'It did not need composing, it came from the heart!' and she tapped her left breast.

She sat back down and glared at them. 'You know that what I say is perfectly just, and both of you have always been aware of what is expected from you. I have allowed you to neglect your responsibilities and run riot, living the life of Riley for far too long. The hour has come for you to do as you are meant.'

'What exactly is it, mummy,' said Valentine slowly, 'that we are supposed to do?'

Harry raised his head, looked at him with bleary eyes, and mouthed the plea: 'Don't'.

'Must I spell it out?' Olivia sighed.

'Indubitably!' replied Valentine.

'I shall do so only when Harry sits up straight as an Avery-Stripe always ought.'

'Please, leave me out of this!' Harry groaned.

'Impossible!' gasped Olivia, 'You are *the* heir! It is your responsibility to continue the family line. That is how it works, no matter how many offspring the others may or may not make; the direct line is linked by the eldest!'

Harry produced from the depths of his being a sound of sheer frustration. His head suddenly swarmed with the unforgettable refrain that he used to have to repeat twice daily; 'Excelsior begat Ambwosius, Ambwosius begat Jewemiah, Jewemiah begat Montgomewy, Montgomewy begat Howatio.' As a teenager, it had driven him half mad as the words swam and looped around in his brain, both day and night.

It had been a regular occurrence for him to wake with a jolt in the small hours to discover his sheets were wet with his cold sweat and realise that he had woken himself by saying it aloud in his sleep. There was no way to escape it. The names ceased to be names, they turned into words with no meaning and these meaningless words soon mutated into strange sounds that haunted him still.

'Don't make such gruesome noises, darling, it is extraordinarily un-dignified. Now, look at me and pay attention,' Olivia ordered.

Lifting his tired head, Harry focused his bloodshot eyes on his mother.

'It is time for you to renounce your imagined nonage, Horatio; no one can stay a child forever. You must accept that you are now a young man and of the age when you should be seeking a suitable girl with whom to settle and fulfil the role left to you by your father.'

'But, mummy, I've had lots of te*ww*ibly nice girlf*w*iends, lots and lots, you even said so yourself, but they were never good enough for you, you f*w*ightened them all away!'

'I concur, you have had lots of *nice* girlfriends, however, not one of them possessed any redeeming qualities. You seem to think that any girl with a vacant head and fatuous face is acceptable but I cannot think of a single one that you have imposed upon us that has been anything other than exactly ineligible.'

'How can you say that, mummy? *W*achael was lovely. I loved her!'

'Rachael?'

'You know, mummy,' said Valentine, 'the one with the telephone.'

'Oh her! No, she was completely unacceptable. She couldn't do anything unless she was relaying her every movement on a mobile. Horrid, horrid invention!'

'Well, you liked C*w*istobel,' reasoned Harry.

'Oh no mummy didn't!' laughed Valentine, 'Mummy absolutely detested Cristobel! She once asked mummy if she had a spare thingamajig at breakfast. I don't know where you were, but mummy died!'

Olivia contorted her face grotesquely at the recollection.

'A spare thingamajig?' queried Harry, and he furrowed his brow.

'Yes, you know,' said Valentine, 'a thingy, a whatsit, a doodah . . . gosh!'

Harry grew progressively more puzzled the further his brother went on searching for the appropriate word, and Olivia's dismay mounted as Valentine's charades became more elaborate.

'Female paraphernalia,' he continued, ' . . . gosh! I don't know, it's not really my field and I'm not saying the proper name in mummy's presence. If you don't know what I mean then you know less about girls than I do. Anyway, mummy was aghast and put right off her kippers. She was furious!'

'Was that the morning C*w*istobel burst into my bed*w*oom in floods of tears then *w*an out of Chinche*w*o and I never saw her again?' Harry asked Olivia accusingly.

'I possess no idea,' she replied, 'I can barely keep track of your fleeting sweethearts as it is, let alone keep record of all of their little upsets. Anyway, you are diverting me from the point; it is imperative that you find a suitable one who will marry you and bear your progenies. I know that men can execute their part well into maturity but the sooner you start the more you will have. What is more, in order to attract the right sort you yourself must be the very sort that they will desire. I admit that you are good-looking but that is not all that matters. You must abandon the Himalayan jaunts, adventures in the Amazon and skiing sprees and so on, eradicate your name from Mad About the Boy's books because modelling really is *infra dignitatem*, and acquire a respectable vocation. A career in the city perhaps, or something medical or legal, so long as it is lucrative. The girl you need will want to marry a man of means. It is a simple *modus operandi* in three parts; the right sort of career equals the right sort of wife, add them together and then multiply – countlessly.'

Harry pushed back his chair and planted his elbows on his knees, buried his face in his hands and groaned.

'Gosh, mummy, it all sounds so very glacial!' said Valentine, 'That equation is so very heart chilling. I must say that I am not terribly sad that it doesn't pertain to the second-born because I'll never be any good at multiplication. In fact, from what I can remember of the Avery-Stripe rules and regulations, not much responsibility falls on the spare to the heir at all!'

'You are monumentally mistaken, Valentino. It is up to every child to repopulate the family, there can never be too many Avery-Stripes and it is what your father wanted. However, I am aware that you are indulging in practices of an alternative lifestyle and enjoying all of the trappings that go with it, progenies, sadly, not being one of them. I have many acquaintances on the continent who share your predilections but that has not prevented them from pairing off with eligible others of their sort who can provide for them, or from making a success of themselves in the worlds of theatre and fashion and interiors.'

'I see,' said Valentine, as he mocked contemplation. 'So, correct me if I am wrong, but you are telling me that I am exempt from the duties of reproduction because I am enjoying a homophilic existence. Though, as such I really ought to obtain a lot of currency by marrying well or by prancing about on stage, creating glorious evening gowns and throwing scatter cushions about the place.'

'Oh, Valentino, you do know how I so despise facetiousness,' withered Olivia.

'I am simply putting it in plain and simple terms, mummy, so as best to recognise what it is that you require from us both, and I think I do.'

'Good, darling, I am delighted. And what do you say?'

'Well, a great many words spring to mind, mummy, such as bourgeois and *mercenaire* and *arriviste*. And here's a another one you'll have heard of, 'snob', or as it is said in Latin, *sine nobilitate*, as I believe that translation to be particularly apropos to you. Another rather long one is megalo-maniac, but there I shall stop for I shouldn't like to offend anyone.'

'You forgot to say c*w*ackers,' said Harry.

'Verily!' replied Valentine.

'I fail to see how the two of you cannot comprehend the supreme urgency of the situation,' said Olivia.

'Oh, yes,' said Valentine, 'and what of this impending destitution and penury that you foresee in your crystal ball, mummy? I have heard of no such dire straits from Gubsy or Gretchen.'

'Gubsy, you must remember, is an old man and not conscious of the realities of modern life or of inflation,' said Olivia. 'He has no notion of the cost of things in today's world because he leaves the financial running of the household to Gretchen, and goodness only knows if she can be trusted. I am quite confident that from wherever it is that she hails she is most certainly of questionable stock. She does, after all, possess a singularly gypsy aspect and everybody knows that they are a light-fingered race.'

At this juncture Harry intervened and revealed an all too rarely glimpsed mettle that was buried deep inside him.

'Mummy! I will not hear a word said against G*w*etchen! I am appalled that you would even suggest something like that! I am ashamed to hear you talk about a woman who is like a . . . '

Harry faltered. Olivia was only too cognisant of which word was to follow and stopped him in his tracks with a glare and he surrendered without a struggle.

Witnessing Harry's miserable defeat stirred within Valentine a strong sensation of fraternal allegiance that he was unable to ignore.

'Gretchen is utterly honourable, mummy,' he said, 'and you know that to be true. If you really considered her untrustworthy then I cannot believe that you would have ever let her play any part in your beloved progenies' lives. And as for Gubsy, I think you sorely underestimate his judiciousness. He is still a man that possesses great power of mind. To insinuate that he is anything less than completely *compos mentis* is in my opinion inexcusably impertinent to the highest degree!'

Olivia was astonished to be spoken to in such a manner; it was not so much what Valentine had said as how he had said it, and she was unsure as to whether or no he was mocking her.

'And until the time that either Gubsy or Gretchen brings to my attention any financial difficulties, as I am certain that if there were any then they would, then I refuse to believe that any such thing exists and it is all just a fabrication on your part!'

Though grateful for the touching loyalty displayed by Valentine, the situation was becoming altogether rather too heated for Harry. He could not bear to listen to his mother and brother's caustic exchange for very much longer. He craved harmony and equilibrium, as he had experienced in the Himalayas where he had absorbed himself in the beliefs of Tibetan Buddhism. In an effort to recapture even just a taste of that tranquillity, he withdrew from the pocket of his jeans his lotus mala beads and sought solace in meditation.

'Are you accusing me of mendacity?' asked Olivia with severity. 'For I assure you that I do not possess a single deceptive bone in my body, and it distresses me to hear that you suspect that I might.'

'What I am accusing you of, mummy,' answered Valentine, 'is selfish motives.'

'Selfish motives!'

'Yes, you know, having reasons for behaving in a way that will be of benefit to no one but yourself.'

'I am perfectly aware what the term means, Valentino, however I would like you to explain how it applies to me!'

'Certainly, mummy, I simply mean that you only had the one big house to sell and you can spend the proceeds of a sale just the once. You seem subsequently to have discovered other ways and means but now find yourself so embarrassed that you have to suffer the Ritz, and it makes impeccable sense to you to command Harry and me to get well paid jobs of work so as to supplement your dwindling income!'

Olivia reeled in shock at the ghastly things that Valentine was saying, not just because they were ghastly but also because they were accurate. Somehow, he had neatly compressed almost every aspect of the past sixteen years of her life into two sentences. She was indeed in need of financial assistance, and had sometimes resorted to desperate actions, but this was something to which she simply would not ever admit. However, she felt that the real tragedy was the part he left out; she really did want to see Monty's dream of the resurrection of the Avery-Stripes' glory days brought to fruition. She would never feel atoned until she felt the prospect was set in motion and it galled her to realise that perhaps her children did not consider her aspiration bona fide.

'I absolutely refuse point blank to listen to another moment of your nonsensical imaginings, Valentino!'

'I do not consider what is perfectly palpable to be nonsensical imaginings, mummy!'

'All that is perfectly palpable, Valentino, is that the veracity of what I say is wholly evident, the family is in desperate need of a fresh injection of income. One only need look about the house a very short while to realise its stark state of disrepair.'

Valentine stopped to deliberate what Olivia had said and let his inner eye make a swift tour of Chinchero; the damp wall in the dining room, or maybe it was just constantly cold to the touch. There was the leak in the conservatory. The drawing-room ceiling had that disconcerting crevasse. Unknowing guests were always kicking the loose floor tiles in the entry hall out of place. One could no longer describe Gretchen's kitchen as fitted since most of the cupboard doors refused to shut properly. Gubsy's bedroom doorknob frequently came off in his hand and it took great efforts with a screwdriver on the other side to rescue him. The wallpaper in both Olivia and Corny's bedrooms was peeling rather dramatically and Willy had cracked glass in nearly all of her windows. The light switch in Harry's bedroom was hazardous, and when using the stairs that lead up to his own bedroom Valentine always had to be mindful of the third step if he did not wish his foot to penetrate an airing cupboard. There was a broken bidet, two lavatories had flushing issues, every bathroom had a severe case of mildew, and supposedly the rafters in the main roof were riddled with woodworm but no one dared go up there as the scuffling of little paws and scratching claws could often be heard coming from within. Now that he considered it, the list of defections seemed endless and he had to agree that what he had hitherto regarded as charming imperfections were, in fact, cause for concern.

'Yes, mummy, I admit that Chinchero has seen better days but I still think that it is for Gubsy to raise the subject if it is something that bothers him as it is his house, not yours, in fact much of the time you are not even here. Therefore, I remain strictly resolute in my conclusion that your motives are purely self-serving. Further, mummy, I find it intensely disturbing that you are so easily able to discuss so openly such matters as *money* and in a manner one might expect only from a true vulgarian, because it is jolly vulgar of you to suggest that I should marry for something as shallow as money. I feel it only fair to tell you now that if ever I do marry it will be because I am in love with a boy because he is beautiful and *not* because he is rich!'

'So, not only am I told that I am dishonest and selfish but I am also to be accused of vulgarianism! You are exceedingly fortunate that I am a woman of extreme tolerance and compassion; if your father were here today, he would thrash you to within an inch of your life for such malevolency and insolence. I also shudder to think what he would have made of such an epicurean son that laid claim to such aesthetic desires; he would be ashamed of you, and surely you cannot be so naïve as to think that marrying a person for their looks is in any way prudent?'

Valentine felt shocked to the core that his mummy would resort to such base tactics in their altercation; To suggest that his daddy would ever feel anything other than great love for him, or thrash him, was something that he refused to contemplate; he was his daddy's little popinjay.

'You're daddy's little popinjay', Monty would whisper in Valentine's ear as he bounced him on his sturdy corduroyed lap. Valentine had loved the stingo scent of the whispers that were so ticklish he would wriggle and squirm. Monty would tickle him all over his body, causing Valentine to laugh so much that on one occasion he had lost control of his bladder. Even then, Monty had not been cross with him. Valentine did not get a thrashing; all he had received was a playful smack on the bottom for being so naughty, and a fresh pair of pyjamas in exchange for his soiled ones. Monty would always tell Valentine that he looked like a royal prince in his pyjamas on the nights when, instead of the astringent Nanny Cook, it was daddy who put him to bed.

Valentine would hold clumps of his daddy's thick golden hair in his little fists as he watched with fascination the big fingers and thumbs fumbling to fasten the small buttons of his pyjama jacket: 'There we are little popinjay, you look like a royal prince ready for bed!'

Monty would throw him up into the air, catch him in his strong arms and spin him around the bedroom before tucking him up to the chin under the warm blankets. He would then switch on the nightlight and kiss Valentine on the forehead, and say, 'Sweet dreams, little popinjay'. On occasion, Monty might even stay the night because too much beer in his belly made him immobile, and those were the nights that Valentine enjoyed most of all.

Valentine looked up the word 'popinjay' in the dictionary a few years after Monty died, and upon discovering the definition, he concluded that if his daddy had loved him for those qualities then his love was irrefutable. Therefore, he felt that he had *carte blanche* to do whatever he wanted with his life, especially if what he wanted to do was to be a princely popinjay in pyjamas every single day.

'Daddy would not ever have thrashed me! He never laid a finger on me in anything other than love! And if what I am and what I want makes me an epicurean with aesthetic desires, what of it? I am confident beyond doubt that daddy would have approved. Besides which, I am not the first Avery-Stripe in possession of such a disposition. You are forgetting Millie Avery-Stripe.'

'The life of Maximilian Avery-Stripe is not one to be held in high esteem, Valentino!' said Olivia, desperately restraining herself from raising her voice, 'His dead body was found in an opium den in Shanghai.'

'Chengdu, actually, mummy, and that is not all that he did, he also happened to collect over three-hundred species of rare and exotic butterfly.'

'Oh, Valentino! You drive me to distraction! Yet again you are diverting; do you or do you not think there are things in a spouse that are more important than the way they look?'

'I should think that decent etiquette is a strong contender, but no, aesthetics are principal!'

'Your heterodoxy is heinous, Valentino!' snapped Olivia, 'I imagined you to possess some common sense!'

Valentine was horrified: 'Gosh! I possess common nothing, mummy!'

Under the table, Olivia dug her fingernails into her forearms. The room fell quiet as she and Valentine stopped to catch their breath. With locked horns and eyes, they evaluated their opponent before battle recommenced but the gradual sound of strange murmuring that grew more apparent diffused the intensity of the situation and they turned in bewilderment to its source.

Head bowed, Harry was slumped forward, giving the impression that all of the bones in his body had gone soft. He was systematically rotating his beads as he reiterated an unusual series of sounds.

'What on earth are you saying, Harry?' Olivia snapped, 'You look absurd! Sit up straight and stop being silly, this is a serious state of affairs!'

Harry fell silent and hesitated a moment before raising his head, and wearing a refreshed and somewhat dazed expression, he said, '*Om Mani padme hum*, is what I am saying, mummy. It's a mantwa that Buddhists chant when they meditate. It helps in stwessful situations and it's bwilliant. I love it.'

Olivia felt a hot rush of blood quickly rise to her head and she held her breath as if about to be pulled under.

'It certainly seems to have done the trick, Harry, you look to be as fresh as a daisy!' said Valentine, sincerely impressed with the metamorphosis.

'Thank you, Valentine,' smiled a flattered Harry. 'You are a good bwother.'

'Gosh! Thank you. So are you. We missed having you here, you know. It's not quite right with only three of us.'

'Thank you, Valentine. I missed you too.'

Having heard quite enough of the insipid intercourse between the brothers, Olivia interrupted with a demand to know whether or no Harry had absorbed all that she had taken great pains to say and what exactly he, being the eldest, intended to do about it.

'Yes, mummy, I heard evwy word.'

'Good.'

'But I'm afwaid that I can't help you. Not in the way that you want at any wate. You see, I weject western matewialism and am only intwested in the Bodhisattva Ideal, attaining enlightenment and finding nirvana for evwyone and ending the cycle of birth and webirth.'

Harry's religious revelation rendered Olivia speechless. She stared at him, unable to take in what he had said. She looked at him in disbelief. Surely he was joking and just teasing her but this was not like him at all. No one was as earnest as Harry.

Nevertheless, joking or no, it was transparent that she had been unsuccessful in conveying the crucial obligation of his position. She felt more deflated by his meek response, even if it did sound ridiculous to her, than she did by Valentine's maddening imperiousness.

Valentine himself found that his estimation of Harry had increased tenfold; by basing his rejection of their mother's demands on his newfound beliefs and a quest for personal spiritual development, Harry had, in Valentine's opinion, executed a masterstroke of pure genius. It also had the added gratification of baffling, as well as silencing, her.

'Ha-ha, Harry! And how does your eating scrummy sausages fit in with your new beliefs?' tested Valentine, unable to resist playing devil's advocate.

Upon hearing the question, Olivia's ears pricked up. Perhaps Valentine had found a thread for her to pull, and thus unravel Harry's cover and she looked at him expectantly.

'If meat is what is on the table it would be wude to wefuse and would not benefit the animal as it is alweady dead. To weject hospitality is an offence,' he answered, matter-of-factly.

'Gosh! They do sound a civilised bunch!' said Valentine, 'Just think of all of those dogmatic vegetarians out there who choose to be so purely for the sake of being a nuisance and not because of any religious convictions. They should all convert to the Bodhisattva Ideal and then we wouldn't have to worry about what to put on their plates! I am so happy that the sect you have chosen to join is one so aware of the necessity of both decent manners and of meat-eating. Aren't you, mummy?'

Although as pro-etiquette and anti-vegetarianism as Valentine, Olivia did not feel joy over Harry still being able to enjoy a roast, even if he only could do so out of politeness.

She was simply overwhelmed by her sons' evasions of her requisitions and asked herself how she would ever be able to honour Monty's wishes when their two eldest amounted to nothing more than a twit and a pansy, leaving her with the two youngest who were little better than a frump and a mute. She reasoned that there had to be a resolution to the predicament, but for the time being she felt too fatigued to do anything other than admit temporary defeat and dismiss Harry and Valentine, for she felt unable to persevere in the face of their puerility.

Eyes screwed shut, she said: 'It is unarguably apparent that our conversation is getting us nowhere tonight. It would be fruitless for us to try to make any progress with it when we are all so incredibly tired. Please vacate the room immediately.'

Olivia's surrender filled Harry with relief, and Valentine felt victorious, he had hoped that her return would have been a happy occasion as her presence was best described as patchy. However, these sporadic appearances were precisely why he refused to have her dictate his life, and he felt perfectly just in making his stand despite the wretchedness of having to do so.

'Good night, mummy,' he said, and he rose.

'Good night, Valentine,' she replied, eyes still screwed, 'And good night, Harry. I am certain that you are exhausted after such a long journey.'

'I *weally* am, mummy, I know I shall sleep like a log and I have to be up at the *cwack* because Cosmo is coming *vewy* early.'

Olivia's lids flipped open, and Valentine froze in the doorway. He dropped his arms theatrically, gasped and expelled, 'Gosh! Really not? Not that Neanderthal! But why and whatever for? *Must* he?'

Harry was genuinely confused at Valentine's reaction. He was unable to understand how anybody could dislike somebody that he liked. In fact, he had difficulty in grasping why it was not possible for everybody to get on amicably.

'But, Valentine,' he reasoned, 'you like him *w*eally, I *w*emember you laughing at some of his jokes so you must like him a bit.'

'I certainly was not laughing at his jokes; I was laughing at him! That does not mean I like him! He is an out-and-out oaf and he eats like a hog!'

Harry looked as if he had taken this as a personal slight and pushed out his lower lip.

Olivia had quietly absorbed the unpleasant news that fairly eclipsed what had been troubling her a minute earlier. She had her own reasons to be just as unhappy with Harry's announcement as Valentine did, more so in fact, but she said to him, 'We mustn't be derisive of family, no matter how distantly related they are. Blood is blood and kin is kin.'

'Vastly distantly related, mummy,' exclaimed Valentine, 'the only ancestors we share with him are Excelsior and Olympia. He is to us the equivalent of what a chimpanzee is to a human. Worse even, because he is an Oxley-Stockman, and none of the Avery-Stripes proper have ever thought highly of the Oxley-Stockmans!'

'I do,' said Harry, 'and you get on *w*eally *w*ather well with Flick,' he reminded him.

Valentine tutted. 'Out of the lot of them she is the only one that is occasionally palatable, but even she is a dipso-nympho, and they all have those ridiculously small heads!'

'*W*eally? I've never noticed they all have *w*idiculously small heads, you are just being *w*ude.'

'Actually, Harry,' said Olivia, 'Valentine's observation is accurate. I too have noticed it; just look at the photographs and paintings and you will see for yourself that they each possess alarmingly undersized craniums.'

Harry was confused and began to wonder if the two of them were telling the truth and not just pulling his leg, for he did have a rather gullible nature.

'Disturbingly miniscule!' exclaimed Valentine.

'Yes,' said Olivia, 'and their backs are hunched.'

'Gosh, mummy! It is true! They are! They are not chimpanzees, they are gorillas!' said Valentine, and mother and son looked to each other and, unable to contain themselves, they burst into fits of laughter over their relations' abnormalities. Olivia then pointed out that the Oxley-Stockmans seemed also to have incredibly short and spindly legs, and their laughter became hysterical.

After applying some thorough deliberation, Harry could see that what they were saying was not without foundation. The Oxley-Stockmans did appear to be guilty of these physical misdemeanours, all except the last. Harry was keen to point out that they were not all quite so deformed, and said, 'No, only Esmé has all of those att*w*ibutes, the others' legs are normal.'

The mention of Esmé Oxley-Stockman had a sobering effect on Olivia and Valentine, for they considered her excruciating, and their laughter came to an abrupt end.

'Yes, you are quite correct, Harry, only she has such legs,' said Olivia, 'but as I was saying, there are more important things than one's appearance and I for one shall be only too happy to welcome Cosmo to Chinchero. For how long will he be staying?'

'*W*eally not sure, mummy, he's actually coming to collect his f*w*iend *W*upert at Heath*w*o, he is flying in f*w*om Af*w*ica. I've not met him, but Cosmo says he is g*w*eat so I said they can c*w*ash on a couple of matt*w*esses on my floor for as long as they like. I have checked it with Gubsy and he says it is all *w*ight because there are al*w*eady too many people in the house anyway.'

Valentine was distressed to hear that there would be two of them. He was sure that the unknown Rupert would be as beastly as Cosmo, and the worst of it was that they were to stay for an indefinite period. How could Gubsy have agreed to it?

'It's all arranged then. How lovely!' said Olivia, masking her real feelings behind her crocodilian smile. 'It is a sorry shame that I have to be out most of the day tomorrow, and I am not certain if I will be returning until quite late but I am positive that I shall have the pleasure of seeing darling Cosmo and meeting his exotic sounding friend soon enough.'

'Well I shan't be running away anywhere!' said Valentine. 'Chinchero is my home and I'm not going to be pushed out of it by a pair of dis-agreeables. I shall go about my business in my usual manner and hope that their presence will not inflict too much on my existence!'

With that, he span on his heels and made his offended departure from the dining room and all of its unpleasantness as hastily as he was able. He did not notice Willy curled up in a not very small ball behind the globe drinks' cabinet in the drawing room.

CHAPTER 5

The Magpie Quartet

Although Valentine's small turret bedroom was on the uppermost level of Chinchero and he always slept with his head deeply ensconced in a mass of cushions with the blankets pulled right over, he could not believe that anybody could sleep through the rowdy arrival of Cosmo and his friend.

He listened to them grapple in the gravel with Harry as they performed the rough-and-tumble play fight that seemed to be a mandatory ritual for some boys when greeting one another, and he tutted. He did not have to dig himself out from his violet scented sheets and consult the clock to know it was still far too early to contemplate daylight, and was glad when the boys went inside and simmered down so he could enjoy a few more hours dreaming.

Valentine's dreams were eventually brought to a rude end by the caco-phonous cawing of a murder of magpies that had congregated on his roof, but he did not mind this noise quite so much as the one made by the boys for he felt an affinity for the debonair bird that had a penchant for shiny trinkets. He wondered how many were up there and had a fancy that it was four, and this happy promise made him feel ready to surface to the land of the living.

The first part of him to emerge from the depths was his delicate hand as it groped its way around the disarray of bric-à-brac that had pleased his eye sufficiently to have the honour of living on his bedside table. His hand finally found the large hexagonal box it sought and he flicked the switch at its base. After a few moments of clicks and whirrs, the top of the box retracted and a precious pirouetting ballerina slowly emerged and proceeded to rotate to the accompaniment of a tinny rendition of Tchaikovsky's *Dance of the Sugar Plum Fairy*. Having set his scene's music in motion, Valentine slowly pushed away his blankets, theatrically stifled an exaggerated yawn and languorously stretched the kinks from his limbs.

Unseeingly, because of the black silk scarf that he wore as a blindfold to outwit all peeps of light, he reached for a violet cream from a porcelain dish on his bedside, popped it in his mouth, crushed it between his molars and used his tongue to rub it all about his teeth and gums, for it was

70

infinitely nicer than toothpaste. Only then did he remove the blindfold and open his eyes to the glorious day.

The summer sky was cloudless and cyan, the sun shone magnificently and dazzled through grandmother Araminta's vast collection of Murano glass ornaments that Valentine had claimed and positioned on high shelves all along his windows, and it filled his room with a mass of brilliant colour. He gasped with delight as he marvelled at the spectacle, as if it were new to him, and decided that not even Cosmo could impair such a day, but that still did not dissuade him from his plan of snubbing.

He heard the front door slam, followed by a haphazard crunching of gravel and the squeak of the bicycle shed door, he jumped out of bed to see who it might be and hoped that it was Cosmo departing.

The view from Valentine's bedroom window provided him with a grand vista, and employing a pair of antique mother-of-pearl opera glasses, he espied, between Araminta's ornaments, Corny getting out his fire engine-red bicycle. Valentine watched him wheel it to the front gate then set it down and open the gate, cycle through, get off, put it down again, close the gate, get back on and whizz down the Avenue.

Good old Corny, off in a hurry to spend his pocket money, laughed Valentine, and began to waltz about his room with an imaginary partner to the *Dance of the Sugar Plum Fairy*. He sashayed and whirled faster and faster until his universe became a kaleidoscopic blur of coloured glass, sunshine, and the butterfly corpses of great uncle Millie's collection with which Valentine had adorned his walls. The music came to a gradual end and he was somewhat relieved, for the early exertion inflicted a rather nauseating effect on him. He heard the slam of the front door once more and leapt to the window to observe through the opera glasses his mother wearing a colossal pair of sunglasses, and hooked in her crook was the ever-present crocodile Birkin. Valentine wondered if her swift clicking stride down the garden path was because she was late for something or because she had meant to escape from the house hours ago and had found herself having to interact with Cosmo.

Valentine recoiled at the notion and then he removed his Tricolore pyjamas. Wearing not a stitch, he decided his face was in no serious need of a shave and that it was too lovely a day to suffer the toil of towelling after bathing, so he chose instead the easy option of a full body spray of violet scent. Then, because it was a day for simplicity and not one that called for the complication of stripes, he dressed himself in a patternless pair of freshly laundered and pressed pale pink pyjamas, and with some violet pomade, he dressed his hair into the style of his namesake; Rudolph Valentino.

Admiring his reflection in the toothy ferro (which, upon discovering it in the cellar, he had originally thought to be a particularly lethal sword until regarding the bow of the gondola chandelier) Valentine believed his ablutions adequate and attire appropriate, and felt prepared for anything that might happen. He took a fancy to the large conch shell on his bookshelf, held it to his ear, heard the sound of faraway seas and believed it to be the perfect companion for the day.

He took care to avoid the third step when descending the stairs and strummed his fingers across the strings of Olympia's gold harp that he met on the landing. Out on the west terrace, stood Gretchen wearing a sombrero and, with secateurs, she was painstakingly pruning the abundant wisteria. Valentine was glad because it meant that the coast was clear to find something enjoyable to eat.

The ruckus and pungent odour of illegal substances that emanated from Harry's room prompted him to hasten to the kitchen where, upon arrival, he invaded the larder. Its floor was ice cold beneath his bare feet and he rummaged about in search of cake and was happy to find a marmalade one in an old biscuit tin. He set it down on the table and unleashed a spectacularly evil-looking knife, which he pretended to slice across his slender neck and he laughed quietly to himself as he cut an eighth of cake and devoured it. In the refrigerator, he made the pleasant discovery of a half-full bottle of champagne, he extracted the silver spoon, raised the bottle to his lips and let the lovely bubbles dance down his throat and fizz up his nose, more than thrice. He wiped his mouth with the back of his hand that still held the fierce knife, licked his lips, and startled when the Bakelite telephone bell rang.

Tutting at his jumpiness, he amused himself by not answering the telephone and instead, picked up the conch that he had placed next to it. He held the conch to his ear and said hello, enquired who it was that was calling, and laughed again. The telephone bell, however, was persistent, and he felt he had to give in to its demands though to do such a thing was an anathema to all in his family. He rolled up his pyjama sleeve, lifted the receiver in a no-nonsense manner and spoke into it.

The caller was Geraldine Strap, mother of Agatha, wanting to talk to Mrs Avery-Stripe about the wickedness of Wilhelmina. Valentine promptly asked if she could please hold and that he would see if his mother was at home. He placed the receiver on its side and called out for his mummy, opened and then closed the kitchen door, waited a space, opened and closed it again, and retrieved the receiver.

'Yes, hello, who is it?' Valentine clipped, in Olivia's voice. 'Ah, yes. Mrs Strap. I was wondering when I would be hearing from you as the strength of an apology lessens the longer it is left, and I feel quite certain that if left too late they cannot be considered kosher.'

Valentine held the knife and used it as a looking glass in which to inspect his teeth as he smiled at his mischief. 'Yes, yes. It comes as no surprise to me to hear that Agatha is unwell, Mrs Strap. I am quite confident that had I been as venomous as your daughter seems able, then I too would be feeling sick with shame and feverish with remorse. However, I dread to think of what further disgrace a young lady might inflict upon her family without the deterrence of penitence.'

As he listened to Mrs Strap's warble start to heighten, he used the knife to create a thin dancing slash of bright light on the kitchen cupboards by deflecting the rays of sun that were bursting through the window. 'Yes, indeed. I do consider it savage behaviour, but please do let me assure you that Wilhelmina is quite beside herself with the trauma of having been pushed to it. I believe that it is of some comfort to her when I put it that her reaction was nothing less than perfectly natural, for no one of any honour would tolerate hearing someone acid-tongue one's family. In fact, it has taken me many hours of handholding and tear-wiping to convince her that any person of pedigree would deem her retaliation as utterly unerring; for when one encounters such a filthy mouth one cannot help but feel that it deserves to receive a thorough washing out with soap. If, however, there is no cake of soap at hand one makes the most of what is, and if that happens to be manure, then so be it. Morally objectionable language merits such punishment!'

He accentuated his exclamation by holding aloft the knife and thrusting it down with a violent stab into a stack of cork placemats, where it remained erect upon being relinquished. The volume of Geraldine Strap's rejoinder was so ear-splittingly shrill that Valentine had to hold the receiver at arm's length. It was then that he noticed that Willy had come into the kitchen through the backdoor; he did not know for how long she had been present but her wide smile told him it had been long enough.

He put his finger to his lips to ensure she stayed shushed and then beckoned her over so they could share the pleasure of hearing the torrent of language that ranted from the receiver. Skulls conjoined, Valentine and Willy suffocated their giggles with their palms, but Mrs Strap's crossness soon became monotonous. Yet, before boredom consumed the siblings, the tantrum tapered and Valentine resumed his role.

'Am I to understand, Geraldine, for I feel that I may refer to you by your Christian name now that you have broken the ice of our acquaintance with such scurrilous vocabulary; am I to understand that you do not find yourself able to apologise for your daughter's misconduct?'

At which point, Willy snorted into her hand and Valentine flapped his wrist at her. 'Oh dear. I must admit, Geraldine, that I am most disappointed. I always feel that almost any quarrel can be resolved if one is fortunate enough to be dealing with persons of civility. Oh dear. This is indeed distressing. I am sorry to say to you that I do not feel capable of continuing to converse with a character so lacking in the consideration of others.'

Another piercing earful of unpleasantries volleyed out into the kitchen and forced Valentine to interrupt: 'All that remains for me to say is goodbye, Geraldine. I sincerely hope that you never feel the need to communicate with me again unless you miraculously manage to employ a decent sense of decorum. Further, may I suggest that until that happy day arrives you lie down in a dark room somewhere silent, for I fear you sound as if you are about to give yourself a hiatus hernia.' And without further ado, he replaced the receiver in its cradle and it went *pling*.

'Horrid thing!' said Valentine, in his own voice again. 'I do so hate talking on the telephone!'

Before he knew what was happening, Valentine had the wind pushed out of him by Willy's ursine embrace that was so enthusiastic, it lifted him to the tips of his toes.

'Oh, Valentine, you are wonderful!' and she rubbed, with affection, her cheek against his chest.

He used his fingers to try to prize her strong arms from his diaphragm for he felt on the verge of asphyxia.

'Let go, Willy,' he wheezed, 'you are breaking my skeleton!'

Willy released him. He steadied himself by gripping the back of a chair, and recaptured his breath. 'Aren't you glad you didn't carry out your threats of Chinese burns now,' he said, smoothing out the creases from his pyjama jacket.

'I should jolly well say so! I admit I wasn't certain you'd keep your end up but that was silly of me. You are an utter trump, and I don't think she will ever telephone again after the lashing you had mummy give her!'

'It was rather whippy I suppose? But that's how mummy talks so I wasn't being altogether too fraudulent, was I?'

'It's how you talk as well sometimes, Valentine, and the way you do her voice and hold yourself just like her is quite scary. Oh! If mummy knew!'

Roars of laughter came from the floor above and Valentine tutted.

'Have you seen them yet?' he asked, and jabbed the uncorked knife in the direction of his displeasure.

'Oh no, not yet. Gretchen said they went to Harry's room directly after their arrival and haven't peeked out even once,' said Willy, with no small sense of disappointment, for she was very keen to see Cosmo, whom she secretly regarded as an absolute dreamboat.

It did not take Valentine much to deduct that the cause of the piquant perfume that permeated from Harry's room was also the cause for the boys' concealment and, that too, of their laughter. He was just about to illuminate Willy when he noticed that her appearance was somewhat awry and her cheeks most markedly dappled with varying shades of blush.

'I say, Willy, that's a pretty *dress* you have on,' and he ruffled her lilac puff sleeves that were dotted with posies of peonies. 'Where ever did you find it, and why are you wearing it?'

'You're not the only person who goes down to the cellar, you know!' answered Willy, defensively. 'And if you didn't know, it is a scorcher of a day and . . . this is a very light material practical for work in the garden when it is so hot and you sweat buckets!'

The thought of sweaty garden workers filled Valentine's head with visuals that did not include his sister or anyone else of her gender. His imaginings did not last very long however because his eyes fell upon the trug of Sweet Williams that appeared to be the only evidence of Willy's toils in the garden. He was on the precipice of pointing this out when the upstairs rumpus was heard to escape onto the landing, and the sound of six heavy feet bounding down the stairwell saved Willy from any further interrogation. Her face lit up and Valentine leapt into the larder, pulled the door to, leaving it ever so slightly ajar, and found himself eyeball to eyeball with a skinned rabbit.

'Hello, rabbit,' whispered Valentine, 'I didn't see you here before. You look delicious,' and then he remembered why they would be eating rabbit the next day. He pushed this thought from his mind and strained to hear the conversation between Willy and the boys in the hall but to no avail.

They seemed to talk for an inordinate length of time, and Valentine felt his feet start to hurt with the cold of the floor. Just as he realised that it was ludicrous to be lurking in the larder with a dead rabbit and an immense knife and that he was not going about his day regardless, the boys went into the drawing room and Willy returned to the kitchen and called his name. He pushed open the door and stepped out onto the sun-warmed flagstones and the pleasure this provided caused him almost to swoon.

'Valentine, what were you doing in there?'

'Seeing to things! What are the boys doing?'

'They're going to have a game of cricket in the garden and I think I will watch them. Do you want to?' Willy asked, barely able to contain her excitement.

'I can't think of anything more dismal!'

'Oh well, see you later, and thanks so much for taking that call. I owe you a favour,' and she skipped gracelessly out of the kitchen.

'Wait!' he called after her, 'You haven't asked what mummy's serious talk was about. Don't you want to know?'

'Oh no, not really,' Willy sang over her shoulder, 'I'm certain it's nothing that concerns me!'

Alone again, Valentine was bothered because he had planned on spending time in the garden, but now that it contained three boys hitting a ball about, he had to reconsider. He decided that the side-garden, accessible from the back door and quite separate from the main garden would do just as well. He would lie in the shade of the pair of Conference pear trees and have some more marmalade cake and a pot of tea.

Realising that Gretchen was certain to soon return to her kitchen, he set to work and took out his favourite crockery, the one with the geishas, and put it on a silver salver along with his conch. Boiling water and cutting cake was the height of Valentine's culinary ability, but it was not long before he was out in the side-garden and had established himself on the luscious green grass. He filled his mouth with cake, and stretched out supine. The sun pushed through the branches of the pear trees and poked him in the eyes, forcing him to roll over onto his front. He poured himself a cup of earl grey, dropped in three lumps of sugar, stirred it with a silver spoon that made a delightful *tinkle*, blew delicately on it and then sipped. Now a dandelion caught his eye, and he plucked it to appreciate its beauty at close range.

'Poor thing. So pretty. Yet they say you are a weed. Such a glorious yellow though! At least they have dignified you with a decent name, *dente-de-lion*, teeth of lion. ROAR! Quite a regal ring when you reflect.'

He twirled the stem in his fingers, and discovered, under its head, a ladybird, and he gasped, 'Dear little ladybird!'

He sat up, persuaded the insect onto his palm and tossed the dandelion onto the salver.

'One, two, three, four, five spots. You are five years old! Dear lovely little ladybird.'

Presently, he felt a tiny sharp sting and realised that the ladybird had bitten him, and he gasped again. He was outraged that she should bite him when he had been saying such nice things. He raised his other hand and clapped to crush her. The horrid mess this created made him feel quite ill and he wiped his palms on the grass to rid himself of it.

'Unpleasant beast!' he said, and he took a gigantic bite of cake and rendered himself recumbent again.

The dots of sun through the branches of the pear trees were still too bright for him to look for long at the cyan sky so he screwed his eyes. To his annoyance, he realised that in so doing he heightened his other senses and consequently accentuated the noise of boys' thwacks of leather against willow. With a tut and a moue, he reached for his conch and held it to his ear, blocking his other with a finger. Thus, he could imagine he had washed ashore after a frightful storm and he the only survivor of a shipwreck.

It was an exotic island, with the most tropical flora and peculiar fauna and perhaps a volcano, yes a smoking volcano, and a majestic waterfall too. The natives were few but immensely strong and disarmingly beautiful and exclusively male. They wore bones through their noses and little grass skirts that barely served their purpose, and spent their days diving for oysters for supper and pearls. They would all think Valentine a wonder with his milky skin and verdant eyes, and would proclaim him King of the island, no; Emperor was nobler.

He did not yet know of his fate, as he was still semi-unconscious amongst the jetsam. Slowly though, the blazing sun colouring the insides of his lids coral, and the crash of waves upon the shore, were reviving him, and in a moment he would lift his lids to discover his new situation.

'What has happened to me?' he thought to himself. 'Gosh! I feel wretchedly achy and why has the handsome tea clipper ceased to rock and sway on the ocean wave, and why is it that I cannot hear the flap and billow of silky sailcloth yet I can still hear the briny sea. Whatever can have happened to me? This is most curious. I must slowly open my eyes and orientate myself to my predicament.'

Upon doing so, all he could see was the wide expanse of sky marred only by a few boughs of a rather tall and unusual plant that produced a mysterious fruit that the people indigenous to the island had named pear.

As he played the game of gazing up and studying with astonishment the oddness of this foreign vegetation, he was once again agitated by the sun and, all of a sudden, he became aware of a little dot that was hurtling toward him from a very great height. It came at him at such velocity that he did not have time to contemplate moving let alone physically doing it. Which was just as well because the little dot that fast grew into a normal sized cricket ball hit the grass with a loud *tock* just to the right of his head, bounced over it and ended its journey with a crash in his crockery. The pear tree branches that had been disturbed by the plummeting ball shed some of its embryonic produce, they plopped to the ground and bruised themselves, and foliage fluttered close behind.

A leaf landed on Valentine's nose as gently as a kiss and it was this, as well as the echoes of smashing china, that brought him out of his daze. He sat bolt upright and his eyes widened with horror as he surveyed the damage done. The salver was swamped with earl grey, and his teacup had cracked into two perfect halves, as had its saucer, and the matching teapot had been de-spouted. The devastation stunned him senseless. He felt too traumatised to consider what his immediate reaction should be and the shock had so slackened his jaw that he could not manage even the tiniest tut.

If, however, the sight of the disaster was proving too much for his senses to digest then what he was to see next would be enough to dynamite him into a state of sensory overload because presently he became conscious of a large pair of bare feet planted next to the swamped salver. His eyes travelled up the length of two powerful legs and over the muscular torso and strong arms that led up to a set of broad shoulders and thick neck, and then they settled upon the most overwhelmingly beauteous face that they had ever encountered.

The stranger was staggeringly beautiful to Valentine, for he was the embodiment of all the physical attributes that he considered necessary to create the ideal image of man. He was Adonis, he was David, Apollo, and Antonius of Bithynia, and he was so positively pulsating with rude health that it was almost an offence. He looked to Valentine exactly like one of Il Duce's fascist athletes in the Stadio Dei Marmi, made human; his skin was caramel, his eyes were forget-me-not and his hair was the colour of highly polished gold. Valentine's mind was instantaneously devoid of any distress; he felt his heart swell and his entire being sang out with the purest and most magnificent, all consuming, quixotic love.

He was so awestruck that he could not at first gauge where this beatific vision of exquisiteness had appeared from; it was as if he had descended from the heavens inside a cricket ball. Valentine was able to do nothing but look up at him in adulation and gasp, 'Gosh!'

The object of his admiration rewarded him with a magnificent grin, hunkered down on his haunches, and fingered Valentine's china. He looked with consternation at the ball in the breakages and said, 'Crikey! I'm sorry; it's my fault. Cosmo's bowling and I'm batting and hit the ball too hard. We all watched it fly over and heard the crash. Harry's fielding but said it was my hit so I should fetch it.'

Valentine heard all of the words but did not listen to them; he was too busy concentrating on the movement of the beauty's lips and the proximity of his body.

'I'll glue it,' said Beauty.

'What?' asked a love-struck Valentine.

'The broken china. I'll superglue it.'

Valentine looked at the half of delicate teacup that Beauty held gingerly by the handle with his thick fingers. 'Only if you let me watch you,' he cooed and reached up, stroked Beauty's hair and looked deep into his eyes.

Beauty bestowed him with another grin and then, upon seeing the conch, he grabbed it and looked at it in amazement.

'Crikey! I've not seen one of these in a long time,' he said, examining the shell whilst letting Valentine play with a lock of his hair. Then, much to Valentine's dismay, Beauty jumped to his feet and said, 'Let's see if I can still do it.'

Beauty raised the conch to his puckered mouth and produced a high-pitched trumpet sound not unlike that of an elephant call. It resonated through Valentine, thundered into him, and he saw Beauty metamorphose into the merman god Triton rising up out of the Aegean with a mass of salty spray and creating huge walls of waves with his oceanic horn. Valentine felt overcome with exuberance, and it was all that he could do not to lose consciousness.

Grinning, Beauty had the conch turn a somersault in the air and caught it. 'Learned that in Hawaii, ' he informed Valentine.

Valentine stretched out his arms to him. 'It was unspeakably heavenly!' he exclaimed, and waggled his hands to signal he required assistance to rise.

Beauty complied with what Valentine considered the utmost gallantry, and his spirits soared to even greater heights with the realisation that

Beauty was also a gentleman. Not letting go of Beauty's hand, he asked how he had managed to produce such a glorious sound: 'I have seen it in pictures and read about it in mythology, but did not know it could actually be done!'

'You have to make a little hole in it, like this one. Can you see?' said Beauty, and he raised the conch closer to Valentine's face.

'Gosh! Yes, I see! Still, I am not certain that I could manage it. It looks a very strenuous thing to do, and I am not as strong as you look to be.'

The arrival of Harry, Willy and Cosmo interrupted Valentine's coquetry. They came jogging around the corner from the main garden to investigate what had given cause to such an alien sound. Willy rolled her eyes at the inevitability of the scene. She could not have predicted in precise detail that they would find Valentine and Rupert standing hand in hand under the pear trees and inspecting a giant white shell together, but she knew Valentine's tastes and she knew his ambition. Cosmo scoffed and Harry looked somewhat perturbed but chose to ignore it.

'Did you hear that incwedible noise?' he asked.

'Yes!' said Valentine, with pride, as he beamed at Beauty, 'He was blowing my conch! Did you ever know that it really could be done and not just in books?'

Cosmo stepped forward and used the cricket bat to separate the joined hands. He sneered at Valentine who looked at Cosmo's shrunken head with feelings of contempt. He observed that Cosmo's monobrow seemed to have increased in density as if to compensate for the premature absence of hair on his undersized scalp. His ears looked to have grown even more cauliflowered since last he had seen him and the general aspect was that of a hunky caveman dragging his knuckles in the dirt.

Valentine was at a total loss as to how Harry, so good-looking, and Beauty, so beauteous, could associate with one so abhorrent to regard, even if his every pore did exude a feral masculinity that he knew those lacking in refinement sometimes considered to be alluring. He was disturbed to reflect that Willy was one of those incomprehensible people.

Beast said to Beauty, 'I see you've met my pansy cousin Valentine then.'

Rupert turned to Valentine smiled and, in a mellow tone, said, 'Hello, Cousin Valentine, I'm Rupert Bringsley-Beer.'

Valentine responded with an excited gasp and the exclamations, 'Hello, Rupert Bringsley-Beer! I am so happy to meet you! I am not his cousin! I do not even like him! But I *love* you!'

Rupert's cheeks dimpled with amusement.

'Oh, Valentine!' whined Harry, and Willy sniggered.

Defiantly unflustered, Cosmo picked up the tea-soaked cricket ball, dried it on his shorts, and said they had a game to be getting on with.

'Better find yourself a different fox to hound,' he whispered to Valentine giving him a brutish slap on the back, 'C'mon chaps!' and he flung the cricket bat on his shoulder and stalked off back to the main garden with Harry close behind.

Valentine was distraught at the thought of losing sight of Rupert. He could of course watch him play cricket, but that would mean a compromise with Cosmo, and Valentine was adverse to that idea. He reached out for Rupert's hand but realised that it was in vain; Rupert was Cosmo's friend and looked the sort to need to be doing something that required physical effort. Valentine resented that he had hardly been given adequate time in which to sufficiently enmesh Rupert.

Rupert looked at him with an expression that suggested a reluctance to continue cricketing but Valentine supposed that it was done so only out of courtesy.

'Why don't you come and watch with Willy? Or we can make two teams and you can play with me,' offered Rupert, for he considered getting to know Valentine a bit better to be something he would quite like to do.

'I'll play too!' interjected Willy.

The notion of playing with Rupert entertained Valentine for a flash but then the crushing dilemma crashed on in and he again wished for a way to wheedle a more satisfactory Saturday afternoon.

The answer to Valentine's wishes arrived in the form of Corny rushing in through the side gate and stumbling to his knees. He was positively rapturous, there was chocolate or toffee or both smeared on the area around his mouth, and he was flourishing a flier. Valentine took it from him and learned that that very day the local community was holding its annual summer fête on the Green. Lots of lovely things seemed to be going on there; arts and crafts stands, a white elephant stall, a tombola, fairground rides, Punch and Judy, a steel drum band, a fancy dress parade, a beer tent, Pimm's and strawberry and cream teas.

Perfect! thought Valentine.

'Gosh! What fun!' he said to Rupert and Willy, who had been reading the flier over his shoulders. 'But why aren't you still there, Corny?'

Corny pulled a theatrically sad face, pushed his hands deep into his pockets and then withdrew them, turning his pockets completely inside out to demonstrate that he possessed nothing but lint and a pathetic looking lollipop.

'Gosh! Pocket money all gone?'

Corny replied with a melodramatic nod.

'C'mon, Rupert! What's the delay? Valentine won't and can't play cricket and we need you,' hollered Cosmo, as he and Harry re-entered the side-garden.

'Change of plan, Cosmo,' said Valentine. 'We are all going to this,' and he presented him with the flier.

Cosmo snorted disparagingly, 'A fête! Do you want to go to a bloody suburban fête, Rupert?'

'Might be good, there are rides,' answered Rupert, in what was fast becoming apparent to Valentine, his customary easygoing manner.

Harry was aware of Corny's longing to return to the fun of the fête and he felt that he really should live up to the role of big brother especially as he was so reluctant to fulfil the one of son and heir. 'And there's a beer tent,' he pointed out.

Unconvinced, Cosmo realised that Willy was his only prospective ally. 'What about you?' he said to her, 'It looks like it's for children and old people. Do you think we should go?'

'Of course Willy wants to go!' interrupted Valentine, 'She always wants to go to the summer fête. Why else would she be wearing such a pretty dress? For you, do you suppose? Willy loves the summer fête and looks forward to it every year, don't you, Willy?' and he made eyes at her to remind her of the favour she owed.

Feeling rather bulldozed, but also fearing the possibility of the awkward alternative of staying home alone with Cosmo; a situation which would undoubtedly render her inarticulate with romantic yearning, Willy mustered as much enthusiasm as she was able, and said, 'Oh yes, I should love to go. Mr Punch is such a bully, but really I think it is quite hilarious when he throws the baby out of the window and hits Judy over and over and over again!' She blushed fiercely and all of the boys fell silent and looked at her in surprise. Gosh, thought Valentine, I really must teach her how to fib with conviction.

'Glorious!' he said, 'It is unanimous! We are all going to the fête, Corny!'

Corny leapt up and punched the air, Cosmo looked immensely peeved and Willy felt decidedly sheepish.

Valentine took Rupert's hand in his, 'Will you wait here while I fetch my espadrilles?' he asked.

'Sure, I don't think the fête will be as fun without you,' replied Rupert.

The response sent Valentine's heart aflutter as he danced through the kitchen and into the hall to collect his espadrilles from the drawer in the Victorian hall-tree.

Gubsy, who could no longer easily manage the stairs, shuffled out of his bedroom on the ground floor. Gretchen was behind him, she still wore her sombrero, and Remarkable sat on her shoulder. Upon seeing Valentine sat on the bottom step, Gubsy stopped his shuffle and whacked the newel post with his cocobolo cane.

The impact of wood on wood made Valentine jump but he sang, 'Good morning, Gubsy! Good morning, Gretchen!'

'Morning? Is it still morning?' asked Gubsy of Gretchen.

'No, Mr Bartholmoo, time is now half of twelve.'

'I thought as much, I thought as much. Not much of a one for mornings are you, Valentine?'

'Actually, Gubsy, I've been up for simply hours and hours! You just haven't seen me before now, have you?'

'I will not tolerate lies in Chinchero, young man! Now tell me, what was your mother's talk about?'

'Gosh, all quite silly really!' said Valentine, getting to his esperdrilled feet and veering himself out of the reach of Gubsy's cane. 'Mummy wanted to talk to us about you.'

'About me?' asked Gubsy, narrowing his eyes and gnashing his false teeth, 'What about me?'

'Yes, about your money.'

'My money!' he spluttered, and banged his cane on the loose floor tiles, causing them to scatter.

'Yes, Gubsy, and its diminishment.'

Gretchen slowly shook her head and sounded a small snort.

Gubsy was beside himself with rage and his entire head turned purple. He looked as if he would explode, and he did. 'My own money! She wants to discuss my own money! My own money is my own business; it is none of hers! The audacity! The sheer impudence!' and as he exclaimed his outrage, he rotated on the spot, quite like Valentine's Sugar Plum Fairy ballerina, only rather different for obvious reasons.

Remarkable fanned out his wingspan, flapped wildly and squawked a riot. Gretchen had a formidable task on her hands to try to placate Mr Bartholmoo and his bird, and angrily she pushed Valentine out of the house. The front door slammed behind him and he stood on the front step to wonder for a space why he had just been so puckish, it certainly had not been to provoke reaction from Gubsy or Gretchen or even Remarkable but there had to be a reason. He had an idea that it might have had something to do with his mother's mendacity but he pushed that irksome thought from his mind and decided to think of nothing but Rupert.

He noticed Corny's red bicycle lying in the gravel as he skipped round to the side gate, he pushed through and though he was conscious of all of those that stood in the side-garden, he saw only Rupert, who smiled at his return, and Valentine asked, 'How many bicycles do we have, Harry?'

'*Weally* don't know. Why?'

'Lets all ride bicycles to the Green!' Valentine exclaimed, 'I bet you look good on a bicycle, Rupert, and I bet you can go ever so fast!'

Rupert laughed and said, 'Yes, I'm pretty good on a bicycle. I once cycled from Edinburgh to Southampton.'

'Gosh! Really not!' said Valentine.'Is Edinburgh so beastly?'

'Ha-ha! No, it was just to see if I could.'

'Gosh! You simply must have the most super powerful quadriceps!' said Valentine, and thought it was one of the most astounding feats that he had ever heard of. He beamed at Rupert. He marvelled unabashedly at him. Rupert returned his looks with one of amused amiability, and Valentine felt that it was plenty for the present.

The next thing he felt was identification with a victim of whiplash as Cosmo grabbed him and escorted him through the side gate.

'C'mon, Valentine, we've a bicycle for everyone!' Cosmo shouted. Then he said in a low voice, 'I'd drop it if I were you, he's not one of your bloody sort.'

Though Valentine hated to lose sight of Rupert, he submitted to the rough handling of his person with the decision that he might as well let Cosmo carry him.

'Imbecile,' Valentine whispered, 'I don't care what he is. I'm not prejudiced.'

Cosmo set him down on the gravel where he and Harry had wheeled out five more bicycles. He stared hard at Valentine, who had already turned to seek Rupert, and seethed over his arrogance; he knew the family put it down to Valentine being the great-great grandson of Excelsior, but this explanation did little more than rankle Cosmo who was also a descendant of the very same man, and moreover, he believed, of better and more substantial matter. A descendant that Excelsior would most certainly have been proud of, rather than the effete and fey Valentine. Cosmo considered himself to be far more of Avery-Stripe stock than Valentine deserved to be, and he found it intolerable that he was considered less so simply because he lacked the proper last name because he was linked to Excelsior through a female, Fortunata, his eldest child, and well known to have been Olympia's favourite.

CHAPTER 6

The Summer Fête

Four Avery-Stripes, one Oxley-Stockman and a Bringsley-Beer each had a bicycle that more or less corresponded with their respective sizes and set off in formation down the Avenue to the Green. Valentine cycled behind Rupert to afford himself the journey's best view, and the hot summer air gradually filled with the jolly sound of Jamaican steel drums playing *When the Saints Go Marching in*, the chatter of people and the merry-go-round's bells.

As they leant their bicycles against the railings, Valentine surveyed the scene on the Green and was dismayed that his vision of genteel bourgeoisie pleasantly drinking tea was, in reality, a frenzy of Hogarthian ropiness. He could not remember it being so busy in previous years and surmised it was because of the extraordinarily good weather. The crowd and the dinginess was not something that appealed to him but he supposed that if he confined himself to his brethren, with a particular proximity to Rupert, then he would be out of harm's squalid reach.

Thus fortified, he walked into the throng of it, all the while ensuring that Rupert was no less than kissing distance but the *hoi polloi*'s limbs, off-spring and pet animals seemed to enjoy creating a veritable jungle in his path. He noticed with admiration Corny's genuine obliviousness to the tangle, and watched him look about in delight and trample on people's paper plates, demolishing their clotted creamed scones and upsetting their teas with his dizzy gait.

Valentine turned to Rupert but was shocked when, instead, the offensive face of Cosmo met him.

Cosmo put his gargantuan hand on Valentine's slight shoulder and gripped it, 'Don't worry,' he said, 'they will all think your bloody pyjamas are part of the fancy dress parade.'

Valentine was resentful that someone so bridge-and-tunnel would deem his community, no matter how basic some of them may look to be, not sophisticated enough to realise that many people of sunnier climes would often roam about town in pyjama suits.

'Gosh! And don't you worry; I am certain that when they see you they shall suppose you are in a gorilla suit and award you first prize!'

He wriggled free of Cosmo's grip to join Rupert who somehow seemed to have no trouble fitting in and simultaneously shine like a beacon of heavenly light in a sea of seediness. Rupert was talking to Harry, and Valentine employed a gazelle like grace to sandwich himself between the sanctuary of their bodies, though with a decided tendency toward Rupert.

Willy, whose dimensions could create clear paths with ease if she were not so self-conscious, observed with some envy Valentine's agility. Then to her surprise she saw her mother in the distance behind him and brought her sighting to the others' attention. Valentine peeked around Harry and saw that it was indeed so. It struck him as unusual because the situation was not his mother's sort of thing at all. She sat beneath garlands of Union Jack bunting at a trestle table quite close to the Pimm's tent. Two of her cronies were with her and not one of them looked very happy to be there.

Quite without questioning their decision to do so, Olivia's children made their way over to join her. It would be most impolite not to acknowledge one's mother at a fête. Quickly, Olivia applied to her face a mask of affection for her twit, pansy, frump and mute progenies and her distantly related pinhead. She could not suppress a genuine interest in the stranger, not because he was beautiful but because she detected pedigree.

'Auntie O!' Cosmo boomed heartily as he bent down and enveloped her in his strong arms, 'Stunning as ever! How are you? Can't remember the last!'

Olivia was not pleased at having her deportment disturbed but managed to crocodile smile up at him and say, 'Oh but darling, how splendid to see you!'

She presented him with a reluctant air kiss on either cheek: 'It really *has* been simply too long! How is Esmé? How is Quentin? And darling Flick? Oh but really, I do appear to have embarrassed myself most unashamedly and dispensed of etiquette most deplorably! Let me introduce you to my exceedingly excellent friends; Nina and Sophie.'

Valentine felt that these two harpies leering up at Cosmo and over at Rupert certainly provided proof that his mother was entirely sincere in her claim that looks are of no importance. He thought Nina Frethell a doppelganger for Dix's *Sylvia Von Harden*, but wearing an allegedly gratuitous eye-patch in place of the monocle, and hirsute Sophie Babbington, who was the proprietor of a luxury dog parlour, looked like her clients' pre-groom.

However, this testimony to Olivia's tolerance of unsightliness did little to humble him, for he knew that she associated with the duo purely because they had both married very badly and divorced very successfully with alimonies that supplied them with the wherewithal as if on tap yet still they claimed to exist on the breadline.

Valentine regarded the mercenary divorcées with disdain and when they had finished pressing their withered lips upon Cosmo's cheeks he introduced them to the beauty that they could not ever buy.

'And this is *my exceedingly excellent* friend Rupert,' Valentine said, taking Rupert's hand and swinging it joyfully.

'*Your* friend!' said Olivia, 'But I thought he was Cosmo's?'

Valentine looked to Rupert, 'Well, he's mine too, aren't you?'

'Crikey, yes!' Rupert said with his magnificent grin.

'Hello, Rupert,' said Olivia, 'I hear you shall be staying in Chinchero for a spell. Please do make yourself at home and do not mind Valentine too much; I am afraid he has a tendency to be somewhat overbearing.'

Harry and Cosmo had managed to collect a chair for each of them to sit around the table, though Corny was much too busy turning his special acrobatics all over the place to make use of his. The flash of Olivia's eyes when Cosmo withdrew his heavily pregnant wallet from his pocket went unnoticed and he asked everyone what they would like to drink.

'You may *not* have a Pimm's, Wilhelmina,' said Olivia, 'You are much too young!'

'I am seventeen, mummy!'

'Exactly. You may have lemonade.'

Willy folded her arms and slumped back in her chair with a fierce scowl, and Harry, Cosmo and Rupert went to fetch the drinks. Valentine lit a cigarette and half listened to the desperately vile things his mother's companions said, whilst he watched with amusement Corny drain the dregs of Pimm's in the neighbouring tables' abandoned plastic cups, and he waited for the glory of Rupert's return.

Olivia bled what remained of the Pimm's in her cup, fished out a slice of orange and sucked out the alcohol. She wondered why Willy had put on a dress but she was glad of it, even if it was ill-fitting it was rather pretty and she hoped that Willy would continue to dress as a girl. She looked at Valentine and felt nothing but irritation that he had ventured out of doors to parade in pink pyjamas on the Green.

Leaning forward she said to him in hushed tones, 'You embarrassed poor Rupert most dreadfully, Valentino. You must realise what is and what is not acceptable behaviour. One day you shall expose yourself to mortal peril if you are not cautious.'

'Don't be silly, mummy,' interposed Willy, 'Rupert is a decent chap. I think he likes Valentine, and anyway Valentine can take care of himself.'

'Thank you, Willy,' said Valentine, 'and I do not think I am exposing anything other than cordiality. He is our guest and I am treating him accordingly. It is just pure coincidence that he also happens to be the boy I shall marry.'

Willy chortled, though Valentine was not joking.

'Don't be preposterous, Valentino!' Olivia spat, 'He is transparently not of your persuasion and not likely to permit your pawing his person for very much longer, so be sensible and cease.'

'He doesn't seem to be minding at all, he is nothing but smiles,' argued Valentine.

'Anyone with half a mind can see that he is high!' hissed Olivia.

'So am I!'

'Valentino!'

'I am high on love. He is lovely and I shall marry him because he is beautiful!'

Olivia looked full of exasperated disapproval.

Each of the three boys returned with a pitcher of Pimms, and poured a cup for everyone, save Willy and Corny who had to settle for lemonade.

Rupert sat, unhesitatingly, next to Valentine and smiled at him.

'Gosh, Rupert!' said Valentine, 'Look how many strawberries you have! You are lucky! I do so love strawberries and I don't have more than one in my cup!' and he looked at his drink histrionically.

'Would you like one of mine?' offered Rupert.

'Gosh! May I? Oh, yes please! That would be glorious!' exclaimed Valentine and was excited to watch Rupert employ his caramel fingers to extract a strawberry.

Rupert pulled one out, smiled triumphantly and gave it a quick generous lick before dropping it into Valentine's cup.

Valentine felt a rush of exhilaration jet through his body as he was titillated to bits by the lick and he looked at Rupert in mock astonishment.

Rupert grinned and his forget-me-not eyes gleamed playfully.

'Scoundrel!' Valentine declared, quite breathlessly, 'You ought to kiss my strawberry!'

Rupert leant close and whispered naughtily into Valentine's ear, 'I ought to eat your strawberry.'

Valentine gasped at Rupert's taste for cheek and was about to whisper a reply when Willy grabbed his wrist so tightly that it caused him to spill a little Pimms and nearly to yelp, but she did not let go.

Willy was looking straight ahead in pure terror.

Irritated, Valentine turned to discern what exactly had caused such a reaction yet was unable.

'Gosh! What is it, Willy?'

Rupert was the only other at the table aware of Willy's terror but was equally as nonplussed and remained so even when without the use of her lips she enlightened Valentine to its source, 'Mrs Strap!'

'Where?' asked Valentine, rubbing his released wrist.

'Just there, straight ahead, standing by the white elephant and wearing the biggest straw hat!'

'You mean the mass of floral fabric and faux pearls, attacking a brick of Victoria sponge with a plastic fork, and talking at the vicar?'

'Yes, her.'

'Gosh, now I know why she spoke as if she had a mouth full of cake. She looks never to eat anything else!'

'She's headed in this direction, Valentine,' panicked Willy, 'Do something please!'

Valentine saw that Mrs Strap and the vicar were definitely meandering toward the vicinity of the Pimm's tent and he grew rapidly aware of the impendent sticky state of affairs and thought it wise to make themselves scarce.

He interrupted the conversation Cosmo and Harry were having with the divorcées and his mother, and said, 'Gosh! It really is too beastly basking and I feel that I am starting to cook in this direct and harsh sunlight! I do believe I shall have a wander and see if I cannot locate some kindly shade or a friendly breeze.'

'I'm coming too!' said Willy.

'Glorious!' said Valentine, 'I shall be glad of the company. Would you care to join us, Rupert? There seems to be an awful lot of things to see and do and I am certain you are simply itching for a poke about.'

'A poke sounds good to me,' said Rupert, rising, for he felt sure that he would have a much better time with Valentine than he would with the ladies.

Valentine motioned for Willy to stand hidden behind Rupert, though even Rupert's well-built form was incapable of entirely hiding her expanse from view.

'Yes, of course, darling,' said Olivia, 'We can't have your sensitive skin scorch, crust and peel,' and she looked up at Valentine with some confusion. It was not like him to want to wander when he had a perfectly decent seat but the idea of his absence was not wholly disagreeable to her.

However, the thought of him alone with Rupert with only Willy acting as chaperone was not one that sat well with her, thus she turned to Harry and Cosmo and said, 'And why don't you go too? And do try to ascertain the whereabouts of Cornelius; wherever he is pandemonium is certain to be fast on his heels.'

The children bade their regrettable farewells, and telling Olivia that they would see her back at Chinchero they departed, and in Valentine and Willy's case, the exit was brisk.

The exodus presented Olivia with an immediate sense of calm. She was relieved to be only with her contemporaries and she filled their cups to the brim with Pimm's. Her serenity was to be short-lived however as the three of them soon became conscious of a small gathering of people looking in their direction. At the centre of the gathering was a woman in a dress that appeared to be very much homemade, and though this woman did seem somewhat familiar to Olivia, she could not furnish her with a name. Therefore, it came as quite a surprise when the woman cast her a glance seething with undiluted malevolence to the accompaniment of much sound of distaste from her companions.

Valentine and Willy took temporary refuge in the tent of creamed teas and let the boys go on ahead. Valentine turned to her and under the mass clatter of crockery he said, 'Gosh! That was close!'

'Too close for comfort,' she replied. 'Do you think Strap will see mummy?'

'Maybe. Mummy's not instantly recognisable in her clever disguise of immense sunglasses.'

'Anyone can see it's mummy, no one else dresses so severely.'

'I shouldn't stew, Willy, just be glad that we are not in the soup of it. But speaking of disguises, I do deem it sage for you to don this.'

He picked up a discarded mask of a chimpanzee that some child had left on a chair and handed it to Willy.

'Really not!'

'But you must! Do you think if Strap sees you she will be full of happiness?'

'What about you? You told her she sounded like she was going to have a hiatus hernia!'

'Not I! Mummy did. Come on, Willy, you have to wear it or things might get very sticky.'

Willy pulled a face like thunder but realised that Valentine was wise and she put on the mask.

'Glorious!' said Valentine. 'Now stroll about a bit so I can evaluate the effectiveness of the disguise.'

Willy obeyed and took a few steps back and paced about. Valentine's consequent laughter caused the surrounding people to turn from their teas and witness the strange sight of a rather healthily plump girl wearing a too tight but pretty dress and monkey mask, stamping her feet and shaking her fist at a skinny young man, dressed in pink pyjamas, and laughing hysterically.

'I will take it off if you don't stop laughing!'

'It's for your own good, Willy,' said Valentine, wiping away his mirthful tears. 'You know that. Now you can enjoy the day without worry. Anyway, I must locate Rupert, are you coming or do you want a banana?'

'Oh, Valentine!' she howled, and followed him out through the other side of the tent.

Harry, Cosmo and Rupert were with Corny; he was sat on a wooden stool and having his face painted like Spiderman's. His excited squirming was not letting the face painter have an easy time of it, and Harry was trying to hold him still whilst he used his spit on a paper napkin to wipe clean Corny's ice-creamed hands.

'You are a dirty *w*ascal!' admonished Harry as he smiled at his little brother.

Corny replied with a silent laugh and a knocking of his knees.

'Keep still, *w*ascal, or you'll *w*uin the *w*ed bits.'

Rupert was filling his beautiful face with a gigantic hotdog and holding a stick of candyfloss that he presented to Valentine, as he correctly supposed it to be a thing that he might quite like.

The gift seemed to Valentine to be overflowing with romantic sentiment for the fluffy spun sugar was the precise same shade as his pyjamas. With feelings of unbridled passion he plucked a piece of the pink cloud and put it in his mouth before blowing Rupert a candied kiss. The recipient made out as if its landing on his cheek were something to make him swoon.

Cosmo arrived from the hotdog stand with one in each hand and his monobrow shot up when he saw the strange addition to Willy's ensemble.

'What on bloody earth!' he boomed.

Harry looked up and was just as taken aback by the monkey mask; he rose and asked, 'Willy! Why are you wea-*wing* that?'

Unsure of what to say, Willy's smiling chimp face looked at each of them in turn.

Valentine managed to contain his laughter and he explained, 'She may look silly but she is in fact being very clever, aren't you, Willy?'

The chimp hesitated before slowly nodding, and Valentine elaborated; 'She is protecting her skin from the rays in the glasshouse effect due to the holy ozone layer. She advised me to wear one too but I said I couldn't possibly permit anything to hinder my view of Rupert.'

He turned to Rupert and, quite as if rehearsed, they cocked their heads at each other and smiled like fools. Cosmo did not look very happy that his friend seemed not only to be accepting of Valentine's peculiarities but also to be enjoying them, and even quite encouraging of them.

It was then that Valentine felt something limp and bony from behind slide up his left arm pit and he shivered. The limp and bony thing possessed the power to force Valentine to describe a half circle and he found himself facing the local vintage pederast, Brian Pavilion, wearing a panama hat and an exquisitely cut ivory linen suit that draped elegantly on his lanky frame, which stood like a tall reed blowing in the wind.

'My dear! However are you?' said Brian in his voice of lavender velvet, and he made a display of scanning Valentine from head to toe.

Valentine was a frail and pale schoolboy who dressed only in black when he first met Brian, who at the time he addressed as 'Mr Pavilion' for he had been Valentine's art teacher.

Art lessons had been the only ones that Valentine had attended religiously. Mr Pavilion would wax lyrical about Leonardo, Raphael and Michelangelo, and would seem to take great pleasure in chastising, with his rude tongue, the better-looking boys who he felt were not paying him adequate attention. Best of all though were the classes when Mr Pavilion would bring to school one of his many nephews, and have them disrobe to give his pupils lessons in life drawing.

On these occasions Mr Pavilion would commend Valentine on his technique and proclaim that his eye for the superior beauty of the male physique showed great promise.

Occasionally they would bump into each other in the grounds of the park across the road from the school, smoking cigarettes whilst trampling through the denser areas when really they ought not to be. Mr Pavilion would always look a shade awkward and Valentine would wonder why his teacher was not reprimanding him for leaving the school premises, but they always spent a civil time exchanging pleasantries on a bench.

After a few of these meetings, when autumn turned into winter, Mr Pavilion suggested that it would be sensible to converse in the warmth of his cosy mews house not so very far away and Valentine agreed that it sounded a very nice thing to do for the chill was rather biting.

In Mr Pavilion's cottage-like home they would sit, smoke, and drink tea and he introduced Valentine to the world of pornographic filmography and to the art of a Finnish man named Tom. Valentine learned of chickens and bears, of demonstrative goings-on in men's saunas, of the glory of holes in walls, and of using another man as if he were a marigold. Consequently, Valentine's mind felt warped but he coped by placing his new knowledge in boxes at the back of his brain.

Soon after Valentine abandoned his formal education, Brian's vocation as art teacher ended. The two endings were unrelated; Valentine had grown too bored with school to attend and the school dismissed Brian due to his having performed a lewd act with a life model in front of his pupils. Brian decided that he had no desire to associate with children ever again, so upon receiving an unexpected inheritance from his maiden aunt he opened a small gallery – Pavilion Pictures – in the Terrace and sold the work of local artists. It did not make him much money but the windfall was such that he could afford to keep the place running more as a hobby than for business, and every year his gallery had a stand at the local fête where he and Valentine now stood.

'Simply glorious, Brian, and you? You are looking achingly well I must say,' said Valentine, as he finger fed himself pink floss.

'Thank you, my dear, you are too kind to an old cadaver! But you must tell me, my dear, who are those three strappers with you?'

'The tall one with the beard and trying to control Spiderman is my brother Harry, the hulking ugly ape talking to the chimp is cousin Cosmo, and the heavenly adonis is Rupert, but keep your hands off him; he is the love of my life and I intend to take him up the aisle.'

'Don't you worry, my dear; this jaded fairy you see before you is no longer interested in pretty youths. Your beloved Rupert need not fear me. No, the one that you say is ugly is the one that has my dusty loins a-leaking!'

'Cosmo? You surely jest? He is repulsive; if he visits me in my dreams I wake up screaming!'

'Oh, I quite disagree. What you are calling ugly is evidence of an abundance of testosterone. He is a handsome brute and I should like to make him bite the pillow.'

'I can assure you that you would most certainly have a tussle on your hands doing whatever I dread to think you'd like to do to Cosmo.'

'My dear, what you are saying has me tense with turgidity. I insist that you send him my way! I shall be at home this evening with only a chilled bottle of vino for company. Do tell him to pop by and that I'll show him my box of magic tricks.'

Unpleasant, but not entirely unamusing, visuals filled Valentine's head as he imagined the sort of things perverted Mr Pavilion might like to do to Cosmo.

He laughed and turned to determine whether Rupert was still within reasonable reach. He was just a little way over; he and the others were standing by as Corny was trying to loop a hoop at the end of a long stick through the hook in the head of a yellow rubber duck. Harry and Cosmo seemed to be discussing something quite uninteresting, and Willy's chimp face kept looking over her shoulder. Only Rupert was paying attention to Corny's efforts, and it melted Valentine's heart to see the encouragement he was giving him.

He looked back at his ex-educator, and said, 'Brian, you are simply incorrigible. I love you. But I really must go before I lose the others.'

Brian placed a tapered hand on Valentine's cheek and looked at him tenderly.

'Yes, my dear, you must. If you love him you must catch him and never let him go, hold on to him with all that you have got!'

'You don't need to worry about me; I'll get what I want,' Valentine said, defiantly.

Brian smiled gently and retrieved his hand, 'Oh, I know you shall, my dear.'

Valentine looked to Rupert again, who was cheering Corny's win of a goldfish in a small bag of water, whereupon he went to get what he wanted.

He heard Brian call after him, 'Don't forget to keep up the drawing either, you always did show great promise!'

In little more than a hop, skip and a jump, Valentine was back amongst his fold. Corny's smudged Spiderman face bore a proud smile as he held aloft his prize for Valentine to commend.

'Gosh, Corny! Well done you, what a glorious goldfish you have there!'

'He managed it after only three go's,' said Rupert, ruffling Corny's hair as he beamed at Valentine.

'Only three? Gosh! That's much better than I could ever do! I think that we should name your goldfish Gloriana!'

Corny was very pleased with the choice of name, and he grinned at Valentine and Rupert through Gloriana's water.

'Who was that queer old coot you were talking to then?' Cosmo wanted to know, and so did Harry, 'Yes, who is he?'

'Queer old coot!' exclaimed Valentine, 'and he said only the loveliest things about you!'

Cosmo did not look pleased.

'And you know who he is, Harry, he's my old Art teacher, you remember him don't you, Willy?'

The chimp mask nodded and Valentine started to wonder why the disguise has rendered her as mute as Corny, that was, until a particular stall caught his attention; 'Haberdashery!' he exclaimed, and he leapt over and eyed the sewing paraphernalia with wonderment.

There seemed to be hundreds of wheels of different coloured ribbons, some were striped, some possessed spots and others had little motifs such as cherries and four-leafed clovers, and one was in the design of a tape measure and he thought this to be a most charming idea. He then examined the rows of boxes that contained buttons of every shape and size and tried to decide which was his favourite. His deep deliberation was halted when Rupert pressed a hand upon the small of his back and asked, 'What are you doing now?'

'Gosh! It's my Achilles heel; I always go weak at the knees over haber-dasheries!' Valentine said as he continued to rummage through the boxes.

Rupert grinned. He did think Valentine funny and he admired his disobedience to be anything other than he was, it was as if he moved in his own orbit.

'Aha! Here it is!' exclaimed Valentine, and he extracted a buttercup yellow button.

'Is it a special one?' asked Rupert with curiosity.

'It is my favourite button! And it is yellow. I *love* yellow,' Valentine said and held it up between his finger and thumb, 'Isn't it a gay little one?'

'It's a very gay little one,' agreed Rupert, smiling and took it from him to appreciate it. Valentine turned his attention from the button to Rupert's face but suddenly he heard a *clang*, *whiz* and a loud *bong*.

Harry and Cosmo had found the Test Your Strength striker, and Cosmo had just hit the bell at the top of the nine-foot climb, where it said 'Heroic'. Cosmo wore an expression to tell everybody his achievement had required the minimum effort; he handed the big mallet to Harry and collected his prize of a token for a free beer. Harry was not quite so good; he managed to knock the puck up to 'Mighty', but that was not 'Heroic', so the bell did not bong and he did not win a beer.

'That was *weally wubbish*!' said Harry, displaying his best catwalk pout.

'Rupert! Gosh, Rupert! I bet you could bong the bell so very easily!' whispered Valentine.

'Watch me,' Rupert replied, certain of his ability, and Valentine considered that he would not miss Rupert exhibiting his strength for all of the gay little buttons in the galaxy.

Rupert poised before the striker with confidence. He gripped the mallet and looked to Valentine and said, 'Are you ready?'

'Raring!' exclaimed Valentine, stood between chimp-masked Willy and Spiderman-faced Corny.

Rupert then focused his attention on the task in hand, swung the mallet behind his head, and then flung it back in a tremendous arc bringing it down on target with an almighty *clang*, the puck whizzed as if fired from a cannon and it struck the bell with an explosive *bong* as big as Ben's.

The spectators cheered and Corny punched the air. Valentine did not know whether to faint or shriek but he felt on the very brink of both for Rupert was indisputably Heroic and deserving of a medal and not just a beer token and he told him so.

'You weren't disappointed then?'

'Disappointed! Why would I be? It was glorious!'

'Crikey, because I was aiming to shoot that bell to the sun for you!' stated Rupert.

Valentine gasped.

The next resounding bong announced that Harry had achieved the status of 'Heroic' on his second attempt, which was just as well for although Harry did make a very good model it was as a happy one and not one that pouted. Now that each of the three boys had won a beer token it was time to claim them and because Valentine certainly did not want to set foot in a beer tent he told them that he, Willy and Corny would wait for them by the coconut shy.

As they waited, Corny held Gloriana up to his eyes, danced on the spot, and through the water, he observed Valentine take out a cigarette from his silver case and light it.

He could see Willy too, wearing her chimpanzee mask and looking all about her. Then he admired the flawless blue sky. He saw four magpies glide through the air; he followed their flight that led his eyes to the return of the boys with their beers.

'How many tokens did you win?' exclaimed Valentine upon seeing that they each carried two plastic pints.

The trio grinned at him and Cosmo boomed, 'One for each! You don't think we could enjoy our beers and watch you bloody die of thirst do you?'

'But I don't like beer and those cups are grotesque!'

'Well, tell Rupert that; he bought yours.'

'Gosh, thank you, Rupert!' said Valentine full of happiness, but received the giant cup in both hands and peered at the rancid colour of its content.

Rupert laughed, 'Just give it a go. It'll put hairs on your chest!'

Valentine did not wish to possess a hairy chest, he liked his smoothness but because he did not want to reject anything that Rupert gave him, he raised the cup to his mouth and sipped gingerly.

'You like it?' asked Rupert, amused by Valentine's behaviour.

'Divine!' lied Valentine, who braved another sip of the horrid stuff whose only redeeming quality was being ice cold, and a grinning Rupert took a big gulp of his own.

'You don't drink beer with your bloody pinkies sticking out!' jeered Cosmo.

'I'll do whatsoever I desire with my pinkies!' snapped Valentine.

'You should dwink it like Corny,' explained Harry. 'Look!'

They all watched Corny down his beer like a dipsomaniac. Valentine was not certain that Corny should be drinking beer at all and turned to Willy to see that she had not had any of her's. She was unable to drink from a cup because of her mask and realising this, Valentine said, 'Willy needs a straw. She can't drink her beer with her sun-mask on.'

Harry rushed back to the beer tent and when he returned, he gave Willy a straw that she fed through the chimp's mask and proceeded to drain her beer rather rapidly.

Harry, Cosmo and Rupert finished their beers quite quickly and they decided that to throw a wooden ball at a coconut was an irresistible activity. They set their empty cups down on the grass and sauntered over to the stall. Valentine believed he had done a decent job of drinking an inch of beer so he put his almost full cup down with theirs and followed Rupert. Willy trailed behind still sucking her straw, and none of them saw Corny throw his empty over his shoulder and pick up what Valentine did not want, for he had developed quite a taste for the stuff.

Coconut shying seemed to be trickier than it looked. Cosmo's technique was admirable but he had yet to succeed in knocking one off. He was not swallowing this easily and started to bluster at the stall owner that he had nailed the nuts to their posts. Fortunately, Rupert stepped forward with the idea that his hard pitching would excite Valentine. He limbered up, concentrated on the coconut in question and putting his entire body into it, he snapped back his arm, whipped it forward as if a slingshot, and the wooden ball hit the coconut with a *thwock* and it fell, causing Cosmo to scowl.

Although becoming accustomed to Rupert's physical prowess, Valentine was still enraptured at watching his demonstrations. His delight doubled however when the stall owner told Rupert to choose one of the helium balloons as his prize because Rupert decided on a shiny pink love heart for Valentine, who received it with a coy laugh.

Corny looked at the balloon with envy but was soon sated when Cosmo managed to hit a coconut with his fifth throw. He let Corny pick a round Spiderman balloon to match his face of which he was unaware had smudged to such a degree that the red and black paints had transmogrified into a muddy cloud, yet no one could look quite as blissful as did he with a fish in one hand and balloon in the other. Harry had also been triumphant on his first attempt and he proudly gave monkey-masked Willy a balloon in the novel shape of a big banana. Valentine found this very funny and told Harry his naughty streak was showing. Willy's huffing reddened her décolletage and Harry's look of pleasure turned to one of confusion. Corny came to Harry's rescue, he grabbed his wrist and tried to pull him in the direction of his outstretched arm that was pointed toward the bouncy castle.

'Ha-ha, *w*ascal! I'm much too big to go on that; I would get in *tw*ouble.'

Corny's countenance became one of extreme woe.

'But look,' said Harry, 'here is two pounds, I'm sure that's enough for you to be allowed on,' and he pressed the two gold coins in Corny's clammy hand. 'But give me your goldfish and balloon. You can't take them with you.'

Whereupon, Corny entrusted his treasures to his big brother before running off in a zigzag toward the castle.

Cosmo decided that he too felt the need for some vigorous bouncing and Harry and Rupert required small persuasion to join him on the dodgems. Willy shook her head when asked if she would come, and Valentine was not at all sure it was something that he would like either. Harry handed Corny's fish and balloon to Willy to hold, and he and Cosmo got into a dodgem each.

'C'mon, Valentine, I bet you'd really enjoy bumping about,' encouraged Rupert as they stood at the side with Willy.

'Gosh! I am quite certain I would not! Someone would be bound to bash hard into my rear and send me flying into the air! Besides, I've never driven a car.'

'It's not like driving a real car!' laughed Rupert, 'C'mon, it's fun. You'll like it. You can get in my car; you're slim enough to fit.'

'And you will drive?'

'Yes, I'll drive. C'mon, it's starting!'

'And I won't go flying?'

'Not if you hold me tight.'

'Hold this, Willy!' said Valentine, giving her his love heart balloon.

Valentine stepped onto the oval graphite floor and instantly felt transported to an entirely different plain of loud metallic music and garish flashing neon lights. Rupert grabbed his hand and pulled him over to an available car.

'It's yellow, you love yellow, don't you?' said Rupert.

'Verily!'

'Good. Quickly get in.'

Rupert sat behind the steering wheel and nodded at the space into which Valentine was supposed to squeeze. It was going to be a snug fit, Valentine thought happily.

'Quickly!'

Somehow, Valentine managed to climb in and realised he was so heavenly squashed against Rupert that it would take the battering from a very big ram to dislodge him. Rupert's firm grip upon the wheel turned his caramel knuckles white, and he, Harry and Cosmo were engrossed in telling one another how very hard they were going to bump each other. Presently the horrid music became horribly loud, Rupert pushed his foot down hard on the pedal and they were off.

'Hold tight!' he shouted, and the first big bump from behind gave Valentine good reason to do just that because Cosmo had hit them hard and the jolt was quite unpleasant. Rupert laughed and worked the wheel to turn and they crashed into Harry

From that moment, and for what seemed an unnecessarily extensive length of time, the violent bumping of dodgems rendered Valentine's head rather like a pig's bladder on a stick and he held on tight to Rupert.

'Are you alright?' shouted Rupert with concern.

'Gosh, yes! It's glorious fun!' Valentine said loudly, with as much poise as his position would permit.

Rupert shouted, 'Good!' and he grinned.

Valentine had not meant that the bumping and crashing was glorious. The gloriousness to which he referred was their intimate propinquity and he squeezed the strength in Rupert's arm. He was close enough to see the pores in Rupert's skin and the small grooves that formed when his mouth morphed from a grin into one puckered in determination as he applied full force to the pedal. He could see the separateness of each eyelash and brow hair, and the miniscule nick in front of his ear where he had cut himself shaving. Even at close quarters he could not discern any evidence of an imperfection and therefore he believed that he could exist very happily simply regarding any part of Rupert's exquisite anatomy.

Gradually the cars slowed down and the ride was over. The music lowered and the air filled with screams and cries. There was a space of confusion as the exact origin of the noise of upset was not immediately apparent but with a start Harry realised that the commotion came from the castle, he leapt out of his dodgem and sprinted over. Traumatised children were jumping and falling off the castle onto the rubber mats and into their parents' arms, their hysterical faces were tear-streaked, snotty and red, some of them were trembling and inconsolable as their mothers tried to discern what was the putrid substance on their clothes and in their hair. They could think of only one thing it might be, and sure enough, it was.

It was astonishing to see how much vomit Corny had managed to create. It was the consequence of all of the chocolate and ice cream and toffee apples on which he had spent all of his pocket money. Then on top of that had been the hotdog and the many dregs of Pimm's and two pints of beer. All of it in his excited belly, shook up by the wild and manic bouncing on the castle. He had thought it would just be a belch but when he opened his mouth an awful lot more had erupted. The other children had screamed and managed to slip and slide out to safety but as he was unwell, he was unable to escape and had remained flipping and skidding about in his mire of spew until Harry jumped in and carried him out.

Corny's brothers and sister, and Cosmo and Rupert, encircled him and made a fuss but it fast became apparent the he was nothing worse than a trifle shocked, albeit rather slick with sick that was fast drying in the fierce sun. Harry quickly stripped Corny down to his underpants, threw his soiled clothes in a rubbish bin, and poured a bottle of water over his head to get what he could out of his hair. The chilled water did little to improve the state of Corny's painted face, and it made him shiver terribly so Harry pulled off his polo shirt, wrapped it round him, and picked him up.

'It's al*w*ight, *w*ascal. You mustn't t*w*emble,' he soothed, as he gently rocked him and rubbed his back.

Aware of their audience, Valentine turned to face the masses and with an air of nonchalance, he procured a cigarette from his silver case and lighted it. He scanned the faces in front of him and cast an arrogant glare at any person that dared view his family censurably, yet he could quite clearly hear their whispered disparaging comments about Corny.

He wished to approach each individual and give them a thorough dressing down. He could hear them saying the word 'special' and he wanted to tell them all, 'Yes, Corny *is* special, he is an Avery-Stripe. Who pray tell are *you?*'

Rupert joined him and took his hand. He viewed the crowd with Valentine, and tightening his hold, he said, 'Crikey!'

Valentine turned to Rupert, looked at him in wonder and in love, smiled and replied, 'Gosh!' Whereupon, they all took one last look at the fête, decided that they had exhausted their use for it and that it was time to return to Chinchero.

Upon exiting the Green, Willy removed the monkey mask to reveal that it had indeed protected her face from the harmful rays of the holy ozone layer, but the sun had coloured the surrounding exposed areas of her head an angry red, thus creating a queer balaclava effect. She stomped her foot on the mask and ground it into the grass. As the others collected the bicycles, she grabbed Valentine's wrist and pulled him aside.

'Ouch, Willy! Do loosen your grip. You know I'm physically delicate,' he said.

'Uncomfortable, is it? I bet it's not as uncomfortable as wearing a blasted plastic mask in the scorching sun for hours!'

'It worked, didn't it?' he said, as he wriggled his wrist free and rubbed it, 'Strap didn't see you did she?'

'No, but it was sweltering hot and the whole time I had to watch you getting close to Rupert whilst I looked a fool!'

'You didn't look a fool. Lots of people were wearing masks!'

'They were all children!'

'And anyway, what's wrong with my getting close to Rupert? Are you jealous?'

'No.'

'Gosh, I know! You were jealous because you wanted to get closer to Cosmo.'

'No!'

'And you felt you couldn't because of the mask, but that is just so silly! Consider all of the intimate encounters the masked Venetians had during their carnivals! In fact, it should have been of assistance rather than a hindrance when you reflect.'

'Oh, do shut up, Valentine!' said Willy, whose blushing caused the disappearance of her balaclava for a flash.

'And another thing,' said Valentine, 'how do you expect to get closer to someone if you don't talk? Why weren't you saying anything?'

'Well, if I had spoken someone might have recognised my voice and then my disguise would have been for nothing!' said Willy, exasperated to have to explain the patent.

'I had not thought of that, Willy. That was incredibly shrewd of you,' said Valentine, delighted at the notion that she really had thought her disguise so convincing, and not realised that it had been transparent to anyone that knew her that it was simply Willy wearing a mask.

It was not much later than four o'clock, and the sun, though no longer at its summit, was still merciless and caused each of them to sweat profusely. They cycled home in silence with the hubbub of the fête still banging on their aural drums. Harry insisted that Willy travel between him and Cosmo because she did look somewhat off-colour, and Valentine and a balloon-festooned Corny flanked Rupert who, much to Valentine's admiration, cycled with one hand in order to carry Gloriana in the other.

Whilst the boys put the bicycles back in the shed, Willy stood before Chinchero and looked up at her mother's bedroom window. She turned to Valentine and bit her bottom lip.

'Don't worry, Willy,' he said, calmly, 'I'll tackle mummy, if necessary.'

He felt gratified when he saw relief flicker in Willy's eyes but he was soon distracted by two colossal hands grabbing and gripping very hard his upper arms from behind.

'Gosh! What is it that so invites people to handle me with such hostility!' he wailed as he writhed.

'You'll tackle mummy, will you?' jeered Cosmo, squeezing harder. 'Over what, eh?' and he jiggled Valentine's frame as if he were no more than a rag doll.

'Let me go this instant!' Valentine ordered as he wriggled, but Cosmo only laughed.

'Unhand me now, you brute!'

Cosmo's grip grew tighter.

Valentine ceased his wriggling as it only worsened his discomfort. He looked down at his hands and saw that his veins were aggressively prominent, and the sight alarmed him.

'Ouch, Cosmo! Do let me go!'

Because Valentine's tone suggested a plea, Willy became rather anxious and called for Harry who, with Rupert and Corny, was still putting away the bicycles. Harry looked in frustration at the antagonistic relationship between Valentine and Cosmo, he pushed a hand in his pocket and toyed with his beads to calm himself, whilst Rupert and Corny rushed over.

'Let him go, Cosmo, can't you see you're hurting him,' said Rupert.

Cosmo sneered and said, 'Come to play the hero have you? Tell me, why have you taken such a liking to him? Is there something I don't know about you?'

Though Valentine's pain was increasingly unbearable, he thought that he would also like to know the answer to Cosmo's question.

'You're being a bully, just let him go,' reasoned Rupert, 'He's half your size; try picking on me instead,' and he squared himself up.

'Ha! I'm starting to think you might like that!' Cosmo guffawed, and the two of them eyed each other pugnaciously.

Valentine was uncertain as to whether his feeling of light-headedness was due to Rupert's gallantry or to the blockage of blood but he experienced instant relief when Cosmo released his iron grip and yelled out in pain.

Valentine turned around fast and saw three balloons climbing the sky behind Cosmo bending his leg and clutching his foot. Corny dropped something in the gravel, ran behind Valentine and peeked out at his big cousin who he had just struck with a broken brick.

Hopping, Cosmo nursed his painful foot in both his hands. He was in shock. He was wearing only a pair of very old deck shoes and the soft leather provided little protection from brick blows. He looked at Corny in astonishment until his rage rose, forgot his foot and lurched forward in fury.

Corny cowered behind the physically insubstantial shield of Valentine whose reciprocal instinct for fraternal defence afforded him the courage to stand his ground. Fortunately, the intervention of Rupert rendered the bravado unnecessary as he pushed himself in front of Valentine, clutched Cosmo by the shoulders, and held him at bay.

'Back off, Cosmo!' warned Rupert.

'That bloody little devil! I will murder him!' roared Cosmo, as his small head seemed fit to pop and he fought, with all his might, to triumph over Rupert's superior strength, 'He damn well could've crippled me! I'm going to smash him to bloody smithereens!'

'Don't be a dolt!' said Rupert, 'He's just a boy!'

'And he was showing great honour by defending his brother!' Valentine exclaimed, 'I wish he had broken your cumbrous foot! You, after all, have virtually broken two of my elegant limbs!' and he demonstrated, with a charade and whimper, how he was unable to raise either of them much more than just a little bit.

Harry came up from behind and hooked his arms under Cosmo's to restrain him.

'*Welax*, Cosmo, we had better have a look at your foot. It might not be ve*wy* bad and I don't think mummy would like it if you smashed Corny to smithe*w*eens.'

Harry's calm tone managed to subdue Cosmo and he desisted in his efforts. He looked at Corny, who was peering out from behind Valentine, he looked at Valentine who was looking back at him around Rupert, and lastly he looked at Rupert and seemed to appear somewhat ashamed of himself. He turned to Harry and growled, 'Let's go inside.'

Harry led the way, unlocked the front door and Cosmo limped behind him.

Concernedly, Rupert asked Valentine if his arms really did hurt very much.

'Gosh, they're not too bad, though it was painful and they do feel a tiny tender but I am not quite as weak as all that,' answered Valentine, blithely, as he rubbed them through his pyjama sleeves.

'I know, but he is a Rugby Forward and, well you . . . crikey, just let me see,' said Rupert, as he held Valentine's right hand and pushed up the sleeve that was rather loose on the lithe arm to expose what possible harm may have been done. He was dismayed to regard that the modest bicep was chafed and red raw, and proceeded to bare the other which appeared equally as upset.

Valentine was surprised to see quite how unpleasant it looked, and said, 'Gosh! It really is an awful bore to be made of such sensitive stuff!'

Corny and Willy inspected the injuries, he made a sorry face, and she asked Valentine what he would do about them.

'Nothing whatsoever,' he replied, 'I admit it is rather unsightly but it shan't remain forever.'

'How does this feel?' said Rupert, cradling Valentine's upper arms in his palms and massaging them with his thumbs.

Valentine looked up at him and theatrically swooned.

'Exactly like I'm a strawberry in need of a kiss!' he gasped tremulously and threw back his head.

Upon hearing Valentine's notion, his siblings knew he was quite all right, and Rupert, gazing at Valentine, was amused and on the verge, when Gretchen appeared.

'What is goink on?' she demanded to know, as she took in the scene of her wards with some confusion but no surprise except regarding that of Corny's face.

Valentine was rather annoyed that Gretchen had quashed his chance of a kiss, and irritably he said to her, 'Nothing very much. Why?'

Grudgingly, he removed himself from Rupert's hold.

'Why is everyone be-ink so upset? Master Cosmo he is limpink. Miss Willy she is lookink so sickly, and why is Master Corny's face so diskustink? Where are his clothes?'

'Long story, Gretchen,' said Valentine, 'but to summarise, Cosmo had a brick crush his foot. Willy is nauseated because of a sun mask. Corny is wearing face paint, and his clothes are covered with sick in a rubbish bin.'

Gretchen shook her head, snorted, and said, 'I see all of these goinks on are all around but you are not touched.'

Valentine was rather taken aback, but then Rupert stepped forward, 'Actually, that's not true; take a look at his arms.'

Gretchen looked at Valentine's arms and immediately her mien metamorphosed from one of reproof to another of concern, and she asked, 'How is happenink? Who is doink? I see clearly the prints of hands.'

Valentine told her that it was absolutely nothing.

'I am not stupid-head, Master Valentine. I can see someone has been unkind. Is true you are naughty boy but if I am startink to think maybe perhaps somebody is beink physical with you because you are not a boy that likes beink with kirls then this is makink me ankry!'

'Don't worry, Gretchen,' said Rupert, 'Valentine will always be safe with me around,' and the certainty with which Rupert delivered the statement ensured him a place in Gretchen's good books.

Valentine had often heard tell of one's heart skipping a beat but he did not think that it was a thing he had ever undergone, not properly, at least not before hearing the sweet words that had just passed Rupert's lips. He repeated in his mind the romantic revelation that Rupert intended always to be around to keep him safe. This prospect filled him with felicity and he was ripe with the urge to somehow marry Rupert on the spot.

Yet with no wish to rush into matrimony without the correct procedures, he managed, with a gargantuan strain, to gather himself and say, 'Yes, Gretchen, you should have seen him! He came to my rescue immediately.'

'And Corny too!' added Willy.

'Gosh, yes! And Corny too!'

'Well done, Corny!' said Rupert, ruffling the boy's shock of hair.

Corny looked immensely cock-a-hoop.

Gretchen wondered what exactly had happened, but felt it wise not to ask. Instead, she turned her attention to matters of a practical nature, and told Willy that she must have a lie down if she was feeling 'nauseatink'.

Then to Corny, she said he looked 'diskustink', and that he must wash his face and get dressed before supper. She ushered him through the side gate and claimed Gloriana, 'I must find a better home for it.' she said.

Though Valentine considered the idea of a separation from Rupert to be torture he too deemed it decent to toilette before supper, therefore he bade him a rather melodramatic adieu. Rupert reciprocated the dread of the division most charmingly, and Willy cast Valentine a worried glance regarding his tackling of their mummy, but whilst he sped up the stairwell this issue was entirely absent from his mind because it was jammed with nothing but zeal to return to Rupert.

Thus it came as quite a shock to collide with Olivia before Olympia's gleaming harp.

'Gosh, mummy!' he said, with a gasp, 'I did not see you there! What are you doing lingering on the landing?' Then he remembered that she might be cross because of Mrs Strap: 'How are you anyway?' and he braced himself.

Olivia grimaced but not because she had suffered an interaction with Mrs Strap, though still she could not calculate why the woman had glared at her so hotly on the Green. The reason for her grimace was that the sudden appearance of Valentine had caught her unawares whilst she had again been comparing the actual Starfish with the painted one and she had barely adequate time to hide it from him.

In fact, the time was insufficient because although she managed to replace the ring in its pouch, as she fled from the portrait, the pouch itself had refused to comply with her desire to hide it in her Birkin and instead chose to fall on the landing floor as if to reunite with its original owner's harp. Yet Olivia was blind to the reunion and so too was Valentine and, with the Starfish at his feet, he wondered the reason for her grimace.

'Perfectly well thank you, darling, why ever would I not be?' Olivia asked.

'Gosh, I don't know; I suppose you just seem slightly irked.'

Olivia searched for a motive to be irked.

'Your behaviour irks me, Valentino!'

'My behaviour is exemplary!' he protested with relief.

'I mean your behaviour with the big boys; it can be a perilous thing to push provocativeness too far.'

Valentine was in two minds how to accept his mother talking to him as if he were still a little boy; on one hand it annoyed him to be patronised, but on the other it appealed to the Peter Pan in him.

'Gosh! I'm not scared of the big boys, mummy, and anyway, Rupert has said that he will look after me always!'

'He has?' Olivia asked in astonishment.

'Yes!' said Valentine, bouncing on the balls of his feet and nodding delightedly.

Presently, Olivia abandoned all thoughts of the Starfish as she concentratedly wondered if a union between her pansy and his new playmate may not only transpire to be possible but also of lucrative benefit to the family.

'What do we know of his people? Are they comfortable?' she asked, snappily, 'What I mean to say is; do they *prosper*?'

'Gosh, mummy! I possess no inkling whatsoever!'

'He *is* called Rupert, I know,' she said, 'and that does suggest that they may be decent. However, an acceptable name does not always a silver spoon in a newborn's mouth make, but I do admit that he does seem to radiate that golden glow of the very rich.'

'Gosh! You know I couldn't care a fig for his family or financial situation, they could be penniless peddlers and I would not care; he is too beautiful for money to matter.'

'Your superficiality saddens me, Valentine.'

'Pot and kettle, mummy! Anyway, I thought you were out for the day; why are you here?'

'Because, darling, it is my home!' said Olivia who had, in fact, arranged to dine with Nina and Sophie but must now cancel for she should certainly break bread with the family in an effort to better evaluate Rupert. 'Further, my previous plans have unfortunately foundered yet fortunately Gretchen is cooking one of her incredible Indians of which I am so very fond and for which I must now get ready.'

She strode toward her bedroom door and twisted its knob, 'Bye-bye, darling!' she chirruped, for she edged on elation over Valentine's potential partnership with a boy of probable means.

Valentine regarded his mother's closed door and he tutted because she was more concerned over Rupert's capital than his beauty but then he smiled because she had evidently escaped any dealings with Mrs Strap. His happiness was such that he chose to celebrate it with a brush of his fingers upon the harp strings. The resulting plings pleased him but not so the stab in the sole of his foot.

'Gosh! Ouch! I only just divested my espadrilles!'

He looked to the cause of the discomfort and discovered, on the carpet, a small velvet drawstring pouch that was new to his eye. He wondered what it might hold, and was on the verge of investigating when he heard Rupert's distant laughter, and he filled with anguish: 'Gosh! Whatever am I doing? Rupert awaits me! I must hasten or he shall start to miss me terribly, begin to wonder my whereabouts, and fear for my safety!'

Mindful of the third step, he skipped to his turret, lifted the lid of a cylindrical black and shocking pink Schiaparelli box that had once housed a hat in the design of a lady's topsy-turvy shoe, and dropped the velvet pouch amongst the bibelots therein. Then he extracted, from a drawer, an immaculate pair of scarlet and heliotrope striped silk pyjamas, for the events of the day had rather sullied his pale pink ones, before departing for the bathroom where he would shave and soak whilst at the same time smoke like a cheery chimney.

CHAPTER 7

Leo Rex Aureus

The stupendously appetising smell pervading the hot air that escaped into the dining room through the open French doors invaded Valentine's nostrils as he entered unnoticed. All were in attendance and captivated by the plethora of Gretchen's multi-coloured curries and various accompaniments, for they rendered them giddy with gluttony.

Valentine positioned himself in a pose that he considered comely and teeming with poise, so as to best display how soap-shining he was from his indulgent submersion, and how suave he was to regard in his silk pyjamas, and exclaimed to all, though with his gaze glued directly upon only one, 'Hello, everybody! What a glorious evening! Don't you think?'

Rupert greeted him with a broad and beaming grin, 'Crikey, yes!' whereupon Valentine circumnavigated the lacquered table and proffered him his hand.

'Miss me?' he coyly queried.

In a tone to suggest surprise at the question, Rupert replied, 'Crikey, lots!' He received Valentine's hand and gave it a convulsive squeeze, 'You were gone so long that I was starting to worry!'

'Gosh! You are lovely! But you shouldn't have worried; for here I am; and as you can see I'm as safe as can be! At least I am now I'm next to you! I shall always be safe with you, isn't that true?'

'Very true!' was Rupert's smiling reply and the pair regarded one another with unabashed affection.

Olivia was pleased to witness the obvious fondness Rupert felt for Valentine, providing, of course he possessed means. However, she was not happy with the seating arrangement; there was not available space for the pair to sit side-by-side, and now that she was considering inciting their intimacy, she ordained that Willy relocate.

At first, Willy felt rather put out but upon realising the reason, and that her new situation would be adjacent to Cosmo, she became benevolent. Nevertheless, she would not yet allow herself total happiness; she must ascertain from Valentine whether or no he had successfully 'tackled' their mother who had made no references to Mrs Strap but that meant nothing;

she might only be biding her time before detonating. Therefore, when upon orbiting the table, Valentine created a slight collision as he took Willy's seat, and whispered to her, 'Oblivious,' she enjoyed such an overwhelming sense of exoneration that she smiled quite idiotically at Cosmo when she sat next to him.

Cosmo did not notice her smile; he was too busy scowling at Valentine and his queer performance, Harry saw this, and gave Cosmo a firm nudge. After the attack on Cosmo's foot, Harry had had to explain to him that if he wanted a pleasant stay in Chinchero it would be best not to upset Valentine, for if Valentine got upset then so too would Corny, and then, in turn, so would Gretchen, and that would have an effect on Gubsy whose house it was. Therefore, it would be wise, because life would be considerably calmer, and Cosmo's stay infinitely more pleasant, if he did not give Valentine grief, even if Valentine did, sometimes, like to try.

Thus, for the sake of his best friend Harry, Cosmo had promised to be tolerant, and he would not complain about how Gretchen had bound his foot in bandaging uncomfortably snug, nor would he make a meal of how it hurt to walk.

So it was that nine people, of varying degrees of congeniality, sat at the Indian feast set before them and presently hungrily delivered it to their mouths. When the gastronomy tantalised their taste buds, they each sighed with satisfaction and showered Gretchen with praise.

'It is indeed delightfully delicious,' managed Olivia, 'And may I also compliment you on your costume, Gretchen, it is so very vibrant.'

Gretchen, passing the saag paner to Harry, and dissuading Corny from dropping grains of pilau into Gloriana's bowl, wondered if Olivia was being unpleasant or had genuinely forgotten seeing her dressed in her green, with gold detail, sari, and sporting a bindi on several occasions for such was her apparel whenever the meal was Indian.

She gave Olivia the benefit of the doubt: 'Thank you, Mrs Olivia, your kind words are kood to hear, but you have seen before my sari many times I think.'

'No, no. You are mistaken, I am certain that such a sight would stick in my psyche,' said Olivia as she forked a tandoori king prawn, and Gretchen, now having had the unpleasantness confirmed, wondered if it had been deliberate.

In truth, Olivia could recollect the sari and though she thought it affected, her annoyance was more about the presence of a goldfish at supper; the toucan perched upon Gubsy's shoulder was bad enough!

'It's an amazing sari!' said Rupert.

Gretchen placed her hands over her cheeks to cover her blush.

'Thank you, Master Rupert. Is nothink special but is somethink I like to wear.'

'You look *wavishing!*' asserted Harry.

'I'll say!' said Gubsy.

'And gloriously apropos! What with our Indian summer's day, not to mention the curry!' exclaimed Valentine, enjoying his chicken tikka masala, and he pressed his bare foot onto Rupert's under the table, and made eyes at him to which Rupert responded with his grin.

Presently, Cosmo elaborately masticated a bhaji without the thought of closing his mouth. The sight and sound of this did not escape Valentine's notice, and he winced at the disregard of propriety. He noticed also that Willy was gazing at Cosmo quite as if she considered his table manners exquisite, and he simply could not fathom it for the sickly lip-smacking sound was, to his ears, torture.

He considered, for a space, that he could request that Cosmo kindly shut his mouth but then he regarded, upon Rupert's forearm, some red scratches. They looked painful and were fresh for Valentine was certain that he would have realised them in the dodgem.

He made a moue of sympathy, touched the scratches, and asked how they came to be.

Rupert grinned at him, 'Remarkable had a stroll on me, look, there's more on my shoulders,' and he pushed forward the one closest to Valentine.

Valentine gasped at the slight latticing upon Rupert's caramel skin.

'Gosh! You vicious thing!' he declared, flung out his arm and pointed at Remarkable whose response was a baffled squawk.

'You dare speak to Remarkable in such a tone!' admonished Gubsy.

Valentine ignored Gubsy. 'He's literally lacerated you!' he said to Rupert, and made big eyes at the little nicks.

'Crikey! It's nothing,' laughed Rupert.

'Nothing?' exclaimed Valentine with incredulity, 'It looks to be agonising!'

Rumbles of laughter came from Cosmo, and an appalled Valentine told him that he would very much like to know what the joke was.

'Those piddling little scrapes really are nothing to Rupert, is what the bloody joke is,' said Cosmo. 'If he felt them at all he'd have no more than thought them ticklish!'

'Gosh! How uncaring you can be!'

'No, really!' grinned Cosmo, 'Rupert's got far worse wounds than that!'

Valentine looked questioningly at Rupert, and he wondered what Cosmo might mean; 'far worse wounds'? What horrific defacement might Rupert be hiding?

'Show them, Rupert,' coaxed Cosmo. 'Show them your mutilation, show them how you really know what it is to be scratched!'

Valentine was in a serious state of discomfort by this point. He observed that Rupert was looking mildly abashed, and his head crowded with nightmare visions of what Rupert's embarrassing 'mutilation' might be.

'Crikey Cosmo! Talk about putting me on the spot!' said a red Rupert, 'I'll show them if it shuts you up!' and he rose to reveal.

'Oh gosh!' thought Valentine, 'He's going to show! Can I dare to look or bear to know?' and holding his breath, he watched Rupert remove his vest, and was thankful that it was his vest and not his shorts, for he was uncertain that he could stomach a more southerly sight of distress.

Rupert stood before them all, stripped from the waist up and twisted his tremendous, tan and taut torso to exhibit both his back and his front, and he hoped that what he had to show did not cause Valentine any disturbance.

As it was, the muscularity in motion moved Valentine to such an extent that he did not at first see the cause of the others intake of oxygen. Presently, he discerned two sets of quadruple parallel scores fixed in Rupert's flesh; one set near the centre of his back, and another, quite shorter, upon the left of his heroic pectorals.

'But what was this?' Valentine asked himself in astonishment as his jaw dropped to the floor. He stood to scrutinise the curious markings, whereupon he came to learn that whatever had created them had cut quite deep. They seemed to have healed many moons ago but still the lines of scar tissue were pale and not caramelised like the surrounding skin, and no golden hair could grow from the formation on Rupert's chest, though of course, his beautiful back was hairless.

Valentine touched the sinister strips with his finger tips, and asked, 'But what happened?'

'A lion happened!' announced Cosmo.

'A *lion*!' cried Valentine, and Corny's silver fork plopped to the bottom of the fishbowl as he stared at Rupert with wonderment.

Mindful that she might be wise to express an interest in anything regarding Rupert, Olivia smiled benignly, and though she doubted the likelihood, she asked, 'Is this so?'

Rupert said yes; it had been a lion that had happened.

Valentine was awash with awe, 'Gosh! Really not? But why ever would a lion attack you? Where were you? Did you manage to overpower the beast and slay him? I'll bet you did! I'll bet you killed the beast with your bare hands just like Heracles, or did you use a jolly big club? Gosh!'

He felt fit to faint with the excitement of it all; Rupert was incredible – he could slaughter lions! He ought to be proud of his wounds and wear them like medals. They were *not* mutilations!

Cosmo burst out laughing and Rupert grinned because he had once more provoked Valentine's admiration, but he said, 'Crikey, Valentine! It wasn't like that at all!'

Now Valentine was confused, he could not perceive how a clash with a big cat could end without at least one death – surely, it had not ended by Rupert shaking him by the paw!

'You must've maimed him at least!'

'It wasn't a him, it was a her,' said Rupert. 'So actually it wasn't a lion but a lioness, and her name was Chephirah, and we were the best of friends.'

'Friends with a lion?'

Rupert began: 'It was my gap year and I wanted to do something good, you know, something to help, and I wanted to travel, be somewhere hot. My dad, he told me about his buddy, Dylan, known him since school, who lives in Kenya, running a sanctuary for lions that are hurt or ill. He nurses them back to health and then releases them back into the wild, or sometimes, if they never fully regain their strength, they stay in the sanctuary. I thought it sounded interesting, and it wasn't something anyone else I knew was doing.

'I'd been there almost a month when I spotted a young lioness, Chephirah, on my patrol. Crikey! She was a mess! She could barely walk, she had a nasty bites on her hind legs; been in a fight or something, so, of course, she couldn't hunt, and she was practically starved to death. So we took her in.

'In a few months, she looked in pretty good shape again, so they examined her and found that though she was getting better, she wasn't ready to be released yet. I was glad because I was a bit lonely out there. Not much to do at night, and no one to talk to really. Dylan is a great guy, but not much of a talker.

'But it was okay because I had Chephirah, I loved talking to her. I would just talk and talk to her, night after night, lying under the stars, and she would listen, I mean, not just hear but listen, and she would just gaze at me. Her big cat eyes seemed so wise, full of love and so gentle, that it was hard to believe that she could kill.

'It was frustrating having to talk to her through the bars, but I had to, but every night I would get a little closer to them, closer to her, and before long, it was like we were practically lying side by side. No one else knew; it was our secret – mine and Chephirah's.

'But soon she got restless. She started pacing up and down as I talked to her. Never took her eyes off me though. Sometimes she would push her nose through and stare at me, as if she was looking right into my soul. I was so tempted to reach out and touch but I just couldn't do it.

'Then one afternoon, I heard that four of the cats were being released the next day, and that Chephirah would be one of them.

'Crikey! I was down about that! I mean, it was amazing she was healthy again, but who was I going to talk to after she went?

'That night I found it hard to talk. I think she understood, and we sat for hours just looking at each other. I stayed out there longer than I ever had before, the sun started to rise, and I knew I had to go. I stood up and told her goodbye, that I wouldn't see her again, and for the first time, she didn't seem to understand me, and that's what did it.

'I couldn't hold it back; I just cried and cried. I took hold of two of the bars, and lent my head against the one in-between, and I bawled like a baby.

'Next thing I knew, Chephirah was up on her hind legs, with her paws up on the bars I was holding. She was massive! Towering over me! I should've been scared but I wasn't – her eyes told me not to be, they told me not to cry.

'Suddenly, she pushed through and grabbed me, pulling me forward. She rested her other paw on my chest, and pushed her nose through and licked my face and hair.

'I don't think I ever felt so safe and comforted before. It was amazing! We stayed like that for at least five minutes, but then somehow we both knew we had to say goodbye.

'It was when she let go of me that her claws sunk in. It wasn't on purpose or anything, I mean she could've killed me if she wanted, it was just like when a regular cat scratches you by mistake. It hurt like the dickens I can tell you! My shirt was ripped in the front and back, and I was bleeding lots.

'I tried cleaning it up myself with some alcohol, but Dylan found me and went crazy, but he fixed me up, and he had to admit it was pretty amazing!'

Upon finishing his lion tale, Rupert looked both proud and embarrassed.

'That *weally* is amazing! C*ww*umbs! You are *weally* lucky, *W*upert!' said Harry.

'I don't think I've heard the full version before,' Cosmo said, sneering, 'You always left out the bits about lying under the stars and staring into souls whenever you told me.'

'I've a lion in my bedroom,' announced Gubsy, 'Brother Sebastian shot it.'

'Oh! What a wonderful and magical story!' said Willy. 'But so sad too! Did you ever see Chephirah again?'

Rupert sighed. 'No. I wasn't allowed to go and watch her be released because they thought it might not be safe. Anyway, I was all bandaged and stitched up by then.'

'Oh! How wretched!' sympathised Willy.

'Actually, that's why I have just come back from Kenya. I said I was going to visit Dylan, but really I wanted to see if I could spot Chephirah in the wild, but I couldn't find her.'

'How romantic!' Willy said, with a swoon, 'Isn't it romantic, Valentine?'

For a space, Valentine was inarticulate; all manner of sensations consumed him. From the very first, he had been strongly alert to Rupert's physical beauty and over the course of the afternoon, he had learned also of his gallantry, of his generosity, kindness and protectiveness. Yet now to see Rupert at such close range in a state of semi-nudity and to discover that he possessed scars made by a royal animal, induced in Valentine feelings of explosive amour, and to learn the specifics of the liaison with a lioness was the very summit, for from it, Valentine learned of Rupert's deep sensitivity.

It was patent to Valentine that Chephirah too had been aware of Rupert's finer feelings, and that is why she had been so gentle with him, as she might with one of her cubs, thereby, Valentine reasoned, rendering Rupert a lion amongst mere men.

Presently, Valentine viewed Rupert as a lion-man, a *golden* lion-man – no, better than that! – a golden lion-*king*! He told himself that he was in love with a golden lion-king – of course he was; had he not always possessed a predilection for the superior? – and he was tremulous with delight at the notion of their impending betrothal!

Valentine, clasped his hands to his chest and sang out, 'Gosh! I do! Oh! I *do*!'

Such a histrionic response from Valentine was nothing out of the ordinary in the eyes of his closest kin but Cosmo could not contain a scoff.

Rupert was rather surprised but nevertheless pleased at Valentine's unexpectedly zealous reply.

He placed a palm upon Valentine's nape, laughed, and said, 'Crikey! *Thank* you!'

Olivia now felt empathetic in the extreme toward Valentine's penchant for beauty, for Rupert was beautiful. Harry was good-looking but she considered the fine specimen before her to be quite something else, though she was pleased when he put his vest back on for decorum was imperative always – especially at the table.

Whilst listening to Rupert's experience, she gauged also that he was stupid – for who else but a person of supreme stupidity would put himself within such easy reach of a man-eating mammal? However, she did not consider stupidity to be much of a hindrance in a man; Monty had been devoid of too much brainpower, and she had found that to be very agreeable.

Quickly, she ticked a mental checklist – civilised; tick, witless; tick, and, for Valentine's sake, beautiful; tick – so far, so good. However, there was, of course, the vital component she had yet to ascertain; was Rupert rich?

She made the decision to discover immediately the form of his financial situation, for she would not waste any more time in binding a bond betwixt the boys if it transpired that Rupert was poor – in which case she would have to do all within her power to quash the crush so that Valentine could look to fry fish of bigger fortune.

Holding Rupert in her steely gaze, Olivia said to him, 'It is a very impressive story and indeed, also most amazing, but I cannot help but think of what worry and cause for concern you must have inflicted upon your poor parents. I can only imagine that they were deeply distressed and so far away too! In fact, from whence do they hail, and may I ask, what it is that they do?'

Harry grimaced and Valentine shuddered, and they both felt that they would like to tell Rupert that he need not reply, but realising that saying so would only sound rude they said nothing.

Gubsy ground his false teeth in fury, and loudly asked Harry if he knew how long his mother might be staying.

'*W*eally don't know, Gubsy,' came Harry's whispered reply as he tore himself a chunk of peshwari naan.

Valentine watched with ardour Rupert wipe with a white linen napkin the bhindi bhaji from his lips, and cleanse his palate with a gulp of water.

'Yes, they were worried,' answered Rupert, 'Mum was really upset and wanted me to come home right away, but Dad trusted Dylan's opinion that I was all right, so that was all right.

'From whence do they hail? Well, Mum's Austrian and Dad's a Brit, comes from Salcombe, that's where I grew up too, but he lives down under now.'

Austrian! – thought Valentine – that is quite like German! Virtually Aryan! Small wonder he is so breathtaking and blonde!

'How exciting to be of foreign extraction!' he exclaimed.

'And your mother? Where does she live now?' asked Olivia, thinking that it would never do if Rupert came from a broken home.

'Oh, she doesn't,' said Rupert, twisting his napkin, 'She died six years ago.'

Valentine's heart broke as he saw the sadness sweep over Rupert's face. He touched him on the shoulder, and said, 'I'm so sorry, Rupert.'

As if a spell had been broken, Rupert's countenance brightened and he beamed at Valentine.

'It's okay really, Dad remarried, and Nicole is the best step-mum ever! Only problem is she's from Australia.'

'Well, I have heard that Australians are quite charming really,' consoled Willy, piling her plate with salmon biriyani and Bombay aloo.

'Ha-ha! Crikey! No, that's not what I meant. I mean, she didn't want to live here, so Dad moved out there, and I can't think of Brisbane as home.'

'Gosh! Yes, and it's so very far away, isn't it?' said Valentine. 'I've seen it on the drinks' cabinet. Have you ever thought of visiting him?'

'Oh, I've been out there lots; Dad and Nicole are the only family I've got, apart from my cousin Izzy, so it's great seeing them, but it's not home.'

'Gosh! You have been *all* the way over there?'

'Crikey, lots of times!'

'Gosh! You are so very lucky! Did you ever see a kangaroo?'

'Ha-ha! Yes, one or two.'

'Gosh! You have seen and travelled so much!' said Valentine, wishing that he could see some foreign places.

'Yes, I'm lucky but England is home.'

'Hear! Hear!' boomed Gubsy.

'You say that, Rupert, but you've been all over the bloody place,' said Cosmo, 'Since you left school I don't think you've stayed put for more than six months at a time.'

'No, that's not true; when Mum died I stayed with Dad in Salcombe for two years and helped him with the business.'

Olivia saw her chance to enquire again the nature of his father's business, but missed it when Willy asked, 'Where else have you been?'

'Yes, do tell!' said Valentine excitedly.

Rupert smiled and said, 'Whew! Crikey! I guess Cosmo's right; I have been all over. Let's see, well, you already know I've been to Kenya and Australia, and of course, we'd often go as a family; my mum, dad and me, to Austria to visit my oma and opa; that's how you say granny and granddad there.'

'What funny and adorable names!' chortled Willy.

'I *love* oma and opa!' gushed Valentine, imagining them to live in a cottage made entirely of gingerbread with cuckoo clocks all over the place, 'Where else have you been?'

'Well, I think I told you I've been to Hawaii, didn't I, Valentine?'

'Gosh, yes! Gosh, mummy! Rupert blew my conch just like a horn!'

Olivia was not sure how to swallow this piece of information and decided to ignore it.

'Where else?' asked Willy, who had almost forgotten entirely the existence of her curry.

'*Hmm*, the usual places in Europe; Italy, Spain, Portugal and France, and I've been to Toronto and Los Angeles and Ipanema too, working on beaches and in bars.'

Valentine gasped, 'Can you mix Grasshoppers?'

'A grasshopper?' Cosmo boomed.

'Don't ask!' said Harry, 'It's an impossible d*w*ink to make.'

Cosmo then said it sounded like a made-up drink.

Valentine executed an extreme tut and Rupert said, 'Actually, it is a genuine drink, and if you have the ingredients then I can make it for you, Valentine.'

'Gosh! Glorious!' Valentine said, rapturously, 'Where else have you been?'

'I think that about covers it,' answered Rupert as if sorry to disappoint.

'So many places!' said Willy. 'Where do you think is loveliest of all?'

Rupert did not hesitate in saying that England was the loveliest, which triggered another 'Hear! Hear!' from Gubsy.

Olivia was beside herself with impatience. Usually she would have no qualm whatsoever in interrupting her children's imbecilic chatter, but mindful that it remained to be seen whether Rupert's people possessed means she bit her tongue. She now saw her opportunity to persevere with her probing and she snatched at it.

'Yes, England really is most lovely; I'm certain that your father would not bring himself to leave it for anything other than love. But tell me, how did the move affect his business? Is it one that he is able to operate overseas? What, in fact, is his vocation?'

'Like a bitch with a bone,' Gubsy growled into his tarka dal.

Olivia's offspring, even Corny, were each aware that much hinged on Rupert's response. If it was one that failed to meet their mother's expectations, then she could conceivably make matters sticky for the pair, even if Valentine was, more than the rest of them, capable of conquering her opposition.

With bated breath, they awaited his words, and Rupert, as if aware of the weight of his reply, let the ormolu clock strike its eight chimes in the next room, before smiling and saying, 'My dad deals in property.'

The siblings heaved a collective sigh of relief; they could all but hear the churn and swirl of bricks and mortar spinning in their mother's mind as her eyes seemed to grow greener with the notion of wealth.

Having no interest in the financial status of Rupert's father, Valentine felt rather fed up that his own mother was being so unrefined. Therefore, he endeavoured to divert the discussion.

'What's Salcombe like? I should love to go one day!' he said.

Rupert turned to Valentine and dazzled him with his smile.

'Salcombe is beautiful, you would love it. Lots of sailing, and lots of shellfish, and the summers are amazing, almost Mediterranean, we even get dolphins sometimes.'

'Dolphins! Gosh!' swooned Valentine.

'And your father,' interposed Olivia, 'does he possess properties in Salcombe?'

'Yes, he's got a few there,' Rupert replied, 'A couple are right on the estuary, and another has an amazing view of the sea, and two more further inland.'

'A sea view!' said Valentine, bursting with excitement, 'Gosh! How glorious!'

Olivia too, considered it glorious, for she felt certain that a sea view situation in Salcombe would be worth something in the region of a million or two, or three, and perhaps even four, and what was more, it was not the only property; Rupert had referred to five.

'And what does he do with these properties? Does he let or sell them?' she asked.

'Well, he lets some of them; the ones he doesn't want to sell. The others, sure, he sells them. That's how he makes money; he buys a place, renovates it, I mean makes it amazing. I've helped with some of them, though not the ones in Australia, and then he sells them at the right time for a profit, then buys a bigger place to renovate and sell.'

'He certainly sounds to be a very shrewd man, and I always find that to be a most admirable characteristic,' said a sated Olivia, for she now had no hesitation with the decision that she was very well pleased with the prospect of a connubial connexion betwixt the boys. She would grant Valentine his prince charming whose golden glow she had been right to suspect was not due solely to his being beautiful but also, and probably predominantly, because his father had money – even if it was new and he did not sound to be 'smart'.

'Thank you, Mrs Avery-Stripe,' said Rupert.

'Oh, darling! I insist that you call me Olivia!'

'Crikey! Then, thank you, *Olivia*.'

'You are, indeed, most welcome, Rupert,' and with that, Olivia exposed to him her canines before returning to her plate.

CHAPTER 8

A Glorious Idea

There descended upon the table a silence most welcome for it signalled that Olivia's investigation was complete. Moreover, the conclusion had met with her satisfaction and would hopefully render her less spiky.

Rupert nudged his knee against Valentine's. Their eyes met, Rupert rolled his, which forced Valentine to stifle a laugh with his napkin for he felt quite dizzy with happiness.

The sensation reminded him of how he would feel whilst drinking that last glass of champagne before oblivion kicks in and inhibition is disposed of, thus making the idea of swinging from the chandelier seem a very clever one.

However, he was wise enough not to try any such acrobatics on the crystal gondola suspended over what remained of their Indian supper, and instead he pushed back his seat, rose, and exclaimed, 'Gosh everybody! I have just had a most glorious idea!'

Upon learning that Valentine had had one of his 'glorious ideas' Corny mirrored his action by jumping up and looking extraordinarily excited despite not yet having learned precisely what the idea might be. He was sure that it would be a good one though; one that would involve untold amounts of fun, and he was beside himself with the thrill of anticipation.

Olivia wished that Valentine were not quite so fond of exclaimed statements and scenes.

'Do sit down, darling, you are exciting Corny,' she said.

'Gosh, mummy! My idea is one bound to make Corny simply explode with excitement!'

Hearing this, Corny felt full of panic, and flung his arms over his head to brace himself for his explosion.

Harry, physically coaxing Corny out of his cower, asked Valentine, 'Well, what is your glo*w*ious idea?'

Valentine basked in being the centre of attention for a moment, and then declared, 'My glorious idea is that we ought to have a most marvellous party! A birthday party! For Corny's sixteenth!'

'Oh! What a good idea!' said Willy, 'I really think we ought!'

'A ve*w*y good idea!' agreed Harry, 'Would you like that, *wascal*?'

The rapture that these words induced in Corny virtually destroyed him. He did rather feel quite like he might explode, and his appearance became that of one who had just learned that his wildest wishes would come true all at once as he grasped spaces of air above his head and hopped like a mad thing with its feet on fire.

He looked fit to rocket up to the moon but Olivia knocked loudly with her spoon.

'I do not think it to be such a 'glorious' or 'good' idea!' she said to them, 'There will be no party.'

Corny and Valentine returned their bottoms to their seats with deflation, and the table turned to Olivia with dismay.

'But, mummy! Why ever not?' Willy asked.

'Well, for one thing, Wilhelmina, there is not enough time to put into action the according arrangements.'

'We've two whole weeks, mummy! That's plenty!' Valentine remonstrated.

'Oh, you think so, do you, darling?'

'Indubitably!' he replied. 'Do not worry, mummy, I'm certain no one shall expect you to assist.'

Staring hard at him, Olivia wondered at his audacity. Had she not approved of Rupert? Was that not enough? It would appear that it was not, for now he wished to have a party, and she possessed the intellect to deduct that the party he had in mind would not be a simple affair. She knew that his vision would be something verging on a ball, and this was a notion that did not sit well with her because balls meant people and she was not fond of people; further, balls cost money, of which she had little to none, and, moreover, where, exactly, would they hold this ball? Surely not Chinchero?

'That, Valentino, is not the issue!' she said in strangled tones.

'Well, whatever is the issue then?' asked Valentine, 'Just look at Corny, mummy, he is disturbed!'

Corny was the very image of wretchedness weeping and sniffing pathetically.

With his arm around Corny, and wiping away the tears as fast as they fell, Harry said, 'I *w*eally think you should *w*econsider, mummy, it is his sixteenth after all, and I can't *w*emember the last time he had a birthday party.'

'I didn't have a sixteenth birthday party!' said Willy pitifully.

'Gosh! And I didn't have a twenty-first!' added Valentine. 'And that proves the point that we are in desperate need of a party!' and contorted a look of anguish on his face that he turned to Rupert.

Olivia now felt herself immensely embarrassed in front of Rupert, and said to her children, 'I very much regret appearing to be a wicked witch but I am thinking in practical terms, and would very much like to know where it is that you had in mind to hold this party?'

'Gosh! Well, here of course! Right here at Chinchero! Where else?' said Valentine.

'And that is precisely why your "marvellous party" idea is not practicable, darling.'

During the discourse between Olivia and her children, Cosmo and Rupert had considered it best to keep quiet, but from Gubsy and Gretchen came gnashing and snorting.

Olivia's last comment pushed the gnashing to a crescendo and Gubsy demonstrated his loss of patience by slamming on the table his large, liver spotted fists, and roaring, 'I'd like to know what *precisely* is not *practicable* about Chinchero!'

Unaccustomed to being directly addressed to by Gubsy, Olivia faltered; his fury reminded her so of Monty's, but even Monty had not ever appeared to blow steam from his ears when in a rage – perhaps that would have come with age.

She tried to articulate to him her definition of practicable, but was unable to find a diplomatic way to say she thought Chinchero on the point of collapse, especially when he glowered at her in the intimidating way that a bull would red, and she produced only sounds of a wheezing sort as she sought the elusive words.

Her discomfiture made Valentine want to create mischief, and he realised that if he could channel Gubsy's fury in the right direction it would be the making of the marvellous party.

Thus, to stoke the fire, he said, 'I think what mummy is trying to say, Gubsy, is that she considers Chinchero to be in a . . . what was it she said? . . . Oh, yes! "A stark state of disrepair" and therefore, I imagine, she considers it too tawdry for a party.'

Olivia looked at Valentine with incredulity, and Gretchen decided that she had heard enough; she would not sit and be insulted and she started to clear the table, gratefully accepting Rupert's assistance.

'Valentine!' reproved Harry, 'Don't cause twouble!'

With a tut and a moue, Valentine quietened. He knew that he perhaps had been a little too naughty, but what he said was true; his mother had spoken those exact words. Besides which, he told himself, Corny really ought to have a marvellous party!

'A stark state of disrepair?' Did you say that? Did you say that, eh?' Gubsy bellowed at Olivia.

Having prevailed over her initial shock of Gubsy's rage, she saw him now as nothing but a bully, and this, combined with her annoyance with Valentine's troublemaking, roused within her the confidence to tell the old despot the exact extent to which she judged Chinchero to be incredibly dilapidated.

As she catalogued the various and numerous eyesores and malfunctions, she seemed to increase in magnitude and her children grew increasingly ashamed with each addition to her extremely long list that consisted of everything from hinges that squeaked to ceilings that were fit to fall on their heads at any moment.

She was fearless and she was relentless, and then finally, when she was satisfied that she had not overlooked a single flaw, she silenced herself and glared at Gubsy defiantly.

Gubsy held her glare and he marvelled at it. He marvelled at her shamelessness, and, for a flash, he admired it, and in that flash he saw a spark of the reason why his nephew had fallen for her – besides her once exquisite looks.

Nevertheless, he would not let her win. She may possess pluck but he was an Avery-Stripe and it was his house, whereas she was a mere baby-maker for the family and a non-paying lodger.

'I am gravely offended!' he boomed.

'I am simply telling you what is plain to see!' she said, still seething.

'It is an insult that you have not brought any of this to my attention before now!' he continued to boom. 'You know that my eyesight is not what it once was, and for you to take advantage of that is beyond the pale! And if you think for one moment that not informing me of them until this late hour is going to prevent a party for the young'un then you are mistaken!'

To say that Olivia looked astonished by Gubsy's response would not convey adequately her appearance of severe surprise. The last thing she had expected was to be admonished for not complaining sooner, and on top of this, Gubsy, despite being made fully aware of the dereliction, was all for the party.

'Oh! Gubsy!' squealed Willy, 'You mean there shall be a party?'

'Why, of course,' he replied, 'there was always going to be a party.'

'Oh! How wonderful!' she said, running round the table to cuddle his rotundity.

'Hu*ww*ah!' said Harry, 'You hear that, *w*ascal? There will be a party for you!'

A loud *squelch* came from Corny as he slurped up the runny snot that his grief had caused to seep steadily from his nose. He triple blinked his teary eyes dry in surprise, and not knowing who to embrace he settled on hugging himself whilst laughing in animated silence.

Rupert's return from the kitchen, where he had been busy helping Gretchen with the dishes, and a pudding of sorbet the flavours of mango and mandarin that he now set before each of them, caused Valentine to feel just as joyous.

'Gosh, Rupert!' he exclaimed as Rupert sat back down next to him, 'We shall be having the marvellous party after all!'

'Crikey! That's amazing!' Rupert enthused.

'Don't you think? Gubsy said we might! And, oh! It *will* be marvellous, won't it, Gubsy?'

'Indubitably!' boomed the great uncle, 'But your mother is right about one thing.'

'Oh?'

'We are short of time if it's going to be done properly and I won't have a party if it is not done properly.'

'Gosh, no!'

'And the first thing that needs sorting is all, or as many as possible, of the things that your mother has been too lazy to bring to my notice before now. I will not have people thinking Chinchero's a ruin.'

'Excuse me, Mr Avery-Stripe,' said Rupert, for just as Gretchen had heard Olivia's list of grievances so too had he, and not one of them was a thing that he could not fix, 'but I could help with all of that.'

Everyone looked at him with interest, and Gubsy, somewhat perturbed as he had misunderstood the proposal, said to him, 'Out of the question, young man! The Avery-Stripes do not accept charity! I can easily afford to pay for repairs myself!'

Slightly reddened over the misinterpretation of his offer, Rupert clarified, 'Crikey! Actually, I meant that I can do all those jobs for you.'

'Gosh! Really not?' exclaimed Valentine.

'Could you? Could you really?' said a pleasantly surprised Gubsy.

Rupert, relieved that the confusion had been tidied, said, 'Sure, pretty much. I mean all of the minor stuff anyway. I mean, there's not enough time before your party to fix any major structural problems if there are any, but I can definitely fix the minor. No problem at all, it's all easy stuff; I've done tons of stuff like that working on my dad's houses.'

'Could you mend my windows?' asked Willy excitedly.

'I can put new ones in, sure; easy!'

'Ooh!'

Gubsy beamed at Rupert and announced that he was 'a very handy fellow to have about the house indeed!'

Olivia thought it ridiculous; to have Rupert labouring in the house as if he were a common factotum was not what she had had in mind for him. She was vexed beyond belief that the family could not see that he was only being polite and did not expect them to take him up on his offer. She was certain that they would not see him for dust after this; she considered her vision for Valentine doomed.

'I can re-paper your walls too, if you'd like, *Olivia*,' Rupert smiled at her.

In an instant Olivia's anguish lessened considerably, and she replied; 'Oh, but darling, that is too much!'

'I insist! And Gretchen's kitchen cupboards too!'

'Master Rupert! That would be amazink!' glowed Gretchen.

Harry and Cosmo watched as everyone looked at Rupert in adulation. It made Harry wish that he were as good with his hands, but just as Monty had been, he was all fingers and thumbs when it came to DIY. Cosmo was resentful that Rupert might be casting him in a bad light for he had no intention at all of getting to grips with manual labour.

'Look here,' said Cosmo, 'I'm all for lending a hand but I don't think I can with my foot.'

'Gosh, Cosmo! I wasn't aware that Rupert would be renovating with his feet!' exclaimed Valentine, causing Cosmo to fume and scowl.

'Well, if you think you can get it all done in time for the party, I'll pay you good money, young man!' said Gubsy to Rupert.

'Crikey!' Rupert replied, 'There's no charge, I'd be happy to do it; think of it as my contribution to the marvellous party, and my payment for a place to sleep.' For something inside him was saying that he would enjoy a prolonged stay in the home of the Avery-Stripes.

'*Payment for a place to sleep!*' repeated Gubsy, 'Let me tell you now, young man,' he said, wagging his finger, 'you are my guest! And there will always be a bed for you here!'

'Gosh, yes! *Always!*' emphasised Valentine, elated that Rupert's residence was concrete, and Rupert was also.

'Crikey! Thanks, Mr Avery-Stripe!' said Rupert, 'And don't worry; I'll get the jobs done in time; two weeks isn't it?'

'Yes! Two weeks tonight! June 22!' said Willy.

'Bravo!' boomed Gubsy, 'Jolly good! Jolly good! Then the house will be perfect for the party!'

Valentine's head simply span with magnificent ideas of how the party ought to be, and said, 'Might it be a fancy-dress party, Gubsy?'

'Certainly not!' was the swift rebuke.

'Gosh!' said Valentine, dejected but not defeated. 'How about a masked ball?'

'Ridiculous suggestion!' was the retort

Valentine thought it most unfair for the party had been his idea, but upon regarding Rupert, he realised that a masked ball would not be so glorious really, as it would hide from view his beautiful face, and Valentine wanted very much to show that off.

'I certainly do not want to wear a beastly mask ever again in my life!' said Willy.

'If I'm to foot the bill for this party then it's to be done my way!' announced Gubsy. 'And I won't be having any of your namby-pamby ways, young man! Masked ball! Fancy dress, indeed! Not a bit of it!'

To this, Valentine could not help but elaborately tut, but his pique petered out when Rupert squeezed and jostled his knee to cheer him.

'I remember well the sorts of parties my parents had, they were sophisticated affairs, and that's just the sort we'll be having,' continued Gubsy.

'Oh! What a lovely idea!' exclaimed Willy.

Valentine considered Gubsy's decree. He pondered it and his mood became merry once more.

'Gosh! You mean to say the chaps are to wear white tie and tails?' he asked eagerly.

'I think that would be appropriate,' affirmed the great uncle.

'And the ladies chic dresses and sparkling tiaras and to be simply dripping with diamonds?'

'Certainly!'

'Not everybody possesses diamonds and tiaras, Valentine,' interjected Olivia.

'Then they must get some if they are to expect entry!' he cried.

Olivia felt hopeless in the face of Valentine's lackadaisical relationship with reality, and realised that there was nothing to be done but accept that his ball would be held, and she knew, without a flicker of uncertainty, that it would somehow evolve into calamity.

'And we will not be having any inane modern music. I like Elgar and I like Strauss!' said Gubsy, adding emphasis to his statement with knocks of his dessertspoon on the table.

'Gosh! With proper dancing with partners?' Valentine queried quite breathlessly.

'Only villains and drunks dance alone!'

'Gosh! And what to drink?'

'Champagne, of course! Lots of it!'

With every word that he heard, Valentine found himself in deeper accord with Gubsy's concept and could quite clearly see that the entire event was to be nothing short of a shimmering gala that was to sparkle and glisten so very brightly that it would outshine the stars and devastate the moon into darkest oblivion!

He decided that absolutely everybody must receive an invitation.

'I shall organise the invitations!' he exclaimed. 'And the glorious stiffies that I shall give everyone will be so hard to resist that they will all be bound to come!'

'Valentine!' Harry censured.

'They will!' argued Valentine. He turned to Rupert, and said, 'And although you live here now, I will give you a stiffy too.'

'Crikey!' said Rupert, 'Thanks! I look forward to getting it; I'll definitely come!' and he grinned.

'The tragedy of the reality,' said Olivia, who seemed to simultaneously address everyone and no-one, as she licked her spoon before letting it *clank* into her empty silver bowl, 'is the awful lack of lucky people to whom Valentine can *give* a stiffy.'

Olivia had a point, for the Avery-Stripes were many things but not one of them was popular. It was not so much that they were disliked but more that they all either suffered from a superiority complex or were so insular because they had each other, or both, and therefore, did not much feel the need for 'people'.

Valentine refused to accept entirely the truth of his mother's statement by mentally hunting people to whom he could give stiffies. Presently, upon overturning a psychological stone, he thought of his cousin Flick, and triumphantly, he said, 'I am positive that cousin Flick would love a stiffy!'

'Felicity?' asked Olivia with astonishment, for only twenty-four hours ago Valentine had referred to her as a dipso-nympho.

'Yes, Flick, Felicity,' he said, and he asked Cosmo, 'Where is she? She'll come!'

Cosmo had loved his little sister Flick when they had been children together but now they were older they had gone their separate ways and he considered her ways strange. He supposed he did still love her really, even if she was a trifle *outré*, but he had not an iota of an idea where exactly she might be, and was not sure he wanted to speculate.

'Not exactly sure,' he replied, unhelpfully.

'Hmm, I'll track her down!' said Valentine with determination. 'There you go, mummy, Flick'll come!'

'If Flick comes,' said Olivia, 'you won't need anyone else; you could fill the Albert Hall with her *charisma* alone!'

Cosmo scowled at Olivia's acerbity but feeling he had to agree he said nothing.

'And Corny will invite his fwiends too,' added Harry, as Corny writhed ecstatically in his lap.

Olivia had not thought of that. She lowered her lids and prayed for mercy as she imagined the arrival of a minibus load of Corny's like-minded friends.

'I'd like to invite my cousin Izzy too, if I may,' said Rupert. 'I'm not sure she'll come; she's so shy, but I know she'd like to be asked, and maybe I can talk her into it.'

'You can invite any damn person you like, young man!' Gubsy boomed.

'Gosh! Do make her come! I should love to meet her!' said Valentine, wondering how his dear and sweet sounding, shy and soon to be cousin-in-law might look – a female Rupert perhaps? She was bound to be beautiful, he thought, and then he asked, 'Does she have a tiara?'

'Ha-ha! She might; I'll ask! And I'm sure she'd love to meet you too,' said Rupert.

That Rupert's cousin might attend the party set Olivia's mind in motion. Might Izzy be someone suitable for Harry? Had not Rupert alluded that she may be in possession of a tiara? But would it be one of real diamonds or merely imitation? Olivia would have to investigate and she started to hope. Perhaps this party will prove provident, she thought.

'What about you, Willy?' asked Valentine, 'Who will you invite? I'm counting stiffies in my mind.'

The faces that the question caused Willy to contort whilst she pondered who she might like to ask produced in Olivia the desire to warn her of the disastrous consequence if there was a change in the wind. Yet before she could voice caution, Gubsy cleared his throat, and boomed, 'Ask anyone you wish, dear girl, but I trust you not to choose that Strap wench you dunged up – ha!'

As if served a sudden slap to the face Willy startled, and Valentine's gasp was incredible.

Olivia's confusion at the comment and the subsequent reactions fast led to a dawning of what she had not hitherto known; and this rising of the sun illumined a great many things, but before she let rip she sought confirmation.

'Who is this Strap wench of whom you speak?' she asked Gubsy, tersely.

'Eh?' he responded, as he grinned approvingly at Willy, for he still liked to laugh about the seeing to she had administered the blasphemer. 'Oh, just a nasty little miss that chose to taunt Willy with a defamatory doggerel. But don't worry yourself; Willy set her right and filled the brat's face with fertiliser on the stable floor! Oh! Ha-ha-ha! When I think of it! Oh dear! My word! Ha-ha-ha!' and he wiped from his face the tears of mirth that the recollection had induced.

Thus, the cat was out of the bag and set amongst the pigeons and Olivia, now aware that the woman who had cast such vehemently con-temptuous glances at the fête was Geraldine Strap, felt herself to be on the precipice of a paroxysm of satanic rage.

The gathering observed how she seemed about to self-ignite. All were confused as to why, save Willy whose petrification had rendered her immobile, and Valentine, who thought it wise to keep his lips zipped.

Olivia turned slowly, and she zapped virtually visible razor-beams of bone-penetrating wrath at her daughter.

Clever Corny indulged his idea to grab Gloriana and run to another part of Chinchero and hide, and Gretchen hastened to chase him with a napkin to make his face nice again.

Willy braced herself for the shrieking influx of imprecations she felt sure would shoot forth from her bloodthirsty mother for she looked fit to spit far worse than feathers.

However, Olivia somehow summoned a form of otherworldly power and managed to find the discipline not to combust, for she had no wish to cause a scene the likes of a kitchen-sink drama in the presence of Rupert.

Therefore, her verbal response was not at all incinerating but positively glacial to the point of freezing, and when the words of her question to

Willy; 'Is this correct?' snaked from her mouth they sounded so cool as to be sheathed with sinister icicles.

Stiff with fear, Willy was without verbal ability and looked to be hypnotised by the cold enquiry.

'I repeat, Wilhelmina, is this correct? Did you, or did you not, orally exploit the Strap girl with equine excrement?'

Harry was dumbfounded, and fondled his beads, whereas Cosmo revealed that he considered the notion amusing by emitting an involuntary guffaw, and they both looked to the rigid Willy between them who acknowledged her mother's suspicion as being spot-on with a reluctant and tremulous nod.

Olivia's response was to give the impression that she had the ambition to vacuum the entire room and its contents up through her nasal passage and, in a voice so sharp it might cut with a swift slash, she said, 'All is crystal clear to me; for the very first time I see, and it deeply distresses me to an inconsolable degree, the deplorable and despicable daughter you are! You are a very evil, exceedingly vicious and wretched little girl and I wish you to vacate my vision this very instant!'

Poor Willy, humiliated before Cosmo, and mortified beyond imagination, stared with shock at her hostile mother who held her pose and awaited her vacation.

Gubsy did his best to intervene: 'I say! Just who do you think you are! In my own home!' But Olivia would not suffer him this time and with no small amount of aggression, put up her hand to silence him.

'Get out of my sight! Go to your room!' she seethed at Willy who still had not displayed any suggestion of motion.

'Gosh! Mummy!' tried Valentine in a reasoning tone.

Immediately, Olivia swivelled to face him, displayed her teeth, and all but hissed to caution his encroach.

Without looking at anything other than into space, Olivia galvanised her request with a chill and calm, 'Leave. Now. And do not even consider violating my vicinity until you manage to scrape together some semblance of how a young lady ought to be.'

Promptly bursting into tears that sprayed in every direction, Willy hauled herself to her feet and trudged out of the room.

Upon the sad departure, the dining room was so hushed that one could have heard a pin drop, but instead they listened to the sobs and heavy footfalls of the evictee slowly climb the stairwell and cross the landing until came the sound of the shutting of her bedroom door.

Gubsy gnashed and glared at the woman whose poisonous presence he could no longer tolerate, then postponing his port, he wished the boys a very pleasant evening and shuffled off to his wing chair to turn *The Times* into a tent.

Thus, there remained only Olivia, her two eldest, Cosmo and Rupert, and the air was thick with tension.

Olivia took it upon herself to diffuse the atmosphere; she flared into the very embodiment of ingratiating deference, and said to Rupert: 'My deepest and most absolute apologies, darling! Whatever must you think of such a frightfully unrefined and feral family? I simply dread to deliberate and shudder with the sheer shame of it! I most sincerely hope you can find it in yourself to forgive our fearful foulness and forthrightness!'

'Please, don't worry about it, Mrs . . . ' he started.

'*OLIVIA*!' she shouted.

'Crikey, sorry, *Olivia*, Please don't worry about it. I don't want any special treatment, but, Willy; do you think she's all right?' asked Rupert.

'Please do not talk to me of her!' said Olivia in a comparatively less agitated tone.

Valentine, not wanting to seem anything but virtuous in the eyes of Rupert, exclaimed, 'Gosh! But could you credit it, mummy?'

Olivia regarded him with confusion, and asked what he meant.

'What I mean, mummy, is that all Willy did was defend the family name! And it appears to me to be wildly unjust that any Avery-Stripe should be admonished purely because the Strap girl has a taste for traducement!'

'Traducement?' questioned Olivia.

'That's just what Gubsy said, isn't it? A 'defamatory doggerel!' A rude rhyme! About our family, no doubt! And it would seem to me that Willy did right in setting her straight! Don't you think? Gosh! When I think of the anguish the Strap inflicted upon Willy, why, I could simply spit – but I shan't – couldn't you?'

'I *never* spit, Valentine, as well you know, but could it not be the rude rhyme was merely making fun of Willy?'

'Willy?' he exclaimed as if scandalised, 'A person would have to be unbelievably base to base a rude rhyme about Willy! I adamantly refuse to believe such a simpleton to be in existence!'

Valentine continued, 'And though I cannot fathom a person being quite so puerile, I can believe that they might be as malevolent to mock our good name! I wholly believe that Willy did the honourable thing and dealt with the dastard in the most apropos way!'

Rather carried away with his notion of liberating Willy, Valentine roused the rabble about the table: 'Willy did right! Don't you think, Harry? She stood up to the bully! She would not be intimidated, would she, Cosmo? She stood her ground and single-handedly saw to it that the Strap might, henceforth, mind her manners! I do believe manners the very basis of civilisation, don't you, Rupert?'

Valentine's rabble opined that they supported his rousing, and Olivia found herself to be in acquiescence.

'I rather fear, mummy, you might have to offer Willy your deepest and most absolute apologies. I wonder if she will accept?' said Valentine, feeling a tingle of delight.

Olivia however, felt nothing but regret, and a mental reflection revealed to her that Valentine's view carried veracity. She realised now that she had been rather hard on Willy who had performed just as she had been raised, and revered the name of Avery-Stripe, and with no small amount of reluctance Olivia had to admit that an apology seemed to be in order, moreover; Rupert might regard her as a very petty and pretty low-class sort if she did not.

Thus, in the confines of her mind she cursed a thousand times, and resigned herself to the idea of eating humble-pie for breakfast for she could not face it immediately, and she said: 'Yes, darling, poor Willy, I was a soupçon strict I suppose, so I shall say sorry in the morning.'

'Why not now?' demanded Valentine.

'Because, Valentino,' she replied, as she eyed her Tiffany wristwatch, 'it is late, and I am tired; I simply must sleep; tomorrow is an important day for all the family.'

Valentine and Harry remembered their father and that tomorrow was the day for their annual visit to his graveside.

'Furthermore,' Olivia went on to say, 'though I concur Willy is not entirely guilty, for she did honour our name, she did not act as a lady ought, and I dread to think of what further disgrace she might inflict upon us without the deterrence of a little penitence.'

Valentine was momentarily shocked to hear his mother use almost the exact same phrase he had when pretending to Mrs Strap that he was she.

Quickly though, his accuracy tickled him, and it provoked him to say, 'And don't you think, mummy, that it would be a glorious idea to make Corny's party as marvellous as can be so to display to all the glory of the family even if only to rub the Strap's nose in it? I *really* think you ought to invite *everybody* in your little black book but her!'

This caused Olivia to smile quite as she had not in a long time. 'I possess no such "little black book",' she said, 'but I do think it an excellent idea, I shall see who I can dig up. The family deserves a sensational celebration, for we are, after all, the Avery-Stripes! Good-night, boys!'

And as if she had been but a mere reverie of questionable quality, she vanished from the room in the blink of an eye.

Olivia's concord made Valentine realise that the wretched tumult had been well worth it, for now there really would be a marvellous party. He experienced a delicious sense of triumph and he laughed internally. He felt that he could quite easily stay awake and dance and talk the entire night, especially if it were in the company of Rupert whom he knew to enjoy talking beneath a starry sky, and then Valentine thought of the west terrace.

On close and sweat-making summer nights, such as it was that very night, the Avery-Stripe children were in the habit of sleeping outside, though not in the garden as that would be unseemly and savage. However, they regarded the west terrace suitable for alfresco slumber as it was not ground level and vigorous wisteria hung in pendant clusters from the trellis all around, thus creating thick floral walls to prevent prying eyes.

Valentine suggested to Rupert that he might like to go there, and Rupert met the suggestion with alacrity. Unfortunately, Harry did too, and therefore so did Cosmo, which rather dashed Valentine's design.

He decided that as intimacy with Rupert was not imminent, he would knock on Willy to ask if she too would like a night under the sky, but though he knocked several times, and called to her through the door, there came no reply.

Valentine tutted. He very much wanted to inform Willy of the recent turn of events and that she could expect, quite miraculously, an apology from their mother.

'Pwobably best to leave it, Valentine,' said Harry, leading him away from the door, 'she's pwobably asleep anyhow.'

'*Hmm*,' said Valentine, doubtful of his brother's probabilities, but then he remembered the wisterian chamber and his overcrowded date with Rupert therein, and he was instantly devoid of worry over Willy's misery.

The warmth of the late evening was quite astonishing and deciding the climate appropriate, Gretchen had gathered many mattresses, light blankets and plump pillows and cushions on the terrace and created a sumptuous nest for the brood.

Corny had helped with the greatest excitement and looked forward to the arrival of the others. However, as he lay with his head upon a pillow and waited, he watched Gloriana endlessly circle her bowl and soon he became powerless to resist falling off into the lovely land of nod.

It touched Valentine's heart to see his sweet little brother seraphically asleep, and he sat upon a tasselled cushion adjacent to Rupert who greeted him with a broad smile.

'No Willy?' asked Rupert.

'Later, I hope,' he replied.

Rupert then proudly presented Valentine with a glass meant for a martini, into which he had poured, with a flourish, a cool pale green mixture that he had created at the globe drinks' cabinet.

'Gosh! A Grasshopper!' Valentine exclaimed, 'Thanks ever so very much!'

'Drink it and tell me what you think,' said Rupert, encouragingly.

Valentine placed the rim to his lips and sipped. The concoction washed over his palate and he knew that he was in heaven. He smiled at Rupert as he savoured the sensation of the creamy nectar seeping down his throat.

'Absolutely ambrosial!' he gasped, and Rupert grinned triumphantly, whereupon Valentine adopted an orchestrated sprawl, sipped his cocktail and enjoyed Rupert kneading his thigh with microscopic movement whilst watching him watch Cosmo construct something relaxing to smoke.

'You've got a lighter, haven't you, Valentine?' said Cosmo, when his job was complete. Willy's absence did not seem to bother him in the least.

Valentine rose to present his lighter, and upon doing so he beheld the product of Cosmo's labour and much to Cosmo's annoyance, he plucked it from him. Valentine marvelled at it and wondered how it could be that a pair of clodding hooves had the ability to form a thing of such exquisiteness for surely the formation would require a supreme delicacy of digits.

He held it up high to better examine it in the light from the lantern above, gasped and exclaimed, 'Gosh! Cosmo! Who ever would have guessed of your niche! Such artistry! I'll bet you're wizard at origami! Have you tried it?'

The idea of burly Cosmo practicing the Japanese art of paper folding caused both Rupert and Harry to laugh, and the surly artist snatched it back and took a flame to it.

'Don't be a bloody fool; course I've not tried bloody origami!'

'Gosh! Well, maybe you ought. You could start tomorrow and make some dear little things!' Valentine replied, and rendered himself recumbent again.

Filling his lungs and holding his breath, Cosmo scowled hard and said that he did not think so, and Valentine, with a tut, said he thought that to be a very sad shame.

Harry was next in line to appreciate Cosmo's artistry, and as he languidly exhaled, he said to Rupert, 'You've *weally* got your work cut out for you, you know. All the work a*w*ound Chinche*w*o in only two weeks, but Gubsy and G*w*etchen think you're a b*w*ick, and so do I, and I'll help with what I can but I'm not ve*w*y p*w*actical at all.'

Rupert replied that it was no problem; he liked being busy.

Valentine was next to indulge in the smoke, though to him the taste was not nearly as nice as an ordinary one, and he said: 'If anyone can fix it all and fix it all so fast, it's Rupert, Rupert'll fix it all, I just know you can, can't you, Rupert?'

Rupert squeezed Valentine's ankle and confirmed his faith in him. 'Of course I will. I promise I will,' he smiled.

Valentine had inhaled enough; he passed it to Rupert, and gushed, 'Gosh! Glorious!' before letting his form flop back on his mountain of cushions.

Oh! He did feel rather queer! And regarding Rupert mingled with his queer feelings a lazy gaiety that he very much desired to display but the delicious lethargy induced him to indulge purely in the pleasure of watching the object of his desires.

He heard, but did not listen to, the boys' conversation for it all sounded to be nothing but loud murmurs and random bursts of laughter. Cosmo had quite obviously put a lot into his handiwork, and its sickly, pungent scent created a heavenly and heady aroma as it suffused the peppery honey mixed with vanilla fragrance of the wisteria, whose vines Valentine now watched entwine Rupert's body.

Notions of a carnal nature claimed him as he saw Rupert now transform into the Celtic semi-cervine deity Cernunnos; lord of the wild things, of vegetation and fruitfulness, and god of lust and masculine fecundity. He fancied he saw grow, from his crown, a pair of powerful and virile antlers that he was desirous to clutch whilst Rupert bucked as a stag in a rut in the dark hot forest where it was always night but they would never sleep.

Valentine woke suddenly; he had fallen asleep after all. At first, he was not certain of his location. He viewed the stars in the sky sparkling, for the lantern was no longer alight, and the clammy night air was disconcertingly still. He sat up, looked about, and made out in the silvery-moonlight the forms of sleeping bodies that were breaking the silent night with their gentle snoring.

It was with great chagrin that he saw Rupert on his side, face turned away, his beautiful body rising and falling with the steady breaths of one in slumber.

'Bugger!' thought Valentine, for he did not want to wake him; it might not be a thing that Rupert would welcome.

Irrevocably vexed he settled back on his improvised bed, closed his eyes and tried extremely hard to concentrate on falling asleep.

Presently, he heard the sound of someone shifting. He lifted his lids and saw that it was Rupert, and he gladdened because that might mean he could at least see his face.

When Rupert had achieved his re-positioning, he settled for a space, and then slowly opened his eyes.

Valentine stopped breathing; he felt silly at being caught watching him, but his worry vanquished when he saw how the light from the moon illuminated the brilliance of Rupert's broad grin.

Valentine required no more incitement; he smiled back and nodded toward the door, and Rupert replied with a nod of his own.

Slowly, quietly, they pushed away their sheets and, careful to make not a noise, Valentine led the way.

Chinchero was silent but for the distant tick of the ormolu clock, and the landing was close to pitch black; only the golden shine of the Olympia's harp was visible.

Unsure of their destination, Rupert took hold of Valentine's hand and heard the whisper, 'Be mindful of the third.'

As Valentine pushed his ribboned key in the door, he all of a sudden remembered the raucous caws of the magpie quartet atop his turret roof that morning, they had heralded to him the arrival of a boy.

He felt full of happiness when he considered the inaccuracy, for who had arrived was far more substantial than a mere boy; he was Adonis, Apollo and Triton, and the hero Heracles, he was his royal protector; Leo Rex Aureus, and his horny lover Cernunnos.

He was Rupert, and he was beautiful – through and through – and Valentine loved him, more than yellow, more than Grasshoppers, more even than violets, and he was going to marry him.

He led the smiling Rupert into his turret, closed the door, and then came the sound of his key turning the lock; and thus commenced the end of Valentine's Day.

CHAPTER 9

Montgomery's Deathday

The night had been cruel to Olivia. She spent most of it letting her eyes wander through the cracks in the ceiling of her four-poster until the crack of day crept into her room. She was certainly exhausted but not too aggravated for she did not suppose anyone to have much chance of repose on such a night.

All of the previous day she had felt agitated, not simply because her children were infuriating and not just because of Cosmo's presence either, but also because she had found her entire day to be an odyssey of ordeals upon her nervous system. One minute she had felt on fire, the very next discombobulated, and then almost as if full of despair, and that would never do.

She resolved to ignore the despair. The hot flushes and muddle-headedness, she told herself, were surely something quite ordinary for a woman of her age. These too she decided to disregard for she was loathe to admit that she was ripening because she did not want to have aged a single day since the departure of Monty.

Exactly sixteen years had passed since last she had lain with him. Sixteen years since she had seen him, that long night, when he had sought her reassurance and she had all but bitten off his head. It disturbed her still.

Her one moment of respite, the one chink of light in her otherwise dark night, was when she had heard the small squeak of the door to the west terrace – where she knew the boys to be – and Valentine's whisper; 'Be mindful of the third.'

It had made her smile for a while, for Valentine, quite possibly, could have bagged the beau of whom they both had been dreaming.

Yet the important thing was for Harry to wed and breed but he was so ineffectual that he needed an aggressive shove rather than a gentle push. Perhaps Rupert's cousin Izzy will be right for him, and the more Olivia considered the marvellous party the more she thought it wise.

If only Monty were still alive then everything would be altogether quite different, but surmising that he would have been proud of Willy's sense of Avery-Stripe honour, she steeled herself for the apology she knew had to be made that very morning. She wanted the family to be in solid union when later they went to his resting place.

It was then that she fell asleep, just for a few sweet hours, and when she woke, her Tiffany told her the time was ten. She climbed out of the four-poster, gave her hair a thorough brush, pulled on her kimono, and as she descended the stairwell, she pinched her cheeks so to look something akin to decent for breakfast.

She journeyed to the dining room via the drawing room, where she found Valentine and Rupert sat upon the chesterfield.

Although relatively appropriately dressed in charcoal and black striped satin pyjamas, Valentine seemed to be glowing almost as brightly as rich and golden Rupert, whose natural glow was accentuated by his daffodil yellow t-shirt that exhibited, quite pleasantly, his physical form.

'*Good* morning, mummy!' exclaimed the radiant pansy, 'Just have a look at what Rupert is doing for me!'

What Rupert was doing was carefully applying superglue to Valentine's broken geisha teacup and firmly holding it in place. He had already tended to Valentine's spout, and the teapot stood quite restored upon a sheet of newspaper spread over the coffee table on which also stood two flutes of orange liquid that sparkled.

Rupert beamed, 'Good morning, Mrs . . . Olivia. I'm just fixing Valentine's china before I start on the house, because I broke it by accident,' he explained.

'With a cricket ball, mummy!' added Valentine, 'I'm certain I shall never again love the game of cricket quite as much as I did in that moment!'

Rupert took his eyes off his application, and the look that flashed between the pair seemed to heighten their luminosity.

Happy with the realisation that Valentine had obviously filed his claim, Olivia decided to ask if they had had a good night.

'A glorious night, mummy, thank you!' Valentine chirruped, for his aesthetic desires certainly had enjoyed a night's indulgence.

'Yes, thank you, Olivia,' replied Rupert with a blinding smile, 'and you?'

'Oh, a splendid night, darling!' she lied, 'And now I simply must have something to eat. Have you two already breakfasted?'

'Yes, mummy, we have, and gosh! You should have seen the pile on Rupert's plate! So much bacon and so many eggs! Simply heaps and heaps of eggs! Mountains of them! And sausages too! And toast!' enthused Valentine who thought a boy with a big appetite in the morning to be thrilling, 'More even than Cosmo has! But without the horror show,' and he grimaced.

Rather sheepish at having eaten so much, Rupert apologised but Olivia insisted it only right to have a hearty breakfast, 'though I'm afraid I shan't be eating nearly so much,' she said.

'Gosh, mummy, I ate nothing at all!' said Valentine in a theatrical tone, 'Rupert and I have been up for hours but when we went for breakfast I was put right off because Cosmo had quite obviously already had his because there were crumbs in the butter *and* butter in the jam!'

Whether it was the idea of Rupert's heaps of eggs, Cosmo's eating deficiency or the distress of crumbs in the butter and butter in the jam, Olivia presently felt queasy.

'So now all I think I can manage to swallow is Bucks fizz!' said Valentine, and he took a healthy sized sip, 'Rupert too!'

'Champagne for breakfast?' asked Olivia, disapprovingly.

'Gosh! It has orange juice in it and that's breakfasty! And Gubsy's still at the table, and by the smell of it, having haddock.'

The fishy smell suddenly seemed to be all about her, and Olivia, fast finding the thought of food entirely rank, decided that she too would breakfast on champagne but without the addition of vitamin C.

She called to Gretchen to fetch her a flute of it and Gretchen complied most stonily with the opinion that Olivia ought only to 'drink 'buzz fix' like the boys.'

'Champagne for breakfast, mummy!' mocked Valentine.

Olivia justified her decision with the claim that Monty would have approved, whereupon she traversed the Axminster, and through the conservatory to stand at the open doors to the garden and let the green of it soothe her weary eyes.

It was a generous garden, much larger than most in the area, and awfully verdant. All along the edges, topiary tamed the hedges into neat lines and topped them with imperial cones and spheres. In front of the hedges there were beds jam-packed with rose bushes, so that amongst all the green there was a wild abundance of red for Gubsy decreed that England's roses should always be coloured just so.

There were other flowers too; wisteria from the west terrace cascaded the rear of Chinchero, and jasmine wove herself through and over the cottage arch – that led to the side-garden – by the cupid fountain (which was more of a piddle, to be frank). Up and across the pergola, under which was a wrought iron loveseat, climbed jasmine and met with honeysuckle and wild clematis that overwhelmed the gazebo and most of the brick wall at the far end.

On one side of the gazebo was a rockery and on the other there was a pond, and behind it there were cherry blossom trees that were breathtaking when they bloomed and showered the garden with their confetti afterwards. Looming large over the wide expanse of lawn – which the family liked striped for obvious reasons – was a grand oak. In the strong arms of the oak was held the tree house, and beneath it a coup, in which lived the chickens – Pernickety, Impossible, Tenacity, Hysteria – and the useless rooster – Farinelli – who could not *cock-a-doodle-do*.

Olivia stood in the hot sun and enjoyed the sharp taste of her cold champagne. She regarded it a sensible thing to have for breakfast after all, for when she looked at Corny, lying on his tummy on the striped lawn and muttering in the spotted dogs' ears as they each peered into Gloriana's bowl, he did remind her of Monty but strangely it did not hurt.

There were Harry and Cosmo too, lurking behind the gazebo, sending up smoke signals and she deemed them imbecilic to think she could neither see nor smell their habit. Harry had better be on decent form for the cemetery, she thought, she would have a word with him, but not before seeing Willy. But where was Willy?

Olivia about-turned, and in the drawing room she asked Valentine if he knew of Willy's whereabouts, but Valentine said he possessed not an inkling, and, now that he thought of it, it was rather peculiar as he had not seen her since her expulsion.

Presently, Gubsy, having had his haddock, appeared, and trundled over to his wing chair for a doze.

'Uncle Bartholomew, have you seen Wilhelmina?' asked Olivia.

Gubsy would not even face her, and landing in his chair, he said to Valentine, 'Tell your mother that I have not seen Wilhelmina, and that if she wasn't so careless with her children then she mightn't misplace 'em!'

'Gubsy says that if you weren't so careless . . . ' began Valentine.

'Shush, darling! Gretchen, have you seen Willy?' Olivia asked Gretchen who had just walked in with Gubsy's *Times*.

'No, Mrs Olivia, I have not seen Miss Willy,' she replied, and she also thought it odd, 'I will knock on door,' and off she went to investigate.

'I don't think she even came down to breakfast!' said Valentine, 'And it's not like Willy to miss a meal!' He turned to Rupert, and asked, 'Have you seen Willy?'

Rupert said that he had not.

'Gosh! Think of the big gaping hole left behind without any Willy to fill it!' exclaimed Valentine.

'You are pushing my patience, Valentino!'

Biting his tongue, Valentine opened his silver case for a cigarette.

Olivia felt panic rise and grip her to the very marrow; what if Willy had run away? Today of all days!

Gretchen's return brought news that Willy was not in her room and that her bed was still made.

Olivia's psychological alarm bell rang, and she rushed to the garden to ask the boys if they knew where Willy might be.

Corny began to look all about the garden as if it were a game of hide-and-seek. Harry had been walking, and Cosmo limping, back to the house when the question came; Harry had not seen Willy, and Cosmo thought it tremendously droll to make a trumpet of his hands and through them bellow, 'Willy! Willy! Have you seen my Willy?'

His bellows were so loud that they were quite audible in the drawing room and gave Valentine cause to tut.

Out in the garden however, they made apparent Willy's whereabouts, for the casement windows of the tree house shut with a loud slam, and joyous to have successfully sought, Corny jumped and pointed to the tree.

Though relieved that Willy had not strayed far, Olivia still felt irritation that she had hidden in a tree and as it was not a place that she intended to venture, she ordered, 'Do go up there and tell her to come down, Harry. I've something to say to her.'

Harry was obedient and Olivia watched him climb the ladder, push open the trap door in the tree house floor and stick his head through for what seemed too long a time to convey so simple a request.

As Olivia waited she listened to the mumbled exchange that came from within Willy's hiding place, and she felt a wave of heat sweep through her.

Her wait was eventually put to an end when Harry backed halfway down the ladder, then turned to jump the rest, and with a furrowed brow, he explained, 'Well I t*w*ied, but Willy *w*efuses to come down and says if you want to talk to her, mummy, then that's just your jolly *w*otten bad luck – her words not mine!'

Many words of the four-letter variety wanted to blast from Olivia's mouth; apologising was one thing but to climb a tree was beyond the call of duty – especially today! But what choice had she?

'*Ugh!*' she said, before climbing the ladder to make amends and she pushed against the trapdoor that gave with a *bang!*

Ten years ago, Harry had the idea to build a '*twee house*'. He had had a tree house when he was small, quite a splendid one in fact, and he thought it a shame for his siblings not to enjoy the same sorts of adventures that it could bring.

It was fortunate that Gubsy's garden possessed a tree capable of holding a house, but unfortunate that Harry was without the manual dexterity necessary to build one. Therefore, with the aid of his earnings from a modelling job, he paid a local company, who made such things, to realise his idea.

Aged eleven, Valentine thought himself rather too refined for tree-dwelling, but upon seeing the shirtless young men constructing Harry's house he did not think himself too refined to spend hours in the garden with the excuse that he must put to use the bubble-pipe he had found in the cellar.

Neither before nor since had he blown so many bubbles and he was glad when one of the workers encouraged him to take an interest in the erection. Valentine considered, and decided that he would quite enjoy decorating the interior. The worker told him to let him know how he would like it and that he would see what he could do.

Thus it came to be that once the building work was complete, the same company, for a moderate extra fee, furnished and decorated the inside of the tree house to be exactly as Van Gogh's painting of his bedroom in his yellow house in Arles – though naturally a version of half the dimension.

It was in this replica of the room that Willy had spent her night. She had gone to her own room just as Olivia had ordained, but after a while of suffering the heat, for her windows were so cracked that it was hazardous to try and open them, she realised that she could no longer bear it.

Valentine's invitation to sleep amongst the wisteria was tempting, but she chose to ignore him as he too had been naughty, though somehow, and quite inevitably, had escaped their mother's castigation, and this induced in Willy a hatred for him.

She waited until she was certain the coast was clear; the boys were out on the terrace, her mother running a bath, and not a sound came from downstairs.

Quietly, she crept out of her captivity and as best she was able, she slinked down to the hall, whereupon Gretchen started singing something foreign in her kitchen.

Into the drawing room Willy darted, and started when she saw Gubsy in his wing chair, but was relieved to discover he was asleep. Quickly, she grabbed a banana and an orange from the fruit bowl and escaped through the conservatory out into the garden, and scurried up the ladder to the house in the tree.

Once inside, she searched in the murk for the saucer of candle stubs and found them under the table, and in the table drawer, she found the box of lucifers and struck one. There were seven candles in all and she lighted each of them before draping a cloth in front of the window so that no one from the house might see.

Oh, the candles truly did give a lovely light! It was a comfort and rather cosy even on such a warm summer's night. She settled back on the bed and looked about at the state of the place. It was Corny's place really and full of lots of his things but it was still quite tidy. She had not before seen his collection of spiders and beetles kept in old preserve jars with gauze lids held in place by rubber bands, and though Willy was not a delicate girl she did not like the idea of them being in the room where she would sleep so she covered the creepy-crawlies with an old rag.

On the floor next to the bed was a pile of decrepit books such as *Treasure Island*, *Twenty Thousand Leagues under the Sea*, and *The Lion, the Witch and the Wardrobe*. She picked up the last and skipped to her favourite part to pay sweet Mr Tumnus a visit.

It was just as she sat down to tea with Lucy and the faun when she heard laughter from the west terrace. She recognised Harry's laugh, and knowing the other to be neither Valentine's nor Cosmo's she surmised it came from Rupert, and this brought to an end her literary dip. She slammed the book shut, and scowled with the knowledge that Valentine had obviously made a joke at Cosmo's expense.

'Oh! Viperish wretch!' thought Willy of Valentine, to have maintained in their mother's eyes his innocence when he had been such a fibber! He had enjoyed it too, she was certain of that, pretending to be Mrs Avery-Stripe, and then making her wear the monkey mask! And now he was having a lovely time under the stars with his beloved Rupert and being a beast to Cosmo.

It was most unfair! Cosmo at least paid attention to Valentine and despite having tried her very best to appear attractive for Cosmo he did not even seem to notice her, whereas Valentine all but had Rupert eating out of his hand. She just could not calculate how he did it.

She could not either work out why their mother deemed him so important. Willy was well aware that he had a knack for self-promotion but that did not explain why he had been involved in their mother's serious talk of which, from her concealment behind the globe drinks' cabinet, Willy had heard nearly every word. From what she understood the aim of the conversation was to whip Harry and Valentine into getting jobs of work and producing progenies, and any fool could see that to expect either from Valentine would be futile if not utter madness. It was reasonable to ask them of Harry, and she was in full agreement that it was his duty, though she saw no reason for him to hurry.

It had been terribly upsetting to discover that her mother considered it nothing that concerned her. Surely, after Harry she ought to be next in line to wed and breed. Yet it was patent that she was not considered capable of such an impossible mission, because as Willy had often suspected, her mother really did regard her to be so useless and so very ugly that no man in his right mind would ever want anything to do with her!

Considering this cold, hard and horrid fact, she let the tears that she thought she had exhausted, roll down her plump cheeks. Her mother would never think her a lady, Valentine had replaced her with a new best friend, and Cosmo would not ever desire her. She knew that they thought her, at best, a second-class citizen, and more likely, simply a big fat nothing.

She would not spend another moment under the same roof as them. She no longer wanted to be part of the family. Certainly, she would miss Gubsy's cuddles, Corny's sweetness, Gretchen's cooking and Harry's gentleness, but she could no longer live with any of them. Thus she resigned herself to a life of a spinster with the books and insects for company. She would wait for death to claim her where she lay, and it was with these sorry thoughts that Willy's sobs shook her to sleep in a tree.

A fierce thirst woke her. Her tongue felt shrivelled. She looked about and wished she had thought of bringing some water to drink. Remembering the orange, she grabbed it, and with her thumb, she punctured it then placed her lips upon the resulting wound. She sucked it, and squeezed it very hard and drained every drop. It was delicious, and so too was the banana, and she concentrated on the deliciousness of her fruit to hold misery at bay.

Her efforts were successful for a space but then came Cosmo's trumpet. She was relieved that it had not taken the family all day before they realised her absence but when she heard Cosmo bellow 'My Willy!' it sounded so mocking, as if it were a ridiculous thing that she might ever be his, that she shook with rage and then shut, with aggression, the windows to block out his witticism.

Moments later, the trapdoor opened, and up popped Harry's head. She was glad it was his and not anyone else's.

'Hullo, Willy,' he said happily, 'we were all wond*w*ing where you were! What are you doing up here? I've not been up here fo*w*ever!' and he looked around at the idea he had had a decade ago, 'Still looks p*w*etty good, I *w*eckon!'

Willy inspected her new home in the light of day, and though it was rather on the small side, she considered if she saved for a camping stove, some pots and pans, and a tin kettle, that it might make a nice little home, if Corny did not mind.

'Hello, Harry,' she replied, 'Well, I'm up here and this is where I will stay!'

'*W*eally?' he said with surprise but was also flattered that she liked it so much, 'Well, mummy wants to see you; she has something to say to you.'

'Like what?'

'*W*eally don't know. She didn't say. Come down and find out.'

'Oh no! I am not ever coming down!'

'*W*eally not?' Harry asked with astonishment.

'Really yes!' said an unbending Willy, 'You can tell mummy that I shan't ever come down and if she wants to talk to me then that's just her jolly rotten bad luck!'

'C*w*umbs! All *w*ight! I'll tell her that.'

'Thank you.'

'No p*w*oblem! See you later!'

'Goodbye.'

'Goodbye.'

Harry's head vanished and he shut the trapdoor.

Willy flung herself, facedown, on the bed and managed some more tears; now she really had to live in the tree house!

Olivia regretted not having thought of putting on some shoes before venturing up a tree but then she realised she possessed no shoes suitable for such an excursion – why ever would she? She had not ever climbed a tree before and it was her first time in the children's tree house. Once inside she considered it larger than she had supposed and though she had heard tell that it resembled quite remarkably the Dutch painter's bedroom she was impressed that it still bore a likeness, even if a somewhat squalid one.

She found Willy lying in a dishevelled heap on the bed with her face pushed into a pillow. Willy did not acknowledge her mother's arrival.

Olivia steeled herself and said, quite breezily, 'Good morning, Wilhelmina, what a delightful place! But do let's return to Chinchero, hmm?' and she wrung her hands as she waited for a response.

None came; Willy merely breathed heavily into the pillow.

Silent for a space, Olivia surmised that it may well transpire to be quite a chore to lure Willy back down, therefore, utilising a chewed-up pencil, she removed a banana skin from one of the little chairs so she could at least sit. She wished she had a cigarette.

'It is a lovely day, darling, why don't you come and see?' she tried, and then added, 'Quite soon we shall have to dress for Daddy.'

Willy decided that she would not be going to see her daddy for she was no longer part of the family. They must go without her and she hoped they would soon so that she could swipe supplies from the larder. She wished that her mother would leave now for even to hear her voice was an unendurable ordeal.

Olivia perched on the uncomfortable chair and grimaced at Willy's broad back. 'Gruesome girl!' she thought, 'Articulate!'

'I cannot converse with your rear end, Willy,' she said in a definite tone, 'And until you sit up and talk to me I shall remain where I am; even if it takes all day!' and she prayed this would prompt a response, but all that came was a muffled *harrumph*.

'Well?' asked Olivia, but Willy said nothing; she would not talk to her mother. She would not sit up. Not ever! Not even if it did take all day!

Thus, a state of stalemate ensued for they both refused to budge.

The situation might have stuck if Olivia had not decided to investigate a rusted tin of throat lozenges, for upon removing the lid, and discovering it to be a bumblebee mortuary, she shrieked so piercingly that the window glass might have cracked.

Unable to resist discerning what had produced such a scream, Willy elevated her head and looked at her mother's horrified face as the swiftly discarded lozenge tin of apian corpses clattered on the wooden floor.

'What is it, mummy?' asked Willy with alarm.

'Nothing, darling, nothing at all,' replied Olivia, grabbing at her dignity, 'Just some horrid things! But, ah! I see you have been feeling sad.'

Olivia's description of her daughter's appearance was accurate, and to hear it was of no surprise to Willy. However, had she had made use of the looking glass she would have felt shock at quite how sad, for her face was pockmarked with pillow crease, and bulbous from blubbing, and her hair was a veritable nest of an exceptionally untidy crow.

Willy found her tongue, and assertively said, 'Yes, mummy! I *am* sad! And it is because of you!' and in a fairly decent impression of both her great uncle and her father, she glowered at her mother.

Noticing, with a modicum of surprise, the similarities, Olivia realised that the moment for contrition had come; she had to say sorry, but somehow the word jarred in her gullet because she did not in fact feel it, what she felt was a distant relation of remorse.

'Darling . . . ' she tentatively began, 'listen to me, darling.' Willy continued to glare. 'Darling, are you aware that last night was simply my momentary misinterpretation of the matter of your spat with the spiteful Strap and that you know me to be really rather riddled with remorse at realising the reality of the incident?'

There, I have said it, thought Olivia, but Willy said, 'What?' for though Willy thought her mother might be saying sorry, she was not certain and could not either quite believe it.

Olivia displayed the palms of her hands, and with as wide eyes as possible, she reiterated, 'I am *remorseful*!'

'Remorseful?' said Willy confusedly.

Oh! Idiot girl! thought Olivia, she knew Willy's schooling to have been not exactly top-notch, but that was no excuse; surely, she must know the definition of the word; or was she just being trying? Either way, Olivia realised she must hold her temper if she was to successfully coax, and though it stuck in her craw, she managed to expel, 'Sorry, darling.'

Still, Willy believed her ears to be deceiving her, and asked again, 'What, mummy?'

Having said the word once, Olivia felt she could repeat it, and as if on overload, she said; 'Sorry. Sorry, sorry, sorry, darling, I am very sorry, sincerely and most seriously sorry. I am sorry.'

'Really not!' Willy was incredulous.

'Yes, darling. Very. Valentine explained to me, after you left the table, what must have happened, and so that is what I am.'

'He did?' asked Willy, feeling much cheered up that Valentine had been loyal after all, and she wondered what he might have said this time.

'Yes, darling. Now I see that you were purely doing just as you ought, and honoured the family name. I am pleased and proud, and what is more; I condone your actions; the horse-mess thing, I might even have done the same.'

'Oh, mummy!' and for a space, Willy was very happy and forgiving of her severe mother, but then she remembered how she viewed her with regard to her place in the family's pecking-order, and why it was seen as insignificant.

'Yes, darling, so do let's stop being silly and get out of here. We must get ready for Daddy,' said Olivia, relieved that she had done her bit and that they could now advance.

'No, mummy. I shan't get out of here.'

'Why ever not?'

'Because I shall stay here and live here and not with a family that considers me irrelevant!'

'But you can't live in a tree, don't be absurd! You can't live in a tree, eating bananas,' and here Olivia pointed to the peel, 'like a chimpanzee!'

Though she did not know it, this was the worst thing Olivia could have said. She had no notion that Willy had spent the previous afternoon donning a chimp mask, but Willy thought her to be making fun, and with a loud howl, she grabbed a pillow and proceeded to savagely bite it whilst emitting a shrill and hysterical cry.

Olivia looked at Willy and was distressed at the sight. She asked herself, 'Is she insane? What she did to the Strap girl was not exactly normal, and then she says she wants to live in a tree and now this!' She wondered if Willy was certifiable. She considered who to call in such a case, and if it would entail a straitjacket and padded cell. Oh, the humiliation she would never live down!

Momentarily, Olivia was fairly scared, but then she gathered herself and refusing to entertain the possibility of lunacy, she smacked Willy, quite hard, on the face.

The smack did the trick, and after a flash of shock, Willy was once again normal though still her tears streamed. She clasped the cheek that Olivia had hit, and spluttered, 'Wh . . . wh . . . why did you hit me? You hit me! Ow!'

'You left me no choice, darling. It was for your own good. Now tell me, why do you not want to live with the family? Are you not proud to be an Avery-Stripe?' asked Olivia as gently as was possible, for she feared instigating another passionate frenzy.

Willy snuffled and rubbed dry her eyes with the pillow.

'Oh, mummy, of course I am, you know I am! That is why Agatha Strap deserved what she got! I love the family but I know it considers me a joke and not to matter very much at all!'

Wondering how she might have drawn such a conclusion, Olivia asked her, 'Why on earth would you think that?'

'Because of you, mummy!' Willy cried, 'You said your serious talk was nothing that concerned me, but I heard it, mummy! All about family and money and marrying and multiplication, and you don't think I have anything to do with it, but I do! And I can marry! I can marry the right man for the family! But you don't seem to think so, and I know why!'

Although somewhat taken aback by Willy's admission that she had eavesdropped, and of her eagerness to marry the right man at only seventeen, Olivia disregarded these qualms, and said, 'Of course I think you can marry the right man for the family; it is important that you eventually do, and I hope and trust that you someday shall!'

'Oh, yes, you hope that I shall but truthfully you think that I cannot, and that is why you did not include me; you think me to be nothing but a fat joke that no man might ever want!' accused Willy.

'Oh, darling! You do say the most ludicrous things!' said Olivia defensively.

'Ha! Exactly! Don't you see? You think me ludicrous! Ludicrous and fat, you think me so fat you wonder how I managed to squeeze through that trapdoor and a miracle that the tree has not collapsed under my weight! You think I'm fat and a foolish joke, a frump with no chance at all because you don't even think I could ever even be a lady, you said so last night!'

Olivia admitted to herself that she did wonder how much weight the tree could withstand.

'Oh, darling, don't be . . . I mean, of course I don't think you're fat! You are certainly not fat!' she said, placing her hands on Willy's face and supposed that somewhere it hid cheekbones. 'You are simply what I would call nicely-padded; the right side of comfortable! Not skin and bone like me!'

'*Humph*! But you still think no one will marry me because I'm a frump!' pouted Willy though pleased to be 'nicely-padded' and not fat.

'Wilhelmina Avery-Stripe! I can completely and in all conscience confirm to you that I have not ever, not even for a moment, considered you to be anything even remotely resembling a frump!' stated Olivia with all the conviction she could muster.

Willy gazed at her, and she wished she could believe her, and she wished it were true.

'But, mummy,' she sniffed.

'Yes, Willy?'

'I *am* a frump!'

'No, you most certainly are not!' snapped Olivia.

Willy stood and regarded her reflection in the looking glass. She was shocked at the sight.

'Oh, but, mummy! I *AM*! Just look at me! I am a walking haystack of mess!' and she yanked at the bird's nest on her head in an effort to detangle it.

Olivia looked her up and down, and realised that diplomacy could be pushed only so far, and said, 'But that dress was so pretty yesterday. You ought not to have slept in it. You should wear dresses more often. Girls who are not frumps wear dresses, not corduroys, and they wear pretty shoes, not boots. And make-up too, because soap is not enough. And they brush their hair, they have it styled in a salon and not hacked at home like the boys. That is how not to be a frump.'

Akimbo, Willy looked Olivia in the eye, 'So I am a frump?'

Olivia cleared her throat and spat it out; 'Put it like this, darling, you've room for improvement.'

'It's all your fault, mummy,' Willy sighed.

'Mine! But how?'

'You're never about! I live with boys, so how could I learn to be graceful and feminine? And don't say Gretchen!'

Olivia wanted to say that femininity was a natural occurrence, and to point out that her absence seemed not to have hindered Valentine's acquaintance with it one bit, but instead she said, 'Well, darling, you never displayed any interest in the matter before, but it's never too late to become a lady. I'll help you, and we shall start today!'

'Truly?' said Willy hopefully.

'Why ever not, darling? Besides, daddy will love to see you in a dress. I'll find you something nice to wear (though she wondered as to what) but we had better get a move on,' encouraged Olivia, for not only was she keen to place her feet on solid ground, and eager to visit her husband, she was also glad that Willy had at last begun to embrace femininity.

'And what about Corny's party?' asked Willy, 'I must have something just wonderful to wear for that!'

'Naturally, darling, of course you must, and you shall!' then Olivia paused before asking, 'But, for whom? Is there a boy you would like to ask?' and she dreaded to contemplate the calibre of boy Willy might like, for though still far too young for anything serious, it simply would not do for her to associate the family with someone unsavoury.

Willy turned to hide her sudden blush; she did not want her mother to guess the object of her affections to be Cosmo. It would be far too embarrassing and certainly be considered amusing or unacceptable and probably both.

'No, mummy, no, there's no one in particular; I'd just like to look nice from now on,' said Willy as casually as she was able, before facing her mother again, and adding, 'Besides I must be the sort of girl that the right sort of man would like to marry, isn't that right?'

'Precisely!' confirmed Olivia, for though she would not entertain the idea of a marriage before at least twenty, she presently decided it high time that Willy start stepping out with boys of good breed and she began to think of any eligibles that people she knew might know, and how she would add the cream of them to Valentine's stiffies.

Willy was mollified; now that her mother had revealed that she considered her merely 'the right side of comfortable', and would assist, and take seriously, her ambition to acquire a suitable husband, who she would expose to be Cosmo at such time as she had captured him with her imminent femininity, she was ready to rejoin the family.

She took a last look at the room where she had spent the night, and though it was a good place and just right for a boy like Corny, it was no place for a lady, and she said, 'Come on, mummy, let's get out of here.'

'A splendid suggestion, darling, yes, let's.'

Like a shot, Olivia disappeared, and with her feet firmly back on terra firma, she filled with happy relief whilst she watched the descent of Willy's big behind.

CHAPTER 10

The Ancestors

'Hooray!' cried Valentine, as Harry circled the cemetery with the Jaguar, 'We are here!'

The journey had not seemed long to Valentine who had whiled away the miles daydreaming of Rupert, but as soon as he saw the wrought iron railings, he readily dispensed with his dreams for it was time to see Daddy.

'Do try not to make the situation of visiting your father's grave sound to be a jolly Sunday school picnic, Valentino!' said Olivia, irritably.

'Sorry, mummy.'

Olivia narrowed her eyes, sat in silence for a space, and then suddenly, she clutched her breast, and said, 'Harry!'

He seemed not to hear, so again she said, 'Harry!'

'I'm twying to park, mummy!'

'Never mind that!' she rebuked, for she was panic-struck, 'You remembered the roses, didn't you?'

'Yes, mummy, the woses are in the boot!'

The response quelled Olivia, for the roses were from the garden; Monty had hated shop-bought flowers. He had thought them common.

Corny had certainly considered the drive a long one; no one had spoken and though the scenery had been variable, and Gloriana ever fascinating, his long sleeved shirt and trousers felt so restrictive and he was itching to stretch, to run, to hop, skip and jump.

It was with a supreme strain of effort that he waited for Valentine to alight before he burst forth from the car, and all but tap-danced on the pavement to celebrate his freedom.

'Seize the fish, Willy, darling, before Corny drops it,' said Olivia. 'The last thing we need is it smashing and slashing his wrists and throat.'

'But, mummy!' Willy whined.

'Seize it!' Olivia snapped.

Willy reluctantly obeyed and watched, with envy, Olivia receive, from Harry, the red roses of which there were thirteen; one for each year of marriage. She started to think that perhaps her mother might not be taking seriously her aspiration after all, despite her loan of the black wrap dress that Willy now wore, for a flower bouquet was infinitely more feminine than a fishbowl, and she scowled.

'Give it to me, Willy,' said Harry, having hoisted Gubsy out of the car and onto his feet, 'I'll ca*wwy* it.'

When composed, the Avery-Stripes penetrated the sun-drenched necropolis, and Olivia, in her inky sleek Chanel suit, skyscraper heels and widow's veil, and her mind crammed with memories of Monty, solemnly led the cortège. Gubsy's protracted locomotion dictated the procession be a slow one, bar Corny who clambered over the conglomeration of monuments. Eventually though, they reached their destination.

The plot was a mishmash of headstones, some large and lordly, others understated and refined, but all were a gleaming white granite, and possessed much ornamentation, each of them particular to the death it represented. There were knots to mean marriage and unity; calla lilies to signify beauty; poppies symbolised eternal sleep, and a lamb denoted a child's innocence. Bugles and crossed swords for military deaths, rifles for huntsmen, stone dogs indicated loyalty and fidelity, and broken columns commemorated the early loss of a patriarch.

Between two such columns stood the largest stone, a formidable plinth, a good five-foot in height, and on its apex stood a gargantuan granite Peruvian Booby, head bowed, beak to breast, in eternal grief. Engraved on the plinth was 'AVERY-STRIPE', and below it was the family maxim, *Nil Desperandum*.

This master stone was in honour of the mother of them all, Olympia. The cause of her death was crapulence; she just would not stop eating. Food was her comfort and her friend, moreover, Excelsior liked her fat, he loved it in fact, but in the end, it cost him his wife, for her arteries simply could not withstand the waste produced by the mammoth mounds she would devour. They contracted and restricted, and eventually, entirely prevented her glutinous blood from pumping her large, loving heart. Thus, upon achieving a mid-morning consumption of Mrs Beeton's Roly-Poly Jam Pudding, majestic Olympia, at the tender age of forty-five, suddenly expired.

Excelsior became a widower in 1886, and he was to live another thirty-nine years before he passed away peacefully in his sleep. He died a content man because despite having cushioned on top of his wife his four youngest daughters – Honoria, Isadora, Bedelia and Cornelia, their lives claimed, respectively, by consumption, syphilis, an electrical storm and a chandelier – and the eldest – Fortunata – having disavowed him shortly after her mother's death for which she blamed him, he still had his son, Ambrosius, who had delivered unto Excelsior the extensive family he had always desired. For together with his elegant wife – Angelica – spoiled and charming, Ambrosius, had produced eight children, of which the six eldest were boys.

First to arrive, in the opening year of the twentieth century, was Jeremiah, followed in 1902 by Maximilian, then eighteen months later, came Sebastian, after him a three-year respite, then there was Olivier. Some more years went by, and in 1910, yet another boy, Bartholomew, and fast on his heels, a mere ten months later, Valerian, who came with the added delight of a twin sister, Victoria, and two years after the twins, last but not least, and eighth in line, baby Octavia.

Excelsior was beside himself with uproarious joy with the army of boys, and the girls were rather nice too, and he announced to all and sundry that his beautiful daughter-in-law was so aptly named for she had proved herself to be nothing but a genuine angel.

This collection of eleven Avery-Stripes lived together in luxury and splendour in Excelsior's Ballestas, and they were pompous and they were smug, and so very pleased with themselves for being so superior to the masses, including the alienated Fortunata, for whom they felt nothing but deep disdain, for she had married a common cow farmer named Mr Oxley.

Excelsior did not reign for long over his new brood however, for he died a decade and two years after the arrival of baby Octavia. His relations found that instead of celebrating his centenary, they were mourning the loss of their strict and proud patriarch, and on a snowy morning in January 1925, they lowered his corpse into the frozen ground to unite with Olympia.

He left everything he possessed to his adored Ambrosius, but what he took with him was good fortune, for not long after his departure did the family start to founder, and their fate went awry. Not one of them appeared destined to see as many years as had Excelsior and in the most unfortunate ways they started to drop like flies.

The first to join the family underground, at the age of twenty-three, was Sebastian. He had gone to Tanzania because he said he very much wanted to shoot some lion, and within two days of his arrival he succeeded in shooting *'A cracking great big one, father!'* he wrote, *'Can't wait to bring it home and see the look on mother's face!'*

That was the last that the family heard from Sebastian because the day after the date on his letter, he was trampled to death on the Serengeti plains by a stampeding herd of blue wildebeest. Accordingly, Angelica's face when shown the leonine carcass was nothing in comparison to her horror upon seeing the destroyed one of her formerly brawny and beautifully golden son.

Two years later, the next to go was Octavia. Aged fifteen, she was no longer a baby but still considered so by the family. With her peaches and cream complexion and pale-gold ringlets, she was pretty and she was vain. She could not pass anything that possessed the power to reflect without pausing to pose. Not a looking glass, a night window or a shiny surface escaped her ardour. She would even admire herself in the silver cutlery at mealtimes.

The water of the wishing-well in the apple-orchard provided her favourite reflection. There she could gaze at her other self, framed by the clouds in the sky and the apple blossom, and it would look to her so romantic.

One afternoon however, her narcissism got the better of her, as she was unable to resist leaning forward and planting a delicate kiss on her watery image. She lost herself in self-love; she lost her footing too, and tipped over the edge. There was a *splash* followed by a *crack*. Baby Octavia broke her neck on the bottom of the well and quite a few hours passed by before the search party discovered her stockinged legs jutting out at a most improper angle.

Maximilian's departure came soon after. He had a passion for butter-flies. Ever since a little boy he had found them enchanting and would often be seen prancing about the grounds with his butterfly snare. He captured many of the common garden variety, such as the Painted Lady, Red Admiral, Brimstone and Comma, whilst still in his teens, but then he felt his collection should stretch further a field.

Thus, he packed a valise and set off on his adventures abroad. His quest to broaden his rabble of butterflies carried him to quite all four corners of the world, on which he amassed swarms of them, each prettier to his eye than the last; the Two-tailed Pasha, the Morpho, the Zebra Longwing, some Swallowtail and Asian Grass Blues, the Lesser Fiery Copper and Levantine Leopard and Pomegranate Hairstreak, all added to his grand collection.

Ultimately, Maximilian's wanderlust led him to China, and in Chengdu, he discovered that though he loved his butterflies, he learned to love more the pleasures of smoking opium which fast became his favourite pastime in which to indulge whilst concealed in dens of iniquity where he soon felt his health start to wane.

Yet he possessed the power of mind to realise his decline and wired to his brothers to come rescue him. Jeremiah dutifully went but he was too late, for Maximilian's addiction to the fermented juice of unripe poppy pods had already brought about his dark and delirious death at the age of twenty-nine.

For the four years following the loss of Maximilian, the Avery-Stripes managed not only to retain their number but also to make two additions.

Jeremiah had wed a stunning 'filly' of admirable personal means. Everyone agreed that Araminta was indeed 'jolly good fun' and what was more, she was acceptable. Together, the happy couple produced the bonny and bouncy baby boy, Montgomery, and for a while, self-satisfaction returned to the family, for the heir's heir had had an heir.

But in 1936, a mere year after the latest arrival, Excelsior's own baby boy lost his life.

Ambrosius had decided that to celebrate their Ruby year, he and Angelica, should go to Berlin for the Olympic Games, and though she was not a big fan of sports, she thought it might be quite an interesting thing to do because Germany seemed the place to be as Mr Hitler's ideas were, to her mind, so very sound.

As it transpired, the impressive show of athletics swept Angelica quite away, and she admired in particular the looks of the hosting country's competitors. This lack of patriotism did not go unnoticed by Ambrosius who angrily decreed that they no longer watch the Games, and instead explore Berlin's surrounding countryside.

In their little open-top MG, they sped around and could not help but fall in love with the beauty of rural Germany, and on one such of these motoring jaunts, when Ambrosius was driving particularly fast, a seagull in flight felt the urge to empty his bursting bowels.

Understandably, the shock created by the falling waste hitting his face, with an almighty *splat,* caused Ambrosius to lose control of the wheel, and within seconds of the bird's release, the car swerved and crashed into an evergreen and catapulted the couple to their crippled ends.

The remaining Avery-Stripes were stunned at the news, and Jeremiah had been promoted to head of the family at far too soon an age but he was glad of his wife and son and of course his surviving siblings.

Mr Hitler's sound ideas soon brought on the Second World War, and naturally, the Avery-Stripe men were honour bound to serve their country. All four went off to fight but two of them were never to return. Whilst performing lookout duty, Able Seaman Olivier fell from the crow's nest and after the plummet of seventy-five feet, he met his death upon the deck with a loud *thud*. A propeller cut short the life of squiffy Flight Sergeant Valerian when, on solid ground, he rotated face first into its high-speed revolutions and was consequently hacked into bloody strips of flesh.

After these two losses, only five of the family still breathed, and Ballestas seemed to have lost its life too, in fact, it seemed to Jeremiah to be full of nothing but death. What was more, he could no longer maintain the building or its grounds for the war had cost him both money and domestics.

He made the decision to sell and to divide the proceeds between himself and his remaining brother and sister; he kept half, and to them he gave a quarter each, whereupon Bartholomew purchased a large gardened, five-bedroom house in Chiswick (Chinchero) and Victoria was happy to live in a sizeable mansion block apartment in Kensington.

With his half, Jeremiah bought an imposing townhouse in Belgravia, where he and Araminta tried to enjoy the benefits of a London lifestyle that she had come to love during the war years. He was too depressed to try for another child, and sent Montgomery to boarding school, alternating his holidays between his uncle and his aunt.

Thus was the situation of the Avery-Stripes in 1945; a mere shadow of its former glory, of which Bartholomew and Victoria went to great pains to educate their nephew who listened with studious attention and resented that he had been born too late.

His parent's abandonment of him made Montgomery a very angry individual. He was hopping mad that they had no interest in their heir beyond that of a generous monthly allowance. He was furious that they had yielded so readily to the fate of the family, and had he known just how hopeless they had become he would likely have hammered with his fists the reminder that Avery-Stripes 'never despair' into their skulls.

Jeremiah and Araminta had indeed become most hopeless – hopeless alcoholics. They were a mess, and would cavort about town as if a couple of children indulging every whim, attending every party, buying any silly expensive thing that caught their eye and all the while holding in their hands a glass – if not a bottle – of something sparkling. They were ghastly and superior creeps, and before too long, the stiffies stopped coming.

The lack of stiffies however escaped their attention for they had discovered a place that they liked better than London and spent as much time there as was possible.

They had fallen in love with Venice, and had they possessed any sense at all they would have relocated but as they had none they stayed always at the Luna Hotel Baglioni. They spent their Venetian days rising at noon, then drinking and lunching before shopping for extravagant souvenirs; Araminta developed a penchant for Murano glass and purchased all manner of it, including a gondola-shaped chandelier.

The nights saw them continue drinking until they were morons that liked nothing better than to don dominoes and run and scream through the maze of narrow backstreets and kiss and touch in dank alcoves.

It was on one of these intoxicated nights of imbecilic passion that the pair had the idea to embark on an intimate gondola ride for 'what naughty fun just to steal one!'

They had no notion of how to operate the Italian rowboat but Jeremiah said it was certain to be just as a Cambridge punt, and shortly after the small hours, they chose one at random, climbed aboard and unmoored it from the striped pole.

For a while, they simply drifted, full with the excitement of derring-do and the luxury of having the Grand Canal quite to themselves. Eventually, Jeremiah decided to put to the test his punting skills but found the gondola to be remarkably 'un-punty' and could not fathom how to work the remo in the forcola, but this was of little concern to them for it was fun to go with the flow as they opened a bottle of Dom Perignon.

They soon found themselves at the basin belonging to Saint Mark, whereupon Araminta exclaimed the divine sight to inspire her to dance. Her delightful moves rendered her so dizzy that she inevitably tripped and then plopped overboard. Without hesitation, Jeremiah jumped after, and thus, the dipsomaniac double act duly drowned.

Upon receiving the tragic news of the watery demise, Bartholomew telephoned to Victoria who said she would 'be over in a jiffy', and hurriedly put on her Schiaparelli hat in the design of a lady's topsy-turvy shoe.

Her haste was such that she clean forgot the lift to be temporarily out of service, therefore, when she stepped through the divided doors she plunged down the shaft until meeting the malfunctioning mechanisms with a bone-crushing *crunch*!

Poor Bartholomew found himself not only in the sorry situation of having to organise a treble funeral but also to be the last man of his family's generation still standing. In little more than three decades, the Avery-Stripes had suffered ten departures, and in 1955, only he and his nephew remained.

Yet Bartholomew had a cast-iron faith in the fresh-faced beneficiary; he knew that determined young Montgomery would sire a new generation of Avery-Stripes, and in this, he was not wrong. He only wished that he had not had the sad task of burying him also a mere quarter of a century later.

Regarding the familial stones, and reading each name in turn, made Gubsy's eyes swim. He felt riddled with guilt at having survived so much longer than all but one of them; only Excelsior lived to see as many years, and Gubsy had not achieved anywhere near as much as he had. Though not through lack of effort, and this too, shamed him, for muster as he might, he had never been able to bring to a lady's table anything better than a serving of boneless pork.

He now looked to Montgomery's heir, Harry. He was good-looking and sure to get a good wife, but still so young, he had plenty of time to repopulate, though a wriggle on would not hurt. Gubsy was glad to have them all under his own roof, for in some ways, it was as the family had been when he was one of the youngest.

Montgomery's monument was a broken column and bore the emblem of a huntsman's rifle. Before it, Olivia genuflected and placed, at its foot, the red roses from the garden. He had loved that garden; they had spent many pre-marital evenings there sitting on the loveseat beneath the pergola where he had impressed her with tales of his family and she had fallen deeper in love.

She tried to derive solace from the idea that he was now as one with those that he had so revered, but she found herself without the ability to do anything other than yearn his return.

She wanted to throw herself on his resting place and with her bare hands to dig and claw at the earth, then rip at the walnut box in which he lay and reclaim him in her arms.

It was impossible for her to perceive his robust body to be anything other than bursting with virility; she considered him to have merely ceased to breath. With her tears and kisses she would revitalise him and he would live again to look after her and tell her she need neither worry nor fear what to do or how to get by. All these years later, she still was unable to feel capable; she craved his pig-headed resolve for it would provide the solution to all of her anxieties. She craved too his touch, which had not in every instance been ham-fisted. Ultimately, she desired purely to be with him, to prove to him her love, and to receive his forgiveness.

As it was, Olivia did not endeavour to exhume her husband for she reasoned such an exhibition to be Mediterranean, and because she was English, the best she could manage was to stand stiff as a rod, and the most emotion she would permit herself to display was a civil tear. Slowly, she lifted her widow's veil and delicately dabbed with a white handkerchief to prevent her sentiment from streaking her expressionless face with mascara.

She contemplated the idea of withdrawing, from her Birkin, Olympia's Starfish and presenting it to Monty, as if to appease him, however, knowing such an unveiling would incite interrogation as to the explanation for the ring's procurement she refused to entertain the urge with what she considered an unsurpassable strength of discipline.

Oh! She needed a cigarette; she needed a drink! She pictured darting behind Olympia's headstone and downing Monty's flask of whisky and smoking cigarettes until blue in the face, but she could not; she must remain composed. She gathered herself, concentrated on their progenies, and tried to gauge what their thoughts might be.

She could not determine what was happening in Corny's head, but there he stood, looking as if one of the stone angels made mortal for the bright sun upon his white-blond hair created a tangible nimbus.

Corny was at a loss what to think; the muddle of stones with the family names he knew bore some relevance, especially that of his father. He had had explained to him that some of the stones were for relations like Gubsy, but that confused him further; if that was the case then why were they there or he not with them? He knew that the stones were for dead people and he thought he knew what that meant, but when he tried to imagine what it meant not to be alive, his brain began to hurt.

Making a supreme effort to appear wistful, as she surmised it an appropriate stance for a lady on such an occasion, Willy found that she could not feel it as sincerely as she wished. Naturally, she was sad to have no memory of her father whatsoever, but she wondered how she was to mourn someone she could not recollect.

The thing is to think of him, she told herself, and thus she commenced, and considered how it might be if he were still alive; might then they have stayed at the old house, that she could not either remember, and how might that be? Would they have been a happier family? Would Mummy

be nicer? Would Daddy have loved her? Would he have thought her a
lady or a frump? Would he even have liked her at all?

Willy concluded that as she would never know the answers, or if they
would make much difference to what had since transpired, she might as
well not think at all, and decided it best to pay her respects by attempting
to appear wistful. It was then that she began to consider whether Cosmo
might ever think her a lady.

Olivia could not interpret the look upon her daughter's face. She knew
Willy had a desire to be ladylike – an undertaking, Olivia considered, of
epic proportion – so why was it she seemed to be at great pains
of concentration as if trying to calculate a particularly problematical
mathematical sum. Did she really believe Monty's graveside to be a
suitable location for mental arithmetic? Olivia shuddered to think, and
turned instead to Harry, to whom she now stepped over in a single stride,
and slid her hand into his.

But Harry did not at first realise Olivia's presence for he was miles away
with thoughts of Monty, but unlike his mother's memories, his were not
romantic. In fact, the more Harry thought about his father and his idea of
how a family ought to be, the more he realised how different they were to
his own. When he was a little boy they had never seemed to do anything
together. He could not recollect a time when his parents inhabited the
same room unless custom dictated otherwise. In fact, his father always
seemed to be out killing most days, whilst his mother would invariably be
napping if not shopping.

Even on holidays they never did anything as a family. He had memories
of skiing with his father, though his father would always find fault in his
technique, and his mother, with a tiny Valentine in tow, would roll herself
in furs, and lounge in bars.

He could not remember his parents even to hold a conversation. They
would have a meagre exchange of words at mealtimes, but if ever the talk
went beyond the bare minimum it would be because his bumptious father
had decided to deliver an orotund monologue to which his mother, to all
intents and purposes would listen, but her green eyes would glaze over.
Harry did not blame her though; it would always be a dreadful bore –
shoot this, kill that, hunt it, hang it, pluck it, skin it, gut it, eat it and Avery-
Stripe, Avery-Stripe, Avery-Stripe, family, family, family, *burp*; yawn!

When Harry had heard he was to have a little brother he was very
excited because it would be someone to play and have adventures with –
because though he loved Nanny Cook, she was no good at playing or

adventures. Moreover, a brother would be someone with whom to share his parents and the burden of their father's expectations.

Valentine certainly did prove fun to play with, and no sooner had he started to talk had he shown an ability (that Harry and his mother seemed not to possess) to charm the jollity out of his overbearing father who would dote on Valentine and his infantile verbosity.

Harry was grateful for Valentine's knack of wrapping his father around his little finger as it took the heat off him to a degree, but sooner or later, his father's attention would focus on him again, and though this focus was no longer constant, now when it came, it came with ferocious force.

'Don't you think for one moment, young man, that this lessens your load!' Monty would roar at him, 'Valentine is patently a thorough Avery-Stripe; one only has to see his certitude when he sings about being a little teapot to know he's bound to play his part without any trouble! However, you are the eldest; that is how it works; you know the score. Now, say it!'

Knees knocking, Harry would look up at his powerfully built father, at his florid face, and obediently he would repeat, 'Excelsior begat Ambwosius, Ambwosius begat Jewemiah, Jewemiah begat Montgomewy, Montgomewy begat Howatio.'

Though the rhotacism was not unknown to Monty, he always gave the impression that it was a shocking insult as if he thought it should have somehow magicked away overnight and he would accuse Harry of faking the impediment purely to humiliate him. It would push Monty to a state of virtual spontaneous combustion, and like a large man-sized natural disaster not dissimilar to a small tornado or hurricane, he would abuse and destroy quite anything in his orbit. He even punched through a panel in a wardrobe door and broke his three middle fingers in the process, and it was only because his arm jammed in the demolished wood when he tried to retrieve it that Harry had the opportunity to run for cover.

Harry was fortunate on that occasion but seldom would a day pass that his father did not curse and swear at him at foghorn volume and threaten to cut out his 'spastic tongue' if he did not stop his 'verbal wetardedness'.

Aged eight, when prep school became his new home, Harry was glad, for it meant he would not have to see his father except during the holidays, and even then he would sometimes spend the duration with Cosmo's family.

Four years later, when Gubsy broke the news that Monty had met his maker because of a defective gun, Harry had discovered that though he was not happy to hear it, he was not unhappy either, and that made him feel sad. That and Valentine's silent distress that lasted a week, little Willy too, she did not understand, and their mother pregnant with Corny, all these things induced in Harry a sadness, but he could not say that he was upset that his bullying father had blown out his brains. Harry always told himself, that when his time came, he would, with utter certainty, be a loving and sharing husband, and a kind and gentle father; for his own had shown him exactly how not to do it.

Harry now looked at his siblings and felt glad that his father had done at least three good things in his life. He wished that his mother had not taken it upon herself to try to pick up from where he had left off, but was grateful that she had not the inclination, or perhaps merely lacked the physical ability, to be as heavy-handed. Yet presently he became aware of her hand holding his.

'Inspirational, darling?' Olivia asked.

Harry turned to her, 'What, mummy? So*ww*y, was miles away.'

'Of course you were, darling,' she said, patting his forearm. 'I was wondering if the sight of the site might incite within you a stirring of motivation?'

The question was, to Harry, one of great exasperation; she was nagging him still! He really had hoped he was safe behind his shield of the Bodhisattva Ideal, but he now realised it insubstantial, and that his mother would soon choose to slash through it as effortlessly as a mâcheté would silk.

'Sti*ww*ing of motivation?' he echoed.

'Yes, darling . . . all of your family are here! You see before you your heritage; does it not encourage a passion to propagate?'

Harry was unsure how to respond. He mentally scrambled for a deferential reply but Olivia's look of expectation served only to stall him, and he was relieved when came Valentine's exclamation, 'Gosh! I should think it glorious fun to be dead!'

Upon arriving at the plot, Valentine had gazed longingly at his Daddy's column, so bright white in the sun, and he appreciated it obviously having recently received a thorough polishing by the cemetery people.

'Hello, daddy!' he telepathically said, 'It's your princely popinjay in pyjamas! Regard how still I have not changed very much since last you were here! I'd like to think I'm somewhat more sophisticated to the ways of the world, but I'm still your little popinjay, and forever shall be!'

Valentine was certain that Monty would always recognise him, no matter how many years might pass before their jubilant reunion. He was confident that when his time came the heavens would open and his daddy's strong arm would reach down and together they would live as radiant saints in blessed bliss.

Here, Valentine stopped his thoughts for a space to consider how much fun saintly virtue might be, and deciding it to be not very, he wondered if the fate of the wicked might be more so. In a flash, he concluded that as his daddy had always enjoyed a roaring good time it seemed to him accurate to assume that they would share eternity in the heady abyss of Beelzebub.

'Gosh! What fun might that be!' he thought, and imagined how he, with his daddy, would ride bareback double upon a black cold-blooded stallion called Caligula whose hooves would be as terrific thunder when they galloped at fearsome speed through and over the deep valleys and steep ridges of fiery Hades.

Gosh, how nice it would be to once again feel his daddy's rough tweed embrace, and to touch the scratch of his golden stubble! And what fun it would be for they would surely attend decadent balls with the likes of Wallace Simpson and Mussolini, the Borgias, the Romanovs and Andy Warhol!

The exciting prospect was such that Valentine found it too much of a labour to hold his tongue and abstain the exclamation, 'Gosh! I should think it glorious fun to be dead!'

Olivia's eyes bore into him, and had she possessed the powers of Medusa he would have transformed into quite a novel tombstone.

'What an irretrievably idiotic idea!' she snapped at him.

Valentine was impervious to her scorn, 'When I'm gone, I should like to be buried right next to daddy, and I want nothing but violets to grow all around. I *must* be buried in pyjamas, and on my stone there must be engraved a little Popinjay bird! No need for names; daddy will know me!' With that, he bounced on the balls of his feet and felt proud of his decision.

'You are being ridiculous and disrespectful!' spat Olivia with disdain.

'Gosh!' said Valentine with surprise, 'But its best you all know. I might go at any time at all, and it will help knowing just what I want. Isn't that so, Gubsy?'

Gubsy had been worlds away when he was brought back by the question, which he needed repeating.

'The ninny's right. It all helps,' he said in a quiet voice before raising it, and adding, 'However, make damn well sure it's not any time soon . . . *any* of you children! Most especially you, young Harry, you've things that need doing, eh?'

'Yes, Gubsy,' mumbled Harry, and internally he groaned.

Willy had been viewing Valentine with puzzlement, and she asked, 'But why a little Popinjay bird? What's the significance?'

Upon receiving Valentine's proud explanation, Willy wondered some more and asked, 'Mummy, did daddy have a special name for me?'

The group turned to Olivia, and presently she noticed the sun soaked world turn grey as clouds of the same colour dominated the sky. Though it was still warm, she felt a chill down her spine; she was not used to pandering to her progenies. However, she did have the answer, and with a thin smile, she replied, 'Yes, darling, of course he did. He called you his 'little Willy Wonka.'

'Oh!' said Willy with some disappointment; she did not consider it the nicest name, and it certainly did not conjure up images of femininity.

Corny trespassed Olivia's personal space, and gazed up at her with eyes like saucers full of anticipation, for he too wanted to learn his special name.

She looked down at him as a supercilious cat might an irreverent mouse, and told him, 'You were his "jammy little dodger".'

Corny was thrilled to bits with the information, though, with a furrowed brow, he wondered what a jammy little dodger might be.

A silence of an awkward type followed – surely, Harry had one too? Why was she not telling?

'What about Harry, mummy?' said Valentine, 'What did daddy call him?'

'But don't you remember, Harry?' reasoned Willy, 'Valentine remembers his.'

Olivia was at a loss what to say, she could conceivably invent a moniker but that would hardly be true to her husband. Monty had considered it an unsuitable thing for Horatio to possess; his heir was to be honourable and sensible, and a silly baby name just would not wash.

Harry knew he had none, and he knew the reason. Yet it did not bother him; he would rather have had no name at all than have suffered his father's bullying for his first dozen years.

'Well?' asked Valentine and Willy in unison.

Kismet was kind to Olivia because, as if in a flick of a switch, the tiny drops of rain she had felt on her face became a thorough downpour.

'Gosh!' exclaimed Valentine, and Willy cried, 'Bother!', as they both ran with Harry back to the car, 'I'll fetch the umb*w*ella!' he called over his shoulder to Olivia.

'What the deuce!' boomed Gubsy watching the children flee.

'*Ugh*!' said Olivia, and called out: 'Bring me the umbrella, Harry!' for the vigorous rain hindered her hearing.

Valentine and Willy bundled into the backseat as Harry produced some blankets and a large umbrella from the boot. He tossed the blankets in at the damp pair.

'I'll be *w*ight back; don't go anywhere!' he said, and he rushed, with the umbrella, to his mother and great uncle.

'Where does he imagine we might go?' asked Valentine of Willy.

'Thank you, darling,' said a sodden Olivia to Harry, 'Do fetch Corny; he's being a fool!' and she held the umbrella to shelter both herself, who could not run in heels (and never would anyway) and Gubsy who could not run if his life depended upon it.

Harry found Corny still stood by the plot. He had decided it fun to face the sky, open wide his mouth and catch inside it as much rain as was possible.

'C'mon, *w*ascal! You're getting d*w*enched!'

He grabbed his little brother and his goldfish and carrying them, he made a dash for the car.

With the wet children safely inside, they towelled off with the blankets and wiped the window to watch through a space their mother and Gubsy's snail-like approach as they avoided puddles and huddled beneath the umbrella.

'Gosh! I think I simply have to laugh!' said Valentine and he did, so too did Willy, and, in his own silent way, Corny.

Despite himself, Harry smiled also, for it was hard not to when seeing his nagging mother have her decorum pushed askew, and he waited until having to brave the rain again to help fit Gubsy into his seat.

Harry had spent more than an hour washing the car that morning as Cosmo looked on, for he could not help with his foot, and seethed and scowled. His cantankerousness only slightly lessened when the car was spotless and gleaming from bumper to boot because Harry then suggested that they relax with a smoke behind the gazebo.

Whilst relaxing, Harry had explained as peaceably as possible: 'It *w*eally is just a family thing, you know. I mean, *w*eal family, oh, I mean you are weal family too, but I mean family of my dad. We aren't going there to see Excelsior. You and I can do that another day, but today it's just for my dad.'

After sending off the family with a hefty whack to the Jaguar, Cosmo watched it motor down the Avenue and turn the corner. As he limped into Chinchero, he thought to himself, 'Bloody family!' before remembering that they did not quite see themselves to be that. If they did then they would have welcomed his company, in fact, they would have insisted upon it.

It was true that Monty had not been his father but he had been raised to call him Uncle, even if that did somewhat compromise factuality. Moreover, the plot was not only the resting place of Excelsior but also that of Olympia, and on top of that, Cosmo just happened to be the great-great grandson of her favourite child – Fortunata – and it was not Cosmo's fault that Excelsior had not felt the same way.

Excelsior and Fortunata had never enjoyed the pleasantest of relations; he thought her impertinent, and she, accurately, accused him of tyranny, and after Olympia passed away she could not tolerate even to be in the same room as him. She made no secret of her belief that she thought him wholly responsible for the death; his cruelty, and his fondness for feminine fat, had Olympia employ food to please him and fundamentally stuff herself as if for foie gras.

Forswearing Excelsior and his expectations, Fortunata married a humble cow farmer and was henceforth known simply as Tunny Oxley, and she did not ever again set eyes upon or speak to her father or siblings.

Tunny died a decade before Excelsior, and when her daughter Hattie heard of his death, she had in mind to put to an end the family rift, and thought she might do even better if she could push her own ambitious (and illegitimate) daughter Ursula upon young Sebastian Avery-Stripe.

The Avery-Stripes would not have it. Though Ambrosius was curious what had become of his eldest sister and her subsequent issues, he did not deem a union between the two families at all appropriate for they were rather too rustic and his father would not ever have approved of such a misalliance.

Poor Ursula was heartbroken for she had fallen entirely for Sebastian, but as fate had it, a hunting accident in Africa put an end to his life not more than three months later. It was all to the good though, for soon afterward Ursula met her heaven-made match in a charming, if somewhat unctuous, Tarquin Stockman, and within a year, they wed, thus creating the name of Oxley-Stockman.

Tarquin was a man of great financial comfort and pumped much of his currency into Ursula's cow farm, making 'Oxley-Stockman' a beef of good repute, and it was not long before the Avery-Stripes held parvenu Ursula in decent regard though still at arm's length.

Mr and Mrs Oxley-Stockman had but one child, a son named Quentin and he was the apple of their eye though he was a slimy little wretch. When he came of age, he joined the family's meat firm and watched the wealth grow as steadily as that of his cousin Monty's drained, and he was happy, for he knew of the ancient fissure.

Quentin made a wife of a Miss Esmé Rufkin; together they were a most complacent pair, most notably as guests at the wedding of Monty and Olivia in 1967, and the following year both couples had delivered unto them their first-borns; Montgomery begat Horatio, and Quentin begat Cosmo.

Cosmo had learned of this family history from his Granny Ursie in the Oxley-Stockman pile, Stakely Manor. She had always retained a bee in her bonnet over Ambrosius Avery-Stripe's derisive rejection of her – 'Not good enough for his shining Sebastian! Served them right he was trampled to death!' she would say – and then harp on about how she had shown him who was superior to whom when she had married her Tarquin and made lots of meaty money when Ambrosius was living off the remains of funds harvested from bird-droppings!

'Bird-droppings were his life and bird-droppings were his death!' Granny Ursie would cackle, and then add, 'Avery-Stripes! I wouldn't give tuppence for the lot of 'em!'

Her grandson would though. Cosmo was in awe of them when a little boy. To hear of Excelsior's grand wealth thrilled him and to learn how great-great-granny Tunny had turned her nose up at it all angered him, for though the Oxley-Stockmans were now far richer than the Avery-Stripes they did not possess such a rich and impressive history. The tales of the peculiar departures were as exciting horror stories to him, and he wished his father as hardy as Uncle Monty and his mother as glamorous as Auntie O. He knew he would far rather have been born an Avery-Stripe, than an Oxley-Stockman for still he saw them as the roots, trunk and crown of the family tree, whereas he was of the branch that they would have liked to sever.

He revered them, yet at the same time, he despised them their self-assured sense of superiority. It rankled him that their confidence seemed to them an entitlement bestowed at birth despite how they might turn out to be, for they were all of direct lineage.

It was with irritating thoughts of how even Valentine – in fact, most especially he – possessed the unshakeable arrogance, that Cosmo limped toward the drawing room.

Rupert was inside. He had laid dustsheets on the floor, draped more over the piano and chesterfield, and was erecting an A-frame in preparation for the reparation of the ceiling crack. Cosmo stood in the doorway and watched Rupert ascend the ladder, and utilise a paintbrush to remove loose matter from the fracture. Puffs of white dust and bits of plaster appeared and seemed to take Rupert by surprise and he stopped to remove, with his upper arm, the chalky powder from his face.

Seeing Rupert's trifling hindrance made Cosmo smile and think how his friend was a fool to have offered to renovate Chinchero, and gratis at that! Yet Cosmo's smile vanished when he considered Rupert's motives, and it vexed him to think that it was either because he wanted to ingratiate himself to the family or because he had shown, what Cosmo considered to be, a shocking liking for Valentine and wanted to remain near him.

Upon hearing that Rupert needed collecting from Heathrow, Cosmo had decided most certainly would grant the favour with the suggestion that they stay for a while with his nearby relations whereupon he would flex over them the muscles of his supremacy.

It would also be good to see Harry, he was certain that his two friends would get along. He was positive that Rupert would regard Valentine with as much disdain as did he, and to make the pansy feel uncomfortable in his own home certainly had an appeal.

He thought it a brilliant idea at the time but Valentine had somehow managed to drive Rupert to disclose a partiality entirely revelational to Cosmo.

He simply could not tolerate that Rupert possessed such a repellent skeleton in his closet that had only come out after so many years of shared companionship. Rupert had not hitherto exhibited any such tendencies. He was normal, he played sports; he scaled mountains, went white-water rafting, he was not scared of anything, nothing fazed him, he was fearless, he was as a man should be. He had had girlfriends, pretty ones. When Cosmo had met him on a fishing holiday in his teens, Rupert's girlfriend was the best-looking in Salcombe, and he could not believe that Rupert was capable of such duplicity, especially when he considered the many post-rugby game showers they had shared. On one hand, it embarrassed him to think of Rupert's eyes on his anatomy but on the other it was humiliating to consider that if Rupert's eyes had so ventured then why did he fail to show any sign of appreciation. Not that Cosmo wanted appreciation from one of his own gender – of course he did not! However, the fact that Rupert had expressed none made him consider his physical shortcomings and when he wondered what Valentine might possess that he did not, he felt disturbingly beta to the pansy's alpha.

Still, this uncomfortable thought did not conclude a satisfactory explanation in Cosmo's mind, for no matter how great Valentine's attribute might be it would count for nothing because surely he was yin to Rupert's yang. To consider the alternative conjured a visual more horrifying to Cosmo than the original, yet try as he might, he was unable to locate a sounder rationalisation because he could not compute how anybody might otherwise fall victim to Valentine; it was not as if he had about him anything else that a chap that likes chaps might find attractive.

Surrendering himself to that thought, Cosmo found there was no option but to swallow the logical fact that Rupert was a slave to the sausage – worse yet, the sausage of Valentine! And knowing his cousin as he did he was not surprised to learn that as soon as he was aware of the power he possessed he had brandished it and hypnotised Rupert into supreme acts of folly such as redecorating the family house! Cosmo found he felt a little bit sorry for Rupert, but more than that, he actually praised The Almighty for not having bestowed upon him such an endowment as Valentine's (no wonder the pansy was conceited!) for then who knew what Rupert might have attempted in the showers! The very idea made Cosmo sick to the pit and his burly build shuddered.

'I'll wager you wish you hadn't said you'd do it now,' Cosmo said, with a sneer.

Rupert had been too involved in his endeavour to realise Cosmo's presence, and seeing him at the door, he smiled, and replied, 'Oh, hello! I'm already making a mess, but, no, not at all, it's no big deal. I made a list with Gretchen before I went to the shop and it's just lots of simple things, and you know I like to keep busy. Want to help?'

Cosmo limped closer. 'No thanks, I can't with my foot.'

Rupert looked down at him and made an indent in his blond brow: 'Yes, it's too bad how that happened,' then he resumed his work.

Cosmo did not care for Rupert's tone. He took hold of the ladder, shook it and said, 'Besides you're a big enough dupe for the both of us.'

Rupert grasped the top rung.

'Crikey! Don't be a dolt!'

But Cosmo merely accelerated his action and laughed up at him. Rupert abandoned the ladder and asked Cosmo what he thought he was playing at.

'Me? What am I playing at? What about you! You've got your feet nicely under the table here, haven't you?'

'Crikey, Cosmo, I thought you'd be glad! I'm just fitting in!'

'Oh, I bet you're bloody *fitting in*, especially with Valentine!'

'What's that supposed to mean?' asked Rupert, setting his jaw, 'What's your beef?'

Cosmo considered Rupert's use of the word 'beef' to be a dig at his family's fortune, therefore he grabbed the front of Rupert's daffodil-coloured t-shirt and pulled him near.

He leered at him and demanded, 'What exactly did you get up to last night? What were you doing in Valentine's room? *Sleeping*?'

Rupert regarded his hostile friend and thought his question irritating. He was at a loss as to why Cosmo should believe he had a right to know, and considered the bellicose bodily contact unnecessary.

Calmly, he asked, 'Why would that be any of your business?'

The response seemed to Cosmo to be dripping with condescension, he had not heard Rupert talk in such a way before; he sounded quite like Valentine, and it filled Cosmo with revulsion.

'It's disgusting that's all, how Valentine's hypnotised you into dancing to his gay tune, and when I think what you might have been doing all night . . . why, it makes me want to bloody vomit!'

This was too much for Rupert to bear and though violence was to him an anathema, he considered Cosmo's bigotry to be begging for it, thus with one swift move he put to use his muscle and socked him hard in the nose.

The unexpected punch hurtled Cosmo to the floor and he took the ladder with him, for it transpired not to possess the power to break his fall but it did have the strength to whack him in the mouth on their shared descent.

The crash and clatter awoke the dozing Remarkable, and he contributed to the commotion with loud and maniacal squawks.

Presently, Gretchen arrived. The racket could be heard from her kitchen, and upon seeing bloody-mouthed Cosmo tangled in the collapsed ladder and an incensed Rupert looking down at him, she sighed and felt foolish to ask, 'But, what is happenink?'

Rupert did not want to lie, yet felt the truth too bad, therefore, he replied, 'I asked Cosmo if he wanted to help, but it turns out he can't with his foot and then this happened.'

Gretchen quietened Remarkable and looked at the golden young man whom she liked very much, and though she knew there was more to the story, she accepted his explanation for she did not like the bloody young man nearly so much.

She watched Cosmo, watery-eyed and clutching his nose, shake off Rupert's assistance to rise, she snorted, and shook her head.

'I think perhaps you should get up, Master Cosmo, and I will look at your bleedink,' then added he was to be a brave boy for the alcohol would make his mouth 'stink'.

On his feet again, Cosmo, furious at the pain in his face and ashamed of his fall, did not know quite where to look or what to do with himself for he was somewhat disorientated.

Gretchen conveyed him to her kitchen and said, 'You are so accidental, yesterday and today, foot and mouth! What will tomorrow brink!'

Cosmo glowered at her, and spluttered, 'It's my bloody nose too! I think it's broken!' and he decided he had no intention of staying another day to be looked down upon and constantly attacked, and that when Gretchen had tidied him he would be making a telephone call to his father.

Alone again, Rupert set right the ladder. He was relieved to find its descent had not caused any breakages other than Cosmo's lip, and had narrowly escaped a collision with the Steinway. As he climbed back up to the ceiling, he stopped midway and looked at his fist that clenched the brush. It felt quite sore, though surely not as sore as what it had hit, and certainly, he would not let such a minor injury prevent him from rendering Chinchero perfect for Valentine's marvellous party. With that, he picked up from where he had left off, and whilst he brushed, he whistled the tune of Tchaikovsky's *Dance of the Sugar Plum Fairy*.

Upon entering Chinchero, the brilliant smell of roast rabbit filled Valentine with joy, but rapture surpassed joy upon his rushing to the drawing room and finding Rupert therein, regarding the ceiling.

'I am here!' exclaimed Valentine, 'I have returned!' and he tiptoed over the dustsheets toward him.

Rupert spun round, grinned magnificently, and enveloped Valentine in his arms, 'I'm all dusty, you know,' he said.

'Gosh! I don't care, I'll be happy to divest this mourning attire, besides I'm already wet!'

Rupert felt Valentine's damp shoulders and rubbed them.

'Did you have a . . . I mean, how was it?'

Enjoying the enfoldment, Valentine did not move an inch except to close his eyes.

'Gosh, yes! It was glorious; I love seeing daddy.' He stopped to think, and pulling back a little, he looked at Rupert in earnest, and asked, 'Where do you suppose to be most fun, Heaven or Hell?'

Rupert corrugated his brow to consider, when Olivia appeared with the chastisement: 'Do not say such things, Valentino! Rupert will think you a heathen!'

'Gosh! Do you think me a heathen, Rupert?' asked Valentine, and received a whisper that Rupert was uncertain as to what exactly one was.

Olivia stalked into the drawing room to survey the ceiling, and was pleased to find that Rupert had filled the crack admirably.

'Already it had made an incredible improvement,' she said to him.

'Thanks!' said Rupert, 'Just need the mud to dry completely and I'll paint over it tomorrow.'

'It looks so smooth,' said Willy.

'I'm imp*w*essed!' said Harry.

'I knew all along Rupert would do a first-class job of it!' Valentine exclaimed, holding his handyman's hand.

Corny looked, with astonishment, up at the ceiling, and Gubsy, who had only just arrived, involved himself in the inspection, and boomed: 'By Jove! Jolly good! Jolly good!'

Pleased with the reactions, Rupert told them that he had also, with underwater sealant, fixed temporarily the leak in the conservatory for the water's precise point of entry is easier to locate when it is raining.

Gubsy beamed at him, and said, 'In your clever hands, young man, Chinchero'll soon be good as new, and then nobody . . . ' here he turned to Olivia, 'shall be able to *nitpick!*' and he gnashed his false teeth.

Olivia's response was to regard him distastefully, for had she not brought Chinchero's derelict state to his attention then Rupert would not ever have offered to see to them.

Presently a teardrop of rain dripped from her soaked satin camellia atop her widow's veil, and trickled its way along her hairline. It was a reminder that her appearance was fairly sodden and not at all respectable, so to Rupert she said, 'Your craftsman capabilities are indeed highly commendable, but if you will please excuse me for now I simply must change into something less miserable,' whereupon the rumble of distant thunder accompanied her hurried leave.

In the dim light of her bedroom, Olivia removed and then briefly examined the rain-specked garments of Chanel before throwing them on the four-poster. Would they ever be quite the same again she wondered, and she hoped that Gretchen knew a trick.

Dressed in only her black lingerie, Olivia viewed her reflection in the Venetian looking-glass. She liked what she saw and considered that Monty probably still would too, for unlike Excelsior, he had liked his ladies lean, and she let down her hair.

She rolled down her stockings. They were too damaged to wear again, she screwed them into a ball and tossed it to the floor. She removed her bustier and panties and then she remembered her pearls, and not ever having enjoyed being naked without Monty, she quickly put on her kimono and looked out of the window at the never-ending torrent.

The depressing sight brought to her mind the possibility of a cold and she decided that she would have a bath before it claimed her. She approached her door, turned the knob, opened it, and in perfect timing with a flash of white lightening, she gasped with the shock of fright.

To Olivia it was not at first apparent that the barbarous ghoul in the hall was Cosmo, for he had now transmogrified into something so monstrous as to make his former self seem comparatively dainty. His eyes were an indigo-black, his nose had swollen to almost twice its ordinary size, and across its bridge, and another on his lip, was a bloody butterfly-stitch that the flash of nature's electrical light had caused to look very sinister.

Recovering from the nasty shock, Olivia propped against the door and she clasped her throat. Eyes screwed, she gently rolled her forehead against the woodwork as if it soothed her, and hissed, 'Do not ever do that again, Cosmo, you look hideous and scared me half to death!'

Cosmo's surprise that Olivia should feel to be the suffering party when it was he who wore butterflies caused him to raise his monobrow but he quickly desisted because it hurt his face.

'I don't doubt I look hideous!' he snarled, 'I've a cut lip, a broken nose and two bloody black eyes, but I'm sorry if that offends your delicate constitution!'

Olivia rolled her head to face him, and sighed, 'What happened?'

He would not answer. He did not want to say. It was humiliating and he was sore at the whole situation.

'What happened?' she repeated, straightening her stance, for she was no longer scared.

'A bloody silly accident with the ladder is what happened! But never mind that. I've come to tell you I'm off; I'm going back to Stakely Manor.'

'Already?' asked a relieved Olivia, 'But you only just arrived! I thought you were staying for an indefinite period,' and she wondered if it might not be true but then she saw his leather travel bag at his feet.

'I was and now it's definitely come to an end,' he said defiantly, folding his arms across his puffed-out chest.

'Oh dear. Well, it has been a pleasure, darling, do drive carefully in the wretched rain.' She squinted her eyes, and continued, 'You are safe to drive, aren't you?' fearing he might say no.

'Ha! You can't bloody wait to see the back of me, can you?' he accused.

'I don't know what you mean! It has been a delight!'

'What I mean is since I got here you've not once looked me in the eye until now!'

'Fantasy!' she snapped, 'You are imagining things!'

Cosmo laughed disparagingly at her. 'Typical woman!' he said, 'Typical, typical, bloody, bloody woman!'

'I shall not be spoken to in such a way!'

'You were all sweetness and smiles in Paris; laughter and charm, and looked at nothing but me until you got what you wanted and then you drop me like a hot brick!'

'Oh, Cosmo! Last week seems so very long ago! So much has happened! Besides, I refuse to believe that you for one second considered it to be anything other than an amicable transaction; nothing more, nothing less, and well you know it. So do desist your amateur romantic dramatics!'

Cosmo scowled at her as best he was able, he squared his shoulders and employed his build to squash her against the door.

He leered down at her, 'Oh, come now, Auntie O! You're the actress; you enjoyed very much what I wanted!'

Experiencing again Cosmo's uncomfortable proximity, his smell and his size, flashed into Olivia's mind the recollection of their premeditated meeting.

He had stayed in a hotel near Notre Dame, and she at the Ritz. She would not entertain the idea of being seen visiting the hovel in which she imagined his abode to be, and nothing would have induced her to invite him to hers.

Instead, they met in the fourth arrondissement for a supper of moules marinière in a brasserie that he deemed decent though she thought it tawdry. After which they went for a late night stroll along the Seine, and that was when the reason for the rendezvous arose.

Outrage had filled Cosmo when Olivia said she would neither go to his hotel nor take him to hers. His outrage fast fused with impatience and merged into lust, whereupon spying the narrow street of the fishing cat, he all but carried her halfway through, and there, in the most torrid fashion, he insisted himself upon her.

The memory of the sordid ordeal fired Olivia with fury, and she glared up at him, looking as if about to jump at his jugular and sink in her teeth.

'Step back this instant!' she demanded. 'Do not delude yourself to consider you possess the power to intimidate me! If you try to bully me, I shall . . . I will . . . '

'What? What shall you do?' Cosmo asked, lasciviously, bending his legs so their faces were on a level, 'Tell me what you will do to me; I must know!' and he pushed himself closer.

Trapped, Olivia fought hard the urge to rearrange his leering and swollen face with her strong fingers, and in a steely voice, said, 'I shall break more than your nose and I will feed them to the chickens!'

The cutting comment wiped for a moment the lewd smirk from Cosmo's face. He pulled himself to his full height and though it hurt to do so, he roared with laughter.

'Take a bloody look at you, up on your hind legs! You are brilliant, Auntie O! You'll never change . . . and I hope you never will! Small wonder I always wanted you, and now that I've had you, I'm happy. The fact that you might've enjoyed it too is neither here nor there, and you're right, we both got what we wanted. I hope you'll treasure it as highly as I always shall the memory of our "transaction".'

Olivia felt both demeaned and furious. She trembled with profound rage but since Cosmo had backed off physically she refused to lose further face by any rash behaviour that might degrade her; she was, after all, an Avery-Stripe, and he a mere Oxley-Stockman.

Therefore, she simply said, 'As well you might treasure the memory. I paid over the odds, hand over fist, in fact. My one consolation is that the part you played in my half of the exchange was so shamefully insubstantial and of such blessed brevity as to be entirely eradicated from my mind!'

Cosmo regarded her with surprise for a space.

'And to think I bloody waited to see you before leaving! I've been ready for over an hour. So here I am, but you don't seem very interested in what I have to tell you. I am disappointed!' and he tried to pull a face of woe but it was hard to with his nose in the state that it was.

'You've told me goodbye!' she replied, 'and in a most un-gentlemanly manner I might add, but goodbye, I can't say I shall miss you!'

He laughed at her again, and said, 'That's not it at all! What I want to tell you is that I telephoned Pater to let him know I'm homeward bound, and do you know what he just happened to mention?'

'Naturally not!'

'Ha-ha! What he told me made me smile, he said that my stupid mater is going out of her mind because she can't seem to find Olympia's Starfish! Tearing Stakely Manor down, he said! Ha! So that's why I say I hope that you'll treasure it!'

The news did seem to enhance the lustre of her possession of the ring for Olivia did so despise Esmé.

She looked to Cosmo, smiled, and then said, 'You are dishonourable, and I trust that your dishonour shall prevent you from educating Esmé as to the location of the Starfish.'

Cosmo replied with a sneer, 'You really think I might tell her? But then I'd have to explain *why* I gave it to you! And I'd be sure to lose my allowance, not to mention my inheritance! It's our secret, and I don't want Harry to find out either – he'd never understand.'

Olivia looked at him with feelings of disdain mingled with amusement before saying, 'Well, goodbye, Cosmo. I expect I'll be seeing you again quite soon enough,' and she proffered her cheek.

'Goodbye, Auntie O,' he said, and he kissed her a moment too long for her liking.

She pulled away. 'Do drive safely, darling,' she said, and quickly gave his freshly broken nose a vicious tweak and stepped back into her room, slammed the door, and liberated a tinkle of laughter upon hearing his outraged *Ow*!

Cosmo grimaced his un-pretty face and blinked his black eyes that the tweak had caused to water. He grabbed his leather travel bag and limped down the stairwell, and he sneered at Olympia's portrait as he considered how very much his Auntie O had coveted the Starfish. He could also remember his drunk Uncle Monty (thinking himself out of earshot) remonstrating with the painting how the ring was rightly his.

However, when Olivia had suggested the tryst, Cosmo was not convinced that her real reason was that she wanted the ring but, in truth, was because she wanted him as much as he always had her.

Well, *always* was not quite true. Certainly he had when puberty struck, and all through adolescence too; the idea of sharing intimacies with his aunt would keep him up all night, and work him into such a fever that there was no option other than to remedy the situation with the only solution he had at hand.

He strongly suspected she had secretly enjoyed attentions that – after the passing of Uncle Monty – he had been careless to conceal. He understood the difficulty she obviously underwent in admitting to herself how greatly she desired him. Not because they were family – for indeed they shared not a drop – but because, no matter what his mater and pater might say, she was a lady to the bone and always would honour the memory of her husband.

Except for this one time, something had made her weak, and understandably, she was lonely after so many years without the touch of a man, and who better to run to than her potent nephew? Naturally, she was no longer the looker she had once been but still, she possessed considerable physical charm, and for the sake of nostalgia, Cosmo was powerless to the proposal. If she wanted to dress it up as a silly transaction then he would do her the courtesy of humouring the pretence.

All he need do was steal the Starfish from his mater. It would be an easy thing to do because Esmé was careless with her jewellery for rather than store them in the safe box she stuffed them all into the drawers of her dresser. Cosmo simply waited until an evening his parents went to play bridge, and after a few minutes of searching, he found the ring, removed it from its original box, placed it in a small black velvet drawstring pouch, and telephoned a Paris hotel to make a reservation.

Then, when walking along the Seine at midnight, he presented his Auntie O with the Starfish that she examined for a moment – as if to check its authenticity – and dropped it into her Birkin, whereupon she made the breezy request that he hail her a cab for she simply had to sleep *alone*. Consequently, Cosmo saw red.

This red was not purely one of rage, though it certainly played a part, but mostly one of lust teased to the point of no return. He considered her a game old bird and no mistake, for her refusal to fulfil their collaboration in either his or her hotel was, to his mind, an obvious indication that she desired an altogether more deviant culmination. Therefore, to prove he was more than equal to the task he pulled her into a narrow side street where she put up a rousing tussle to thrill him further and he demonstrated to her the extent of his virility in two minutes and thirteen seconds.

In those one-hundred-and-thirty-three seconds every one of his juvenile yearnings were unleashed and never before had he felt so thoroughly powerful and intrinsically male, as if for the very first time he knew precisely what it was to be a man, and believed he would have gladly laid down his life for his amatory aunt.

She, however, did not seem to be quite so moved by the experience despite, whilst postcoitally hoisting her knickers, claiming to be 'inordinately impressed, darling' before stepping into the street, magicking a cab out of nowhere, and disappearing into the Parisian night.

He had tried reaching her at the Ritz several times the next day and the one after, but each time the concierge told him either that she was out or had expressed the wish not to be disturbed. It was then that the revelation struck him that she had manipulated him, as one might a pawn, in her plan to procure the ring, which he now saw with clarity, had been her sole goal all along.

At first, this did not sit well with him for the more thought he applied to the episode the more his eyes opened to the fact that it was not he who had exerted his power over her, but she over him. But then he considered what power was that, other than the only one woman had over man, namely the power of seduction, and like a clever little minx, she had exerted her feminine wiles with expert proficiency. Why, she had even almost succeeded in eluding her part of the exchange!

With this shrewd realisation fixed firmly in his head he mulled it over until he came to the conclusion that as she had behaved exactly as a lady of the night and knowingly cheapened herself before him it returned to him his power and furthermore, provided sterling proof of his superiority to the Avery-Stripes. This belief gave him cause to sneer (how he would have loved to tell Granny Ursie and hear her approving cackle!) not to mention to feel the pleasure of certain stirrings.

Each of Cosmo's cousins were in the drawing room, and Rupert was also.

'I'm off! I'm going home!' Cosmo boomed.

The group greeted his appearance and announcement with feelings and sounds of disgust and surprise mixed with relief and distress.

'Cwumbs, Cosmo! What happened?' asked a concerned Harry, 'and you can't weally be going so soon?'

Grief-stricken, Willy rushed over to the man of her dreams, and in a tremulous voice, she proclaimed he looked awful, and asked whatever had happened, and should he not stay until better, did he really have to leave? All the while, she mentally prayed, 'Make him stay!'

Cosmo glanced at Rupert with embarrassment evident in his eyes; he hoped he would not divulge to them the true cause of his injuries.

'Was trying to help with the ceiling, but bloody toppled from the top of the ladder. No good for anything with my foot!' Cosmo explained, 'but I'll be all right; not the first time I've been hit in the honker, but hurts like the bloody dickens! So, I'm off home. Need to rest and all that!'

Rupert said nothing; he already felt guilty for using his fist, and did not wish to further injure Cosmo's pride.

More protestations came from Harry and Willy, and Cosmo thought with annoyance how they both made all the right noises now but neither of them had requested his presence at the cemetery. Why should he stay when they did not truly perceive him to be one of them?

He noticed Corny with his fish, sat at the summit of the ladder, gazing down at him in horror.

Valentine also saw Corny's alarm, and said to him, 'Gosh, Corny! Why are you looking at Cosmo that way? I don't know what all the bother is about. He doesn't look to me to be any uglier than usual.'

'You beast!' cried Willy.

'Don't be wude, Valentine,' whined Harry.

Cosmo, however, appreciated that Valentine was at least constant in his attitude.

'Right, I'm off!' Cosmo said and performed the perfunctory chap-hug with both Harry and Rupert. 'Goodbye, Valentine, Corny and Willy,' he said and then limped out of the drawing room with Harry close behind.

'G-g-good-b-bye, C-cosmo,' replied a distraught Willy who felt as if her entire world had ended.

'Buck up, Willy,' consoled Valentine. 'He'll be back long before he's welcome!'

Willy regarded her hateful brother. Her eyes cracked with red and already brimming.

'You are pure evil!' she said to him, and gasped with shock at her own words. She paused and then gathered her strength to scuttle out to the hall for one last glimpse of her beloved.

'Gosh!' said Valentine to Rupert and Corny. 'So I am to be an evil heathen from now on! Well, this evil heathen is simply starving for his Daddy's Deathday rabbit! Glorious fragrance, don't you think?'

Corny replied with an audible lick of his lips and rubbed his tummy with such vigorous circles that he and Gloriana would also have suffered an altercation with the ladder had Rupert not prevented it with a swift and steadying hand.

Through the stained-glass window, Willy watched a green Harry hold the umbrella over a red Cosmo as he climbed into his muddy-wheeled BMW.

As if in imitation of the falling rain, uncontrollable tears streamed over her podgy cheeks; she did not know when she would see Cosmo again. Worse still, all he had known her to be on this visit was a girl in a chimp mask dismissed from the dinner table and bedding in a tree! None of which had the power to captivate even the most desperate.

Cosmo motored off, Willy choked with a sob and buried her face in her hands until Harry came back in, whereupon she flung her arms round him and bawled.

'Willy! Do not c*w*y! Please t*w*y not to c*w*y!' said Harry in soothing tones, and stroked her back: 'Cosmo'll be fine; he's even tougher than he looks, you know.'

Willy convulsed, and then she whimpered, 'Do you think he'll still c-c-come to the m-m-marvellous p-p-party?'

Harry pondered. '*W*eally don't know, but I don't see why not.'

This seemed to mollify Willy somewhat.

Harry was touched that she had such a soft heart, and he enjoyed, for a space, her warmth but then he suddenly had a thought, and said, 'C*w*umbs! I hope Cosmo can d*w*ive with his foot!'

To say the least, Olivia was happy Cosmo had gone. His surprise presence in the home had been an awkward one for she feared that he might mention Paris to the children and was grateful that he had not.

She was quite capable of regarding the unpleasant method she had employed to extract the ring to be nothing but necessary. To possess Olympia's Starfish was to her mind well worth it and she was certain that Monty would have approved, for it had been just the one time and it was in the name of Avery-Stripe. Besides, Monty was dead therefore nobody sane could construe it to be extramarital, though in her heart she would always be his wife and she knew that the ring's retrieval had set in stone her devotion to him and his ambition for the family.

She wished she had been able to present the Starfish at his grave but realised it had been wise not to. She must, however, look at it now. Gaze at its glimmer, marvel at it sparkle, and appreciate her achievement.

Wrapping tight her kimono, Olivia sat upon the four-poster, and delved into her Birkin. Her excitement built as she groped for the feel of the velvet pouch.

Annoyed that it eluded her, she narrowed her eyes and put the bag on her lap to view where her hand ventured but still it seemed impossible to locate amongst the accumulated paraphernalia therein.

Expelling a sigh of exasperation, she irritably turned it upside down and emptied its contents on the bed. All manner of trappings descended; cigarettes, scent, spare underwear, and Monty's hip flask, along with compacts, lipsticks, a hairbrush and pages ripped from *Vogue*, all fell in a heap, and when all had fallen she began to dig deep.

She searched through it once, then once again and that was when an awful thought crossed her mind and sweat broke from her brow, but she looked a third time and a fourth.

Presently, she paused, and realised it futile, for quite patently she had placed it elsewhere, though she retained no recollection of having done so.

She looked on her bedside, fumbled through the jumble on her dressing table, and rummaged in each tallboy drawer, but it was not in any of those places.

She balled her hands into fists, hammered them on her head and commanded, 'Recall, darling! Recall!'

A moment passed, and then she realised that if she could not locate it then maybe it was not lost, and if it were not lost then that would suggest that somebody had stolen it, and only someone who knew she possessed it in the first place could steal it!

She leapt to her window just in time to see Cosmo leave and she was immediately cognisant that he had stolen it back. Small wonder he came to visit so soon and left so soon after, it made perfect sense!

However, could she really be certain of his crime? How would she ever know? She could not possibly ask him, and even if she did and he had, he would unlikely confess.

Alternatively, perhaps he did not have it, maybe it still was somewhere in Chinchero, but if she combed, would it be in vain? Would Cosmo all

along watch her desperately try to locate something he had sticky-
fingered?

Olivia was powerless to the distress of her predicament. She collapsed
to the floor and grabbed at her Chanel to suffocate the primordial scream
that erupted as if from hell.

CHAPTER 11

Willy's Fitting

It was patent to Valentine that the very first thing to fix were the stiffies, and as luck would have it, on one of his recent ventures into the depths of the cellar, he had happened upon several boxes of the necessary stationery. Thus, for a concentrated three hours, Valentine sat at the écritoire, and with ink both the colour and scent of his favourite flower, he applied to the task his exceptional calligraphist skills by manipulating a flight feather of a long ago swan.

When he had embellished every stiffy, he presented one for Rupert to admire, though he would not let him touch it for his digits were greasy from oiling scores of hinges.

'Crikey! Very nice!' Rupert enthused.

Valentine, though flattered, was not sated, 'Gosh! Thank you, but what do you think of the wordage? Is it, perchance, a touch too froufrou?'

Whereupon, Rupert took another look and read aloud: 'The Avery-Stripes cordially request the esteem of your most gracious and noble presence at Chinchero for a most Marvellous Party to celebrate the gloriously joyful occasion of the sixteenth anniversary of the nativity of handsome Cornelius from the honourable hour of eight of the clock on the 22nd sun of jaunty June.'

Valentine flipped the stiffy to show Rupert the reverse.

Your expectations from the fine family, in their immaculate place of residence, may include, amongst other things, gallons of champagne, divine victuals, charming ornamental decorations apropos to the circumstance, and orchestral delights! Our simple expectations from you; the gentlemen; white tie and tails, the ladies; breathtaking gowns and jewels (tiaras are glorious) and from all; sparkling wit and tons of bon ton! Time of carriages yet to be decided.

'Crikey!' said Rupert with a grin, 'The words are amazing! I can't wait!'

Valentine was gratified, he knew that his phrasing was fitting but to have it confirmed and appreciated by Rupert filled his cup of happiness.

'Hits and sets the right tone, don't you think?'

'Yes, it's just right! And it smells of violets too.'

'It's the ink! Glorious, don't you think?' said Valentine, and he waved the grandiose stiffy under Rupert's nose.

'Mmm, glorious!' Rupert agreed.

Valentine desisted his flapping, and said, 'All I need now is an awful lot of lick for the envelopes shan't seal themselves, but their taste is so vile!'

Rupert considered and keen to help he offered his tongue, but Valentine told him he did not wish to get it horrid, therefore, he positioned Corny on the ottoman and had him stick out his.

This seemed to Corny a wonderful pastime and he was quite disconsolate when they had finished. However, he cheered up immediately when given the task of licking the brass head of the stamp bearing the family crest and motto, before each time Valentine pressed it into a wax puddle on the back of every envelope.

According to the ormolu clock, it was midnight when their toil was complete, and an exhausted Valentine said to a dehydrated Corny that very early in the morning they must purchase, from the postal office, a block of stamps and then feed the jolliest pillar-box they can find.

With that, he and Rupert made certain that Corny brushed his teeth before tucking him into his blankets with Gloriana on his bedside, then they retired to Valentine's turret and locked the door.

Corny could not sleep for he was full of excitement. He did not know if it was the theatrical summer thunder show or the prospect of his party that produced his restlessness, but no matter how persistently he tossed and turned, or counted sheep until he ran out of factual numbers, he just could not nod off.

He wished that someone were still out of bed, for though Gloriana was to him precious, and her circular laps and unblinking eyes riveting, he craved the company of humans and their voices.

He arrived at the astute conclusion that as Valentine and Rupert had stayed up with him so much later than the others then they were the ones most likely still awake.

Removing, from beneath his pillow, his battery-torch and clicking it on, Corny slipped out from under his blankets, sneaked into the hall and following the path of his torch, he crept silently up the stairs – mindful of the third – to Valentine's turret.

It seemed strange to him that though there poked from under the door a line of bright light there came from within not a sound. He decided sadly that they were probably asleep and that one or both of them were scared of the dark. If that were the case he did not wish to wake them with a knock, but just to confirm his suspicion he crouched and peeked through the lock and was puzzled by what he saw.

For framed by the keyhole, Rupert was recumbent on the bed, his head tilted as if inspecting, for a great length of time, a new ceiling for cracks. This in itself was not puzzling, but the crown of laurel leaves in Rupert's golden hair did look rather queer, and queerer than that, although the point of view made it hard to tell, the crown looked to be his only item of clothing!

Corny blushed, and decided quite definitely that the game of undressed musical statues was not one that he fancied playing. Therefore, without further ado, he stole downstairs and back into bed where he tried to outstare Gloriana until he could no longer resist a deep and sound sleep.

Quite soon, the party's guests got their stiffies, and as a consequence the Bakelite behaved most uncharacteristically by ringing off it's hook which resulted in Gretchen being run off her feet, as each time the bell rang she was obliged to drop whatever busy thing she was doing (for the family would not answer) and add names to a list.

Much to Olivia's distaste, Harry was in possession of a mobile telephone, and on this he received a call from Cosmo who had called to boom, 'face feels much better, but still bloody black and blue and nose'll never be the same, but I've lost count the number of times I've crashed my conk! Anyway, pater, mater and I are all coming, and a friend of a friend got me a number for Flick, if you'll pass it to Cousin Valentine.'

It cheered Harry to hear that all the Oxley-Stockmans would be in attendance. Well, all of them if Valentine got through to Flick, and he went to deliver to him the writing paper upon which he had penned the number.

En route, he spied Willy sat upon a wicker peacock chair, looking wretched amongst the wisteria on the west terrace, as she plucked petals from a daisy. Harry did not like to see her so down in the mouth and he decided to share with her the news of Cosmo's coming.

'Hullo, Willy! What do you suppose?'

Willy did not feel up to supposing much other than she might not ever again see the man for whom she was plucking so to determine the requital of her romantic feelings. She supposed them one-sided, and the final pluck confirmed it. Subsequently, she supposed that she would never receive the opportunity to rectify the tragedy.

She let the demolished daisy fall to the floor, and in response to Harry's question, she replied, in a tone heaving with total dejection, 'I am sick and tired of supposing!'

'C*ww*mbs, so*ww*y,' said Harry, 'I'll just tell you then.'

And as he divulged to her the happy tidings, the colour that had been lacking from her cheeks swept back and returned them to their natural apple that he did like to see.

Willy's world now seemed full of potential, and mindful there existed little less than two weeks to metamorphose from frumpy caterpillar into enchanting butterfly, she resolved to concentrate her undivided attention and devote all of her energy to the endeavour. Yet, with this, she required assistance, and recollecting her mother's offer of succour, she braved herself to ascertain its validity.

Olivia still had not managed to locate the Starfish. There was not a single inch of her bedroom that she had not searched. Several times, she had scoured the stairwell, in particular the landing between the ground floor and first, for signs of the ring, because the last time she could remember holding it was when she had compared it to the painted one in Olympia's portrait. Yet no matter how often she returned, she did not ever find it lurking in the shadows from the risers on the treads or wedged beneath any of the rods that secured the red runner.

She looked to Olympia's portrait, at her Starfish and fat face, and she felt to be as enraged with her as Monty had always been.

'You overweight imbecile!' she mentally screamed at the ancestor, 'Had you given it to Ambrosius and not your cow farmer's wife of a daughter I would not now be driven to distraction. I *demand* that you tell me where it is!'

The half expectation of a reply brought to Olivia's attention her close proximity to insanity. Thus, it required of her a great power of strength not to rip the painting from the oak panelling and smash it over the newel post and instead, merely to reach up and administer a sharp slap to the cheek of the innocent bison.

Willy arrived in time to witness her mother's unwarranted attack on the beast.

'Mummy!' cried Willy, 'Why are you smacking the bison?'

Olivia startled and span to face her daughter at the top of the stairwell.

'I thought I saw some sort of insect, darling,' she explained as she dusted her hands together, 'but probably just dust,' and she proceeded to descend as if certain of her destination.

'Mummy, wait!' called Willy, and she ran down to the spot that Olivia had vacated.

Olivia froze, screwed her eyes for a space and irritably wondered what Willy might want for she had little time for nuisances.

She turned and grimaced, 'What, darling? I am presently somewhat otherwise occupied.'

Willy frowned.

'The Marvellous Party is to be soon, mummy, and you rather said that you would help ladyfy me in time, so I was quite hoping we might start.'

Olivia knew that Willy was correct but she had no time for silly pursuits when she had to find the ring.

'Oh, darling, it's not difficult; brush your hair, wear a nice dress and say the right thing at the right time. It's no great secret. You can do it, or did I raise a perfect fool?'

To say that Willy was disillusioned would be inaccurate; in her heart she had not truly believed that her mother might have meant to keep her word, yet that was paltry recompense. Therefore, she persevered, 'But you said you would help, up in the tree. You said so!'

Olivia displayed her palms to command silence.

'Please do not patronise me, darling, I am well aware of what I have and have not said; I require no reminding. Further, I ask you to cease your hysteria, which I might add is not appropriate behaviour in a lady, for it is blindingly patent that it is I that must remind you that I did indeed aid your ambition with the loan of my black wrap, and it suited you very well. Moreover, I believe a little black dress to be the initial essential of every young lady's wardrobe and now that you have one I have started you off nicely, but you must not ever forget that less is more; ostentation is seldom anything other than unforgivably offensive, so don't get greedy!'

Willy grasped the balustrades and glared hard at Olivia.

'So, it's true; you will not help me because you do consider me a frump beyond hope and that I'll never find the right man to marry for the family!' She trembled with rage and envisaged doing harmful things to her mother. 'It was all words to trick me out of the tree! I should have known it; you have always been full of piecrust promises!'

The combination of fearing another maniacal outburst such as the one in the tree house, and the accusation of trickery, forced Olivia to realise it wise to abide by Willy's desires, though, of course, not first hand for she did not have the time.

She walked to the foot of the stairwell, looked up and peaceably said,

'My piecrust promises are concrete, darling; I am a woman of her word. It simply breaks my heart that you feel to be so lacking in allure that you require relief, however, leave it to me, darling, all will be well.'

'So you really will help?' asked a doubtful Willy.

Olivia shook her head and crocodile smiled, 'No, darling, I have some-one much better in mind.'

Valentine recklessly skipped down the dangerously steep steps to the stone floor of the cellar. It was a journey that he made at least twice a day almost every day of his life; therefore, he had no fear of misjudging and breaking bones. Yet Willy was hesitant and, from the top of the stairs, she peered into the murky abyss.

'Come on, Willy!' she heard Valentine call from out of the dark.

'I daren't!' she replied.

'Why ever not?' came the disembodied voice.

'I'm certain to fall!'

'Gosh! Don't be silly! You've been here before . . . just hold onto the rail!'

Willy grasped the rail and uneasily descended into the dim and dank depths. Before her eyes became accustomed to the lack of light, she shuddered in the damp coolness, and sniffed at the unpleasant camphor aroma in the air.

Suddenly, from around the corner, Valentine appeared carrying a candle the light of which illumined the cellar's archaic cobwebs and its dust made from decades of dead skin cells.

'Gosh, Willy! What took you so long?' he said, seeming in his element.

'I just don't like this place as much as you,' she replied, and felt her dislike was such that it warranted an affirmation; 'I don't like it.'

Valentine could not understand how anyone could fail to love the cellar. It seemed to him that he was the only one that took pleasure in it, but glad not to have to share, he did not complain.

'Can't we turn on the light?' asked Willy, reaching for the switch.

'No!' cried Valentine in horror, 'You'll ruin the ambience; it's much nicer by candlelight, besides, I've a surprise for you. Come with me.' and he disappeared around a corner.

Willy withdrew her hand from the light switch and hurried after him, rubbing her bare arms as she went, for the damp chill gave her goose pimples. In the gloom, she saw strange silhouettes of a zebra rocking horse and a vast Taj Mahal birdcage, whilst the climbing shadows of a stuffed bald eagle, a penny-farthing, and a long-limbed Jack that had jumped his box seemed to reach out as if to cause her harm.

She began to wonder whether Valentine might very much mind if she were to scurry back upstairs when he stopped and said, 'I am certain that what you shall see behind this door is bound to make you scream!' and he stationed her before it.

The door was warped, its coat of paint heavily cracked, and above it, mounted upon the wall, was a great thick branch around which was coiled a gargantuan Indian python that though long dead looked to regard her with malicious intent, daring her to cross the threshold.

Willy was worried. She considered that Valentine may be playing a sinister game and had ideas of imprisoning her with some evil form of spectre, and she watched, with terror, as he pushed open the door and its hinges creaked with an eerie sigh.

Inside the room the pungent odour of moth camphor was concentrated and horrid but beyond that, Willy saw in the light of the mass of candles that there was nothing to fear. Rather, the sight that met her eyes was nothing short of wonderful. For in the centre of a crowd of woodworm riddled Chippendale wardrobes and antiquated trunks, was a seamstress dummy wearing an exquisite tea-length gown of pure white; the pearl beading of its boned bodice travelled in twisting fronds over the taffeta skirt that a bounteous tulle petticoat caused to billow with such voluminosity that it resembled a spectacular hemisphere of sumptuous froth.

Valentine set down his candle, leapt over to the dress and ruffled its hem to demonstrate its buoyancy.

'Light as a feather!' he declared, 'It will be as if floating in a glorious cloud, don't you think?'

He regarded the garment with a holy reverence, and went on, 'I think that if I were of female persuasion I should wish to live, die and be buried in this dress and never would I feel troubled by anything!'

Willy considered the dress worthy of a bewitching fairy tale, and it stole her breath, for most certainly it would render the wearer irresistible. Unfortunately, she was not convinced that quite anybody was deserving of such delightful apparel.

She raised her hands as if in fear of the dummy, and gasped: 'But I could not ever wear it! It is too . . . *beautiful*! I would make it look awful!'

Valentine stood akimbo, and expostulated, 'Gosh! Utter rot!'

'No, Valentine, it's not rot,' Willy said, landing her large behind on a particularly large trunk, 'It is the most beautiful dress I've ever seen, but I'd look like Nellie the Elephant.'

Valentine was scandalised at Willy's meagre amount of self-esteem. Somehow, he had to inflate her ego, or at the very least grant her with the ability to appear confident, even if it transpired to necessitate the employment of a psychological shoehorn.

'I'm sorry, Willy, but I've such a strong aversion to self-pity that it borders on a serious allergy liable to bring me out in hives! So I'm likely to itch and scratch and get so very fractious that I shan't be responsible for the consequential incidents if you do not *fermé la bouche* and *écoutez-moi*!'

Valentine's French orders inspired Willy to protest but before she could she was shocked at his next command.

'Now,' said Valentine, 'Pretend I'm Cosmo.'

'Why should I want to do that?' Willy wanted to know.

'Don't be silly, Willy, we both know the reason why, though I must say I shudder at the thought and it aches to try to understand.'

Willy folded her arms and scowled at him.

Valentine was undeterred: 'All right, so now I am Cosmo. I'm a wretched and wounded boorish bore with pea-sized skull and . . . '

'You beast!' she howled.

'Gosh, sorry, just feeling my part!' he smirked, 'Anyway, I'm Cosmo, and I have you all to myself at The Marvellous Party. We are sat quite close and I've just brought you over a drink, even though mummy wouldn't like it but mummy'll never know because she's busy somewhere doing something or other. Anyway, we're sat as close as close can be, and then I lean even closer and quietly I say to you in my very deep voice . . . '

Here, Valentine rose and positioned himself adjacent to Willy upon the large trunk and bringing his mouth near to her ear, he adopted a bass style of speech: 'Why, Wilhelmina, you look to be infuriatingly ravishing tonight! I cannot begin to imagine how I have not noticed before now just how captivating you are! Have I been blind all of these years? Oh! What a bloody silly bloody sod I have been!'

Staring into space, Willy bit her bottom lip.

'At any rate, my darling,' Valentine went on, 'at last I can see you! You have given me my eyes! The only thing that could possibly make me feel to be any happier than I feel to be presently, sat with you and holding your precious hand (he took hold of Willy's hand) would be if you were to let me take you away from this mad, albeit marvellous, party and make of you my bloody wife!'

Willy triumphed in letting her imagination believe that Valentine really was Cosmo, that all he said was true and that he wanted nothing quite as much as to be her husband. She sensed every trace of sorrow evaporate and be replaced by an utter bliss that created a fizzing wave that swept her to a higher plane of existence, where she felt herself to bloom quite like an early spring flower fresh out of the thawed earth, and reaching out to the most burly bee, hungry for her honey exclusively!

'Freeze!' snapped Valentine, 'Do not bat a lid!'

Willy returned to reality but, obediently, she did not move a muscle.

'You look veritably incandescent!' Valentine exclaimed, 'Quite as if you own something wonderfully glorious that everybody wants but only you possess!

'You must remember exactly how you feel presently, physically and emotionally!' instructed Valentine, 'Be mindful of the facial muscles you are using and how it feels, and memorise that too, and practice it until it becomes a mask you are able to apply in a flash, because it really does look to be quite endearing!'

Willy unstuck her face, looked at Valentine and blushed.

'Really not?' she asked, as she hid her shyness with her hands.

'Really yes!' he replied.

'Oh, *really* not?' she said in total disbelief.

Sounding an exasperated tut, Valentine said, as he pulled away her hands, 'Gosh! Yes really! Honestly, anyone would think you had no sense of self-worth whatsoever! It is very cross making, and you must at least seem to be confident of yourself even if you are not! Can you do that?'

Willy did not think so. It sounded like a conundrum.

'I'm not sure that I can. How is that possible?' she asked.

Valentine illuminated her: 'The thing is to convince yourself of it, you must believe it and then others will too. Your new face positively melts the heart. Surely that gives you some confidence?'

'Well, yes, I think so,' she softly murmured.

'Gosh, Willy! Be certain of it. Simply say, "Yes, it does!" as if you mean it.'

She straightened her back, concentrated, and repeated with assertion, '*Yes*, it *does*!'

'Glorious! Well done, Willy!' enthused Valentine, 'Now, when I click my fingers I want you to put on that pretty face again.'

'But, Valen . . . '

Interrupting his own name, Valentine made his fingers *click*, and ordered; 'Face!'

Willy was silent and at first nothing happened.

'Oh, Willy!' moaned Valentine, 'Remember Cosmo wants you because you look to possess something glorious that everybody desires!'

With immense effort, Willy recollected how joyful the idea of Cosmo's advances had made her feel, and she mentally reiterated; '*I possess something glorious that everybody desires . . . I possess something glorious that everybody desires . . .*'

Valentine watched the transformation and considered how Willy really did look to glow from within. He believed himself to be watching a rapid reconstruction of the ugly duckling fairy tale and it filled him with satisfaction.

'Glorious!' he exclaimed, 'That wasn't so very hard now was it?'

'No, not at all,' Willy replied with inert lips.

'Gosh! You must let your face move!'

'No, not at all,' repeated Willy, this time with her lips.

'And with plenty of practice you shall soon be able to conjure it up in an instant!'

'I do hope so, Valentine.'

'Piece of cake!' cried Valentine, 'Anyway, the time has come for you to divest yourself!'

Willy was incredulous. 'You mean that I should remove my clothes?'

'Verily!' he replied, 'Not everything though, of course not *everything*; you should retain your undergarments. Then we shall try on the dress and see exactly how *un*-awful you look!'

'You bully me as if you think you might win the fight, Valentine,' she said, 'but we both know I'd beat you hands down!'

'Gosh! Don't be ridiculous! As if I would threaten you with anything physical! You are quite right that you'd win hands down if it came to fisticuffs, but my choice of weapon would be mental, and that sort of damage is harder to heal.'

'You viper!'

'Needs must when the devil drives!'

'Very well, I shall divest! I would have anyway.'

Whereupon Willy began to unbutton her cheesecloth blouse.

'I shall avert my vision!' Valentine said, turning around.

Much huffing and puffing ensued as Willy disrobed and fumbled at the hooks and eyes in the bodice of the gown, and she surmised it a trial akin to the threading of a needle whilst wearing mittens.

'Whatever is the matter?' asked Valentine facing the wall and trying to guess what she might be doing.

'I can't get the blasted thing undone!' Willy cursed.

Tutting, Valentine ignored her protests, and after some seconds of nimble fingering he had it unhooked.

'Thank you,' she said, defending her modesty with crossed arms, 'Now, turn back around.'

Granting her wish, Valentine watched Willy's struggling shadow on the wall.

'Gosh!' he said, 'You really shall look so glorious! Also, I have found satin opera gloves, with little pearls at the wrists, and a feather fascinator, all of them white! And so are the kitten heels! It is *so very* exciting!'

Barely able to contain his excitement, for he was determined to prime Willy as one might a young debutante for her coming out ball, Valentine span around and expected to find her ready, but still she was fighting her way into the bodice and so far only her arms had managed to poke through.

'Gosh!' he exclaimed, 'You look incredibly funny!' and he laughed.

Willy desisted her efforts in order to stamp her foot and cry; 'Do *not* watch! I need more time!'

'Sorry! Sorry!' said Valentine, and again faced the wall.

Willy was not quite sure she was going about the business in the right fashion. It seemed to her astonishing that something that looked such a dream was, in fact, an outright nightmare to manage.

Eventually, the dress was on her person, but with the hooks behind her, they were double the trouble to manipulate and she asked again for Valentine's assistance.

'Gosh! You look to be magical!' he exclaimed, 'Jaws will drop!' and he darted behind her to secure the hooks.

Willy girned, 'I haven't said I'll wear it to the party yet!'

Willy certainly wanted to however, for though she had not focused on her reflection, the corner of her eye had spied flashes in the mottled looking glass on the other side of the room, and they had pleased her very much.

'Do suck in, Willy!' begged Valentine, as the meeting of the hooks with their eyes seemed to be one unlikely to happen.

'I am sucking in!'

'But you can't be!' he argued.

'I am!' she insisted.

'Harder then!'

Willy tried her very best to suck as hard as she was able but to no avail, and Valentine, feeling his fingers start to strain as the exertion threatened to snap them like twigs, temporarily surrendered to the struggle and let go.

'Gosh! What a bugger!' he said with annoyance.

Willy was crestfallen. She had come to believe that no other dress would do. That Cosmo would find it impossible to resist its charms. It was to be her talisman and without it she would be hopelessly lost.

All too easily she resigned herself to the notion that wearing the dress was an impossible aspiration, and that she was destined to only ever wear clothes fit for a frump, for that was what she was, a plain and simple frump without a whisper of a chance of being anything else.

Screwing her eyes to stop them from leaking, she said, 'I knew it wouldn't fit. I knew it from the first. I'm not meant to wear it. I am just too fat.'

The words flabbergasted Valentine. He would not allow it, neither the defeat nor Willy's self-loathing.

'What on earth do you mean "too fat"? You are not too fat! The silly dress is too small!'

Willy smiled pathetically at his kindness, and replied, 'No, it's me that is too big; I need to lose some of this flesh. It is revolting.' She demonstrated with a wobble of her arms and tears started to stream.

'No, no!' Valentine insisted, and laboured another attempt at bringing together the hooks with their eyes, 'You are not too fat. You possess generous breasts, hips and thighs, and your bottom is merely ample, and correct me if I am wrong but aren't chaps supposed to think curves on a woman to be alluring? Is that not what makes a woman a woman? I mean, stick thin ladies can be sinfully chic but don't most men like to bury their face in mounds of mammary?'

He grabbed Willy's mounds of mammary from behind and squashed them in to see if that might promote the connexion but though it helped, it was still a good inch shy.

His solution was to apply extra force to his squash whilst Willy covered her face and indulged in an abundant howling of disconsolation.

Presently, they heard a *clip-clop*, and Gretchen appeared. She was wearing her clogs, and in her arms, she carried a bundle of soiled linen.

'What are you doink?' she asked with alarm.

Willy was too involved in her sobs to acknowledge her, but Valentine said, 'Ah, Gretchen! We are trying on Willy's dress for The Marvellous Party, but it is stubborn to my solitary endeavours. Perhaps if you squash I can hook?'

Except to remove Valentine's hands from Willy's breasts, Gretchen quite ignored him, put down the linen and said, 'Oh, Miss Willy! What a lovely dress you are wearink! It looks so kood on you.'

Willy's howling came to an abrupt stop. She looked at Gretchen and wondered why she was talking such rubbish.

'Are you making fun of me?' she cried, 'It does not look good on me at all!'

'Of course I am not makink fun!' stated Gretchen, 'Never am I makink fun! It does look most kood on you; you look like very fine younk lady!'

'Really not!' replied a startled Willy.

'I told you so!' said Valentine.

'You think perhaps I am lyink?' asked Gretchen, shaking her head with dismay, 'Never am I lyink!' and she appeared to be quite hurt.

'Oh no, Gretchen!' cried Willy, who would not dream of hurting Gretchen's feelings, 'I do not mean I think you are lying! I just mean that I do not think that I look a very fine lady!'

'You must not be pullink and tukkink at it, Master Valentine,' said Gretchen smacking away his hands, 'It is very delicate material and you will break it.'

She put her head on one side and looked closely at the problem. 'Is true, is not perfect, but is only needink little alterink. This Kretchen can do.'

'Truly?' asked Willy, daring to hope it so.

'Of course I can!' replied Gretchen, 'When first I come to Enkland, I work in factory and all day I am stitchink. Is not a think you forket how to do!'

'Gosh, Willy! Gretchen'll fix it! Hooray!' Valentine cried.

Willy perked up immediately and she wiped away her tears.

'Oh, Gretchen! You truly are an utter trump!'

Gretchen looked sternly at the pair, the naughty boy and sensitive girl, their faces aglow with delight. No matter how old they and their brothers might get, and whatever nuisance they were bound to be, she would always see them as children, not as her children but as children that needed her, and she would not ever fail them for she loved them all.

Presently, she folded the pair into an ungainly embrace that took them by surprise, and she exclaimed, 'Kretchen will make it fit like a klove!'

'Hooray!' cried Valentine once again and did not seem to mind very much the hausfrau tousling his hair beyond redemption, 'You shall captivate one and all, Willy!'

Willy felt full of happy anticipation, for though she dared to believe that the dress would successfully metamorphose her from a frump to a lady capable of captivating one and all, she was only interested in the one and his name was Cosmo Oxley-Stockman. Consequently, she required no amount of imagination to appear as if she possessed something glorious that everybody desires!

CHAPTER 12

The Anniversary of the Nativity
of Cornelius

The early morning sun streamed in through the window, traversed the new aeroplane patterned wallpaper, danced upon the water in Gloriana's bowl and eventually reached the sleeping boy.

The light agitated Corny's face to a pucker and he drew the blanket over his head. Then he threw it back. Suddenly, his eyes opened wide. He sat bolt upright, spread out his arms to welcome the day and laughed his mute laugh, for today was his birthday!

He jumped out of his bed and cavorted about his bedroom in much the way he imagined a Native American tribe might about their totem pole when celebrating some sort of conquest. With this in mind, he moved his chair over to the wardrobe and retrieved, from its top, his rainbow-coloured feathered headdress.

Thus crowned, he returned to the centre of his room in a single leap, and continued his cavorting until he wondered the time. He grabbed his Mickey Mouse alarm clock but the magic of Gloriana's eternal laps distracted him. He grinned hysterically at her and rapped his fingers on the glass, and then set about the serious task of trying to determine what time Mickey's dislocated arms told him, but no matter how thoroughly he furrowed his brow he could not calculate and soon gave up.

Water sloshed from the fishbowl as he gambolled down the stairwell. He dashed into the drawing room and felt troubled by its lack of people, dogs and bird. Where was everybody? Was it still too early to be awake? He decided to sit beneath the Steinway and wait for someone to arrive.

It was not now so comfortable to sit on the floor as someone had rolled up the Axminster to store in the cellar until tomorrow and the parquet had been highly polished for the party. It astonished him to see the wide expanse of space that the cut-pile rug's removal had created, and he marvelled at its sheen.

As he shifted his weight from one buttock to the other, his eyes wandered and he noticed with interest that the double doors to the dining room were shut. The ormolu clock on the mantelshelf chimed some sort of time and its occurrence instigated in him an instinct to investigate.

Drawing the bowl to his bare chest, he crept out from under the piano and straightened his war-bonnet before tiptoeing toward the closed doors where he cupped an ear to hear whether there might be someone within. He dared hardly breath for fear that it might blanket a revealing sound, and just as his lungs felt fit to burst he heard an excited whisper followed by a sharp *shush!*

Realising with delight that someone else was awake, he twisted the handle and pushed open the door to discover who it might be, whereupon he found the room to hold his entire family, Gretchen and Rupert, and, in unison, they exclaimed, 'Surprise!'

The gathering certainly did surprise Corny. He took a few steps back and his gleeful grin became almost a comic exaggeration as they sang to him, as tunefully as possible, the words to *Happy Birthday to You!* whilst the dogs and Remarkable accompanied with barks and squawks.

Upon the song's climax, Corny found himself festooned with confetti, the contents of party poppers and long curly strips of coloured paper and his excitement was such that he looked on the verge of a spasmodic seizure.

'Quickly! The bowl! Get the bowl!' ordered Olivia, seeing it start to slip.

Harry swiftly saved Gloriana and settled her on the table.

'Ha-ha, *w*ascal!' he laughed, bending down to give Corny a big birthday hug, 'You weren't expecting that, were you?'

Harry piloted him toward the chair at the centre of the great lacquered table and Corny could scarcely believe his eyes at the bounty it held. Not just the collection of brightly wrapped packages, but also the tempting array of food, most especially the leaning tower of pancakes, and he beamed at clever Gretchen who knew just what his favourite breakfast was, which she now commenced to serve.

'Thanks, G*w*etchen!' said Harry, 'I'm *w*avishing!'

Gretchen smiled at him and sagely said to them all, 'I think perhaps we all have a little to eat before openink kifts,' and no one disagreed for it all looked so delicious.

'Gosh! What a lot of presents you have, Corny!' enthused Valentine as he gratefully received, from Rupert, a top-up of breakfast tea in his good as new geisha cup, 'You are so very lucky!'

Corny, with a mouthful of pancake and chin drizzled with syrup, picked a random present and generously offered it to Valentine who laughed, 'Gosh, no! They are all for you!'

The rebuff slightly puzzled Corny but he did not let it bother him and instead considered how kind Valentine was.

'And that specific one is from me,' added Olivia, annoyed that Corny's intelligence was so lacking that he readily gave away his own birthday presents willy-nilly, 'It is particularly precious!'

Corny's interest was aroused when he learned that he was to receive something particularly precious. He was not sure that he possessed such a thing and, eager to open it, he crammed the remains of his pancake in his mouth and reached out but Gretchen pulled back his sticky hands, and told him to first finish chewing.

The sight of Corny's bulging cheeks as he hurried to complete his consumption caused the others to laugh.

'Look at the young'un go!' chuckled Gubsy.

'Careful, *wascal*, you'll do yourself a mischief!' warned Harry.

Narrowly avoiding a mischief, Corny successfully swallowed it all, and set about the ripping of wrapping.

He considered himself a most fortunate boy for his family were so very generous, and each present seemed to him so wondrous that he could not consider how anything might be better until he opened the next; a chemistry set, a spy kit and a padlocked treasure chest that bore the pirate skull and crossbones insignia.

Another present was a small human skull that though quite disturbed him at first soon pleased him when told it was not authentic and that it was to serve as furniture for Gloriana. He dropped it in her bowl and she promptly disappeared through its mouth and emerged from an eye socket. He also received, for Gloriana's bowl, a miniature replica of the remains of the *Tempio dei Dioscuri*, an assortment of small shells and a 'No Fishing!' sign.

Gloriana's unblinking countenance displayed little reaction to the additions but she did not hesitate in exploring as each new one plopped in. It seemed to Corny that her home was now a perfect kingdom and he wished that he could somehow join her.

As if having predicted the desire, Harry now gave his present. He knew that Corny could not yet tell the time, and with the idea of encouraging him to learn, had bought for him a digital watch capable of resisting water to the depths of two hundred metres. Corny insisted that he wear it immediately, and when he had fastened the strap, he thrust his hand in with Gloriana to ascertain the legitimacy of its claim. Indeed, the digits indicative of the passing seconds continued to count, and as he watched the numbers climb, he jogged with joy on the spot.

Only the present he had offered to Valentine remained; the one from his mother, and as he loosened the ribbon, Olivia said to him, 'I fear it may prove anticlimactic after so wonderful a watch, but nevertheless, it is of significant sentimental value.'

Corny tore away the paper to reveal a small leather bound box. He experienced some difficulty in releasing the catch but upon doing so he lifted the lid and found inside another, but not at all modern, wristwatch.

'It was your father's,' Olivia told him.

Peering at it, Corny sat down slowly. He felt overwhelmed for he had not ever owned anything that had belonged to his father and he was too in awe even to touch it.

Harry leant over and looked at it too. The wristwatch was smart, yet quite small; he could not imagine the strap ever having been big enough for the wrist of his bullish father.

'*Weally?*' he queried, 'Was it *weally* dad's? It doesn't look his size.'

Olivia's patience felt pushed by her eldest son's dimwittedness, and in a tired tone, she said to him, 'It is not meant for a fully grown man; it is a wristwatch for an adolescent boy.'

The explanation made sense to Harry, and Olivia continued, 'Of course, I did not ever see him wear it, but I am certain that Uncle Bartholomew remembers it.'

'Do you, Gubsy? Do you remember daddy wearing it?' Willy wanted to know.

'If it is the one I am thinking of then indeed I do,' Gubsy replied, 'May I see it?' and he received the wristwatch from Corny.

Gubsy scrutinised the pale gold face with Arabic numerals and subsidiary dials for date and seconds, and he was gratified to see that it was still a handsome piece. Of course, he remembered it; he remembered it well. He should do, as he had picked and paid for it . . .

Gubsy had felt somewhat Machiavellian in his method but after the previous year's disappointment, he did not want his nephew to suffer further dejection, and upon taking him for a birthday luncheon at the Savoy, he realised, with some sadness, that his scheme had proved sagacious.

Young ruddy-cheeked Monty was not surprised to receive no written salutation from his ever-absent parents. However, the arrival in the post of the stylish Dunhill wristwatch with the dedication; *To Montgomery on his 16th, from father and mother with affection,* induced in him such a strong sense of jubilation that the champagne that accompanied his Dover sole luncheon was close to redundant.

Jeremiah never did know of the deed though he came close to it; Montgomery had made up his mind to telephone his parents to thank them for the gift, but though it frustrated him not ever being able to reach them it filled his Uncle Bartholomew with relief.

Gubsy did not feel he had done wrong by his brother, in fact the watch was as much for his sake as it was Montgomery's, for he liked to justify Jeremiah's disregard of familial duty on his inability to cope with the war and its consequence of having to sell Ballestas.

Seeing Gubsy inspecting the back of the wristwatch, Valentine excitedly piped up, 'Is there an inscription?'

Gubsy did not react, he was too lost in emotion but Olivia said, 'Yes, there is.' and she whipped the wristwatch from the old man's liver spotted hands and passed it to Valentine. Willy and Rupert flanked him and peered over his shoulders as he read in his head.

'Gosh! What a glorious present!' he exclaimed, now dangling the wristwatch in front of his face, 'But to think daddy was ever so small!' and he wondered if it sat well with him to acknowledge the obvious reality that his father had not always been a big golden bear of a man. With that thought, he handed it to Harry.

It was curiosity and good manners that drove Harry to read the inscription as he realised he was doubtful to like it, and sure enough, he was right. Of course, when he had turned sixteen his father was no longer about, and that had rather suited him, but this evidence that his father's own father had been one so generous and full of kind thought, made in his mouth a bitter taste. '*With affection*' it said: when had his father ever shown him any sign of affection? The closest instance had been with the back of his hand. Not wanting to hold the wristwatch a moment more, he returned it to the new owner, and said, with a smile, 'You're a ve*w*y lucky boy, *w*ascal; a p*w*oper g*w*own-up watch!'

Corny screwed his eyes in an effort to decipher the curlicued italics of the inscription but soon surrendered and turned the wristwatch over in his palm. He considered it a very good present, one he was proud to possess. He thought the description of it being 'particularly precious' accurate, and he grinned at it.

Casting her mother a quizzical glance, Willy wondered why they had not known of the wristwatch before, and asked why she had not given it to Harry or Valentine on their sixteenth birthdays.

The question nettled Olivia, and she enlightened everyone to her solicitousness.

'Naturally, I might easily have presented it to either. But after careful consideration I came to the conclusion that as both boys were fortunate enough to have benefited from an actual acquaintance with their father I held it in safekeeping until the time came for it to be bestowed upon his posthumous child.'

'I'd have bwoken it anyway,' said Harry, who would not ever have worn it.

'And I do not like the bondage of time strapped to my wrist!' declared Valentine.

Olivia was pleased that her boys had backed her up, and she asked Willy, 'And do you suppose a young man's wristwatch appropriate attire for a young lady such as yourself?'

'Obviously not,' murmured Willy, somewhat humbled.

'In that case, I am certain you shall allow me the luxury to believe that my reasoning was right!' said Olivia in her tersest tone as her forbearance was close to cracking.

Olivia's justification for waiting until Corny's sixteenth to unveil the watch was, in fact, fictitious. In truth, she had forgotten entirely its existence and had found it at the back of a drawer whilst frantically hunting her bedroom for the Starfish for the umpteenth time.

The search had driven her to such desperation that she had resorted to opening old jewellery boxes she had long disregarded and upon discovering the vintage wristwatch, she considered it provident for she could not afford the time or money to find something else for Corny.

That the ring still eluded her caused her a great maelstrom of ire. On numerous occasions, the thought of taking a crowbar to every floorboard in Chinchero had flashed through her mind, and there was not a person in the house whom she had not at some point suspected of theft. Any of them might easily have probed her Birkin without her knowledge! However, applying rationality to the possibilities forced her to deduce that each was without foundation; Uncle Bartholomew was too slow. Gretchen valued her job. To suspect Harry would be akin to suspecting one of the dogs. Valentine would have made no secret of the acquisition. Willy would not dare. Corny would not care for it and Rupert was too rich to have to steal. Therefore, her commonsense told her, 'No; none of them would have taken it,' and although her irrationality begged of her to interrogate, she would not dream of it, for that might easily toss her from the frying pan into the fire of humiliating explanations.

Her mind returned to the day after she had come back from Paris – she had not left the house other than to attend the summer fête. Thus, under the pretence of a strange desire to walk the dogs, she embarked upon an exploration. She retraced her exact route, letting her eyes travel each paving stone, every tree root and along the gutters, until she arrived at the Green where she realised her search futile as any litter-picker would have inevitably pocketed such a valuable find.

With that in mind, and after some deliberation, she visited the police station. Maybe some improbably virtuous type had handed it in and it was simply waiting for collection. It was too much to hope; the sergeant had not even heard the likes of quite a ring. Therefore, she filled in a form that asked, what she believed to be, many idiotic questions, and then she sketched a competent illustration to compliment her literature.

Departing the station she came to consider that for the time being there was little else she could do and it filled her with annoyance. Her annoyance heightened when it came to her attention that she now had to walk all the long way home; for she would not deign to set foot upon a dingy double-decker and sit with the proletarians.

Continuing her journey along the Terrace, she encountered a jewellers and it set in motion her psychological cogs and wheels.

She had not eradicated the possibility of the ring's disappearance being the fault of Cosmo. In fact, the more consideration she applied to its likelihood the stronger the probability came to be, but with the option of a direct accusation being one she refused to use she realised it better to coax from Cosmo a confession.

The bell that sounded a twee *ting-a-ling* as she entered the jewellers jarred her, as did the unnecessarily seedy appearance of the man stood behind the counter. Yet mindful of her scant means she overlooked his outer shell and employed every charming ploy she had at her disposal to extract from him what she desired at the most minimal expense.

Not more than thirty minutes later, Olivia caused the bell to grate her nerves a second time, and once more in the fresh air she expanded her lungs, for the shop had been nasally offensive, but she was proud of her achievement. Seedy Mr Creswell, though she had been encouraged to call him Colin, had reassured her that a duplicate Starfish would be ready in time for her ailing aunt's birthday.

Olivia had gushed with gratitude and told him how very happy the old woman will be to see again the ring that her fresh-faced husband had given her just a week before losing his life in battle so very many years ago. She told him that it did not matter that the stones were not real as it was the sentiment that counted.

Colin guaranteed they would be so convincing that only an expert might tell, and of course, she should think of it as a favour although a dinner date would be most charming.

Such flattery had caused the retiring Olivia to blush, and she promised that as soon as she returned from visiting her aunt in Washington, D.C. and quite a few other relations in many other States too, that they might perhaps go for a bite.

Corny was now eager to wear his father's old wristwatch, and removing his hand from Gloriana's bowl he proffered both the watch and his dripping wrist to Harry.

'You want to wear dad's watch instead of the new one?' Harry asked, disappointedly.

Shaking his head, Corny clasped his hand over the diver's watch. He did not want to swap it for his father's; he wanted to wear both.

'I think he wants to wear both,' suggested Willy.

Corny confirmed with a spirited nod.

'Ha-ha! All *wight*, give me your *wist*.'

'Gosh! Don't put them on the same one, Harry!' cried Valentine.

Harry stopped what he was doing, appeared nonplussed, and asked, '*Weally*? Why not?'

'Because,' said Olivia quite amazed at having to explain, 'now that Corny is wearing the waterproof watch, he is liable to plunge his arm in water every time that he sees it and daddy's watch is valuable and therefore not fit for such submerging,' and she wondered why she ever thought it wise to give it to Corny. That said, she could not foresee herself ever again attending an Avery-Stripe sixteenth.

Presently, Harry saw the obvious sense in a watch on either wrist, and adorned Corny accordingly.

'Now that you have a digital and an analogue you shall soon be able to tell the time!' exclaimed Valentine before adding, 'If you feel so inclined.'

Not many people would believe themselves presentable in a costume consisting only of a Native American war bonnet, underpants and two watches, but Corny did not care, indeed, all he cared for at that moment was to obtain a speedy ability to tell the time. His head pivoted from one watch to the other, then back again and then back, over and over, faster and even faster, until dizziness influenced him to slow down.

'Mind yourself now, young'un, or you'll bring up breakfast,' chuckled Gubsy.

Olivia narrowed her eyes and wondered what, in fact, was the time. She glanced at her Tiffany and gasped. 'The people for the garden will arrive at any moment, and I've to be at the salon in an hour!'

'Oh yes! And me!' Willy exclaimed.

'Yes, darling, and you,' said Olivia, and remembered, with some irritation, that it was to be a mother and daughter outing as the new young lady required touching up.

Olivia rose and wrapped her kimono tight.

'Happy birthday, darling,' she said, kissing Corny's cheek. 'So much to be done, and already it is eleven o'clock!'

With wide eyes, Corny watched Olivia leave the room and he wondered why she had ruined it for him when he had almost worked it out.

CHAPTER 13

Preliminaries

Not so very long ago Valentine would have watched the attractive men who had come to work in the garden, but now that he had Rupert they were lucky to have entered his consciousness at all. Still, the absence of his attention did not compromise the quality of their labour, and though they had been late in arrival their departure was sooner than had been anticipated.

The external dance floor the labourers created by slotting together many dark wooden panels looked good and worked the space well. At each of its corners was a wrought iron pole, and they were linked at their tops by strings of red and orange Chinese lanterns.

'Gosh, Corny! How clever!' exclaimed Valentine, stepping out from the conservatory and prancing onto the floor, 'It is like a giant wooden jigsaw – though only of square pieces – and really big, I mean, I did not imagine it to be quite so large!' and, in yellow pyjamas, he started to spin.

Corny spun too, and then accepted Valentine's invitation to dance. They waltzed, after a fashion, across the dance floor from the corner by the cottage arch to its diagonal neighbour by the gazebo, and then to the corner by the tree house and over to the last. Quite soon, they felt sick of dancing, for they had both eaten a great number of pancakes, and when their exertion came to an end, they received a round of applause from Harry and Rupert.

'Isn't it glorious?' gasped Valentine, quite out of breath, 'And so very big!'

The two older boys joined the brothers on the floor, though not to dance, purely to inspect.

'Yes, it is big,' agreed Harry, 'but it should be, so people have *w*oom enough to dance. Ha, *w*ascal, you're *w*eally sweaty!' and he wiped the sweat from his little brother's brow.

Valentine turned to Rupert, 'Shall we dance tonight?'

'I'm not sure,' Rupert teased, 'I'm not an amazing dancer.'

'Gosh!' said Valentine, with some distress that he soon overcame with a solution; 'Don't worry, I'll lead; you'll be fine!'

'Maybe,' said Rupert with a grin.

'I don't think I'll be dancing at all,' said Harry, 'I'm te*ww*ible at it; I've got two left feet.' He looked down at them with dismay and wished that one of them was right.

Neither Valentine nor Corny could quite believe the lack of enthusiasm, and Valentine said, 'Gosh! What a pair of party-poopers you are! You don't have to be expert ballroom dancers!' and taking their hands, he drew them together, 'If you take turns being the man, you'll soon get the hang of it.'

Harry and Rupert looked awkwardly at each other, and then looked to Valentine.

'*Weally?*' asked a dubious Harry.

'If you are both so lacking in confidence it will be good to get to grips with it together!' Valentine declared, and keen that Rupert should fast learn how to lead, he proceeded to position him appropriately, 'Harry, you shall be the lady and . . . '

'But there's no music!' Harry interrupted because although he liked Rupert and thought him a very decent chap, he did not like him so much that he wanted to dance with him.

'Harry's right,' added Rupert, 'we can't really dance without music,' for though he would certainly dance with Valentine at the party, he did not feel right doing it with Harry.

Just as Valentine was about to advise them to use their imaginations, Gretchen, who had been observing from the conservatory, saved the uncomfortable dance partners from further embarrassment by calling out, 'I am needink everybody to help! There is no time for dancink, this you can do later!'

Harry and Rupert filled with relief, but Corny had been looking forward to seeing the big boys dance together – even if it might look a little queer – and Valentine sounded an irritated tut.

'And no time for naughty bullyink, Master Valentine!' Gretchen informed him as she wagged a finger.

Valentine sounded a second and louder tut.

'Now, everybody ket inside!' said Gretchen, hurrying back to her kitchen, 'So much to be doink! So much to be doink! *Dancink!*'

'Come on, *wascal*,' said Harry, 'best go see what needs to be done,' and they jumped off the floor to jog after her.

Valentine was inclined to sound a third tut, and he said to Rupert, 'Gosh, well, I suppose I shall have to dance alone, even if Gubsy says only villains and drunks do that; perhaps I'll make the most of it and be both!'

Rupert grinned. He took hold of Valentine's hand, raised it up high and persuaded him into a flourishing twirl before bending him backward in an elegant curve.

The unexpected activity sent Valentine's world into a dizzy whirl of garden, and before he knew quite what was happening, the gazebo was topsy-turvy with its apex pointed down toward the cloudless sky. He would have happily remained in the position but wishing to see Rupert's beautiful face, he reached for his neck.

Giddily, Valentine gazed up at Rupert; his gilded hair, forget-me-not eyes and gleaming teeth, all of which seemed more dazzling than the sun in the surrounding sky, and he said, 'Gosh! So you will dance with me?'

Exhibiting his ability to retain his wide smile whilst speaking, Rupert replied, 'Crikey, I was only teasing, Valentine! Course I'll dance with you!'

'Jackanapes!' exclaimed Valentine, with an excited gasp.

Rupert added, 'Anyway, that wasn't really dancing.'

'Gosh! I'm not certain what else you might call it, but whatever it was, I loved it! Will you do it again tonight?'

Presently, a look of the utmost earnest claimed Rupert's face. He said, 'I've told you so many times, Valentine, I'll do *anything* you want!'

Valentine smiled and said nothing. He let his hands explore the strength in Rupert's arms, and he was thrilled that despite the prolonged pose they displayed no sign of tiring, and though he knew very well Rupert's Heracelean stamina, he coyly asked, 'Am I not getting heavy?'

'No,' stated Rupert.

Whereupon, he brought his face closer to Valentine's, their breath became one as less than an inch separated their lips, and then came the interjection of Gretchen: 'Time for hanky-panky is not now! I am needink you inside!'

Rupert was steadfast and had seen to every one of Olivia's gripes about Chinchero, and more besides, in time for The Marvellous Party. The entire family felt much better not to have a gash in the drawing room ceiling, and when it rained, they found to their amusement that they would instinctively circumnavigate a phantom champagne bucket in the conservatory. Rupert went on to re-grout the bathrooms, fix the temperamental flushers and install a new bidet. After that, he measured Willy's windows for new glass and oiled nearly a hundred hinges. Gubsy's knob would never again come off in his hand and the tiles in the entrance hall had been perfectly re-laid.

Then, after a thorough wash, he painted the exterior of the house; first, he primed it, and then applied two further coats as Gubsy watched on grinning, intermittently banging his cocobolo cane, and booming, 'Jolly good!'

Whilst waiting for each coat to dry Rupert painted the drawing room, and within four days all paintwork was complete.

One morning he took Corny to choose new wallpaper for his bedroom (peculiarly, Olivia said she did not want hers re-papered after all, as it was in an embarrassing state as it was) and the following night Corny spent a good hour shining his battery-torch on his four walls emblazoned with aeroplanes both archaic and newfangled.

Rupert then threw Gretchen's kitchen into temporary disarray when he emptied all of the well-stocked cupboards in order to re-secure them. When he had finished, the newly aligned units were so stable that neither nook nor cranny had a ghost of a chance of ever again appearing.

'They're strong enough to swing on,' he said to Gretchen who was so pleased with the facelift she replied that she might have 'a little swink later on maybe, perhaps.'

When the glass for Willy's windows arrived, he removed the old ones and the gunky putty with a knife. Then, with Harry's nervous but necessary help, he installed each gleaming new pane with brand-spanking new putty. The new installation had Willy feel her bedroom was now virtually palatial and she would stare at the glass that she polished daily and would dream of being Cosmo's wife in a house full of such sparkling windows.

Rupert fixed Harry's light switch hitch in a flash; two naughty wires were naked and pushed up against screws causing shocks with each flick. This was remedied by turning off the mains supply for five minutes, cutting the wires down to size and strapping them with tape.

'Cwumbs!' said Harry, 'Thanks! I was getting pwetty sick of being electwified evwy night!'

Rupert then looked at Valentine's third step. Carefully he pulled up the carpet and discovered the tread demolished.

'Gosh! I've no inkling!' said Valentine, when asked how it had happened, 'It's been that way forever! But I think daddy used to court and woo up here, and he was a big bear of a man . . . maybe he got cross and stamped his foot because of some awful girl?'

'Crikey! Never mind; it's easily fixed.'

'Gosh, glorious! But can you make it creak rather loud? That way I'll hear the approach of impinging snoops!'

So it was that Valentine's third step went from one to avoid to one that simply creaked. Rupert successfully achieved this by laying a new tread that was tread-able but used some nails not exactly suitable, therefore creating a creak quite audible. Valentine was overjoyed.

Next, Rupert climbed a stepladder, pushed open the hatch up into the main roof and pulled himself inside, flashing his corrugated caramel stomach on the way.

The sight caused Valentine to swoon, and he said to Willy, 'Cosmo has a bit of a beer gut doesn't he?'

'I hadn't even noticed!' Willy fibbed. She thought Cosmo's little belly 'sweet'.

'Ha-ha!' Valentine said, then called up to Rupert, 'What's up there?'

Rupert's face appeared, and in a matter-of-fact tone, he said, 'Squirrels.'

Brother and sister gasped at the horror of it.

'Really not?' said Willy, 'Are they up there now?'

'No, they must be out foraging, but it's definitely a squirrel's nest.'

'Greys, I'll bet!' said Valentine, 'Horrid American ones that are chasing away all our dear little English reds! Trap them and we'll eat them!'

Rupert looked with intrigue at Valentine – the genteel boy who displayed, on occasion, a voracity for gore.

'You savage!' Willy wailed at Valentine.

'Gosh! Not I! They're the terrorists! We'll eat them! Sautéed squirrel!'

'Valentine,' said Rupert, 'I don't think we should eat them.'

'I'd like to know why not?' asked Valentine, thinking that they ought to taste quite like lovely rabbit.

'Well, they're vermin and probably rabid and I don't think you should eat anything that's not clean,' Rupert said as he lowered himself down.

'But I'll trap them for you,' he reassured Valentine, whose head filled with pictures of heroic huntsmen even if they were sadly not to consume the kill.

Much to Valentine's displeasure, not only would the vermin be spared the chance to grace his supper plate, they were also spared their lives, for though Harry knew them to be foreign he insisted on treating them to a jolly motor jaunt to the countryside.

'We might at least have charged them the price of their tails for the use of our loft!' Valentine exclaimed, and with chagrin, he felt his tummy suffer the denial of squirrel.

The family assumed that having completed his odyssey of rectifications

Rupert would help with the rest of The Marvellous Party's preliminaries. Fortunately, he was of an ilk so easygoing that he did not view the attitude to be one of liberty; in fact, he did not view it at all except with an eagerness to make someone happy.

This is not to say that the genuine Avery-Stripes remained inert, far from it. Indeed, all but one of them (Olivia) contributed to the effort. Gretchen could not call to mind there ever before being a time when each of her wards provided a hand in some shape or form. From top to bottom, every surface, both vertical and horizontal, came under scrutiny and not an inch went untouched by an implement designed to dust, buff or suck.

They polished all the windows, and every looking-glass to within a hair's breadth of their lives, and inflicted the very same treatment to the entirety of herringbone parquet that floored every ground level room, except the tiled entrance hall and Gretchen's flagstone kitchen, and those they duly scrubbed.

All the hard labour was well worth it; for the day before that of Corny's birthday – luckily the longest day in the year – they had between them successfully transformed Chinchero, that had not so very long ago been considered ramshackle, into a place in which they might easily entertain people possessed of blue blood.

The brief idea to employ a catering company to supply the party's cuisine mortified Gretchen, and she quashed it with the assertion that she was more than capable of furnishing the shindig with plenteous fare. The abashed family bolstered further her determination by explaining they had only thought it a fearsome feat for one person to feed over one hundred and did not want to put her to unnecessary strain. Gretchen had shaken her head slowly and snorted at each of them with the confidence that she would surpass expectation. She did not care for the notion of her family eating anything prepared by strangers.

Gubsy had ordered a great quantity of good quality dead animal from Harrods, as well as other necessary sundries including stacks of sturgeon roe and crate upon crate of his favourite champagne, and Gretchen spent almost the entire night before the party working away in her kitchen constructing vast armies of blinis and the garnishes for canapés of many varieties. She eventually retired at four in the morning only to surface at seven in order to continue and to be ready with pancakes for the birthday breakfast. This celebratory meal provided her with a welcome respite and after that, there were the final adjustments to Willy's dress, and then the resumption of preparing things for consumption, including, of course, Corny's cake.

Shortly after the departure of garden labourers, and mindful that Mrs and Miss Avery-Stripe were suffering at the salon, Gretchen called upon the boys to manage the final tweaks instead of gallivanting in the garden.

Here, Valentine came into his own, sat upon the chesterfield to second-polish the giant silver punch bowls, and delighted in delegation whilst Gubsy snoozed beneath *The Times*.

Much relegation of superfluities to the confines of the cellar Valentine deemed mandatory, and he had the boys place a plethora of inessentials, such as the bellows, coalscuttle, hearth-brush and poker, ornamental photograph frames, a fair amount of ethnic ashtrays, exotic baubles, foreign souvenirs, in cardboard boxes in the cellar.

He ordained the removal of defunct stiffies from the mantelshelf and had the ugly ormolu clock and rhinoceros horns brought to a lustrous shine. These, however, remained in place as they formed a smart foreground to the (delicately and reverently dusted) portrait of Excelsior.

Also to be temporarily stored in the cellar were the chickens and Farinelli in the vast Taj Mahal birdcage; for they would only get in the way of the party, and were unlikely to much enjoy the fireworks.

Fortunately, all the space needed for the new additions below stairs became available by the extraction of forty red velvet cushioned gold chairs, positioned in pleasing places about the garden in groups of four and five. Each set of chairs shared between them a collapsible table of teak covered with a cloth of snowy-white damask that Valentine beautified further with elaborate centrepieces of grapes, foliage and bloom.

Draped from the flat roof of the tree house and reaching down to touch the very tips of the grass below (and conveniently concealing from view the evacuated coup) was one half of a pair of extraordinarily large flags. The flags were identical and had graced a great number of festivities held by the family in their heyday. They were of good quality crimson silk, and on them was woven in large black gothic script 'AVERY-STRIPE' above their crest of a Peruvian Booby stood upon a chevron, and below that, again in gothic script' '*Nil Desperandum*'.

More outside decoration came in the form of miles of wide silk ribbon in every colour available, hung in garlands from tree house to cottage arch to conservatory to topiary to gazebo to pergola and back to tree house. Following the silk route was sturdy twine on which hung scores of Chinese lanterns to compliment the ones around the dance floor.

Gubsy was adamant that he would not permit modern music in Chinchero and its grounds, and as he very much liked and insisted upon Elgar and Strauss, had hired a musical octet whose repertoire included compositions by said composers. These instrumentalists were to play in and around the gazebo, and hopefully, their music would meet with a satisfaction that provoked the guests to dance. Failing that, there was always the Steinway or the newly unearthed gramophone and vintage vinyl that still sounded remarkably well.

At seven post meridian, Willy stood before the full-length three-panel looking glass in the main bathroom. In there, she could view, from many perspectives, the reflection of herself looking like an immense dollop of whipped cream in the expertly modified gown of white.

Her accessories of feathered fascinator, opera length gloves and kitten heels, added what she believed to be extra sophistication, and having had her hair smartly bobbed at the salon, she felt herself superior to a mere lady and rather fancied, that despite her podge, her appearance was that of a perfect princess.

Bringing her face close to the glass, she removed the lid from the lipstick Olivia deigned to spare, twisted the base and applied to her mouth a crude shade of red. She stepped back to indulge a minute more the admiration of her new urbane façade and considered how captivated by it Cosmo was bound to be, before she hastened to Valentine's turret with the idea that she lacked a pearl necklace.

Valentine could not call to mind a boy to look as unbearably beautiful as did Rupert in his hired white tie and tails. Up until then he had seen him wear nothing more than t-shirts, vests and shorts, and though these articles possessed the advantageous attribute of revealing much of Rupert's flesh, none exhibited his virile figure quite as magnificently as did the evening attire.

The vision caused Valentine to gaze at Rupert in rapt adoration and mentally debate whether or no he might look more glorious dressed just so than he did without a single stitch.

'Gosh, Rupert,' he gasped, 'you really are impossibly beautiful!'

Rupert reddened, 'Crikey! Thanks, but I don't look as suave as you do. I'm too big to be suave.'

Thrilled at having received confirmation of his suavity in Great Uncle Millie's tails, Valentine wiped excess violet pomade from his hands with a linen cloth, appreciated his reflection in the ferro for a flash, and considered how very slick he did indeed appear.

He lit a cigarette, and argued, 'But you're not too big at all. You're the perfect size, and look to be a movie star!'

'You're the movie star!' insisted Rupert, as he sat next to him on the bed, took his hand, and grinned.

'Rudolph, perhaps,' Valentine replied, and popped a violet cream in his mouth, and another in Rupert's – who patently thought he meant the reindeer and not Valentino.

The look of confusion was endearing to Valentine, he ran his fingers through Rupert's golden hair, twisted a forelock, and swallowing his cream, he said, 'Gosh!' and was on the precipice of telling Rupert, yet again, how beautiful he presently looked to be when the loud creak of the third step signalled the approach of an impinging snoop.

Valentine sounded an annoyed tut, and called out, 'Who is it?' a split second before the snoop knocked.

'Oh!' said Willy, 'It's me!'

'Gosh, Willy! What is it?'

'I want to show you how I look!'

'I'm still getting dressed! I'll be down soon!'

'But I need to ask you something, *please*?'

Unable to ignore Willy's pleading tone, Valentine turned his key and opened the door to regard Willy looking quite wonderful.

'Gosh! Glorious!' he said.

'Truly?' Willy asked with a blush, as she gathered the bountiful skirt and performed a shy revolution.

'Truly!' Valentine confirmed, 'Doesn't she?' he asked Rupert, who beamed accordingly, and enthused, 'Crikey, yes!'

'And I must say I do like your little bob!' said Valentine, 'But anyway, I'll be down soon,' and he started to close his door.

'Wait!' Willy cried, and planted her kitten-heeled foot firmly in the doorframe.

'Gosh, what?' Valentine cried, looking with agitation at her foot and he stamped one of his own, 'I'm busy getting ready!'

'I need jewels don't I?' she explained, 'You said all the ladies ought to be wearing them to the party and the pearls on my dress don't count! Have you got any?'

Now exasperated beyond imagination, Valentine told her to wait, and he grabbed his Schiaparelli hatbox of bibelots and pushed it in her arms.

'Look in there, there's bound to be something, but do not wear anything obvious or it'll ruin the look and I'll take it away, and remember there's still the nosegay and the corsage; I'll help you with those when I'm down-stairs, all right?'

'Oh yes! Quite all right!' Willy exclaimed.

She was amazed at her luck for an entire hatbox of the kind of trinkets Valentine was inclined to magpie would surely hold something at least as splendid as a string of pearls. She hugged it, gushed with gratitude and gambolled down the stairwell, to explore the treasure in her bedroom.

Locking his door, Valentine turned to Rupert, looking beautiful as he ever did, and said to him, 'Gosh! Now, wherever were we?'

At five minutes before the honourable hour of eight of the clock, the Avery-Stripes plus their honoraries, gathered before Chinchero. Each of the boys looked smart in white tie and tails, with buttonholes of gardenia. Corny wore the extra adorns of his two wristwatches and war bonnet that he refused to divest, and he clutched Gloriana to his chest. The three ladies of the house were splendid in each their own way; Olivia's outfit of red heightened her regality; Gretchen was grand in a royal blue bolero over a no-nonsense gown of the same colour, and Willy wore her white ensemble with the added accoutrements of a gardenia nosegay and corsage.

The front garden had been decorated also, but not to the same degree as the one at the back. They had neatly raked the gravel, from the trees hung further Chinese lanterns, and a length of red plush carpet was unfurled to bridge the journey from front gate to porch. Draped over the façade of Chinchero was the second half of the pair of immense family flags so that none of the invitees might mistake which house held the soon to be Marvellous Party.

A mahogany occasional table was set before a red rosebush, and on this occasion, it held the gramophone. Rupert turned its handle, and after some crackling, Rossini's *La Gazza Ladra* burst forth from the horn that resembled a giant flower of burnished brass. The music filled the summer air and climbed up high. The family agreed that it did add a touch of nobility.

CHAPTER 14

The Marvellous Party

They posed as if for a family portrait, and Valentine exclaimed, 'Now, everybody smile! Remember we are Avery-Stripes!' and, like savages, they each exposed their teeth toward the garden gate, ready to welcome their imminent and in a few cases, some thought, unwelcome, Marvellous Party guests.

Olivia's smile was one of satisfaction, for seedy Colin Creswell had created a replica Starfish so identical she was quite convinced that if she still possessed the original she would unlikely be able to distinguish one from the other.

Certainly, she had played a key part in the achievement, for without her detailed description success would never have been possible. Nevertheless, she had bestowed upon Colin her undying gratitude and filled him with an unerring certitude that on her return from the United States they would absolutely dine.

'Ropey wretch!' she thought of the generous jeweller. She shuddered to think of having ever again to suffer his presence, though naturally, that would not ever happen, and now she smiled to consider what Monty might have done to the man if he were about. Why, he would have pummelled him to a paltry pulp for his assumptions!

For the hundredth time that day – which was her average amount for that time of day – Olivia wished that Monty were still about. Then she could show to him how very well the Starfish suited her, even if it was a fake.

She reassured herself that she was soon to possess the genuine when Cosmo revealed his wrongdoing. Her idea was to exhibit discreetly to him, in the close vicinity of his parents, the fake on her finger to provoke a reaction. The plan was foolproof because knowing that he had stolen the genuine he would either boast of his felony, or, and rather more likely, he would simply sneer at her inanity. Either way, with her suspicion confirmed she was confident of retrieval because once a cat was caught she had a wide variety of ways of skilfully skinning it.

She would not wear the Starfish for the entire duration of the party because someone else would be sure to recognise it and ask questions.

No, the ring was for Cosmo's eyes only. She had cast it a final glance in her bedroom before removing it from her finger and paid extreme attention to exactly where she placed it in her Givenchy clutch, for she would loathe losing the replica also.

Valentine poked Willy, and whispered, 'Face!' whereupon she endeavoured in its application. The impending arrival of Cosmo and family was a thing that caused a feeling of great nervousness in Willy, and it seemed to her that the butterflies in her belly were having a riot. She did feel captivating in her enchanting gown but her confidence was not such that it averted sweating shakes.

'*I possess something glorious that everybody desires . . .* ' she told herself as she regarded the gate with trepidation.

Unbeknownst to Willy, she did indeed possess a glorious thing of which at least two were extremely desirous, and had she possessed any notion of the peril in which the possession placed her then she would have great reason to worry.

For earlier, filled with elation over Valentine's unexpected generosity of allowing her not only to explore the array of goodies in his hatbox but also to borrow, within sensible reason, a bauble, she had emptied the hoard in a heap on her bed.

The vast collection of valuables dazzled and shone as if piles of piratical plunder. She pushed her fingers through the gamut and gloried in the feel of it. Certainly, there was a string of pearls, and upon picking it, she discovered that it was a great long one and that there were two. The second was shorter, and just the right length, and she fastened it around her neck. She contemplated her reflection and was pleased with the effect the pearls provided, but still she needed a proper jewel.

There were cameos and lockets, earrings, brooches and bracelets, all of which sparkled with stones. A pair of emerald teardrops she considered delightful but then there was the problem that she had unpierced ears. She recognised, from his portrait, Excelsior's ruby-headed gold pin and thought it a shame that she could not wear that. The bracelets were nice but as she was to wear a corsage, she did not think them right. A cameo brooch depicting Leda and the Swan appealed to her but she was uncertain as to where exactly one would pin it. There were many splendid rings with stones of different shapes and sizes, however all were too small for any of her opera-gloved digits except for one of tiny sapphires that she managed to squeeze onto her right pinky.

This ring of blue stones was charming, and though Willy would have wished for something less modest, she was mindful that both her mother and brother had warned her against ostentation, therefore she deemed her selection of the pearl string and sapphire ring sufficient.

It was then, as she gathered the bounty of spoils to return to the hatbox, that she saw a little black velvet drawstring bag. She had not noticed it before as it had hidden in the glimmer. She wondered what it might hold and instantly satisfied her curiosity and loosened the string.

What she extracted from the bag provoked from her a gasp of outright astonishment because never before had she beheld such a heavily encrusted ring. A glittering white diamond sat in the centre of five more shimmering stones; each was a different colour; there was red, next to green, then purple, and then orange before blue and little diamonds that sparkled like tiny stars surrounded these five.

Willy did not know it to be Olympia's Starfish, and in her naivety, she whispered in awe, 'Like a magical flower!' and wished that she might wear it. Investigating it for size on her wedding finger, she was amazed that the silver band seemed as if made for it because the fit was perfection.

Beholding her bejewelled hand in the sunlight that shone through her gleaming windows, she marvelled at the stones' sparkle and promptly fell in love with each of them. As she gazed, a slight recognition of the ring danced through her mind, but she was too enthralled to speculate where she might have seen it before. She did stop to wonder why Valentine did not bestow the object with the exaltation he lavished on far simpler things for, of course, she did not know that with his head jammed with the joys of Rupert he had neglected to even penetrate the pouch. She was thankful that he did not seem to care for it, and she supposed that it might perhaps be nothing more than costume jewellery. Yet this little mattered to her, because real or no, she doubted anybody else at the party could rival such rocks.

Nothing would dissuade her, she had made up her mind; she would wear the ring to the party. Her mother and brother would unlikely consent, but she would not tell them. She would lead them to believe her additional ornamentation was nothing more than the simple string of pearls and the humble cluster of sapphires. Only she would know of the ostentatious ring she would hide beneath her beribboned nosegay of gardenias.

The glamorous group grinned at the garden gate for the entirety of *La Gazza Ladra,* and when the needle finished its journey along the spiralling groove, sounding nothing but crackles, they all let their aching faces relax and wondered why no one had yet arrived.

A sudden crash came from the kitchen and Gretchen hastened to see what had happened, and knew that she had been wrong to leave the hired waiters without her supervision.

'Crank the wheel and play it again, Rupert,' said Valentine, 'There's something about its tune that appeals!'

Rupert was compliant, and once more Rossini influenced the air as the family resumed their respective poses.

'I wonder who might come first,' said Willy, through her smile.

Valentine, through his, replied, 'I don't much care whom. I'm only really interested in three of them; Izzy, Flick, and Brian, the others are superfluous.'

Corny looked up at him and his eyes conveyed his feeling of shocked dismay upon learning that Valentine was not excited to be meeting his friends as well.

'Sorry, Corny, your people too, of course,' amended Valentine.

'If any of them are superfluous,' spoke Olivia through her strained smile, 'It is the Oxley-Stockmans! I cannot calculate your reasoning for requesting their presence!'

'Gosh, mummy! I had to! Verily, they are undesirable but we really ought to show them how the Avery-Stripes still reign supreme, besides which "kin is kin"!'

Valentine's reasoning produced a concurring guttural rumble from Gubsy followed by a gnashing of false teeth, and then he went inside for he no longer wished to wait on late arrivals as if he were nothing but a butler.

Olivia was not convinced of Valentine's logic, and she wished that the Oxley-Stockmans were not coming. She could not surmise why they had accepted, unless to parade their imagined superiority, which she supposed to be the most probable explanation. She hoped that they would not arrive before many others so she might quite easily avoid too much of their presence. But then, whose presence was she to find pleasing?

A moment later, the first recipients of their hospitality appeared, and though neither Nina and Sophie nor their grim spawn filled Olivia with pleasure, she considered that it could have been worse.

'Welcome, darlings!' she exclaimed as she air kissed her two dearest friends and forced a smile at their children, 'How very well you all look!'

Valentine contemplated his mother's outrageous lie. To his discriminating eye, her people looked nothing of the sort. In fact, each of them pushed the boundaries of acceptable exteriors much too far for his liking, and he felt fairly astounded by their nerve.

He was convinced that Nina, who had somehow reached the conclusion that a dress of distressed denim was fitting for the occasion, had worn her eye-patch over her left at the fête, and now it concealed her right. He wondered what had persuaded her to think its embroidered eyeball becoming. Moreover, he deliberated as to why she reputedly had feelings beyond the appropriate love of a mother for her son – Josh – who looked as if sculpted from lard, and his gelatined-spiked hair was actually quite frightening.

Valentine's opinion of Sophie's appearance was not much better; she had dressed as, he imagined, a dogmatic hippie might. True, she had some stunning stones about her throat but they did little to distract from her beard.

He had not before met Sophie's twin-daughters Polly and Jessica. He regarded their tissue-thin skin – that those of heavy smoking parents seemed often to possess – and their feeble bone-structure and thoroughly bleached hair, and he questioned the factuality of their reputation, for he found it hard to believe many boys really had suffered at their hands to award them with the lofty prominence of promiscuousness.

Yet when he noticed their decidedly brazen scrutiny of Harry, he thought that the boys might not have much say in the matter, and decided that he had better watch his brother's back. Then, when he saw the girls unabashedly ogle Rupert, he considered the damage capable of creating with a caviar fork, and feared for their throats if they dared lascivious bids.

'Not a patch on you, Olivia!' Sophie toadied, 'Oh! No offence, Nina!'

'None taken, Sophie,' said Nina, and cast her a malevolent glance with the eye she had decided to display, 'Olivia always surpasses herself.'

Gratified by the praise, Olivia decided that her friends were not so appalling after all, and though she was inferior to them in wealth, she considered herself more than a cut above them in terms of class and liked it when they reminded her that this was something of which they were well aware.

'Thank you, darlings, it's nothing really, but one likes to try,' she insisted before looking awkward with the realisation that she ought to introduce her children to those of her friends.

'Not all of them are your children!' said Nina, eyeing Rupert.

Olivia laughed self-consciously, 'Oh no! How silly of me! Rupert has become a regular and much loved feature in Chinchero, but he is not, in fact, one of my own!'

Noticing the licentious twins again leering at Rupert, Valentine placed himself protectively before him, and said to them, in a territorial tone, 'But he is, in fact, *my* own!' and held their insolent stares until they had the sense to avert.

Presently, Nina pushed forward her oleaginous son, who had, all this while, been gripping a cellophane wrapped bunch of carnations and slimily smiling at Willy who had noticed it, not liked it and endeavoured to ignore him, but was now unable.

'These are for you,' he squelched, and thrust them toward her, 'You look . . . um . . . ' He screwed his face for a space before hit with the recollection, and continued with confidence, 'you look to be a perfect lady!'

Willy was aghast and regarded him with revulsion before turning to Olivia and applying to her a look of undiluted rage then turning once again to the buttery boy and his feeble bouquet.

The revelation that anyone might deem the squib of a dork an appropriate suitor shook her to her very foundation. Did her mother really consider her incapable of capturing a better husband? Clearly, she did not for it was obvious she had instructed the blob exactly what best to say.

Looking at him, Willy found she could not prevent herself from feeling a modicum of pity for the lowly beast, but she could not accept his flowers as she would appear foolish with two species of bloom and would not relinquish her nosegay for fear of revealing her magical flower. Even without the magical flower she thought carnations a poor exchange for gardenias.

'Oh, help!' thought she, 'He could not be less like Cosmo if he tried!'

Help came in the form of Valentine's interposed arm. He too had realised their mother's lack of faith in Willy, and filled with chagrin, he set about a rescue.

He seized the inferior flowers, and said, 'Gosh! So very nice of you! Yet there seems to be some misunderstanding; it is not Willy's birthday but Corny's! And I don't think Corny much cares for carnations, do you, Corny?'

Corny answered with a resolute shake of his head.

Valentine went on, 'But I'm certain we can find a home for these and, by the looks of it, rather fast before they totally decompose,' and he grimaced at the patent petrol-station purchase.

A strong sense of gratitude for Valentine's gallantry engulfed Willy, but neither Olivia nor Harry were impressed. She snatched the substandard flowers – which, to tell the truth, she too considered offensively miserly.

'What a splendid spray, Joseph!' she said to Josh, and she gathered her strength to inhale some sort of agreeable odour from the flowers but smelled only parsimony.

'Willy is indeed a very lucky lady, and I know just the very place for them, but first, if you will all please come through to the garden.'

Olivia ushered Sophie, Nina and their unpleasant offspring. 'Do come too, Harry, darling,' she said, 'You must put these in something,' and she pushed at him the objectionable bouquet with the presumption that he realised that the something was a bin.

Corny cranked the wheel of the gramophone to enjoy, for a third time, the sound of Rossini, and just as the crackles metamorphosed into music there came also a raucous honking of a car horn; Brian Pavilion and a bevy of chaps of the same bent had arrived.

The inverts numbered four but sounded more as they whooped, 'Toodle-pip!', 'Toodle-oo!', 'Cheerio!' and 'Goodbye!' with unsuppressed hilarity at their mysterious chauffeur as he motored away. It was plain to see that the gay quartet had already imbibed in some festive spirit. Each was dressed in accordance with Valentine's stiffy, and their accoutrements of conical party-hats, a magenta feather boa, and a kazoo did not prevent them from looking achingly debonair.

They turned in unison to face Chinchero and they exclaimed, '*Ooh!*' and '*Ah!*'. Brian opened the gate, sashayed up the red carpet, with the others behind, and he melodiously cried, 'My dears! How ever are you? Such a splendorific vision you all are! And Chinchero, my dears! Chinchero!' and he performed a theatrical show of regarding the flagged façade. So too did his mini-entourage.

'The flag!' shrieked Peter, a particularly small one of Brian's people, and he stretched wide his short arms in an effort to exemplify its enormity.

'The red-carpet!' screamed corpulent and jolly Jolyian and flourished his magenta boa as he danced a little jig upon the runner.

'The lanterns!' cried a rather lined but still handsome in a silvery way, Gerard, and he aimed at the Chinese lights a series of buzzing blows on his plastic kazoo.

'The vision of loveliness!' Peter cried regarding Rupert, and he pointed at him.

Recognising Valentine's blonde betrothed, Brian smacked away little Peter's pointing hand.

'Out of bounds!' he said to Peter, who met the news with a mew of disappointment.

Corny gaped at the new group, the realisation that his family had hired clowns pleased him immensely, though they were rather well dressed clowns, and he supposed that they might be comical conjurors. In either eventuality, he considered them with wondrous awe.

Brian looked down from his great height at the boy in his headdress, and said to his friends, 'Now, this is the birthday boy!' and he flapped his elegant hands about Corny.

The friends all gasped with delight and, as rehearsed, they sang to Corny his second *Happy Birthday to You!* of the day. It was no more tuneful than the one he had received at breakfast but sung with considerably more brio, and though he was somewhat perplexed as to why they replaced the words 'happy' and 'birthday' with the single one of 'hippopotamus', he liked it very much.

Brian extracted, from a pocket, an envelope and handed it to Corny. It contained a card depicting a spectacled bear enjoying marmalade, and inside it, a note portraying the ruling sovereign and the figure fifty.

Corny had not ever before possessed red fiscal matter, and its high number caused his eyes to pop because he now thought himself to be a boy of exorbitant means.

'Brian! How very generous!' exclaimed Valentine.

'My dear, but a mere trifle! And I feel I must admit that at my ripe age it is hard to imagine what children might enjoy these days so I consider my gift to be somewhat of a cheat!'

'Corny, appreciates it very much, don't you Corny?' said Valentine, and the birthday boy looked amazed at the notion that he might be anything but abundantly appreciative.

Brian laughed at the transparent success of his present, but upon regarding Willy, he suddenly stopped, for her attire induced a recollection.

Willy wondered why Mr Pavilion's mirth ended so abruptly when he looked at her. It did little to bolster her confidence, and then he gasped, and cried out, 'Meringue!'

'How rude!' Willy retorted, and her cheeks blushed with indignation.

'No, my dear! I am laden with meringues!'

'Are they catching?'

'No, my dear, they are Martha's,' he said, and picked up, from the gravel, an immense paper bag.

Upon peering into the bag and seeing that it was indeed laden with exquisite meringues, Willy was appeased, though only marginally for the fact that her dress reminded him of the cakes still remained.

Martha's meringues were famously good, and Valentine described to Rupert how their scrumptious central gooeyness was unrivalled.

'Crikey!' said Rupert, 'Sounds delicious!' and he licked his lips in an entirely un-self conscious manner.

'Delicious!' echoed Peter at Rupert, and licked his own lips.

Valentine refrained from making a moue at the little man, and chose instead to tolerate the admiration of his beau's beauty, and he said to Brian, 'Is Martha not coming?'

Brian sighed, and replied, 'Alas, my dear, I fear not! I begged and I pleaded and all but bribed her too, but she would not for she so dislikes the pretence of communal camaraderie, and being as sweet as she is, and wishing to cause no offence, she sent, in her stead, a million meringues!'

'Gosh! Glorious! But it's no communal party!' said Valentine.

'No communal party!' cried Brian with amused incredulity, 'You try telling that to Geraldine Strap! She is severely aware that all but she got a stiffy, and though secretly frothing she insists she has long held tickets for *Madame Butterfly*! I said to her, I said, "The opera? On a Saturday? I did not know you were so suburban!". She did not like it.'

Presently, a new arrival at the gate appeared, and it was not one that Valentine wished to greet for she was aggressively dull and quite strictly Catholic. Fortunately, Harry reappeared just in the nick to receive her, and Valentine exclaimed that he and Rupert would show Brian and his kind through to the garden.

Though the party was far from full swing the turnout was estimable by a quarter to nine, and those that believed that to arrive late was a fashionable thing to do were surely on their way. The garden had always enjoyed the best of the evening sun, and what with it being the precise middle of summer, it still beamed its wondrous warmth stupendously.

Gubsy sat; proudly filling every inch of his wing chair that Harry had hauled onto the striped lawn, for though the golden chairs were upholstered they were less than pleasant to his great uncle's large behind. Between Gubsy and the dance floor was the freestanding perch upon which rested Remarkable looking noble with his gold ankle chain to render him safely earthbound.

Valentine capered out to the garden, bestowed upon an exotic waiter Martha's meringues, and he sang, 'Mummy! Meet Brian, Peter, Jolyian, and Gerard! Brian, Peter, Jolyian, and Gerard, I present to you my mummy dearest!'

All at once Peter, Jolyian, Gerard, and to a lesser degree, Brian, fell over themselves in an effort to ingratiate Olivia with flamboyant flatteries and she watched them flap and fawn but did not listen. Naturally, she had met their sort before and was not unaccustomed to the adulation they lavished upon her, though the compliments confused her for she could not comprehend why any man would so gush if they were not in pursuit of physical intimacies and she deliberated as to whom might miraculously fall for Willy. Admittedly, she had been unfair to push forward the greasy Frethell boy but she had merely meant him to be something on which Willy might cut her teeth. Besides, she could not have told Nina of the search for a suitable without appearing to deem him acceptable, but then again the carnations were an insult! Olivia was glad that now Nina could see (with one eye anyway) in Rupert the standard of man fit for the family, and that her globular son possessed less than a breath of a chance and hoped that the realisation slapped Nina's face with a sharpness of reality sufficient to sting for days.

Steadily, the garden filled with fresh arrivals. Along with the aggressively dull Catholic – Rowena Whitaker – who everybody was eager to avoid for once she had you cornered she was as if a leach sucking away one's will to exist, came her sons – Edward and Oscar. Valentine knew that these two were also for the benefit of Willy, but though one went to medical school and the other studied law, and they were of decent looks, they both possessed their mother's mammon of monotony. Moreover, Valentine remembered his daddy not much liking Catholics and he wondered how his mother might have been so foolish as to forget the fact.

After the charismatically challenged Catholics, Mr and Mrs Frobisher arrived, and by comparison, they seemed magnetic, though in truth, the best that one could say of them was that they were non-offensive, unless ramblers of the walking and not the talking sort caused one distress, but it would have been impolite not to invite one's immediate neighbours.

Then came Hugo Pargeter and he was a handsome widower who had a keen eye for Olivia though she would not entertain him for he was not

Monty, and had only received a stiffy because he had an equally hand-some son – Giles – who had just secured an admirably waged job of work in the city.

Sadly, Giles was not very discriminatory, and he immediately engaged in an interaction with the twins for he had already sullied himself with them and his stressful vocation caused him to enjoy a sure and easy opportunity, especially when it was two for one.

Willy could plainly see the attraction in Giles with his square jaw and camel lashes, but she was not bothered in the least that he looked straight past her, for just as Hugo was not Monty, neither was Giles Cosmo, and Willy had her sight firmly fixed. She wondered why Cosmo had not yet come and she started to fear that he might not at all. She fingered her secret ring beneath her nosegay, reminded herself '*I possess something glorious that everybody desires . . .* ' and staged her face with captivating confidence to mask her worry.

Though exhilarated by the attendance, and his trove of boons amassed in the entrance hall, Corny was quite concerned that none of his friends had arrived. He and Harry waited patiently at the porch and played Rossini on a loop, when suddenly the birthday boy's people came all at once in a minibus, just as Olivia had predicted, and accompanied by two tired looking elders to provide supervision.

Upon the happy sighting of his comrades, Corny jumped and caused the mass of contents in Gloriana's bowl and Gloriana herself to spin violently.

Oh! He was so glad to see them! He rushed to the gate to greet; there was Jeremy, Liam, Arthur, Daniel, Daisy, Marcus, Bertie and tiny Petal. Each of them bounced out from the undersized bus and gambolled into the front garden to meet their host. The mute group beamed at him and hugged him until he appeared to verge close to a cataclysmic eruption of euphoria.

He lead them through Chinchero and out into the garden where they each looked in wonder at the festivity and goggled in astonishment as the plunging of Corny's arm into the frog pond seemed not to matter at all to his smart new digital watch, though the planktonic algae certainly soiled his sleeve.

By this time, the sun had gone to bed. In his place hung the silvery moon and she shone her mysterious light upon that which the becoming glow from the Chinese lanterns could not. More people came and soon the garden was crowded with them; sat on the golden chairs in groups about the damask clothed tables, and dotted about in bunches by the cottage arch and cupid fountain, the rockery, pergola and gazebo. The continental waiters in jackets of white weaved about balancing vast shining salvers bearing blinis and bellinis that created a high-spirited gaiety and did indeed induce, what some might call, dancing upon the designated floor to the *Champagne-Polka*.

Ignoring completely the nature of the music, bearded Sophie was trying to relive the 1960's with a terrible effort at the Twist with Peter who could not help transforming his little twists into excited twirls. Dashing Gerard disposed of any decorum he might possibly normally possess by frisking, in a rather too risqué manner, with cuddly Jolyian. Between them, they had snared, with the feather boa, a deeply traumatised Catholic Oscar Whitaker, whose ears suffered very close and continual kazoo blasts. One-eyed Nina danced rather too intimately with her unctuous son, and the rambling Frobishers swayed systematically.

Frolicking amongst the bedlam were some of Corny's friends that seemed already to have indulged in too much effervescence, and in the epicentre was a florid Gubsy stomping with ferocity as if in an effort to extinguish a small fire.

Rupert tightened his hold of Valentine's hand and enquired if he would care for a Grasshopper.

'Gosh!' Valentine exclaimed, 'I do believe that even if I tried extremely hard I would not think of many things I should like more! One can actually get quite tired of champagne cocktails!'

Rupert smiled, 'Then I'll mix a whole shaker of them for you.'

'Gosh! And I shall invent a thousand ways in which to thank you!'

'Crikey! In that case, I'll make two shakers!' said Rupert, with a broad grin, and with that, he advanced toward Chinchero with the aim of creating for Valentine an entire cloud of Grasshoppers.

As Rupert worked his way through the crush, Valentine admired his heroic form, and then his world filled with smoke for suddenly standing next to him was Brian gesticulating an extraordinarily long cigarette holder.

'Gosh! Brian! I did not see you there!' said Valentine, extracting from his silver case a cigarette for himself.

Brian cast him a wry glance, and said, 'Of course you did not, my dear! You were far, far away in the land of love! Do tell me, is it still the same? More years than I care to count have passed since I last fell in it!'

Valentine sighed and declared that the place in which he found himself with Rupert could not ever before have been as glorious.

'Well done you, my dear!' said Brian, sucking hard on his smoking apparatus. 'I am perfectly thrilled to see you have him wrapped around your pinky and fixing you cocktails without your even having to ask; I am impressed!'

'Gosh! His fixing cocktails is but the tip of the berg!' replied Valentine and proceeded to boast of all the glories that Rupert possessed.

To hear of Valentine's rapport with Rupert was music to Brian's ears, and his eyes could see very clearly the sincerity of his perfervidness. However, whether it be Brian's sagacity or only the cynicism formed by his own less than idyllic history, he had a sudden sense of foreboding. He possessed half a mind of putting it to Valentine that he would be wise to be wary of losing himself altogether, for according to his book of knowledge, nothing was more enervating to overcome than a trampled heart, but Brian was loathe to rain on such a impassioned parade. He hoped for the sake of Valentine that the affair would prove steadfast, and resolved to be at hand if it transpired that Rupert was a Romeo.

Olivia, though she had to confess the *Champagne-Polka* cheerful, would not ever have deigned to dance, and as she looked upon those that willingly made fools of themselves, she marvelled at their debauchery. She noticed Valentine, stood at the other side of the dance floor, and, with a modicum of envy, she regarded how firmly tucked his hand was inside of Rupert's, for it brought to her mind how much she missed Monty. If he were present then she most certainly would dance with him.

Presently, she underwent the repellent experience of an unexpected whisper in her ear. She startled and felt tremendously vexed, first by the assumed familiarity of the whisperer, second by the realisation that it was Hugo, for he was a man that she simply could not abide. Never before had she encountered such a vain poseur as he who provided perfect proof that charmers were seldom, if ever, charming. It was true he was handsome in the way that some men grow to be, but his knowledge of it, and his fantasy that he was irresistible to all womankind, was to her intolerable, and she was intensely galled by his audacious invitation to dance.

Executing her crocodilian smile, she said, 'Hugo! Darling! I'm so very sorry but I'm afraid I'm obliged to decline your request for I've promised my first dance to my son.'

Which particular son she did not divulge for mindful that Hugo may well prove persistent she had three of them with whom to improvise her evasion.

As she watched Hugo strain to swallow the unaccustomed rejection and slope off, she shot poison tipped spears of contempt between the blades of his shoulders, and wished Monty's fist in his impudent face.

For a space, she mentally argued whether she was shocked more by Hugo's impertinence or by his idiocy not to realise that his getting a stiffy was because of Giles, the location of whom she now wondered. She hoped that he was enjoying an interaction with Willy, and as she sought his situation, she snatched a flute.

She spied a little girl sat upon Uncle Bartholomew's wing chair. The girl was so small that not only were her feet unable to reach the lawn but neither did her circumstance permit her knees to bend for she was deeply ensconced.

The little girl was, in fact, fifteen years of age but looked to be years younger, and her name was Petal. The name was appropriate for she was indeed as delicate. Up until a moment ago, she had been running about the garden with Corny and the others but was now enjoying a pause and was jiggling Remarkable's gold chain.

Upon seeing the tall and elegant lady in red, Petal thought that never before had she seen someone so glamorous, and hoped that when she became a grown-up she would look just the same. Presently, the lady returned the gaze and Petal became shy but somehow found it impossible not to smile.

Olivia wondered why the girl stared and smiled so strangely at her, but then all deliberation vacated her mind when she saw, grouped behind the wing chair, Giles squeezed between the twins with six hands feverishly groping, and three sets of lips seemingly knowing no bounds.

The conduct struck Olivia as dissolute and in every way indefensible. Had they no sense of decency? The occasion was a celebration of a young man's birthday, yet they chose to regard it as an opportunity to behave in a manner so offensively orgiastic it was akin to a spit in the face! She could not comprehend the lack of discrimination in Giles, not to mention his absence of acumen, for his decision to associate with the harlot twins when he might have Willy on a plate displayed a startling shortcoming of both. Olivia had specifically requested Valentine ensure Giles get a stiffy, for out of all the potentials, he, with his new and lucrative line of work, was whom she had uppermost in mind for her daughter's first foray.

Now, Olivia felt her blood boil to such a degree that it threatened to bubble over. However, she retained her composure with the resolution that if Sophie could not keep her daughters on a leash then she herself would somehow have to smack into them a sense of respect. Slowly, the rage dissipated, but before it left entirely there erupted a final flash of it that forced her hand that held her flute to clench too tight. The destruction of the crystal glass sent sinister shards flying.

Slightly shocked by the unintentional detonation, Olivia was surprised to find that though her palm was wet and fizzing, nothing had pierced her flesh, and she licked the champagne from her hand quite in the way a cat has a clean.

No one witnessed Olivia's momentary loss of self-possession but the inconsequential Petal; she had seen it all.

Despite her shyness, Petal, because of her admiration of the elegant lady, had offered her a small smile. With that smile, she wished to indicate how very glamorous she thought her to be, for even if she were able to communicate with words, the mere idea was too intimidating to consider, but she had to convey her appreciation somehow. Therefore, she smiled.

The lady looked furious with the smile and her eyes had appeared as red as her dress, and she froze, still as a statue, and suddenly she made her drink explode!

Petal was scared, and terribly upset. Why did the lady not like her? She decided that the lady was not very nice after all, even if she did look glamorous, and upon seeing her lick the broken glass from her hand as if granules of sugar, she decided that the lady was, in fact, a witch!

Still Willy and Harry waited in the front garden for the arrival of the Oxley-Stockmans. Flick had come noisily, and after a brief dalliance with Harry – with a mystifying reference to mayonnaise – and a compliment cast at Willy's dress, had swept into Chinchero with no mention of her family.

'Where is he?' wondered Willy, now fearing that Cosmo might not come at all. Everybody else (bar Izzy – whom Rupert had warned might be too shy to attend) had arrived, and time was ticking.

Brother and sister stood in silence. They had ceased to crank the gramophone, and listened to the sounds of The Marvellous Party that travelled from the garden. Both felt they really ought to be part of the revelry but were reluctant to abandon their responsibility of receiving. Besides, the Oxley-Stockmans were family.

'Cwumbs! I hope nothing tewwible has happened,' said Harry, stroking his beard.

Willy's worry escalated; the thought that something terrible might have happened to Cosmo before she had the opportunity to captivate him was a thing too tragic to contemplate!

'What sort of terrible thing?' she asked with alarm.

Harry pouted and contemplated possibilities, 'Well, if Cosmo's dwiving and his foot's still dodgy they wun the wisk of cwashing.'

'Crashing! You mean dead?' Willy wailed, and edged on the point of nervous collapse.

'Cwumbs, no! Not dead! Just a little cwash, into a twee, or a pillar-box, or maybe another dwiver,' said Harry, and felt rather pleased with his imagination. 'And then they would have to swap addwesses.'

'But why? Who with?' asked Willy.

'The other cwasher. That's what you do,' said Harry, wisely, 'But maybe they just bwoke down and are waiting for woad wescue, and that pwobably takes a while on a Saturday night.'

Absorbing Harry's theories, Willy pictured Cosmo at the wheel of his muddy BMW with his parents in the backseat, and mentally pictured that because of his foot, he had crashed into a tree, pillar-box or another driver.

She then had the horrible idea that the other driver might easily be a girl of fantastical loveliness for whom Cosmo would instantly fall, and have at hand good reason to see her again to discuss vehicle reparation, and thus endeavour a romantic pursuit!

Perhaps the feeling had been mutual and this very moment the crashers were sat in a hotel bar and toasting their engagement!

Fearing all hope was lost, Willy could no longer wait for a man who had likely spurned her, and she asked Harry, 'Would it be all right if I went through to the garden for a while?'

Harry furrowed his brow, 'Quite all wight, Willy. Go and have some fun . . . besides you ought to show off your dwess, you weally do look vewy pwetty.'

Though several had flattered her appearance that evening, Willy realised Harry's sentiment the most sincere. In fact, he made all the others sound like fibs. It touched her and she wished, without hope, that Cosmo might come to touch her too.

'Thank you,' she said, quietly, 'and you look very handsome.'

Flashing a smile, Harry replied, 'Thanks . . . now go and show off . . . and tell Corny I'm sowwy to be missing his party but I'll be out soon.'

'Of course! I'm sure he understands, but I'll tell him anyway.'

With that, Willy gathered her gown and trundled into Chinchero.

In the midst of the hall, a charge of Corny and his people racing at breakneck speed from the kitchen through to drawing room and out toward the garden virtually toppled Willy, but she steadied herself and cried, 'Corny!'

Corny came to halt, turned his feathered head and displayed his excited and sweaty face to his sister. He was having the best birthday he could call to mind!

'Harry says he'll be out soon, all right?' said Willy.

Nodding his head as if he desired to rid himself of its encumbrance, Corny signalled that he understood, and then jumped high as a kite before dashing out to join his friends.

At least he is having a good time, Willy thought, and she considered that of all present he was the one most deserved of it as it was his birthday. After catching a waiter and asking him to ensure Harry receive some champagne, she landed her behind on the second step of the stairwell, causing her skirt to balloon, and brought forth the sigh of one entirely devoid of expectation. Her heart felt as if twisted and wrenched from her body, and her eyes struggled to blink away the stream of sadness she felt welling.

Cosmo was not coming. She just knew it. She realised they had been fools ever to believe that he would. He was probably laughing at them all this very minute, most especially the recollection of the fat frump in the monkey mask.

All she desired to do was climb the stairs, tear off her dress and forget her 'facial staging', for they were both redundant, and cry herself to sleep, but she could not. It was Corny's party and for him she must persevere. Besides, Harry was right; she should show off the fairy-tale dress that Gretchen had so painstakingly altered. Tomorrow, however, she would return to her usual apparel and sport some comfortable jeans and plaid shirt, and renounce the impossible dream of becoming a lady, for without the opportunity of obtaining Cosmo what point was there?

She decided to put on a brave face, and resolved that one last time she would convince herself . . . '*I possess something glorious that everybody desires . . .* '

She placed her nosegay in her lap and enjoyed the exquisiteness of her secret ring to promote a sense of happiness within. '*I possess something glorious that everybody desires . . .* ' she mentally repeated whilst stroking her magic flower.

If Willy had chosen to sit further up the stairwell, she might have noticed her great-great grandmother plucking her golden harp beneath the bison, and learned that her magic flower was, in fact, a starfish, Olympia's Starfish. However, had someone pushed the portrait in her face she most likely would have remained oblivious, for her application to the task was one of such dedication that no earthly thing might penetrate her absorption.

Olivia, of course, was entirely capable, but Willy was ignorant of her sudden presence until came the strangled and terse question from behind; 'What on earth are you fiddling with like a bone idle buffoon with no thought for anyone but herself?'

Willy's concentration cracked in an instant and crashed at her feet. Grabbing her nosegay, she leapt up, and with her heart in her mouth, she looked with fear at her mother.

'Nothing, mummy, nothing! Just my nosegay . . . it's so pretty you see,' she fibbed and hoped it convincing.

Narrowing her eyes, Olivia did not look confident of the reply.

With a design to deflect, Willy asked, 'What were you doing upstairs?'

Though Olivia pulled a face of horror, and said, 'I do not believe I am answerable to you!' Willy was relieved to have achieved in distracting her from her magic flower.

'If you must know,' Olivia went on, 'I was using the lavatory. Does that sit well with you?'

'Yes, of course, mummy, but . . . '

'There is a "but"?' Olivia demanded to know with no small amount of incredulity in her tone, 'I should love to learn the basis of this "but"!'

Willy had filled with regret the moment the 'but' passed her lips, however, she tentatively elaborated, 'Well, there is the downstairs loo. Why go all the way upstairs?'

Olivia snapped her neck as if she were the recipient of an unexpected slap.

'I refuse to justify to you, or anybody else for that matter, my thought process behind the water-closet I choose to use! It is not a thing a lady ought to discuss!'

With that, she descended the remaining steps and positioned herself uncomfortably close to Willy.

'You *are* a lady, aren't you? Or was that a fleeting fancy?'

Stifling a gulp, for her mother's unusual proximity rather unnerved her, Willy replied, 'Yes, mummy . . . I mean, no . . . it was not fleeting; I *am* a lady, I *truly* believe I possess something *glorious* that *everybody* desires!'

The strange response silenced Olivia and she brought her face an inch closer to Willy's to inspect her for physical evidence of insanity, and thought, 'I possess something glorious that everybody desires' – what sort of imaginary world might Willy believe herself to inhabit, and might her madness escalate into something apparent to all? Again, just as she had in the tree house on the anniversary of Montgomery's death, Olivia pictured scenes involving straitjackets and padded cells for Willy, and humiliation for the family, and it scared her. There was nothing for it; Willy must marry before the bats in her belfry bred to such a number that she became completely ineligible for matrimony. There was no time to waste.

Willy's unease grew to such a degree that she believed she might pop with terror, yet a shock of relief ran through her when Olivia, in a surprisingly pleasant tone, said, 'Darling, that is indeed the most wonderful piece of news I have had the pleasure to receive in a very long time. Come, let us go to the garden and discover who might desire the patently glorious thing you so transparently possess.'

'Oh, no, mummy!' Willy wailed, as Olivia piloted her through the drawing room, 'There are not any boys here that I like! I merely meant that I felt to be a lady!'

Olivia tightened her grip on Willy's exposed shoulders and unintentionally dug her nails deep into the fleshy upholstery.

'Obnoxious and spoiled girl!' she thought to herself and contemplated the amount of effort to which she had gone for the sake of procuring prospective boys, and now Willy believed herself too good for any in attendance!

Olivia would not have it. She would not permit her machinations to prove pointless. She would force Willy on Giles, and pull the right strings to ensure at least an engagement, and was sure she could count on Hugo for assistance if she gave him a bone.

Penetrating the crush, Olivia smiled at the guests, and hissed in Willy's ear, 'You quite obviously overlooked Giles Pargeter. He is precisely the right sort of man for the family, so in the name of Avery-Stripe, snare him and make your parents proud!'

The pain of Olivia's claws in her bare flesh made Willy want to howl, yet presently finding herself pushed face-to-face with a sozzled Giles sandwiched between kissing twins, she managed to suppress its development.

Giles and the twins looked at the sudden appearance of Willy in slight confusion and the girls looked on the brink of protestation but before they had a chance to spit acid, Olivia stepped in.

'Girls! So sorry I've neglected you!' she sang, 'I am excruciatingly glad you could come and so sorry, that at your awkward age, it must be such a bone-crushing bore. But never fear, I'm here to remedy that with the sort of *girly* chat I'm certain you adore!' and she presented to them, cradled between the fingers of one hand, two champagne cocktails.

In her other hand, she held another flute for herself, and through the aid of physical intervention, she managed to separate Giles from the twins who looked greatly irritated by the division and stared at the flutes thrust before them.

'But, mummy, may I not have one of those? I've never had a champagne cocktail,' said Willy.

'No!' snapped Olivia, with rather too much venom before repeating, sweetly, 'No, darling, these are special ones just for Jess and Poll, I'm having one too, whilst Giles takes you for a turn on the floor.'

Willy wished that the world might swallow her whole for she felt her mother's manipulations to be mortifying and screamingly crass. She looked to Giles and he looked to her also, yet it was plain to see his lack of focus for he so swayed with the fill of alcohol it was as if he were at sea. He did not even appear to have heard Olivia's words.

Quick to rectify, Olivia twisted the twins' fingers around the flutes, and turning her back on them, she applied herself.

'Giles! ' she said, and straightened his Windsor knot.

Recognising his name, Olivia's captive pivoted his head toward her, and said, 'Ye*sh*?'

'Giles, so lovely to see you . . . I remember when you were a very little boy running about naked and thinking it ever so funny! Such a naughty boy!'

Giles looked both bashful and proud.

'And look at you now!' Olivia went on, 'A man of the world, and a very handsome man too, I might add, and so very clever with such an important new career!'

Giles issued a moronically flattered chuckle and quite seemed to enjoy Mrs Avery-Stripe handling his too wide Gucci tie but also looked as if it were all that prevented him from folding into an intoxicated heap.

'*F*ank-you . . . Mrs*h*. Ave*wy*-*Schtw*ipe,' he said and all but batted his camel lashes.

'No need to thank me, Giles, darling, but I should very much appreciate you dancing with Willy,' replied Olivia.

'Wha*aa*?' said Giles, confusedly.

'My daughter,' Olivia clarified, and clamping his square jaw in her hand, she turned his attention to Willy. 'She's desperate to dance with you but simply too timid to ask but I know that you will oblige,' and repositioning his face back to hers, she added, 'Won't you, darling.' without the inflection of a question, for it was no such thing.

'*Umm* . . . ' was the sound Giles made as he swivelled his eyes toward the plump girl in the preposterous gown, or were there two of them?

'*Umm* . . . ' he sounded again, and viewed two sets of wanton and seething twins.

'*Umm* . . . ' and he returned his eyes to Olivia who seemed to him to possess a dozen of them, each of which narrowed to emphasise his lack of choice in the matter.

'*Hmm?*' Olivia said, and wet her thumb with her tongue to wipe from his mouth the marks left by the twins' cheap lipstick.

'*Umm* . . . ye*sh*,' Giles said with surrender.

Releasing his head, Olivia bore her teeth, and exclaimed, 'Darling! Such a gentleman!' and, with that, she manoeuvred him so he could clearly see his destination that was the dance floor, hooked Willy's hand in his crook, and push-started their journey with a shove.

For a space, and with a sense of satisfaction, she regarded their ambling progress, and smiled at Willy (scowling at her pushy mother over her shoulder) before turning and focusing her attention upon the transparently livid twins.

'Well, girls, *do* tell me all your gossip! I'm certain you two possess a veritable library of lewd tales!'

Neither girl looked eager to regale, nor even to talk, and seemed to find it a sorry enough situation merely to stand near their mother's friend, and other than to swig their champagne cocktails and chew gum, they let their feeble jaws hang slack with the idea that it made them appear a thing called cool.

Olivia could not care a fiddlestick whether they conversed or not, in fact, not would be nicer, for she was unable to believe either possessed anything resembling intellect, and though imbecility was a quality she considered advantageous in a man she thought it disastrous in a woman. She did not feel irritated by their insolent stares for she knew they could not help their lack of breeding, and she hoped only that they might soon exhaust their flutes because until they had, she could not be certain that they had swallowed the strong and fast-acting laxatives she had dropped into them.

*

Valentine's adoration of Rupert brought to Brian's attention their shared proclivity and it provoked him to ask, 'My dear! I simply must enquire as to the whereabouts of your splendidly brutish cousin. I really had hoped and assumed he might be here. I shall be sorely frustrated to learn that my hunger may have to suffer dissatisfaction!'

'Cousin Cosmo!' exclaimed Valentine, with revulsion, and was somewhat surprised that Brian still carried a torch.

'Yes, my dear, he!' said Brian, 'At least I believe so, though I am flawed in the recollection of names but more than make up for the deficiency with my dexterity with a man's anatomy.'

Valentine winced, not at the notion of Brian's adroitness but of his ambition to apply them to his caddish cousin.

'Gosh! Well, he did get a stiffy and said he would come though I can't say I shall mind very much if he does not.'

Whereupon, Valentine looked about the vast array of questionables present in an effort to reassure himself that the party was still devoid of Cosmo. It was then, that above the considerable racket, he became aware of a surmounting sound that though he had not heard it earlier he had done so on many an occasion before. The hysterical pitch of it was unmistakable and the moment he was mindful of its maker, out through the crowd squeezed the person he had often thought to bear, in the nicest possible way, an uncanny similarity to an overjoyed pygmy-hippo; Flick Oxley-Stockman.

She was a vision of yellow, though the dress appeared to be a diminutive hospital-gown (albeit one cut to display her heaving bosom) and had she educated Valentine that it indeed was, he would not doubt her for such was her existence. The term 'dirty stop-out' might easily have been invented with her in mind, or else the word 'vagabond' would serve just as well. That is not to say that she was without a home, merely that she was so incompatible with her parentage – Esmé in particular – that she chose not to dwell in their abode.

Instead, she opted to enjoy the kindnesses of strange and not unwealthy gentlemen. She had developed an unfailing pattern, of which she was not altogether aware for her perception was often addled, of occupying a fresh acquaintance's sofa or spare bed for two or three weeks after having met them at some sort of bash, before relocating, for a matter of months, to the bed of a chap claiming to be in Debrett's or the best friend of someone awfully famous, then finding herself again on a sofa.

At this point, she would hit upon another suspicious man, or discover she was in desperate need of a stretch in a sanatorium for her liver demanded mercy as she possessed an aptitude for emptying cocktail cabinets in an exceedingly short space of time. There she would dry out for as long as was tolerable and then abscond to resume her social loop the loop with deft aplomb.

Valentine did not know at which point of her coiling navigation Flick currently was, for when he had caught her on the telephone, he had been brief and she close to incoherent, though he surmised it to be an agreeable point, for her countenance was in bloom and displayed no discernable cracks. True, her tousled rich-brown hair gave her the appearance of having been dragged backward through hedgerow, but he believed the look to be intentional, for her lips and nails were flawless.

Flick emitted a sound akin to that of a foxhunting bugle (perhaps purposely because of the octet's current delivery of *The Ride of the Valkyries*) and throwing back her dainty head, she flung herself with wild abandon into the arms of Valentine who embraced her enthusiastically.

'*Dahling*!' she joyfully cried, and buried her face in his chest – for even in her Westwood heels she was still far from tall – and inhaled, '*Mmm*! Violets! *Lummy*! Super to see you! But you are a bounder!'

'Gosh! Me? But why?' demanded Valentine, for he considered himself as un-bounder like as could possibly be.

'Yes! You! An utter bounder! You did not tell me it was a party, and though I'm not adverse it does rather dash my hopes for a jolly good *ketchup*!'

'Gosh, but I did tell you! And anyway you look to be attired entirely appropriately for a party!'

'That is because I have just left one, not a very good one, but in '*Ker-nickeds-bridge*', with a Wall Street banker but I appear to have mislaid him during the cab journey,' explained Flick and she downed the dregs from her flute whilst simultaneously plucking another from a passing salver.

'Gosh! You are careless! Though also very sweet to be wearing yellow!' said Valentine.

'Oh, *dahling*!' she purred, 'You know I know you love yellow! And do admire my fantastic rock!' and she proudly presented a gigantic yellow diamond nestled in her plunging cleavage.

'Gosh! Colossal!' exclaimed Valentine, with admiration.

'Isn't it *lummy*? Some Iranian chappy forced it on me and I dread to wonder why!'

'Best not to I should say!' he advised.

'You are wise, *dahling*, and I shouldn't think I'll have much trouble doing that with all the dishy chaps here! First, I met Harry at the door and his handsomeness always makes me mayonnaise, then there was a simply scrummy chap mixing cocktails, and he all but made me lubricate! I asked him what he was making and he told me Grasshoppers! So I said no thanks very much, and seeing lobster claws I said I'd have a Lobster martini!'

Flick was greatly tickled by her own comedic genius and through her chortles she continued, 'He told me you were out here, so out I came and fighting through I saw yet another dish with lashes so long he made mine feel positively stumpy!'

'That must be Giles Pargeter,' said a nettled Valentine, 'and he *is* a bounder with a taste for tat so I shouldn't touch him, the scrummy Grasshopper maker is Rupert and *mine*, and really you should not refer to Harry in such a way!'

'Don't be a prude!' Flick argued, 'You have to admit he's a dish! Besides he looks just like Excelsior, and you and I often looked up at his portrait and discussed how saturating he was!'

'I do admit they both are handsome, but my issue is not your appreciation of Harry, merely your applying mayonnaise to him, and I certainly deny calling Excelsior saturating!' insisted Valentine irritably, for though he had vague childhood memories of thinking his ancestor striking, he felt decidedly nauseated by Flick's crude phraseology.

Brian absorbed the familial exchange with amusement. Successfully, he calculated that Flick must be sister to the brute on whom he was waiting, and considered her a delightful scream (though a drop de trop) and endeavoured to make himself known.

Brian's doing so struck Valentine with the realisation that he quite probably stood between the two most perverted people present, with the possible exception of the twins, and he longed for the return of Rupert so that his situation might feel less seedy.

No sooner had his longing breached acceptable bearability did Rupert reappear. With him, he brought close to a gallon of Grasshopper decanted in a crystal receptacle, and three cocktail glasses, two of which were empty and the third contained something observably putrid. It was coral in colour and creamy in consistency with little black pellets floating about, and out of the sickly spume emerged a red antenna, crusher claw and leg of a lobster.

Though Rupert beamed proudly, Valentine was aghast, grimaced grotesquely, and asked, 'Gosh! Whatever is that? It looks to be revolting!'

Flick's ear-splitting scream of hilarity blanketed Rupert's reply.

'My Lobster martini!' she excitedly cried and then howled with such extravagant laughter that it was practically apocalyptic.

Now aware of the caper, Valentine viewed Rupert with adoration anew. It touched him deeply that he had done something so silly. He gazed at him with adulation, tangled together their fingers, and as they both supped at Grasshoppers, he felt as if he were floating.

Quite soon, the ice was broken, and Flick learned that Rupert had long been a friend of her brother. She wondered aloud as to why their paths had not before crossed, but upon hearing that the boys most often met on foreign shores and usually to perform activities of an athletic sort she found the explanation, for she was fond neither of abroad nor of sport.

'But I have heard lots about you,' Rupert reassured her, and she screamed as if the revelation was orgasmic.

Upon the cessation of the ringing in his ears that Flick's piercing-cry had induced, Brian issued a comparatively sedate shriek because his height afforded him a luxurious line of vision, which presently filled with the appearance of Cosmo at the threshold of the conservatory.

As if requiring assistance to resist stampeding toward the root of his shriek, Brian grasped at Valentine, heaved a sigh and dreamily gasped, 'My dears! Ahoy, the handsome brute!'

Employing the aid of Rupert's broad shoulder for leverage, Valentine saw, over the heads of the crowd, that it was indeed so; Cosmo had come! His aspect was commanding for his build suited the wearing of evening attire, but not quite as grandly as his arrogant sneer suggested he believed it. His black eyes, though not so dark as they had initially been, were still reasonably raccoon, and this shading promoted the prominence of his monobrow, and though his nose was most likely still slightly swollen it was possible to see that the sock had rendered it roman.

Flanking him were two people of equal, if not more so, monstrous manifestation; Quentin and Esmé Oxley-Stockman.

Quentin's face was wizen and furnished with shifty eyes, too close together for comfort, and devoid of white. A hooked beak was his nose and an ugly little gash served as his mouth. He possessed the Oxley-Stockman undersized skull – which retained but a solitary lock that he coloured black as night and lacquered in a curlicue over his ashen scalp – and a formidable hunch that coerced his withered frame into an elaborate stoop.

Equally as nefarious, though quite at the opposite end of the degenerate spectrum, for excepting her substandard legs that were disturbingly embryonic, Esmé's configuration was as copiously bulbous as a bacterial boil in critical need of a prick. Even the lids of her tiny eyes looked to bulge, and they protruded from her distended face that emerged from her plethora of chins. Her shoulders and torso were frankly goliath and her arms also. The contradictory proportions between her upper body and lower lent to her the redoubtable silhouette of an American football player, and her hairstyle in the shape of a helmet heightened this likeness further. The trio of Oxley-Stockmans appeared to be exerting an extreme amount of effort in contorting their faces to exhibit flamboyant looks of pained contempt as they stood in the conservatory door and viewed the hustle and bustle before them.

'How horrifying!' Valentine exclaimed and involuntarily shuddered. He quickly purified his eyes with Rupert, his hero, whose beauty would shield him from the unsightliness.

Rupert was not entirely comfortable with the coming of Cosmo either, for their last encounter had proved less than amicable.

A haze of confusion swallowed Flick as she absorbed the varied reactions to the new arrival whom she could not see for her legs were too short. She wondered who might produce a response of lust in one, horror in another, and perturbation in the last, and simply had to ask, 'But who is it?' and looked to be electrically shocked when from Brian came the breathless answer; 'Oh my dear! It is your beefy brother!'

Immobile as an ancient ruin, she said to Valentine, 'Cosmo is here?'

'Verily!' he replied.

Flick's intake of oxygen was incredible.

'You invited him?' she said with astonishment.

'I am afraid so . . . and in my folly, your parents too!' admitted Valentine and he teemed with regret.

Suddenly agitated, Flick hopped from foot to foot (quite out of time to *The Blue Danube*) and frenetically flapped her arms, causing her incalculable collection of metallic bangles to jangle with irritation.

'Hide me, *dahlings!*' she cried, and much to the annoyance of a motley group of guests sat at a table, she tried, in vain, to clamber beneath its damask cloth, but to no avail; small as she was it would not provide refuge. Therefore, she chose to conceal herself behind the brawn of Rupert where, from her oversized handbag, she produced a bottle of vodka, tossed its cap over her shoulder, and slugged it neat.

*

244

Willy supposed that she might easily dispense the burden of Giles, and instead dance with Gubsy who had evidently forgotten his adage that only drunks and villains dance alone and was stamping in the centre of the dance floor. Yet she considered, that of all boys present – siblings excluded – good-looking Giles to be the most agreeable. Be that as it may, it was close to impossible to dance with him, most especially to *The Ride of the Valkyries,* for he was far too inebriated to summon the dynamism required, and she found herself virtually hoisting his square frame. He did display a measure of masculinity, however, when Josh possessed the audacity to ask of him if he might cut in.

'Go dan*sch* wi*v* your mummy, little boy, I *f*ink she*ez* your only chance of luck tonight and it take*sh* a real man to handle Willy!' Giles slurred at Josh who instantaneously looked humiliated and did indeed run back to his one-eyed mummy.

'Oh! That was good!' thought Willy. Certainly, it was not the most romantic sentiment ever expressed, but it got the message across and did verge on the chivalry a gentleman ought to bestow upon a lady.

With that in mind and the splendid sound of Strauss' *Blue Danube* now underway, she encircled Giles' girth to maintain his verticality, and waltzed him wildly. Her ecstasy at having had her lady-likeness confirmed was such that she did not notice the difficulty her partner's feet were having keeping up with her bouncing steps for they did nothing but slip and trip, nor did she notice, that though he smiled at her, his face gradually grew green.

Presently she heard a voice that infiltrated her attention, and it was the booming and arrogant one of Cosmo. Initially, she could not credit it, and wondered if she even dare to dream the possibility of his presence when she had so thoroughly convinced herself of its unlikelihood. Continuing to manoeuvre the legless Giles, in circles about the floor, she braved it and arched her neck to determine, between the heads of her fellow dancers, whether or no her prince had truly come.

Then she saw him! He was standing between his parents and talking in loud and proud tones to Harry at the entrance to the conservatory. The sight of his billiard ball head made her own feel quite as light as a paper-bag of feathers. Mindless of all else other than Cosmo she abandoned Giles, whose form consequently met the floor with an unceremonious crash at the feet of a startled Gubsy, and she flew on the wings of love toward her heart's desire with the thought; '*I possess something glorious that everybody desires . . .* '

*

Having decided there was nothing to fear with Rupert and his beauty so near, Valentine had composed himself to such an extent that by comparison a cucumber would not seem at all cool. Rupert smiled down at him. He no longer felt uneasy over the arrival of Cosmo and he realised the reason was Valentine and his sudden nonchalance, and the two of them regarded each other with such feelings of romance that between them they looked to possess just one wit.

'Oh! Auntie O! Super to see you!' Valentine heard Flick say, and he saw the approach of his mother.

'Gosh, mummy!' he said, 'Wherever have you been?'

'Hello, Flick, darling,' Olivia said, and deigned to pat her niece on the head as one might a precious shih tzu, 'Thirsty, I see.'

'Rather!' exclaimed Flick good-humouredly for her hurried imbibing had successfully anaesthetised the dreaded presence of her parents.

'I have been here at the party, of course!' Olivia said to her puzzled son, 'Where else might I have been?'

'Gosh! I've no inkling, and shouldn't like to hazard,' he said, and before Olivia had a chance to castigate, he plucked a sprig from her hair, examined it and then dropped it. He did not either permit her to provide her explanation that upon sighting the arrival of Cosmo and his parents she had stealthily skirted in the shadows and pushed through topiary toward Valentine for she considered him best qualified to dilute the terror.

'What do you suppose, mummy?' asked Valentine and he supped his Grasshopper.

'Oh, Valentine!' she exclaimed with exasperation, 'You know I loathe games!'

'Gosh! But it *is* a party!' he justified.

Olivia grabbed Valentine's wrist just as he was lifting his Grasshopper to his lips and caused a slight spillage.

'Gosh! Ouch!' said Valentine, for the fake diamond in the middle of the pretend Starfish – now twisted upside-down around Olivia's finger – did dig in rather fiercely.

'I am in no mood for nonsense, Valentino! You must tell me what to suppose!' she tried her very best not hiss at him.

'Gosh, mummy! It's only a game!' he said, reclaiming and rubbing his wrist, and he wondered what had hurt it quite so much, 'If you really want to know what to suppose then I shall tell you!'

'Please do!'

'Well, it's nothing really except that Cousin Cosmo, Uncle Quentin and Aunt Esmé have arrived,' he told her.

'Have they, darling?' Olivia replied, breezily.

'I know, mummy, it's not very exciting, in fact, I should say it borders on boring, and that is why I thought I'd brighten the dullness by making a game of it.'

'Well, darling, I suppose I needn't remind you that it was you that issued the stiffies.'

'You suppose right, mummy, I must admit it was not my most intelligent moment but I feel more than capable of ignoring them.'

'I wish I could, *dahling*!' said Flick, wiping away some fresh spirit from her chin, and she brandished her bottle before downing some more.

Olivia did not feel able to disregard the Oxley-Stockmans either. She was the Avery-Stripe matriarch, and must make Monty proud, moreover, there was the small matter of the stolen Starfish with which she must confront Cosmo. There was no hurry, however, and for the present she supposed that she could bring herself to suffer the fatuity of Valentine for at least his insouciance temporarily soothed her.

No sooner had she calmed herself with the notion of postponing a reunion with the relations, did she apprehend, with much irritation, that Brian was signalling their position to Cosmo by way of flourishing his white handkerchief.

Brian spun and swooped upon Valentine, used the same handkerchief to wipe the exhilaration from his brow, and said, 'My dear! The brute doth cometh hither!'

'Gosh! Brian!' withered Valentine with a tut, 'I wish you had not done that!' and he slugged at his Grasshopper.

Olivia was in accordance with Valentine's sentiment but suddenly the Oxley-Stockmans, accompanied, somewhat perfidiously, by Harry and Willy, were horribly close. Esmé blinked her tiny eyes twice, all but snuffled her button-mushroom snout, and in her voice that suggested several plums in her gob – albeit tinned and long past best before – she shouted, 'Olivi*ahh*!'

CHAPTER 15

The Oxley-Stockmans

Though no big fan of submitting oneself to drastic dental surgery purely in the name of vanity, Olivia believed that in Esmé's case it would not only be cosmetic but also a mercy. The black and jagged little teeth she had displayed when shouting were the stuff of nightmares. Nevertheless, Olivia, rose above the dental disaster – and that too of Esmé's shocking green sequined batwing frock that clashed so spectacularly with her elegant one of red – and in a gracious tone, she said, 'Esmé, darling! How lovely!'

Esmé managed to make the sound of a disgruntled sow.

'And Quentin too . . . hello!' Olivia went on, and received, from the human helix, a kiss so dreadfully wet that it shivered her spine, 'And Cosmo . . . how delightful! I'm so glad your face shows sign of improving! I simply cannot tell you how very happy I am that you have honoured the invitation with the same sense of propriety with which it was sent.'

Cosmo sneered and bowed to kiss the cheek his pater had not, and though this kiss was dry it was no more pleasant, for his nose was larger than it had previously been and it was an obstruction he had yet to learn to surmount.

'Gosh! I say, Cosmo!' said Valentine, upon seeing the uncomfortable kiss and surmising the reason, 'Your honker looks to be practically Wellingtonian!' and his giggle formed a ripple in the Grasshopper he raised to sip. His mirth was short-lived however, as Cosmo – not because he had the presence of mind to turn the other cheek, but because he had always admired Arthur Wellesley – said to him, 'Thank you, Cousin Valentine.'

'Gosh!' said Valentine, exhaling smoke, 'You're quite welcome, I'm certain,' and he managed to temper his vexation with the imagining of the swollen protuberance suffering the same fate as the one possessed by Lord Elgin, whereupon he felt able to face Esmé and in a high falsetto voice, say 'Hello, Aunt Esmé!'

Esmé did not like Valentine; never did and never would, she had thought him a queer little boy and the amplification of this quality in young adulthood caused her great offence.

She blinked her piggy eyes at Valentine, grimaced, and turned to Olivia,

'Traffic was diabolical! Thought we might not ever make it! Easy to forget the nightmare of London! And to have to journey to the suburbs makes it even more ghastly! Can't fathom how you can stick it here! If Monty could see you now he'd think you bananas!' With that, the top half of Esmé's head flipped open, and out came her laugh, 'Ah-h*ahhahhahh*!'

Quentin wrung his lengthy hands and stretched his ugly little gash of a mouth into a thin line to exhibit his appreciation of Esmé's extraordinarily good sense of humour. Conversely, he had about him an ingratiating streak and in defence of his cousin he said, in his hiss, 'Esmé, you are so naughty! And so silly not to remember that Monty's rusticity was simply a pose; it never really suited him, and it never convinced, he was a city boy at heart, but I'm certain he would love to see the festivities the Avery-Stripes have managed to assemble for Cornelius!' Whereupon, he stretched out one long arm and performed an encompassing wave over the festivities that Esmé viewed as if she had not been cognisant of it upon their arrival, and granted it a *grunt*.

Olivia could not even begin to count the very many ways in which Esmé and Quentin so succinctly jarred her deep-seated desire for decorum. She realised that her welcome had been solar systems from sincere but sincerity was not the issue, nor even a necessitation, no, all she deemed necessary was basic etiquette, yet these two seemed to possess little to none, and what was more, appeared to revel in creating an exhibition of this sorry lack.

'Oh, darlings!' she said to them, 'I cannot tell you how it warms my heart to hear such generous reminiscences of Monty from old *acquaintances*. You are accurate, Quentin; it was a pose, or to be more precise, a labour of love, for Monty strongly believed no place better than the country for bringing up small children, and readily forsook his own preferences so that they might have bucolic beginnings. I need not tell either of you just how important family was to him. But the funny thing is he practically revelled in rurality after a while, so you are correct, Esmé, he might well think me to be 'bananas' to return to the city were it not for Bartholomew because Monty most certainly would wish the children to have a paternal figure of consequence.'

Olivia presented Quentin a crocodile smile. Then, over and above his hunch, she viewed Cosmo, and his grimace provoked her to persist with the assault. 'And these stones! What splendid specimens!' she said of Esmé's emeralds and she curved her hands around Esmé's bulging throat as if about to commit strangulation. 'I do envy you! Where ever did you get them?' she asked, knowing full well that they had once adorned the vulturine neck of the decrepit Ursie Oxley-Stockman, except on her the earrings had not stretched her lobes like plasticine and the necklace had not resembled a garrotte.

Esmé was mildly appeased and shouted, 'Yes, I'm rather proud of them! They belonged to Quentin's mater, and perhaps I ought not to say it, but I do think they suit me better then they ever did her!'

'Well, they certainly are excellent emeralds. Such stunners they are, Esmé darling, and what a boon to have a husband whose mother could bequeath upon you so many marvellous minerals! As you well know, both Monty and I always admired your particularly ravishing ring of rocks, I forget its name now, was it Jellyfish?'

Esmé so puckered her face with resentment that it seemed to retract into her head as if by some internal force of suction. Olivia had touched upon an extremely raw nerve. For though Esmé talked less of the loss than when first she had been aware of it, she still on occasion exploded with an anger which even the dismissal of two long-serving domestics she suspected of theft had not lessened.

Keen to pacify his wife, Quentin made the grand effort of patting her on the shoulder with the tips of his fingers and he emitted a drawn-out noise similar to a creak of a coffin lid.

'Darling, I am sorry, how silly of me! It is, of course, *Starfish*!' said Olivia, 'So beautiful! I should so love to see it again someday soon!' and she felt over the moon for not only had she managed to cause Esmé upset she had also derived from her reaction that if Cosmo had retrieved the ring at least he had not returned it to her.

Looking and feeling as uncomfortable as if any boy could possibly be, Cosmo scrabbled for a diversion, and unable to think of one better, he boomed, 'Rupert! I say, Rupert old chum! Bloody brilliant to see you!' And he pulled Rupert into a hearty hold before stepping back to survey how much his appearance had changed during his time of separation. 'You look bloody brilliant, old chum, old pal, old buddy!' then served him a hefty whack on the back to prove their masculine and platonic relationship.

Rupert was amazed by the embrace, yet being of a naturally amicable disposition, he smiled, 'Crikey, Cosmo, how are you? I'm glad your bruising's gone down.'

Cosmo sneered. The double-dealer was mocking him, taking glory in the damage he had caused purely to defend pansy ways, why it made him feel sick! Still, it was of little significance, the important thing had been to distract his mater's mind from the matter of the missing Starfish, and he had succeeded.

'What! Rupert here?' Esmé shouted as she rotated her entire mass on her nimble legs, for the solidity of her thick neck did not permit her head to turn independently.

Upon regarding her son's beautiful friend, her little mind filled with bewilderment, and so too did the shrunken skull of Quentin. Neither of them knew of any social connexion between the appealing Rupert Bringsley-Beer and the Avery-Stripes, except through Cosmo.

'I say, if it isn't young Rupert! What on earth brings you here?' said Quentin and he tilted his head on one side as if the process might provide the answer.

Before Rupert had a chance to answer, Esmé believed she had joined the dots and discovered the explanation, 'Of course! You are a chum of Harry! You were all in St. Moritz before Christmas!' and she champed her teeth with the pleasure she derived from her deduction.

'No, Auntie Esmé, I didn't go on the *Cwesta Wun twip*,' Harry interjected, 'I was saving money for my *twek* in the Himalayas.'

'Himalayas!' Esmé shouted, 'Hogwash, Harry! You were in St. Moritz! I distinctly remember Cosmo telling me!' for she refused to be contradicted, 'Did you not, Cosmo?'

Cosmo's grin had frozen, he was reluctant to disagree with his mater but he was in no position to avoid it, 'No, mater, I did not; Harry didn't come, only Rupert, Piers, and Garth.'

The vision of the Oxley-Stockmans besetting Rupert was not one that suited Valentine very much, most markedly the detail of Cosmo's hand upon Rupert's shoulder. Therefore, entrusting his Grasshopper to Harry, Valentine brushed away Cosmo's hand, viewed down his nose the horrid aspects of Esmé and Quentin, and said to them, 'Rupert is with *me*.'

'You?' exclaimed the pair.

'Indubitably!' answered Valentine, and after reclaiming the Grasshopper, he lifted his hand that was neatly inside of Rupert's to display that they were so conjoined, 'And I, very much, with *he*.'

Both Esmé and Quentin looked stunned for the plain and simple reason that they were. Their world suddenly seemed quite different from the one they had inhabited hitherto – as if in a blink of an eye cataclysm had struck and sent their diminutive minds reeling.

First to recover was Esmé, and though she found the notion of Rupert possessing such an affinity implausible she had to admit that Valentine's claim looked very much true. He and Rupert were more than holding hands, they also beheld each other's full concentration and were gazing at each other like love's young dream.

With great effort, she managed to retain all food matter in her gut to shout her disapproval, 'I have always suspected you to be a pansy, Valentine, and have always considered it tragic, but to learn that you actually practice your deviance is a ghastly embarrassment to the family!'

Presently, Flick, having heard quite enough of her mater's small minded-ness, stumbled out from behind Rupert, clutching the neck of her nearly empty bottle, and in a surprisingly sober-sounding voice, said, 'Mater! Next you will be saying you have always suspected the world to be round! *You* are the embarrassment! And to say that Valentine is practicing is preposterous! Everybody can see that he is already perfect!'

Here, Valentine and Rupert sandwiched her and they all felt as if in a lovely tin of sardines.

'Felicity!' exclaimed Quentin, with shock at her sudden emergence and backchat, 'Such sass and disrespect I cannot disregard!'

'That's not my name, pater!' called out Flick.

'Felicity?' asked Esmé, looking all about; she refused to acknowledge Flick's presence, not just at the party but in general, for not only was she disapproving of Valentine's predilections, Flick's manner of living dis-enchanted her also. Her feeling was such that on many occasion she had entreated Quentin to cease Flick's allowance, but though more often than not he kowtowed to Esmé's demands, in this instance he would stand firm and merely halved it.

'Felicity? Felicity? I see no sign of the girl, is she here?' said Esmé, as she performed the charade of trying to recognise her daughter's face in those of strangers.

Cognisant that she was in no position to preach the merit of maternal affection, Olivia still felt antipathy toward Esmé and her disregard of her own flesh and blood. Admittedly, she herself often struggled with negative thoughts over her four offspring and many a month might pass when she might not see even one of them, but never would she deny them! The very idea of it shamed her! However, upon reflection, she surmised that Esmé's behaviour was no surprise, for had not Fortunata – matriarch of the Oxley-Stockman branch – disavowed the original Avery-Stripes, and Esmé most certainly adhered to the tradition. This exhibited to Olivia a distinct lack of loyalty and to her mind this deficit was despicable because loyalty was a quality she revered above all others. To consider that this creature devoid of such a trait had moments ago reproached Valentine and accused him of bringing embarrassment to the family filled Olivia with so great a rage she was unable to hold her tongue.

'Esmé, darling,' she said, but Esmé did not hear for she was too busy appearing discombobulated over the mention of Flick.

'Esmé!' Olivia reiterated with surmounting annoyance and grabbed one of the woman's beefy arms.

Subject to the unexpectedly strong grip and victim to Olivia's claws, Esmé was unable to persist with her sham; she yanked free her limb, regarded her assailant with irritation, and shouted, 'What, Olivi*ahh*?'

'Esmé, darling, I am certain that somewhere in the recesses of your heart you shall hit upon a hint of maternal empathy and therefore bring yourself to understand that as a mother I cannot allow you to speak to my son in such a manner. The way Valentine chooses to exist and with whom is entirely natural and in no way tragic or deviant. It is the way of the world and nothing to create the emotion of embarrassment in anyone other than a person possessed of marked puerility, and though I am aware that the provinces are bursting with bigoted bumpkins I am scandalised to consider that you may be one of them.

'Further, I feel certain that if you were to classify one of my children having formed a union with a boy as charming, as I realise you know Rupert to be, as *ghastly*, then you would be hard-pressed to convince any person of any sense of your sanity. Moreover, you speak of the family as if you were part of ours, and to my knowledge, you are not, never have been, and never shall be, anything even resembling an Avery-Stripe!'

Esmé was outraged to the core. She somehow inflated her upper body, and shouted, 'Most certainly I am not an Avery-Stripe, I am an Oxley-Stockman! And in my opinion the family tree that binds us ought to be pared down!'

'Oh! I beg of you!' cried Olivia, tossing her hair over her shoulder and lowering her face on a level with her stout opponent, 'Bring me an axe so I might strike the first blow!'

Both ladies were momentarily speechless as they struggled to be next to locate the harshest words with which to wound. However, the interception of Willy brought the tumult to halt. She could not bear to see her mother wrangle with the mater of her beloved, for its escalation may well conclude in the catastrophe of her fondest dreams. Therefore, mustering her pluck, she approached her aunt and, as sweetly as possible, fearfully said, 'Look,

Auntie Esmé, that table is free, let's please sit down, you must be awfully tired after the terrible journey!' and successfully she manoeuvred her.

Though irked not to have tasted blood, Olivia was quelled by Esmé's obvious relief. Her pleasure doubled with the disobedience of Quentin who ignored Esmé's instruction to sit because he wished to greet Bartholomew for whom he had a foolish proposition.

The altercation had provoked the pumping of Olivia's adrenalin, and finding herself mercifully devoid of any person's attention for a space, she un-snapped her clutch to procure a cigarette. In the midst of her procurement, her serenity ceased when, again, she played victim to a vulgar whisper, and on this occasion, the culprit was Cosmo.

'What a corking little scrapper you are, Auntie O!' he said in his lowest bass, and he made at her the sort of face she considered in serious need of a smack.

'Oh, it's you,' said Olivia in a tart tone, 'I'm surprised you possess the nerve to approach me after bombarding us with that woman that is your abysmal mater.' and she snapped shut her clutch with a curt *click*.

Cosmo pouted, 'But Auntie O, you were pretty bloody abysmal too, I'd say more so; mater didn't stand a bloody chance! And though I'm all for girls scrapping there comes a time when girls ought to grow old gracefully.'

Stepping back to cast her eyes over Cosmo, Olivia appeared full of deep thought for a flash. She then gave the impression it was futile and brought herself close again.

'Really, darling, in my attempt to imagine what conceivable comprehension a below average blip of a boy might have garnered of girls, I find myself hovering hazardously close to the misfortune of a migraine.'

Cosmo felt humiliated. Again, he considered the possibility of his deficiency in the department of pants, and he began to think that when next in the rugby showers discrete glances would be necessary to determine how he measured up.

Gauging Cosmo's uncomfortable thoughts, Olivia liberated a tinkle of laughter. The release gave him cause to scowl, though it vanquished upon her request that he see if he might be very clever and find a flame for she was well due a smoke.

Cosmo's show of whacking his hands over each of his pockets in search of a light seemed to Olivia lamentably lewd. She wondered if it was intentional, and considered the very idea of his performing what he might perceive an exhibition of eroticism, especially to the overture of *William Tell*, to be laughable. She managed to restrain herself however for it was no time for mirth, indeed it was one ripe for gravity, for the moment had come for her to reveal Cosmo's criminality.

After much self-flagellation, Cosmo realised that he was without a lighter and it rankled him for he would need one later in private. He cursed and turned to seek a source – he did not want to be so incompetent that he could not even light a cigarette!

A moment later, he returned with a lighter made of plastic, and with his thumb, he made it flick a flame.

'Well done, darling,' Olivia said and kept her eyes on his as, slowly, she raised her hand, which held the cigarette, and wore the now right-side-up faux Starfish.

Cosmo registered no recognition and purely looked inordinately pleased with his ability to produce fire.

Therefore, ignoring the lavender twists that expelled from her flared nostrils, Olivia pumped her suction to tease the flame. The process illumined the sparkle of stones so spectacularly that she quite saw their reflection in Cosmo's eyes widened in horror.

Yet, Olivia did not interpret his augmented eyes to indicate horror but simply his astonishment at seeing the Starfish which he knew to be fake because he had reclaimed the authentic, and was incredulous of her ridiculousness therefore would at any second laugh and confess his crime, whereupon she had him trapped and thus, would make him pay.

Regrettably, Olivia was about to discover that her hours of ingenious contriving had been a monumental waste of time.

'You bloody fool!' Cosmo boomed.

He threw the lighter to the lawn, grabbed her wrist, and yanked it down. He looked about to determine if he had attracted attention.

Satisfied that he had not, he turned to Olivia and in a hushed tone, repeated, 'You bloody fool! What on earth do you think you are doing wearing that right under my mater's nose! Why if she saw it she'd string you up by your toes and have my guts for garters!'

Quite in shock, Olivia was without verbal ability and wished to shriek for his grip created an intense pain – only her prevalent desire to preserve her dignity prevented her from doing so.

She clenched her teeth, and hissed, 'Release me this instant!'

'Only after you remove the ring!' was the snarling response.

Cosmo held Olivia's wrist at such an awkward angle that even if she felt so inclined she could not have obeyed his order without the risk of dislocation.

'I shall remove the ring when you do as I say!' she spat, 'Or perhaps you might prefer one of the hundred odd people present to espy our predicament? For I assure you I shall delegate the delivery of an explanation to you!'

Realising that they were indeed surrounded by a great number, any one of which might suddenly sight their situation, Cosmo relinquished his grip and hoped that his aunt would be sensible. The ecstasy that came with the release from Cosmo's iron grip almost caused Olivia to vomit, but this was not something she would allow, and she wished simply to cap his knees.

She twisted, with her left fist, the skin about her right wrist in order to soothe it, and said, 'Are you totally without restraint or reason? You quite easily could have snapped my arm! And how would that have made you feel? Like a big powerful man, *hmm*? Barbaric little bully! '

'Just take my bloody mater's bloody Starfish off, you bloody stupid woman!' Cosmo growled at her, and cupping a hand over her exposed shoulder he squeezed with a degree of pressure to suggest that if he so chose he could easily crush it.

Momentarily, Olivia stood rooted with incredulity, for though Cosmo's new clench was less than pleasant it felt nothing worse than the caress of a lover for he had enlightened her to a disclosure of distressing magnitude.

Olivia calculated that even if Cosmo's undersized cranium had been packed with grey-matter he would still lack the proficiency to stage such a performance merely to cover his tracks. No, his reaction to the ring was genuine, his shock sincere! He truly believed that she wore the original, and her audacity to do so in the presence of his parents provoked in him an eruption of upset panic and had taken the form of brutality. As plain as the broken nose on his face, it was patent to see that Cosmo most categorically had *not* stolen the Starfish!

'All right, darling, all right!' Olivia said in the tranquil tone she had managed to summon, 'I was simply teasing.'

She removed the ring, deposited it in her clutch, snapped it shut and smiled at him as he released her from his simian grip.

'Please do try to wipe the worry from your face, darling,' she said, 'the wrinkles will come soon enough as it is, and anyway I was quite convinced you would be glad to see the Starfish. I distinctly remember during our last tête-à-tête your entreaty that I treasure it and I merely desired to display to you my outrageous honour to own it.'

Cosmo sneered so hard that it looked close to splitting his lip.

'I am sorry that it transpired to ignite your dynamitic temper, darling,' she went on, 'sincerely I am, but you must realise it practically impossible to permanently pander to a person possessed of such a preposterously piddling wick!'

With that, she pivoted and slinked into the crowd. She was unsure of her destination only that it was away from Cosmo. The carousal surrounding her was a colourful blur of blazing lights and grotesque faces distorted with ribaldry merging into one mass as each produced its own particular brand of badinage. Through it, she advanced to the unoccupied drawing room where she stood at the Steinway and gazed, with consternation, at the portrait of her great grandfather-in-law.

'Where is it, Excelsior?' she telepathically asked him, 'Tell me where it is! If anyone is aware of the ring's location, then, darling, it is you! For the sake of Monty and his children, please tell me so that I may return the Starfish to the Avery-Stripes!'

It was to no avail; Excelsior would not furnish her with enlightenment. Instead, he leered hubristically down at her.

Olivia looked about the vacated room and experienced a torrid flash of fever. She felt weary and despondent, yet simultaneously alive, as if she harboured a small fire that manufactured a fearsome heat that consumed her and created a sense of ominous nausea, and she was certain that the sensation was the result of the mystery of the Starfish.

Possessing no idea how best she might proceed, she desired nothing more than to retire and chase dreams of Monty in their four-poster. However, upon eyeing the ormolu clock, she surmised that even if it was not quite accurate, it was still much too early to abandon her guests – for no matter how indecorous some of them may be she was the cream to their dregs, and should endeavour to raise the tone.

Therefore, she essentially accosted a waiter and hastily imbibed two flutes of champagne, and affecting a visage of *noblesse oblige* she returned to the party with a plan to have Hugo fawn.

Olivia's parting comment regarding Cosmo's 'piddling wick' had served to him a figurative kick to his vitals, for though she was not fully aware of it being so sensitive a point, it most certainly seemed to him that she knew all too well. It stunned him senseless for a space and by the time he regained his grip she had disappeared. He was not sure what he would have said to her in any case, and though hugely relieved that she had secreted the Starfish before his parents had noticed it, his apoplexy was insurmountable.

Uncertain how to contain his anger, he made a brusque about turn to see upon whom it might be unleashed, and consequently had squashed into his furious face the surprise of confectionery.

'Oh! My absolute dear! What a mess! What an *Eton* mess!' exclaimed Brian Pavilion who endured great pain to restrain a tickled smile. 'What a mess of Martha's meringues! If only she knew of the happy fate of one her splendid creations! Oh, jammy meringue!'

Obviously, Cosmo was not exactly enchanted to be creamed in the face by the antiquated fairy. He wanted to roar, he wanted to push his thumbs into Brian's jugular and watch him flap and flail until he could no more. He wished also to do the same to Valentine, who stood aside, employing no effort whatsoever to mask his amusement, nor either did Flick, and this pushed Cosmo's mercury further. With them was Rupert, and though his presence did little to simmer Cosmo's temper, it did inhibit him from carrying out a violent demonstration.

Brian whipped out his handkerchief and made to undertake the task of tidying Cosmo's face but Cosmo would not have it – who knew what bacteria the handkerchief might carry!

'As there were a limited number of messes, I rushed over to ensure that you have one of them,' Brian went on, 'and then, my dear, disaster! I am so dreadfully sorry, my dear!'

Cosmo collected the cream from his face with his vast palms and wiped them on his flanks. He felt sullied by Brian. He glowered at him, and could not prevent himself from rather too loudly growling a word one might also use to describe a bundle of sticks meant for fuel.

With chagrin, Rupert regarded Cosmo who suddenly seemed somewhat sheepish and obviously feared a second sock. However, superhumanly suppressing his urge to issue such a rejoinder, Rupert proudly asked Valentine if he should like to dance.

'Gosh! Should I like to?' exclaimed Valentine, 'I should positively love to!'

Thereupon, the Grasshopper escaped Valentine's grip as Rupert masterfully transposed their situation to the dance floor to elaborately sweep and spin him off his feet to Khachaturian's melodramatic *Masquerade waltz*.

Cosmo considered the dancing pansies an improper spectacle and he scowled but Flick interrupted his thoughts.

'Golly! What a beastly bounder you are!' she said, and then seized Brian who was giggling, though only to hide his horror at Cosmo's vocabulary, and together they swaggered to the dance floor.

'Who does she bloody think she is?' Cosmo wondered of Flick, 'She's the bloody black sheep!' and he grimaced as he watched her make a fool of herself with Brian as they cavorted to the octet's strain.

Presently, Cosmo deemed the idea of dancing not a completely bad one, for suddenly he spied an identical pair of girls. He had not noticed them before, and the brevity of their skirts and their chemically treated hair signalled to him their possession of little to no virtue. He focused his attention and reached the conclusion that though they were far from stunning neither were they absolute hounds, and when he received from them matching and inviting smiles, he made his way over, carrying with him a stirring in his loins.

A moment later, Willy appeared on the spot upon which Cosmo had just stood. She had escaped the hard labour of listening to Esmé's scathing critique of the party and left her with Rowena Whitaker, whose aggressive dullness was just deserts.

Willy had wanted to ask her aunt why she wished to stay at a party that she considered so dire, but gathering from allusions, she surmised her uncle to be endeavouring upon a mission involving Gubsy. Willy could not think what it might be, and neither much caring nor needing to know, she did not question it. All she cared about was Cosmo, and pondered where he was. Therefore, directly fleeing Esmé, she pressed through the crush in order to locate him as quickly as was possible.

It was the shine of the moon upon his scalp that told her of his situation, and hurriedly pushing a path toward him she became mindful of her carriage, rubbed her magic flower under her nosegay, and staged her face with the mantra, '*I possess something glorious that everybody desires . . .* '

Yet, too late! Exactly as she arrived at the desired location, it was in time to see Cosmo entwine the tawdry twins in order to escort them to the dance floor.

Willy's world fell apart. She wanted to cry, she wanted to dig a hole in the ground and scream into it, she wanted to curl up and die! It was then, however, that she caught sight of the family flag, and its adage not to ever despair, whereupon she determined not to cry, scream, or curl up and die, and considered the disposal of her rivals a better solution but was unsure how to achieve it.

She thought of Valentine immediately, but upon viewing his whirling with Rupert that she dare not intercept, she thought of her mother.

Casting her eyes about, Willy soon found her, draped over Gubsy's wing chair, necking flutes, blowing smoke rings, and paying no mind to Hugo Pargeter's dogged cajolery.

'Mummy!' said Willy.

'*Hmm*? Oh, hello, darling, sorry, I was quite worlds away. Oh, hello, Hugo, you here too?' said Olivia, and she smiled at the exhausted lothario, 'I was just enjoying watching our two boys dominate so delightfully the dance floor, do they not look to be divine?'

The two boys to whom Olivia referred were, of course, Valentine and Rupert, and though their dancing was not exactly delightful (as it was far too elaborate for such a sedate word) it was indeed dominating because Rupert's baroque handling of Valentine was so munificent that the others upon the floor had no choice but to make way.

'Yes, mummy,' agreed Willy, though she thought the boys rather too acrobatic, 'they do look to be divine, but isn't it a shame about the others?'

Olivia threw her a questioning glance, therefore Willy particularised: 'I just think that Cosmo really ought not to dance with two, don't you think someone should intervene?'

'Oh, darling,' replied Olivia, viewing the surprising survival of the twins twirling beneath Cosmo's arms, 'I shouldn't worry; I'm quite certain the threesome shan't prevail.' And upon seeing one of the girls clutch her tummy, she estimated their departure to be imminent. 'Anyway, darling, what happened to Giles, and, moreover, where is Harry?'

'Oh . . . I . . . ' faltered Willy, for she could not account for the fate of Giles, whom she had so rudely abandoned, without sounding to be vastly unlike a lady.

Fortunately, Gretchen arrived with an interjection to fish Willy out of the soup.

'I would like to know also where is Master Harry; soon is eleven o'clock – cake time – and all children should be in karden.'

The family had agreed that the cake's presentation should be at the precise time of Corny's birth; 11.06 post meridian.

Olivia's sigh of exasperation created a large cloud of smoke.

Irritably, she said, 'I cannot be expected to perform the role of both hostess and nursery maid, therefore I suggest that somebody else put themselves to good use and hurriedly hunt down Horatio if birthday cake so looms upon the horizon!'

Suddenly, a trio of Babbingtons pushed past, with hirsute Sophie ushering her wanton twins before her, both looking to be in a severe amount of intestinal unease. The three of them rushed into Chinchero only to exit it at the front door and run down the red carpet toward their own toilets.

Their coerced departure was opportune for it momentarily greatly lessened Olivia's irritation, and quite to the mystification of Willy, Gretchen and Hugo, the success of her secret scheme caused her to laugh unrestrainedly.

CHAPTER 16

A Most Enchanting Discovery

The mounting hostility between his family and the Oxley-Stockmans made Harry feel awkward and produced in him a desire to disappear before the situation worsened. He was glad when Corny came to his rescue.

Corny grinned up at him; his eyes spinning, as he tugged the coat-tail of his big brother whom he wanted to come and play. Harry suffered no dilemma whether he might prefer to party with Corny or endure familial discord, therefore, directly returning to Valentine his Grasshopper, he slipped away.

Pushing through the partiers, Harry paused to watch, with pride, how pleased Corny was with the water-resistant watch whose endurance he demonstrated again with several lunges in the pond. Consequently, they leapt over the pond and squeezed between gazebo and topiary – snagging their finery on the rosebushes – ending their journey in the haven beneath the pergola.

Inside were Corny's people, dashing helter-skelter, and Gloriana sat precariously upon the loveseat. Harry considered it a shame that they felt the need to segregate themselves from the grown-ups, but could quite understand, and besides, they looked to be enjoying superior fun in their hideaway. Promptly, he joined in and chased them, ran with them, let them overpower him and pull him to the floor to tickle him until he could bear it no more. He rose with a struggle, and celebrated his victory by dangling Corny upside-down.

Corny enjoyed this immensely and, in this instance, more so than usual for he liked his friends to see the excellent big brother he had. Inevitably, he wished Harry to turn each of his friends topsy-turvy too.

Harry complied, and, one by one, held each of them the wrong way up; they all thought it wildly funny and laughed silently. Then came the turn of little Petal but she did not want to be turned on her head; not just because she was worried that her knickers would show but also it seemed to her too fearsome. Therefore, Harry tucked his hands under her arms and lifted her as high as was possible without pushing her head through the vegetational ceiling. Petal wriggled a little and liked a lot to view her friends from such a height, but quickly signalled her yearn to return to planet earth with a gentle kicking.

Harry was pleased to see the happiness he could create, but upon settling Petal down he realised that his shirtfront was wet with the sweat produced from the horseplay, and though the evening was balmy it was not so warm as to render the dampness pleasant – he would have to find a fresh one to wear.

Once he had stationed Gloriana safely on the bedside table in Corny's impressively tidy bedroom, Harry went into his own which was not so tidy. In his wardrobe, he found a fresh shirt which, although not exactly a dress shirt and not devoid of creases, was white and it was clean, moreover it was dry, and quickly he changed into it.

He then remembered he was unable to knot his bowtie, for he was all fingers and thumbs and he kept tying them up in the process. Valentine had knotted it for him earlier, and realising he needed again his or some other nimble-fingered person's assistance, Harry made his away across the landing to descend the stairwell. Before the harp, he noticed that the doors to the west terrace were open, and upon investigating the reason, he made a most enchanting discovery, for amongst the wisteria was a girl whose pose was such that he was unable to view her face yet her shapely nape, bathed in moonlight, told him that she and he had yet to interact for the very first time.

He wondered, as he watched with mild amusement, why she chose not to join the party and to instead hide and peep through vines at the revelry below. Slowly, she inched about as if trying to locate a better point of vantage and in so doing, her naked shoulders oscillated with an alluring fluidity that captivated Harry.

Stepping out onto the terrace, he purposely let his foot tread with a degree of definiteness with the aim to alert her to his presence; however, she did not hear it. Undeterred, he paced about a bit, but still she did not react, therefore, he summoned all his derring-do, and travelled three generous steps forward placing him in a position so near to her she could not fail to realise his existence – yet still she was unaware.

Harry marvelled at how close by he was without attracting her attention and then because his invisibility allowed it, he began to appreciate her sweet countenance presented in profile as if a cameo.

Again, he admired the contour of her neck; graceful as a swan's, and exposed for she had coiled her light gold hair into a loose French roll, liberated strands of which strayed in spirals to frame her face. Her skin was translucent, and the whites of her wide blue eyes exquisitely clear and gave to her the appearance of a little girl lost, which even her seemingly affronted tip-tilted nose could not counter. He considered her cheeks to be the colour of the palest pink flowers, and decided her chin, though inarguably weak, indicated a calming disposition. In fact, her entire delicate stature did, and he felt very much that he should like to kiss her upon her Cupid's bow lips, but possessing neither the nerve nor presumption, what he bestowed upon her was a shock of fright when he said, 'Hullo there.'

The start gave the girl cause to gasp and rip leaves from vines between her slender fingers as she flinched, and immediately, Harry was ashamed of his inadvertent surreptitiousness.

'So*ww*y, so*ww*y! I didn't mean to scare you!'

Slowly, she shook her head to signal that he had done no such thing but her large watery eyes and absence of words said otherwise. This dearth had Harry wonder if she might be one of Corny's friends although she was quite easily ten years his senior, and Harry's feeling of guilt heightened. He gently placed a hand upon the pearl whiteness of her shoulder, which was silky smooth to his touch, and led her to the bench.

'Please, sit down, I *w*eally am most d*w*eadfully so*ww*y.'

And once they were seated he decided to brave it and ascertain her powers of speech.

'Can you tell me your name?' he asked.

For a space, she appeared confused by the question and seemed to have trouble in breathing, but just as Harry began to worry, she calmed, and in the sweetest tone he thought he had ever heard, she said, 'I*th*y.'

He looked at his enchanting discovery, and though pleased she possessed vocabulary, he considered it perhaps somewhat limited for 'ithy' was not a name or a word and sounded to be simply a sound, thus, at the risk of appearing rude, he repeated, 'Ithy?'

Colour swept into the girl's cheeks, and with her pristine teeth, she bit her plump lower lip.

'I'm *th*orry, I have a mo*th*t terrible li*th*p,' she said, and consequently undertook to speak her name in a way in which he might understand by saying, 'I*ff*y,' and 'I*vv*y.'

'Oh!' said Harry, with a laugh for he now knew her name: 'Izzy!'

'Ye*th*, I*th*y,' and she blushed more furiously, and said, 'I'm *th*orry I can't even *th*ay my own name without *th*ounding *th*illy.'

Presently, Harry's smile disappeared for he felt wretched with the idea that she might think him to be laughing at her, and he did not hesitate in a rectification.

'Well, you mustn't think that; I've got my speech impediment too.'

'You do?' she asked, and looked at him with surprise.

Harry mirrored her look for he could not quite believe that she had not noticed.

He promoted their proximity, and whispered, '*W*ound and *w*ound the *w*ugged *w*ock the *w*agged *w*ascal *w*an!'

Izzy suddenly smiled at him, at his disclosure and their connexion, she heightened their intimacy, and replied, '*Th*he *th*ell*th* *th*eath*h*ell*th* on the *th*eath*h*ore!'

Harry felt struck by the realisation that the many times girls had insisted his rhotacism was attractive were genuine, hitherto he could not consider it possible, but listening to Izzy's engaging lisp his heart was wide open to the notion.

Naturally, the attraction lay in far more than just her lisp, of course, he had yet to get to know her, but what he saw appealed to him greatly. Her aura of gentle innocence seemed, to him, to counteract all of the dissension in his world, and he desired nothing more than to lie with her and soak up her antidote to the poisons created by inharmonious people.

He then noticed that she looked at him expectantly, and he remembered his manners.

'So*ww*y, *w*eally *w*ude of me! I'm Ha*ww*y. I can't *w*eally say my own name either!'

'Oh dear!' said Izzy with a smile.

'Why "Oh dear?" ' he wanted to know; he had not said 'oh dear' to her 'ithy'.

'Well, you have it wor*th* than me; if you are Harry Avery-*Th*tripe!' she said, in a playful tone.

Her impishness tickled him.

'*W*eally, I do!' he laughed, ' "How do you do? My name is Ha*ww*y Ave*w*y-St*w*ipe."! But how did you know I'm Ave*w*y-St*w*ipe?'

'Well,' she started to explain, 'thi*th* i*th* a birthday party for Valentine'*th* brother Corny. And Rupert did tell me they have another brother called Harry, *th*o really I am pre*th*uming that'*th* who you are!' and she looked to consider her powers of deduction to be incredible.

It took Harry a few moments to unravel the tangle of confusion in his mind, however he eventually managed it and discerned that enchanting Izzy was the cousin of Rupert who had warned that she might be too shy to attend. Harry was glad to see that she had not surrendered to such feelings of timidity, not completely at any rate; she was hiding herself away after all, but if that meant he had her for himself, he did not think it a shame as he would like to keep her for his very own.

Yet, he could not gauge whether she might feel an urge to reciprocate his yearnings for she simply sat and regarded him as if waiting for what he might next say or do. Quickly, he scrambled for words, and said, 'Yes, that *w*eally is who I am! And I think I know who you are too!'

Izzy giggled, and asked, 'Who am I?'

The giggle delighted him, and, smilingly, he told her, 'I should say that you are the cousin of *W*upert! And that would make me say 'Oh dear' too, because there is an S in B*w*ingsley-Beer, so you have almost as much t*w*ouble as I do!'

Harry felt very clever and wished to claim a kiss as a reward but she thwarted his triumph with an uncontrollable fit of giggles.

'No! My name i*th* not Bring*th*ley-Beer! It i*th* Merryweather-Vane! And there i*th* not a *th*ingle letter e*th* in that! *Th*o there! *Th*illy *th*au*th*age!'

Her victory over the handsome boy induced her to clap with delight.

Harry did indeed feel himself to be a silly sausage but he did not mind so long as his silly sausageness could cause her such pleasure.

'But you are right,' she admitted, 'Rupert i*th* my cou*th*in, maternal cou*th*in, *th*o that'*th* why we have different name*th*.'

Pleased to be half-right, Harry said, 'You *w*eally have a lovely name, Izzy Me*ww*yweather-Vane, I love it!'

'Thank you,' she said with a blush, 'I like your*th* too, Harry Avery-*Th*tripe.'

Whereupon the verbally hindered pair regarded each other with feelings of affection that neither of them cared to conceal.

For a moment, Harry toyed with the idea of drawing her face close to his so that they might kiss but as forthrightness was not a natural component of his psychological make-up he instead, in an uncomfortably affable tone, said, '*W*upert is tops! I mean he is an absolute b*w*ick! You should have seen Chinche*w*o two weeks ago, he has t*w*ansformed it d*w*amatically!'

'Oh! He i*th*!!' she agreed enthusiastically, 'He i*th* *th*o good at fixing thing*th*! And he love*th* it here too! When he called me, he talked almo*th*t non-*th*top about Valentine! I *th*uppose I really ought to meet him but I'm a little bit *th*y to go down*th*tair*th*. When I arrived the front door wa*th* open *th*o I ju*th*t walked in*th*ide, but when I *th*aw *th*o many people out*th*ide

I felt *th*y, *th*o I quickly ran up the *th*tair*th* and when I *th*aw out here, with all the beautiful wi*th*teria, I con*th*idered it a good pla*th*e to *th*ummon my courage!'

She paused for a space and tried to prevent her face from reddening but it was of little use and Harry thought the dappling of her flower-like cheeks to be charming.

'And that'*th* when you found me! I hadn't been here very long and wa*th* ju*th*t taking a *th*neaky peek through the vine*th*, and I *th*ay, i*th* that your brother Valentine that I *th*aw Rupert dan*th*ing *th*o wonderfully with?'

Harry was dumbfounded. Izzy's childlike candidness seemed to him as sweet as the first chirrup of birdsong at dawn, and he felt almost without the ability to do anything other than regard her in rapt adoration.

Somehow, though somewhat in a trance, he answered, 'P*w*obably . . . yes, it p*w*obably is my b*w*other *W*upert is dancing with; they are p*w*actically insepe*w*able.'

'Oh! I ju*th*t knew it wa*th*!' she joyfully exclaimed and again clapped, 'Oh! They do dan*th* together *th*o *th*plendidly and look to be *th*o happy! I really *th*ould go down and *th*ay hello and I think with you with me I would not feel to be at all *th*y!'

'You want to go down to the garden?' asked Harry with disappointment, because though he was thrilled to learn that Izzy would derive confidence from his presence, he still very much wished to stay situated in seclusion just as they were.

'Don't you think we *th*ould?' she replied, and knitted her delicate blond brow.

Harry could not bear to see her look so disquieted.

'Yes, of course!' he said as he rose and steeled himself, 'And I'd be ve*w*y p*w*oud to escort you and int*w*oduce you to ev*w*ybody!'

Izzy seemed to fill with rapture and gazed up at him in such a way that led him to think himself a very fine and noble man.

'Oh! You are *th*o *th*weet!' she exclaimed, and rose also but being a good head and shoulders shorter than him she still had to raise her face and she all but glowed in the light of the platinum moon.

'*W*eally, it would be my pleasure!' said Harry.

'I'm *th*o plea*th*ed! I'm much too nervou*th* to do it all alone!' she said, 'But let me fix your tie for you fir*th*t.'

Izzy applied her dainty fingers to the bowtie Harry had forgotten entirely, and knotted it beautifully.

'Perfect!' she said.

Presently, Gretchen appeared, 'Master Harry! All over I have been lookink for you!'

'Cwumbs! Sowwy, Gwetchen, I didn't wealise!' said Harry, hating to avert his attention from Izzy but being well-bred enough to always look in the eye whom he addressed.

'Is okay, Master Harry,' said Gretchen, suddenly realising her inopportunity and feeling somewhat guilty for her favourite to meet a mate was a much cherished hope of hers, 'but soon is time for cake.'

'Weally? I didn't wealise it was so late,' Harry replied.

He turned to Izzy once more and smiled, though he wondered how late she might stay and hoped it to be very.

'Yes, already is quite late! So please come to karden very, very soon!' and with that, Gretchen left them in peace.

'Who wath thee?' asked a bewildered Izzy.

'That's Gwetchen,' explained Harry, 'She wuns the whole house weally. She's bwilliant.'

'How nithe!' Izzy said and looked into the middle distance as if she saw a flower fairy.

Harry took her hand in his. 'Shall we go down?'

'Oh yeth!' said she, whereupon the pair went into the house.

At the foot of the stairwell, leaning against the newel post was a decidedly inebriated Giles sporting a magenta feather boa and conical party hat. Stretched out before him were his legs, and in his hand, he held a close to empty champagne bottle. He was out for the count with his camel lashes unified, square-jaw nestled on his chest, exposed because his shirt was raffishly unbuttoned, and a string of spittle, drooling from the kazoo in his lips, was tangling in his chest hair.

'Oh dear!' said Izzy.

'Yes, weally oh dear!' agreed Harry, and wondered how the boy had escaped Gretchen's notice.

A more disturbing vision sat upon the hall tree. For there was one-eyed Nina and curled in her lap, was Josh, his face slicker than usual with his spout of tears.

Pressing through to the drawing room, Harry noticed both hands on the ormolu clock pointed to ten, therefore he calculated there to be still plenty of time before the presentation.

'What a handthome gentleman!' said Izzy, coming to a standstill and pointing at the portrait above the mantelshelf.

'My G*w*eat-G*w*eat-G*w*andfather Excelsior,' Harry educated her.

'Ex*thelthi*or,' she repeated and looked at the painting, then at Harry, then the painting, and once again, at Harry, 'You are identical! Although, you do look much ni*th*er.'

'Thanks ve*w*y much!' said Harry, gladly, for he realised she had inadvertently called him handsome.

Then, because he realised Izzy's alarm at suddenly seeing Ridiculous' long and rude tongue, he hastily led her through the conservatory and together they stepped out into the garden and The Marvellous Party.

Valentine's sensation of riding a golden stud on a merry-go-round of romance suddenly ceased, and wondering the reason (for the *Radetzky March* was far from over) he steadied his head to focus upon Rupert and saw that he appeared to brim with happy surprise.

'Gosh, Rupert!' said Valentine, writhing in his arms, 'Why stop now?'

'Crikey!' said Rupert, as if not hearing him, 'Izzy actually came! I really didn't think she would!'

'Izzy is here?' gasped Valentine with excitement, and tried to look over the heads of the other dancers at the spot where Rupert's line of vision appeared to point.

'Yes! It's amazing!' Rupert said with a grin, 'C'mon! Come and meet her!'

Before Valentine had a chance to say 'Gosh! I should love to!' he found himself transported and watched Rupert embrace a girl so pretty that it teetered on silly.

The family resemblance was remarkable to Valentine. Naturally, any-body could see that both cousins were blonde (though her hair was not so gleaming a tone of gold as was his) and their eyes were the precise same shade of forget-me-not blue. After that the superficial similarities ended, for he was muscular and caramel whereas she was sylphlike and milky, but despite these discrepancies, nobody could deny their shared mien of goodness so prominent that one might easily believe their DNA to possess the remedy for every human degeneracy.

Mirroring one another, Harry and Valentine held the hands of their respective blondes; the heir his Merryweather-Vane, and the spare his Bringsley-Beer, and the spare exclaimed to the Merryweather-Vane, 'Gosh! You look to be a snowdrop!'

'A *th*nowdrop!'

'A snowd*w*op is a good thing.'

'An amazing thing!'

'A most glorious thing!' exclaimed Valentine, 'But why are you not wearing a tiara? Rupert assured me you had one, and pretty as you are I do think it a shame you've not got a swarm of diamonds upon your head!'

'You are so *wu*de!' said Harry, 'So*ww*y, Izzy, it's just his way.'

'It*'th* quite all right,' said she, using both her hands to flap a cool breeze upon her reddening cheeks, 'I am *th*orry, Valentine, it i*th* my fault; Rupert did a*th*k if I might wear my tiara, and I did con*th*ider it but I'm *th*uch a *th*tickler that I couldn't po*th*ibly wear it before I'm married.'

Valentine looked at her with curiosity, 'You mean to say one oughtn't to wear a tiara before one is wed?'

'Not really, no,' Izzy replied, as if guilty of some horrendous misdemeanour.

'Gosh!' said Valentine, whose interest in tiaras suddenly skyrocketed, 'How I should love to have my very own sometime soon!'

Rupert bestowed upon Valentine his magnificent grin that he then turned to Izzy, and the beautiful pair embraced once again.

'Oh, Rupert!' she said with a giggle, 'You are cru*th*ing me!'

'Ha-ha! Sorry!' he replied, 'It's just so amazing to see you!' and he looked to grin as hard as he was able.

Presently, Rupert's blindingly sunny countenance transmogrified into one that forecast a storm and it came in the form of Cosmo.

'Hello, chaps!' he boomed at the boys, then in a slightly softer but painfully lewd timbre, 'And hello chappette!' he said to Izzy at whom he believed it appropriate to elaborately leer.

Izzy could not help but shrink, and upon spying the shrinkage Valentine felt toward her both empathy and amity.

'Who might you be, missy?' Cosmo said to her.

Harry put a protective arm about his enchanting discovery but did not feel able to vocalise caution to Cosmo, therefore, the pansies built a buffer.

'She's my cousin and her name is Izzy,' said Rupert, squaring himself up.

Valentine added, 'And certainly she is not called 'missy', you despicable ape of awfulness!'

Cosmo displayed his palms in mock surrender.

'Sorry! Sorry! Please don't hurt me!' for his fill of drink had muddled his mind to the fact that Rupert most definitely could. 'Well, I'm charmed to meet you is all I can say,' he said to Izzy, and stuck out his hand to shake hers.

Then Willy came. She halted abruptly before her brethren, florid faced and panting with her chest heaving. She looked first at Cosmo, quite like she wanted to wallop him with her nosegay for his evasion, and then turned her attention to Izzy. It rankled Willy immensely that the will o' the wisp wore a dress effectively identical to hers, and she gawked at the slighter rendering with vexation. It did not either soothe her spirits that Cosmo had so obviously made a beeline for her pretty rival, but she was soon placated upon regarding Harry's bearing; she knew Cosmo could not and would not ever pilfer from him. Still, Valentine mouthed at her the word 'face' whereupon, with a hidden fingering of her magic flower, she applied it instantly.

Presently, Olivia sauntered over. Upon her face she wore the mask of benevolence for her spirits were as if electrically charged with expectation since sighting Harry with the alien girl possessed of an air of acceptable standing and, transiently, the missing Starfish seemed superficial.

'Hello, darlings,' Olivia said, 'I do believe that it is actually turning out to be a party not a million miles from marvellous, would you not agree?'

'Gosh! Yes, mummy, I couldn't agree more so, at least on the whole!' exclaimed Valentine, regarding Cosmo.

'Yes, well, darling, every silver lining must have one,' Olivia concurred, 'and sometimes even three!'

Crocodile-smiling, Olivia then focused on Izzy as if not having been hitherto aware of the conceivable fiancé for the heir, and she said, 'I regret, no one has yet seen fit to tell me who you are.'

'So*ww*y, mummy,' said Harry quickly, 'Izzy, please meet my mummy, and mummy, this is Izzy; *W*upert's cousin.'

'No! Oh, but how wonderful that you made it!' exclaimed Olivia.

Izzy performed a modest curtsy which Olivia appreciated for the girl ought to display reverence if she might marry an Avery-Stripe. Then when Izzy raised her blonde head and displayed her placid and un-enlightened face, Olivia could all but hear the peal of wedding bells for it was the type of aspect that had always appealed to Harry. Her buoyancy somewhat sunk, however, when Izzy opened her mouth.

'Oh! Mr*thth* Avery-*Th*tripe! It really i*th* a mo*th*t marvellou*th* party! Thank you *th*o much for inviting me!'

The malformed tongue sent a river of dismay through Olivia and she contemplated what Monty might say about the lisp of a girl whom she suspected he would otherwise consider acceptable. Would he wish sigmatism in the blood especially when paired with rhotacism, and run the risk of producing a litter only able to say Ave*wy*-*Thtwipe*?

Greatly regretting having no way of telling what Monty would think in such an instance, Olivia realised the decision was hers, and considering the shortage of options and wishing Harry would hurry, she concluded that if Izzy satisfied adequately all other areas the impediment need not be such an issue. Besides, speech impediments were not necessarily hereditary, and even if they transpired to be then this time she would insist upon surgical procedures.

'You are most welcome, darling, but I insist that you call me Olivia; Rupert always does and we quite consider him to be family therefore, henceforth, so shall we think of you too.'

Rupert grinned, and Izzy said, 'Oh, how ni*the* of you! Thank you, Olivia!'

'That is, indeed, quite all right, Izzy,' said Olivia, 'and am I correct in thinking that Izzy is an abbreviation?'

'Why! Ye*th* it i*th*!' Izzy replied and regarded Olivia as if she possessed a great power of intelligence, 'It i*th th*ort for I*th*adora!'

'What a lovely name, darling,' said Olivia, 'I *do* approve,' and certainly she did for she considered the four syllables a happy harbinger.

Now Corny arrived looking full of nothing but worry and woe.

'What's *w*ong, *w*ascal?' asked Harry, with some apprehension.

Corny answered the question by circling his arms before him to demonstrate the mysterious disappearance of Gloriana.

'Oh! So*ww*y, I put her up in your bed*w*oom before anything te*ww*ible happened,' Harry said sheepishly, and then added, 'but don't wo*ww*y, she's safe and sound.'

Corny brightened immediately and possessed not a care in the world, what was more, his birthday party was still in full swing and he knew he had yet to receive his cake, and its imminence was to him a thing of great excitement.

Feeling much better about his fish-napping of Gloriana, Harry too contemplated the cake for he very much wanted to experience further intimacy with Izzy but did not think it feasible until after the blowing out of sixteen candles. He then remembered the hands of the ormolu clock claiming it to be ten-to-ten, and with Corny's permission, he utilised the diver's watch to learn the correct time.

'C*w*umbs! Not long now!' Harry said enthusiastically to Corny who jumped for joy and dashed off.

'What a *th*weet boy!' Izzy said to Harry.

'Yes!' Harry said, proudly, 'But he *w*eally is a *w*ascal!' Whereupon he and she made eyes at each other and hers produced in him an inability to eschew just a snatch of seclusion.

'Let me take you away f*w*om here,' he whispered in her darling little ear.

Her *retroussé* nose tickled on his boxed beard when she whispered in reply, 'Where *th*all we go?'

He had not considered this detail but the octet's commencement of Johann Strauss' *Kiss Waltz* inspired him and reinforced his desire.

'Come with me,' he said, taking her hand in his, 'I know the perfect place.'

The place he had in mind certainly was perfect for amatory intentions, and indeed many moons ago Monty had also thought it fitting when wooing Olivia, though at that time the pergola had not been so enshrouded with foliage.

Stepping inside, Harry was happy to find it vacant and so was Izzy. They faced each other and both filled to the brim with infatuation. Holding her dainty white hands in his lean and tan, Harry did not feel the need for conversation, only to kiss, and thinking it right to start with her fingertips, he pressed them to his lips.

'Oh, Harry!' she whispered, quite taken by his chivalry to which she was unfamiliar, for most boys she had encountered were beastfully forthright.

'Yes, Izzy?' he asked, not desisting with his kissing but letting his brown eyes swim in the blue waters of hers.

'I am *th*o plea*th*ed that I came!'

'I *w*eally am too!'

'To think that almo*tht* I didn't!' Here she shut her lids, 'And then I might not ever have met you!'

'And I wouldn't have met you either!' he replied, now kissing her palms that seemed to him not ever to have known any form of industry, and he liked it very much for it was as if kissing cool satin.

Presently, Izzy trembled causing a vibration that Harry felt upon his lips, and with some alarm, he ceased his display of affection, and concernedly asked, 'What is *w*ong? Are you all *w*ight?'

'Oh ye*th*!' she replied, opening her eyes from which appeared tiny tears that trickled and then settled upon her cheeks like delicate raindrops.

'*W*eally not! You are c*w*ying! Why are you sad?'

'I am not *th*ad, Harry,' she whispered.

'But then why cwy?' he asked with confusion. 'Please twy not to cwy,' he said with caring, and wiped away her tears with the back of his finger, 'I feel so vewy happy to have met you!'

Izzy blinked, and regarded him elatedly.

'You are *tho thw*eet! And *th*uch a *th*illy *thauthage*!' she said, with a gentle giggle.

'*W*eally? Why?'

'They are tear*th* of happine*th*!'

'*W*eally?' asked Harry, believing it to be the loveliest thing that he had ever heard, for never before had he known of such a phenomenon and the spectacle of it was, to his mind, a marvel.

'Ye*th*!'

'Because why? What's the *w*eason?'

'Becau*the* you! You're the rea*th*on!'

'*W*eally not!' insisted Harry reddening but half daring to imagine it true that he might provoke such an enchanting emotion in so enchanting a girl.

'Really ye*th*!' she assured him, placing her hands upon his beard and taking pleasure in its tickly prickliness, 'I think you are ravi*th*ing!'

'*W*avishing?' he exclaimed with incredulity, for he could not believe himself to be so. 'Me?' he said, and he shook his head, 'But I think *you* are the *w*avishing one!'

'*Th*top it!' she said, taking back her hands to cover her face, 'You are tea*th*ing me, it i*th* not ni*the*! I will blu*th th*o furiou*th*ly and mo*th*t likely faint!' and she started to sway.

Panicking, Harry secured her arms with his, and said, 'You mustn't faint! Do you want to sit down? Would you like a d*w*ink?'

'Oh no,' she whispered, 'I *th*all be quite all right pre*th*ently.'

Harry did not relinquish his grip, rather, he strengthened it; instead of endeavouring to steady her, he persuaded her to vacillate to the sound of the octet's music, and soon he quite magically forgot his two left feet and piloted her into a spiralling waltz.

Round and round, Harry danced with Izzy beneath the floral canopy, and smelling her fragrance, he reasoned that no flower might ever hope to emit so intoxicating a scent. He experienced a warm wave of desire for her rise within him; he delighted in the lissomness of her physique and derived comfort in her meekness for it gave to him a sense of equilibrium. There was nothing for it; he simply could not bring himself to bear a moment more an existence in which his mouth was separate from hers. He was unable to fight it and neither did he wish to try.

With a finger, he lifted her weak chin, then brushed aside a stray lock of her hair and tucked it behind her ear. With a hand upon the small of her back, he drew her near; she was fragile and he loved her for it. His blood quickened and it surged, and his heart felt fit to burst with the urge to be with her, to belong to her and her to him. He watched her eyes close, the lips of her ineffably sweet smile parted and slowly he touched them with his own.

Yet no sooner had the tips of their tongues touched, causing both he and she to feel to be a single entity, did the kissing melody rudely stop and transmute into the tune of *Happy Birthday to You!* Whereupon the pair ceased to kiss, slackened their embrace and regarded each other quite as if the sound was that of a doodlebug.

Harry, though loathe to break their moment of passion, took Izzy's hand, and together the lovers fled their Eden to join everyone in singing felicitations and bear witness to the appearance of the breathtaking birthday cake.

CHAPTER 17

Remarkable's Hegira

Approximately three foot in height, and consisting of four tiers, the birthday cake was chocolate in flavour and cyan in colour, but for the orange that made up a great troubling of marzipan goldfish. These almond-paste water vertebrates festooned the undulant ganache, some were even plunging and jumping from one tier to the next, and each of them looked to smile with the fun of it all and seemed not to mind one bit the fizzing from the mass of sparklers rising from their sea.

Two intrepid waiters placed the titanic cake between the pair of gleaming bowls of watermelon punch upon the large table next to the conservatory, whilst the singing crush formed a crescent and watched Gretchen glow with love for an ecstatic Corny as she handed to him a chased-silver cake-knife.

Corny gazed up at her and felt full of adoration for the woman who so brilliantly looked after him. Quite ignoring his cake for a moment, he pounced and encircled his arms about her, and squeezed with all his might.

His gratitude brought a tear to Gretchen's eye. She wiped it away, and said to him, 'Is time for cuttink cake, Master Corny, and do not forket to make wish!'

The music stopped and not a person made a sound, all eyes were on Corny as he endeavoured to summon a wish. He looked to his siblings and though each of them smiled, not one of them offered wise words – not even Valentine.

Corny grinned back at them, and suddenly had an idea of what he would love to have. He placed the knife atop the bottommost tier, screwed his eyes tight, and wishing as hard as he was able, thrust down the blade.

His swordsmanship met with claps, and cheers of 'Hurrah!', and his siblings embraced him unreservedly.

Now there came, from the bottom of the garden, an immense *BANG*! Then, from atop the pergola, rockets shrieked as they volleyed high on up and reported crashes that hammered almost as loudly as the whopping bangers whilst rainbow coloured catherine wheels whirled their revolutions with hisses and spits of sparks spraying all about. Immense dazzling spiders, palm trees and bouquets exploded in the black sky but dwarfed in comparison to the golden brocade crowns with white strobing stars that looked to resemble an alien invasion. Roman candles blasted crossettes of ruby and lapis lazuli, squibs created epic emerald waterfalls, and electric-tangerine lances inscribed, in large cursive characters, '*CORNELIUS*'.

The spectacular show struck Corny with colossal awe for he considered it to be more magnificent than literally anything, yet it was not until he saw his name in flames that the revelation of the display being in his honour struck him also.

Corny's happiness heightened further when the octet began to play the music of the can-can and he darted to the dance floor to demonstrate to his friends the proper manner in which a person ought to high-kick to the tune. Not one of his friends possessed an inability to master the manoeuvres within minutes.

The dance floor rapidly filled with excited partiers having a crack at performing the provocative dance. Whoops, shouts and cries of exhilaration burst forth, most particularly from the fairies – especially Jolyian who had traded his feather boa for Giles' Gucci tie and was flourishing it elaborately. The Frobishers moved as if dodging bullets aimed at their feet and seemed to not ever known such hilarity. Hugo danced with Nina, for he could not persuade such silliness from Olivia, who smiled to see the billing and cooing of Harry and Izzy by the cupid fountain.

Willy, with her head fizzy with bubbles, spun like a top. She manipulated her gown with mad inhibition, cavalier to the prospect of her under-garments, and reckless of not behaving exactly as was expected of a lady. However, and somewhat ironically, her indecorum provoked a completely unexpected response from Cosmo. For quite full of fizz himself and also seeing no other suitably aged female bar Flick, and moreover considering Willy to look fun, he seized her hefty waist with his gargantuan hands and elevated her as if she were weightless. He bounced her all about, giving her cause to feel like a prima ballerina and to believe, beyond a doubt, her possession of something glorious.

Corny then encouraged his friends to join him in gathering the grapes from each table (whilst mischievously helping himself to half-filled and neglected flutes) then to toss the grapes toward the toucan so to marvel at his talent to catch. Remarkable did not once disappoint, and everybody thought his routine of catching, strutting, ruffling and posing to be stupendous.

Gubsy too, appreciated Remarkable's exhibition, which he just about managed to watch over the hunch of Quentin who had not desisted in his sycophancy since his arrival. Gubsy had thought it only natural for a person to want to brown nose an Avery-Stripe, but upon catching Quentin cast a sly glance across at Esmé, he suddenly realised that something shifty was quite clearly afoot.

The gradual growth of his suspicion of the relation's flattering possessing an objective accelerated when Quentin – rubbing together his long hands, for he was sure he was paving his way effectively – said, 'Of course, nothing I have seen here tonight can quite compare to the handsome portrait of Great-Great-Grandfather Excelsior.'

'*Humph!* Handsome does not even begin to describe the picture,' Gubsy boomed through his cigar smoke, 'It is majestic, I tell you! It conveys the might and charisma of my own grandfather impeccably; captures his spirit to a T! Why, you can almost sense him in the room! Even his lizard looks like you could touch it!'

Quentin now put it to Gubsy that he had a proposal for him. Not liking in the least the sound of it, Gubsy immediately demanded to know the exactness of the proposition, and upon learning its high level of despicability, his rage transcended volcanic. He raised his cocobolo cane, and sounding a warlike roar, brought it down like a bolt of lightening upon the reprobate's freakish hump, and then served a strike to his piteous, though evidently hardy, skull.

Quentin's terrified shrieks violated the ears of everyone. Even Cosmo, engaging in a secret and relaxing smoke in the front garden, heard them. Corny also heard them from within the tree house where he had decided was the best place for him now. His birthday had been excellent; he could not remember a better one nor either could he imagine the future to hold another just as good, but following his last spurt of activity with the can-can, the exciting events of the day had finally exhausted him. Therefore, he thought it best to enjoy a little rest in the tree house. As he drifted off, the shrieks entered his consciousness but not so aggressively as to prevent him from fast falling into a deep and drunk sleep.

Gubsy was obstinate in the slaughter of Quentin. He beat him mercilessly and would not relinquish his iron grip about his screeching prey's neck no matter how it wriggled and shrieked.

'What! What!' shouted Esmé, whose spindly legs propelled her over to her distressed husband in an instant. 'What are you doing to him? Let him go you lunatic!'

'Never!' boomed the assailant, impervious to her wrenching, 'Not till I've beaten the living daylights out of 'im!'

Yet Gubsy was not to achieve his ambition because Rupert and Harry intervened; Rupert courageously caught the cane, and hooked an arm around Gubsy, and Harry heroically prized Quentin free, and peaceably said to Gubsy, '*W*elax! T*w*y to calm down, whatever can be the matter?'

'The blighter offered me money!' roared Gubsy, now further enraged by his restraint, 'Money for my own painting of my own grandfather! He wanted to buy it!'

A collective sharp intake of breathe was sounded by the Avery-Stripes, whereupon Gretchen smartly claimed Gubsy and steered his passage to his wing chair where she would set about his mollification.

'I am inestimably astonished by your supposition that such an insult would not incite monstrous irritation in any Avery-Stripe!' snapped Olivia, staring with unfathomable contempt at Quentin, snivelling like a wretch and tentatively kneading his inflamed hunch and scalp.

'Stripes!' hissed Quentin, 'I fail to see what leads you to think you are so special! Shacked up in a squat in the suburbs with no more than a pittance between the sorry lot of you! You are all wasters clinging to your past!'

'Gosh! Listen to the bitterness of the glorified knacker's yard foreman!' exclaimed Valentine.

'I demand that you hold your acid pansy tongue!' shouted Esmé.

'Who said that?' said Valentine with pretend confusion, and he looked all about him to mock Esmé's earlier snubbing of both Flick and himself.

Whilst he performed the pretence, his eyes searched the party (that had now returned to its festive mode) for Flick, to ascertain her appreciation of his quip.

He would not find her however, for she was hiding with a bottle beneath the tree house behind the family flag. She felt full of shame over her parentage and was drowning the feeling as fast as humanly possible.

'Gosh! Where can Flick have got to,' said Valentine to Rupert, 'Gosh, well, never mind! Let's just dance before the marching of the Radetzky comes to a halt!'

'Harry, darling,' said Olivia, sharply, 'I shall go inside and will return only when you have eradicated the regrettable relations – all three of them – for if I so much as smell an Oxley-Stockman on the premises I will not be held responsible for the catastrophic consequences!' Whereupon she swiftly turned and strode toward Chinchero with firm thoughts of carrying out a massacre if need be.

'Ewadicate!' exclaimed Harry, not thinking himself capable of such a thing.

'Calm yourself, Harry!' said Esmé, sneering at what she considered to be his feebleness. 'We came only to offer financial assistance which your family so obviously requires but your pride prevents you from admitting! Keep the nasty picture! Come Quentin; let's find Cosmo and depart!' and she chomped her evil little teeth.

Suddenly, Willy appeared, distraught at the prospect of their departure because her efforts at being a lady had only just begun to reap a reward; Cosmo's manly operation of her upon the dance floor had sent her heart aflutter and her hunger for him had soared up to the stars. If he were to leave now, and under such horrific circumstances, she feared that those few moments in his arms would transpire to be the zenith of their involvement.

It was with this thought that she abandoned her nosegay and dignity; she threw herself at Esmé's feet, and cried, 'Oh no! Please don't go! Mummy doesn't mean it, not *truly*!'

The stridency of her plea was such that Olivia heard it. She stopped dead in her tracks by the conservatory, and questioned Willy's will to live. How did she dare contradict her!

Esmé looked down at the girl and thought her absurd in her dress, but appreciated her display of humility.

'Stand up, child, stand up straight!' and she coerced the verticality of Willy but at the same time pushed her away. 'I understand your shame, and I pity you but it is time for us to leave, I consider myself mad for having come in the first place! Quickly, Quentin! Don't dawdle!'

Quentin was not dawdling, in fact he was not moving at all; he was rooted to the spot with solid shock and unyielding to his wife's corporal pressuring.

'What, Quentin! What is it?' Esmé shouted with irritation and then filled with perplexity over his countenance elongated with disbelief.

Quentin's rigidity allowed him only to extend a finger and point directly at wailing Willy busily involved in ruining her excessive blue eye-shadow in an effort to blockade her blubbing.

Initially, Esmé could not comprehend why her husband's shrivelled heart was so touched by the waterworks, but on closer inspection, she grasped the cause of his distraction. Indeed, it also claimed her entire concentration, and caused in her a great sensation of disturbance, for on Willy's ring finger was the vanished ornament of Olympia!

Esmé's ensuing shout was of such volume as to be virtually Jurassic; 'My Starfish!' she blared, and bounded upon Willy with no sense of restraint whatsoever.

The shout resounded through the air and, immediately, Olivia reappeared. She wondered if it could be true, and, if so, how? It was no time for speculation however, and without delay, she set about releasing Willy from Esmé's fierce grip.

'Release my daughter this instant!' Olivia snarled, with her nose all but jammed against Esmé's snout whilst her claws wrenched against her trotters.

'The little bandit has my Starfish!' returned Esmé, employing her heft to bulldoze Olivia out of the way.

'Fiction!' Olivia snapped.

Whereupon Esmé yanked Willy's arm and produced, before Olivia's astounded eyes, the elusive ring.

'Imitation!' Olivia cried, strongly suspecting it to be the genuine.

Poor Willy was in agony and felt to be the quarry of two ferocious animals; she was in total shock that Esmé should think her magic flower to be Olympia's Starfish. To be sure, she now realised it similar, but Valentine would not ever treat an heirloom with such nonchalance.

'Ouch! Ouch! Do let me go!' she cried, 'You are really hurting my finger!'

'Silence! Thief!' ordered Esmé, 'How dare you steal from me!' and she tried in vain to extract the piece from Willy's digit for it had jammed against the fabric of the opera glove.

'I did not steal it! I swear it!' sobbed Willy, as she collapsed in a heap upon the lawn.

'Harry! Harry! Assist Willy! She is under attack!' Olivia ordered her eldest.

'Please, Aunt Esmé,' said he, 'I'm sure there has been a te*ww*ible misunderstanding,' but his words of reason proved ineffective.

Esmé suddenly gave a violent tug, divesting Willy's arm of the glove by way of pulling it inside out, painfully robbing her of the ring and giving her cause to shriek.

Blanketing her ears with her hands, Izzy breathlessly gasped, 'Oh plea*the*, *th*top it! *Th*top it! I cannot bare it!' and true to her word, she promptly lost consciousness, thus claiming Harry's full consideration.

'Valentine! Valentine!' called Olivia, but he could not hear her for his ears were full of Strauss on the dance floor.

'Ah*ahh*!' exclaimed Esmé triumphantly, though success still eluded her for she could not tease the Starfish out from the reversed glove.

Olivia snatched at the empty arm and there commenced a tug-of-war during which was exchanged all manner of unpleasantries. Nevertheless, Esmé's brawn prevailed, whereupon she foolishly held the tip of the ring finger and aggressively whipped the glove so to coerce it to cough up.

'Careful, Esmé! Not so hard!' advised Quentin, who had felt it wise to leave the seizure to his wife but now believed her handling too vigorous. Olivia was in full accordance; the ring was not indestructible, and one should not handle a thing so valuable with such carelessness.

'Inveigle it, imbecile!' Olivia spat, and posed to snatch the Starfish as soon as it appeared.

Yet Esmé was heedless and her rashness resulted in the sudden slinging of the ring. It described a generous arc in the air, where, mid-flight, its stones reflected the Chinese lanterns and momentarily dazzled, before plummeting and landing somewhere on the other side of the dance floor.

Olivia, Esmé and Quentin each sounded a gasp of horror and hastily pushed through the dancers to find it first.

At that moment, the ring found itself in the possession of an altogether new owner. One that did not think it to be a starfish but simply a star for it had fallen from the night sky and hit her on her head. Petal could forgive its hostile arrival though, for it was so very sparkly in the grass. She picked it up and marvelled at it; she was not sure she had ever before seen such a wondrous thing and believed herself a very lucky girl to be hit by a shooting star, and she smiled at it.

Presently, her delight was interrupted by the appearance of the beautiful witch who earlier had sent glass splinters flying. The witch was then joined by Quasimodo and then came Nosferatu. The three of them seemed to be searching rather frantically for something, and Petal was slow in realising that the something was the shooting star!

The evil trio slowly descended. They each smiled to trick her into trusting them but Petal was not so silly as to fall for the ruse; she knew that they required the shooting star to put into action some terrible calamity, perhaps even international catastrophe!

With the understanding that only she could put a stop to their dastardly plot, Petal grasped precisely what she had to do and that it must be done fast for they were almost upon her.

She looked to the toucan. She knew he was her friend because earlier she had released him from his bondage, and she believed him good because his beak really did seem to be a very big grin. In fact, as she looked at him now he even winked at her. It was all that she required to be convinced he was on the right side and, as best she could, she threw to him the shooting star, just as she had the grapes. Her aim was not perfect but the bird was clever and, leaning forward, he successfully caught it.

Neither Olivia nor Mr and Mrs Oxley-Stockman wished to waste time punishing the girl for they each had foremost in their mind the desire to rescue the Starfish from Remarkable. He regarded them defiantly as they closed in on him and gave them cause to cower when he suddenly fanned out his wings.

'It's all right,' said Olivia, 'He is on a chain.'

'Get away from Remarkable, you villains!' barked Gubsy, sat in his chair, and he reached for his cane.

'Is this the chain?' Quentin enquired, holding, between a finger and thumb, its loose end.

'Get away from him I say!' demanded Gubsy.

He struck Esmé hard on the behind but she was oblivious and only cursed crudely when Remarkable evaded her clutches and took flight.

Bent backwards, Valentine saw, beyond Rupert's golden glow, Remarkable loop the looping and thought perhaps that his many Grasshoppers were causing him to hallucinate.

He double blinked, gasped, and exclaimed, 'Gosh! Look there!' and he pointed into the air.

Setting Valentine right, Rupert looked up and saw Remarkable's revolutions directly above.

'Crikey!' he said.

Within minutes, the entire lot upon the floor desisted their dancing to witness the flight of the exotic bird.

Gubsy was beside himself, and boomed, 'Remarkable! Remarkable!'

Olivia, Esmé and Quentin pushed through, stretched out their arms, and cried out, 'Remarkable!'

Whereupon everyone present called out to the bird, 'Remarkable! Remarkable!'

Remarkable was having the time of his life. It was good to stretch his wings and feel the wind in his feathers. He soared through the sky, first in circles, then in a zigzag fashion, and believed the spectators quite right in proclaiming him remarkable.

He zoomed toward the moon, higher than he had ever before been, then descended, corkscrew style, back to the party and alighted the roof of Chinchero. He click clacked his talons across the tiles, as he sauntered the roof's decline, perched upon the guttering, and peered down his long beak at the crowd looking back up at him.

'Remarkable! Remarkable!' they continued to call.

Remarkable wanted to squawk that he would return when he was ready but remembered his beak contained something most unlike a grape, though pleasant to hold nonetheless, and decided that, for the present, his situation suited him very well.

'*Ugh*!' said Olivia, under the chorus of Remarkable.

'I wish I had my Purdey!' grumbled Esmé, 'Then I could shoot the bird down!'

'Do you have a gun on the premises?' Quentin asked Olivia before emitting a scream as Gubsy's cane struck him on the skull again.

'If anyone gets shot it'll be you!' Gubsy boomed.

'Silence fools!' snapped Olivia at everyone, 'We must lure him down gently! Call to him, Uncle Bartholomew!'

Gubsy looked up at his pet and made the sound, 'Kik-kik-kik-kik.'

Remarkable merely tilted his head on one side.

'Kik-kik-kik-kik,' called Gubsy again, this time with more feeling, 'Come down to papa! Kik-kik-kik-kik!'

Presently, the entire conglomeration joined in; 'Kik-kik-kik-kik! Kik-kik-kik-kik! Kik-kik-kik-kik!' but Remarkable only ducked up and down to the rhythm.

It was then that Cosmo reappeared. Somewhat muddleheaded due to his smoke, and wholly mystified by the scene.

He scratched his scalp, and said, 'What on bloody earth are you all doing?'

'It's *W*emarkable; he's up on the *w*oof!'

'Ha-ha! What?' boomed Cosmo.

He stepped out into the garden, saw it to be true and was unable to suppress his hilarity.

His laughter caught the attention of Esmé and she bore down on him.

'Where have you been? You stupid boy! Just when I needed you most!'

'Sorry, mater,' he returned, smiling but cringing, 'Just out the front taking a breather, that's all.'

'Well, pull yourself together this minute and get up there!'

'What!'

'Climb up to the roof and catch that bird!'

'But why would I do that? What do you care for that bloody bird?'

'I couldn't give a monkey's for the bloody bird! It's the Starfish I want; it's in its beak!'

'Gosh!' said Valentine, with an excited gasp, for the thickening of the plot thrilled him.

Cosmo could not quite believe the misfortune of the Starfish, and he looked to Olivia for confirmation. Her countenance convinced him entirely.

Suddenly he came to life. 'I'll need a ladder!' he boomed.

'The only one tall enough,' Valentine chirruped, 'is beneath a gigantic pile of paraphernalia in the cellar, it'd take hours and hours to unearth! Why don't you scale the wall instead? If you're very cautious the wisteria *might* bear the strain!'

Cosmo looked to the vines that climbed Chinchero, and considered the risk.

'Crikey!' said Rupert, 'It'd never hold him!'

'Yes, I'll admit it does rather court disaster,' said Valentine, with a smile.

'Oh please, don't do it!' begged Willy.

'He must!' Olivia, Esmé and Quentin remonstrated.

'I think your best bet is to go up to the west te*ww*ace, and t*w*y to push th*w*ough between the t*w*ellising and climb that d*w*ainpipe,' suggested Harry with pride at his practicality.

'Can't we just telephone the fire brigade?' pleaded Willy.

'Gosh no!' said Valentine, 'No time for that! Remarkable might take flight at any moment or simply swallow!'

Both Olivia and Esmé sounded a loud and empathetic gulp.

Cosmo tore into the house.

Out on the west terrace, Cosmo found that he could not push between the trellising for the gaps were too compact with ramulose wisteria. He proceeded to pull at it and endeavoured to sever the branches with his bare hands but found it impossible. Sweat cascaded down his forehead, soaking his monobrow and seeped into his eyes, as he considered the consequences if he did not rescue the ring.

He pulled off his tailcoat, yanked loose his bowtie and used it to mop his scalp and eyes. Cursing a thousand times, he felt to be an utter duffer as he clambered over.

Pugnaciously regarding the toucan, Cosmo growled.

Remarkable responded with a look of mild disdain and a guttural rumble akin to a chuckle that filled his pursuer with rage.

Yet, mindful of his precariousness, Cosmo gingerly straddled the broad pipe with his thick thighs as best he could and continued his climb.

'Hooray!' most of the party guests cried upon seeing Cosmo surmount the wisteria.

'Hooray!' they cried again, when he hugged the downpipe.

'My dears!' sung Brian to his people, 'What a wonderful rear view!' whereupon each fairy tittered.

'Oh my goodness! Oh my goodness! Do be careful Cosmo!' called out Willy.

Esmé turned to her, and shouted, 'If anything happens to my Starfish I shall hold you responsible!'

The dictum struck Valentine as puzzling: 'Why should Willy be to blame?' he wondered.

'I am *th*cared *th*tiff that he will fall!' panted Izzy.

'Don't wo*ww*y, Cosmo won't fall,' Harry reassured her with uncertainty and revelled in her embrace.

'Oh! But why? Why is it my fault?' wailed Willy, 'Truly, I did not steal it!'

'You expect us to trust the word of a common pilferer?' hissed Quentin, 'Esmé is right, we shall sue if we lose the ring!'

'Oh! But oh! Oh! Oh! Oh!' Willy cried and jumped up and down, thus ballooning her gown as if she supposed she might then float up to her beloved, 'Really and truly I did not steal it!' and she felt the wish to biff the horrid pair in their horrid faces for they seemed not to care in the least about Cosmo's predicament.

'Of course you stole it! How else do you account for it being on your finger?'

Willy ceased jumping. She loathed to confess before Valentine that the ring was one of his, for now he may not ever see it again and instead would see nothing but red. Yet she could not lie, and moreover, she desired to direct her attention to the welfare of Cosmo.

'I tell you, I did not steal it! It was given to me!'

'Given to you! Whom by?' Esmé asked with outrage.

Olivia also very much wanted to know from whom. Up until that point, she had not considered how Willy came to possess the Starfish, for the distraction of its retrieval was all consuming, but now with the question asked she listened with the greatest of interest.

'Well, *um*, yes, *um*, sort of,' Willy stammered, 'It's on loan from Valentine.'

'Valentine?' Esmé boomed.

'Valentine!' Olivia gasped and kicked herself for not having known all along.

'Me?' the accused exclaimed, 'I retain no recollection!'

'*Um*, well, you wouldn't, not specifically I mean,' said Willy, knotting her gloved fingers with her others that were nude. 'It was in your pink hatbox, in a little black drawstring pouch bag thing. I'm sorry. You told me not to wear something showy, but I did, and now it has probably gone forever! I'm sorry! So truly sorry!'

With that, Willy pushed through the guests to take sanctuary next to Gretchen and together they looked up at the bird and the brute.

'Oh, Gretchen! I am scared for Cosmo!' she said.

'Blast the boy!' Gubsy retorted with a gnash, 'I want Remarkable!'

Valentine's mind ticked overtime. Presently, he recalled his discovery of a black pouch at the foot of Olympia's harp and the revelation hit him that it had held the Starfish. But how did it come to be there? he wondered, and then he remembered his mother's fumbling with her Birkin as he had sped up the stairwell to make his early evening toilette. She must have dropped it! Whereupon he questioned her attainment, moreover, her methods, and swiftly he surmised the transpiration of something severely dubious.

'Your deviancies seem to know no bounds!' Esmé shouted at him, 'Not only are you a pansy but you are also thief!'

Valentine cast Olivia a glance and saw fury in her eyes but also the request that he not direct any attention toward her, and though not cognisant of her reasoning, he chose to comply, for he felt to be full of Avery-Stripe camaraderie. Moreover, the notion of making mischief was not one that he found to be disagreeable.

He gathered his equipoise, and said, 'I assure you Aunt Esmé, though I am guilty of many things and far from pure as the driven snow, I am most certainly not a thief!'

'Do you deny you had the ring?'

'Indubitably, I do not, for I cannot lie!'

'So you admit you are a thief !'

'Gosh, Aunt Esmé, please do not worsen the situation by embarrassing yourself with grand displays of stupidity!'

Esmé and Quentin gasped at his cheek.

'Please allow me to elaborate,' said Valentine as he pushed out, from his lips, a pretty puff of smoke. 'To steal the Starfish it would have been necessary for me to know precisely where you kept it. And though I am not certain, I imagine that to be in a bank or else somewhere in Stakely Manor, and having no way of entering either, at least not without your knowledge, I put it to you that it was beyond my powers to have stolen it. Further, I say to you, though it really is painfully patent for any fool to see, that only someone with habitual access could have done so undetected. In other words, I suggest to you that the crime was committed from within. *Id est*; an inside job. Indeed, it is more than a suggestion but a pure and simple point in fact. And my certainty of this fact is based on the rock solid reality that at the very same time the Starfish was presented to me so too was the crook's identity.'

'Yes?' said Quentin, and Esmé said 'Who?' as they leaned in closer, for they both felt to be rather involved in the telling of a whodunit.

Valentine sounded a close to earth shattering tut, and with an exasperated sigh, he said, 'Quite obviously Cosmo.'

'Cosmo!' Esmé and Quentin cried with horrified surprise.

'That's the chap,' Valentine confirmed.

'Why on earth would he give you the Starfish?' Esmé demanded to know.

'Gosh!' said Valentine, 'This is where we venture upon a territory of supreme fragility.'

He contorted his countenance to exhibit an emotion of unease, and squeezed Rupert's hand to tell him to play the game. Accordingly, Rupert responded with a face of mock concern.

Valentine went on, 'I am afraid to unveil to you all the shock revelation that Cosmo is possessed of leanings alternate to the norm and quite identical to mine. But brace yourselves for there is more; he is also controlled by an overriding feeling of fondness for me, and in his endeavour to seduce me into submitting to his desires, he forced upon me the stolen Starfish!'

Valentine pressed against Rupert's chest, and cried, 'But you must believe me when I say that not for one moment was I ever tempted, so you must not even think of demanding satisfaction by throwing down the gauntlet and duelling at dawn with pistols and epées!'

Rupert held Valentine close, he glowered up at Cosmo, and cursed, 'The swine!'

Internally, Olivia said '*Ugh!*' for she considered Valentine's flamboyant pretext credulous only to a cretin.

'*W*eally not, Valentine?' said Harry, dubiously.

'Really not what?' Valentine asked, annoyed that Harry might blight the subterfuge.

'That *w*eally doesn't sound like Cosmo to me!'

'I was just as surprised, Harry!' said Valentine, but before he had a chance to embroider, Izzy intercepted.

'Often it i*th* the one*th* you lea*tht thuth*pect,' she said with wisdom. 'My father had a friend who had a neighbour who wa*th a* bodybuilder with tattoo*th* and a bulldog, and every night my father'*th* friend li*th*tened through a gla*th* at the wall to the *th*ound*th* of him enjoying *th*odomy!'

Harry was not sure what he felt about Izzy's story but he had faith in her integrity. Therefore, though somewhat puzzled, he began to accept the exposé of Cosmo as possibly gospel, and as he visibly did so, Olivia's eyes widened with disbelief at the degree of his susceptibility.

Not so ready to believe were Mr and Mrs Oxley-Stockman.

'Complete hogwash!' Esmé stated.

'Total piffle!' announced Quentin.

'Oh I am certain it does not sit well with you,' said Valentine, in a carefree tone, 'but I'm afraid I cannot furnish you with anything other than the truth for I've not the imagination for another explanation, and I suspect neither do you.'

Esmé and Quentin both looked to engage upon the process of rumination.

'You could always ask Cosmo to elucidate,' Valentine suggested, 'but considering his hitherto clandestinity, I'm confident his reply will be packed with fudge.'

The pair cogitated further.

'Gosh!' said Valentine with a laugh, 'As if I even want the silly ring! If I did then would I really have treated it with such negligence?' and, with that, Valentine was victorious.

'Cosmo!' shouted Esmé, at a volume akin to a nuclear explosion; she all but wished again that she had brought her Purdey, 'Catch that bird this instant!'

'I'm doing my bloody best mater!' Cosmo hollered from his perilous situation.

Whereupon, Quentin sounded a long hiss, unfurled his curled form (creating distinct sounds of cracking cartilage) and extending his sinuous arms skyward, he howled up to his son, 'If you return without the Starfish I shall skin you alive!'

Having successfully ascended the downpipe, Cosmo, by way of utilising the guttering for leverage, hoisted himself atop the gradient roof. He was wise enough to know that to look down was a certain recipe for vertigo therefore he refused the instinctive urge, yet it was impossible to ignore the obvious fact that he was three floors up with the chimneys and treetops on a level, and he without the luxury of a safety-harness or net. The babble and blurting from the audience down below hindered his focus further, and far from the first time that day, he cursed his stupidity.

His curses did not stop there: 'Bloody woman!' he muttered in reference to his aunt for being so careless with the Starfish that it should end up in a beak!

'Bloody bird!' he growled at Remarkable, 'Just come to me and I'll see to it that you get a first-class stuffing!' and, on his hands and knees, he advanced with stealth.

'Softly-softly catchee monkey,' he whispered beneath his breath.

Then he sounded 'Kik-kik-kik-kik' with as much affection as he could muster, and reached out.

Remarkable regarded Cosmo's futile efforts with amusement. It entertained him greatly to see the difficulty he endured to achieve an equal footing, when he himself had simply to flap. It tickled him that with every inch his pursuer progressed he had merely to hop to the left, with no fear of falling, for his limbs were of the superior sort, and easily escape his reach. Teasingly, he clicked a talon on a tile a message in Morse that those in the know would decipher as, 'You utter duffer!'

Though unaware of its exact meaning, Cosmo decoded it as offensive and it fired his fury. He decided to discombobulate the bird with a hearty chuckle as if it were all a big game. Indeed, Remarkable momentarily let down his guard and narrowly missed an unexpected swipe.

Bird and brute looked at one another.

'C'mon, be a pal and let me catch you,' said Cosmo, in as amicable a tone as he was able. Remarkable refused with a ruffle of his feathers.

Presently, Cosmo no longer cared for his safety and wished only to achieve his object. Therefore, throwing caution to the wind, he lunged forward to grab Remarkable as he would a rugby ball.

Obviously, the game of rugby would be quite a different sort if the funny shaped ball possessed the ability to fly, and as if to verify this point, Remarkable rendered himself airborne just in time.

Too late, Cosmo recognised his greatest act of utter dufferism, lost his balance and found himself hanging from the guttering, clinging on with his fingertips for dear life. His sense of stupidity heightened upon the reappearance of Remarkable, perched upon the roof again, and reiterating, with a talon, his message in Morse code.

The majority of guests filled with terror and they all edged away from Chinchero, for not one of them welcomed the prospect of being crushed by a hunk. Yet Willy did not seem to think it such a dismal fate, and immediately she positioned herself to catch him.

'Cosmo! Oh Cosmo!' she cried, with tears in her eyes, 'Hold on tight! Please hold on tight! Somebody save him please!'

Her consequent screams bordered on hysterical.

'Harry! Rupert! Plea*the* do *tho*mething! Plea*the*!' begged Izzy.

Accordingly, with the plan to seize Cosmo from a window, Rupert raced inside, and Harry chased after him.

Had Valentine known of Rupert's valiant intention he would have been worried, but as it was, he felt nothing but peckish for cake. He squeezed through the petrified mass and helped himself to a slice.

'Gosh, Willy, you really ought to try this; it truly is scrumptious!' he said between mouthfuls, for never would he talk during, 'Though perhaps a trifle too viscous.'

'You beast!' Willy wailed at him, 'Can't you see what is happening?'

'Indubitably,' he said, peering up at Cosmo. 'Look, he's trying to reach your bedroom window. If I were you, I'd rush up there. Think of the reunion!'

With that, Valentine turned and sought Rupert, for he had for him a slice of cake, though he did not get very far before came an almighty curse from up above.

Cosmo had lost his grip, and he plummeted, with a ferocious *whoosh!* before landing, with a resounding *thump!* in a rosebush.

His downfall influenced the table upon which sat most of Corny's cake and a generous remainder of watermelon punch, and they avalanched and inundated him, with the silver punch bowls sounding like cymbals.

Willy, along with everyone present, issued a sharp gasp, and she immediately threw herself upon her prostrate, motionless and considerably icky beloved.

'Cosmo! Oh, Cosmo!' she screamed regarding the malformed angles of his upper limbs, but unconscious Cosmo could not respond to her slaps or cries.

'Crikey! Don't move him!' Rupert shouted down to her before he and Harry disappeared from the bedroom window.

'Gosh! Is he crippled?' exclaimed Valentine, whereupon Izzy collapsed at his feet for he could not catch her with his hands full of cake.

Neither of Cosmo's parents felt traumatised by the possibility of his paralysis. Indeed, they sensed not a thing but disgust for him, his exposed perversion, and squandering of the Starfish, now airborne, destined who knew where, for Remarkable's sense of culpability had sent him soaring into the firmament.

Esmé and Quentin looked to the recently revealed and messy pansy prone in a rosebush, and then to the inconsolable Willy, Quentin hissed, 'If that creature, who is no longer my son, has any sense at all, he will not wake up, and if he does, you may tell him to consider himself disinherited!'

'We shall telephone Pritchard to see to it first thing Monday morning!' Esmé shouted.

Whereupon, Mr and Mrs Oxley-Stockman, linked arms, and departed with their noses in the air.

'Remarkable! Remarkable!' bellowed Gubsy in the midst of the silent party guests, and he fell to his knees to watch, through his waterworks, the platinum moon-framed silhouette of his pet flying away.

Gubsy's bellows reverberated in Olivia's ears; she too wanted to scream the bird's name, to catch and kill him and reclaim the ring. Her violently palpitating heart however thought only of Monty; she had failed him further, though through no real fault of her own, and she wished to find him in their four-poster where she would beg his forgiveness. Yet she knew that even if Monty did miraculously manifest in their marital bed he would unlikely show mercy because, just as she had calculated, The Marvellous Party had ended in calamity, and, quite patently, the time had come for carriages.

CHAPTER 18

Interims

'Crikey! What do you suppose?' asked Rupert, returning to Valentine's turret with a breakfast tray laden with the appropriates.

'*H'm*,' was the thoughtful sound Valentine made whilst enjoying breakfast in bed for the third consecutive morning since The Marvellous Party.

'I know!' he said, with a smile, 'I suppose us to eat *all* our meals in here from now on!'

Rupert grinned at him, and converging their propinquity beneath the violet scented sheet, he played mother with the geisha teaware.

'Crikey, yes, that would be amazing! But no, I'll tell you, Gretchen says she saw the Frobishers, who said they thought the party to be the most fun they ever had! She said it makes them think twice about moving but they really do want to move to the Cotswolds.'

'Oh good,' replied Valentine, with a feeling that he had been asked to suppose something rather disappointing. 'I did not know they were moving. I wonder who might be our new neighbours,' and he did indeed look to wonder.

'Well, they've not put it on the market yet and that's just it; they think the work I've done here is amazing, so they've asked if I can do some things in their house to spruce it up! Isn't that amazing?'

'Yes, I suppose so,' said Valentine with a moue. 'But I hope it isn't lots of work; I don't like to share you.'

Rupert laughed. 'I don't think it is, but you know I like to be busy, and anyway, you won't be sharing me; I'm all yours!'

'Glorious!' exclaimed Valentine, very much liking his holding, and he dipped a corner of his toast into Rupert's tea.

'You're savage!' Rupert said with a grin.

'Verily feral!' Valentine concurred in a teasing tone, whereupon Rupert seized him and the pair proceeded to tussle.

'Careful! Careful of the lion!' cried Valentine, with a laugh; he did not think that he should return the hide of Great Uncle Sebastian's lion sullied with stains – strawberry jam or otherwise.

*

Gubsy possessed not a clue that Sebastian's lion had left his bedroom. At least not until Gretchen brought the absence to his attention, but it was of little concern to him as Remarkable was still AWOL, and that was Tuesday.

'Do not be worryink, Mr Bartholmoo,' Gretchen said, 'Remarkable is clever bird, I think perhaps maybe he enjoys a little holiday and be comink home soon akain.'

Gubsy was not convinced.

The following morning, after days of disposing debris, Gretchen finally returned Chinchero and the garden back to its former order. She was considering what to do with the Gucci tie when the toucan crash-landed on the lawn, and nonchalantly wandered back into the house looking only slightly the worse for wear.

'Mr Bartholmoo! Mr Bartholmoo!' Gretchen called out as she and the bemused Dalmatians danced about the bird, 'You must come see!'

Gubsy's grumpy face instantly lifted upon seeing Remarkable saunter across the Axminster and mount his perch.

'Rotten scallywag!' Gubsy boomed as his eyes brimmed.

Remarkable nuzzled his head against his master's shoulder to beg forgiveness for his decampment.

'Kik-kik-kik-kik,' sounded Gubsy stroking Remarkable's feathers with a forefinger – there was nothing to forgive.

To exhibit his gratitude of Gubsy's clemency, Remarkable opened wide his sunset beak, emitted a raucous squawk and waggled his long grey ribbon of a tongue.

There was, however, no sign of the Starfish.

Corny was just as pleased about the homecoming and his consequent efforts at cartwheels in the garden were impressive but nevertheless stopped when a happy Harry grabbed his ankles.

'Hu-*ww*ah, *w*ascal! *W*emarkable came back! Isn't it b*w*illiant?'

Upside down, Corny nodded his consonance enthusiastically and thrashed about wildly when Harry spun him.

'Such a *w*elief for Gubsy!' said Harry setting Corny down, 'And for me! I wouldn't have felt *w*ight leaving ev*w*ybody in the lurch. He came home just in the ve*w*y nick.'

Corny looked, with suddenly watery eyes, at his eldest brother; he had forgotten that Harry was to go abroad again.

Sheepishly, Harry furrowed his brow, and he said, 'I'm so*ww*y, Corny, but I *weally* have to go. I *wealise* mummy says modelling is *infwa dignitatem* but a chap's got to earn a *cwust!*'

He hugged Corny close and requested that he be a good boy. Of course, Corny would be good but still he filled with sadness as he watched, through his tears, Harry hoick on his backpack in the hall, stride with uncustomary purpose to the garden gate, and disappear down the Avenue.

The catastrophic fate of the Starfish still seemed to Olivia unreal, and during snatches of sleep, (for since the debacle, insomnia tortured her) she would dream not only of Monty but also that she wore the ring.

Then she would wake with a jolt and curse the sticky fingers of Valentine. Her every atom sorely wished to haul him over the coals for his thievery, but mindful that he would then inquire how it came to be in her possession in the first place she realised that to raise the subject would be unwise, and she was astonished and thankful that he had not probed her predicament. Moreover, she was appreciative of the brazen veil that he had cast over the truth of the transaction, for if he had not then she was certain that the Oxley-Stockmans would have carried out their threat of legal proceedings and thus opened the box of Pandora.

'But what might happen when Cosmo comes out of his comatose condition?' she considered with dread, and wondered if, upon discovering his destitution, he would decide to spill the beans regarding their Parisian tryst.

Certainly, his version would illustrate him as innocent and depict her as villainous; a scenario which Quentin and Esmé would be all too willing to believe, and inevitably sue her for every penny she did not even possess!

The very notion caused her to sweat as she pictured a steep declivity into poverty. Even more terrifying to consider was the family's ascertainment of her ignominy employed to attain the ring – surely, they would disown her, or at the very least, she would lose their respect. Therefore, she prayed that Cosmo's coma would transpire eternal as the thought of his resuscitation caused her to vomit almost hourly.

Nothing and no one could induce Willy to leave Cosmo's hospital bedside. Neither the kindly Doctor nor militant Matron could persuade her, for when they tried, her hysteria was so prodigious that they considered it wise to permit her persistence, and when even the oceans of coffee she imbibed could not keep her awake, she would sleep in the uncomfortable armchair at his side.

Most of the time she was alert, at least to some degree, and with bloodshot eyes she would stare at Cosmo's lids and prey for a flicker, but there came none.

Time for her was now non-existent; her only realities were he, she and his bed. She spoke to him continuously – though she was cognisant most of her words were codswallop – she told him that she loved him and longed to hold his hand but was unable for both his arms were in casts and elevated. She would regard his face and its strong features. She desired to kiss his lips (which even then slightly sneered) with a hope of revivifying him as if in a fairy tale, but she did not dare. Whereupon she would wonder if their current situation might be the most intimate they would ever share and came to consider that perhaps she wished he would not ever regain consciousness so to render the status quo everlasting. Then she would fill with shame at her wicked thought and stifle her unreserved sobs in the bedclothes.

Naturally, Valentine did not feel troubled by any of his relations' circumstances. He thought it glorious for Harry to spread his handsomeness. So too was it glorious for Willy to spend her every earthly hour in the presence of her heart's desire, toward whom Valentine had not ever before felt so amiable.

Valentine was a trifle riled, however, that for almost two weeks he had possessed the ultimate heirloom and not even known of it. Then he would ponder the shenanigans of his mother, but quickly he would fill his head with lovelier notions.

When not indulging lovely notions, he would enjoy almost quite as much the thrill of tutting at the twee décor and tat belonging to the Frobishers (away for a fortnight's ramble in the Pennines) whilst Rupert painted, hammered and drilled. But the pastime of vigorous tutting soon became lacklustre, therefore he decided to locate Corny because he was always a good fellow with whom to while away the hours.

Thus, for four days, Valentine and Corny virtually lived in the cellar. Together they rifled through the Chippendale wardrobes and antiquated trunks to see what wonders they could wear. Their costumes promoted games with names such as *King Ludwig II of Bavaria and Charlie Chaplin go on safari*, and *Drunken sailors discover the joys of transvestism*.

Eventually, they exhausted the desire to dress up and instead chose to make magic potions with Corny's chemistry set – but naturally, they wore white coats in their laboratory that was the tree house. Unfortunately, though their concoctions in test-tubes were glamorously coloured and fizzed or glittered, no one, not even the Dalmatians, despite being told of their medicinal powers, could be persuaded to sample them, and there was little fun to be had watching insects simply drown.

Then Corny all but begged that they create stink bombs and, much to Valentine's reluctance, they made a dozen. However, upon accidentally dropping one, the tree house became uninhabitable in an instant, and it ended their avocation of genius inventors after only three days.

So began their travels with Lemuel Gulliver courtesy of Jonathan Swift, in the comfort of the gazebo, Valentine read, Corny listened, and they both drank lots of lime cordial. The exploits enthralled Corny to such an extent that when luncheon came he was quite impatient that Valentine would not rush his food so to continue.

Finally, on the sixth day, a Saturday, when in the land of Houyhnhnms, Rupert, as was usual, joined them for the midday meal and announced that his work at the Frobishers' was complete, and what with the weather being so amazing, he suggested that the next day they picnic in Richmond Park.

Corny responded with animated enthusiasm and Valentine said, 'Gosh! Glorious! Let's!'

Three weeks had passed since the flight of the Starfish and instead of resigning herself to the loss, Olivia felt feverish all around the clock, and this nettled her for she liked to believe that she was intelligent enough to be philosophical.

She watched Gretchen heave a wicker picnic-hamper of inordinate magnitude filled with delectable homemade provisions, which together with the gramophone, Rupert placed upon the folded blanket in the backseat of the Jaguar, and at a quarter-to-ten, he, Valentine, Corny, Gloriana and the Dalmatians motored fourth on their jaunt. Olivia waited until Gretchen also left Chinchero, and immediately she went to the kitchen. There, she pulled out a chopping board; on it, she spread a section from *The Sunday Times*, and then brandished the heavy-duty metal mallet used to render meat tender.

She tightened her kimono about her waist, from her pocket she produced the pretend Starfish and placed it upon the paper. She regarded it for a flash and felt full of chagrin as the paste stones sparkled in the sun that streamed in through the window. Nonsensically, she blamed her entire situation on the dishonest object. This, however, was her aim; to channel her rage and release it, and with her rage now summoned, she raised the mallet and commenced to smash the impostor to pieces.

Quite soon, she smiled to see the band gratifyingly warped and the stones nothing but sorry granules of imitation. Momentarily, she considered her sanity, then quickly she experienced a sense of calm and she celebrated her achievement by parcelling the destruction in the newspaper and depositing it in the bin.

'Counterfeit!' she said to the ring, as the bin lid shut with a *clang*.

She dusted off her hands and decided to open a bottle of champagne. She would have preferred a pot of tea but refused to brew as that was Gretchen's job.

Upon entering the drawing room, to drink on the chesterfield and look at magazines, the presence of Gubsy and Remarkable came to her attention. It annoyed her for she wanted to be alone, yet she would not retreat from the room in which she wished to withdraw.

'Uncle Bartholomew,' she said to acknowledge his existence, and she established herself upon the chesterfield.

Gubsy made the sound, '*Humph*!' shook the money section of *The Sunday Times*, and gnashed. He was full with infuriation over Olivia, not because she had somehow fiddled with his grandmother's Starfish (indeed, he had no clue of the dramas surrounding it as his attention had focused solely on the maltreatment of Remarkable) but because she remained in Chinchero.

'What was that noise coming from the kitchen?' he suddenly demanded to know, 'More renovations?'

'Ants,' answered Olivia, peeling the foil from the bottle top.

'Must've been great whopping ones!' he retorted, and eyed her with scepticism.

'I was killing them,' said Olivia, not meeting his eye and instead concentrated on unscrewing the wire about the cork.

'*Humph*!' sounded Gubsy again, regarding her disdainfully before returning to his paper and gnashing, whereupon Remarkable, sat upon his perch, produced his guttural rumble and eyed her just as hatefully as had his master.

Olivia could tolerate Remarkable no longer. Since his hegira with the Starfish, and subsequent effrontery to return empty-beaked, she had wanted to reincarnate him into a novelty shoehorn. Now his derisiveness pushed her further than she was prepared to permit and she was unable to resist the desire to punish him corporally.

With the bottle of champagne, she zeroed in on the avian being preening his plumage, and with her thumbs, she carefully coerced the cork. The emancipation created a satisfyingly loud *pop*, and Gubsy jumped as if bitten, but that was the closest the cork came to physical harm. It missed Remarkable by a mere inch, hit instead the mantelshelf, ricocheted into the open Steinway, and, upon its strings, went *pling*, *plong*, *pling*, *pling*.

For a moment, silence prevailed until Remarkable realised his near miss and squawked and flapped as if a riotous maniac and broke the spell of shock cast upon Gubsy.

'Devil woman!' he boomed at Olivia. His countenance was beetroot and pulsated obscenely, 'Mark my words! If ever you try anything like that again I will personally kick your bony seat from here to Kathmandu!'

'Butter fingers, darling, so sorry,' said Olivia, displaying her manicured extremities, and mentally cursed her botched job as she filled her flute.

The remainder of Olivia's day was uneventful, she considered it just as well for she was exhausted from the exertions of obliterating jewellery and attempted bird-murder, and midway through the champagne, she tired of month old magazines and fell asleep on the chesterfield. Not even Gretchen could stir her with Sunday roast; the thought of food was abhorrent to Olivia.

'No, Gretchen, not even honey!' she was forced to curtly reiterate, for though she was hungry it was for something she could not put her finger on, despite it being on the tip of her tongue, and because the scent of roast-something perturbed her innards, she relocated to repose upon the four-poster.

Little less than an hour had passed when a persistent knock on her bedroom door awoke her.

'Who is there?' she called out with irritation, for she had not slept so well in weeks.

'Hullo, mummy, it's Ha*ww*y,' came the reply.

'Oh, darling, you're back. Very good. Welcome home, I suppose.'

'Thank you, may I come in?'

'No!' she said, 'I am sleeping! I'll see you later.'

'How much later?'

'Oh, darling!' she said with exasperation, 'I require rest! Please go away or I shall never!'

There followed a pregnant pause, and, relieved, Olivia endeavoured to drift off once more, but then Harry spoke again, and this time rather assertively.

'No, mummy, you *weally* must let me talk with you; I've something ve*wy* important to tell you. If I can't come into your bed*woom*, then, all *wight*, I'll wait in the d*wawing woom*, but it is something you will want to know so I'll go down now and fix you a d*wink*.'

Olivia heard his footfall across the landing, and she sat bolt upright. A plethora of possible situations ran amok in her mind. She filled to the brim with dread, and panic seized her, but nothing could stop her from hurriedly dressing in Dior and departing for the drawing room to discern the reason behind Harry's categorical insistence.

CHAPTER 19

Harry's Confession

Harry's requirement to pose for clicking cameras on the continent possessed not a drop of reality; it was simply the best story he could conjure to cover the factuality of his leave of absence. That he had deluded his family, and Gretchen, greatly bothered him, therefore, riddled with remorse, he returned to confess his crime. He was apprehensive, to say the least.

With the assumption that the entire family would be home on a Sunday evening, he timed his arrival to meet them *en masse*. However, upon learning from Gretchen that each his siblings were elsewhere, he realised it probably best that he first face the senior relations as they were the most likely to condemn.

Awaiting the arrival of Gubsy and his mother, he fixed three stiff drinks at the globe drinks' cabinet. He swiftly downed one and directly made another that he nursed in his nervous hands as he perched upon the edge of the chesterfield. He eyed the ornamental table lighter in the design of a scarab beetle, and wished that he smoked cigarettes for he had heard that they produced a soothing influence upon the nerves and his were currently fiercely a-jangle.

Still uncertain how easiest to make his admission he decided to use his short spell of solitude to figure it out. He considered it wisest to start from the very beginning, and thus he endeavoured upon a mental unfolding of the truth.

In his head, the commencement of his stealth coincided with its apex for he was unable to remove the visual memory of Corny and his woebegone countenance as he bade him farewell at the garden gate, for guilt had viciously tugged at Harry's heart. At the underground station, he wiped dry his eyes and purchased a ticket to Paddington, for his destination was not abroad, his destination was Bath, and his motive was not modelling but to further his familiarisation with his enchanting discovery.

As the train whooshed along the tracks, he felt his spirits gradually lift with the knowledge that he would soon be with the girl with whom he had fallen so unutterably in love, then, upon locating Izzy's house in the Circus, he utilised the *fleur-de-lis* knocker, and no sooner had they embraced did their lips lock and his every molecule soared with a sweetness of ecstasy untold. Yet, much to his disconcertion, Izzy recoiled.

'I'm *th*orry,' she said, 'I cannot ki*th* for very long as I've a bea*th*tly *th*ummer cold, *th*o it'*th* hard for me to breathe. I wouldn't want you to catch it.'

'C*w*umbs, Izzy!' Harry replied, smiling at her rosy-tipped nose, 'I'd suffer anything to be with you; the last few days have been *w*eally d*w*eadful without you, so *w*eally I don't care if I get bunged up, but now I am here, I will look after you!'

With that, Izzy filled with girlish glee, and joined at the hips, the pair's elegant torsos arched, thus lending to them the appearance of involved swans. They regarded one another with romance, before kissing again, and crossing the threshold.

The front door shut and the *fleur-de-lis* went *clack*, Harry set down his backpack and instantaneously felt as if he had entered a parallel universe of peacefulness for though he was no expert in feng shui, it seemed to him that the house had uppermost in mind the importance of serenity and equilibrium. Never before had he felt so imperturbable, not even amongst the Tibetan monks. The walls would not permit voices raised in anger, the atmosphere would set to soothing any feelings of upset as soon as they threatened, and combined with the refined furnishings, the place reflected perfectly the invitingness of Izzy to unwind. Consequently, during their tea of Darjeeling, finger sandwiches, scones, cream and jam, that is precisely what the entwined two, cradled in an ivory satin Regency sofa, chose to do.

Situated thus, Harry learned much about his enchantress. He watched her open up as if a fragile flower, and listened to her sweet cadence, as slowly she revealed herself.

Her father had been a Doctor of Science, and her mother (elder sister to Rupert's) a moneyed Austrian, and Izzy, their sole offspring, was delivered to them considerably late in their lives. Indeed, both her parents' deaths were ones associated with advanced years, and at the age of twenty-one, Izzy was an orphan with nothing but the charming house, a sizeable inheritance, Rupert, and her dream of becoming a world-class ballerina, this last however came to an end upon her being thrown from a temperamental mare.

Without her beloved parents, Izzy, though no longer a child exerted her childlike ways. She purchased three pedigree cats – Shelley, Keats and

Byron – and two porcelain dolls – Lady Bathsheba and Princess Tabitha. Izzy would lose herself entirely dressing her dolls for tea parties at which the three of them would enjoy civil conversations and have a delightful time, unless she invited also her teddy bears who were often downright rude. Izzy would not ever chastise the bears however, for she loved them dearly because without them, her dolls and her cats, she was quite alone, except for her cook, but even Cook quite scared her. Naturally, Izzy could always make a telephone call to Rupert if need be, but he was often overseas and her shyness caused her to shrink from the possibility of being a nuisance.

Blushingly, Izzy admitted to Harry that she could not imagine anyone to suffer quite as much from loneliness as had she since the departure of her parents half a decade ago.

'*W*eally not?' asked Harry with dismay for, due to his siblings, he could not envisage such isolation, indeed he had often craved it but never to such a harsh extent, and that delicate Izzy had had to endure it swarmed his heart with sadness.

'Ye*th*, really,' she replied, with tragedy in her tone.

'But what about f*w*iends?'

'I have none!' said Izzy, as her tear ducts produced pristine drops that traversed her colour-heightened cheeks.

'Please, Izzy, you must not c*w*y,' Harry implored, and borrowing her little lace handkerchief, he tended to her tears.

Izzy convulsed pathetically. She held his hand upon her cheek, and then kissed its palm.

'I am *th*o happy that you de*th*ided to come!'

'There was never any question; I've wanted te*ww*ibly to be with you!'

'Really not?'

'Yes, *w*eally!'

'Oh, you are *th*o lovely!'

'It is you who is lovely!' Harry insisted, 'And I shall never let you be lonely ever again!'

'You *th*an't?'

'Not ever! I am your f*w*iend! In fact,' said Harry, with utmost earnesty, 'I would like ve*w*y much to be your *boy-fwiend*.'

Izzy froze with shock; never had she dreamed to meet such a gentle and handsome man who would like to be her boyfriend; hitherto, all her suitors had been rowdy oiks whose rough-and-tumble deeds intimidated her sensibilities.

'You would?' she asked, quite with disbelief.

'C*w*umbs, Izzy! Ve*w*y much! A chap would be c*w*azy not to! So may I?'

'Oh! Ye*th*! It would be *th*o ni*th*e!' said Izzy, and all but burst into tears once again.

She abandoned herself to their increasingly intertwined embrace, and Harry filled with exhilaration. He quite surprised himself at his instigation to utilise the Regency sofa in an uncustomary manner, and together they surrendered to the impassioned fever that so consumed them.

Their romantic souls converged into one, and forgoing supper (except for a midnight excursion to the refrigerator for cold chicken and piccalilli) they furthered and firmed the merger until long after the remains of the day ebbed away. Then, in an interwoven pose of passion, they fell fast asleep in Izzy's bed as soft as a blessed cloud.

They awoke at the crack when the sun rudely intruded the bedroom, but neither of them minded its presence in the least, and continued unreservedly with their unification and, again, stopped only when Harry was '*w*avishing'.

Izzy was glad that being a Thursday, it was the cook's day off, but discovering the cupboards quite bare, she fed the cats before the enraptured pair, set off, hand in hand, to Sally Lunn's, for a luncheon of buns.

The subsequent incidents were but a glorious haze in Harry's mind but he remembered feeling proud as a peacock to promenade through the streets of Bath with Izzy's hand hooked in his crook. He possessed flickering images of Jacob's Ladder upon the Abbey, and the grand curvature of the Royal Crescent too, but foremost in his memory was the sight of Izzy skipping beside him, in her blue cotton dress, and of her palpable loveliness.

Employing Ockham's razor, he surmised that their meandering stroll delivered them to a purveyor of hot air balloons because no other explanation could support their eventual occupation of such a contrivance.

Despite there being a dozen others in the basket, Harry and Izzy, embroiled in their ardour, felt to be quite alone as the grand balloon floated in the firmament a good one-thousand feet high. The Georgian city looked as if it were a town for toys, although the inhabitants appeared to be insects, the River Avon was a sinuous ribbon of blue, and the surrounding country a verdant patchwork quilt. It was blissfully quiet, save when the pilot periodically opened the blast valve on the burner to flush fierce flames that sounded with an almighty roar, whereupon Izzy would emit a pitiful mew, conceal her little ears with her dainty hands and seem as if tortured.

Oh! How her delicate disposition penetrated Harry's soul and produced his very core to burst forth emotions of fantastic affection and tenderness that gave to him a warm and more wonderful feeling than he had ever before been able to imagine in his life!

Each time the roar came, he pulled her ever closer for he wished to envelope her entirely, and he felt as if he held in the palm of his hand, the most exquisite, timorous and somewhat wounded songbird. The beat of her sensitive heart was as if a violent pound upon a bass drum, through him it reverberated, and he marvelled at its magnitude; that such raging palpitations could come from one as frail and as flimsy as a dandelion clock.

Presently, Izzy transposed her line of vision from the panoramic view to meet his, and produced the loveliest of smiles. Harry instantly experienced an acceleration of his own heartbeat, quite as if the organ might abruptly explode. Suddenly his oral cavity felt as parched as ancient parchment with every drop of erstwhile saliva as dry as the ink upon it, when the realisation struck him that he could not ever be the boyfriend that Izzy so rightly deserved for his dissatisfaction with the role would render it insufferable.

He regarded her intently and concentrated upon her now tranquil demeanour. Determinedly, he considered the circumstance and definitively arrived at the ultimate solution. He was unsure whether he possessed the necessary pluck but upon seeing her omnipresent vacant expression that so gripped him to the very marrow it provoked him to summon it. He felt his hands and brow saturate with the cold sweat of trepidation but somehow he successfully gulped down the gargantuan lump in his throat, and lower his mouth on a level with her ear to issue four words that the blast of the fiery burner so cruelly blanketed.

'*Tho*rry, what?' Izzy asked in her loudest possible voice as she cupped her hands over her ears and appeared traumatised.

Harry nervously repeated his request and received only a response of bewilderment from Izzy who could not hear through cosseted ears. His unease did not prevent him from smiling at her predicament for a space before gently taking her graceful wrists and applying little pecks of love to her lobes, and again, he reiterated. Unfortunately, so did the burner, quite continuously. Rather aberrantly, Harry cast the pilot a derisive glance, but still the flames roared so to fire the balloon higher.

Harry lost his patience; he could not wait for the expulsion to cease, and he repeated once more, very loudly, his question to Izzy – wincing due to her exposed ears. His shouting tone was unnecessary however, for the roar suddenly quietened, thus throughout the Kingdom (at least partially) reverberated Harry's proposal to Izzy: 'WILL YOU *MAWWY* ME?'

Harry paused his narrative as he recalled precisely the tension upon his nervous system at that particular instant that seemed never-ending for Izzy's response could not come too soon.

Olivia, sitting alongside Harry upon the chesterfield, regarded him with her jaw on the floor; that he finally possessed the sagacity to abide the family's need to marry someone suitable astonished her, moreover so did his mettle to apply to the endeavour such explicit alacrity, and it was on tenterhooks that she anticipated the continuation of the account of his venture.

'Well then, spit it out, spit it out!' Gubsy boomed from his wing chair, 'I expect she said "yes"!' and he gnashed his false teeth with feelings of satisfaction rather than displeasure, for no news could be better than the betrothal of the heir, other than his reproduction.

Harry's countenance now transmogrified from one of apprehension to another of undiluted joy as he rekindled the remembrance of Izzy's response.

Her pupils had dilated to such a degree that almost no blue was visible and looking midway between a somersault and a swoon, for her mind's eye saw partying pixies and her mental ear heard the magical laughter of mermaids, she hesitated only to catch her breath before flinging her shyness out of the basket and her arms about his neck, and she exclaimed, '*Thi*lly *thau*thage! Ye*th*, of cour*the* I will! Oh, ye*th*, ye*th*, ye*th*!'

Whereupon, their fellow passengers and the pilot all cheered as the freshly affianced pair duly, and most thoroughly, engaged in a kiss of unrivalled passion.

'Yes,' Harry said, staring into space as if he himself still could not quite believe it, 'Izzy said yes.'

Silence dominated the drawing room for a spell but it was broken when the ormolu clock chimed. Gubsy rose and exuberantly boomed, 'Bravo! Bravo my boy! Jolly well done, you've bagged a sterling popsy there and no mistake; she's got a fine English complexion and a pretty ankle, and by the sounds of it, she's not short of blunt! Hats off to you m'boy! My own grandfather would be proud!' And he beamed up at the portrait of the ultimate patriarch.

Olivia too felt fit to pop with pride at Harry's achievement; Gubsy was right, what with the house in the Circus and her 'sizeable inheritance' Izzy certainly did sound to possess a wealth of fiscal matter, which, after all, was what the Avery-Stripes needed so to nurture its multiplication.

'Yes,' Olivia thought, 'finally he is toeing the line with someone exactly eligible, and the means make the lamentable lisp but a bagatelle.'

Her satisfaction was such that she plain forgot her malaise, and abandoning her usual cool decorum, she embraced her firstborn with an enthusiasm that nominally knocked him for six.

'Colossal congratulations, darling!' she sang, 'I could hardly be happier! Not only would Excelsior be proud but Daddy would be also, and of course, I am overwhelmingly delirious with delight!'

Harry looked over Olivia's head and saw, stood by an unimpressed Remarkable, Gretchen glowing in a poncho. Harry wanted to know what she thought, for though he would not admit it consciously, her opinion was of greater importance than that of his mother.

'Oh, Master Harry!' said Gretchen, 'I cannot remember last time I feel so klad to hear such kood news!'

She made to hug him yet Olivia would not have it and all but hissed at her for she did not care to share the moment, and thus Gretchen settled for a stroke of Harry's boxed beard and basked in his affectionate smile as he took her hand in his and squeezed it.

'We must toast the engagement!' declared Gubsy, importantly.

'Champagne, Mr Bartholmoo?'

'Of course!' he replied, and with that, Gretchen hastened toward her kitchen.

Suddenly flustered, Harry said, 'Gwetchen, wait!'

Gretchen stopped in her tracks and looked at him with quizzicality, as did his mother and Great Uncle.

'I haven't told you ev*w*ything yet,' said Harry, and his unease grew faster than their curiosity.

'Oh, darling!' laughed Olivia, jostling his arm good humouredly, though she sensed a foreboding, 'Surely it can't be anything as bad as all that!' but she feared what it might be and prayed that Izzy was not penniless.

'Well, no, it's not bad, not *w*eally at any *w*ate,' said Harry with a forced smile designed to mollify for he was fearful of her subsequent reaction.

Nevertheless, he persevered. His anxiety prevented him from beating about the bush and he confessed that he and Izzy were more than engaged and were actually, and, very happily, 'Al*w*eady ma*ww*ied.'

Bracing himself for the influx of protestations, Harry effectively cowered under Olivia's glare, and though he would have dearly liked to drain the remnants of gin in his tumbler he did not dare. Both she and Gubsy looked to be shell-shocked because for once they were in concurrence and were aghast at Harry's having wed without the family's knowledge, presence, or seal of approval.

'Well, I'll be!' said a deflated Gubsy as he sunk into his wing chair, ''Pon my soul . . . quite beyond the pale!'

Gretchen shook her head slowly, though not with disapproval, only disappointment. She felt sorry for her Mr Bartholmoo, and she presented Harry with a sad smile, for she would liked to have attended the ceremony, but still she was happy for him. Her hurt face cut Harry to the core and he was relieved when the ring of the front doorbell summoned her.

'You *eloped*?' said Olivia, with unadulterated disdain, 'Oh, Horatio! If your father knew, he would simply spin in his grave! The shame! The dishonour! How undignified! How improper! How could you, Horatio? Overridingly, *why*?'

And she continued to regard him with distaste, pitied his obvious unease and considered how regrettably unlike Monty he was.

Her final word echoed in Harry's mind. He buried his face in his hands and gripped tight in an effort to oust the query but to no avail – the word '*Why*?' bounced about in his brain.

It was the moment he had been dreading. He had known all along that it would come. Even when he made the decision to admit to the family his covert wedding he knew that they would ask why, but he had had to confess and now he found himself with nowhere to hide. Their reaction to his secrecy was bad enough, what might happen when he furnished them with his justification? He wished that he could escape, or at least there might come a distraction, and then, quite as if on cue, Valentine capered in with Corny, Rupert and the dogs, and with them was a panicky Izzy.

'Gosh!' Valentine exclaimed, pushing her forward, 'Look whom we found loitering outside!'

Whereupon, Olivia applied to her unexpected daughter-in-law a face not meant to strike as much fear as it so patently did, and said to her, 'Good evening, *Mrs Avery-Stripe*!'

*

Oblivious to the sudden tension in the drawing room, Valentine declared, 'Gosh! It simply was a most wonderful picnic! I don't mean the victuals, but they were delicious, Gretchen! But, oh! The sunshine in Rupert's golden hair, and Corny's too! And dappling the Thames as Rupert rowed our boat with the gramophone playing! And climbing enormous trees! Rupert lifted me! Then Rupert and Corny kicked a ball about and I made them daisy chains – look!' he drew attention to the boys' pretty adornments, 'Glorious, don't you think? And then we came home and found Izzy whom said she was passing from Bath!'

Here he paused to view Olivia because he was certain she would agree that passing from Bath was quite preposterous, but then he read her face, frozen with disparagement, and his garrulousness ceased with the surprise of her words he just now realised.

'What did you say, mummy?' he asked with confusion and regarded an anxious Izzy with puzzlement.

'I'm *th*orry, Harry,' Izzy said to her husband, 'I really wa*th* waiting out*th*ide!'

Harry leapt up and sprung toward her.

Taking her hands in his, he said, 'It's all *w*ight; I was just about to get you anyway, I have told them now. Well, mummy, Gubsy and G*w*etchen at any *w*ate, and ev*w*ybody is ve*w*y happy about it!'

He turned to Olivia a face that read, '*Please* be ve*w*y happy about it!'

Olivia assessed the situation. To be sure it was a shock to the system, though admittedly not one entirely sinister for now, more so than at The Marvellous Party, she was able to evaluate the girl, and though she deemed her demeanour pitiable she was comely, and her well-groomed appearance left one in no doubt that she was indisputably rich. Perhaps richer even than Rupert, and he too was a reason for blessing the marital knot, for if she were to object and revile he would unlikely retain the desire to associate with the family himself.

'Moreover,' Olivia considered, 'is elopement really so awful? Would Monty truly have minded?' Upon weighing it up, she calculated the answer to be a negative one because though the surreptitious nuptials were far from proper the main thing was that Harry had married someone suitable; that was what Monty had wanted, and inevitably, the two would become three and then four and hopefully more, and each of them Avery-Stripes!

'Happy about it?' said Olivia, before sharply sucking in air through her teeth, 'I adjudicate *happy* an inadequate adverb as my emotions edge exceedingly close to ecstatic!'

'Oh, thank you, thank you, Mr*thth* Avery-*Th*tripe!' said Izzy, gushingly, and looked as if about to fall to her knees so to kiss the feet of her mother-in-law.

Sensing such a display, Olivia swiftly adjusted her position, and insisted that Izzy address her by her Christian name, for she still considered the lisp irksome and she pictured scalpels.

'And you, Gubsy?' requested Harry with hope.

Gubsy was powerless to the prettiness of the new family member. Her porcelain skin and dewy blue eyes penetrated and shattered what he suddenly deemed his archaic sense of protocol and he found that he could not blame young Harry for snapping up the popsy *tout de suite*, for in his shoes he would have done just the same.

'Soonest wedded, soonest bedded,' Gubsy told himself, and, of course, to his mind, bedding meant breeding, and he very much wanted to hear the scamper of tiny Avery-Stripe feet before he went to meet his maker.

Therefore, grasping the armrests of his wing chair, he jubilantly boomed, 'Welcome to the family, my girl! You're a very fine addition, a *very* fine addition indeed!'

Consequently, Izzy planted, upon his ruddy cheeks, kisses of thankfulness.

Now Valentine piped up: 'Gosh! You got married?'

'Ye*th*!'

'Gosh! Really not?'

'Yes, *w*eally! And we leave for our honeymoon first thing tomo*www*ow! '

'Crikey!' said Rupert, with a blinding grin, 'Congratulations, Izzy!' and he embraced her, 'Congratulations, Harry!' and he shook him by the hand, 'Amazing news!'

'Well, this is a bit of a bolt!' said Valentine, slowly sensing something askew, 'When did all this happen?'

Again, Harry found himself having to explain his escape to Bath, but this time it was different; Olivia and Gubsy's acceptance made it easier, however, what made it awkward now, was admitting his deceit to Corny who so far had expressed little reaction to the revelation.

With wide eyes, Corny had absorbed the reality of his eldest brother's situation over the past two and a half weeks and he filled with sadness; Harry had lied to him! Also, he had chosen to spend his time with someone else when he had only just recently returned from the Himalayas after an absence that had seemed to Corny an eternity.

Corny very much liked the look of Izzy; he empathised completely with

Harry's attraction, but he was mindful that now married there would be less room for him in Harry's life. He tried to feel grown-up about it and reason that still he had Valentine and Willy (though since Cosmo's drop, her presence was rare) and with that he was moderately successful, but still Harry had lied and it was impossible for Corny to hide his hurt feelings.

'I'm so*ww*y, *w*ascal, *w*eally I am!' said Harry, hunkered down on a level with his little brother who had taken refuge beneath the Steinway and was receiving consolatory licks from the dogs. 'I'm *w*eally so*ww*y I lied but you must be a little bit happy for me, surely?'

Corny wanted to ask why his brother had lied.

Fortunately for Harry, Corny was mute and therefore unable to voice the question to which the answer was, 'Because of mummy; if she had known where I *w*eally was she would have got her hopes up and meddled and p*w*obably *w*uined ev*w*ything!'

No one could be certain what thoughts ran through Corny's mind, but then Izzy, believing herself entirely to blame, minced toward the piano. She crouched next to her husband and bestowed upon Corny her ineffably sweet smile which he could not help but diminutively mirror.

'Hello,' she whispered, and he regarded her thoughtfully. 'I am *th*o happy to have you for my little brother because I don't have any *th*ibling*th* of my own, and together we can play lot*th* of game*th*!' Here, she clapped her hands with delight. 'And I do like your dog*th*! I have three cat*th* at home, and doll*th*, and *th*ome very naughty bear*th*, but I am not a*th* lucky as you to have a beautiful goldfi*th*!' Whereupon, she daintily tapped a fine finger upon the glass of Gloriana's bowl cradled in Corny's lap.

Izzy's admiration of his fish provoked Corny to think her a very nice person. He wondered how it might be not to have a brother or sister and only toys and he pitied her. With that, he decided that he was willing to share Harry with her, especially if it would make Harry happy, and he presented her an enormous smile. He presented to her also the fishbowl to hold as he crawled out from beneath the Steinway, and once on his feet, he circled one arm about her waist, the other about Harry, and pulled them together in a heartfelt and congratulatory hug.

Because Valentine increasingly suspected an exact and shady reason for the sudden betrothal he was determined to gain confirmation. He had no qualms with direct questioning but realising the answer might produce upset in some and consequently prevent honesty, he set about removing the person most susceptible to shock.

'Glorious!' Valentine exclaimed, 'Now that everybody is so very happy I think it only apropos to drink champagne! In fact,' he said to Gubsy, 'I'm surprised not to see any!'

'I already suggested a toast, you jackanapes!' Gubsy retorted with a gnash, 'Gretchen, Champagne!'

'Of course, Mr Bartholmoo!' she said, and hurried to her kitchen.

'But what about Willy?' asked Harry.

'Gosh, she's in hospital!'

'*Weally* not?' said Harry, concernedly, 'What happened? Is she all *wight*?'

'Indubitably not!' Valentine replied, 'Galaxies from it! She is insane and won't leave Cosmo's side for a moment, and just stares at him like a lovelorn fool!'

'*Cwumbs*! You mean Cosmo's still unconscious?'

'Verily!'

'*Cwumbs*!' said Harry, 'Do you think we should still go on our honey-moon?'

He turned to Izzy, and looked doubtful, whereupon she looked fearful, but before she could respond, Valentine interjected, 'Gosh! We could all go on your honeymoon and he'd be none the wiser! You'd be silly not to go!'

Izzy flushed with relief, and Harry, rather tentatively, said, 'Yes, I suppose you're *wight*.'

Presently, Gretchen reappeared with the squeaky tea wagon upon which rattled three bottles of champagne in ice and eight crystal flutes. She thought that Corny should be allowed to toast Harry's marriage and was pleased when Olivia acquiesced, and was further pleased when Valentine, uncharacteristically, assisted with the distribution.

'Voila, Gubsy!' Valentine said, handing him a gleaming flute, 'Now hold it steady, but tilt as I decant.'

'I am well aware how to hold a glass, you ninny!' Gubsy boomed and proceeded to gnash.

He stopped grinding, however, when the ninny poured the cold fizzy drink directly upon his rotundity thus drenching his shirt and trousers.

'Gosh! Gosh! Hold it still!'

'Rapscallion!' roared Gubsy, and he reached for his cocobolo cane to administer a sound hiding.

Valentine jumped out of harm's way.

'Gosh!' he cried histrionically, 'I was trying to fill you but you jiggled so!'

'Blasted scoundrel! I'm soaked to the skin!' boomed Gubsy, as Remarkable squawked.

Shaking her head, Gretchen approached sodden Gubsy from behind his wing chair, and placated him.

'Come, Mr Bartholmoo, we must change shirt.'

'Nonsense!' he argued angrily.

'I am not askink, Mr Bartholmoo,' she said assertively, 'I am *tellink*!' And she persuaded him to his feet, 'You ket so krumpy when you catch kold!'

'It is July!' he retorted, as she ushered him toward the door.

'And you no lonker are such a younk man who can sit drippink!'

Gubsy's discharge successful, Valentine was now able to put his thoughts into words though they did not take long to convey for he was able to express them quite succinctly with just the one: 'Shotgun!'

'Shotgun?' repeated Harry and Rupert in unison.

'*Th*otgun?' echoed Izzy.

Corny, naturally, said nothing and supposed it a new game which he was unsure how to play. Yet Olivia cottoned on immediately and she hoped that Valentine's conclusion was accurate because though it would heighten the indecency of the situation it would matter little if Harry had already sown the seed for the next generation, and she prayed and expectantly waited for the outcome.

'Ha-ha! You two!' Valentine said to the new Mr and Mrs Avery-Stripe, 'You can't expect to fool us all into thinking your hurry to marry was based purely on lust!'

'Valentine!' said Harry in an admonishing tone.

'We married for love!' insisted Izzy with a pout.

'Gosh! Yes, I know you love each other! From tip to toe, you're both covered in it, anyone can see it, and I think it glorious! But you can't deny it's suspicious when you marry so soon, and in secret, and so I suppose I am correct in thinking there's a lovely little bun baking in the oven!'

Izzy's countenance contorted with absolute horror at the accusation.

'Crikey, Valentine!' said Rupert, 'Steady on!'

'Gosh! There's no shame in it! I think it glorious!'

'What's glo*w*ious?' asked Harry, with genuine bewilderment, 'I don't follow.'

'Don't be dense, darling!' said Olivia, acerbically, whilst sipping her champagne.

'Gosh, Izzy!' exclaimed Valentine, 'Please don't be upset! You can admit it now Gubsy's gone. I think it simply wonderful that you're *enceinte*!'

Izzy emitted a small shriek, and flinging her arms about Harry, she cried, 'Oh *th*top it! *Th*top *th*aying it! Plea*the* make him *th*top it, Harry!'

Harry looked to Valentine as sternly as he was able.

'Yes, you must stop saying it!' he said, and wondered what 'it' was.

'Please, Valentine,' added Rupert, 'you're upsetting Izzy,' though he was confused as to why her upset was so considerable.

'Gosh! I'm sorry,' said Valentine, who would gladly drink dishwater if Rupert requested it. 'I have stopped. I didn't mean to distress anyone.'

'It'*th* all right, don't be *th*orry,' whispered Izzy, 'I'm *th*orry too,' and she pushed her sniffing and tip-tilted nose against the comfort of her husband's shoulder.

'Will somebody please explain to me what's going on?' pleaded Harry, 'I am *w*eally *w*ather confused!'

'Darling!' said Olivia with exasperation, as she downed the remainder of her drink; she was annoyed at the inaccuracy of Valentine's suspicion, and, moreover, Izzy's pathetic response. Harry's slow-wittedness did not help either. 'Darling, what Valentine is so subtly suggesting and your wife so sorrily swallowing, is that your scurry down the aisle was for morally imperative reasons.'

Harry flinched as Izzy expelled a short sharp scream in his ear, and he continued to look entirely nonplussed.

'*Ugh*!' said Olivia, 'He was saying that he thought you had got Izzy pregnant!'

'*Cw*umbs! *W*eally not!' said Harry with a groan, and he filled with dismay.

Izzy whimpered into his arm, he stroked her soft hair and squeezed her bare shoulder to comfort her.

Though uncertain what had caused the sadness, Corny knew that he did not like it, and he stroked his cheek upon Izzy's hand.

Rupert also bolstered her: 'Please don't be distressed, Izzy, Valentine didn't mean to upset you.'

'I swear on my daddy's death I really didn't!' said Valentine, experiencing an unfamiliar feeling called shame and he was glad of Rupert's strong grip on his hand.

Olivia regarded the tableau unsympathetically; to her mind, the sight was pitiful, and to hear Valentine talk about Monty in such a manner provoked within her a sensation of resentment.

'Is the girl made of straw?' she asked herself, 'To suffer upset so easily! Has she no grit?' and she wondered if Izzy might be an entirely *un*suitable addition to the family, for what hope was there of the ineffectual pair creating anything better than a litter of milksops?

Izzy's delicate frame gently quivered against the bulwark of Harry's as she dried her eyes on her little lace handkerchief.

'Oh, Harry!' she said in a small voice, 'Thi*th* i*th* no good; I under*th*tand it i*th* difficult for you to tell them, and perhap*th* if I were *th*till out*th*ide you would have by now but really I *th*ould do it a*th* the problem i*th* mine.'

'No, Izzy, it is not a p*w*oblem, and whatever we have we share, I shall tell them now, I *w*eally was about to when you came in.'

'Oh, Harry!' cried she, and clung to him as if he were a mast upon a foundering clipper.

'Oh, Izzy!' he replied, and looked to her with his brown eyes full of explicit devotion.

'Oh what?' exclaimed Valentine, who could not bear the suspense, 'This is too tenterhooking! So do tell!'

'Yes, darlings,' said Olivia, slowly surmising the situation with horror, 'the tension is intolerable, so one of you, and I don't care who, illuminate immediately; secrecy is repellent to me!'

The newlyweds regarded each other, their expressions conveyed their deep love and tenderness that then transmuted to trepidation upon facing Olivia.

Harry swallowed hard, and said, 'Well, mummy, it's like this . . . '

But Izzy interrupted, 'I *th*all do it, Harry. Let me.'

'If you *w*eally insist, he said, with admiration and some relief.

'Ye*th*, I do in*thith*t,' she replied, and gingerly she stepped toward the chesterfield upon which she then sat and courageously sandwiched the hands of her mother-in-law between her own.

Olivia looked at her with astonishment whilst the room held its breath.

'You *th*ee, Mr*thth*. Avery-Th*tr*ipe,' Izzy began (Olivia lacked the patience to amend) 'your wonderful *th*on – my wonderful hu*th*band – Harry, ha*th* made me the happie*th*t girl in the world. He ha*th* *th*aved me from loneline*th* and filled me up *th*o much with hi*th* love! Before I met him I wa*th* an empty void and *th*o very *th*ad but he ha*th* given me love, *th*own me joy, given me contentment and made me *th*o very happy to be alive again!'

Here, she looked shyly at Harry blushing most furiously beneath his boxed beard, and then she went on.

'There i*th* nothing in the world I would not do for Harry; I would *th*wim ocean*th* and cro*th* desert*th* ju*th*t to make him happy, but there i*th* one thing I cannot do for him. I did tell him before we married *th*o plea*the* do not think I am di*th*hone*th*t or *th*neaky, but when I wa*th* twenty-two, not long after I lo*th*t my parent*th*, I had a hor*the* acc*th*ident. I wa*th* thrown in the air and cra*th*hed in a broken heap, and *th*o I could not ever become a ballerina becau*the* I broke my back and my pelvi*th*, and though they fix*th*ed me with *th*teel rod*th* I cannot ever . . . ' and she looked down in shame as her tears now flowed freely, 'I can *never* have babie*th*.'

'Oh, Izzy!' said Harry, as he hurried over to hold her, 'It's all *w*ight, *w*eally it is; I love you so much, you're all I need!'

Rupert was shocked. Of course, he had known of the incident with the horse and of Izzy's subsequent surgery but he was unaware that it had rendered her sterile.

'Crikey, Izzy! You should have told me; I never knew!' he said, and from behind the chesterfield, he held her with Harry.

'Gosh!' said Valentine, 'I feel such a perfect ninny now!' but he looked to Corny and wondered if he too was considering Izzy's internal metal and of fun with magnets.

Corny, however, looked perfectly distraught. Never before had he heard something so tragic and he sought solace beneath the Steinway so to have the dogs lick him silly again.

As the disclosure sunk deeper into Olivia's psyche and begin to take root, her essence seemed to fizz with an electricity that fried and charred her every membrane. Harry so patently possessed such low regard for the family and its expectations that it bordered on hate. Indeed, it was contempt, contempt and ire, for why else would he rebel against it so antagonistically? To wed a barren bitch was tantamount to mutiny!

Olivia felt the desire to tear away her own flesh, to strip off and strew her skin and sinew to show to Harry her now stagnant blood. She wished to rip out her heart and wring it in his face because he had killed it.

Yet somehow, she dissuaded herself from creating such a scene, and instead turned to Harry, and coolly inquired, 'You knew of this before exchanging vows?'

Not such a fool as to find comfort in his mother's outward placidity, Harry realised it merely foreshadowed a ferocious rage at the connexion's inability to produce an heir, but he did not care; he loved Izzy.

'Yes, mummy, I knew,' he said in a tone that implied nonchalance, 'Izzy told me on my ve*w*y first night in Bath,' and he thought back to their shared intimacies upon the ivory-satin Regency sofa, smiled and then kissed his wife on her flower-like cheek.

Olivia looked to the weeping girl between the consoling boys and considered the emotional manipulation she had patently employed to trap Harry who always had been susceptible to the hardships of unfortunates – especially when pretty and vacant.

There then flickered through Olivia's mind the notion of committing murder that she did not extinguish for it brought to her a glimmer of hope. She needed a plan if she were not to despair. After a respectful period of mourning Harry would still be of an eligible age. Moreover, he would then be rich and widowerhood might even furnish him with the edge that he so sorely lacked.

Cognisant, however, that such an endeavour would require supreme meticulousness; Olivia made the decision to deflect any motivation she might possess.

Thus, she said, with as much sensitivity as she could summon, 'Do try not to be too down in the dumps, Izzy, darling. You are lucky, it is a blessing; children are always disappointing. And I'm doubtful that my invertebrate son could create, if anything, little better than a child of chaff.'

Izzy, her husband and her cousin each bore a countenance that displayed their varying degrees of disbelief, but to these Olivia was blind, all she could see was the wisdom in a swift exit from the drawing room before saying something that hinted at homicide. She retrieved her hands from Izzy's, and rose.

'Now, darlings, I must leave, I'm concealing the commencement of a cataclysmic headache, and simply must lie down before I drop! But well done for getting married, I'm certain you shall share very many happy years, and do enjoy your honeymoon!'

Whereupon, she vacated the drawing room but not without first snatching a bottle of champagne from the tea wagon.

The ormolu clock upon the mantelshelf struck the hour six, and when the chime's subdued echoes silenced, Valentine, though well aware of his mother's masquerade, exclaimed, 'Gosh! She rather seemed to take that on the chin, don't you think?'

Harry looked concurringly at his brother; he agreed that on the surface, she had accepted the news with good enough grace, and for that, he was grateful, but still he knew that the torrential storm was but only beginning to brew, and from that, he thought it sage to flee – there was still plenty of time to tell Gubsy of the break in lineage.

'She *weally wather* did!' Harry said, trying to sound as if he believed it.

'Oh ye*th*,' said Izzy quietly, as slowly her tears diminished and she dabbed her runny *retroussé* nose, 'I am *the*rtain it wa*th* a na*th*ty *th*ock and to all intent*th* and purpo*theth the* wa*th* quite ni*the* about it, but I do wi*th the* had *th*tayed *th*o we could tell her we might adopt one day.'

'Olivia is an amazingly nice lady!' said Rupert, stroking his cousin's white shoulder, 'She'll be an amazing mother-in-law, her family is very important to her, I think she would even kill for them!'

Valentine surmised Rupert's estimation of his mother accurate, and was immensely pleased to hear he thought her good in-law material, but the idea of adoption did not sit too well with him; blood is blood and kin is kin, he thought to himself.

Yet to cheer Izzy, he said, 'Gosh! I shouldn't be thinking of offspring anyway, not now you are married and can wear your tiara every single day!'

Izzy's demeanour completely transformed from distress to delight and she looked quite as if she had seen a unicorn.

She gasped, and realising that Valentine was right, she said, 'Ye*th*! I really could! Though perhap*th* not *every th*ingle day!'

'Gosh, I would! I would wear it even in the bath! You must at least wear it every day of your honeymoon! Gosh, how I wish that I had a tiara!' Valentine exclaimed, and made every effort not to look at Rupert as that might appear crass, but Rupert certainly looked at him with a grin.

Harry looked to Izzy. Her apparent childlike gaiety at the realisation that she could now wear with legitimacy her mother's tiara caused his heart to surge and sing with love for her.

'I think it a ve*wy* good idea, we must b*w*ing your tia*wa*!' he said, enthusiastically.

Presently, Izzy relinquished any feeling of upset, and exclaimed, 'Oh, Harry, we mu*th*t get home quickly *th*o I can pack it, I had forgotten all about it!'

Immediately, the group transposed themselves to the front gate and began bidding their farewells.

Harry drew Valentine close to kiss him and whisper, 'So*ww*y to leave you in the lurch with mummy, and I *will* tell Gubsy when I *w*eturn, unless you want to tell him for me? I just don't think Iz . . . *I* could hack it today.'

'Cowardy custard!' Valentine whispered in reply, 'Don't worry about mummy; she shan't give me any bother, and Gubsy's a piece of cake!'

Harry released Valentine, and glowed with gratitude.

'You be a good boy, won't you, *w*ascal?' he said to Corny, and pulled him into a hug that little helped Corny's efforts at holding back his tears.

The excited newlyweds now got into a black cab, and then came Gubsy bounding, as best he could, down the garden path.

'What the deuce!' he boomed.

'Chee*w*io, Gubsy! Goodbye ev*wy*body!' shouted a very happy Harry, waving from behind his equally happy wife.

'*Th*ee you *th*oon! Ki*th*e*th* for you all!' she cried, and motioned her delicate hand as if caressing the cheek of a child.

'Koodbye! Koodbye!' said Gretchen with joy over their happiness.

'Bon voyage!' exclaimed Valentine, as he threw pretend confetti.

'Have an amazing time!' trumpeted Rupert through his cupped hands.

'Reprobates!' hissed Olivia, peeking at the departure between her bedroom curtains, 'Enjoy your time together!'

As the cab motored down the Avenue, Harry leant his lean and long torso out of his window, and he called out, 'Send my love to Willy! And Cosmo can have my *w*oom when he wakes!'

With that, Harry climbed back inside, to kiss, with an intense passion, the new Mrs Avery-Stripe, whilst his family watched them disappear into the distance.

CHAPTER 20

Beastly Limbo and Wonderful Arousal

For twenty-two days, Willy had stared at the spaghetti of tubes inserted into adamantly comatose Cosmo as they each played their part. Every day, she blushed and screwed her eyes when the nurses sluiced and swabbed his every nook and cranny. Every two hours, she watched, with hope, that he might wake when manoeuvred to prevent bedsores, and every minute, she listened to the uninterrupted *beep* of the machine monitoring his heart and she tried not to mind that it did not skip a beat when she whispered, in his cauliflower ears, 'I love you'.

The situation seemed to her eternal and maddening, for though she could see, through the window, people leading lives apparently conventional, she could not envisage it ever being so for herself or Cosmo. Then, when not garbling nonsense in an effort to probe his subconscious, she would look into the middle distance and wonder if one might legally wed a victim of coma and then she would cry at the notion of such miserable matrimony.

Her tears would cease, however, when the notion of matrimony carried her mind to the subject of rings; the Starfish to be exact, and her head would hurt when wondering precisely what had happened at the culmination of The Marvellous Party. As she recollected the event, it made little sense to her, and she felt as if trying to fit together a puzzle that lacked several pieces of significance.

She knew that the ring was Great-Great-Grandmother Olympia's Star-fish, and she berated herself for not having realised it from the first. She knew also that it had come from Valentine's hatbox, but she was unable to reason how he had come by it and why he had treated it with such indifference. She could not either calculate why Mr and Mrs Oxley-Stockman would punish Cosmo so severely as to disinherit him when he had shown true valiance in his attempt to rescue the ring.

Naïvely, Willy, after weeks of fruitless wondering, considered it worth-while simply to ask. Therefore, from the waiting room, with the pockets of her jeans weighed down with the contents of her piggy bank, she braved the payphone so to sound the Oxley-Stockman telephone bell.

'Stakely Manor!' Esmé shouted in her rotten tone.

'Oh! Auntie Esmé!' said Willy, trembling with trepidation as she rattled the coinage in her pocket, 'It's me, Willy. How are you?'

'Who-*ooh*?'

Willy paused to think; Auntie Esmé was either extremely scatty or she was going to be intentionally awkward, but Willy would not be deterred. 'It's Wilhelmina, Auntie!' she said, amiably.

Now Esmé fell silent for a space, and then shouted, 'Wilhelmina? As in 'Stripe?'

'Yes, Auntie, Wilhelmina Avery-Stripe. How are you?'

'Quite incredible!'

'Oh! That's good!'

'It is quite incredible that you possess the gall to call!'

'Oh!' said Willy, sadly realising the misunderstanding. 'Yes, well, *um*, it was unfortunate.'

'Unfortunate, you say!'

'Well, yes, it was, I mean *is*, very, very unfortunate, and that is why I am calling, to try to fix things.'

'Have you my Starfish?'

'Oh no, I don't.'

'Then the situation is irreparable beyond a hope! Do not disturb me again unless you find my Starfish. Goodbye!'

'But, Auntie Esmé! I need to ask you some questions! Please!'

'Questions! You dare to question me? As if *I* were under interrogation?'

'*Um*, well, I have to, you see, I can't ask Cosmo, can I?'

'Who-*ooh*?'

'*Cosmo*, Auntie Esmé! I can't ask him what happened because of his condition.'

'What?'

'He's still in a coma! I really thought mummy might have told you!'

Then Willy realised it a perfectly silly thought.

'Oh, Auntie Esmé! I am certain it's all just a terrible mix-up. Won't you please come and see him? Maybe he will respond to your voice.'

There followed a monumental hiatus.

'Auntie Esmé? Auntie Esmé?' said Willy, and thrice knocked the receiver on the wall with the thought that the line had died, but then upon placing it against her ear, she heard Esmé shout, 'I sincerely hope no one is labouring under the misapprehension that Quentin and I will be footing the medical bills; Cosmo is no longer covered by our insurance!'

'Oh! But Auntie Esmé!' Willy blurted in a highly emotional tone. How could she be so heartless?

'But nothing! I refuse to acknowledge any connection with a son that panders to pansies! And I repeat, do *not* disturb me again unless you locate my Starfish! Goodbye!'

With that, Willy reeled in shock at the sound of the *click* followed by the *burr* of Esmé's harsh telephonic disconnection and obdurate severance of her son.

Willy stared in disbelief at the receiver before slumping into a conveniently-placed plastic chair. Her mind's eye spun in a hypnotic spiral as she considered Esmé's horridness and pondered her words, and then she came to wonder what 'panders to pansies' exactly meant. Whereupon, she filled with suspicion and decided to make the Bakelite bell in Gretchen's kitchen ring so to quiz the pansy she knew best.

'Miss Willy! Oh, Miss Willy!' said Gretchen upon answering with exhilaration as just a moment hitherto she had been bidding Harry and his surprise wife farewell. 'It's such shame you are not beink here, I have such kood news to tell!'

'That's very nice, Gretchen, but can it wait? I need to speak to Valentine.'

'But of course,' said Gretchen, her disappointment apparent, 'I will ket Master Valentine, it is right that he tells you, I think. Hold please!'

Willy filled with regret over her curtness and listened to the muted sound of the ormolu clock chiming a quarter until covered with Valentine's chatter as he approached the Bakelite.

'Gosh, Willy! What do you suppose?' he asked, quite breathlessly.

'I suppose I have a question for you!' she said with assertion.

'Gosh!' said Valentine, flummoxed at the deflection for a flash, 'Well I suppose it to be a very important one for you to telephone. Can you give me an inkling?'

'Oh, you are so annoying, Valentine! I will not give you a clue! I shall just ask it!'

'Gosh! How un-thrilling!' he said with a sigh and a tut, 'Very well, fire away!'

Willy paused to think how best to put it and her conclusion was thus: 'What would you say is meant by panders?'

'Gosh! Well . . . I should say it means a group, I forget the collective noun, probably something silly like a blush or cupboard, of large black and white, bamboo eating bears from China facing extinction. Why?'

'No! Valentine! That's not the panders I mean!'

'The dear little red pandas like raccoons then? I don't know much of them, I believe they hail from the Himalayas, so you'd be better off asking Harry but he's just left, oh, Willy! It is very exciting! But anyway, why the sudden interest in pandas?'

'I do not mean pandas but pan*ders*! *Ders . . . ders . . . ders!*'

'Oh!' said Valentine, experiencing an enlightening, 'That's quite different! Why do you ask?'

Willy explained, 'Because Auntie Esmé said something queer about Cosmo pandering to pansies and it's why he's been disinherited!'

Valentine's enlightenment heightened.

'Gosh! That does sound very queer! I wonder what she might mean.' for he had not the heart to confess to Willy his besmirching of Cosmo's character. 'I suppose she might mean his eyes,' he said, helpfully.

'His eyes?'

'Well yes, you know, he had black eyes, quite like a panda though more like a raccoon – *in fact*, rather like a red panda!'

'That doesn't sound very likely to me! Anyway, it doesn't explain the pansies bit either!'

'*H'm*, yes, you are right,' said Valentine before emitting a theatrical gasp.

'What, Valentine?'

'Just a terrible notion, that's all!' said he.

'Well, what?'

'Well, it could be that Cosmo's been biffing pansies in the eyes and making them look to be pandas!'

'Oh no, Cosmo wouldn't do that!'

'Gosh! Wouldn't he? He got me all black and blue not so long ago, remember? Perhaps it's a habit and Esmé found out and is so very ashamed as to find it so intolerable as to cut him off! Gosh! It smacks of fact to me!'

'Oh, Valentine! Really not! It can't! Cosmo's a bit grumpy but he's not as beastly as all that!'

'Well, I'm quite certain he can explain when he wakes . . . has he stirred at all?'

'No, he hasn't.'

'Oh dear,' said Valentine, 'I suppose we might not ever know, but I shouldn't worry, Willy, Esmé is likely talking tosh!'

'I don't think that she was talking tosh, she sounded very angry and serious!'

'Gosh! I don't doubt it; her existence alone is taxing!'

'And it really is shocking that she doesn't give a hoot about Cosmo and only about her Starfish!' added Willy.

'Really not?'

'Really yes!' Willy confirmed, and then put forward the question, 'And I'd really like to know how you came by it in the first place.'

A pair of nanoseconds passed before Valentine answered.

'Oh, I happened to find it.'

'Find it?' said Willy, sceptically, 'But where?'

'Why on the floor of course, in the hall to be precise but anyway that Starfish was pure paste! Not the real thing at all, and so I kept it.'

'What?' responded Willy with great incredulity, 'Then why didn't you say so at the time!'

'Gosh, well I tried at first but nobody listened and then it all became so dramatic that I hadn't the heart to dispel!'

'You viper!' Willy howled.

'Not I!' he argued, 'I'm not the one so silly as to lose my head over a vintage ring that's not even the real thing!'

Then, to swerve the conversation, he said, 'Anyway, what do you suppose? Oh no, don't try, I shall just tell! Harry got married!'

'Really not?' replied a successfully swerved Willy with surprise.

'Really yes!' exclaimed Valentine, 'To Rupert's lovely cousin Izzy! Glorious, don't you think? They just left for Bath, just moments ago, then they're off on their honeymoon tomorrow, *with* a tiara!'

'Are you fibbing?' asked Willy, suddenly doubting his word.

'Me! No, not at all, it's absolutely gospel! It belonged to Izzy's mother and she can wear it in public now that she is married – isn't it romantic?'

'Yes,' said Willy in a joyless tone, 'It's very romantic. Anyway, *um*, I must go now. Send my love to Corny and Gubsy.'

'Verily, I shall! Harry sent you his too! *Do* take care won't you, Willy?'

'I shall, Valentine. Goodbye.'

Willy returned the telephone receiver to its cradle and unceremoniously burst into tears.

Of course, she was happy for Harry but it did seem to her beastfully unfair that he could so speedily marry, when for years, she had pined for Cosmo who had not once shown her an inch of reciprocation, and now he was in a coma because of an imitation starfish! And so Willy cried and cried as she trundled down the corridor to cry some more into Cosmo's bedclothes.

According to Cosmo's subconscious, his fall did not end in a rosebush but he had, in fact, penetrated the earth, and, as if down a giant rabbit hole, continued his descent deep into the nether world.

Like Alice, he could have thought, 'Curiouser and curiouser!' Only his adventure brought to his mind a different childhood memory of nocturnal chimney sweeps dancing across the rooftops of Victorian London, beneath an ostentatious display of fireworks, except the dancers were not chimney sweeps but people that he knew.

There was Willy galumphing about in an outlandish gown designed as if for a wedding, her heft wobbling rather like agitated jelly, and her face contorted by an ominous smile. Harry was waltzing with a luminous and frail creature that looked as if from heaven, the pair of them mutually besotted. Equally as besotted was Rupert, but he was not dancing but bounding about in mad pursuit of a string of grotesque sausages flourished by Valentine who was prancing in a most tormenting manner.

Yet these individuals, troubling as they were, did not cause Cosmo quite as much anguish as did the howls from his pater and shouts from his mater threatening to flay him alive, whilst they wielded cutthroat razors and sharpened the blades with swift strokes over leather strops.

He heard also the laughter of Olivia, quite hysterical and rather musical for it was the tune of the can-can, it taunted him and made him feel insignificantly small, that is to say if he existed at all and of this he was not sure. Each time he tried to gauge his aunt's expression to determine whether her mirth was in malice or merely flirtatious, an enormous pair of wings, as black as midnight, would swallow him, talons scratched at him, and a blindingly bright beak made to gouge his eyes. Desperately, he tried to shield his face but his arms felt heavy as stone, in fact, his whole body did and he wondered how he could feel so very weighty when he was so small.

His weight hurtled him deeper underground, though all about him were the stars, the moon and fireworks and amongst them, he was searching for something, though he was uncertain what that something was, only that his life depended upon its salvation. He hoped that he would realise the something when he saw it but his concentration was powerless to his heaviness, the feathers, fireworks, sausages, threats, mad laughter and the disconcerting chant of the many that went 'Kik-kik-kik-kik!'

And it was in this alternative reality, this beastly limbo, that Cosmo had dwelt since his misfortune at The Marvellous Party. Suddenly however, with neither rhyme nor reason, his plummet came to an abrupt halt and momentarily he hovered in his oblivion before levitating, at first only tentatively, then gradually with more certainty until quite soon his escalation accelerated with exceptional rapidity.

The unnerving inhabitants of his hell and their accoutrements swept from his mind as if by a passing cyclone, and their departure further increased his buoyancy. There remained the haunting chant 'Kik-kik-kik-kik!' but even this was to fade and just when it had diminished almost entirely it mutated into a different sound, a *beep* . . . *beep* . . . *beep* . . . *beep* that did not come from below but from all around. With every heartbeat, it grew louder and its monotony became so irritating that it forced Cosmo to open his eyes.

Naturally, his sense of orientation was awry but soon he became aware of his hospitalisation, though he possessed not a clue as to why. He did not remember his fall, in fact, all memory of The Marvellous Party was now wholly erased from his conscious mind, and he regarded his elevated arms in casts with shock.

'What the devil!' he said, and instantly realised the penetrating tubes, 'What the devil!' he said again.

Presently, the blubbing sound, of which he had hardly been aware, ceased, and Willy, whose genuflected pose had hidden her from view, became all that he could see.

'Oh, Cosmo!' she cried, and looked in as much shock as he felt to be for she hardly dared to believe in his resurrection, though she required little reason to cover his face with unbridled kisses. 'Oh, Cosmo! You are awake!'

'Of course, I'm bloody awake!' he said, with some annoyance, as he could not restrain her impassioned display with his arms in casts but eventually she stopped simply to stare at him through her happy tears.

'You must tell me what happened, Willy! Why am I here?' he demanded to know.

'Oh, Cosmo, you had a fall! You've been in a coma!' she explained, and once again dove in to smother him.

'Stop it, Willy! Bloody stop it, I say!' and he tried to dodge his little head away, 'I've been in a bloody coma? How long?'

'Three weeks!' she said, and made an effort to restrain herself, 'Three horrid and beastly long weeks that seemed forever! Oh, Cosmo! I was so scared you might not ever wake up! Oh, Cosmo!' and she pulled the cord to alert the doctors and nurses to his wonderful arousal.

Though every inch of Cosmo's body was in discomfort, no part hurt quite as much as did his brain as he tried in vain to swallow his situation.

'But what bloody fall? When did it happen?'

'From the roof of Chinchero, at The Marvellous Party!'

'What the dickens was I doing up there?'

'Trying to catch Remarkable.'

'Why was I bloody doing that? And what marvellous party?'

Willy now regarded Cosmo concernedly, it was of unparalleled relief that he had come round but he seemed not retain any recollection of his mishap. She wondered if this was normal and thought it wise not to overload him with information.

Therefore, in a mollifying tone, she said, 'Oh, none of that's important now, the main thing is that you are awake, oh, and Cosmo, I am *so* happy!'

Endeavouring still to locate his bearings, Cosmo looked about his room and asked, 'But if I've been here three whole bloody weeks then where are my cards and presents? Have I been left for dead? Are you the only bloody one that's been here?'

'Oh no, Cosmo, not at all,' said Willy, though his surmise was not too far off the mark, 'Gretchen has been here everyday, look at the lovely peaches she brought today!'

'Gretchen!' he said, with surprise, 'What about my pater and mater? What about Harry?'

'Oh, Harry did visit the first few days but then he went away and now he is married to Izzy!'

'Married!' Cosmo said with even greater surprise, 'He got married? I must've been in a coma longer than three weeks! And Izzy who? And where *are* my bloody parents?'

Willy was at a total loss for words. Many times, she had envisaged his awakening and pictured it no further than their passionate embrace for she had dared to dream it to rouse within him dormant feelings of affection for her. She had contemplated neither his inevitable questions nor the answers. She wondered how she could brace him for the revelation of his disinheritance, and she filled with relief upon the timely arrival of the militant matron.

CHAPTER 21

The Ramification of the Parisian Tryst

Upon departing the drawing room, as calmly as she was able, Olivia, with the bottle of champagne, ascended the stairwell (mindful to avoid eye contact with the harp-plucking Olympia possessing the Starfish) and entered her bedroom.

She slammed the bottle down on her dressing table with such force that the jumble on it jumped. Then she drained all her energy not to scream like a banshee (for she did not wish the family to hear) and only to hiss like a tail-tugged cat, and score the closest post of the bed until wrath depleted her, whereupon she collapsed supine on her side of the four-poster and gasped to recapture her breath.

Now, less possessed, she spoke to the ghost of Monty laid next to her.

'I am sorry, my darling, so very sorry, I have tried my best, my absolute best, with our ridiculously raw materials, but Horatio, oh my darling, Horatio! He has spurned his function and wedded an infertile!

'But all is not lost, my darling, I shall not ever despair! My only regret is that your heir leaves me no option other than to make of myself a murderess! I shall *not* let the lisping limpet hinder the lineage, for I, and not she, *never she, I,* am Mrs Avery-Stripe!'

The sound of crunching gravel diverted her attention and upon hearing Valentine's exclamations she peeked between her curtains to view what might be happening in the drive and she witnessed the newlyweds' valediction.

'Reprobates!' she hissed at them, 'Enjoy your time together!'

She then turned away from the window, divested herself of her Dior and climbed into bed with the champagne. Her head contained oceans of memories of Monty, and in them she swam as she drank the fizzy anaesthetic, considering the villainy first of Valentine for stealing the Starfish that she had so sullied herself to seize, then of Harry to marry so mutinously as to push his mother to murder, until finally she fell fast asleep.

*

When she woke it was with a start, for though she had not eaten in a while, she felt the violent need to vomit, but she brought up only bile that she deposited in her wastepaper basket.

Her head spun with malady, she felt weak and knew that she must eat. She was ravenous for something but she still could not determine precisely what. Wondering the time, she consulted her Tiffany which told her it was half-past-nine, therefore, she decreed to venture downstairs to somehow discover the cure for her overwhelming craving.

The morning light that streamed in through her window did not dissuade her from believing it still the previous evening and that she had no more than a cat-napped, for she was too involved in knotting her kimono.

The light in the drawing room did not either alert her to the new day because Gubsy, sat in his wing chair, flipped down *The Times* and unabashedly scrutinised her arrival.

His examination was such that she abandoned her idea of inquiring his thoughts on the barren couple, and she said only, 'Uncle Bartholomew.'

To which he replied, 'You are getting fat!' whereupon he returned to the news, whilst Remarkable eyed her contemptuously.

Olivia stood frozen with shock. It was not Gubsy's hostility that so stunned her (she was well used to that) but the suggestion that she had gained weight. She knew that she was svelte and to say otherwise was nothing less than a certain sign of insanity, or in his case senile dementia. With that comforting conclusion, she entered the dining room where she would wait for Gretchen and consider what to consume, and upon doing so the reality of morning dawned upon her, for sitting at the lacquered table laden with the trappings of breakfast was a solitary Valentine drinking the appropriate tea.

'Good morning, mummy,' said he, returning his teacup back into its saucer with a *clink*.

Olivia was agape, and she gasped, as slowly she sat opposite him.

'Is it, darling?' she asked.

'Well, in fact, not,' he replied. 'Quite the contrary really; Rupert's next door discussing his manual labour with the Frobishers back from their ramble. Apparently, other people are there too whom also require work in their horrid houses, and I just know he shan't say no because I know he likes to be busy and so I am really rather rankled!'

Simultaneously, he sounded a tut and made a moue, before adding, 'And Corny is with him too.'

'No, darling,' Olivia said, with some exasperation, 'I meant, is it really morning?'

Valentine viewed her queerly for a flash, then he looked at the sunshine through the French windows, heard the ante meridiem avian chirruping, surveyed the items upon the table, and declared, 'Indubitably!'

Surrendering herself to the verity, Olivia poured herself a cup of tea, and said, with sigh, 'Really, darling, I am most discombobulated, I could have sworn it was still yesterday evening.'

'If that's the case,' Valentine replied with scepticism, 'why are you wearing your kimono?' and he checked the jam for butter before applying it to his toast in a manner to imply that nothing could be more laborious.

'The idea that one's apparel should be dictated by the time of day carries less than little weight when said by a person who exists permanently in pyjamas,' spat Olivia, and she raised a brow as she lifted her cup to her lips.

'Gosh, mummy! Little wonder you are in disarray; it is most unlike you to be so incisive before noon!'

'*Ugh!*' said Olivia, spluttering her tea so demonstratively that it dribbled down her chin, 'What is this dishwater, darling? Surely not tea?'

'Indubitably tea!' Valentine exclaimed with irritation, as if his own fair hands had picked the leaves, and he motioned like a maniac for her to obliterate the chin trickle.

Olivia obliged, then peered suspiciously into her cup and wondered why its contents tasted so vile. Had Valentine played a trick and substituted sugar with salt?

'It tastes disgusting!' she stated.

'Gosh, mummy! Some words really ought not to be bandied about at breakfast!'

'I refuse to mince, darling! If a thing happens to taste disgusting than I shall certainly call it disgusting!'

'Well then eat something nice to take away the *disgusting* taste of the *disgusting* tea! Have some jam!'

'No, darling, I couldn't, the very idea of it disagrees!'

'Gosh! Disgusting tea and disagreeable jam! What about some disgraceful bacon?'

'I really could not!'

'Disreputable sausage?'

'Certainly not sausage!'

'Well, mummy,' said Valentine, after listing all the breakfast foods he could call to mind, 'you've exhausted my suggestions, except for the one that you might not even be hungry.'

'Darling!' she said to him in a hushed tone that indicated abject desperation, 'Never before have I felt as fiercely famished as I do exactly now! But the crux is I cannot locate precisely what for and everything else makes me want to vomit!'

Aghast, Valentine was about to tell her that that was what he just might do if she continued to use such vocabulary but then Gretchen appeared wearing a muumuu.

'Kood mornink, Mrs Olivia!' she said joyfully, 'Is such kood weather to be koink away for honeymoons!' and she grinned from ear to ear, 'I am so happy for Master Harry, and you must be also still very!'

Olivia believed Gretchen's manner mocking and she considered a double murder for a moment until realising Gretchen might not have heard about Izzy's infertility. She glared at her with annoyance nonetheless.

'Mrs Olivia?' said Gretchen with a frown, 'Are you not happy?'

'Gosh!' Valentine interjected, 'Mummy couldn't be more so! Yet, alas, her happiness is hindered by her serious hunger for something she cannot name!'

Gretchen looked at Olivia as she might a frail infant. Slowly, she shook her head.

'This is no kood! Breakfast is most important meal of day; everyday you must eat breakfast like a kink! Tell Kretchen what is you want.'

Olivia merely shrugged her shoulders and looked forlorn, whereupon Gretchen named numerous dishes.

'Not even honey with yokhurt?' she said finally.

'Gosh no, Gretchen!' exclaimed Valentine, 'Today honey is dishonourable and yoghurt dishonest!'

'Well, I cannot think what you can eat,' said Gretchen with serious concern, for she did not want to think of anyone going hungry and neither did she like being unable to provide. 'I will ko to kitchen and see what else might be.'

With that, she made her way toward the kitchen door but then she suddenly stopped, turned, and with eureka effectively emblazoned across her face, she said, 'Mrs Olivia! Could you eat kedgeree?'

Olivia regarded Gretchen with a greater sense of elation than she had felt in a very long time; the foreign woman really did earn her keep, for the rice, egg, and fish dish was the solution to her situation.

'Oh, Gretchen! You are a saint!' Olivia exclaimed, 'Kedgeree is exactly what I crave! I feel I could eat a trough of the stuff!'

'Kood! Kood!' said Gretchen, with a triumphant smile. 'I will make you lots!' and she hurried into her kitchen.

'Immense gratitude, Gretchen!' cried Olivia, and she turned to Valentine and grinned a toothier grin than that of the crocodile mounted upon the wall behind him; at last she could feast on something that would not induce her stomach to somersault!

Valentine, however, was not so rapturous; distant memories had suddenly sharpened and cast an illumination.

Quite clearly, he could recollect his crisp Nanny Cook explaining to him, as he straddled his zebra rocking horse in the nursery, 'The reason mummy is eating "troughs" of kedgeree is because anticipatory ladies often crave specific plates,' and, 'Yes, Valentino, I am quite certain that she craved plates when you were in her tummy. Now, do dismount Zebadiah, it is well past your bedtime!'

Another clear and altogether more joyous recollection, from later on that same evening, was straddling a strapping corduroyed-thigh and enjoying daddy's hearty and stingo-scented laughter at his question, to which came the reply: 'Mummy did "crave plates" with you, in fact, it was kedgeree too, just like with little Willy Wonka and Horatio. It's a new family tradition, I suppose! Anyway, little popinjay, enough chatter! It's time for me to tuck you up!'

The two recollections caused Valentine to contort his countenance with an astonishment that he did not conceal from Olivia whose own face slowly lost its smile as she wondered the root of his apparent perturbation.

Naturally, Valentine was aware that for his mother to inhabit again her kedgeree-craving state then somebody, and certainly not daddy, had sown the seed to situate her so.

'But whom?' he mentally asked, with severe concentration.

Then, as his psychological cogs and wheels collaborated, a stupendous squall of facts spiralled into a vortex and as each gravitated toward its sphincter, his hidden and ugly notions apropos her doubtlessly shady methods to procure Olympia's Starfish rammed on in.

The penetration struck him with the dire misgiving that in exchange for the ring an interaction of the most unsavoury sort had transpired between his mother and one of the Oxley-Stockman men.

'But which?' Valentine asked himself.

He knew only of two, and his rumination brought him to the conclusion that Quentin would not ever, if indeed, he even could. Yet Cosmo was certainly capable, moreover, Valentine could recall several occasions when Cosmo had slyly cast his mother impiously lewd glances.

The idea of such a union made Valentine feel sick to the core, not so much over his mother's dearth of propriety, for he knew that to be erratically lax, but to compromise herself explicitly with Cosmo so warped his constitution that he began to reject the reality and to deem his deduction ridiculous.

However, wishing to ascertain whether or no she had committed such a sin, he gathered as much equipoise as he was able, poured himself a fresh cup of disgusting tea, and calmly inquired, 'Gosh, mummy! Are you burdened with a bastard baby?'

The query was, to Olivia, a horrific blow; Valentine's obvious contemplation had disconcerted her certainly but she had not dreamt it would result in so objectionable a question. Nevertheless, despite her insufficient girding, she retained a detached demeanour, and put up a defence.

'What an imbecilic idea, darling,' she coolly said. 'Why do you suddenly suspect everyone expectant? Is it a new fad? And "bastard" at breakfast, Valentine? I find your behaviour hypocritical.'

'Gosh! Not everyone!'

'No, darling, just your mother and your brother's new wife, which I might add was incomprehensively idiotic; they'd hardly time to create the complication!'

'Gosh, mummy! You call conception a complication! You, above all others, perhaps even Izzy, wished such a *complication* to be the case instead of the fruitless fact! You virtually spat venom!'

'I'm quite certain I possess no notion of the argument for your allegation vis-à-vis spitting venom!'

Here, she put up a hand to deflect any further speculations with regard to herself and felt her head flood with the possibility that she may indeed be burdened.

'But surely not!' she mentally reasoned, as she involved herself with the inspection of her place mat depicting Pasiphae *in flagrante delito* with the White Bull.

'How could it be?' she wondered, and then realised she was too long in the tooth for such naivety. However, upon reflection, she conceded that being still the right side of fifty rendered it possible, and what was more, after applying mathematics to her monthlies, the probability multiplied.

Overwhelmingly confused and intimidated by chaotic numbers and calendar calculations, she turned her mind to the physical evidence: her sporadic slumbering, her waves of heat and increasing irritation over everything, the constant vomiting, the alleged weight gain, her antipathy toward tea, and the disability to consider consuming anything other than kedgeree. All were indicative of gestation, for she had suffered the exact same symptoms during the four previous invasions. With that thought, she suddenly realised that in the recesses of her psyche she had known all along that for a fifth time the kernel of a hominid inhabited her being, and Valentine was right; this time the kernel was a bastard – the bastard of Cosmo (for she had conjoined with no other since her husband, and neither before nor during) whom had so foolishly neglected to shroud his insubstantiality!

Momentarily, Olivia managed to push the ramification of the Parisian tryst from her mind and study hard her place mat, but knowledgeable of the bestial pairing's consequential minotaur, it little soothed her nerves. Instead, she raised her head and was surprised at the sight of Valentine, for he had quite escaped her concentration, and to him she said nothing because words seemed futile, and she waited for his inevitable reiteration.

Sure enough, it came. Valentine somewhat baulked at his mother's sudden anaemic appearance, but still he had to know, and so he asked, 'But, mummy, *are* you burdened?'

It was too much for her to bear. She did not wish even to acknowledge the question let alone reply and chose simply to arise as nobly she could and leave the dining room to ascend the stairwell and take refuge in the four-poster.

Upon Olivia's silent departure, there was little doubt in Valentine's mind of what had come to pass for it all made perfect sense. Therefore, directly following a minute's reeling, despite the tinge of sick in his craw, he filled with something akin to awe at her pluck simply to return the Starfish to the family, and he called out to Gretchen: 'Bring mummy's kedgeree on a tray; she's bedridden!' before excitedly galloping up the stairwell.

In an effort to appear tentative, Valentine knocked gingerly upon Olivia's door but before she could call out he misplaced his patience and skipped inside.

'*Ugh!*' said Olivia, with her face in her husband's pillow, 'Go away!'

'Gosh! But, mummy! It's me!'

'I'm well aware who you are! Go away!'

Valentine did not abide. Instead, he closed the door, sat at the dressing table and surveyed the scene. He raised his brows at his mother, face-down on the four-poster, and he blinked. He looked, disapprovingly, at the empty champagne bottle on the floor. He noticed the mess in the wastepaper basket and his nose turned up accordingly.

'Gosh, mummy! You are in a pickle!' he exclaimed.

Olivia startled at his voice; she had believed him absent, and with irritation upon her nerves, and her dishevelled hair straggled over her face, she repositioned to regard him.

In a withering tone, she said, 'What are you still doing here? I demand solitude!'

'Gosh, but, mummy! I've come to be with you!' he replied, 'You've patently had quite the shock and oughtn't to be alone, although, well, there are three of us in here, aren't there?'

Creasing her brow to exhibit bewilderment, Olivia insisted, 'I am wholly mystified by your meaning!'

Valentine sounded a tut and transposed his seat so to perch on the four-poster, and he elaborated, 'You and me and baby makes three!' and he dared to place his hand upon his mother's stomach.

Olivia wanted to scream. She wanted to take Valentine's hand and yank his arm from its socket, but she merely slapped it, and snapped, 'This baby talk is becoming a bore! So do desist!'

Valentine cradled his hand and made a moue.

'Gosh, mummy, why the secrecy? I mean from me! Because though I think it somewhat sordid, you really are ever so intrepid!'

'What are you wittering about, darling?' asked Olivia, feeling the noose about her neck gradually tighten.

'Well, mummy, I mean your enterprise!'

'My enterprise!' she said, shrilly.

Valentine viewed his mother and wondered how long she might maintain the charade and he hoped it not very.

'Gosh, don't let's play silly buggers, I mean your Starfish enterprise, more specifically, to return it to the family as daddy always wanted! I do think it ever so romantic, though the extent of your involvement with Cosmo was a trifle extravagant but I salute your tenacity and now, well, here we are with no Starfish, and I'm awfully sorry about that, but in its stead we have something superior; a new addition to the Avery-Stripes! Hooray!'

Emitting an enormous sigh, Olivia reclined and let her eyes traverse the cracks in the four-poster's ceiling, and mentally cursing, she surrendered herself to the shrewdness of Valentine for she sorely lacked the strength to oppose it.

'You certainly did not inherit daddy's lack of intellect did you, darling?' she quietly said.

'Gosh! Whatever do you mean?' asked a nettled Valentine; his daddy was a deity and not to be disparaged!

'Daddy, darling,' she said, 'possessed more brawn than brain but do not think for a moment that I loved him any the less for it; quite the opposite in fact, yet he was not ever perceptive.'

'Gosh yes!' replied Valentine, excitedly, as he clambered further on to the bed and crossed his legs, 'Daddy was gloriously strong! And I know I didn't inherit that but he did always think me very clever with my tongue, and yes, I indubitably possess a perceptive eye!'

Olivia now looked to Valentine. She noted, with pleasure, his obvious reverence for her husband and decided to reward it.

'Yes, darling, he did venerate your verbosity,' she said. 'And your perceptive eye you inherited from me.'

Valentine swooned at the affirmation of his daddy's love.

'Gosh! I suppose I must've!' and he turned his attention to her tummy, 'I wonder if baby shall too. Of course, although an Avery-Stripe, he shan't be anything like daddy but, with any luck, all he'll get from Cosmo is his small skull, to start with anyway, because I imagine it'd make his advent altogether less of an ordeal. When exactly is his estimated time of arrival?'

Olivia wondered how Valentine was so certain of the kernel's gender but then the reality of the conversation and the gravity of its matter hit her. She broke out in a cold sweat, and cried, 'Oh, but it cannot be true! Monty would murder me if he knew! No! I will not have it!'

'What!' Valentine said with panic, 'But you must have it! You can't destroy it! Daddy would definitely want you to have it; it, *he*; the baby, is divine providence, don't you see?'

'You fool!' she snapped, whilst she started to excavate her Birkin for a cigarette then decided, of course, not to smoke, 'I mean, I will not have the situation!'

She looked at him now with perplexity and this state somewhat calmed her.

'What, darling, do you mean by divine providence?'

Without hesitation, Valentine educated her.

'Gosh, well I think it crystal clear that some celestial chap, perhaps not *Him*, more likely daddy, though I wonder if he might dwell in Hell, or even Excelsior, yes probably Excelsior, foresaw the fate of the family, *id est*, Harry marrying Izzy, and saw that it was *good* because she is beautiful and not poor, and she is quite nice really if a little simple. But, yes, barren! Therefore, something had to be done and Excelsior looked to his people, *us* I mean, and commenced a concentrated contemplation until he saw the solution that was quite obvious!

With increasing excitement, Valentine went on, 'He took Olympia's Starfish, which I suppose you could compare to the star of Bethlehem, and with it, he guided not wise men but his only available vessel, *you*, toward the only spermatozoon whom is of his blood but not of yours, *Cosmo*, to procreate a progeny to bestow upon your first-born in order to ensure the continuation of the Avery-Stripe lineage; Excelsior begat Ambrosius, Ambrosius begat Jeremiah, Jeremiah begat Montgomery and Montgomery begat Horatio! I *do* think it sounds *so* like a biblical passage! And now we must think of a suitable name for Horatio to beget, and we must see that it is *good*!'

Olivia began to thrash about with a reckless rage, and she wailed, 'So that is why you think it certain to be a boy!'

'Gosh! No need to make a musical about it, mummy!'

'A *musical*!' she cried, 'To bare a baby to give to one's son to raise as his own is more tawdry soap-opera than anything, and yet you tell it as if it were a parable!'

'Well, it is rather. Don't you think?' he reasoned.

Olivia screamed into a pillow and then quietened, before saying, 'I refuse to be preached to by a thief! You should not have taken the Starfish from me!'

'I am not a thief, mummy!' Valentine argued, 'I simply found it, and even when Willy wore it I did not know of it, besides if my acquisition of the Starfish was through thievery then what might we call the process that you so honourably employed?'

Olivia looked daggers at him, and realised she could hardly castigate because he did have a point and she started to hyperventilate.

'Anyway, mummy, the Starfish has gone, nobody has it now, not even Esmé, and that is a boon, and so too is Cosmo's disinheritance, though it is rather a shame his coma prevents him from knowing about it. Gosh, by the by, am I right in assuming that Cosmo was unaware of the child?'

'Not a clue, darling.' said Olivia almost dreamily for suddenly exhaustion claimed her.

'Glorious!' said Valentine, 'I must say, Cosmo's coma gets more blessed by the minute; we don't want him interfering!'

'I most certainly do not require further interference from him!' stated Olivia.

'Gosh, mummy! I beg of you to spare me the specifics!'

'Of course, darling.' she said, 'Oh, and darling I never did thank you for coming to my aid that night at the party, I did appreciate it.'

'Quite all right, mummy, you would have done just the same!' said Valentine, and he lay down on his daddy's side of the four-poster to inspect the cracks in its ceiling with his mother.

With camaraderie in the air, Olivia felt comforted and she started to review the situation and contemplate Valentine's solution.

In her mind, she walked around it as if it were a tremendous installation of Art in an otherwise empty gallery, and though she thought it not the prettiest sight, she could not envisage either its replacement or removal; it was there to stay, in fact, it was veritably fixed to the spot.

Then, she considered its soundness, and as she mulled, she came to grasp the sagacity of Valentine's words. They did make significant sense. Harry had married well but for the one flaw, and she was in a position to remedy that flaw, and rather than taking Izzy's life, it would be much nicer to give her one. However, the overriding benefit of the entire scheme was the appeasement of Monty by delivering, to the family, another heir, because that would most categorically set in stone her love for him and her reverence of the Avery-Stripes.

Presently, Olivia experienced a sweet sense of atonement sweep over and through her but only for a flash because there then flickered a shadow of doubt.

'But, darling, what if I transpire not to be burdened? It is only a strong suspicion!'

'What!' exclaimed Valentine, sitting bolt upright and staring at her with wide eyes, 'You mean to say you do not know for certain?'

Olivia winced.

'No, darling, I do not. I did not even think of it until you put it to me!'

'Gosh, mummy!' said Valentine, concernedly, 'We must find out! It would be a terrible thing if the baby is not real!'

Quite to her surprise, Olivia found herself nodding in acquiescence.

'Hand me your Birkin!' Valentine commanded.

Olivia obeyed before asking why.

'Because,' he explained, as he rummaged, 'I need money to buy one of those kits that read your pee!'

Here, he froze for a space, and then asked, 'There are such kits, aren't there? They do exist don't they?'

'Yes, darling, they do,' she said, with a sigh at his patchy innocence, yet thankful for his alacrity to take charge.

'Gosh!' he said, with wonderment, 'How clever!' and then he found her empty purse, 'Oh, mummy! There is nothing!'

'Really, darling?' Olivia said, with pretend surprise.

Valentine sounded a tut.

'Never mind, mummy, I'll find some and then I shall whiz to the apothecary to purchase the pee-reading kit – I'll be back in a jiffy!'

He sprang from the four-poster to put his plan into action, but before he left, Olivia asked, 'How did you guess about the baby anyway, darling?'

'Gosh, mummy,' he said, as he opened the door, 'I'd love to say I'm clairvoyant but it was the kedgeree that did it!'

Whereupon Gretchen arrived with a salver upon which was a large platter of the dish. Valentine snatched it from her and delivered it to his mother before scraping together some hidden notes that he knew of, and borrowing Corny's fire engine red bicycle, he whizzed to the apothecary.

No sooner had Valentine vacated her bedroom did Olivia savagely attack the platter of kedgeree for which she had so long been craving, and as she ingested she reminisced. Certainly, the reminiscences were of Monty, for he was her *raison d'être*, but on this occasion, her nostalgia concentrated upon their first encounter.

She resented so much the ease with which she could recall her poky bedroom in the tiny terraced house belonging to her battleaxe mother in Battersea. It was like a prison cell, except the walls were only chipboard, and upon the walls only lining paper that no more than absorbed the damp it meant to hide. The patches of damp created dirty cloud shapes, and in the candlelight (for her mother often refused to top up the electric meter with the claim that to do so would be decadent) Olivia would dream herself astride the clouds so to escape her horrid existence and live a life of luxury.

Yet, at the age of seventeen, she knew that nothing ever came from dreaming and that she would have to apply herself accordingly if she were ever to realise her ambition. Further, she was cognisant that the journey would significantly shorten, and be less of a labour if she could snare a man, and that whatever else he may or may not be, it little mattered so long as he was wealthy.

Her practical understanding was such that she also knew it impossible to locate such a man in her locality and she was grateful that the no.19 bus, which stopped at her corner, travelled into London's centre and, on its way, passed plenty of smart hotels and bars in which the pickings were rich. But before venturing to any of those places she was mindful that she would have advertise her assets so to sell herself to the highest bidder, and that though her body was beautiful she must adorn it appropriately, for she did not wish a prospective buyer to detect a whiff of her impoverishment or desperation. Therefore, she went against all her better instincts and secured herself a job of work in a local candle factory snipping wicks down to size. It was humiliating and menial but it was a means to an end and, quite soon, she saved enough shillings to purchase a bright red Biba dress that she deemed capable of persuading any decent man's desires.

She was lucky enough to find, in a Red Cross shop, some heels and a clutch that matched the dress perfectly, and upon her first nocturnal foray, she realised, with a smile, that the colour of the bus was also in accordance with the ensemble. Then when she realised that the Chanel scent, stolen from her mother, too niggardly to ever wear it, was the same number as the bus route, she decided the correspondence propitious and decreed never to wear any other.

Fate did not give her an easy time of it however, because though for months she frequented nigh on every sophisticated bar and lounge from Sloane Square to Soho via Mayfair, and met many men of great means all of whom were eager to more than make her acquaintance, none of them measured up to her standards.

Naturally, she would permit them to ply her with champagne because not only would it be rude to refuse, she would look foolish without a drink, and besides she could hardly afford it on her income. But oh! The men that she had to endure! Never had she imagined such a variety of just one mammal! She met them all: the cry-babies, the mummy's boys, the bullying bores, the morons, the misogynists, the narcissists, the seedy lechers, and the geriatric gropers. More despicable specimens than she could ever shake a stick at! She worked hard in her pursuit of money!

That is not to say that she ever acceded to their advances. That was a thing she just would not do, and if they did not like it, well then, that was their misfortune; she would not submit to anyone unworthy for she considered her virgin state a valuable commodity. Occasionally a man would flare up at her rejection, whereupon she would have to rely on the maitre d' or head barman, but as the weeks went by she fast learned to spot the signs of a man reaching the end of his tether and would bolt and relocate. It was a vital talent that she again employed decades later as a widow wandering the continent except that the champagne became cheques and the lounges luxury suites, but never did she compromise her integrity – bar the recent *faux pas* in Paris.

Then finally, after the umpteenth bolt, she realised, with chagrin, that money, though still superior to tertiary, was not of primary importance because she could not ever happily interact with any man unless she loved him or at the very least desired him, and despite being pleasantly surprised at her virtue, the hindrance rankled her. Where might she find a loveable millionaire? She felt as if it were expected of her to surmount Mount Everest, and although it was only half-past-ten, she decided against propping up another bar and chose instead to take the bus home to wallow in her feeling of defeat.

The bus only got as far Sloane Square and went no further due to a puncture and Olivia had to alight. Matters became worse upon her discovery that the only money she had brought with her was enough for two fares; the journey out and the return, and now she had nothing except the annoyance that came with the realisation that she would have to walk. Then her rage all but got the better of her when the heel of her left shoe broke in a crack in the pavement of the King's Road. Yet her rage was nothing in comparison to the hopelessness that so suddenly and power-fully consumed her. She collapsed in a heap in the gutter, and wept at the prospect of an eternity of poverty with her harridan washerwoman mother who did little else other than assert that though her only happy hour was the one spent with a handsome stranger beneath Clacton Pier, the result of it (Olivia) was the bane of her life.

In retrospect, Olivia could now kiss the bus wheel and high heel, for had they not punctured and broken she would not have been so fatefully situated and would never have heard the first words spoken to her by her future husband: 'I say, what's the ruddy matter with you?'

His tone was sonorous, for that was how he spoke, but Olivia considered it simply bellicose and refused to acknowledge him for she had had her fill of portentous posh-boys. Fortunately, though her judgment was not wide off the mark, Monty was also obstinate.

'I said,' he said, with even greater resonance, as he hunkered next to her, 'what's the ruddy matter with you?'

This time Olivia could not ignore him for he blasted his words directly in her ear, and his beer and gamy breath overwhelmed her face.

'*Ugh*! Do go away!' she said, quite pathetically, and without turning to look at her tormentor, she endeavoured to assist his departure with a shove but it transpired impossible for he was too sturdily built and no more than budged an inch.

With a sigh, she withdrew her arm and folded it over the other to create a cradle for her head and there was silence.

For a space, she thought he had given up and gone away on his own accord but then she heard his heavy breathing and felt his eyes boring into her.

'Please,' she begged, 'leave me alone!'

Then came his reply: 'But what's the ruddy matter with you?'

His reiteration induced in her a convulsive quake of infuriation, but she bit her tongue and made the decision to answer the question with the wish that he might then disappear.

'The ruddy matter,' she spoke, with spite into the gutter, 'is that I've had enough! I am tired and want to go to bed but I do not want to go home. I hate my life and I have only just realised that it will never get any better, and so I am sitting here and refusing to go on because everything is so hopeless!'

There was a pause, then she heard him *harrumph* followed by another pause, and then, with his lips against her hair, he said, '*Nil Desperandum*!'

'This man is a moron!' she thought to herself, 'He is now talking foreign!' and she snapped, 'I do not speak foreign! So please move on!'

He sounded an amused grunt, and then said, 'Not ruddy foreign, it's Latin! Means "never despair"; it's the Avery-Stripe motto.'

She considered his talk pure gobbledegook but it drew her in, and for the first time, she turned to him and, with a scowl, said, 'The Avery-Stripe what-o? What is an Avery-Stripe?'

'I am an Avery-Stripe!' he stated, with obvious pride.

Olivia was not sure what did it. Perhaps it was his fierce defiance to be anything but whatever an Avery-Stripe was, because it patently created in him a feeling akin to a Spartan phalanx ready for war, and she surmised it a club worth joining. Or maybe it was his stalwart physique and dogged jaw, or simply his dependable harebell blue eyes, but instantly she was aware of her attraction to him – and it did not either hurt that his aspect was decidedly moneyed.

'You *are*?' she said, in a tone to imply unadulterated awe.

Monty puffed out his barrel chest, and boasted, 'Most certainly am!' then he furrowed his brow, 'And who are you?'

'Oh, I am nothing!' she said with coy self-deprecation.

Promptly pulling his pugilistic face into one suggesting a firm difference of opinion, he told her, 'You are not a thing! You are a very pretty little thing and I'd like to meet the chap that says otherwise!' whereupon he brandished his powerful fist at a confused passer-by.

'Yes,' thought Olivia, watching how easily he hastened the pedestrian's pace, 'he is definitely an idiot, but a desirable one.'

Then when once again their eyes met, he beamed at her, and she said, 'Oh, you are very kind, already I feel slightly *Nil Desperandum*,' and she batted her lashes and wished him to forget her location in the gutter.

'Excellent! Excellent!' he boomed, 'Now come with me, I've lost count the number of pints I've had to-day but they've barely touched my sides, and I want more! So I'll take you to *The Pheasantry*, buy you anything you want to drink and we'll see about making you totally *Nil Desperandum*!'

Oh, how she wished to go with him! But how could she enter any decent establishment with a broken heel?

'Nothing would be nicer but I cannot go anywhere with my faulty footwear!' she said, and held the detached heel for him to see.

He took it from her and viewed it with anger at its sheer impertinence before tossing it over his shoulder and announcing, 'I'll buy you new ones!'

'But nowhere is open now!' she argued, though she wished that she were wrong.

'*H'm*,' he said, and looked entirely baffled by the conundrum of what best to do.

'I shall just go home!' she said, meekly, with a design to hook.

Presently, his face became one of utter astonishment.

'You said you don't want to go home!'

'But where else can I go?'

Again, he looked puzzled, and she realised that he needed steering.

'Do you live around here?' she asked in such a way that it would sound like polite conversation.

Presently, it was plain to see that an idea had occurred to him: 'We shall go to mine!'

'Oh! What a good idea!' she said, enthusiastically, and he roared with laughter.

'I'm not half the halfwit I look, you know!' he said.

Olivia was about to argue that she did not for one moment consider him anything less than highly intellectual when he rose to his feet, picked her up quite as if she was indeed nothing, and, like a groom carrying his bride over the threshold, he transferred their situation to the middle of the King's Road.

'STOP!' he roared at the fast approaching black cab that screeched to a halt just before them.

The driver wound down his window and expressed his annoyance with expletives that Monty ignored and he positioned his pretty little thing in the backseat, pulled her into a bear hug, and boomed at the driver, 'Belgravia, my good man!'

'I apologise in advance,' he then, comparatively softly, said to Olivia, 'Damned ugly house. I'll only live there until I find a wife and then move to the country to breed. It's my parent's house really.'

Olivia's eyes widened as she wondered how ugly a house in Belgravia could possibly be.

Monty misread her, and went on, 'Don't worry, they're dead. Most of us are . . . '

Whereupon, Olive Teasel's Avery-Stripe education began, and as she learned of Excelsior, she luxuriated in Monty's arms, and in the presentiment that she was indubitably bound for a better life.

'Gosh, mummy!' exclaimed Valentine, upon re-entering her bedroom without first knocking, 'That was marvellously exhilarating! The wind in my hair was glorious, though I did sweat just a little bit, but I'm certain I don't know why the apothecarian stared at me so queerly! Anyway, here's the kit – apparently, the most accurate! Gosh, mummy! Are you crying?'

'No, darling,' Olivia lied, and she blinked several times, 'Gretchen must've put in quite a lot of curry powder, that's all.'

Valentine laughed with delight at the sight of the clean platter, 'Gosh! You've eaten all of it! That must be a good sign because there were heaps of it!'

He flung himself across the four-poster.

'Anyway, mummy, you go and . . . well, you know, *use* the kit and I shall await here for your return . . . It is so very exciting!'

Olivia picked up the box and looked at each of its six sides with uncertainty.

'Gosh, quickly, mummy!' said Valentine in an insisting tone, 'I cannot wait to know!'

Realising that procrastination was never worth the effort; Olivia gathered her grit to grasp the nettle.

'Yes, darling,' she said, pocketing the kit in her kimono and twisting the doorknob, 'do wait here, I shall be back directly.'

After finishing his second cigarette, Valentine began to wonder how complicated the kit could be. He had not imagined it to require quite so much time, and as he retrieved a third cigarette from his silver-case and toyed with the idea of lighting it, Olivia returned.

Her countenance and demeanour combined signs of both thrill and fear but as she climbed upon the four-poster, and pulled Monty's pillow near, she was quite as mute as Corny.

'Well, mummy?' asked Valentine on tenterhooks, '*Are* you burdened?'

Still Olivia said nothing and instead she gave to Valentine the plastic indicative stick in exchange for his unlit cigarette.

'Is it clean?' said Valentine, as he peered at it and tried to divine its meaning.

His trivial concern riled her.

'Of course it is!' she snapped

'Oh, good! But what does it say? I can't decipher dots!'

'*Ugh!*' said Olivia, 'It says that I am indeed burdened!'

Valentine accordingly sounded an almighty gasp, and after an inarticulate moment, he exclaimed, 'Gosh! Jolly well done!' and snatching back his cigarette, he asked, 'But is it a blessed boy?'

Olivia viewed him with astonishment, 'What an incredulously idiotic question! We shan't know if it's a boy for weeks!'

'Gosh!' replied Valentine, with some disappointment, 'The kit's not as sophisticated as I had supposed! But still, I just know it's a boy! I can just feel it! A bonny baby boy for Harry and Izzy, and a new heir for the family! It is a *most* glorious thing!'

Doubt claimed Olivia, she recoiled and cried, 'But how can you be so certain that Harry and Izzy will agree?'

'Gosh, now that *is* an incredulously idiotic question!' Valentine said in a matter-of-fact tone, 'Izzy even spoke of adoption after you left, and this baby is family, and so it's virtually concrete!'

'Yes, darling, I do believe you are right.'

'Of course I am, mummy, one only has to apply the according approach!'

With that, Olivia flopped back and sighed with relief; she was grateful that her second-born had inherited his father's obstinacy.

For some moments, silence prevailed but then there came the sound of much crunching of gravel along with Rupert's cheerful tone followed by another not so agreeable because it was a familiar bellow.

The possibility that the bellow's suspected owner was down below struck them dumb, and they strained their ears so better to hear whether or no it was indeed Cosmo. Yet even when they caught, with clarity, the word 'mater', they still were not entirely convinced. Therefore, Valentine tiptoed to the window and peeked between the curtains, whilst Olivia prayed it was just paranoia. The psychiatric disorder was too much to hope for however, and she filled with dread when Valentine gasped and ducked.

'Gosh, mummy!' he exclaimed in a whisper and crawled toward the four-poster, 'It *is* Cosmo! His coma has broken!'

Olivia pulled at her hair, and whispered in reply, 'Please tell me that you are lying!'

'How I wish that I were!' he said, woefully, 'But it is a horrible truth! Cosmo is back with Willy, and both his arms in slings, and looks to be livid!'

Panic seized Olivia by the throat and she possessively placed her hands over her stomach.

'Oh, darling! What am I to do?'

Valentine considered. 'Absolutely nothing! Carry on regardless. Your burden is not yet evident but you can hide up here if you wish. I shan't let Cosmo take the baby Avery-Stripe!'

'Technically, darling, it is more Oxley-Stockman than Avery-Stripe, I'm not blood!'

'Rubbish, mummy! *He* is thoroughbred Avery-Stripe, as are you! How many heirs do you have to produce before you are blood!'

Olivia felt overwhelmed by the surprise sentiment.

In an authoritative tone, Valentine went on: 'Now listen to me, mummy, you must not tell anyone; not of the baby nor about Izzy, and I shall do the rest.'

'But what will you do, darling?' she begged to know.

Valentine bit his knuckle.

'Gosh! I'm not exactly certain but I've an inkling brewing in my mind, and I'm quite confident that everything will come up roses, because never forget, mummy: *Nil Desperandum!*'

CHAPTER 22

The Machinations of Valentine

Valentine discovered the convalescent and furious Cosmo sat upon the chesterfield in the drawing room, and he sickened at the thought that the brute was the biological father of the unborn Avery-Stripe bastard. Next to Cosmo was Willy, who truly looked to possess something glorious that everybody desires as she gazed, with adoration, at Cosmo's disgruntled profile, and held his tumbler of Scotch because he could not with both his arms in slings.

Rupert and Corny were there, Gubsy also but he was asleep beneath *The Times*, and upon Valentine's entrance, Rupert ceased his uncomfortable conversation with Cosmo and grinned.

'Valentine!' he said.

'You've been forever!' Valentine replied – the need to recognise Cosmo's recuperation could wait.

'Sorry,' said Rupert.

'So, do lots of selfish people require your renovative skills?' asked Valentine, and though he enjoyed Rupert's arm placed about his waist, he made a moue.

Rupert furrowed his brow, and apologetically said, 'Yes, quite a few actually,' then he produced, from behind his back, a striped and bulging paper bag. 'Corny and I were in the Terrace and got you these!'

'Gosh! Whatever can it be?' Valentine exclaimed, despite his strong suspicions, and looked inside, 'Gosh! Simply thousands! Thanks ever so very much! I *do* love violet creams!'

'Ha-ha!' said Rupert, with a beaming smile, 'I thought you might!'

'And thank you too, Corny!' Valentine said to his little brother who exhibited a wild hunger for just one of them.

Corny was happily sated when Valentine simultaneously put one in his palm, another in Rupert's mouth, then one in his own, and because he was thoughtful, Corny bit his in half and dropped one of them into Gloriana's bowl for her to eat immediately or save for later.

Standing between his two favourite blond boys, the three of them enjoying immensely their floral chocolates, Valentine turned his attention to Cosmo, and quite as if suddenly aware of him, said, 'Gosh! Awake I see!'

Cosmo was certain that Valentine was at the root of his hospitalisation but his memory was hazy, and so far he had failed to receive an explanation as to what exactly had happened. He glared at Valentine, and wanted to shout obscenities at him. He could not shout however, nor even talk, for Willy had inopportunely placed the tumbler at his lips, and now he was choking on Scotch.

Valentine tutted censoriously. He was glad when Willy wiped Cosmo's face, and he made a mental note to dissuade the baby from such behaviour.

'Sorry! Sorry!' said Willy as she wiped.

Cosmo did not look forgiving, in fact, he seemed not even to notice her.

'Don't say sorry, Willy!' Valentine reprimanded, 'It's far from your fault!'

Willy's response was to look at him with fury.

'Yes, I am awake!' Cosmo finally roared with a fearsome rage that he endeavoured to demonstrate physically, 'And I've some bloody questions to ask you!'

Immediately, Rupert placed himself in a position to protect Valentine if violence were to ensue but it proved unnecessary as Cosmo's slings restrained him as effectively as a straitjacket would. The predicament and fruitless struggling made it close to impossible for Valentine not to smile; he appreciated that the impairment may transpire advantageous. He watched, with amusement, as Cosmo exhausted himself with the effort, and at the same time deliberated not to answer any questions before he learned precisely of what Cosmo was aware.

Eventually, Cosmo gave up his toil, lowered his bald, small and sweating cranium, and cursed profusely.

'I don't understand,' said Valentine.

'What!' Cosmo snarled into his beefy lap, 'What on earth should you be confused about? Have you been in a bloody coma too?'

'I don't understand,' Valentine repeated, 'how you can be so very grumpy when you've just had the most super long, and I assume deep, sleep. Mind you, I suppose that's often the way, don't you think, Corny?'

Corny demonstrated his concurrence with a few nods and some eye rolling.

Cosmo raised his head slowly and looked with murder at Valentine.

'You are something else!' he said.

'Why, thank you!' was the flippant reply.

Consequently, Cosmo again lost his cool and vocalised a few views that bordered on bigoted.

'Crikey, Cosmo!' said Rupert, with feelings of discomfort and annoyance, 'If you can't stop saying those sorts of things then . . . well, just don't put me in a position where I'll have to do it for you.' And he stood over him to amplify his frankness.

Cosmo stopped and regarded Rupert with surprised fear; his friend's shock predilection for sausage, and the lengths he went to for it, suddenly came back to him, and he grimaced and cowered.

Flashing Rupert a look of contrite on Cosmo's behalf, Willy said to Valentine, 'You are a viperish beast!'

Valentine gasped in horror at the accusation.

'You know poor Cosmo has been in a coma all these weeks!' Willy said, and tentatively placed a comforting hand on Cosmo's thigh, 'I don't think any of us can imagine how terrible it must've been, but I'm sure it was nothing like sleeping!'

'Yes, yes!' said Valentine, blithely, 'I am sorry, truly I am! I suppose it's rather strange to be in a coma and then come back, so apologies, Cosmo!'

Here, Valentine risked perching upon the ottoman, placing himself perilously close to Cosmo's powerful legs. He knew it was rather a risk but he wished to learn how the land lay and, besides, he felt no fear with Rupert near, and he asked, 'What was it like?'

'I can't bloody remember!' boomed Cosmo, still desirous to thrash the pansy but not daring.

'Gosh! Really not?' exclaimed Valentine, 'That *is* disappointing! I had supposed you to remember something! But I suppose also you must feel rather muddleheaded. You haven't been awake long have you? You were still sleeping when Willy telephoned yesterday evening. I am surprised they let you out so soon!'

Cosmo was unable to curb the animalistic growl that came from deep within.

'I was not bloody sleeping! And I wasn't in bloody prison either. It wasn't a question of letting me out; I refused to stay there, and the bloody bitch matron couldn't make me!'

The plain truth of the matter was that despite the matron's usual conscientiousness she was already weary of Willy's presence, which mutated from histrionic melancholy to volcanic euphoria upon the arousal of the patient, and he so furious and verbally abusive to the staff, that her forbearance could not withstand it. Therefore, she did not dispute his insistence to leave directly after placing his casts in slings, and was extremely glad to see the back of him.

'Gosh!' said Valentine, 'Well, I must say it seems rather slapdash, I supposed that they were meant to monitor you for a time but evidently not!'

'You suppose a lot!' snarled Cosmo.

'Gosh! I suppose I do! But there's no supposition regarding your somatic health because, excepting your inept arms, you look to be positively in the pink! Don't you think, Willy? Doesn't Cosmo look to be in extraordinarily fine fettle?'

Suddenly, Willy felt ferociously hot, not because the summer's day grew progressively sultry, and she dressed in thick dungarees, but because all eyes were on her and all ears anticipatory of her opinion with regards to Cosmo's physical appearance.

'Oh!' she thought, 'Valentine is such a wretch!' and though she did not now dare cast even a shy glance at Cosmo, she uneasily said, 'Cosmo's as healthy as an ox.'

Her embarrassment heightened upon Valentine's inability to stifle a snigger at her aptly chosen simile.

'Yes! Exactly!' he said to her, 'As hale and hearty and healthy as an ox! Albeit one with two useless limbs but they'll soon be better, I'm certain! However, what concerns me is whether or no Cosmo is entirely *compos mentis*!'

'Cosmo is completely bloody *compos mentis*!' he boomed at Valentine, 'I am in the room, you know! I'm not still bloody unconscious!'

Valentine waved his hand as if the motion might pacify.

'Gosh! Of course you aren't but did they test you when you woke?'

'For what?'

'For example,' said Valentine, and he held up a finger, 'how many fingers do you perceive?'

Cosmo sounded a disdained guffaw, shook his little head, and said, 'Don't try me, little boy!'

The comment encouraged Rupert to reinforce his role of bodyguard. He put his hand firmly on Cosmo's shoulder, and, in a no-nonsense tone, said, 'Tell him how many fingers you see.'

'I see one bloody finger, all right?'

'Glorious!' said Valentine, 'How about now?'

Cosmo told him that he could see three fingers. Then, to harden the test, Valentine displayed two fingers on one hand and three on the other. Cosmo correctly counted five. Next, Valentine exhibited seven digits.

'Seven!' growled Cosmo, through gritted teeth.

'Wrong!' Valentine merrily chimed, 'A thumb is not a finger!'

Setting his jaw so squarely it looked close to dislocated; Cosmo glowered at Valentine and wanted nothing more than to knock him into next week.

'This isn't a test!' objected Willy, 'You are just humiliating Cosmo and bullying him!'

'Ha!' said Cosmo, 'He couldn't bully me if he tried!' but he did feel a trifle humiliated.

Valentine tutted and replied, 'Indeed I am doing no such thing! I am performing a famous and little known examination of mental abilities, so bear with me, I have but one final question. Will you try very hard to answer it, Cosmo?'

'If it bloody shuts you up then certainly!' Cosmo growled, 'And then I've some questions for you!'

'Very well,' said Valentine, 'I shall answer them all when you can correctly tell me how many fingers I held up with my left hand when you counted five?'

Cosmo was flummoxed. Before the question came, he had quite decided that he would not bother to answer but upon hearing it, he realised that he could not for the life of him remember. He wondered if this was normal and was slightly relieved when Willy said, 'But, Valentine, I can't even remember that for certain!'

Valentine turned to her. 'Gosh! Well it's lucky that you're not the testee! Now, come along, Cosmo, how many?'

Cosmo contorted his face grotesquely. He would feel a fool if he did not answer correctly. However, to hesitate was no good either, therefore he hazarded the guess, 'Two.'

'*H'm,*' said Valentine, thoughtfully.

'What?' replied Cosmo, defensively.

'The answer, I'm afraid, was three,' lied Valentine, 'And this reveals to me something quite interesting.'

'Like bloody what?'

'Well,' said Valentine, 'either you are seeing things as if through a looking-glass *or* you possess a disorderly case of discriminatory remembrance, I'm not certain which as of yet but, sadly, both are indicative of the early stages of broken brain.'

Willy gasped, 'Oh no! Are you quite serious?' for though she knew Valentine to tell fibs she also worried for Cosmo.

'Indubitably,' said Valentine.

'Bloody rubbish!' remonstrated Cosmo.

'I sincerely hope so!' replied Valentine, 'But tell me this: how did you travel here?'

'By bloody tube!' Cosmo boomed with impatience.

'Gosh, well that doesn't count; no one would ever forget that!' said Valentine.

Now, he retrieved his silver case and took out a cigarette to disguise his removal from Cosmo's reach with the wish to utilise the scarab beetle lighter.

Then, in a safe position, he asked, 'Why did you come here and not home?' and he braced himself for an explosion that did not come.

'Because my pater and mater are away on holiday; I can hardly go home with only the bloody servants to look after me can I?' said Cosmo with some annoyance that grew: 'Bloody typical! They go on a cruise when I'm in a bloody coma, and I can't bloody reach 'em to tell them my bloody card was swallowed by the bloody hole-in-the-wall! That's why I'm here and took the bloody tube!'

'Gosh, yes! That *is* bloody!' agreed Valentine and he cast an arch glance at his shamefaced sister. 'Little liar!' thought he, and was impressed but pondered her motive.

Presently, Willy piped up, 'And Gretchen told me Harry said Cosmo can have his room.'

'Good old Gretchen!' said Valentine, whilst internally cursing, 'But all this is quite recent. It would appear that though you can recollect what happened an hour or so ago, you possess no memory of just a moment gone, and that is discriminatory remembrance. Therefore, I wonder . . . ' Here, he inhaled nicotine, 'are you able to recall much from before your coma? That is to say, can you remember the events that led up to it?' And he exhaled.

Willy immediately turned to Valentine and pulled a face like thunder; his harassment of Cosmo was horrible, and she suspected him to think it jolly good fun to torment.

'All I know,' growled Cosmo, 'is that I was at a marvellous party and climbed up on the roof to fetch bloody Remarkable!' Cosmo indicated Remarkable, with his head, 'And then I bloody fell!'

Upon hearing his name, the bird opened one cobalt blue eye to view Cosmo and sounded his guttural rumble.

'I'm sorry,' said Valentine, with hesitant hope, 'do you mean to say that you possess knowledge of The Marvellous Party, the attempted rescue of

Remarkable and your subsequent fall, yet you retain no recollection of the events?'

'That's exactly what I'm bloody saying!' Cosmo replied with anger and embarrassment.

'Gosh! How truly awful!' Valentine exclaimed in such a tone that barely concealed his joy; Cosmo seemed completely unaware of the fate of the Starfish, and his muddled memory would certainly make him more malleable.

Valentine regarded his bullish cousin as a lamb to the slaughter, and said, 'Now, let us see if we can't set about filling that beastly void in your brain so as not to let it break. What are your questions?'

'My first question is this,' snarled Cosmo, 'Why did I go up on the roof to get the bird, why me? Why not somebody else? Like you?' he looked up at Rupert, 'Or Harry?' he said to Valentine, 'And who is Izzy? And when are they back from their honeymoon?'

Valentine was astonished at Willy's ability to avoid answering so many questions and he displayed this sentiment by making wide eyes at her before telling Cosmo, 'That is a lot of first questions!'

'Just answer them!' Cosmo ordered.

Then Rupert interrupted, 'Crikey, Cosmo! You know my cousin Izzy!'

'I've heard you talk about her!' he replied.

'You met her at The Marvellous Party!' said Rupert.

'I told you, I don't remember a bloody marvellous party!'

Eager to avoid the onus of answers falling upon honest Rupert's broad shoulders, Valentine said, 'Well, that is whom Izzy is, only now she is Izzy Avery-Stripe, and I'm not entirely certain when they are back. Anyway, what affair is it of yours when they return?'

'Because Harry will tell me the truth! I'm only asking you because he's away and Willy doesn't seem to know anything; she's about as useful as a bloody paddle without a bloody canoe!' said Cosmo, and shockingly he scowled at the girl who had sat at his comatose side for three weeks.

It took great effort for Willy to hold back her tears.

Upon seeing this, Valentine's revulsion for Cosmo almost got the better of him and he considered requesting that Rupert do his worst, but instead, he merely said, 'Well it's clear to see the coma didn't affect your contemptibility! You are still a cad and yet you demand hospitality and answers! Very well! I cannot go against your beloved Harry's wishes that you inhabit his room, but may I remind you that no marriage welcomes a third wheel, so please don't delude yourself with the idea that his molly-coddling of you shall continue! And as for your reasons for climbing Chinchero to rescue the bloody bird, I haven't an inkling though I'm confident it had nothing to do with chivalry!'

Now Cosmo truly did look on the verge of exploding and, in fact, he more or less did with the release of an almighty and bestial roar of rage, whereupon Corny ran for cover under the Steinway, Willy trembled with fear and Rupert bounded over the chesterfield to shield Valentine. Valentine, however, regarded the baseness of the brute with unfathomable abhorrence and a degree of surprise at the duration of the din. The dozing Dalmatians in the garden howled, Remarkable quite lost his grip on his perch and squawked and flapped, and Gubsy's tent of *The Times* fell to pieces with his rude awakening, 'What, in thunder, is the matter with him?' he boomed.

Then Gretchen stormed in with disgust plastered upon her face.

'What is noise all about?' she shouted, quite as loudly, and twisted a dishcloth in her hands as if it were a chicken neck.

Cosmo stopped his noise. His little head, now similar to a tomato, grimaced with a fuming sulk, and his chest rose and fell as he gasped for air.

'You are too bik to be actink like a bik baby, Master Cosmo!' said Gretchen, placing the cloth over her shoulder, and simultaneously calming Remarkable and folding *The Times*.

'Quite beyond the pale!' muttered Gubsy with disgust, 'A chap can't even take a nap in his own house!'

Valentine explained: 'Cosmo's throwing his toys out of his pram because I can't tell him why it was he, and not anyone else, that climbed Chinchero to catch Remarkable! But I suppose now it's because he didn't have a babysitter!'

Gretchen looked to Cosmo and considered him a nuisance. Naturally, she did not think he had deserved three weeks in a coma but he was so accident bound and really should try to be more cautious.

She sounded a derisive grunt, and said, 'Well I am not knowink the reason also but it was brave even if not brainy, so I cannot help you.'

Cosmo dwarfed Gretchen's grunt with a dissatisfied one of his own, and she decided to investigate. 'Master Rupert, are you knowink why?'

Rupert rubbed the back of his head for a moment before Valentine jumped in with the interjection, 'Of course, Rupert does not know! And it is unfair to ask him, he doubtlessly would've done it himself if it weren't for my welfare. I'm quite certain he considers me superior to birds, don't you Rupert?'

Rupert beamed a smile of thanks at his rescue, 'Crikey, Valentine! You know I do!'

Valentine smiled back, and then said, 'Corny, do you know why Cosmo suddenly thought himself to be Spiderman?'

Beneath the piano, Corny stretched his arms out and shrugged to reveal that he did not have the foggiest idea.

'And you do not know, Miss Willy?' Gretchen asked.

'Oh no! I truly don't!' Willy said, with what Valentine considered, too much conviction.

Finally, Gretchen asked Gubsy, 'Mr Bartholmoo, are you knowink why?'

Gubsy emitted a smug *harrumph*, 'I know precisely why!' said he.

'Gosh!' thought Valentine, 'Do keep quiet! Don't remind him of the Starfish!' then he reflected that his great uncle had not once spoken of the ring and he filled with relief.

'Why?' Cosmo demanded to know.

'Because, young man, you are an utter duffer! Remarkable's not such a birdbrain! He came back when he wanted; just a few days later, he just had a little holiday. Didn't you Remarkable?' and he beamed up at the bird, 'Kik-kik-kik-kik!'

Remarkable responded with a proud ruffle of his plumage.

Cosmo looked fit to burst with outrage at Gubsy's accusation and his face started to redden again. Yet this time he did not roar but only writhed rather rudely because suddenly an altogether different exigency took precedence; Cosmo's bladder was filled to capacity.

Therefore, as he squirmed, he said, in a tone that teetered on timid, 'Bloody Hell! I need the bloody lav,' and he displayed, to each person present, a completely sheepish expression.

'Gosh!' said Valentine, quickly calculating that with his cast arms fixed at right angles, Cosmo's trips to the lavatory would prove problematical unless some charitable soul volunteered a helping hand, yet no one seemed enthusiastic.

Fortunately, Gretchen stepped forward to grasp the nettle.

'Ket up, Master Cosmo, I will take you to toilet,' she said as she hoisted him.

Covered with embarrassment, Cosmo surrendered himself to the fact that Gretchen was his only resort. He sincerely had not considered who might tend to his functions.

'Do not be blushink!' said Gretchen, capably manoeuvring him from the drawing room, 'In my life I have seen plenty little soldiers!'

Cosmo's countenance became veritably crimson.

Valentine could not help laughing.

'Gosh!' he said, 'Gretchen truly is a trump! She really will turn her hand to anything!'

His laughter came to an abrupt stop, however, when Willy charged forward, conveyed him to the dining room and smartly pushed his bottom upon a seat. She closed the doors to the drawing room, marched up to him, and shook her fist in his face.

'If you do not stop being beastly to Cosmo I shall make you so sorry!'

'Beastly? I? But how?' exclaimed Valentine.

Willy girned.

'You know exactly how! He's still not fully recovered and you are being horrid to him!'

Valentine met her girning with a tut.

'It is not I that has filled his silly small head with a pack of lies! Though I am impressed, I must say, to think of sending Quentin and Esmé on a cruise is highly creative, and I'll bet they wish it were true, but it's not true, is it?'

'No, it's not,' Willy admitted quietly.

'It's an absolute whopper of mammoth proportions!' Valentine exclaimed, 'I should be ashamed of you but all I want to know is why?'

Presently, Willy's countenance transmuted from thunderous to pitiful, and she fell to her knees.

'I had to tell him something didn't I? I couldn't very well say, "Oh hello, Cosmo, you've been in a coma for three weeks, oh and by the way, your parents have disowned you!" It might kill him!'

'I would have told him precisely that for that precise reason!' stated Valentine, 'But, for your sake, I find myself having to play along with the charade! And on top of that, you also haven't told him that he climbed up after Remarkable to rescue the Starfish, and because you haven't, all of Chinchero has to lie for you! Really, Willy, to vent your vexation upon me truly is quite unacceptable! You've only yourself to blame! After all, you hid the Starfish when you showed me the sapphire ring and pearl necklace that you were borrowing! By the by, I don't believe you've returned them yet and I should very much appreciate your doing so because they are not paste like the Starfish that so upset everyone, and still is because now we are lumbered with Cosmo and he can't even pay his way because his card was swallowed and he doesn't even know why!' Valentine then sighed, 'It is a most sorry state of affairs.'

Willy held her face in her hands and was silent. Her entire sizeable body started to quiver and then to quake.

'Gosh! Don't be silly, Willy,' said Valentine, looking down at her with a touch of guilt, but she did not stop being silly. Her quakes became convulsive and from behind her hands came the sound of tears.

'Oh, Willy!' Valentine said with exasperation, whereupon Willy revealed her sob sodden face contorted with perfect agony.

She shook her head slowly, and choked, 'It is all my fault, Valentine, I know it! You don't have to tell me that! I've thought about it so much! Day and night, hour after hour!'

'Gosh! Really not?'

Willy spluttered violently, nodded and said, 'Really yes! I mean, I don't understand why Esmé and Quentin are being so hard on Cosmo but whatever their reason, if I hadn't worn the ring then none of it would have happened! And now . . . ' she paused to wipe her runny nose on the back of a hand, 'Now . . . ' she said again but the convulsions overpowered her for a moment, 'Now he will not *ever* love me!'

Valentine looked at his miserable and wailing sister who had decided it wise to wipe her torrent of tears on the rug, and he was astounded by the magnitude of her love for such a rake. It was true that she did not know of his interaction with their mother, but irrespective of that, he was still a base brute possessing no more charm than that of a caveman! For a flash, Valentine toyed with the idea of opening Willy's eyes to the creation of the bastard but that would surely break her heart, and worse, she might tell Cosmo.

Instead, he said, 'But, Willy, he called you a bloody paddle! Does that truly sit well with you? How can you bear such boorishness? It really goes against the grain! And do stop rubbing the rug with your face; you'll irritate yourself.'

Willy took his advice, her face did feel sore and her tears stung her chafed cheeks but she did not care, all she cared for was Cosmo, and this was a sentiment that she would not ever abandon.

'I don't mind that he called me a bloody paddle!' she announced with heartrending defiance. 'He can call me a bloody whatever he wants just because then he is calling me something, he is noticing me! I'll do any-thing to be his bloody anything, but not even my Marvellous Party dress attracted him for more than a few minutes when he lifted me up to heaven on the dance floor! Oh! I shall never be happy again – it was the pinnacle of my entire sorry existence and I deserve nothing better than these dungarees!' Once again, she utilised the rug as if a dog cleaning its face rather theatrically.

Valentine was at a loss at what best to say. He considered the golden tone of silence and simply to leave the heaving mass of Willy where she lay but he could not be so unkind.

Yet neither could he offer words of comfort except, 'Gosh, Willy! I suppose we must all have a cross to bear, and you've found yours so soon, and perhaps you've a natural inclination toward martyrdom, but if I were you I'd fix my face and make certain Harry's bed is made, or else Cosmo might be uncomfy.'

Presently, Willy's weeping ceased, she rose to a genuflected pose, and sniffed back her tears.

'Yes, I shall do that. It's important that he is comfortable,' and she trundled toward the kitchen door for she did not want the boys in the drawing room to witness her state.

'Valentine?' she said before she left.

'Willy?' he replied.

'You won't tell about the Starfish, will you? I think Cosmo would hate me if he ever knew.'

'Gosh, Willy!' said Valentine, 'Your secret's safe with me, I swear!'

Willy gave her brother the saddest of smiles.

'Thank you,' she murmured and then left Valentine to reflect.

'Oh, that was Cosmo being cross,' said Valentine to Olivia upon her four-poster a quarter-hour later.

'But, darling!' said Olivia, with anxiety in her tone, 'Why would he roar? It practically shook Chinchero it was so unearthly!'

'Because no one would enlighten him as to why he so stupidly climbed up after Remarkable. It was quite funny really.'

Olivia corrugated her brow.

'But why not?'

'Gosh, well naturally I would not, Rupert played dumb, Corny is mute, Gretchen and Gubsy apparently genuinely possess no inkling, and Willy is protecting him from the horrid truth because otherwise he would hate her and it would break her heart!'

Olivia's head hurt and she asked with dread, 'Break her heart! Whatever do you mean, darling? What's Willy's heart got to do with anything?'

Valentine regarded her incredulously.

'Oh, mummy, you cannot really be so blind!'

'To what, darling?'

Valentine sighed.

'To the fact that Willy is, and has been for such a long time, truly, madly and deeply head-over-heels in besotted love with Cosmo!'

'Really not!' Olivia said with a gasp and grasped her décolleté in horror.

'Really yes!' replied Valentine, surprised at her shock.

Olivia grimaced, swallowed hard, and tersely said, 'If you knew about the crush you should have quashed it; I hold you completely responsible!'

'Gosh, mummy! One can't dictate another's heart!' said Valentine, 'Especially not when it's Willy, she is rigid and shan't be swayed! Besides if he's good enough for you . . . ' and he cocked a brow.

'He most absolutely is not good enough for me!' she cried, 'He was simply a sordid means to an end,' and she shuddered.

Valentine emitted a small laugh.

Its occurrence caused Olivia to forget her vulnerable state for a flash, and snap, 'I fail to see such a sunny side to the situation that I should like to laugh, darling, please do educate me as to why!'

'Oh, mummy,' he said, as he endeavoured to straighten his face, 'it's just quite funny that "the end" has ended with you not owning the Starfish, and Cosmo not remembering it nor even knowing about the superior treasure that stands in its stead!' and he gesticulated toward her tummy.

Olivia involuntarily, and protectively, clutched it.

'He must not ever know!' she cried.

'Naturally not, mummy!' Valentine said, with a tut, 'As if I'd tell him!'

Adequately sated, Olivia added, 'Anyway, darling, I doubt very much that Cosmo has completely forgotten about the Starfish or how it came to be in my hands!'

'Well, we shall soon find out, mummy.'

'How?'

'At supper, of course.' said Valentine.

'I shan't be eating with him!' Olivia said, in a truculent tone, 'In fact, I refuse to leave my room whilst he resides in Chinchero!'

'You must, mummy! We need to see if and how easily his memory is jogged so I can better approach the situation; you need only do it once.'

'I point blank refuse, darling!' stated Olivia, and she folded her arms to display her defiance.

*

Valentine did, however, successfully convince Olivia to dine with the family, and despite her unease, her performance of glib indifference was credible and such that she managed neither to flinch nor retch, at least not too elaborately, upon ingesting something worlds away from kedgeree.

Gretchen had made a delicious supper of chicken and asparagus loved by all except, on this occasion, Olivia and herself, because had she known of Cosmo's toilet trouble, that she had to handle, she most certainly would have chosen a less influential vegetable.

Naturally, cast-ridden Cosmo could not either feed himself let alone dissect, therefore Willy was in her element and sat practically on his knee to cut up his food and deliver it to his surly mouth, and of this, he was entirely ungrateful.

The gathering was most disconcerting for Corny; he could not understand why no one was talking when he or she could, not even Valentine. He wondered what rendered the air so tense because, but for the *click* and *clash* of cutlery and crockery, the gnash of false teeth, and the occasional tut in response to noisy mastication, an eerie silence dominated the room.

Valentine's scrutiny of Cosmo was meticulous; he wished to divine what was on his mind, most specifically toward his mother, and he calculated that though Cosmo asked, 'Do you know why I climbed up onto the roof, Auntie O?' (To which she replied, 'I'm quite certain I possess no explanation for your insanity.') He did not gaze lewdly toward her or seem to suspect anything out of the ordinary.

Valentine was cognisant, however, that Cosmo would unlikely allude to anything deeper than superfluous in the presence of all. Therefore, directly after gooseberry fool, and during Gubsy's doze, he cleverly invented a situation involving a fictitious and fierce frog in the garden so to leave the convalescent and the expectant alone.

Later, upon learning from his mother, cross at the uncomfortable fifteen-minute seclusion with her nephew, that Cosmo had no more than grumbled about his casts and reviled Remarkable, Valentine became confident that the cad was pleasantly and adequately mentally impaired.

The ensuing days proved enjoyably taxing for Valentine. To his mind, the situation was as if a spectacular brainteaser and he revelled in the pursuit of its solution. He discovered that to lie upon the chesterfield, devouring violet creams, and traversing, with his eyes, the handsome face and form of his ultimate forefather, inspired the deepest and most sage deductions. As he approached the predicament from every possible angle, he mentally envisaged each piece of information he had garnered and painstakingly examined them, one after the other, before starting again, and then he would have a nap. Then, upon waking, he would look to see if the pieces had changed shape or exhibited to him a facet hitherto unseen.

Occasionally, an inconsiderate person (most often Cosmo) interrupted his ruminations, and to them, Valentine would declare, 'Gosh! Do leave me be! I am in the process of contemplation!'

However, he did not mind Corny to sit beneath the Steinway and, with wide eyes, wonder at his older brother's inner world.

Gradually, Valentine whittled each part of the situation down to their essential cores, and then he manoeuvred them to see if they might slot together to create an agreeable result, but though the results numbered many they each involved a flaw too substantial to consider the overall outcome acceptable. Yet he would not be deterred; he was resolute in his ambition to succeed, and did not for one moment despair.

Only during the day would he apply himself to the task because as soon as Rupert returned from renovating the community his mind would glory in love and bathe in his beauty, and after supper they would retire to Valentine's turret. Ironically, it was on one such night, no more than a moment after concluding an appreciation of Rupert's physicality, that Valentine experienced an epiphany, and he gasped with shock, and said, 'Gosh!'

'Crikey! What?' Rupert asked with bewilderment.

'Oh, quite nearly nothing really!' Valentine replied, with a smile; he did not want Rupert to know the exactness of his mental endeavours.

'That's all right then!' said Rupert, 'I thought I'd done something wrong.'

'Gosh! You? No, never! You are the epitome of right!'

'Ha-ha! Good!' replied Rupert with a grin.

'Do let's turn out the light though,' said Valentine, excitedly, 'I've a feeling tomorrow may transpire momentous!'

Rupert obliged, and beneath the violet-scented sheets, he pulled Valentine close, completely oblivious to his Machiavellian mind.

Valentine's epiphany seemed to him divine because his head had been somewhere altogether different upon its manifestation, and the further he examined it the more miraculous it became. However, it did possess a slight flaw, though not one that would blemish the conclusion, only that to arrive at the desired destination he would have to place himself in a position of danger.

Yet this was of little concern to him. He considered himself equal to the task, and upon bidding Rupert farewell in the morning, the kiss he received furthered his fortification. The following cups of breakfast tea served to him in his geisha china galvanised his gall and, with a wry smile, Valentine successfully calculated how to safely interact with Cosmo.

The plan would work only in the absence of Gretchen, and as luck would have it, just as Valentine had concluded a psychological cross-examination of his stratagem, she arrived to clear the table.

She said to him, 'I have just knock on Mrs Olivia's door with tray of kedgeree, and now I take the doks for walks and also I go to allotment. I will not be so lonk, maybe two hours tip-tops, so you must tell your kreat uncle when he wakes and wants to know "where is Kretchen?" you can do that, yes?'

Valentine resisted requesting that she write down the instruction lest he was to forget, because he was eager for her departure.

'Gosh, Gretchen! I certainly shall!' he sang, and no sooner had she motored off with the Dalmatians, did he act with alacrity to set his plan in motion.

First, he sat at the éscritoire, where, upon a plain sheet of stationery, he applied his excellent calligraphist ability that stretched to perfect forgery. Upon completion, he folded the sheet into quarters and put it in his pocket along with two-dozen envelopes. Next, he collected, from the kitchen, the Bakelite telephone and carried it up to his turret where he plugged it into an appropriate socket that he was happy to discover was not defunct because the earpiece emitted the reassuring *burr* of a dialling tone. Then he retrieved the envelopes from his pocket, tied them with a lilac ribbon and placed the bundle in the drawer of his bedside table.

Finally, he capered back to the kitchen and located a suitably mundane tea service, filled the kettle with water and boiled it on the Aga. He placed the crockery and a dozen Garibaldi biscuits on a large silver salver, and then, when the kettle whistled, he filled the pot. Green tea was not a favourite of Valentine's, in fact, he quite despised it, but he knew it to be marvellously diuretical, and that was integral to the plot.

He gasped at the weight of the load on the salver when he lifted it and wondered if the tea wagon might be wiser, but upon spying Cosmo and Willy residing in the gazebo he realised wheels were not an option, and he surrendered himself to the burden.

'Hello!' he exclaimed amiably upon reaching the silent pair, 'I have brought something refreshing for us all!'

Willy removed her amorous eyes from grumpy Cosmo, looked at Valentine suspiciously, and asked, 'Why?'

'Gosh! Because it's such a lovely day I thought it would be nice to take tea in the garden, and the green variety not only corresponds with the foliage but also has very many beneficial thingamajigs!' whereupon he set down the salver, felt his arms tingle with relief, and added, 'And I think we could all do with some of those! Shall I be mother?' and he proceeded to pour.

'You're still in bloody pyjamas!' boomed Cosmo.

Gosh, thought Valentine, he truly is befuddled!

'Yes!' he replied, 'They're green too; celery and lime stripes. Glorious, don't you think?'

Cosmo responded with a *humph* that all but blew the contents from the cup that Willy had raised to his face, he then drank from it, and said, 'You ought to dress in proper clothes; it's not bloody night-time!'

Valentine bit his tongue.

'Gosh! There's no doubt about that! The sun certainly does have his hat on today! But tell me, do you like the tea?'

Having imbibed all that his cup had held, Cosmo reluctantly admitted that he did.

'Glorious!' said Valentine, 'Do have some more!' and he topped him up.

Quite soon, the pot was empty and Valentine returned to the kitchen to boil another. Then, not long afterward, he boiled a third. Cosmo consumed most of the green tea because Willy put his needs first and Valentine surreptitiously emptied most of his own cups into the pond. Only Corny caught him in the act and thought it funny. Corny did not drink any tea; the idea of it being green was unappealing and he was more than happy with Garibaldis.

Halfway through the third pot, the tea took its desired effect because Cosmo started to shift and squirm.

'Bloody hell!' he said, 'I need the bloody lav!'

'Gosh!' exclaimed Valentine, and he jumped up, 'I shall fetch Gretchen!'

He ran into Chinchero, and, in the kitchen, he pulled open a drawer, located the appropriate utensil, pocketed it with the forgery, and he waited.

He did not have to linger very long before he heard the sound of Cosmo stamping in through the conservatory, and he met him in the drawing room at the same time that the ormolu clock chimed a half.

'Where is she?' Cosmo demanded, as he jogged on the spot.

Valentine pulled a pained expression. 'Gosh, Cosmo, I cannot locate her, and the dogs aren't about either, so I assume she's taken them for a walk. Can you hold it?'

Cosmo grimaced at the news.

'No, I bloody can't! My bloody bladder's bursting! When's she back?' he shouted at Valentine, and then at Willy, 'How long does it take to walk the dogs?'

Petrified at the situation, Willy made a short series of miniature gasps.

'Not long usually, maybe half an hour. Can you truly not hold it?'

'No, I bloody well can't hold it!' he blared, and started to thrash his cast arms in an effort to escape his slings as if he then might miraculously be able to attend the lavatory unassisted.

'Gosh!' said Valentine, 'Do try to be calm; any physical exertion might place too much of a strain on your internals and make an accident!'

Realising the wisdom of Valentine's advice, Cosmo calmed himself by way of standing as still as a statue, screwing his eyes and taking slow and steady breaths, whereupon Willy shot Valentine a look of thanks.

'But, of course,' said Valentine, 'today *is* Friday.'

Cosmo's lids flicked open, and he regarded Valentine with the wish for an elaboration.

'Oh no!' said Willy, and Corny covered his smile with a hand.

'Oh yes!' said Valentine, 'An allotment day! She could be gone for hours!' and he too concealed a smile. 'Are you really not able to hold it Cosmo? Not even if you sat with your legs crossed, and tried very hard not to consider Niagara Falls, the Seven Seas or even a dripping tap?'

'You beast!' wailed Willy.

Valentine viewed her as if his mouth would not melt butter.

'Not I!' he exclaimed, 'I'm simply trying to talk Cosmo out of releasing an urging and satisfying leak in his pants, unless you volunteer taking him to "the lav"?'

Cosmo instantly turned to her, and though he did not plead verbally, his eyes spoke for him.

'Oh, Cosmo!' she cried, 'I just couldn't!' and indeed she could not for she would most certainly die of embarrassment, 'I'm sorry!' and she ran out to the garden to weep, with shame, in the sanctuary provided by the pergola.

'Bloody bitch!' Cosmo boomed. He could not quite grasp the reality of her denial; usually she was all too ready to assist him with anything, no matter how menial.

'She's not a bloody bitch, Cosmo, she's my sister,' said Valentine in an unvarnished tone, 'Moreover, I quite consider your manners miserly when it is I whom seems to be your only hope of liberation!'

Cosmo looked at him with disgust.

'I'd sooner bloody die than give you the thrill!'

'Gosh! Well, I'm quite certain I couldn't care a snap of my fingers whether or no you soil yourself, just do try to avoid the soft furnishings and Axminster!'

Then, to his little brother, Valentine said, 'Come on, Corny, let's get out the hose and give the garden a lovely, long watering!'

But before the brothers reached the conservatory door, Cosmo sounded an agonised roar, and shouted, 'Bloody all right then! You can help me!'

Valentine turned to him and smiled.

'You are very sensible,' he said, 'But please tell me it's no more than a number one!' and he filled with gratitude when Cosmo signalled an affirmative with a shy nod of his red little head.

CHAPTER 23

The Waiving of Willy

In the bathroom, Cosmo regarded his reflection in the three-panel looking glass and he grimaced. He considered what was about to happen and thought himself an utter duffer. Yet, what could he do? His bladder was in desperate need of relief and the pansy was his only resort. Nevertheless, when Valentine locked the door, he felt disturbingly vulnerable.

Cosmo summoned his bravado, and boomed, 'Just bloody get on with it! I'm sure you're dying to touch it!'

'Verily!' said Valentine, rolling up his pyjama sleeves and stepping up to him, 'I can barely contain my excitement! Now then, I think I know how to do this.'

Quick as a flash, Valentine unfastened Cosmo's shorts and pulled them down to his ankles.

Cosmo shuffled over to the toilet, screwed his eyes, and braced himself for the foraging in his underpants and the consequent grope but was surprised at having to wait.

'C'mon, Valentine! Bloody do it!' he growled, eyes still shut tight, and he pumped the air with his pelvis.

Presently, his cauliflower ears filled with the sound of naughty laughter. He looked over his shoulder and was confused to see Valentine standing in the roll-top bath.

'What the . . . ?' Cosmo boomed, 'What on earth are you bloody doing? I need to pee! Are you going to help me or not?'

Valentine had not considered how funny the sight would be. Soon though, he remembered the reason for the unusual situation, and he sobered up.

'I'm sorry, Cosmo, but I have brought you here under false pretences.'

'What! I need to pee, that's why we're here, damn it!' Cosmo roared.

'Oh, gosh, yes, that's why I filled you with green tea, so you'd need to pee and I could get you alone!'

'What?' said Cosmo, somewhat less aggressively because he suddenly realised that he had no way of escaping and he feared the worst.

'I've brought you here because of Willy,' replied Valentine.

'Willy?' Cosmo uncomfortably asked and became confused.

He quite forgot his urge, and with his dropped-shorts that he was unable to pull up, he bunny-hopped over to the bath for clarification.

'You've bloody tricked me into drinking all that bloody tea so you could take me to the lav and talk about Willy?' he said with mounting rage.

'Verily!' Valentine confirmed.

Cosmo's consequent cursing made Valentine glad that he stood safely in the bath because it was only the beginning.

He waited until the swearwords stopped, and he said, 'I'm afraid Willy's been leading you up the garden path somewhat.'

Cosmo squared his jaw, glared ferociously, and demanded details where-upon Valentine insisted that Cosmo keep quiet during the illumination and to not get too fractious.

Reluctantly, Cosmo gave his word of honour.

With that, Valentine painted a figurative picture of Willy's unfathomable and hidden love for Cosmo so ornate with authenticity that it bordered on tangible, and Cosmo, quite as if he could see the masterpiece, looked into the middle distance, his face a perfect picture in itself, as his little skull filled with light.

'You may now speak,' Valentine said, finally.

Momentarily, Cosmo said nothing.

Then he double blinked, and, in an expressionless tone, said, 'I'll be bloody damned! It can't be true!'

'On my daddy's death, it is indubitably true!' Valentine assured him, 'Willy *adores* you!'

'Yes, yes!' replied Cosmo, cross with both Valentine and himself, 'I bloody see it now; I don't know why I didn't before!'

Suddenly, Cosmo looked disgusted.

'It's bloody ridiculous! She's family and she's just a little . . . well, *young*, girl!'

'She's not so little or young,' Valentine cried out, 'She'll be eighteen in October, practically a grown-up and only ten years your junior, and my mummy and daddy had a discrepancy of a dozen, plus she's not really kin to you; there's a huge bifurcation in the family tree betwixt your branch and our trunk!'

The outburst had Cosmo wonder with disbelief at Valentine's angle; what was he suggesting?

'Anyway,' said Valentine, 'I am getting ahead of myself here, but I now feel confident that I have illustrated to you the motivation of Willy.'

'I couldn't give a bloody monkey's about it!' Cosmo bellowed. 'If she's lovesick for me then that's her affair and she's not the first! Her little girl games don't interest me! Now if you don't get out of there and help me pee then I'll, I'll . . . I will . . . '

'There's not a thing you can do except shout!' said Valentine, 'Your arms are useless so you can't unlock the door and escape, and you can't step into the bath and thrash me because of your shorts, so be still, ignoramus!'

Cosmo made an effort to prove Valentine wrong but found that he was indeed unable to get close enough to cause him physical harm. Therefore, he leaned over the side of the bath as far as he could without falling, and with his roman nose little more than an inch from the neat one of Valentine, he roared again.

'Just you bloody wait you flaming pansy! I'll not be like this forever and you won't always have Rupert around, and then, when you least expect it, I will tear you limb from limp limb, you bloody see if I don't; I will bloody *kill* you!'

Valentine nobly said to him, 'Indeed you will not! Indeed you will, in actual point of fact, fall over yourself to please me when I tell you that only I possess the power to mollify your parents and thus nullify your disinheritance!'

These choice words were to Cosmo as shocking as a million slaps and he could not derive any sense from them; why would his parents require mollification and what disinheritance? No, his mater and pater were on a cruise, Willy had told him so and she never lied!

Now, Cosmo experienced a dreadful dawning; the cash machine had swallowed his card, and what did Valentine mean when he had said that Willy was leading him up the garden path? Then Cosmo realised he still did not know precisely what had transpired at the marvellous party. Suddenly, his little head hurt with the onslaught of menacing questions.

He was at a perfect loss at how to ask them and where even to begin; the only word he was able to produce was a curt, 'What?'

Obligingly, Valentine set about unveiling to him the precise reality of his predicament.

To start with, it seemed to Cosmo that Valentine was telling the tale pertaining to another person because it began in the year 1870 when, upon the birth of a boy, the father presented to the mother an extravagant ring. Then Cosmo learned that the ring was bequeathed unto an entirely wrong recipient, but until he heard that the ring had fallen into the undeserving hands of his own father, Cosmo could not see how it bore any relevance to himself. Then, upon being told that the ring was called a Starfish he felt as if disembowelled because it cast a terrifying realisation that rapidly mutated into a monstrous spectre when his mental image of the ring provoked him to recall the Parisian tryst with his aunt and their exchange. Presently, Cosmo assumed that the cat was out of the bag and that was why he now found himself cut off.

Cosmo shuffled round and sat his beefy rear on the bath ledge.

'Oh, bloody hell! Auntie O!' he said with aggravation.

'What?' said Valentine with pretend perplexity, 'What's mummy got to do with any of this?'

Cosmo looked at him. He was silent for a space then, with little conviction, he said, 'Nothing, nothing. Don't know what I'm talking about do I? Anyway, go on,' and though relieved that he had not been cut off because of his interaction with Olivia, he wondered what was the reason.

'*H'm*! All right!' said Valentine, who realised Cosmo was now mindful of his adventure with his mother but refused to admit that he knew also, and so he continued.

'Anyway, the Starfish, it's very strange because about five weeks ago, in fact, I remember the exact day because it was the day that you brought Rupert into my life, and anyway that was the day when, upon the carpet on the landing, ironically just at the foot of Olympia's harp, I happened to find the Starfish. Naturally, I thought it to be paste, therefore, I thought little of it and just put it in my hatbox where I put all my collection of jewellery.'

Cosmo narrowed his eyes and mentally cursed his aunt her obvious carelessness with the ring, and he filled with foreboding at the power it gave to Valentine for having found it.

'Now, The Marvellous Party!' Valentine went on, 'It really is a sorry shame that you can't remember it, but it *was* marvellous! Well, except for the end, and that was something else! I wonder if you remember getting the stiffy.'

'What?' asked Cosmo with a look of panic.

'Patently not!' said Valentine, 'And that is a shame too because they were exquisite! Anyway, the stiffies said that every lady ought to wear jewels as well as breathtaking gowns . . . do you remember Willy's gown? No? Oh, that *is* a pity! Anyway, it was glorious, and she needed jewels to go with it, and though I did not know it, she, quite unaware of its worth because, as I say, even I thought it to be paste, borrowed it from my hatbox and wore it at the party!'

Valentine sighed.

'Now, I'm not entirely certain how it happened but your parents discovered it and so ensued mayhem, and somehow, and this bit will really interest you, the Starfish ended up in Remarkable's beak and he upon the roof! That is why you climbed up after him, you were awfully plucky to do so, but, of course, you fell and got your coma and the only reason we have not told you is because Willy thinks the knowledge would kill you and, because she loves you, it would kill her also!'

Cosmo started to seethe like a maddened bull.

'You haven't told me yet how you can "nullify my disinheritance",' he said, through gritted teeth.

'Gosh! Yes, now we find ourselves at the crux of the crux!' replied Valentine, and he compressed his back as close to the tiled wall as was possible.

Cosmo looked at his pansy cousin over his shoulder and thought his repositioning ominous, therefore he rose also, and shuffled about to face him.

'Bloody spit it out!' he blared.

'Well you see,' began Valentine, ostensibly unperturbed, 'your mater and pater were completely convinced that Willy had stolen the ring but, naturally, she is no thief, therefore, so as to get her off the hook, I invented a story. I meant no malice, indeed it was just in jest. I did not consider that they would think it true, and that it would result in your utter severance but it did and, subsequently, I find myself holding all the cards, and here I lay them all on the table for you to see, and I trust that you shall agree to my terms!'

Although considerably perplexed, Cosmo was certain he did not like in the least the sound of the explanation. Moreover, what had been said to his parents to cement the dispossession?

Then, upon learning that his mater and pater believed he had stolen the ring to give to Valentine because he was in love with him, Cosmo's fury so burgeoned that he lunged forward to annihilate the treacherous pansy. Yet the endeavour was unsuccessful and he managed only to clumsily tumble into the bath as Valentine nimbly hopped out of it.

Cosmo's roars were infernal, the curses blue and bigoted, and though his ankles were still shackled in his shorts, he kicked out so violently that the toiletries on the surrounding shelves rained down on him, as did the cumbersome showerhead that struck hard his skull with a *clunk*.

'Gosh, Cosmo! Do try to calm yourself!' said Valentine, enjoying the sight of his cousin so firmly lodged that he could not manoeuvre his upper body, 'Lack of composure never solved anything!'

'I will bloody kill you!' Cosmo shouted so hard that he sprayed saliva. Valentine tutted at the discharge.

'But Cosmo, if you do that then how can I tell your parents that my words were pure slander and illuminate them with an innocent explanation?'

There followed a short space of silence, Cosmo calmed, and he sneered up at Valentine.

'You bloody idiot!' he snarled, 'Don't you think I can do that for myself? Why, as soon as I get out of here I'll set them right, you see if I bloody don't!' and he struggled again to rectify his bearing whilst he laughed at his cousin's vanity.

'Yes, I thought you might say that, but tell me, how you would explain Willy wearing the ring?' said Valentine in an unruffled tone, for he knew very well that Cosmo would not confess the truth, 'Besides, there *is* the small matter of my possessing hardcore evidence of your love for me.'

Cosmo gave up the effort.

'What evidence? What do you mean?' he asked with confusion, and watched as Valentine produced a folded sheet of paper from his pyjama pocket, opened it out and held it for him to read.

Cosmo's first thought was 'Why does Valentine have a note from me?' He could not remember penning it, yet the handwriting was undeniably his. However, when he read the words, he knew that it could not be from him because never would he write: '*My sweet Valentine! Bloody hell and damn it all, I love you! What's more, I'll wager this Starfish proves it! At any rate, when you're ready then I'm willing because a chap just can't bloody sleep at night without you! Bloody lots of love, your Cosmo. XXX*'

'Bloody bunkum!' Cosmo boomed, 'I didn't write it!' and he was disgusted at the thought that someone might think that he had.

'But it's your word against mine,' said Valentine, 'And seeing as I've nothing to lose or gain, I'm quite certain mine will carry more weight! All I'd have to do is post it to your parents, along with the many far more explicit billet-doux I have convincingly inked.'

Cosmo considered. Valentine was right; if his parents had already disinherited him, and presumably stopped his allowance, based only on Valentine's story told apparently solely for fun, then a bundle of counterfeit love letters would set the severance in stone, and would reinforce the notion of his alleged perversion. He could not either disclose the reality because his parents would deem that just as reprehensible, besides,

Olivia would deny it and his friendship with Harry would most likely terminate.

The situation seemed to Cosmo so singularly dire that he lacked the energy to roar, bellow, curse, threaten or boom, and felt capable of emitting nothing better than a whimper.

'Gosh, but Cosmo!' exclaimed Valentine, rather dismayed at his obvious despair, 'You must know that I would not ever do it! You are, after all, still kin, albeit distinctly distant, but of Excelsior's loins nonetheless, so I shouldn't like to see you destitute, therefore I am certain we can come to an agreement.'

Whereupon, Cosmo looked at him resentfully, and hated himself for saying, 'I'll do bloody anything!'

Cosmo was relieved that Valentine did not try any monkey business whilst handling his anatomy, though the utilisation of cooking-tongs was rather chastening, and when finally he was tucked away and his shorts pulled back up, he filled with relief, but his anxiety returned when, a few minutes later, he was imprisoned again, this time in Valentine's turret.

He had not seen inside the room before, and except for when involuntarily reflecting what Rupert might revel in, he did not ever imagine paying it a visit. A violent scent of violets was what he noticed first, then the wall of dead butterflies, next, the overabundance of brightly coloured glass ornaments and before them stood an easel. Cosmo was reluctant to consider what perversion the canvas depicted and he was glad that a draped yellow cloth protected his eyes. In the centre of the 'boudoir' was the bed, opulent with cushions and even the hide of a lion, upon which sat the pansy.

'Do sit down! No need to stand on ceremony!' Valentine exclaimed, excitedly.

Cosmo would rather stand but mindful that his fiscal security was now subject to Valentine's whims he lowered his posterior. Accidentally, his foot kicked the ferro and it fell. Valentine made a moue.

'Gosh, Cosmo! Do try not to demolish my room!'

'Sorry,' said Cosmo, humbly.

'Quite all right; I suppose it's not your fault really that you are so unwieldy!' said Valentine, and then, to tease, he added, 'I hope my bed shall withstand the exertion!'

Cosmo flashed him a panicked look.

'What did he have in mind?' he wondered and he nervously asked, 'So, what's the deal? What do I have to do?'

'Gosh, it wouldn't be much fun if I were to just tell you!' said Valentine, 'Far more adventurous for you simply to submit and go with the flow, I think!'

Executing a colossal gulp, Cosmo, to his surprise, signalled his acquiescence with a subjugated nod.

'Yes,' said Cosmo, submissively, and he closed his eyes with the thought that it might be less traumatic if he could not see what was happening, but then he heard a *pling* and Valentine sing the digits used to telephone his mater and pater as he manipulated the Bakelite dial.

'What are you doing?' demanded Cosmo, beneath his breath.

Valentine placed a finger on his lips, and whispered, '*Shh!*'

Cosmo obeyed and watched, with worry, Valentine straighten his posture and apply an eerily familiar mask of noblesse oblige.

Then there was a *click* followed by the shout of Esmé: 'Stakely Manor!' and the confirmation that the world cruise was fiction convinced Cosmo that only Valentine spoke the truth, and he was shocked tremendously when from Valentine's mouth emerged the voice of Auntie O.

'Esmé, darling!' said Valentine, 'Olivia here. How are you?'

Esmé sounded her snort.

'Oliv*iahh*! To what do I owe the displeasure?'

Valentine emitted his mother's tinkle of laughter.

'Yes, darling,' said Valentine, 'I appreciate perfectly your pointedness, and hope only that I shall succeed in softening your furiosity.'

'Furiosity doesn't cover it, Oliv*iahh*! But because we are in the same boat with regard to having the tragedy of pansy sons, though you seem accepting of yours, I shall listen to what you have to say.'

Cosmo was incredulous to his mater's readiness to believe that he of all people was a pansy and his countenance illustrated seamlessly this sentiment, but Valentine did not see it for he was too involved in his role: 'I am indeed accepting of mine; his homophilia at least, but it pains me to admit he is possessed of personality traits that do not sit so well with me and I feel it only fair that I share with you my shame for it certainly sickens me to consider his damage done to Cosmo, you and your family.'

Esmé immediately shouted, 'I demand an explanation!'

'Of course, darling, I shall elucidate you to the best of my ability,' said Valentine. 'It would appear that Valentine has a fondness for fashioning fabrications to match his mind; a very sorry psychological state indeed. Further, his fantasies have harmed your family and for that, I am sorry, but it would seem that he has quite a possessive passion for your Cosmo, so savage that he would say or do anything to keep him from ever interacting with anyone other than himself!

'Indeed, his own sister even!' Valentine went on, as Olivia, 'Because it has also been brought to my attention that your Cosmo and my Willy are rather enamoured of one another, and this is a thing that Valentine will not have! Therefore, upon discovering that your son had it in mind to give to my daughter the Starfish in way of conveying to her his keenness, Valentine sticky-fingered it and hid it in his hatbox!

'Naturally, he did not know that Willy would find and wear it anyway, and then when the ring was in the beak of the bird on the roof, he could only explain to you its appearance with the codswallop that Cosmo had given it to him for the very reason he was to give it to Willy!'

'You tell me that Cosmo is *not* a pansy and did not give my Starfish to Valentine and that Valentine actually stole it from him?' shouted Esmé.

'To my embarrassment that is exactly, darling, what I am saying!'

'But what makes you so certain?'

'One only need see Cosmo and Willy together; they are radiant with a romance that is impossible to invent! Since Cosmo's resuscitation, they have been quintessentially conjunctive and it is beautiful to watch blossom but with my deviant Valentine in the vicinity, I fear it will wither, and much as I love him, as only a mother could, and even then, it so *very* vexing, I do believe he shall mete out more misfortune and prevent the pair from prospering! Oh, when I think of the detriment he has already dispensed I simply shudder with shame!'

'And so you should!' Esmé shouted, 'And I confess I feel some too; Cosmo was told always that my Starfish was his to give to a girl someday! Ah, my poor boy to have suffered so! How is he now? Since the coma?'

'Camping out in Harry's room and currently napping, I believe. It is best to let him sleep for as long as he can because with both his arms in casts it can take quite a while for him to drift off.'

'Both arms in casts?'

'Yes, darling; it is terrible!'

'It is all your pansy's doing! My poor boy! He needs his mater!'

Here Esmé paused and then shouted, 'You say Wilhelmina has been taking care of him?'

'Like Nurse Nightingale!'

'The sweet girl! At least you have her! She is a good girl; very sweet to me at the party, and she telephoned me from the hospital and I was a perfect monster to her!'

'I am indeed very happy with her, darling, but of course now that Cosmo is to return home I realise that she must go with him, for to tear them apart would surely hinder Cosmo's healing and render Valentine's deviousness victorious. That the Starfish has departed is dreadful but the breaking of two young hearts would be completely cataclysmic!'

'Olivi*ahh*!' said Esmé, 'I could not agree more! Wilhelmina *must* come here with Cosmo so they can prosper in the absence of Valentine! You must tell Wilhelmina to pack their bags and expect a car this evening; they must come to the safety of Stakely Manor immediately!'

'You are very wise, Esmé. And I wonder if, in return for my Willy, I might ask a small favour of you?'

'What?'

'That you do not press charges against my son; already he has brought enough shame to the family! It would not help Cosmo's recovery either; what with the inevitable resulting rumours regarding the pansy romance.'

Obviously, Esmé feared such rumours, and instantly shouted, 'You have my word!'

'Immense gratitude, Esmé! I shall tell Cosmo the good news the moment he wakes!'

Then came Esmé's awkward question: 'Does Cosmo know of his disinheritance?'

'Darling, none of us have had the heart; he looks so pathetic in his slings!'

Valentine eyed Cosmo condescendingly and Cosmo reddened.

Esmé's sigh of relief was clearly audible, and she shouted, 'I shall have Quentin telephone Pritchard immediately to reverse it! Immense gratitude to you too for looking after my boy!'

'It was the least that I could do, darling!' said Valentine, with a sly smile, 'Goodbye, Esmé!'

'Goodbye, Olivi*ahh*!'

With that, Valentine replaced the telephone receiver in its cradle. It went *pling* and he went tut.

He rolled his eyes, and in his own voice, said to Cosmo, 'Hook, line and sinker!'

Valentine's ability to hoodwink so effortlessly his mater was, to Cosmo's mind, a marvel. Certainly, it rankled him to a degree but he was over-whelmingly pleased to be un-disinherited.

Yet, he said to Valentine, 'You bloody ignoble bastard!'

'Gosh!' said Valentine, 'I like that! I have been extremely noble and nullified your disinheritance, just as I said I would!'

Cosmo rose and snarled.

'You needn't look so pleased with yourself; I know you only did it to make me take Willy, but I bloody won't! I'll just tell my mater Willy wouldn't, or couldn't, fit in the car! Ha-ha-ha!'

'Nice try, Cosmo!' Valentine said, with a sigh.

Whereupon, he opened his bedside table drawer and withdrew the bundle of empty envelopes tied with a lilac ribbon and fanned himself with it.

'*Mummy* has only to telephone mater at any time to tell of the suddenly discovered sordid love notes you've sent me, and you shall again be cut off!'

'You bloody bastard!' Cosmo roared.

'Gosh, Cosmo!' said Valentine, with mock horror, 'You do love that B word, don't you? And I'm certain you'll soon love Willy too, or at least be effervescently gentlemanly to her for as long as she wants to stay, other-wise, *snip-snip*!'

Cosmo grimaced.

Beneath the pergola prolific with fragrant flora, Willy sat upon the wrought iron loveseat, and tears cascaded down her plump cheeks. She had heard Cosmo's boomed sentiment that she was a 'bloody bitch' as she fled from the drawing room to hide and weep over her inability to assist him in the lavatory.

She just could not have done it, the idea of it seemed to her so very wrong and consequently, despite her three-week vigil at his hospital bedside, regardless of her feeding him, and her monumental love for him notwithstanding, his only feeling for her was hate. Therefore, her generous body convulsed as she sobbed into her soft fleshy arms, her sole comfort were the sweet eyes and gentle hands of her little brother who seemed to see into, touch and caress her agonised heart.

Corny could not quite understand how Cosmo was worthy of Willy. However, because he indubitably loved his sister, he sat with her while she cried out her heart and it looked to him as if the process may prove eternal.

Yet his steadfastness eventually ended with the appearance of Cosmo and Valentine, who together seemed surprisingly congenial, with the still more surprising news from the bigger of the two: 'C'mon, Willy, I know all about you making up the cruise to protect me, but I'm not disinherited anymore, and mater says you're to pack our bags and come to Stakely Manor.'

Valentine kneaded, with a knuckle, the small of Cosmo's back, coercing him to amend his request.

'I mean, *please* pack our bags because I can't with my arms or else I'd pack my own *and* yours.'

Willy viewed a blurred Cosmo through her tears.

'Really not?' she breathed.

'Really yes!' Valentine exclaimed, 'You are to go to Stakely Manor to look after Cosmo because he needs you very much, casts or no, isn't that so, Cosmo?'

'Very much so,' Cosmo affirmed.

Still, Willy was incredulous; how could it be? What an extraordinary turn of events!

'Really not!' she repeated, this time with nervous excitement.

Cosmo corrugated his monobrow and looked to Valentine for guidance.

Valentine tutted, and said, 'Perhaps she'd be more convinced if you were to crash to your knees and ask again.'

Thus, before Willy had the chance to protest, Cosmo crashed and reiterated.

'Really not!' she cried yet again, provoking Cosmo and both her brothers to experience exasperation, 'But aren't I a "bloody bitch"?'

A sudden sense of lowliness stunned Cosmo and caused him to blush. Willy's elation at his invitation was greater than he had imagined it would be. He had not ever before considered himself capable of inspiring such unwarranted devotion, for devoted to him Willy most transparently was.

'You're not a bloody bitch,' he said to her, in earnest, 'I'm a bloody fool for saying it and I wish you hadn't heard it. Fact is, you're a bloody boon!'

The depth of feeling in Cosmo's eyes convinced Willy of his sincerity and she decided to question it no further.

She gathered his little head to her bountiful breast and cried out, 'Oh, Cosmo! I am always here for you! I live to be your bloody boon!' whereupon she smothered his bald scalp with a flurry of kisses.

Cosmo was not used to such demonstration, but despite himself, he grunted good-humouredly into her cleavage, 'My bloody boon; bloody brilliant! But a bloody boon's got to pack bags because the car will be here in a few hours.'

Willy released him.

'Really not!' said she.

'Cosmo is right, Willy,' said Valentine, 'the car will be here before too long, so let me help you find what to take!'

The wheels of the Oxley-Stockmans' Rolls-Royce crunched the gravel of the Avery-Stripes' drive at the honourable hour of eight despite the ugly ormolu clock claiming it was not yet even seven.

'Oh! Oh!' cried Willy, almost hysterically as she watched, through the stained-glass window, the chauffeur approach the porch and tug the doorbell-pull. 'The driver is here! Oh, so soon! I'm not certain that I am ready!'

'You are perfectly ready, Willy!' Valentine exclaimed, 'Well except for this.'

From behind his back, Valentine produced a hat in the design of a lady's topsy-turvy shoe and positioned it atop Willy's thoroughly brushed bob.

'Gosh! Glorious!' he exclaimed.

Regarding her reflection in the hall-tree looking glass, Willy felt she had to agree; with the funny hat, Valentine had dressed her from head-to-toe in slimming black except for a pearl necklace and pebble-grey genuine armadillo handbag.

'Yes, darling, you do look to be very much a lady,' said Olivia, with a degree of sincerity, as she stalked about her daughter and checked for flaws (she would not have Willy derided by the Oxley-Stockmans) 'And pearls are sublimely subtle – you ought to wear them always; they accentuate the whites of your eyes.'

Willy considered the efficiency of her ears; her mother had not only called her a lady but had also paid her a compliment!

She stifled a sob, and cried, 'Oh, thank you, mummy!'

'Quite all right, darling,' Olivia replied, and she sensed a sadness sweep through her as she watched Rupert and the chauffeur elevate Willy's weighty trunk, that Valentine, irritatingly, called a trousseau, and place it in the boot of the Rolls-Royce.

Maybe it was the baby, but Olivia felt unusually maternal, therefore, she protectively gripped Willy's shoulders, and chaperoned her to the front garden.

*

The ensuing goodbyes were wretched, but Gubsy insisted: 'Nonsense! You shan't miss me!' and he pushed a tidy sum into Willy's palm. 'Just in case,' he said in a low tone.

'Oh, Gubsy! Thank you!' whispered Willy, whilst stuffing the notes into her armadillo.

Gubsy replied with a *harrumph* and turned to strike his cocobolo cane against a wheel of the car because he was about to bawl.

Gretchen, wearing a dirndl, somehow sounded a conciliatory snort.

'Mr Bartholmoo, behave yourself! Miss Willy will be back, is not forever, she will need her Kretchen and her Kretchen's cookink!' but she felt that she too might cry when Willy bundled into her arms; it did not seem so very long ago that the bundle was a babe.

Following her goodbyes to the Avery-Stripe animals, Willy asked Rupert to promise that he would look after the vulnerable Valentine.

Naturally, Rupert complied wholeheartedly.

'Gosh! Don't worry about me, Willy! I'm safe as houses with Rupert!' Valentine exclaimed, 'And so long Cosmo!' and to please his sister and tease him, Valentine pulled him close.

'Yes, goodbye, Valentine!' said Cosmo, as amicably as he was able.

Rupert wished Cosmo a fond farewell, and then so did Olivia.

'Goodbye, Cosmo darling,' she said, 'It has been a delight, but I'm certain you'll be happier where you belong.'

Cosmo scrutinised his Auntie O and tried hard to gauge her thoughts but the giant sunglasses she had cleverly worn to hide any hint in her eye that she carried his kernel rendered it impossible.

Olivia's lips now contorted into a crocodilian smile and disconcerted him, but he was distracted when she pushed Corny forward.

'Corny, darling, do tell cousin Cosmo goodbye; it might be a while before we see him again!'

But Corny assertively snubbed Cosmo and scampered off to press against the cushiony snugness of his sister. He squeezed her tight; he pushed his face in her bosom and caused her almost to topple despite her heels being the sturdy spool sort. He did not want to let go of Willy; his sister with whom he had shared the teats of wet-nurse Mrs Bovinus, and he wept because, one by one, his siblings were fleeing the nest.

It was too much for Willy to bear and she began to ruin her mascara.

'Oh! This is beastly!' she wailed, and she removed Corny's feathered war bonnet to kiss his blond head so thoroughly that her generously applied lipstick made scarlet smudges.

Valentine flashed Cosmo a look, and Cosmo was cooperative because he was eager to get home.

Therefore, he said, in not a completely uncaring tone, 'C'mon, Willy, best get going or it'll be midnight by the time we get there!'

Dabbing her eyes with some kitchen-paper courtesy of Gretchen, Willy realised that he was right and that he was the only reason that she would ever leave Chinchero.

She overflowed with happiness, and after receiving a kiss on both cheeks from Valentine and a thin smile from her mother, she climbed into the car and blew her nose loudly as the chauffeur shut the door.

Cosmo got in the other side and eyed her whilst she inspected the contents of the kitchen-paper, and he asked himself, 'How has this bloody come about?' but then she looked at him so sweetly that he responded with a genuine, 'You all right?'

Nodding her head with an enthusiasm that influenced her hat a little, Willy suddenly gasped and turned so quickly that her hat lost its grip entirely. She viewed her family through a pane of glass, pressed her hands against it and read their mouths saying goodbye. Her tears returned and did not stop until halfway down the Avenue when she considered how she would have heard their words had she opened the window.

At the front gate, Olivia and Valentine watched and waved Willy goodbye.

Olivia tucked a hand in his crook, and, through her smiling teeth, she said, 'Well done, darling, you managed it in only five days.'

Not taking his eyes from the diminishing car, Valentine, like a ventriloquist, replied, 'Four days' inspiration and one day's perspiration, I am quite pleased with myself, yes.'

'But, darling,' Olivia added, whilst still smiling at the departure, 'I am astonished you brought yourself to bring about his re-inheritance, and to waive Willy too; I am not at all certain how well that sits with me!'

Valentine faced Olivia, and, moving his mouth, replied, 'Gosh! Don't be myopic, mummy! Willy wants nothing more than to be with him, and if she must be then better that he can keep her in comfort, besides, if she's sage she'll eventually seize it all for future Avery-Stripes!'

Olivia looked at her second born with mock horror then truly smiled.

'You mercenary!' she whispered.

'Not I, mummy!' said Valentine, 'You know I'm disapproving of money, I require only beauty!' and he cast a happy glance at Rupert cheering Corny under the porch, 'I did it for the family!'

'Yes, darling, I do believe that you did,' Olivia said, thoughtfully. 'Daddy would be very proud.'

'Gosh! I know! I did it for daddy, for the Avery-Stripes, quite predominantly Benedictus!'

'Benedictus?' Olivia asked.

'Yes, mummy,' Valentine answered, 'I have named the baby. I do hope you don't mind. It is beautiful and it is ideal, and do you know why?'

'No, darling, why?'

'It is Latin for blessed, because despite being a bastard he is still the blessed Avery-Stripe heir!'

There was a pause. Olivia marvelled at Valentine's ability to simultaneously scheme and name so impeccably.

Then she said, 'Yes, darling, I do believe it a good name.'

Valentine sighed.

'I did tell you that we would see that it was *good*!'

Though Willy was ecstatic at her situation in the Rolls-Royce with Cosmo, she was worlds away as she recollected Valentine's reply to her question posed whilst they had prepared her trousseau in the cellar: 'Valentine, can you explain to me why Cosmo is taking me away from the family?'

'Gosh! What an interesting way of putting it!' he said. 'Taking you away from the family, indeed!'

'Well he is, isn't he?' she returned.

'Gosh! Only in effect; you're an Avery-Stripe wherever you are! But he needs you and you want him, and for you I pulled some strings. Please don't ask for particulars because it's all a bit Byzantine, but when any Oxley-Stockman denigrates my name, and they will, you must say nothing and simply nod. Do you understand?'

Willy had viewed him with uncertainty but she had faith in him and his acumen and, therefore, she knew that however he had managed it, whatever strings had been pulled, it was not without thorough circumspection.

Therefore, she had quietly replied, 'Yes, I understand.'

Presently, Willy sensed Cosmo's eyes upon her. She turned to him, and her face glowed as if she was but a nubile bud blossoming for her bee, in fact, Cosmo did indeed consider her to look as if she possessed something glorious that he very much desired.

'But what?' he wondered.

Patently, she was still in possession of her virtue and though he thought that an attractive quality it was not one hard to come by. No, what she possessed was something altogether more alluring.

Suddenly, he knew just what it was; she was an Avery-Stripe! An authentic Avery-Stripe and not a mere appendix like her mother; Willy was of direct lineage and, what was more, she adored him and wanted to belong to him. That was the glorious thing Willy possessed that was so desirable!

Now, Cosmo cast her an affectionate curve of his lips that caused in her a rapturous rush resulting in a happy blush, and consequently, he felt less sore about the Starfish and was certain that he could hear the approving cackle of his Granny Ursie. She was joyous that her grandson had appropriated the great niece of the shining Sebastian denied her by the supercilious Ambrosius – son and heir of none other than Excelsior Avery-Stripe.

Thus, Cosmo was without a doubt that Willy was infinitely more desirable than any ring.

CHAPTER 24

The Blue Tea Party

Rupert was due to renovate the home of Hugo and Giles Pargeter the following week, but Valentine, without providing much in the way of an explanation, urged that he first redecorate Olivia's bedroom.

Rupert duly complied; he telephoned to postpone the Pargeters, and Hugo politely appreciated the predicament.

'Very well, Valentino,' Olivia said to him, 'I concur that my room requires a fresh lick but I delegate the organisation to you, whilst I, in the interim, shall reside in Horatio's room.'

Then, to Gretchen, she said, 'I trust that the linen has been laundered since Cosmo's occupation?'

'Yes, Mrs Olivia, and even they are not the same sheets!' replied Gretchen with some resentment over Olivia's thankless attitude, despite the troughs of kedgeree she daily supplied her with.

Gretchen could not calculate why, since the departure of Willy and Cosmo, Olivia's hauteur had increased by a great magnitude but she decided it best to turn a blind eye.

The relocation was more disconcerting to Olivia than she had imagined it might be, because though she had spent many nights in hotel suites since her husband's demise she believed that to sleep in the four-poster whilst gravid would render the kernel more Monty. Therefore, to counter this, she slept with his pillow in Harry's bed, and this she did often because she now found an unexpected ability to catch up on all the hours of sleep that she had lost.

Rupert was speedy with his work however, though, of course, still diligent, and in less than four days, Olivia returned to her bedroom and filled with gratitude that Valentine had insisted upon the facelift.

'Thank you, Valentine, darling! And thank you too, Rupert,' she said, as her head hit Monty's pillow, now back in the four-poster, 'It is a tremendous transformation; I am certain to sleep like a saint!'

'Crikey! Thanks, Olivia!' returned Rupert, grinning and slightly blushing, 'I'm glad you like it!'

'Gosh, mummy!' said Valentine, kissing her goodnight, 'We must ensure that Benedictus has only the very best!'

Eyes shut, Olivia smiled, 'You sound just like your daddy, darling!'

'Gosh! Glorious!' exclaimed Valentine, and, with that, he and Rupert vacated her bedroom.

'Benedictus?' Rupert asked Valentine before Olympia's gleaming harp.

'Yes!' whispered Valentine, barely able to suppress his excitement, 'Mummy is burdened with a bastard baby! Don't ask me how, as I've not yet thought of that, but his name is Benedictus and he is to go to barren Harry and Izzy, isn't that glorious?'

Rupert looked nonplussed for a moment but then realised that he liked the idea, and he grinned.

'Crikey! That is amazing!'

'Isn't it!' Valentine replied, 'But do keep the baby under your hat; he's to be a surprise!'

Rupert's complaisant nod persuaded his golden curls to tousle beautifully, and, in turn, they persuaded Valentine to exclaim, 'Gosh! Let's go upstairs; I feel to be a perfect epicurean with insatiable aesthetic desires!'

The labour required at the Pargeters' transpired to be quite demanding of Rupert's time, (Corny's too, for often he would assist) not that he ever renovated any later than five post meridian, and then he would return to Valentine, but the work days multiplied into several weeks.

One morning, over a familial breakfast, Rupert relayed, to Olivia, Mr Pargeter's daily warm regards, that he had hitherto forgotten to deliver. He said that Mr Pargeter hoped that she was well.

Olivia shuddered at the thought of Hugo. Nevertheless, she still believed that Giles would have been an admirable addition to the family, and she made no bones in voicing the opinion.

'Gosh, mummy! Giles Pargeter?' exclaimed Valentine, and close to upset his cup of breakfast tea, 'But he is a dypso-bounder! Surely, you recollect his intoxication at The Marvellous Party, *and* the way he interacted with the iniquitous twins – entirely ungentlemanly! Don't you think, Corny?'

The question posed interrupted Corny's grimaces at the kipper upon his plate, and he exhibited his agreement with a nod.

'Naturally, I recollect!' snapped Olivia, 'But I am certain that his nerves pushed him to drink because, quite honestly, those girls are mercilessly predatory! No man remains safe when they are in the vicinity; I blame the mother to be frank! Giles is a charming boy, *and* his line is lucrative.'

'Oh, mummy! *Money*! I should have known!' said Valentine, disparagingly.

Olivia persevered: 'Good-looking too! You of all people must appreciate that!'

Valentine settled his teacup with a *clink*, touched Rupert's forearm, and exclaimed, 'Gosh! Why would I look at pretty pavement chalkings when I possess a priceless Picasso?'

Rupert halted his beautiful and silent mastication to grin in appreciation, though he did not bear his perfect teeth for he knew that a sighting of chewed food would distress Valentine.

'I was not intimating an intimacy with Giles with you!' said Olivia, tersely, 'I am thinking of Willy!'

'Gosh, mummy, she is with Cosmo!' whined Valentine, exasperated that his mother had not grasped the purpose of Willy's absence was that she would never know of the burden because she would be bound to tell Cosmo; best that they both be kept in the dark.

Olivia pulled a pained expression.

'Precisely! And I'm still not certain the situation suits me; Cosmo's far from favourable!'

'Oh, mummy! Willy's wanted Cosmo for years, besides would Giles *want* Willy?'

Now Rupert, having swallowed, spoke: 'Actually, I see Giles some mornings before he goes to work, and he's talked about Willy a few times; he says he had an amazing dance with her at The Marvellous Party!'

Valentine and Olivia, and Corny, as well as Gubsy and Gretchen, all of them looked at Rupert in astonishment. They each loved Willy dearly but knew that she was not the most graceful girl and, therefore, unlikely to be an amazing dancer, yet Rupert was as honest as the longest day, and, consequently, they considered the possibility of Giles – most particularly Corny who deemed anyone better for his sister than Cousin Cosmo.

Presently, the letterbox made the sound *clank*, whereupon Corny sprang to his feet and left the table without permission. Moments later, he returned with a letter to the family, as if it might be the most exciting thing to have ever happened, and he decided that Valentine ought to read it for him.

'Gosh! Thanks ever so much, Corny!' said Valentine, 'You are my very own Hermes but I wonder if the message shall transpire divine!'

Yet, this he doubted for the envelope bore the address of Stakely Manor on the reverse. Nevertheless, with the ivory paperknife, he proceeded to slice.

'Darling, I would like to know why you should be the one to open it!' said Olivia.

Valentine sounded a tut.

'Gosh! Because Corny handed it to me. And it is addressed to the Avery-Stripes, and as I am spare to the heir, and the heir is elsewhere, I assume the promoted position!'

In the face of Valentine's imperiousness, Olivia resigned herself, as she was too tired to oppose it, and upon seeing the amount of writing paper that the envelope held, she was glad to have escaped the onus of their perusal.

'Gosh! Simply reams!' Valentine exaggerated (the sheets numbered no more than six) 'I shall skim and scan!'

'Gosh! It is from Willy! But on Oxley-Stockman letterhead!' he said with disdain, 'We must send her a box of Avery-Stripe for her to use whilst she still can!'

'Hear, hear!' Gubsy boomed.

'I'm certain she shall use Avery-Stripe for a good few years yet, darling!' said Olivia, 'Anyway, do read it!'

They all watched as Valentine skimmed and scanned, and they wondered what were the reasons for his tuts, gasps, and askew smiles but he would not enlighten them until he had perused the communication in its entirety.

'Gosh! Well, I say!' said Valentine, upon finishing and folding it.

'What do you say, darling?' asked Olivia in suspense.

'What's Willy write?' demanded Gubsy.

Corny was also eager to know and this he demonstrated by scaling the back of Valentine's chair to look over his shoulder.

'Well,' said Valentine, 'either Willy is deluded or fibbing, or she truly is having the loveliest of times and that the Oxley-Stockmans, chiefly Cosmo, are most accommodating.'

Olivia twisted her lips with displeasure as she recalled the boastful style of hospitality that Quentin and Esmé had inflicted upon her and Monty when visiting Stakely Manor in the early years of their marriage. For a family whose main portion of wealth was old, the Oxley-Stockmans acted like pigs in clover, in her opinion.

'How lovely, darling,' she said, then anxiously asked, 'Specifics?' and she wished that she could smoke.

Valentine sighed.

'Lots of long country walks and public-house luncheons apparently, she says the Oxley-Stockman cattle are "so sweet" and she is "in love" with an expectant heifer called Ramona. Esmé takes her shopping in villages and spoils her rotten – Willy, not the heifer – and Quentin talks non-stop about Excelsior, and Cosmo practically moons over her – again *not* the heifer!'

The idea of Cosmo mooning over Willy did not sit well with Olivia, she sensed a foreboding, and so too did Corny.

'Oh, it is so kood Miss Willy is havink a kood time and they are beink so kind to her!' said Gretchen, though she felt a little sad at the thought that Willy might prefer it to Chinchero.

'Of course they are being good to her!' Gubsy boomed, 'They are honoured to have an Avery-Stripe grace their house, and well they know it!'

'Hear, hear!' said Valentine.

'But, darling,' said Olivia, 'I sense you are not sharing it all; she couldn't possibly stretch those few words so far. What else does she say?'

Now Valentine warped his face; an unanticipated occurrence had transpired, and though it might not be cause for any immediate concern, he certainly would have to tend to it post haste.

'What, darling, what?' exclaimed Olivia, as she watched, with worry, his facial contortions.

'Well,' he said, slowly, 'it would seem that last weekend, the Oxley-Stockmans also played host to Harry and Izzy.'

'Oh! Is that all?' said Olivia, with relief.

'Well, yes,' replied Valentine, and he looked at her to ascertain whether or no her nonchalance was bona fide, and, to his surprise, he saw that it was.

The news did not please Corny and he huffily wondered why Harry had not yet been to see him.

'Was Master Harry's honeymoon kood?' asked Gretchen, enthusiastically.

'Gosh! She didn't say! I assume so!' Valentine snottily snapped.

He was irritated that he had failed to predict the possibility of the newlyweds visiting Willy before coming to see the rest of the family, and he was annoyed that his mother did not realise what that might mean.

'Rapscallion!' roared Gubsy, 'Do not ever speak to Gretchen like that again! D'you hear me! Or I'll whip you into next week!'

Valentine cast him a petulant glance, and Gretchen busied herself with the tidying of the table.

'Is okay, Mr Bartholmoo, Master Valentine, he just is missink his siblinks!' and she hastened to her kitchen with six dirty plates.

Gubsy gnashed his false teeth and muttered expletives all the way to his wing chair to reunite with *The Times* and his toucan.

Both the blond boys viewed, with confusion, Valentine make a moue at his mother.

'Do try not to pull such sulky faces, darling,' said Olivia, 'they might stick!'

'Oh, mummy! You fool!' he cried.

'I refuse to be accused of foolery!' she snapped.

Valentine sounded an almighty tut.

'Despite being guilty of it?'

Olivia bore her teeth, and returned, 'I am incredulous to your impertinence!'

'Gosh! And I am incredulous to your ignorance! Consider the possibility that Harry might have told Cosmo of the infertility? Because if he has, how will he explain the arrival of baby Benedictus?'

Whereupon, Olivia gasped in alarm and Corny's eyes widened in wonderment – somehow there *was* going to be a baby after all!

Valentine did not care for bad manners. He decided that because of his annoyance at his mother's delayed reaction to the news of Harry's visit to Stakely Manor he was virtually forced to snottily snap at Gretchen, therefore, directly following Rupert's departure to the Pargeters', he apologised.

Another, and more important, reason for his expressed contrition was to persuade Gretchen from her kitchen in order to utilise the Bakelite. Naturally, had Gretchen known his call was to invite Harry and Izzy to tea she would have gladly permitted it anyway, but she did wish that she had more time in which to prepare.

'Much is to be done by half-of-four, if is to be done properly!' she stated, 'I cannot be bakink cakes faster than they take!'

But still she was pleased and knew that somehow she would cope, and so did Valentine.

'I'm certain you'll manage, Gretchen!' he said, 'You always do, but do make it magnificent! It's to be an important occasion!'

Gretchen agreed that it was important; it was the newlyweds' first formal visit, and she suggested that as it was such a 'kood sunny Aukust summer day' that they take tea on the lawn.

'Gosh! What a gloriously lovely idea!' exclaimed Valentine, 'But I think not!' because though the garden was large, he wondered if the neighbours might overhear the more delicate aspects of the conversation.

Instead, he suggested, 'the alfresco privacy of the west terrace, we'll get Gubsy up the stairs one way or another, because the wisteria is blooming, and what a glorious blue it is!'

After a moment's reflection, he added, 'Actually, Gretchen, let's make the occasion as blue as can be, somehow it just seems apropos!'

And as so happened once in a blue moon, Gretchen thought him 'a very kood and thoughtful boy'.

Pleased with the hue of blue, indicative of a baby boy, that was to infuse the tea party, Valentine recollected his Great-Great-Aunt Isadora's table linen embroidered with bluebells. Perfect on two counts, because, again, blue for a boy and the embroiderer's name was the same as Benedictus' mother to be!

The increasing harmony caused Valentine to swoon but then he considered what might be the table centrepiece; indubitably, the wisteria was beautifully blue and the stitched bluebells also, but the necessitation of another middle flower was monumental, yet there were no blue ones in the garden. Therefore, he braved, once again, the Bakelite to request that Rupert remedy the plight, and to return to Chinchero at four rather than five.

Quite a few hours later, Valentine and Olivia waited in the hall.

'Quelle heure est-il, mummy?' asked Valentine, perched upon the bottom step and wearing baby blue silk pyjamas.

Olivia eyed her Tiffany wristwatch: 'Twenty-past-four.'

She then focused on the looking glass in the hall-tree, and wondered whether or no her ice-blue empire line dress truly did render her visage less wan because she was feeling somewhat peaky, despite, due to kedgeree, no longer vomiting, at least not so habitually.

Valentine said tut as he now rose to peer through the stained-glass window; he knew that Rupert would only be late because Mr Pargeter was being finicky. He decided not to fret however; Rupert would soon come, and if he did not have time to change, it little mattered, because the beautiful forget-me-not blue of his eyes was the best blue that Valentine knew.

'Oh, darling,' Olivia suddenly expelled, with a sigh, 'I am simply on tenterhooks as to what Horatio and Isadora might say apropos Benedictus because I do not share your confidence that they will so readily receive him.'

'Gosh, mummy! You must not worry! I'll see that it is *good*!'

389

Olivia eyed him sceptically, and said, 'I'm also concerned how you will account for the conception; it was far from immaculate and, of course, you can't say Cosmo.'

'Indubitably not, mummy!' said Valentine, 'That would defeat the entire exercise. I shall say that you fell for the charms of a swarthy sailor from somewhere exotic whom now can't be found, but I shall sway the conversation away from Benedictus' roots anyway!'

'*Ugh*!' said Olivia, 'Well, I suppose, under the circumstances, an exotic and swarthy sailor is comparatively palatable.'

'Yes, mummy,' replied Valentine, 'In fact, he *was* rather appealing!'

Olivia cast her second born a cynical smile.

It was then that they heard a key turn in the front door, and there was Rupert bearing a monstrously big bouquet of intensely blue agapanthus.

'Crikey! Sorry, Valentine!' said Rupert, 'Mr Pargeter questioned the cornicing, but I came as fast as I could; I ran all the way to the florists and then here!'

In a single leap, Valentine positioned himself in Rupert's available arm, kissed him, and exclaimed, 'Gosh! Never mind! They've not arrived yet!' and he buried his face in the bouquet to inhale.

'Gosh! Glorious!'

'I'm glad you like them!' said Rupert, smiling.

'They are beyond perfect!' asserted Valentine, and his sentiment heightened upon reading the label of literature that accompanied the agapanthus for the hybrid went by the auspicious name of *Ben Hope*.

Rupert laughed but had to ask why Valentine had not asked for yellow flowers or violets.

'Because it's a blue tea party for reasons I've yet to unveil! Look, I am wearing blue,' Valentine stepped back to validate his claim, 'And mummy is too!'

'Hello, Rupert, darling,' said Olivia, with a forced smile due to nerves.

'Hello, Olivia!' said Rupert, with a genuine one, 'You look amazing!' and he faced Valentine again for further details.

'Everyone is wearing blue on the west terrace; that's where tea shall be. But you best shower as you're all sweaty, and then can you wear blue also?'

Rupert considered, and then said, 'Yes! I can wear blue! I'll shower quickly!' and he loped up the stairwell.

'Gosh, Rupert!' Valentine called after him, '*Do* put the agapanthus in Grandmother Araminta's blue Murano glass vase on the west terrace!

And do try *not* to wash all the paint from your hair and hands; it's robin's egg!'

Beneath the bison, Rupert examined his paint-splattered hands.

'Crikey! I will! And you're right; it *is* robin's egg! I won't wash them hard!' and he continued his hurried climb.

On the precipice of advising Valentine against pushing his luck by bullying big boys, no matter how beautiful, Olivia froze because the front doorbell rang; the newlyweds had arrived!

Accordingly, Olivia patted her hair, composed her demeanour, and applied her mask of *noblesse oblige*, and as she watched Valentine skip to the door and open it, she prayed for the future of Benedictus.

'Hullo, Valentine!' said Harry, whose handsomeness was more evident than usual – observably, matrimony suited him very well. 'How are you?'

'Glorious, thank you!' said Valentine, and received from him, a kiss on each cheek, before bombarding, 'We all miss you of course. And we miss Willy too; she's with Cosmo, you know? Gosh, of course, you know; Willy wrote in her letter that you spent last weekend there. How *was* that?' And he cast a conspiratorial glance at his mother wearing her fixed smile.

Harry replied, 'It was *w*eally good! Such a *w*elief Cosmo's coma ended and it was g*w*eat to see Willy; she and Cosmo are g*w*eat f*w*iends now; it's b*w*illiant!

'But I am a t*w*ifle confused,' Harry went on, 'because Auntie Esmé and Uncle Quentin seem ve*w*y c*w*oss with you but not about the Starfish anymore. Do you know why?'

'Oh, it's all a little complex. Did they not explain?' asked Valentine.

'No. They weren't given a chance; ev*w*y time they seemed to start, Willy would f*w*eeze up and Cosmo would tell them to shut up. It was st*w*ange, but it's good to see Cosmo so p*w*otective and conside*w*ate of Willy.'

'Gosh! Glorious!' exclaimed Valentine, and he smiled knowingly.

'Yes, *w*eally glo*w*ious!' said Harry, 'I think you got your wires c*w*ossed about Cosmo liking boys.'

'I dare say that I did!' said Valentine, 'Esmé and Quentin must be terribly relieved to see that he is so fond of Willy!'

'Yes! They *w*eally te*ww*ibly are!'

'Glorious!' said Valentine and presently decided to acknowledge Izzy: 'Hello, Izzy!'

'Hello, Valentine.' she said, shyly.

Valentine thought shyness a very attractive quality in a lady; it accentuated delicacy, which, to his mind, was the hallmark of prettiness, and just as matrimony flattered Harry, so too did it increase Izzy's pretty jejunity.

Yet, something about her appearance disappointed Valentine, and he was not shy about stating it.

'Gosh! No tiara!' he exclaimed, reprovingly.

Guiltily, as if the absence of tiara was accidental, Izzy placed her fragile hands on her pale gold halo of hair to verify the accusation.

She seemed as if about to cry, and she gasped, 'Oh my goodne*th*! I'm *th*orry! Wa*th* I meant to?'

She looked so pitiful that Valentine cosseted her.

'Not really,' he said, 'but it is a shame, though I am glad you are wearing blue!'

'Oh! Thank you! It'*th* my favourite dre*th*, it'*th* *th*o *th*imple and ni*th*e!' said Izzy, and she glowed incandescently.

Harry defended his wife's right to not always wear her tiara.

'At any *w*ate,' he said, 'she wore it at the Pa*w*is ope*w*a; we saw *Eugene Onegin*, it was b*w*illiant, wasn't it, Izzy?'

'Oh ye*th*! *Eugene Onegin* wa*th* *th*o wonderful!' she replied, rapturously, 'Ex*th*ept when Len*th*ky got *th*ot!' and then she looked as if the duel still caused her upset.

Olivia, now ready to interact with the pair from whom she required salvation, did not hesitate to amend; if Harry and Izzy were to bring up Benedictus then they must brush up on their learnedness, moreover, they had not yet acknowledged her, thus, with each of the three steps required to reach her firstborn, she sounded the correct syllables: 'Oh-Nay-Gin, darling!'

'Hullo, mummy.' said Harry, awkwardly. He hoped that she had now accepted Izzy's barrenness.

He kissed Olivia's proffered cheek, and she elaborated, 'A hard G as in green garden, darling, *not* Egyptian gypsy!'

Neither of the newlyweds grasped Olivia's meaning, particularly Izzy who stared quizzically at her, and repeated, 'Egyp*th*ian gyp*thy*?'

'*Ugh!*' thought Olivia, as she viewed the new Mrs Avery-Stripe's incomprehensibility. 'Is this simpleton truly to be my successor?' she asked herself but swiftly remembered that she needed Izzy and she became cordial.

'Hello, Izzy, darling!' she exclaimed, and kissed the girl's sweet cheeks, 'You mustn't mind me; Harry's mummy often talks twaddle!'

'Oh! I'm *th*ure you do not!' Izzy argued, deferentially.

Olivia awarded Izzy a crocodile smile; she supposed that she was agreeably malleable, and she said, 'What a sweet girl you are, darling, I am certain I shall like you!' Whereupon, she slinked an arm around Izzy's microscopic waist, and cheerily exclaimed, 'Come! Let us ascend the stairwell to take tea on the west terrace of wisteria!'

Everyone did wear blue; Gretchen wore her royal blue gown (but not the bolero) that she had worn at The Marvellous Party, Corny was proud to wear a blue gingham shirt and had insisted upon having a smart side parting in his blond hair, and Gubsy had on a blue cravat. The animals also had a touch of the colour; the Dalmatians had blue satin ribbons tied in bountiful bows about each their necks, another decorated Gloriana's bowl, and a long thin one attached Remarkable to Gubsy's wicker peacock chair. Each of these creatures waited patiently at the table laid for tea on the west terrace.

None of the food was blue (except the decorative icing on the enormous coconut cake that mirrored the tablecloth's bluebells) but there were plenty of triangle sandwiches, squares of honey, buttered crumpets, and two more cakes slightly smaller than the coconut: a devil's food cake and an angel cake – to counter each other. Everything displayed elegantly upon, to emphasise the theme of blue, the Royal Danish porcelain that complimented perfectly the wisteria, Isadora's linen, Araminta's vase and Rupert's agapanthus.

'Do not be putting in so much sukar!' Gretchen told Corny who was not satisfied with only three lumps in his tea.

Corny scowled at the harsh rationing – it was already beyond his bearability not to devour the tempting confectionary, and he wished that Harry would hurry.

It was then that Harry appeared and magicked Corny's scowl into a smile.

'Hullo, ev*w*ybody!' Harry said, heartily.

Immediately, the Dalmatians pounced and set about wetting his boxed beard with their happy tongues. Gubsy and Gretchen greeted him just as warmly, though, of course, not so demonstratively, and Remarkable and Gloriana simply looked at him.

Corny, however, leapt from his seat and almost ruined the entire table for he had tucked the tablecloth into his collar with the supposition that it was one of the matching napkins, but Gretchen caught it just in time.

'Hullo, *w*ascal!' laughed Harry, embracing his little brother. He lifted him up but said, '*Oof! W*ascal! What have you been eating? You are getting *w*eally big!' and set him down again.

Corny grinned at the joke and then flung himself at Izzy.

Being of feather lightness, the ambush unbalanced her and might have rendered her horizontal had Rupert not opportunely arrived to act as a buffer from behind. She looked down at the broad and tan, and slightly blue daubed hands, that close to cupped her teacup-sized breasts.

She gasped, and she blushed, but felt much better when she heard her cousin laugh, 'Hello, Izzy!'

Rupert had also managed to maintain bits of robin's egg paint in his golden hair, and he was wearing a turquoise polo shirt.

Izzy looked up at his beaming and beautiful face.

'Oh! Hello, Rupert! You *th*aved me!'

'Thanks ve*w*y much, *W*upert!' Harry said, gravely, whereupon he held high his delicate wife's hand, and had her rotate so to inspect her for damage as if she were one of her precious dolls.

Izzy submitted to the examination delightedly.

Content that she was intact, Harry kissed her forehead, and solemnly said to Corny, 'You *w*eally need to be more careful, *w*ascal, I can take your *w*oughhousing but Izzy can't.'

Harry's over-protectiveness caused Olivia and Valentine to grimace.

'Gosh! Ridiculous!' exclaimed Valentine, gesticulating toward crestfallen Corny.

'What's *w*idiculous?'

'Corny's hardly roughhouse, he's just happy to see you both!' Valentine replied.

Harry regarded Corny and felt full of remorse.

'I'm so*ww*y, *w*ascal; we're ve*w*y happy to see you too. But you have g*w*own conside*w*ably!'

Now all eyes were on Corny and considered his size; had he undergone an undetected spurt?

Izzy was in no good position to evaluate, so, instead, she said to him, 'I'm *th*ure you will grow into a *th*trong and hand*th*ome man!'

Corny became cheerful again.

Presently, Izzy let her vision absorb the wondrous sight of the abundant wisteria; her one hitherto experience of the west terrace was nocturnal, and the diurnal version charmed her.

'Oh! How lovely it *ith* out here!' she exclaimed.

'B*w*ings back *w*omantic memo*w*ies?' Harry smilingly asked.

'Ye*th*, of cour*the*!' she replied, with a tiny indent in her feint brow, 'I'm not *th*o forgetful a*th* all that! And *th*uch a lot of blue!' she said, sitting down on the bench upon which she and Harry had first compared speech impediments.

'Gosh! I'm glad you noticed!' exclaimed Valentine, smoothing the linen on the table and sat between Rupert and Corny upon the corresponding bench, 'Look; we are all wearing it!'

'Oh, ye*th*!' exclaimed Izzy, and regarded each person present as if they were supernatural beings. She looked down at her dress. 'Even me!' she cried, and then turned to Harry and said, in a tragic tone, 'But not you.'

Harry lowered his bristly chin and saw that she was right; his colours were khaki and white, and then he exhibited a look of blamelessness.

'So*ww*y, I didn't *w*ealise!'

Izzy looked traumatised by the *faux pas* but Valentine declared: 'You are Mr Avery-Stripe! Therefore exempt from the canons of others!'

'Hear, hear!' Gubsy boomed.

Harry looked relieved for a space, yet Izzy's apparent disconsolation over the discordance prompted him to dash to his old bedroom, and to return wearing a snug and tatty aquamarine t-shirt.

'Oh, how ni*th*e!' said an appeased Izzy, placing his hand over hers.

'Gosh! Anyway,' said Valentine, ostensibly disregarding the hint of henpecking and scrutinising the victuals, 'coconut cake, Harry? Izzy?' and he wielded the chased-silver cake-knife.

Izzy nodded eagerly and pursed her Cupid's bow lips, whilst Harry licked his, and said, 'Yes please! I'm *w*avishing!'

Whilst Valentine apportioned cake and Gretchen poured tea, Olivia viewed Izzy. She considered the girl's fragility a patent façade behind which hid a difficult and demanding persona, in short, she was a prima donna, moreover, a deceptive one. Olivia did not like this in the least; the honour of betrothal to Horatio Avery-Stripe should course through the girl's veins to her very core, it should be she venerating him and not the other way around. Why, the girl had no more than to insinuate dissatisfaction for Harry to alter his perfectly adequate apparel!

Olivia wanted to be sick. No, she wanted to slap some respect into the chit. Yet because she required her to mother Benedictus she could not, and this fuelled the fury she had to conceal. Then when Izzy, obviously deceitfully reticently, exhibited to the family, at Harry's request, the matrimonial rock upon her finger, it was plain for Olivia to see the girl's complacency over the vulgarly large diamond, and she wished to snap the pathetic digit.

Valentine did not find the conversation as mind-numbing as did Olivia who, he noticed, said nothing and merely, insincerely, smiled. He was certain that Paris and Venice were more glorious than the newlyweds were able to illustrate and he was a mite jealous when Harry told him they had seen the inspiration for the interior of the tree house in the Musée d'Orsay, and had been on gondolas.

He also noticed Izzy's influence over Harry, and though he too deemed it disagreeable, he reasoned it beneficial to the conveyance of Benedictus but resolved that afterward he would inhibit any further henpecking before it fixed, because as sweet as Izzy might be she was only spouse to an Avery-Stripe (albeit the heir) and not blood.

'Gosh! As big as the Ritz!' he exclaimed, upon Izzy's seemingly reluctant revealing of her wedding ring.

'Crikey! It's massive!' said Rupert.

'Oh!' said Izzy, seriously, 'It'*th* not that big! I *th*ouldn't be able to rai*the* my arm if it were!'

Corny made appreciative eyes at the diamond and believed it as large as one of the sugar lumps of which Gretchen repeatedly told him he could only have three.

''pon my soul! It's a whopper!' said Gubsy, squinting as if he could barely see it, and Olivia pointedly peered.

'Master Harry!' said Gretchen, leaning forward in her wicker peacock chair, 'It is a wonderful rink!' And she viewed him with pride.

Harry blushed behind his boxed beard. He did think it a very good ring, although nowhere near as precious as his wife, and he wished that he could shower her in diamonds, but just the one had drained his reserves.

'Thanks, G*w*etchen,' he said, 'I did p*w*omise Izzy I'd buy her a diamond *w*ing as a wedding *w*ing on our honeymoon; we couldn't find one good enough for the day.'

Izzy viewed him adoringly.

'Oh, Harry!' she said, 'I would be ju*tht* a*th* happy to wear a band of tinfoil!'

'*W*eally not!' argued Harry, 'You must have the ve*w*y best of ev*w*ything!'

'But I have you!' she insisted, 'I don't need anything el*the*!'

Indeed, Izzy meant it, because despite Olivia and Valentine's suspicions, of which she was unaware, her love for Harry was absolute. And had she left it at that, for she had spoken with such impassioned conviction, it might have erased all scepticism, but then she added, 'It doe*th* not matter to me that you have not much money and I have lot*th*!'

Valentine's intake of breathe was incredible, and he deemed the time ripe to bring up Benedictus, and because of Izzy's solecistical remark regarding her fiscal superiority, he would not bother to pussyfoot. Therefore, as soon as Gretchen topped up his tea into which Corny dropped four sugar lumps, and Rupert had stirred it with a silver spoon that went *tinkle*, Valentine held Izzy in his gaze, and, in a civil tone, asked, 'By the by, did you happen to mention to the Oxley-Stockmans your inability to breed?'

Izzy emitted a shriek and pressed against Harry where she trembled and tearfully peeked out at his family – oh, they were not very nice! First, his mother had teased her about hard Egyptian gypsies in the garden, then his little brother had effectively floored her and now his other brother was taunting her about her infertility! It caused her eyes to leak profusely and she wiped them on her husband's shoulder.

Pulling his distressed wife close, Harry shocked Valentine with a look that bordered on hate; how could he so heartlessly broach the subject, surely he knew it would antagonise? Harry then looked to Gretchen, surprise plastered her face, and caused Harry to surmise the news a revelation, and therefore, logically, it would be so also to Gubsy, and it was to him that Harry now tentatively turned and saw that he was unquestionably shocked.

Harry returned his eyes to Valentine and felt full of chagrin; Valentine had promised to tell Gubsy for him, he had said that Gubsy was 'a piece of cake', but never did Harry imagine that Valentine would orchestrate a tea party at which to drop the bomb!

'Well, I'll be!' Harry heard Gubsy say in a deflated tone.

Gubsy was torpid with astonishment. He could not even bring himself to chew and swallow the coconut cake that sat upon his tongue and he let it slowly turn soggy. Neither could he quite swallow the implication of the sterility. Certainly, the knowledge that Izzy was unable to bear children was present in his consciousness, but that the Avery-Stripe lineage was now *impassé* was wholly indigestible.

However, if anyone present was expecting him to reprimand the young couple then they were in for a disappointment, because though Gubsy would not ever divulge it, he too was fertilely incompetent and was no hypocrite. Thus, he also began to weep – tears for his years of humiliation, and tears of heartbreak over the familial cul-de-sac – whilst a disturbed Gretchen endeavoured to console him.

'Oh, Valentine!' Harry dolefully moaned, as he stroked Izzy's head that convulsed upon his chest, 'You are te*ww*ible! Of course, we didn't tell the Oxley-Stockmans; it's none of their beeswax!'

Izzy sounded a gratingly loud sob, and Harry went on with his telling off, 'I'm *w*eally c*w*oss with you! Look, you made Izzy c*w*y again! And Gubsy and G*w*etchen are in d*w*eadful shock! Sometimes I think you have the devil in you!'

Valentine gasped at the accusation, and insisted, 'Gosh! Not I!' and he sipped his tea before it cooled, 'Do you think I have the devil in me, Rupert?'

'Crikey!' said Rupert, uncomfortably; he felt awkward over the scene but sagely sensed baby Benedictus to be the reason, 'I don't know what to say!' He covered his beautiful face with his tanned and blue hands, and decided to sit tight.

Valentine turned to Corny, and, with his eyes, asked him the same, whereupon Corny screwed up his features and shook his head to display his opinion that the devil did not truly inhabit Valentine.

'Gosh! Anyway, that's glorious!' Valentine chirruped.

'What is glo*w*ious?' asked Harry, not hiding his annoyance.

'That you did not tell them about Izzy's inability, of course!' replied Valentine, cutting the devil's food cake and trying not to tut over the pointless waterworks.

Harry viewed Valentine with incredulity. 'Will you d*w*op it please!' he said, sternly.

Valentine began to brandish it: 'Because if you and Izzy are to have baby Benedictus then one of the provisos is that you are to let all and sundry believe that he is the fruit of your loins.'

Then he bit into his slice of cake, and said, '*Mmm*! Delicious!'

The unknown name and mention of having a baby put an immediate stop to the tears. Izzy swiftly dried her face on Harry's t-shirt and then looked at Valentine with wonderment. She gasped because she could not quite grasp his meaning. She gathered that he spoke of a baby which she might have but she could not comprehend how it could be. Her lips parted and trembled as if she wished to produce words yet to no avail, and Harry was just as flummoxed and inarticulate.

Yet Gubsy was able to boom, 'Benedictus! Who the blazes is he?'

'Why!' said Valentine, 'Benedictus is the ensuing begat!'

Gubsy responded with a *harrumph*; the ninny was talking nonsense!

Harry, however, knew just what Valentine meant, and despite having many questions all he could say was, 'Excelsior begat Amb*w*osius, Amb*w*osius begat Je*w*emiah, Je*w*emiah begat Montgome*wy*, Montgome*wy* begat Ho*w*atio, and now Ho*w*atio begat Benedictus?'

'Exactly so!' exclaimed Valentine. 'So what do you say?' he asked the newlyweds, 'You have baby Benedictus to nurture as your own on the condition that you not tell anyone that he is not of your making. And I mean *anyone*, not even the Oxley-Stockmans; they would have a field day if they heard of the hiccough, and that the baby always be called Benedictus because he is a blessing!' He sipped his tea and then added, 'It's Latin!' before returning the teacup to its saucer with a *clink*, and he smiled as lachrymose Izzy became euphoric.

Izzy could hardly credit the proposal, it sounded as if it were a fairy tale but because she sincerely believed in fairies she believed Valentine's tale true. Further, upon speculating from where this blessed baby might come, she fancied Benedictus to be born of a beautiful flower, and she imagined, cradled in its petals, a lovely little pink and giggling amoretto with a kiss curl, and instantly, she fell for him.

'Oh! Ye*th* plea*the*! I agree!' she excitedly exclaimed and clapped her hands delightedly.

She beamed at Harry and hoped he was just as eager but he looked troubled. Indeed, he could not fathom why Valentine would invent such a story. He knew him to be occasionally naughty, but not to such a degree that he would tease so sensitive a girl as Izzy over so sensitive an issue – surely not!

He narrowed his eyes, and said to him, '*W*eally? It sounds like *w*ubbish to me, where is this baby?'

'Gosh!' said Valentine, 'Baby Benedictus is in our very midst!'

Izzy startled and looked all about her as if she might suddenly see a baby appear out of thin air, but Gubsy was not buying it.

He gnashed his false teeth and boomed, 'Balderdash! You can thank your lucky stars that my stick is downstairs, but by Jove, when I have it in my hands, your backside's going to know all about it!'

'Gosh! Benedictus' presence is not balderdash!' Valentine exclaimed, 'Benedictus resides yonder!' And, with a slant of a brow, he indicated Olivia poised upon a wicker peacock chair with her crocodilian smile.

All eyes fell on her, most augmented with astonishment and still some disbelief, but Harry could easily believe the situation that he calculated with uncharacteristic speed.

'Oh, mummy! *Weally* not?' he cried with dismay at the distant lengths to which she would go purely to ensure that he honour his familial duty.

'Yes, darling!' said Olivia, resting her hands upon her abdomen, and she tautened her empire so to exhibit her slight expansion, 'Really!'

Corny scuttled from his seat and placed his hand between hers. He gaped at her and then grinned; she had a tiny baby in her tummy! He was to have a little brother! It was exactly what he had wished for when cutting his birthday cake! His happiness so consumed him that he flung his arms about her neck.

'You are preknant, Mrs Olivia?' asked Gretchen.

Enduring Corny's headlock, Olivia replied, 'I am indeed, hence the kedgeree craving. Thank you, Gretchen.'

'Is no problem, Mrs Olivia,' replied Gretchen, uncomfortably, and she turned to view a seemingly stolid Gubsy.

'Is kood news, yes, Mr Bartholmoo?' she asked, cautiously, but he did not respond. He was busy experiencing the sensation of reeling down a steep decline of sanity. For Olivia to furnish the family with Montgomery's children was an obligation, and much appreciated, but to bring salvation to the next generation was not only a call beyond duty but also a far cry from conventional. But then, what was the alternative?

He now looked askance at the pretty poppet, Izzy, to gauge her emotional state, and never before had he seen anyone look quite so thrilled. Her face was cupped in her hands, but the exposed angle of her jaw made it plain to see her awe, and her little girl lost eyes of blue looked at Olivia as if she were worthy of a liturgy.

Gubsy mulled and wondered who he might be to deny the pretty one her chance of motherhood, and realised that without Olivia's aid the heir would have no begat at all, and that would never do. Of course, this Benedictus chap would not be of blood but none of the hoi polloi need know, and he was, after all, brother to Harry, why the procedure was practically monarchical.

Presently, Gubsy felt, toward Olivia, nothing other than perturbed gratitude, but still he required concise confirmation: 'D'you mean to say,

Olivia, that you've a little'un in you to give to young Horatio in order to continue the line?'

'That is exactly what I say!' said Olivia, whilst persuading a jubilant Corny from her neck, 'I forbid the family to founder!'

'Woman!' Gubsy girned, gnashed and boomed, 'You are a piece of work!'

Harry did not truly wish Izzy to be upset but he thought it preferable to her desiring a baby so manipulatively designed. He knew the odds were stacked against him, however, when she exposed her face, for a ripple of ecstasy visibly traversed her diminutive body, and she emitted a tremulous whimper of rapture.

She clasped his right hand in both of hers, and cried, 'Oh, Harry! A baby! We are to have a *th*weet little baby!'

At that precise moment Harry knew his fate was sealed because the elatedness that so emanated from Izzy's every pore clenched his heart and caused it to violently pump and secrete a substance sweeter than syrup.

'Yes, it *w*eally seems we are,' he said, lovingly, and on both her flushed flower-like cheeks he planted a kiss that caused her to whimper once more.

'But one thing I'd like to know, mummy,' Harry said, in a sombre tone, 'is how you *cw*eated the baby, I mean, who's the father?'

Despite the awkward inquiry, Olivia felt little worry, and she waited for Valentine to illuminate Harry of the swarthy sailor.

Timefully, Valentine sipped his tea and cleared his throat to better elucidate.

'Well, you see,' he began, 'the spawner is somewhat of a mystery!'

Now, all looked to him, Olivia most penetratingly; she did not know that the father was a mystery, but also she did not know that Valentine had since deemed the seaman insubstantial.

'When mummy was abroad, she attended a grand party in a prestigious hotel, and it was full of all manner of exotic ambassadors, continental nobility and transcontinental royalty!'

Immediately, Olivia judged this new interpretation superior to the previous, and consequently enjoyed everyone's eyes upon her.

'And naturally,' Valentine went on, 'at this party, a party to raise aid for foreign unfortunates, there were oceans of champagne! And that was glorious, wasn't it, mummy?'

Olivia, with a fixed smile, nodded accordingly.

'Gosh! Yes, champagne often is!' Valentine exclaimed, 'But, regrettably, mummy drank too much of it, and the next thing she knew she awoke with an awful head in the bed of a sumptuous suite in the hotel, the morning after! And though she was alone, she ascertained, by the state of the sheets, that she had not been so the entire night, and so, therefore, well, need I colour in?'

And he pulled, at them all, a pained expression whilst the listeners mentally reeled, and Olivia psychologically staggered at her supposed disgrace.

'No, no!' said Harry, exhibiting, to Valentine, the palms of his hands, 'You *w*eally need not!'

'Well, I'll be! A bastard sired by a blasted foreigner!' blustered Gubsy.

'Gosh! Yes, probably, but more likely than not a foreign *dignitary*,' said Valentine, 'And that *is* something. Unless it was just a naughty porter with a key!' he laughed mischievously, 'But the fact that the father is likely of rank is another reason to keep quiet!'

'*Ugh*!' said Olivia, 'I can assure you that whoever he was, he was upstanding!'

She scowled at Valentine's heightened laughter.

'Oh! I do not care in the lea*th*t who the biological father is, Harry and I want the baby, don't we, Harry?' Izzy insisted.

'Yes, Izzy, we *w*eally do!' Harry agreed, wholeheartedly.

'Oh! How ni*the*! When i*th* it due?' Izzy asked Olivia, impatiently.

Olivia surprised herself with the amendment: '*He*, darling, is due at the end of February.'

'Oh! *Th*o long!' said Izzy with a frown, and, surprisingly, looked as if about to curse, but, instead, she asked, 'How do you know it'*th* a boy?'

'Gosh! Because everything is blue!' Valentine exclaimed.

Izzy looked thoughtful and decided the explanation logical, then turned to Harry and said, 'Would you like a little boy? Or really *th*ould you like a girl?'

'*W*eally, Izzy I do not mind!' he said, 'So long as you're happy!'

'One of each would be nice!' exclaimed Valentine, 'Might it be twins, mummy?' he asked, teasingly, and reasoned, 'Twins is in the blood; Valerian and Victoria!'

Izzy gasped with excitement at the notion but Olivia quashed the dream.

'Unlikely in my blood, darling, there's no way of telling because, as you well know, I was brought up in an orphanage!' she lied.

'Gosh! Yes, well, never mind,' said Valentine (not caring about his mother's roots because they were not Avery-Stripe) 'Benedictus is a boy, and it's a boy that we need to maintain the name! Speaking of which,' here, he held aloft his teacup and exclaimed, 'A toast! To blessed Baby Benedictus Avery-Stripe!'

The consequent clinks of porcelain, as each teacup kissed, were delightful to Izzy's darling little ears. She regarded everyone present with feelings of fondness and thought them a perfectly lovely family after all. Not only had they given her a handsome husband they were also providing her with a bonny baby boy.

Mentally, she repeated the baby's name, and then, with tears in her eyes, and Harry's hand in hers, she whispered, 'Benedictu*th* Avery-*Th*tripe!'

Whereupon, all who could, cried, 'Hurrah!' and Izzy sighed ecstatically because Harry then tickled her *retroussé* nose with his boxed beard as he kissed her Cupid's bow lips firmly.

CHAPTER 25

Corny's Evolution

With the treaty of Benedictus sealed, all involved were in accordance that no one was to tell Willy. It did feel rather treacherous but because it was imperative that people outside the family never know, they agreed it necessitous and comforted themselves that they might one day enlighten her when she became less involved with the Oxley-Stockmans.

Naturally, this meant that other than via the telephone or by written correspondence, neither Olivia, whose gravidity would soon be patent, nor Izzy, whose lack of it would be just as clear, could interact with Willy pre-nativity. This course of action inevitably raised the question of Christmas when Willy may conceivably wish to return to the family, but then Valentine suggested that under such an eventuality Olivia ought to decamp to Bath for the duration with the pretext that she was again abroad.

This sat well with Olivia; Bath would be a welcome change of scene because the plan was that she would spend her expectant months concealed within Chinchero and she was certain that the confinement would unhinge her. She had not imagined the extent to which a pregnancy pertaining to a lady of ripeness would require particular consideration.

Yet Gretchen was mindful; she purchased and perused every book on the matter, and disregarding her guilt concerning Willy, she effectively became a mother hen toward Olivia by taking her under her wing and to every appointment – obstetrician or otherwise. And Olivia, never really having enjoyed much maternal nurturing, readily submitted to the mollycoddling and was immensely grateful.

Gretchen's extra attention to Olivia somewhat altered the dynamics of the inhabitants of Chinchero. It affected Gubsy most of all, but though he at first felt a little at sea he did not grumble for the new heir was of utmost importance, and, quite soon, he grew used to his independence, in fact, he claimed it made him feel years younger.

In truth, however, it was not so much Gubsy's modicum of self-sufficiency that so invigorated him but the general atmosphere of excited anticipation that permeated the air, because everyone was energised by the prospect of Baby Benedictus, particularly Corny who, much to his mother's mix of pleasure and annoyance, would sporadically kiss her midriff and beam at her.

Rupert grinned at Corny upon one such occasion in the drawing room, and said to him, 'It's amazing to think your little brother is in there, isn't it?'

Corny signalled an affirmative with a firm nod.

Valentine and Olivia were not so pleased, and tutted in unison.

'Gosh, Rupert!' exclaimed Valentine, 'Benedictus is not to be Corny's little brother; their connexion is uncle and nephew, we mustn't make it confusing!'

'Crikey! Sorry!' replied Rupert to Valentine, and then said to Olivia, 'I forgot!'

'Quite all right, darling!' said Olivia, witheringly, 'But do try not to say such a thing outside Chinchero.'

'Crikey, Olivia! I never would!' he said, earnestly.

'Gosh! I know you never would!' said Valentine, and, with a finger, he lovingly curled a lock of Rupert's golden hair.

As if the process was the winding of a key in a mechanical toy, it caused Rupert to grin again, and they regarded each other with infatuation.

The sudden sound of a particularly wet kiss interrupted the loving gaze, and then came Olivia's cry, '*Ugh*! Cornelius, darling! Please do not take this the wrong way, but I look forward to Harry having you for a month; Benedictus and I can withstand only so much kissing!'

Olivia's readiness for Corny's sojourn was nowhere near as enthusiastic as his, and at precisely noon the next day, although the ormolu clock proclaimed the time nine, he sat upon the bottom step and waited for Harry to collect him and Gloriana. After twenty minutes, he became anxious that he was forgotten, and after thirty, he began to mentally argue whether he was more angry than sad but then the front doorbell rang and there was Harry.

'So*ww*y, *w*ascal! T*w*affic is *w*eally jammy!' said Harry, but Corny did not mind; Harry had come and they were going to have an excellent time together!

Nevertheless, when luncheon was over, Corny could not help but shed a tear upon saying goodbye to Valentine and Benedictus. (Of course, he would also miss the others but they were not his siblings.)

'Gosh! Don't be silly, Corny!' exclaimed Valentine, just about managing to abstain from shedding a tear himself, 'You'll have a glorious time! And you have Gloriana, and Harry and Izzy will spoil you rotten!'

He hugged his little brother, and whispered, 'Don't forget to photograph every room; there's bound to be some things we can laugh about when you return!'

After a hearty squeeze, Corny pulled back and grinned at Valentine before bending his knees and kissing Benedictus goodbye.

'See you in October, darling!' said Olivia, with a smile.

Suddenly, Corny seemed serious. He straightened his headdress, and with his pack on his back and fishbowl in his arms, he strode purposefully toward the car.

Harry looked awkwardly at Olivia.

'Mummy, I *w*eally would app*w*eciate it if you would take more of Izzy's calls; she *w*eally just wants to know that our baby is all *w*ight.'

Valentine and Olivia shushed him sharply.

'Gosh, Harry!' Valentine whispered, 'The neighbours might hear!'

Olivia also whispered, but with a hiss, 'The baby is not yet yours, darling, Benedictus still resides within me! Tell her to get a grip and endure! Once he's out he's out and he's yours; he can't go back in!'

'A bit like toothpaste!' exclaimed Valentine.

Harry felt demoralised to a degree, yet replied, 'The F*w*obishers are the only neighbours that might hear and they've a For Sale sign up, and all *w*ight mummy, I'll tell Izzy but it will make her unhappy.'

'*Ugh*! That girl produces enough water to rival a river!' snapped Olivia, 'She ought to see an optician; it's abnormal *and* aggravating!'

'Spastic ducts, probably!' Valentine added, helpfully.

Choosing to let the matter drop, Harry pouted, said goodbye, and got behind the steering wheel.

'*W*eady, *w*ascal?' he said, cheerfully, as he buckled his brother's safety belt.

Corny nodded with definiteness.

'Ha-ha! B*w*illiant!' said Harry, and after starting the engine, he crunched the gravel as he reversed out of the drive.

An hour following Corny's departure, Valentine felt horribly alone, and in raspberry and cream striped pyjamas, he aimlessly paced the Axminster. He gently tickled the Steinway's ivories, and considered it strange that the house seemed so still, so silent, without his mute little brother who would not return until mid-October.

Naturally, Valentine had Rupert, and that to him was invaluable but Rupert was currently renovating the home of Nina Frethell, and afterward would be working at the Whitakers' every weekday from nine-to-five.

Valentine made a moue, and said aloud, 'Gosh! How beastfully rat-racey!'

But, except for a napping Gubsy, no one was present to hear the remark and laugh or condemn.

Presently, Valentine sounded a sigh and produced the loudest tut he was able. He sat upon the ottoman, sighed again and deciding to smoke; he retrieved a cigarette from his silver-case and lit it with the scarab beetle lighter. Then he turned his attention to the portrait of Excelsior.

'Gosh, great-great-grandfather!' he said, 'What do you suppose I should do to kill my solitary stints?'

And because Valentine possessed an imagination, Excelsior ruminated for a flash and then furnished him with a function.

'Well, Great-Great-Grandson Valentino, I suppose that because the devil makes work for idle hands you should exploit him so to embroider some sinfully glorious table linen that symbolises your honourable union with your beautiful Rupert!'

Valentine gasped with astonishment.

'Gosh, Excelsior! That truly *is* a most glorious idea!'

'Indubitably!' replied Excelsior, 'I am full of them! And you really ought to get a wriggle on because you've never embroidered before and you should finish it in time for Christmas, and do you know why?'

Valentine rushed to the fireplace, grasped the mantelshelf, and gazing up at the picture, he cried, 'No, Excelsior! Why?'

'Gosh!' said Excelsior, 'Because it would be a most glorious Christmas present for Rupert, don't you think?'

Sounding another gasp of astonishment, Valentine hopped out of the hearth, and exclaimed, 'Gosh! You are exactly right! It is precisely what I shall do! Thank you, Great-Great-Grandfather Excelsior! Thank you!'

The volume of Valentine's gratitude was such that it awoke Gubsy. He pulled away *The Times,* and boomed the demand, 'What the deuce are you playing at?'

'Gosh! Gubsy! I have been conversing with Excelsior!' Valentine sang with thrill, 'And he has filled me with a most marvellously inspired notion!'

With that, Valentine dashed from the drawing room and left his great uncle to stare fearfully up at Excelsior, and ponder the sanity of the ninny-boy, but he did not dare curse in case his grandfather was, indeed, somehow present.

*

In his turret, Valentine located, upon his bookshelf, *Embroidery for Beginners* and opened it for the first time. He put it to his nose and inhaled; the scent of old books was one that pleased him. Then he flicked to the front to discover the implements he would require. Naturally, a plain cloth and matching napkins were essential and a tambour frame too, and he knew exactly where to find those items in the cellar, but now he realised the importance of a specific type of needle and thread. Therefore, he hurried to the depths of Chinchero to discover if he could remember the location of such objects.

Fortuitously, his memory served him well, and, in a battered oriental box, he found embroidery thread: the imperative colours of blood red, ecclesiastical violet, verdant green and lustrous gold, and the appropriate needles. These items caused his happiness to soar, and it further escalated upon the find of a gilded thimble.

'Gosh! It is a dear little thing!' exclaimed Valentine, modelling the thimble on his finger, 'Now I shall be impervious to the inevitable pricks!'

Thus, with a tambour frame, essential linen, and the oriental box of necessities, he gambolled up from the cellar, whistling *The Dance of the Sugar Plum Fairy* as he went.

He put his new possessions in Corny's bedroom because if he were to keep them in his own Rupert might see them and ask questions, and that would ruin the surprise. It struck Valentine that he could have hidden them in any of his siblings' rooms, and he wondered why he had chosen Corny's but really only to divert his mind from the sad fact that they were all uninhabited. Quickly then, he capered down the stairwell and into the drawing room, where, at the éscritoire, he artfully transferred his designs from his mind onto paper.

To start with, the sketches were elaborate and then he simplified them because, in this instance, he surmised simplicity aesthetically superior. He lost himself quite pleasantly in the endeavour and did not notice the ormolu clock chiming away the quarters and hours.

The following morning, after breakfasting with Rupert and kissing him goodbye beneath the porch, Valentine astonished Gretchen by assisting her to clear the lacquered table. His motive was not to be helpful but because he required the table so that he could spread evenly the high quality white linen and then, with a pencil, apply his sketched designs directly to it.

In the centre of the square cloth was to be the golden sun, certainly circular and simple enough but it was to burst forth beams of light of diverse lengths, some to extend only moderately, others clear to the hem about which he would stitch green thread. The green thread was grass, and from the grass, an abundance of violets would irregularly grow, and they were to climb, quite high, the burning star's radiance.

To Valentine's mind, the purple-blue flowers demonstrably symbolised himself, and their ascension of the beams his adulation of the beautiful and golden sun that denoted Rupert's Apollonian aspect. To emphasise further the romantic conjunction, Valentine would sew at each corner, rather sizeably and flourishingly, the characters V and R, entwined by an ampersand, with blood red thread, for they were effectively family. Naturally, the napkins would accord with the cloth and once Valentine had sketched them, he sounded a sigh of satisfaction and had a pot of tea with jam and bread, before taking the tambour frame and the other implements, and stationing himself in the gazebo where he began to embroider the sun.

Consultation of the *Embroidery for Beginners* book was essential to start with but after deciding to view the practicalities of the endeavour as obvious logic, Valentine was well under way and became enthralled by the meticulous stitching of golden thread. The process was hypnotic and everyday, as if in the blink of an eye, it would magically transport him from breakfast to supper, whereupon he would luxuriate in Rupert's return, and yearn to tell him of his surprise but somehow he succeeded in keeping his lips sealed.

On the tenth day, Valentine completed the sun and its rays, and he looked up and noted, with irony, the melancholy descent of an oak leaf; autumn was approaching, in fact, he could detect its distinct odour. It made him feel quite cosy and, henceforward, he promoted his cosiness by wrapping himself in the great Indian quilt from the drawing room whilst lazy daisy stitching violets in the gazebo.

Occasionally, he would gaze at the oak to regard its yellowing leaves and hard golden-brown fruit, and exclaim, 'Dear little acorns!' and then he would laugh at the Dalmatians trying, in vain, to climb the tree to catch the pesky American squirrels.

The barking was not so amusing, neither was the hysterical hen clucking it coerced, therefore, to blanket the din, Valentine positioned the gramophone on the leaf-strewn striped lawn and played the vinyl of Vivaldi's *Four Seasons* – chiefly the apposite one. The scene and its accompanying score pleased him and he comfortably kept his nose to the grindstone.

He was glad of the gilded thimble.

Eventually, mid-October arrived, and this was made apparent to Valentine only by the return of his little brother in the midst of Vivaldi's *Spring*. Valentine was painstakingly sewing his hundredth violet when, suddenly, he became aware that he was no longer alone. He looked up and saw Corny at the door to the conservatory, watching him, with a grin.

'Gosh!' exclaimed Valentine.

Recklessly, he abandoned the tambour frame and quilt to canter to the centre of the lawn where the brothers embraced.

'Gosh, Corny! I *have* missed you!'

Corny demonstrated that he was also happy by pulling Valentine into a second and prolonged hug.

Valentine was rather flabbergasted because now in Corny's strong hold, he noticed, for the first time, that his little brother was not so very little anymore, indeed, he was becoming quite thickset.

'Gosh, Corny!' Valentine exclaimed, managing to pull away.

Corny regarded him with puzzlement.

'You've spurted gloriously, haven't you?' Valentine replied.

'*W*eally, Valentine!' said Harry, stepping out onto the lawn, 'I told you months ago that he was g*w*owing! Have you only just *w*ealised?'

'Apparently so!' said Valentine, not removing his astonished gaze from his metamorphosing brother, and he surmised Corny's weight now equal to his own if not more.

Presently, Olivia appeared, and her reaction to Corny's growth was greater than Valentine's because the moment she entered the drawing room and spied the bulkier rendering of her jammy little dodger out in the garden she definitely saw Monty. Her shock made her unconscious of her conveyance through the conservatory, she arrived at its threshold, and alighted on the lawn where she gaped at Corny and gasped almost in horror at the remarkable likeness.

Then, quite as if she was not guilty of a great increase in size because of Benedictus, she said, 'Cornelius, darling, you have grown singularly stalwart in stature!'

Her three sons regarded her, and the second born exclaimed, 'Gosh, mummy! Hasn't he? Not so much in height but,' here, Valentine placed his hands on the subject's shoulders, 'he has definitely broadened! What have you been feeding him, Harry?'

Harry looked at him irreproachably.

'Nothing!' he said.

'Gosh!' said Valentine, turning to Corny, 'Did horrid Harry and Izzy starve you?'

Corny pulled an amused face. Of course, they had not starved him; the meals were plentiful. And though Harry's cooking was not as flavoursome as Gretchen's it was infinitely nicer than that of Izzy's cook which, at best, was insipid, nevertheless, Corny always welcomed seconds.

Harry grimaced.

'Cwumbs! Don't be *wid*iculous! We fed him lots, just nothing extwa-ordinary! But he's so full of energy he was bouncing off the walls, and Izzy got fwightened for her dolls, and ve*wy* upset each time he twapped Bywon, Shelley and Keats in the wardwobe, so I took him out for lots of wuns wound Henwietta Park and we played lots of wugby to burn it off. And because he's gwown so big we've bought him lots of new clothes because his were wipping!'

Olivia said nothing but rolled her eyes at the thought of Izzy's frailty. Would she really be a good mother to Benedictus who may well transpire to be more turbulent than predominantly angelic Corny? Olivia knew that there would be a perfectly sound reason for Corny imprisoning the cats (the reason was that they had traumatised Gloriana) and she sighed at the thought of the tears it had undoubtedly created.

'Gosh, Corny! You hulk! Ripping clothes!' exclaimed Valentine, 'But, really Harry! Rugby? That would explain his sudden sturdiness! Do you like rugby?' he asked Corny, and he received an enthusiastic nod, 'Gosh! Well, do try not to turn into our unsavoury cousin, won't you?'

Corny frowned; he would not ever be like Cosmo!

He then searched the pockets of his shorts; his favourite new pair because of its many pockets, and retrieved, along with a great number of conkers, his spent disposable camera. Proudly, he put it in Valentine's hand before placing both of his upon Olivia's swollen belly and kissing it effusively.

The deed practically stunned Olivia senseless for it caused her to vividly recollect her ultimate night with her husband, who, just a few hours before blasting out his brains in a bramble bush, had so kissed her condition with Cornelius, and now Corny was doing just the same.

Yet, Olivia would not succumb to sentiment for she feared that if she started she might not stop, and to her external sons, she said, 'Well, darlings, still Corny is cavalier to the concept of propriety apropos propinquity!'

Only Valentine was able to translate her terminology. He considered it cold and was about to tut, but then Corny suddenly became ecstatic; he had felt the baby quicken! He beamed at Olivia, and in his eyes, she unmistakably saw Monty, yet it did not disturb her, rather, it pleased her; her husband still lived on. It nearly made her weep but instead she smiled at the three Avery-Stripe boys, and, again, Benedictus kicked as if to remind her that her boys likely numbered four.

Corny was confused. Since his return, the family spoke often of his development (Gubsy would frequently boom: 'Stripling's come back a strapper!') but in his head, he was unchanged, and on his head, he wore his Native American war bonnet. He wore nothing else, and alone but for Gloriana, he evaluated his naked form in the three-panelled looking glass in the bathroom.

He viewed himself from every angle. He examined, almost medically, his entire structure, and slowly ascertained the verity of his evolution. On his flanks, thighs and buttocks were feint stripes, and they indicated that his skin had stretched over a bulk that he had not hitherto possessed. Flexing, like a bodybuilder, he smiled at the tennis ball-sized bumps in his arms. He considered it magical that the transformation had taken place so rapidly, and was relieved to realise his aches, that felt like bruises, were because he was growing into a big boy.

Certainly, he was not big like Rupert or Cosmo, and, definitely, he was not tall like Harry, but as he had learned in Bath, he could run just as fast as Harry could and rather easily rob him of the rugby ball, but he liked to think that that was because Harry was kind.

With Harry in mind, Corny jutted his chin toward his reflection and saw that it bore no more than a whisper of a beard. It disappointed him somewhat; therefore, he returned his attention to his muscles and commenced a proper posedown.

Corny knew that he could now physically overpower Valentine without much effort, not because Valentine was kind like Harry but because he was not tough. Yet Corny would not ever use his newfound strength to dominate Valentine, instead he would employ it to defend his whimsical ways just as when he had struck Cosmo's foot with a brick. Corny decided that next time, if there was a next time, he would not need a brick; he would use his fist, and he brandished it before the looking glass, pulled a menacing face and pretended he was a boxer.

Then Corny laughed at himself. He thought it funny. He would not ever punch anyone; the idea was silly because he was a nice boy. However, his countenance again became pugilistic when he considered Cosmo's acquisition of Willy. Corny was aware that Willy had wanted to go to the Oxley-Stockmans, he was also aware that Valentine had somehow engineered it for her, but he was not sure how or why.

Worryingly, Willy had sounded as if on cloud nine when, last week, the family had telephoned to ask where she wanted to spend her eighteenth birthday that had since passed. Her response had been that she wished to remain with Cosmo and that a fuss need not be made. Corny could not understand why the others had accepted it so ungrudgingly and merely sent her birthday presents of Avery-Stripe stationery and a gold brooch. He thought she should return to Chinchero to be amongst her own, and he started to think that if she did not soon, well then, he might just have to intervene – at least when he was able to out-muscle Cosmo, and with a final double bicep pose, Corny forecast that an imminent prospect.

It was now too cold to embroider in the gazebo. Therefore, Valentine sat upon the chesterfield and worked away at his tambour frame. Presently, he was stitching the first *V&R* with blood red thread but intermittently intermitting to regard Corny's photographs of the house in Bath's interior splayed before him.

Upon first seeing them, a tug of war took place in Valentine's mind; he was nettled that there was nothing laughable about Izzy's décor because he enjoyed laughing. Yet there were some aspects of the place that caused him to gasp, and exclaim, 'Gosh!' Most notably the magnitude of Dutch Delft tiles that adorned the kitchen walls, the marble busts of men that he supposed were musical composers, and what appeared to be an original Hammershoi painting of a lady's nape.

'Gosh, Excelsior!' said Valentine to his great-great-grandfather's portrait (for since the commencement of the embroidering the two conversed daily) 'It is good to see that Benedictus shall inhabit a respectable dwelling, don't you think?'

'Indubitably!' replied Excelsior, 'Only the best for my new heir shall suffice, but is not the abode a bit bland?'

'Verily!' Valentine said to him, without having to cast a glance at the photographs for he was in accordance with his ancestor, 'But somehow I feel it right that he not see anything even near nasty whilst a baby, therefore I consider the lacklustre style to be as if visual maternal milk for the bastard's eyes.'

'Valentino!' said Excelsior, in a definite tone, 'I concur with your sagacity!'

'Gosh!' exclaimed a flattered Valentine, 'Thank you, Excelsior. I hear tell that it is an attribute I owe to you!'

The conversation was not covert but Corny came just in time to catch Valentine's last exclamation, he sat next to him and viewed him with interest.

'Gosh! Hello Corny!' said Valentine, now absorbed in his embroidery, 'Look! My primary V! Rather good, don't you think?' Then he looked at him.

Corny responded with an enthusiastic nod; he did think his brother's needlework impressive, but then he repeated his curious countenance almost comically. He cast it first at Valentine then at the portrait and returned it.

'Oh!' said Valentine, understanding Corny's query, 'I was conversing with Excelsior,' he explained, matter-of-factly.

Corny now pulled a face that said, 'Really not?'

'Gosh! Really yes!' replied Valentine.

Now Corny was pleasantly astonished. He was not particularly gullible but though he knew Valentine's words were not always gospel he was eternally ready to believe them because he sensed that Valentine never lied to him, and that was exactly true.

'We communicate daily!' Valentine went on. 'In fact, it was he whom suggested this to me,' and he jiggled his tambour frame. 'I'm quite certain he will talk with you too. Do not worry, you don't have to talk out loud, it can be mental if done very concentratedly, and it is worth it; he is jam-packed with wisdom!'

Corny's jaw dropped at the notion of communicating with Excelsior, without even having to speak words! Immediately, he scrutinised the portrait and concentrated to the best of his ability.

His concentration was broken when Gretchen arrived with a gargantuan pumpkin cradled in her arms, and said, 'Who do you think will be wantink to make terrifyink face in this, Master Corny?'

Consequently, Corny forgot all about necromancy, and he jumped up. He most definitely wanted to make a terrifying face! Therefore, he went to the kitchen with Gretchen, to create the most ghoulish one imaginable.

On his own again, Valentine smiled. He was glad that his growing little brother, who would one day be much bigger, because he did rather resemble Daddy and he had been a big bear of a man, retained such ingenuousness that the carving of a Halloween pumpkin was still a thrilling prospect.

Then Valentine stopped stitching, rested the tambour frame on his lap, and considered that though it was a foreign custom, he really ought to take Corny trick or treating. Thus, upon completing an ampersand, he went to discover if the idea appealed.

Gretchen cut the lid of the Halloween lantern and Corny hollowed it. The pulpiness of the fruit between his fingers was satisfying and so too was the *squelch* when he dolloped each handful of the flesh onto yesterday's *Times* spread upon the gingham cloth. Once the pumpkin was gouged, Gretchen gave Corny a biro with which to draw the template for the terrifying face, and then she set about separating the seeds from the flesh because, with it, she was to make soup.

Corny contorted his own face in an effort to picture what to draw; he wanted to think of the worst one possible but he found it difficult.

He was relieved when Valentine walked in because he knew that he would draw a good one for him to carve, and he was excited when asked if he wished to trick or treat.

'Glorious!' said Valentine, 'And I am certain that Rupert shall too! But fix your pumpkin first!'

Corny held out the biro and made eyes that conveyed his wish that Valentine would draw it for him.

'Gosh! All right then! *H'm*, let me think of a really ugly one,' said Valentine, and, as he thought, he twirled the pen in the air. 'I know!' he suddenly exclaimed, and proceeded to draw a familiar face.

Upon its completion, Corny looked at the pumpkin in wonderment and laughed hysterically, though, of course, silently. Valentine had not disappointed him because it was plain to see that the face was that of horrid Auntie Esmé!

Gretchen snorted and shook her head slowly; Valentine was a naughty boy, but the likeness was uncanny and made it difficult not to smile.

'Very kood, Master Valentine,' she said, 'It *is* diskustink!'

And she handed Corny a sharp knife with which to carve Mrs Oxley-Stockman's terrifying face.

Rupert readily agreed to accompany the brothers on their Halloween outing, but then came the poser of what to wear. Valentine eventually opted to be a dandyish vampire, and Corny wished to be a goblin but, unfortunately, due to his recent growth, his goblin suit was now too small. However, Valentine solved the conundrum with the idea that with dirt from the garden, cobwebs and dust from the cellar, and a noose about his neck, Corny could be a zombie, and if artfully bound in bandages, Rupert would make a beautiful Egyptian mummy – especially with bits of his golden skin exposed between strips.

Thus attired, the three boys ventured fourth to knock on doors and ask for treats for Corny. Gretchen had reminded Valentine that they were to approach only the houses with pumpkins in the front garden. This, of course, was sensible because it was, after all, England, and Valentine certainly did not wish to appear to be a beggar, but it was somewhat irksome that, on average, only one house in ten displayed a pumpkin. Still, within an hour Corny's tin bucket was half-full with penny-sweets, mini chocolate bars, two toffee apples and a disappointing orange.

Corny had wanted his bucket full before they returned to Chinchero but he did not make this desire known because he thought that it might seem greedy, and upon sneakily peeking at other children's meagre rewards, he deemed his bounty ample, not to mention his outfit superiorly scary to theirs. Therefore, with an elaborate yawn and a theatrical shudder, he indicated to Valentine that he should like to go home because it was getting rather cold.

'Gosh! Yes, Corny, I concur!' said Valentine, 'It is quite nippy now, don't you think, Rupert?'

'Crikey! Just a bit!' Rupert replied, with a little shiver and a big grin, 'These bandages aren't covering up very much of me!'

'Gosh, but you do look good!' said Valentine, 'But yes, let's go, it's tricky smoking with fangs.'

The trio about-turned and began their journey, each of them looking forward to Gretchen's steaming soup.

Suddenly, Valentine sounded a gasp, and exclaimed, 'Look down there!'

He pointed down a road that they had not travelled. At the road's bend was a large house and its front garden was virtually ablaze with the glow of pumpkin lanterns.

'Gosh!' said Valentine, 'I really think we ought to visit; they are bound to be munificent!'

And with that, they deviated from their path.

*

'What!' Gubsy boomed so loudly at supper that he sprayed his elevated spoonful of pumpkin soup over the lacquered table, 'You did nothing to serve the Strap right?'

'Indubitably not!' responded Valentine with screwed eyes until he surmised Gretchen had wiped Gubsy's chin clean.

'But, darling, it is Halloween! Revenge would have been entirely right!' said Olivia, between mouthfuls of kedgeree, and she cast a sympathetic glance at Corny; his protruded lower-lip exhibited disappointment with Valentine for not retaliating against the selfishness of Mrs Strap who, despite her big house being elaborately decorated for Halloween, had shut her front door in their faces, most aggressively.

'Verily!' said Valentine, 'And there were many things I could have done, *exempli gratia*, I could easily have pushed their cardboard skeletons halfway through the letterbox and set light to them.'

Corny slammed down his spoon and threw back his head in wild and mute amusement; he wished that Valentine had committed arson!

Valentine continued; 'But that would only have reflected badly upon us. Far more dignified to turn one's cheek. Thank you, Gretchen, that was glorious!'

'You are welcome, Master Valentine,' said Gretchen, collecting the empty bowls and hastening to her kitchen to minister to the main course.

Olivia surreptitiously scrutinised Valentine and considered his conduct. She wondered if he had refrained from exacting a penalty because of Rupert and calculated it likely. Consequently, she deemed Valentine's response to Mrs Strap nobly decorous. He had behaved as an Avery-Stripe ought and charitably disregarded the grubby lower echelon.

Therefore, in an approving tone, she said to him, '*Noblesse oblige*, darling!'

'*Noblesse oblige* indubitably, mummy!' he replied, 'Don't you think, Rupert?'

'Indubitably!' said Rupert, with a grin, and then he said, '*Ahh*! Gretchen, that smells amazing!'

Gretchen beamed at the beautiful boy still in bandages, she set the silver tureen upon the table, and announced, 'Hasenpfeffer!'

Valentine gasped delightedly, 'Gosh! Hasenpfeffer!'

'I love hasenpfeffer!' said Rupert, 'Oma used to make it; I've not had it in years! It's hare isn't it?'

'Yes, Master Rupert,' said Gretchen, stirring the stew with a ladle, 'Hare and wine made with blood – I hope mine as kood as your oma's.'

'Crikey! I'm sure it's amazing!' said Rupert, smiling at the chunks of braised meat in his bowl.

Corny had been wondering what '*noblesse oblige*' might mean, yet no matter how hard he speculated, he could not compute how anything could justify the rudeness of the woman called Strap, and it rankled him. Yet, he forgot all about it upon receiving his hasenpfeffer because, up until then, he was unaware that Gretchen made it using blood and hair. This seemed to him thrillingly in keeping with Halloween, and he could not eat enough of it.

Except for the first of November, because of sickness due to a glut of sweets, Corny's happiness continued, and because Bonfire Night was near, he was excited. It did not matter to him that they would not bother with more than sparklers; the fireworks on his birthday were enough for one year, and, besides, the bonfire was the main thing. They would not have it in the garden, they never did because it would destroy the lawn, instead they built it on the gravel driveway.

The evening before Bonfire Night, Rupert returned from a day's work at the Whitakers' and he brought with him stacks of superfluous planks in a wheelbarrow. Corny was delighted because this auxiliary timber, added to the already sizeable pile of logs and kindling, created a veritable mountain.

All of the following day he rollicked, with the Dalmatians, about the mountain, impatient for night to fall and the fire to start, and he was eager for everyone to finish their supper of wiener schnitzel (and kedgeree) as quickly as had he, but they would not hurry.

Eventually, the time for igniting arrived. Rupert took care of this and the fire soon grew into a behemoth. Its heat warmed the chill autumnal air, and its blaze was so brilliant that all faces were aglow with varying shades of amber.

'Mr Bartholmoo,' said Gretchen, handing him a goblet of mulled wine, 'perhaps you would like some water instead maybe?'

The beads of sweat that cascaded down Gubsy's brow had formed a drip that hung from his bulbous nose, and more were disappearing into the collar of his heavy taupe polo coat.

'*Eh?*' responded Gubsy, taking the mulled wine, 'No, thank you, Gretchen, no water necessary!' And he continued to girn at the flames, his eyes just as ablaze.

The conflagration was equally enthralling to Olivia, but because she did not want to inhale too much smoke (though it did smell lovely) as it might harm Benedictus, she kept her distance, and was kept marvellously warm by the great mink coat that Monty had given to her the Christmas that she was gravid with Valentine.

'Thank you, Gretchen,' said Olivia, receiving a teacup not of tea but of Bovril because recently she had learned to love it, though she hoped its beefiness did not portend that Benedictus was primarily an Oxley-Stockman. Either way, it did taste wonderful, but after her first sip, she became troubled by the absence of Valentine. Corny and Rupert were in plain view, for they stood before the bonfire, yet where was her second born?

Presently, she felt a surge of panic rise within her and a swift kick came from Benedictus.

'Gretchen!' she said with urgency.

'Yes, Mrs Olivia?' Gretchen replied, readily.

'Where is Valentine? I see no sign of him!'

Gretchen also considered the dearth of Valentine disconcerting, but upon looking toward Chinchero, she saw him.

He was not alone.

'Hello, mummy!' he exclaimed proudly, 'Look whom I have here!'

Olivia gasped, first with horror, then with astonishment, at Valentine's companion.

Certainly, it was a guy but no ordinary guy for it was quite an impressive one, and rightly so, for its creation had taken Valentine an entire day. It was half a foot taller than he was and twice his breadth. The burly body was a potato sack stuffed with dead leaves, the stocking limbs were thick with newspaper, and it was held together by an outfit of a rugby shirt and jeans. Most hideous was the head; made with papier-mâché and a small balloon, and it was the ratio between the small head and big body that made it obvious that the guy was Cosmo. The boot polish monobrow and cauliflower floret ears were unnecessary, but they did add to the authenticity.

'Darling!' exclaimed Olivia, 'It's horrible!'

'Thank you, mummy, I did try to make him a realistic as possible!' said Valentine.

Then he held his creation before him, and manoeuvring its arms, he bellowed, 'Bloody bloody! I am bloody Cosmo! Bloody hell! I bloody am!'

Olivia sucked air through her teeth, and relinquishing her cup and saucer for Gretchen to top up, she stated to Valentine, 'I'm quite certain I disapprove!'

'Oh, Auntie O!' Valentine boomed, from behind the faux Cosmo and held up its arms, 'Am I being bloody boorish?'

Then he jumped forward and had the arms flap about her belly.

'You haven't always bloody minded!'

'*Ugh*!' said Olivia, stepping away. 'Do not vex me Valentino!'

She looked as if about to execute a karate chop but then Corny ran over and regarded the guy with awe.

'Do you like him, Corny?' Valentine asked.

Corny was not sure whether to nod or shake his head because yes, he did like the guy, but no, he did not like Cosmo, who the guy plainly was, and he answered with a grin and blow to its stomach.

Valentine placed the guy's hands upon its trunk, and bellowed, 'You bloody little devil! I will bloody murder you!'

Corny thought this very funny and struck again.

'Crikey, Valentine! What an amazing guy!' said Rupert, because he did not recognise who it was meant to be.

Gubsy was no fool; he recognised the Oxley-Stockman head immediately, and though he admired Corny's pugilism, he boomed, 'Chuck the scoundrel on the fire!'

Valentine delegated the honour to Corny who accepted it most enthusiastically. He seized the stuffed figure, bounded over to the bonfire and flung it on top.

He was very pleased with his achievement, and Gubsy boomed, 'Bravo!'

The group watched the flames lick at Cosmo's feet and gradually consume his legs. It warmed Olivia's heart to witness its annihilation. She smiled because it was a good end to a day made happy due to an ultrasound scan, and now, stood between Valentine and Corny, she decided to impart the news. She hooked her hands in their crooks, and drew them near.

'Most wonderful news, darlings!' she said, in a hushed tone, 'This afternoon, upon a monitor, I saw, for the first time, Benedictus' genitalia, and I am rapturous to report that he is absolutely a boy!'

Sounding a tut, Valentine whispered, 'Gosh! Indubitably he is; Benedictus would be rather a queer name for a girl!'

Olivia narrowed her eyes at him.

'Indeed, darling, but until today his gender was indeterminate.'

'Well, mummy, it is glorious news; the begat is a boy, hurrah!' said Valentine.

Corny beamed elatedly.

Olivia said, 'Benedictus really ought to have a sobriquet, just like "jammy little dodger",' she and Corny smiled at each other, 'What might it be?'

Corny made a thoughtful face.

'Gosh! I know!' Valentine immediately exclaimed, 'Bonny little Benny!'

Olivia considered; would Monty have approved?

'Yes, darling,' she said, 'I do believe I like it; your nomenclature is commendable!'

'Verily!' he replied.

Corny looked concurring yet confused.

There then came, from the bonfire, a series of *pop* sounds. They were higher pitched pops than the fire had hitherto made, and it sounded strange amongst the crackles and snaps because it was persistent.

'Crikey!' said Rupert, furrowing his brow, 'I wonder if it's a hedgehog.'

Corny panicked for the prickly beast; he wanted to rescue it, but then Valentine enlightened everyone.

'Oh no,' said he, 'that will be the sound of the popcorn kernels I gave the guy for brains!'

Everyone filled with relief and thought his idea amusing, most particularly Olivia.

She felt the corner of her lips quiver as she watched Cosmo's cauliflower ears catch fire. Then came a spasm in her chest when she contained her hilarity at seeing his head go up in flames.

'It is difficult not to display my delight at the doom of the dastard who so defiled my decency!' thought she.

To aid her endeavour she turned away, but her line of vision met with the Esmé pumpkin lantern alight in the porch, and she was helpless. She abandoned her hauteur and surrendered herself to a mad fit of laughter so contagious that everyone caught it.

The collective merriment encouraged her; she crunched her heels across the gravel to the porch, collected the pumpkin and, with it, stalked over to the bonfire. She looked to her sons for permission, and they assented. Whereupon, she lifted the lantern up high before hurling it into the flames. The effort caused her to emit an '*Ugh!*' and to stagger but her boys saved her and they and she looked at the fate of the Esmé pumpkin.

That it had landed, face down, in the fork of the guy's legs heightened Olivia's hysterics, and as the tears of mirth traversed her cheekbones, her howling laughter filled the night air and sent shivers down several spines in the community.

Yet Corny felt no such chill. He felt only love for his mummy, glamorous in her mink, she looked beautiful; the glow from the inferno danced upon her face, and the burning effigy of Cosmo was reflected in her green eyes that sparkled with the gravidity of bonny little Benny.

The Oxley-Stockmans could go to Hell for all that Olivia cared; Bonny little Benny was her bastard baby boy, not theirs! He was the new Avery-Stripe heir!

That the exhilaration of Halloween and Bonfire Night was over did not prove anticlimactic to Corny, rather, the lingering scent of smouldering ashes brought to his mind the approach of Christmas, and of all days, Christmas was his favourite.

There were two reasons for this, firstly, the presents, not because he wanted to receive them, although that was very nice, but because he could give them. Thus, every night, instead of directly falling asleep upon his head hitting his pillow, he would think very hard about what people might most like to have and he would plan to give it to them because to see how happy each recipient was upon unwrapping made him feel excellent.

This pastime induced in him such excitement that he would become rather hot and have to push away his blankets to let his sweat dry in the chill air, which never took very long as Chinchero was as cold as charity.

The cold was Corny's second reason for his fondness of Christmas Day, because just as the Avery-Stripes abhorred the telephone, they also deemed central heating vulgar, and only on the anniversary of the nativity of the baby Jesus would they utilise their antediluvian system.

Quite everyone else in the family seemed impervious to the damp and raw air that dominated most rooms from late autumn until early spring. Naturally, Gretchen did not notice it in her kitchen where it was always warm, but even outside, her hardiness and eternal industry rendered her immune.

That is not to say that Gretchen considered the Avery-Stripes invulnerable, indeed, she persuaded most of them to wear much-darned and thick woollen socks, thermal underwear and knitted jumpers. She fed them heaps of steaming cinnamon porridge for breakfast, constantly filled hot-water bottles to put in their laps and beds, and boiled endless pots of tea, and this year, also Bovril for Olivia.

Gubsy, however, drank less tea in the cold season and instead imbibed close to a bottle of brandy daily, albeit discretely from a teacup, and was gentlemanly enough to decant measures into its saucer for Remarkable.

The two of them, as was usual, stationed themselves before the fireplace that, until bedtime, was unremittingly roaring and surrounded by dozing Dalmatians whose presence by the Aga was a nuisance during the day. Corny, however, had not the patience to remain before the fire for too long.

Corny considered Harry fortunate to be in Izzy's house where he was certain it would be warm everywhere. He even wondered, for a flash, if he envied Willy but then he decided that he did not; he could not like Cosmo even if it brought warmth; he would rather be cold. Valentine never seemed to mind the cold, he would not wear special undergarments, but cashmere socks were agreeable and a lamb's wool sweater acceptable. He would claim pyjamas effective, the Indian quilt comfortable, and warm-blooded Rupert even more so, and between them the pair drank more tea than a throng of thirsty Chinamen might.

Corny did like tea, just not as much as Valentine did, and he could not drink gallons of it simply to avoid feeling the chill bite at his bare legs. He refused to wear long trousers, they were much too constrictive, and neither would he pull his socks to his knees in an effort to retain bodily heat because it looked silly. Gretchen, however, forced him to wear his old itchy turtleneck.

'I do not care if you are itchink, it is better than to be sneezink!' she said.

And because Corny was unable to remove the now snug garment unaided, he endured it until Valentine took pity, but then Gretchen would always jump out, scold the naughty boys, and make him put it on again. Not even conveniently losing it whilst out and about saved Corny from suffering because Gretchen had wisely sewn name labels in his whole wardrobe and it would always find its way home again.

What was most irritating about the turtleneck was that except for the blistering itchiness it created about his throat, it did not keep him as warm as he would like. Fortuitously, he discovered, whilst running up and down the stairwell in an effort to alleviate boredom and release energy, that to exert himself physically possessed the miraculous and unexpected result of heating him also, therefore, he resolved to exercise strenuously and rather constantly until the return of summer.

Henceforth, Corny woke everyday at the crack and felt full of beans. He dressed in his shorts and turtleneck routinely, yet reluctantly, and directly after a big breakfast, he would ascend and descend the stairwell until he suffered a stitch or received a complaint about the ruckus created by his feverish footfalls. Nevertheless, the activity got him hot and burnt a measure of his energy, and then he would stand before the open refrigerator, or outside, and gulp down a pint bottle of milk.

Next, on the Axminster, before a girning Gubsy, he would perform press-ups and sit-ups until he felt quite sick, and then he would lie still for a while and study where once there was a crack in the drawing-room ceiling, before resuming his drill with renewed zeal.

On his occasional visits to the kitchen due to hunger and thirst, he would almost wish that he might stay because it was so cosy. Yet Gretchen, who cooked more meals than usual in the winter, and this year constantly kedgeree, would quickly chivvy him out from under her feet. This annoyed Corny somewhat, but when naked in the bathroom, he decided that he did not mind because the looking glass told him that, hot or not, his physical labour was far from Sisyphean, as his stomach had become remarkably xylophonic. The similarity amused him. He enjoyed showing Gloriana, sat upon the cistern, how he could punch, very hard, his taut midriff and flinch not an inch, but not for very long because it was too chilly for prolonged nudity.

Sadly, Corny's exercise routine lasted only until luncheon; frustratingly, he was too exhausted to undergo the effort the entire day, but happily, he soon discovered a much nicer way to keep warm in the afternoons.

Initially, his workouts had distracted him completely from the absence of his mother and brother. It was not unusual for her presence to be lacking but Valentine's was disconcerting, and upon consulting his memory, Corny realised that, for the past few days, he saw nearly neither hide nor hair of them before supper when, ostensibly for the sake of Benedictus, Olivia would dine in her mink.

Therefore, he decided to detect their diurnal whereabouts. Almost immediately, he located them in his mother's bedroom. He did not knock, but he did enter with caution, and discovered Valentine, sat cross-legged upon the four-poster, embroidering, and Olivia, seemingly asleep, forming a small mountain beneath the blankets, her head, slightly distended due to gravity, nestled in pillows.

'Hello, Corny!' exclaimed Valentine, putting down his tambour frame, 'Do come in!'

Corny was uncertain as to whether or no he should; he feared that he might be a gooseberry.

Olivia opened an eye a fraction, and sleepily murmured, 'Yes, darling, come in do, but quickly, and close the door directly; I do not like draughts.'

Excited at the admittance, Corny was obedient, and then stood stock-still and grinned at them.

For a space, they both regarded him as if he had something to say but then they remembered his muteness and realised his awkwardness, and Valentine said, 'Gosh, Corny! No need to stand on ceremony! Jump up!'

Setting Gloriana upon the dressing table, Corny mounted the four-poster enthusiastically, though mindful of his mother's condition, and climbed beneath the blankets next to her. He put one hand on the crown of her head and the other upon the summit of the mound of Benedictus. Then he beamed at her; he thought his mummy magical because she could makes babies, and bonny little Benny was to be his little brother!

Oh! Corny was excited! And, oh, he did love his mummy!

Olivia looked to Corny, his tousled blond head rested upon Monty's pillow, and she wondered if he was purposely aping him, but, of course, that was impossible; Corny was posthumous, yet the similarity grew progressively prominent.

Nevertheless, she did not entertain, for one moment, a mental debate; she was conclusively certain that the correspondence sat well with her and she returned his sweet smile. However, one thing displeased her.

'Corny, darling,' she gently said, 'it's rude to sweat.'

Corny looked downcast at his breach of etiquette, but then Valentine said, 'It's his scratchy turtleneck, Gretchen won't let him take it off.'

'Well, I am his mother and I say that he may, and indeed must, divest it post haste before the blankets become wet!'

Much tugging and puffing ensued but eventually Corny was free of the uncomfortable garment. He felt wonderful, as if he could breathe again in just his thermal vest.

'What muscles, darling!' said Olivia, kindly, upon viewing the moderate bumps on his bare arms.

Corny looked proud and considered exhibiting his xylophone, but then Olivia added, 'And your hands, darling!'

Corny lifted his hands and viewed them with puzzlement.

'Gosh! Like daddy's spades!' Valentine exclaimed.

'Astonishingly alike!' said Olivia. 'Yet not yet calloused.'

Her own hands emerged from the bedding and held Corny's, massaged them, and she added, 'Let's try and keep them so soft, darling.'

Corrugating his brow, Corny nodded but he was unsure he would like soft hands if his daddy's had not been so.

'I've some violet hand-cream you may use,' said Valentine, and he returned to his tambour frame, he had only two napkins left to do, 'But anyway, where was I?'

Olivia screwed her eyes to better recollect, and said, ' "She fell head over flipper in love with the beautiful prince upon the noble clipper." '

'Oh, yes!' said Valentine, and with that, he proceeded to tell the story of *The Little Mermaid*.

From that afternoon onwards, the three of them congregated upon the four-poster where Corny enveloped Olivia and they both would listen to Valentine's versions of well-known fairy tales as he embroidered.

Quite soon, Valentine had sewn all four napkins, each identical with sunbeams, grass, violets and a *V&R*. He so enjoyed the labour that he adorned some baby bed linen with blue bunnies and bows for Benedictus. He regaled relentlessly, sometimes with his own fantasies, other times Anderson and the Brothers Grimm, but always heavily peppered with persiflage.

Corny listened eagerly. He marvelled at how Valentine could rabbit so incessantly – such stories he could tell! – and he would pity the unfortunates that required a television set for entertainment.

Olivia did not pay so much attention to Valentine's words. She realised them fantastical and though that was not disagreeable, she was happy simply to hear his voice as she drifted in and out of wakefulness. She could not call to mind a time during her widowhood in which she was so assuaged. That her blessed redemption engorged her, furnished her with a calmness, and, ironically, she felt closer to Monty, despite Benedictus being not of his loins. She surmised the sensation the result of her reposing in their bed, and she considered the attention that her second- and fourth-born bestowed upon her promoted the notion. That the foetal heir resided in the grip of Corny and was aurally aware of Valentine's vocality made him more Monty, and definitely an Avery-Stripe, and, as if Benedictus was aware of the love surrounding him, he would sporadically kick.

This would always cause Corny great excitement. In fact, if Corny did not feel a kick in a while he would become concerned and Olivia would reluctantly press, against her inflation, a warm teacup of Bovril so to coerce a kick and mollify, whereupon Corny would consider his situation the happiest one in the world.

The evenings were just as cosy. Rupert would return from renovating and Valentine's spirits would soar, then every being in the house, be they of two legs or four, feathered or finned, would gather in the dining room.

For the humans not obliged to consume only kedgeree, there would be a warming supper such as goulash, beef stroganov, haggis and daube, a variety of casseroles and oceans of soup, mostly borscht. There was always a steamed pudding, followed by hot chocolate and a game of scrabble or mahjong before bedtime that, because of an increasingly present Jack Frost, was close to ten, despite the ormolu clock striking only nine chimes in the dark and silent house.

Because he wanted to be with the boys, Corny often wished that he might ascend to Valentine's turret with them, but he respected their doubtlessly big boy games. Further, upon recollecting spying through the keyhole, their particular game of undressed musical statues, he surmised himself unready for that at any rate, and one cold early December night he decided to call upon his mother.

He tentatively entered her room with his torch and cast its beam over his face to exhibit his wish.

Olivia gladdened that she now grasped the meanings of his facial contortions, and quite astonished herself with her assent.

Beneath the blankets, they were deliciously warm together, and every night henceforth, Corny lovingly held her in his arms, buried his face in her hair and stretched a protective palm over Benedictus.

Olivia would dream that she was safe in Monty's embrace, and in the mornings would fill with a sadness that it was not so, yet she would smile at the seraphic doppelganger, concentratedly asleep and clutching her close.

CHAPTER 26

Christmas Day

Due to the whistle and clunks of hot water whizzing through pipes, Corny woke earlier than usual. The sound induced in him a thrill like no other because, more even than the jingle of bells, it heralded the commencement of Christmas Day!

In one deft feat, he jumped from the four-poster and then peeked between the curtains with the wish that the world might be white, but, sadly, it was not; the ground was merely frosted, and a frustrated robin indicated that it was also impenetrable.

Corny smiled at Gloriana on the dressing table. He wondered if she might be chilly as her bowl was rather cool, thus, to warm her, he held the glassware to his chest, and then he filled with joy because though he wore only his thermal underwear he felt wonderfully toasty, and he thought to himself, 'It is because today really *is* Christmas Day!'

He looked to his sleeping mother. He considered her mien regal, and despite his longing to rouse and share with her the exciting arrival of his favourite day, he decided it best to let her rest. Whereupon, without further ado or bothering to dress, because, to his mind, the temperature was tropical, he hurriedly vacated the bedroom, with his fish, to discover who else was awake.

Corny marvelled at the seasonal adornments in the hall as if they were new to him and had not been present for some days now. He inhaled deeply the exhilarating scent of the fir branches that interwove and wreathed the pictures, bison head, balustrades, newels, and doorframes. Mistletoe was also present, in case someone required a Christmas kiss.

The evergreen theme continued into the uninhabited drawing room; there, the branches embellished every painting, and the piano and travelled all exposed dado rail. Holly and ivy, hung from the cornicing in smiling garlands, was further beautified with golden bells and bountiful red and green velveteen bows. The biggest bow crowned the portrait of Excelsior. Corny mentally wished him a very Happy Christmas but did not wait for a reply; instead, he regarded, with awe, the mass of pillar candles and poinsettias crowding the gleaming ormolu clock.

In the fireplace were some coal and burning logs ablaze, but only moderately, as a decorative gesture, because the central heating rendered a roaring one redundant, and about the recess hung four stockings stuffed with sweets and satsumas. The stockings bore the Avery-Stripe crest and motto, and they each bore a name: Horatio, Valentino, Wilhelmina and Cornelius.

Corny saddened upon viewing the one belonging to Willy, because although he was happy to see it there, he was upset that she would not be present, preferring instead to accompany the Oxley-Stockmans on the world cruise that she had unwittingly predestined.

He felt his eyes start to well as he recollected the arrival of her letter inked upon the writing paper embossed with the family name, informing them of the voyage and apologising profusely that she would not be about for Christmas. It seemed to him that only he appeared to mind her absence, and he started afresh to wonder why, but then came the peal of sleighbells.

He held his breath and listened carefully, the conservatory door opened and, full with expectation, he spun round. It was not reindeer, however, but Dalmatians, three of them garbed with the sleighbells he had heard, their animated manoeuvrings jangling them merrily.

The cause of the dogs' agitated disconcertion was the astonishing spectacle of an enormous tree entering the garden through the side gate and travelling toward the conservatory, seemingly independently. That Valentine became apparent and directed the evidently blind tree did not dampen their ardour, nor even did the revelation that Rupert, looking like a lumberjack, caused the conveyance. Neither was Corny's surprise curbed because he thought the conifer the most colossal one in the world!

'Gosh, Corny! Isn't it a whopper?' exclaimed Valentine, flinging his duffel coat on the ottoman and kicking off his brogues. His pyjamas were satin and cardinal.

Corny nodded vigorously and hugged his brother heartily, his big blue eyes wished him a Happy Christmas, and he smiled when a winded Valentine replied, 'And a crushingly Happy Christmas to you too, Corny!'

Corny released him, he had forgotten his strength but knew Valentine wiry enough to survive, and they both watched, with anticipation, as Rupert rendered the evergreen perpendicular.

It truly was a marvellous tree, almost as tall as the room and, when fully dressed, it most likely would kiss the ceiling. The boughs and spurs were fulsome with virile health so exuberant that it tempted one to embrace it, yet, being a Norway spruce, the needles were particularly keen, and thus, any physical affection shown toward it would be far from reciprocal.

Gretchen arrived with Gubsy and settled him in his wing chair before transposing Remarkable from her shoulder to his perch. The three of them regarded the immense tree admiringly.

"Course it's not as big as the ones my grandfather would have but it is very fine!' boomed Gubsy.

'A most handsome tree!' said Gretchen, and she rubbed a sprig between a thumb and forefinger, then smelled them, '*Ah*! So refreshink!'

'It is the most beautiful tree in creation!' exclaimed Valentine, because it was a gift to the family from Rupert. 'And if you'll be good enough to fix some buck's fizz, Gretchen, we shall commence to dress it!'

Valentine cranked the gramophone and set the needle on the vinyl so to sound the Christ Church Cathedral Choir, and with Corny and Rupert, he fervently raided the dusty Christmas tree chest on its annual elevation from the cellar.

'I want everything placed perfectly and thoughtfully!' he declared, 'Not slapdash, though the upshot should look as if we simply threw everything at it and that the glorious consequence was fortuitous!'

Both blond boys corrugated their brows because they could not compute how to achieve the ambition, therefore they decided it best to follow Valentine's lead.

Gradually, the tree grew more splendid with the addition of each vintage ornament. Some of the aged trinkets were older even than Gubsy yet retained their lustre, in fact, their seniority heightened their nobility and appeared to boast their superiority of having been about in Excelsior's day – 'Many an Avery-Stripe Christmas we have seen, and many a tale we could tell!' they seemed to say, and Valentine so greatly wished he could hear them that he felt as if his ears might bleed.

Each decoration was positioned with an exact haphazardness. Then four-dozen counterweighted candleholders were hooked upon the bough's extremities; the Avery-Stripes detested artificial lights on something so imperial as a Christmas tree, and just as Queen Victoria had done, when the tradition of the *tannenbaum* first came to Albion, they enjoyed the comelier light created by candles.

Finally, it was time for the finest detail; the ruby studded silver-plate star to crown the majestic tree's pinnacle. Usually the eldest brother lifted the youngest to execute the coronation but in Harry's absence, Corny mounted Rupert's shoulders and all present delighted in the spectacle of the ceremony, indeed, a space less than an inch separated the grand star from the ceiling, and they each marvelled at the victory of Valentine's vision of orchestrated disarray.

'What an opulently ornamented and tremendous tree, darlings!' said Olivia, graciously, upon entering the drawing room, augustly.

'Gosh, mummy!' exclaimed Valentine, 'To Hades with the tree! All discerning eyes would rather behold you! You look to be resplendent!'

'Do I, darling?' replied Olivia, fraudulently self-effacingly, and she meandered toward the chesterfield upon which she alighted gracefully despite the magnitude of Benedictus.

'Truly, mummy, you do!' he affirmed, sincerely, because not since Bonfire Night had his mother worn warpaint, and nor had she dressed to kill since the blue tea party.

To be precise, Olivia's look was not entirely festive for her attire was severe. A sleek avacado cashmere dress accentuated her every sharp angle and gravid curve, a pair of black snakeskin heels provided her with a plinth, and her crocodile Birkin fortification. From wrist to elbow, her arms exhibited antiquated elephant ivory, and about her throat was displayed a virtual African diamond mine received from Monty upon their tenth anniversary.

Corny thought his mother especially radiant with her sphere so patent. He plucked a mistletoe spray from atop the Steinway, and practically assaulted Olivia and Benedictus with his zealous lips.

Much to the others' surprise, Olivia issued no real protestation, other than her perfunctory *ugh!*, and she unreservedly revelled in his man-handling.

She laughed delightedly, and wished Corny a Merry Christmas, then cupped his happy face in her hands and covered it with kisses – his lips received an especially large one and induced him to swoon.

Then Valentine exclaimed, 'Gosh! Now it's time for putting presents beneath the tree, and do let's hurry before Harry arrives!'

The mention of Harry caused Corny to spring into action. He bounded up the stairwell, two treads at a time, and because Olivia called after him to put on some clothes, he hurriedly dressed in his bedroom with the idea that a cricket jumper and a pair of Bermuda shorts was fetching.

Then he rushed to the bathroom to brush his teeth, and remembered that he had not yet washed. Whereupon, he swiftly stripped and hastily sluiced. Whilst drying himself, before the looking glass, he considered his hair too long and not smart, thus he attacked his blond mop with the nail scissors. His hairdressing ability was far from expert but he considered his hacked coiffure becoming, and he grinned with pride at his reflection before punching twice his xylophone and again dressing.

As if in a race, he ran back to his room and threw himself on the floor. From beneath his bed he pulled out several boxes of Lego and one of a defunct Scalextric because behind them were hidden his Christmas presents. He was pleased that he had so much to give, and then, upon liberating the last, he frowned at his wrapping technique, it was not very neat, and he had required two rolls of (electrical) tape. Still, the heap before him filled him with happiness, and gathering in his arms as many presents as he was able, he rushed to the drawing room to place them at the foot of the tree.

Already there were a great number of them, all gaily packaged in bright patterned paper and embellished with ribbons or twine, and each of them tempting Corny to read which of the labels bore his name. Surreptitiously, he cast a glance at those closest as he relieved himself of his own, but because he deemed the deed naughty he did not mind when Valentine interrupted him with the exclamation, 'Gosh, Corny! Your hair!'

Corny leapt up and bashfully brushed his hands over his haircut; he hoped that Valentine thought it a good one.

Valentine viewed him with some astonishment, it was not the first time Corny had cut his own hair but never before had the result been so choppy. Yet it did not look entirely awful, in fact, it was rather endearing, in a savage sort of a way, and because it was obvious that Corny was proud of his effort, Valentine declared, 'Such charming tufts! Quite like lots of cows' licks, I like it!'

Corny beamed delightedly, even more so when Olivia proclaimed the haircut, 'Simply striking, darling!' and caressed his jerky down affectionately.

Gretchen however was not so impressed with the mess of tresses left on the bathroom floor.

Corny hurriedly returned to his bedroom for the second cargo of gifts to distribute about the tree. He was pleased when Gubsy accused him of 'Out-nicking St. Nick!' and he grinned as he dashed up to his bedroom to collect the third and final load.

He felt heady with elation as he sped down the stairwell. The excitement of the day was to him so invigorating it was as if he were aboard a perpetual roller-coaster ride travelling at breakneck speed. Unfortunately, he too was unable to moderate his velocity and upon advancing the drawing room, Olivia exited it, and so as not to collide with her, he swerved, and crashed instead into the doorframe with an almighty *whack*!

The impact sent him reeling.

Olivia shrieked with shock of fright as presents flew and fell hither and thither, and surrounded a supine Corny. She became mindless of her composure, and heedless to the physical hindrance of Benedictus, she instantly descended upon her inert son.

'Corny!' she cried, 'Corny!'

She jostled his shoulders but his head no more than lolled to the left and revealed a bloody gash on his right brow.

'Valentine!' she screamed, 'Gretchen!'

She slapped the boy's cheeks gently.

Valentine and Gretchen arrived with Rupert and Gubsy. The quartet gasped collectively. Olivia considered herself completely responsible and her vocabulary tangled as she recounted the collision. Valentine became histrionic and Gubsy boomed and bridled. Rupert and Gretchen kept their heads however; he staunched the blood flow with a thumb, and carried the casualty to the kitchen, whilst she located the first-aid kit.

Corny's lids flickered during his relocation, they lifted to display a slither of white and by the time his bottom was nestled upon a kitchen-stool, his irises were fully exposed. He was alert but discombobulated by the bustle about him, and then he experienced a stabbing pain as Gretchen cleaned his cut, whereupon he winced and recollected his crash into the doorframe.

He looked to Olivia for sympathy. She barely stifled a maternal sob of relief; he was alive and demonstrated recognition.

'Corny, darling!' she cried, as she knelt adjacent to him and took his hands, 'My fault entirely! Oh, what an abysmal mummy I am!'

He regarded her with confusion; he considered her the best mummy in existence! He then looked at her lovingly, and raised a hand to prevent Gretchen from applying the butterfly-stitch because he wished his mummy to do it.

Never before had Olivia played nurse to her children and she found the occasion both easier and more rewarding than she had imagined possible.

'Mummy's very proud of her brave boy!' she said with warmth, then, scathingly, 'Beastly bloody laceration!' and she kissed its surrounding area, 'Such a shock!'

Corny immediately brightened. He did like to be his mummy's brave boy. It made him feel good inside and the sensation heightened upon swallowing the shot of brandy brought to him by Gubsy.

'He's a tough enough nut to withstand an occasional knock!' said Gubsy, with a gnash.

Corny smiled at Gubsy. He was happy to be tough, and his toughness was such that he did not feel it compromised by wearing his old Christmas halo presently placed jauntily upon his crown by a now relieved Valentine. It only made him beam, and his smile, combined with his wound, made him look like a martyring angel.

Then came the peal of the front doorbell being pulled; Mr and Mrs Horatio Avery-Stripe had arrived!

'Me*ww*y Ch*w*istmas, ev*w*ybody!' exclaimed Harry, cheerfully.

Izzy echoed his sentiments: 'Ye*th*, Merry Chri*th*tmas one and all!'

And then she shrieked at the sight of Corny, his brutal haircut and injury.

'*W*ascal!' said Harry, concernedly, 'What sc*w*apes now?'

Valentine explained the mishap as Gretchen divested Izzy of her astra-khan coat and Harry of his Loden one before she ushered them all into the drawing room for eggnog and mince pies.

'C*ww*umbs, *w*ascal! I'm glad you weren't ca*ww*ying Glo*w*iana,' said Harry, 'That would've been *w*eally much worse!'

Izzy peered worriedly at Corny, she thought the halo misplaced.

'I hope Benedictu*th* will not be a*th* boi*th*terou*th*. I'm *th*ertain my nerve*th* would not *th*tand it!'

'Already the chit is enervating *my* nervous system!' thought Olivia, 'Her remarks are reprehensible!'

'I keep telling you, Izzy, Corny is not boisterous!' Valentine said, sternly, but then he softened when, from her handbag, Izzy produced her tiara and positioned it on her head.

She looked pleased with herself, perhaps because she was proud of her diamonds or maybe for pacifying Valentine so promptly.

Yet the placation was only moderate. To be sure, the tiara was a stunning and enviable piece, and correlated neatly with Izzy's wedding ring, but still she had disparaged his little brother.

Therefore Valentine simply said, 'Gosh! How twinkly! Almost as sparkly as mummy's!' and he indicated Olivia's rocks.

Izzy was somewhat deflated, Olivia was the opposite, and Corny only viewed the tantalising presents beneath the tree.

*

A vermilion and gold damask Christmas cloth cloaked the lacquered table about which the Avery-Stripes assembled. The illumination from the gondola chandelier flattered each of them kindly. It danced upon both sets of diamonds, and heightened Olivia's augustness and Izzy's preciousness, and promoted also the glow of Corny's halo. Harry and Gubsy's eyes reflected the flickering flames, as did Rupert's magnificent grin, and Valentine's satin pyjamas looked lustrous.

The cutlery was gold and engraved with the initials '*E. A-S & O. A-S*,' and their wedding year, '*1858*'. The bone china was white and gilded with '*Nil Desperandum*' and a Peruvian booby stood upon a chevron, and each of the crystal wineglasses brimmed with rich Barolo except for Olivia's, for she would sip champagne, and Valentine had a Grasshopper.

Izzy made an indent in her brow.

'Ought Benedictu*th* really to be drinking *th*ampagne?' she asked.

The impertinence caused Olivia to inhale. She did not deign to respond, but Valentine piped up, 'Indubitably! It is his Christmas day too, besides Bovril must be boring by now and the bubbles will charm him!'

Izzy looked to Harry and accentuated her indent but then Gretchen arrived with a stupendous dead pig, roasted from snout to corkscrew tail, upon a golden platter. Instantaneously, its glorious scent and the appreciative gasps of the assemblage were circumfluous.

'Gosh! What a goliath pig!' exclaimed Valentine, making hungry eyes at it, 'Don't you think, Corny?'

A passionate nod indicated Corny's accordance and bounced his halo. He licked his drooling lips exaggeratedly because it seemed to him that he would happily devour the whole hog, and its apple gobstopper!

Gubsy also grinned with satisfaction at the roast. He adored eating pig but he did slightly hanker for the Christmas dinner of peacock upon which Excelsior had always insisted.

'Yummy!' said Harry, 'What *tw*eats! I'm so *w*avishing, my tummy is *w*eally *w*umbling!'

To emphasise his claim Harry rubbed, with circular movements, his hands on his midriff, as Gretchen produced further culinary delights such as sugar-browned potatoes and others roasted in goose fat, parsnips glazed with honey, carrots glazed with mustard, great mounds of Brussels sprouts and chestnuts, a vessel of red cabbage and a flotilla of brimming gravy boats.

The celebratory repast rendered all with the desire to devour as if ravenous but before they could start to sate, Gubsy was to carve, and this called for patience as he noisily gnashed, and deliberately incised and apportioned the porcine carcass.

They each salivated over the knolls of festive food on their eventual plates and (following a few words about Willy who, according to Harry, was now in 'Bowa Bowa') they attacked them with great avidity.

Even Olivia forsook kedgeree and partook in the Christmas meal, for not to do so would be most rude. She deemed it all delightfully delicious, yet did not restrain herself from seasoning the food further.

'Corny, darling, you are trickling!' she stage-whispered.

Corny pulled a face of puzzlement, whereupon Olivia employed a finger to collect the rivulet of blood that dispersed from beneath his butterfly-stitch, and she sucked at it, not once but several times, until the fluid congealed.

Corny glowed with gratitude; she was such a caring mummy! He cast his proud smile toward a horrified Izzy who could not quite believe the macabre sight.

Olivia realised Izzy's discomfiture and ridiculed her with a furtive wink that caused her to gasp. Valentine caught the wink also and its vulgarity upset him to such a degree that he declared it time to pull crackers.

Cutlery was rested upon crockery, they all crossed arms, and in both hands held the end of a cracker, the other end in their neighbour's, and thus linked, they formed a ring about the table.

'On the count of thwee evwybody!' Harry said, jovially, and, in unison, the group counted: 'One, two, and three!'

In total, eight cracks came almost simultaneously. Novelties, paper-crowns and mottos flew all about; some fell in food, others clinked against crystal and one drowned in a gravy boat but, fortunately, it was only a thimble, and Valentine said that his of gilt was better than a saucy plastic one. The main thing was that everybody won a paper-crown. To wear it was mandatory – tiara, halo or no – and so was laughing at the puns.

'I don't get it!' Gubsy growled with mounting rage.

Rupert tried to explain his joke again: 'The chap's saying that his little amphibian is a small newt, *mi-nute!*'

'No. Still don't get it,' said Gubsy, gnashing his teeth and regarding Rupert as if he suspected he was playing him for fool.

'It's all wight, Gubsy,' said Harry, 'I don't get it either, it's pwobably not even a joke.'

'Not even a joke!' Gubsy rebuked, 'My crackers must have jokes! I won't have it!' He slammed his fist on the table and cursed.

A solitary cracker remained. The idea of saving it for next year was too tragic for Izzy to tolerate. She said she that could not bear to think of its long loneliness, therefore Valentine suggested she and Harry pull it for Benedictus.

'What a ni*the* idea!' said Izzy, as if she saw a shooting star.

'A ve*wy* nice one, Valentine!' agreed Harry, appreciatively.

Alas, the endeavour transpired to be not very nice. Izzy's upper body possessed little more strength than a melancholy sigh, and try as he might to endow equality to the process of pulling an admittedly rather stubborn cracker with his wife, Harry succeeded only in pulling her toward him.

The family watched uncomfortably and Rupert encouraged his cousin: 'Go on, Izzy! You can do it!'

Izzy hardened her resolve and heaved with all her insubstantial might but she lost her grip, and the sleeve of her charmeuse blouson touched red cabbage.

The consequent waterworks were considerable.

'Oh! My blou*the*! It i*th th*poiled!' she cried, and made it worse by massaging the catastrophe with her napkin.

Harry grimaced both at the stain and at the tears, and he tried to comfort her.

'Don't c*wy*, Izzy, its all *wight weally*. Just a little bit of *w*ed cabbage,' and he hugged her but still she wept.

Then he attempted to cheer her by pulling Benedictus' cracker unassisted, but its novelty, that was a penknife, motivated only more tears.

'A penknife! For a baby boy!' Izzy wailed. 'He will grow up to be an a*thath*in!'

'C*w*umbs! *W*eally not!' said Harry, pressing his thumb against the harmlessly blunt blade. 'I don't think it would make any cut at all.'

Gretchen did not like to see such a delicate girl weeping, and she stepped in.

'Come with Kretchen, Mrs Izzy,' she said, enveloping Izzy in her arms, 'I will ket stain out from beautiful blouse.'

Whereupon, Izzy sobbingly surrendered herself to Gretchen who conveyed her to the kitchen where she would reveal the magical powers of white vinegar.

Those remaining in the dining room returned to their plates and ate in silence. The theatrics gave them food for thought and Harry was keen to digress.

'What scwummy buttewy bwussel spwouts!' he said, enthusiastically, and bit into one of the bud-like vegetables.

Evidently the strength of Izzy's hearing was greater than the rest of her physicality because, from the kitchen, she cried out, 'Don't eat tho many bruthel thproutth, Harry; they give you wind!'

Harry blushed beneath his boxed beard. Valentine made a tut at Izzy's impropriety but Olivia smiled.

'Gosh! What's so funny, mummy?'

'Nothing, darling, really nothing at all,' she insisted, and masked her amusement with her napkin, yet her eyes betrayed her.

Corny grinned at her. He was not sure what was funny but he did like to see her happy.

Valentine considered what the joke was, and asked, 'Bonny little Benny an assassin?'

The question caused Olivia to convulse with hilarity; she bit her napkin but nodded to verify the accuracy of the hypothesis. The idea was ludicrous, yet her mirth subsided marginally when she considered the moniker 'Benedictus the Assassin' to sound peculiarly patrician.

The imposing Christmas pudding withstood its purple flames stoically. Its consistency and flavour brought pleasure to every palate and no one could resist a second helping. There followed a game of snapdragon not dared by all, but the derring-do of those who did was a joy to see, and even Izzy became cheerful.

Suddenly, Corny jumped up and leapt over to the French windows to ascertain that darkness truly had descended and was not simply an optical illusion. Upon discovering it to be true, he looked to his family and danced a jig of glee, for now the time had come for lighting the candles upon the tree!

As was traditional, Gretchen drew the curtains in the drawing room and lighted each of the forty-eight wicks whilst the family waited in the dining room. It required a great deal of discipline for Corny not to peek through the keyhole but, superhumanly, he resisted the temptation. His effort was well worth it, for when Gretchen finally signalled, with a little bell, the completion of her enjoyable task, the double doors divided, and there was the Christmas tree in all its candlelit glory that robbed everybody of both vocabulary and oxygen.

The group gaped at it in golden silence until the ormolu chimed a quarter, whereupon, the peace broken, their *modus operandi* of celebrating resumed. They linked hands, slowly orbited the conifer, and solemnly sang *O Little Town of Bethlehem* and created an atmosphere most festal, yet the Dalmatians, under the Steinway, Remarkable, upon his perch, and Gloriana, atop the écritoire, considered the humans psychiatrically disordered.

Of course, Corny did not sing. Instead he admired the number of presents beneath the tree. He calculated there to be a hundred of them, and he began to look for one in particular. He was sure that he had placed it under the big branch pointing to the conservatory but he could not locate it. This troubled him. Therefore, immediately after the closing line of the carol, he did not wait for everyone to sit comfortably before diving into the bounty.

'Ha!' boomed Gubsy, affectionately, from his wing chair, 'Look at the stripling strapper! By Jove, he's an eager pup!'

All watched, with fondness, Corny's frantic search bar Izzy, who cried, 'Careful! You might break *th*omething!'

A tut came from Valentine, sat cross-legged with Rupert upon the Axminster, and Olivia said, 'Yes, darling, do try to be less *boisterous!*'

No one noticed Izzy's response to the remark because then Corny resurfaced, his hunt triumphant, for he beheld a creatively wrapped box which he then hurriedly presented to his mother.

'Goodness, darling!' said Olivia, in an impressed tone, 'How wonderfully wrapped!'

Corny did not respond; the anticipation of what she might think of the present rendered him immobile.

'Such a lot of sticky-tape!' said Olivia, struggling, 'I always stress the serious need for an adequate amount of it,' she added.

Corny stood and started to tug at his cricket jumper. He twisted it as if he wished to destroy it. His heart was racing but he would not permit a breath to pass his lips until his mother deemed the present at least acceptable.

Finally, Olivia conquered the sticky-tape and defeated the paper. The present inside was one that exceeded her expectation of her sweet special son. His thoughtfulness touched her sincerely, his timeliness too, for little more than a drop dissuaded the absolute exhaustion of her final flacon of Chanel No19.

'Oh, darling! Immense gratitude!' Olivia exclaimed, with exposed canines, 'It is exactly what the doctor ordered!'

She grasped his hand and pulled him close. Corny had to stop himself from falling upon Benedictus, but he was thrilled to regard his mother's obvious pleasure and was proud of himself, even if his gift transpired to be medicinal, and he wondered what kind of doctor might prescribe perfume.

'Such an sublime scent!' she said, releasing the stopper and applying the aroma to her jugular. 'Do inhale it, darling!' she said to Corny, and he lifted his head from her breast to do so.

He thought the smell wonderful and that it was especially nice with his mummy's diamonds, that he presently decided she should always wear. He pretended that the fragrance made him dizzy with ecstasy, and Olivia laughed.

'Mummy wore it when she met daddy,' she said, 'He always loved it!' and she smiled and kissed Corny on his forehead, rendering him relatively relaxed with regard to the rest of the day.

Eight pairs of eyes now cast glances at each other and under the tree. The simple strategy of the event was that between each carol and circum-navigation everybody was to open a present consecutively, until they grew weary of trying to sing, and then they would wrestle only with unwrapping.

After a minute's hesitation the bestowing gradually gathered steam.

Valentine also received a flacon; Gubsy gave him a small but expensive one of violet scent with which he was very pleased. Gretchen had clandestinely knitted for everyone mittens and scarves so luxurious that it was a shame not to wear them for long but the heat made by the Christmas tree candles always was surprisingly strong.

Gretchen was at first uncertain as to the sincerity of the excuse but at once realised its veracity upon modelling the gift from Harry and Izzy because it was a sumptuously dense fur ushanka. She tied the cord under her chin and, consequently, her ears felt toasted.

'I like very much!' she said, with a broad grin.

'I'm *weally* pleased, Gwetchen!' replied Harry, 'It will keep you *weally* warm at the allotment because it is *weal* snow-*wabbit!*'

'Never will I take off!' Gretchen joked, and to her credit she tolerated the heat for over five minutes.

When she removed the hat, she admired again its glamorousness, and looked forward to showing it off when next digging for potatoes.

Then Gubsy opened his present from Corny – a box of Montecristo No. 4 – and insisted on smoking one immediately.

The pungent aroma made Izzy uncomfortable. She disappeared behind a curtain and opened a window to breathe fresh air.

'Fan Olivia with *th*ome paper, Harry!' she called out from her hiding place.

'*W*eally?' replied Harry, with some doubt as to the wisdom of such an undertaking but he complied when Izzy cried, 'Really!'

Olivia watched, with astonishment, Harry pick up a large scrap of wrapping paper and cautiously fan her. Irascibly, she snatched it and cast it away.

'Do not be ridiculous, darling!' she snapped.

Izzy gasped when she heard Olivia's rebuff, and the abrupt attack of cold oxygen upon her larynx was so razor-sharp that she hacked dramatically as she revealed herself.

'But think of Benedictu*th*!' she said, wheezingly. 'The horrid *th*igar *th*moke!'

'I assure you I constantly do!' stated Olivia, seethingly, 'And I assure you also that Benedictus is entirely ignorant to the existence of cigars and of fanning! Overridingly, I wonder what the world has come to when a man cannot smoke in his own drawing room without creating hysterics!'

Izzy was silenced and sought refuge in Harry's arms where she bitterly fought back her tears. She smiled weakly when Gubsy desisted puffing purely for her sake. He did not resent the sacrifice too much, rather, he was pleased with Olivia for defending his rights.

He grinned at her, girned, and then gnashed his false teeth before summoning Corny and talking to him in what he believed to be a hushed tone.

Corny happily obeyed Gubsy's instruction and stuck his arm into the tree to extract a red envelope balanced upon a bough. He delivered it to his mother and stood over her, eager to see what was written.

'Thank you, darling,' said Olivia. She smiled at Gubsy, 'Finally my red-letter day has come!'

Gubsy signalled his approval of the quip with a *humph*, and, with the ivory paperknife, Olivia sliced.

Inside was a card. An ordinary Christmas one depicting a snowy countryside, and inside, a message, in Gubsy's gradient hand: *To Olivia, with respect and gratitude, Uncle Bartholomew.*

The words affected Olivia, on their own they were enough of a Christmas present but they were not alone; a cheque accompanied them. The quantity on the cheque was far from meagre, in fact, it was so profuse that she had to blink to believe, but it was unquestionable – the amount was bountiful. It was such, that when relieved of Benedictus, she could again holiday extravagantly without the need to be nice to unsavoury sorts; she might even be able to afford a decent flat somewhere central. The possibilities were endless; with the cheque, the world was once again open to her; in short, Gubsy's gift was the means of independence.

With fluid eyes, Olivia viewed Gubsy with an affection that she never believed she would feel toward him.

Chokingly, she said, 'Uncle Bartholomew, words evade me, but suffice it to say that *immense* is too anaemic to express the extent of my gratitude, therefore I say *gargantuan*!'

The elaborate thankfulness made Gubsy smile warmly at the woman he hoped would take her leave from the family, following the imminent nativity, now that she possessed the wherewithall.

'Your gratitude's appreciated,' he said to her, 'but don't start waxing lyrical, and no displays, or I'll take it back!' and he gnashed.

Motionless, Olivia mentally ordered her eyes to dehydrate and they complied, then she said to Gubsy, 'Belligerent bully!'

Gubsy's retort was, 'Devil woman!'

Valentine considered it the right time to give his present to Rupert.

'Crikey! What amazing wrapping!' said Rupert, smiling at the sheet music decorated with red sealing wax, and then he grinned at Valentine, 'I wonder what it is!'

'Gosh! I suppose you ought to set about discovering!' Valentine excitedly exclaimed.

'Crikey! I suppose I ought!' replied Rupert, enthusiastically, and, carefully, he began.

'Gosh! You may rip it, Rupert!' exclaimed Valentine, full with trepidation.

Rupert grinned again and ripped it savagely.

The ripping of the musical wrapping revealed to Rupert the product of Valentine's painstaking labour of love, and he grinned appreciatively at the linen before unfolding and admiring it.

'Crikey! It's completely amazing!' he enthused with wide eyes to demonstrate his amazement. 'Did you make this?'

'Yes!' exclaimed Valentine, 'Ever since before autumn!'

'Crikey!' said Rupert again, and held the fabric close to examine the meticulous stitching. 'It's amazing!'

Olivia sipped her champagne and revelled in the brevity of the beautiful boy's dictionary; she did love that he was far from the brightest button in the box and was glad to regard his reception of the romantic cloth.

Valentine emitted a whoop of pleasure and explained to the assemblage, though with his eyes glued firmly upon Rupert, the meanings of the sun, the violets and their ascension of the beams – he deemed the *V&R*s self-explanatory.

'Crikey! I'm the sun?' asked Rupert, his amazement augmented.

'Gosh! You know you are!' Valentine exclaimed, 'You are Apollo made flesh!'

As if to corroborate, Rupert beamed beautifully, his grin so tantalising that he indeed looked like an Apollonian starring in a Technicolor advertisement for toothpaste. Valentine was titillated almost beyond bearability and he abandoned himself completely in Rupert's ardent embrace.

'Oh! How *th*weet!' squealed Izzy, inspecting the entwined initials upon a napkin, 'V for Valentine and R for Rupert, how romantic!' She passed it for Harry to see.

'Ve*w*y *w*omantic!' he agreed, 'And b*w*illiant emb*w*oidery, Valentine, I'm imp*w*essed!'

Whereupon, Valentine gave to the couple their present of Benedictus' bed linen.

'Oh! It'*th* exqui*th*ite!' cried Izzy, and appeared as if about to weep.

'*W*eally exquisite! Thanks ve*w*y much!' said Harry to his brother for the present for his soon-to-be-son who also was his brother.

Valentine was so excited by the appreciation of his needlework that he could barely breathe but he managed to say, 'The rabbits are to link Benedictus to his grandfather, Montgomery, whom died because of one! Apropos, don't you think?'

Olivia grimaced; occasionally she considered her second born's stance infuriating, but before she could vocalise her view Rupert stuck his becoming rear in the air and unearthed a present for Valentine.

'Gosh! How exciting!' Valentine exclaimed, upon receiving it, 'I do love brown paper packages tied up with string!'

'Ha-ha! I thought you might,' said Rupert, still smiling, 'Go on! Open it!'

Valentine was quite certain that the package contained a vinyl, it was the precise shape and size of one, he wondered which it might be, and endeavoured not to mind that it was transparently not a tiara.

He was correct on both counts, and was happy because the vinyl was a recording of Chet Baker's *My Funny Valentine*. He gasped elatedly at the obvious thought invested in the idea and, of course, was ecstatic at the patent sentiment that Rupert indubitably considered him his – even if it meant that he was funny.

Immediately, he evicted the Christ Church choristers from the gramophone. He replaced them with Rupert's serenade, and swooned at being his favourite work of art.

'Gosh! I love it! Thank you ever so very much! It is the most glorious thing ever in existence!' cried Valentine, hysterically, and fingered Rupert's golden curls and kissed him quickly.

After enjoying the kiss and grinning, Rupert then presented his cousin with a gift, despite having just given one.

'I'm sorry, everyone.' he said, pushing out from behind the chesterfield a box too big for beneath the tree, 'I know it's not my turn but it goes so well with Valentine's bedding.'

Certainly it did, because inside the big box was an elegant rocking cradle, complete with a canopy, that Rupert had constructed during his luncheon breaks from renovating the house of the Whitakers. The wood was a handsome mahogany and upon each panel 'B.A-S' was neatly chiselled in simple block characters.

Izzy was rapturous. She caressed the cradle and began to cry, and when testing its compatibility with the embroidered linen and discovering it impeccable, her tears became torrential.

Enveloping his emotional wife in his fortifying arms, Harry turned to Rupert, and because he too was touched by the kind-hearted generosity and industry, his eyes moistened, and he said, '*W*upert! It t*w*uly is beautiful; a bed fit for a little p*w*ince! I don't know how you did it, but I love it! Thanks ve*w*y much!'

Izzy produced a high-pitched pant of protestation, therefore, Harry strengthened his hold, and amended, '*We* love it!'

Olivia was undecided whether it was the champagne that Corny kept pouring in her flute, or Izzy's waterworks that made her head feel quite cloudy. She considered the latter most likely, therefore, to digress, she drew attention to the unseemly situation of the young Mr and Mrs Avery-Stripe who, though having received many gifts, had so far given no more than an ushanka.

'I consider it quite curious, darling,' she said, with disdain, to Harry, ' 'Tis not the season to be miserly!'

Consequently, Harry looked uncomfortable.

CHAPTER 27

Felicitous Revelations

Sat upon the chesterfield, Harry and Izzy felt as if under the blinding glare of a powerful spotlight and they experienced a nausea akin to stage fright, nevertheless, Harry girded his loins to illuminate.

'Well, mummy, ev*w*ybody,' he began, glancing at them each in turn, as a red-eyed Izzy held his hand. 'We haven't many p*w*esents under the t*w*ee, it's t*w*ue, but that's because we are spending lots of money buying a *w*eally t*w*emendous p*w*esent that is for all the family *w*eally, and impossible to b*w*ing into Chinche*w*o.'

Silence filled the drawing room whilst the news sunk in to the recipients' minds and they each wondered what was impossible to enter Chinchero.

Corny considered that Harry might have purchased an elephant, but then he considered it unlikely and thought some more.

'A car?' said Olivia, hoping that it was not; she loathed travelling in any vehicle other than Monty's Jaguar.

It was not a car.

'A foreign holiday for the entire family?' ventured Valentine.

But it was not a foreign holiday either.

Much scratching of scalps and rubbing of chins ensued and the sound *H'm* was widespread.

Presently Olivia said, '*Ugh!*' and she snapped, 'Just tell us darling! I do so hate guessing games!'

'May I tell them?' Harry asked Izzy.

'Ye*th*, of cour*the*!' said she, and looked as if she had fallen in love with him all over again.

Harry viewed his suspenseful audience. He stroked his boxed beard bashfully, and revealed, 'We are buying a house!'

'A house!' Gubsy said, with a start, 'What's the family want with another house? What's wrong with Chinchero? Not good enough, *eh*?' and he eyed Harry pugnaciously whilst gnashing furiously.

'Nothing! *W*eally nothing!' said Harry, displaying his palms as if to deflect violence.

A disgruntled Gubsy sounded a *harrumph*, 'Well then, what's this all about?' he demanded to know.

Izzy close to hyperventilated.

'Oh! It i*th* a hou*the*, not for the whole family to live in, only Harry, Benedictu*th* and me, but the whole family will be *th*o happy with the hou*the* that it i*th*!'

Contorting her face quite grotesquely at Izzy's lisp, Olivia asked, 'Why, darling, is that? Which house is it?'

The young marrieds regarded each other for a flash, and smiled somewhat smugly, before facing the family, and, in unison, saying, 'The F*w*obishers'/The Frobi*therth*'!'

Corny's ecstasy at the news caused him to ricochet about the drawing room until, much to Izzy's distress, he flung himself at Harry.

'The Frobishers'?' said Olivia with shock, and Valentine exclaimed, 'Gosh! Really not?'

Gretchen smacked her hands to her face and, from behind them, howled with delight; Master Harry would not be so far away now, he would be only next door, she could still cook and care for him and his delicate wife and, of course, the new baby! It was the best Christmas present that she could imagine!

'*W*eally yes!' Harry assured Valentine, with a big smile, and then said, to a squirming Corny, '*Oof!* You ought to be a *w*estler, *w*ascal!' and grappled him with difficulty.

'Gosh! Glorious!' exclaimed Valentine.

'Crikey! Amazing!' Rupert added.

'Hear, hear!' Gubsy boomed; he did like to have Harry near.

It was clear to see that Olivia had her reservations about the relocation. Unthinkingly, she drew the ivory paperknife blade across her throat.

She viewed Harry piercingly, and in a penetrating tone, inquired, 'When?'

She sincerely hoped that the newlyweds were not so imbecilic as to inhabit her vicinity where Izzy's lack of gravidity would one day be patent and the next she would be promenading with a perambulator. The entire community would question it, and quickly calculate the correct conclusion that Benedictus was not Harry's begat and was, in fact, an obvious bastard. It was permissible for the inhabitants of Bath to possess such knowledge, but *not* for people familiar with the family!

Olivia felt fit to spit but was swiftly pacified upon Harry's demonstration that he was not so dense. Indeed, he almost laughed at her transparent suspicion that he was.

'Don't wo*ww*y, mummy. We shan't be moving before Benedictus.'

Olivia heaved a sigh of relief, and listened to his elaboration.

'Obviously not,' Harry went on, 'Izzy and I have discussed it and the plan is that though the house will be ours at the end of Janua*w*y, we shan't move in until the end of Feb*wu*a*w*y, or whenever Benedictus a*ww*ives, and that is when we will move.'

'Ye*th*!' Izzy interrupted, 'It *i*th practical becau*the* we will have a full month to get the hou*the* looking ju*th*t *a*th we want it. Harry will make lot*th* of trip*th* and make it *th*plendid becau*the* he know*th* what I like, and he will make a *th*weet nur*th*ery for Benedictu*th* . . . '

Harry excitedly added, 'We al*w*eady have the c*w*adle and emb*w*oide*w*ed bed linen *w*ight here!'

Whereupon, Valentine piped up, 'Gosh! And we'll pull Zebadiah up from the cellar!'

'Ha-ha! Yes!' Harry said, 'Your old *w*ocking-zeb*w*a! I *w*emember him, he would be b*w*illiant! Thank you!'

Izzy smiled at the thought of her baby boy upon a rocking-zebra, and went on, 'And then when Benedictu*th* arrive*th*, we will let my paren*th*' hou*the* and move next door *th*o we can all be a clo*the* family! The Avery-*Th*tripes all together!'

Olivia regarded the couple anew and she wondered if she had under-estimated their sagacity or if they had merely experienced a flash of shrewdness. No matter, thought she, the plan sat well with her for certainly it was what Monty would have wanted.

Then she thought of Willy; her placement with the Oxley-Stockmans was awry. Naturally, it suited the status quo but soon that would change, and when it did, when Benedictus was where he belonged, Olivia resolved to recoup Willy and return her to where she belonged also – at least until such time that she could persuade her upon Giles or some other suitable.

Further consideration persuaded Olivia to believe Willy's odyssey with the Oxley-Stockmans fortuitous, for were they not inadvertently providing her with an education by way of showing her the world? With any luck, Willy would return polished with a hitherto absent sophistication that may well transpire to be her making.

Olivia lost herself completely in these speculative notions and was absent-mindedly flicking the ivory paperknife between her upper and lower teeth, creating a clicking that Valentine could not tolerate.

'Gosh, mummy!' he said, 'That's *not* nice; I'm trying to hear Harry tell of his new job of work!'

Olivia desisted immediately. Harry had a job of work? Presently, she was all ears, except to ask him, 'Really, darling? What work is it? A lucrative line, I do hope.'

Harry furrowed his brow a degree, and wondered where his mother's mind had been for he had already revealed his new vocation, yet, patiently, he reiterated.

'Not ve*w*y luc*w*ative no, and only part-time, but it's a job that is *w*ewarding because Af*w*ican elephants are becoming *w*ather extinct.'

'What!' Olivia said, with shock; she could not imagine elephants profitable; it sounded like an entirely *un*suitable career.

'Well, yes for their tusks,' Harry explained, 'And though I'll not exactly be p*w*eventing poaching I'll be helping them b*w*eed because next year the zoo's getting an *W*ussian tusker called B*w*utus shipped over to stud with the cows. It's ve*w*y exciting!'

Harry turned to Izzy, and smiled happily, whereupon she crinkled her *retroussé* nose quite nauseatingly, and cried, '*Th*weet little baby elephant*th*!' and looked as if made of nothing but sickly sugar.

Her sanity turning somersaults, Olivia looked at Harry and wondered again at his wit. What lunacy was this to work in an elephant house?

Distractedly, she tapped the paperknife against her surfeit of ivory bracelets, as she heard, but did not faithfully listen to, him detail his duties of washing elephants with a 'b*w*oom', feeding them 't*w*uckloads' and shovelling their 'exc*w*ement', as if it were a vocation of which mere mortals could only dream. Olivia admitted to herself that she had requested that he obtain an occupation but not ever would she have imagined this – it made modelling seem respectable! No, it was utterly *un*acceptable, and she realised that following the heir's arrival not only would she have to recover Willy, she would also have to ensure that Harry lose his job.

Oh! Was there no end to maternal responsibilities?

Corny was ecstatic that his guess of Harry possessing an elephant was not completely wrong, and he felt proud that Harry was going to make money to look after Benedictus. With the baby in mind, Corny now gave to Harry and Izzy their Christmas present; a sterling silver rattle. The couple took turns in sounding it, and looked very pleased.

Their thanks made Corny shine with satisfaction, but then Olivia asked the question, 'Is it Tiffany?'

Upon investigating the blue box, they ascertained that the baby's toy was, indeed, from Tiffany, whereupon Corny suddenly became the unspoken subject of suspicion because nobody could understand how he could afford such a trinket.

Then, when his gift to Gretchen transpired to be an Hermès scarf, Olivia had to ask, 'Corny, darling, a rude question I realise, but however did you purchase these luxuries?'

There commenced much shifting in seats, for suddenly, in the drawing room, there was an elephant that the family endeavoured to ignore because it spoke of stealing. Corny was not blind to the elephant, and he was crestfallen that his family thought him guilty of such felony.

A feeling of injustice claimed him, and he was undecided whether to feel angry or sad, but then Rupert revealed the truth of it.

'You've been spending your wages, haven't you?' he said to Corny, with a grin.

Corny filled with relief at the rescue, he bit his bottom lip, and nodded zealously at his employer.

Valentine viewed the blond boys with bewilderment.

'Wages?' he said to them, as if he had not ever before heard the word because though, of course, he had, it sounded quite alien.

Corny then aimed his eager nodding toward him, but still Valentine felt baffled, as did everyone else.

With a broad hand, Rupert cupped Valentine's knee, 'Yes, his wages for helping me. You didn't think I wouldn't pay him, did you?'

'Gosh! Of course, not!' exclaimed Valentine, and thought Rupert more wonderful.

Harry was impressed.

'I'm imp*w*essed!' he said to Corny, 'You must be ve*w*y *w*ich by now!' Then he turned to Rupert, 'Thanks, *W*upert, you're ve*w*y gene*w*ous!'

'I'm not generous at all; he earned every penny!' stated Rupert, 'Corny's an amazingly hard worker.'

Whereupon Corny puffed out his chest proudly, and smiled as if posing for a photograph with no clue that Rupert was, in fact, very generous for paying him all money made in any day that they both worked.

It was irrelevant to Rupert that Corny's contribution consisted of not much more than holding an A-frame steady, some sanding, handing over tools, and observing his industry as if hypnotised. The amiable company was enjoyable.

'Gosh! You little grafter!' said Valentine, because though Corny was not so small anymore, he would always be his little brother.

'Yes, darling,' said Olivia to Corny, 'I am delighted by your diligence. Daddy would be too!' and she gave him her present.

Olivia had not been as extravagant with gifts as had Corny because before Gubsy's cheque, she had lacked the financial ability, but still she succeeded to bestow upon everybody something decent.

Valentine was very pleased to inherit his daddy's old hipflask. Harry was not happy to receive his father's cufflink tray for it reminded him of the time Monty had pelted him with its contents, but he managed to hide his displeasure.

More difficult to disguise was his shock revelation that Corny so resembled their thuggish sire. Maybe he had not noticed it before because he consciously blocked the bully from his brain, but upon viewing his mother's present to Corny; a black-and-white framed photograph of Monty aged sixteen, sporting a Norfolk jacket, a broken gun in his crook, and brandishing a brace of pheasants, the likeness horrified him.

Not so Corny; he was delighted to have the resemblance confirmed; were the boy in the picture to suddenly materialise then they would surely pass for twins of the identical sort. However, upon contemplating his reflection in the photograph's silver frame, Corny concluded that though his daddy had been handsome, he, himself, was decidedly handsomer.

The notion so pleased him that he did not notice Harry's horror and only Valentine's present dragged him back to reality. It was a smart and rather worn vintage vulcanised-rubber rugby ball, and with it, Corny wanted to score a try directly, but frustratingly, Izzy's panic at the idea hindered the ambition.

Gubsy bit into a Grand Marnier chocolate liqueur, wielded a fleshy fist at Corny, and boomed, 'Use my mantelshelf for a crossbar, and my own grandfather's portrait for posts, will you? You young ruffian!' and, despite the sticky liquid drooling comically from his lower lip, Gubsy became a vision of fury.

Corny shook his head vigorously; he most certainly would *not* kick a rugby ball at Excelsior!

Gubsy's colouring became beetroot and he burst into thunderous laughter. He demanded that Gretchen give Corny the last sizeable box beneath the tree. The theme of sport now reached its climax with Corny's receipt of Gubsy's very own boxing gloves from when he was a boy and believed a formidable opponent.

Now sporting boxing gloves that inspired him to rip-roaringly jump about the drawing room, Corny socked the air like a hyperactive leveret, causing Izzy to shriek with disturbance; she truly considered Corny an unruly lunatic, and he scared her witless. She pulled her feet up onto the chesterfield and pressed against Harry.

Everyone else thought Corny's excitement amusing (though Olivia did caution his proximity to the candlelit tree) and a gratified Gubsy boomed, 'By Jove! I knew the strapper was a natural! Look at him go! Fluid and powerful!'

Then he informed the family that the gloves, though, of course, a gift, were only symbolic of the real one, which was a fully paid membership to a local boxing club where Corny could hone his skills.

Upon hearing this, the angelic pugilist ceased to jump and sock. Exhilarated and perspiring, he regarded Gubsy, and cast him a stupendous smile. It was an excellent present! And, with that, he set about punching Rupert's proffered palms.

The exertion between Valentine's favourite boys sounded a satisfying *Paf! Paf! Paf!* It pleased him and he was happy until viewing the meagre remains beneath the tree; only a few presents lingered. He made a moue, and crawled over to tut at them.

'Gosh!' he said, disappointedly, as he perused the labels, 'Only Willy's are left; how sad!'

Presently, the paffing stopped, and Rupert replied, in an unsuccessfully blasé tone, 'Perhaps if you look closely you'll find one more.'

Despite deeming it otiose, Valentine humoured him, and splayed the paltry remains about the tree's tripod. Then, on the verge of another tut, he spied, through the density of the bottommost boughs, a bright yellow bow. Upon further investigation, he discovered that the bow decorated a square box of the same colour. He reached out, withdrew it and gasped because the label said *'To Valentine, love from Rupert.'*

'Gosh!' he exclaimed, 'It's for me everybody!' Then he looked to Rupert, 'And it is yellow!'

Rupert laughed, 'That's just the outside. Why don't you open it?' and he crawled across the Axminster so better to view Valentine's opening.

Corny was just as captivated by the moment and hunkered next to him; he hoped that Valentine was to receive something at least as first-class as boxing gloves!

'Don't just stare at it, Valentine!' said Olivia, impatiently, 'Do as Rupert says!'

And she agitated her ivory for she surmised the ultimate gift significant.

Ceremoniously, Valentine pulled the ribbon, and, solemnly, he lifted the box lid from its base. Inside was a violet coloured cloth. Breathlessly, he unfolded it, and, consequently, swayed and gasped at the romantic shock.

Then, in the style of an exalted angel singing *hallelujah!*, he cried out, 'A tiara!'

Reverently, he held it up high and gasped again at the glorious sparkle of amethysts that created muddled posies of violets with silver foliage as shimmering as intense moonlight.

He managed to avert his eyes from the tiara to regard the possessor of even greater beauty, Rupert, who smilingly returned his gaze and, in that perfect moment, seemed to Valentine, to beam brighter than the sun might ever dare to dream. Giddiness claimed Valentine and he descended upon Rupert in a rush of romantic appreciation that rendered them recumbent on the Axminster, where, quite cavalier to their company, they showed that they were sweethearts.

Though bemused by his brother's excitement over something a princess might wear, Corny was thrilled to see it and he thought Rupert increasingly excellent. He proceeded to jump with joy until Olivia asked to see the tiara, whereupon he endeavoured to pick it up from the floor but was unable due to the gaucherie of his gloves.

Therefore, Harry handed it to her, and said, '*W*eally a b*w*illiant tia*w*a, *W*upert! You're ve*w*y lucky, Valentine!'

The sweethearts looked up at Harry. Rupert grinned and thanked him, and Valentine replied, 'Gosh! Kismet, Harry! *Not* luck!'

Olivia scrutinised the tiara as if questioning its quality but that was not her reason, rather, it was to admire its artistry and, moreover, to revel in the patent proof that Rupert possessed commendable means, despite his predilection for manual labour, and was not shy of spending it on Valentine. Further, with its presentation, Rupert demonstrated his indubitable love for him.

Olivia smiled at Valentine.

'Darling, it is divine, but please do let me see how it becomes you,' she said, and passed it to him.

Valentine clasped it to his chest and removed his paper crown. He looked to Rupert, and because he knew that one might only really wear a tiara when one possessed a husband, he tentatively asked, 'May I?'

Rupert smiled at the endearing query.

'Crikey! Of course; it's what it's for!'

With that, Rupert took the tiara, and respectfully coronated the bowed head of Valentine whose imagination correspondingly filled with the famous march of Mendelssohn.

Valentine raised his face, and flush with blissfulness, he beamed at his betrothed. 'Gosh! Glorious!' he said, breathily; he required no looking glass to realise how well the tiara became him.

'Verily,' said Rupert, and then he kissed him.

'How ni*the*!' said Izzy at the romance, and she blushed with happiness.

'Hear, hear!' Gubsy boomed, because though he thought the tiared boy a perfect sissy, he put him in mind of his equally sissy brother Maximilian.

All presents given, except Willy's spattering, everyone was exhausted and pleased with their new possessions, whether it be a tablecloth, tiara, rugby ball or scent. They now looked to the dwindling candles that, with the spiky boughs, cast arachnidan shadows upon the flawless ceiling.

The dozing Dalmatians under the Steinway, the crackling fire and the ormolu clock's languid internals, made the only sounds. Doubtlessly, the clock's extremities were inaccurate, yet Olivia deemed the moment ripe for the Christmas speech, which, since Monty's departure, was her duty, at least until next year when Harry really ought to, because of Benedictus. This would be Olivia's final time, and despite her torpor, she would correctly deliver it before the candle wax melted and electricity was necessary.

Accordingly, she touched tenderly the thirty-one week old mound, before raising her arms. She shook them to excite her ivory, thus making a sound quite skeletal, and to the room, she regally said, 'I request succour so to elevate!'

Corny rushed to promote her. Proudly, he watched her imperious advance toward the fire to stand before Excelsior.

Olivia clutched her diamonds, caressed the heir, and with a commanding veneer, she cast her glassy-green eyes over her people, coughed genteelly, nasally inhaled, and began: '*Mille noveni centum sex et nonaginta* has been a tremendously turbulent *annus* for the Avery-Stripes, but I am happy to say *ordo ab chao!*'

Here, she condescendingly translated for Izzy (disturbed by the Latin word for six), 'Out of chaos comes order!'

Then, Olivia placed both hands over Benedictus, and faced her external progenies, Gubsy and the Apollonian.

'A most providential order, for the imminence of Benedictus perpetuates the duteous destiny of the family, therefore I christen this year *annus mirabilis!*'

'Hooray!' Valentine cheered, and Corny looked jubilant despite not knowing what all of Olivia's words meant.

Now, she exhibited her palms in an effort to appear humble.

'I insist that I receive no reverence for simply serving my station! My only wish is that we give thought to those whom are not present; oceanic Willy for one, and naturally, my much missed Monty . . . '

Momentarily, she faltered and blinked back her tears.

To scaffold his mother, Valentine exclaimed, 'Gosh, mummy! I feel daddy daily!'

The sentiment strengthened Olivia, and she persevered.

'We must also give praise to our nonpareil patriarch for our Christmas Day of such wondrous and felicitous revelations!'

With that, she stood in profile and looked up at Excelsior with veneration.

'Hear, hear!' boomed Gubsy, whereupon everyone respected the Christmas tradition of the minute's silent regard of the Avery-Stripe supreme whilst he hubristically sneered down at them all.

Then, just as Olivia considered the cruel curl of Excelsior's lips that furnished also Cosmo's countenance, and she wondered if Benedictus might inherit it, the peal of the front doorbell broke the deferential silence.

As if the peal caused an ancient curse to suddenly come to pass, all those present froze; Olivia's pose petrified with the abysmal realisation that a person possessed the effrontery to call uninvited. Certainly, she would not deign to discover the reprobate's identity, and she chose to believe it an urchin playing the game knock-down ginger.

A moment passed.

Olivia snapped her neck with annoyance, gathered her equipoise, and resumed, 'Felicitous revelations . . . '

Again, the bell interrupted.

This time it was relentless. The family could no longer ignore it; the Dalmatians lifted their heads, even Remarkable opened an eye.

Forming small fists, Olivia brandished them before her enraged face, cursed crudely, and demanded that Harry, 'Ascertain the dastard's identity! Inform him of my utmost disgust at his impropriety, and see him on his way, violently!'

Harry would be obedient – at least partially.

He rose, and replied, 'All *w*ight, mummy, but I won't be *w*ude; it might be a hung*w*y vag*w*ant.'

His theory made Izzy gasp with horror, and Valentine exclaimed, 'Give him Brussels sprouts!'

'Make haste, Horatio!' Olivia snapped, and covered her ears, for the adamant peal was punishing.

Therefore, Harry hastened from the drawing room, and Valentine, obeying Olivia's next command, closed the door, and put his eye to the keyhole to view the villain undetected.

'Not a whisper!' Olivia hissed at the room.

Corny nodded to display his compliance; he would not say a word, and he hugged his rugby ball.

Valentine aligned his sight with the keyhole, but not so close to the door as to touch its knob with his tiara. He watched Harry open the front door, and a wisp of wintry air stung his eyeball.

He winced, blinked, and whispered, '*Ouch*!'

'*Shh*! Who is it?' Olivia hissed, whilst rubbing Benedictus for comfort.

'I cannot see!' Valentine returned, 'Harry is an obstacle! Gosh! Whomever it is, is now embracing him, *and* she has chipped nail varnish!' and he sounded a tut.

Izzy became upset at the idea of a strange woman embracing her husband, and was about to weep when Valentine jumped up, and whispered, 'Gosh! It's Flick! And Harry's permitting entry! Quickly! Quickly!' he said to his mother and Izzy, 'Into the dining room!'

Olivia immediately understood the need to hide. Yet Izzy was not so sharp, and asked why she should do such a thing.

'Because,' snarled Olivia, snatching the girl's wrist, and forcing her to her feet, 'You are patently *un*-pregnant!'

Presently, Izzy experienced enlightenment, and the Mmes Avery-Stripes fled into the dining room, closing the double doors behind them.

Their exit was timely for just as the doors to the dining room shut, Harry opened the door to the drawing room. Eerily, each Christmas tree candle simultaneously expired because of a gust that entered through the suddenly open conservatory doors; someone had escaped to the garden. In their rush, they had abandoned a rugby ball, and it bounced beneath the Steinway to nestle amongst the now only slightly disturbed Dalmatians.

But for the moderate blaze in the fireplace, the drawing room was pitch-dark. Then Harry flicked a switch and there was light – horrid and unflattering electric light. It was most unkind to Flick, though, to be fair, she seemed not to have made much of an effort to look comely on Christmas day anyway. Her hair was dramatically wild, that is to say, more so than usual, and her mascara was haphazardly streaked across her dissipated and impish face. She wore a shabby wax Barbour jacket, six-sizes-too-large, and mud-encrusted wellingtons.

In short, she looked wretched, and she was sniffing and shivering so demonstrably that her bravado's only hope of disguising it was ambitious. She viewed the drawing room decked so festively, the wrapping paper debris, the opulent tree and stacks of new possessions, and trying hard to look happy, she said to Valentine, '*Dahling*! Super to see you! Love the tiara!' then she spluttered, and burst into tears very loudly.

Uncertain how to handle the outburst, Valentine said, 'Gosh!' Rupert said, 'Crikey!' Harry rubbed his boxed beard, and said, 'C*ww*umbs!' And Gubsy boomed, 'What the Deuce!' because he thought the exhibition to be plain bad behaviour.

Fortunately, Gretchen ministered to the miserable girl. She enveloped her, and said, 'Miss Flick! Do not be cryink! Today is Christmas Day and you are with family!'

Whilst she stroked Flick's untidy hair (with difficulty, as it was terribly knotty) Valentine, Rupert and Harry looked uncomfortable until told to 'Ket a klass of brandy.'

Whereupon, Harry went to the globe drinks' cabinet, Gubsy gnashed and Remarkable ruffled his plumage.

The drink fixed, Gretchen placated Flick and eased her upon the chesterfield with the Indian quilt. She successfully divested her of the wellingtons but could not persuade her to remove the Barbour.

Sipping the brandy, Flick smiled sheepishly and regarded those that regarded her, which was everyone.

'I'm so sorry to ruin your day,' she said to them.

Harry and Rupert politely argued and insisted that it was super to see her too, and then no one said anything and felt dreadfully awkward.

Exasperated, Valentine sensed a foreboding, and because his mother should not be hiding, he determined to find the underlying cause of it before suggesting that Gretchen put Flick to bed.

'Gosh! I say Flick, I do so love that you always make a spectacular entrance and never fail to attend an important occasion!' he said, excitedly.

The flattery pleased Flick. She could not fight a smile.

'Oh, *dahling*! You know I only do it to give people something to talk about! Their lives would be so dreary otherwise!'

Valentine laughed, extracted a cigarette, offered her one which she declined, and expelling lavender smoke, he drew close to her.

'So, what's the latest? Or should I ask whom?'

Flick's smile now faded, and she made a little frown.

'Did I tell you about my Wall Street banker?'

'You might've mentioned him at The Marvellous Party but I don't recall his name.'

The frown became more prominent.

'Eric. He was called Eric.'

'Gosh! Much too dreary for you!' said Valentine, 'I don't wonder that you bolted, or did you simply ditch? Which was it? And is that why you are here now?'

Flick lowered her glass and creased her face. She shuddered before tearlessly sobbing. 'Oh, *dahling*! I'm in such a jam! I didn't love Eric at all; I didn't even like him very much! Oh! He was a beastly bore! And that idiotic Texan twang! He spoke like a cartoon! But I needed him, he was going to take care of me; he was so rich you see, and still is, I mean; that hasn't changed. Only everything else has, since this morning, I mean!'

And her sobbing persisted.

Many questions hurtled through Valentine's mind; he was not sure which to voice and those to avoid. He looked to Harry to see if he might know what to say, but upon seeing his flummoxed face, he realised the notion futile. Rupert's fixed smile, though still beautiful, was equally useless, Gubsy seemed able only to gnash, and Gretchen looked on concernedly.

Luckily, Flick elaborated on her own accord: 'This morning was wonderful, well, quite, if one assumed that I loved him and didn't think him just a kind and rich fool, but then, suddenly, at breakfast, I noticed his friend's cigarettes, had a recollection and *everything* turned upside-down, well, right-side-up really, and I had to tell Eric the truth. He was not cross, just sad, and so I had to leave. I didn't say goodbye, except a note; I wrote; '*Goodbye. PS thank you and sorry.*' I couldn't find my coat or shoes by the door so I took this,' here, she stroked the Barbour, 'It's his, and his wellingtons; they are so big; it's not true what they say about feet because he was practically an acorn!'

She grimaced at Valentine and he tutted.

'I knew that I had to come here but I didn't want to ruin your day so I've been wandering around until I thought it was a suitable time to call and tell all, but now I'm here, I'm scared stiff!'

Directly on the other side of the double doors, the Mmes Avery-Stripes listened intently. Flick's obviously upset tone induced Izzy's eyes to well, she pressed her fingertips to her lips, and her tip-tilted nose twitched sympathetically. Olivia, little more than the distance of a breath from Izzy, scowled to signal she had better keep quiet and not cry.

Olivia was furious with Flick for her dramatics, intrusion and ramblings.

'Just bite the bullet and spit it out, darling!' she wished to scream, but though she held her tongue she was uncertain how much more of Izzy's feebleness she could tolerate.

Then, as if her thoughts had telepathically travelled, she heard Valentine say, 'Gosh, Flick! Do stop rambling and bite the bullet!'

There followed no words, only a minute of silence, except for a metallic jangle of bangles, then came gasps, and Valentine exclaimed 'Gosh! You kept that well hidden!'

Olivia's feeling of frustration furthered.

Before the Steinway stood Flick, the shed Barbour in a heap at her feet revealed her heightened resemblance to a pygmy-hippopotamus: she was fubsier than she had ever hitherto been, and it was obvious that her engorged belly was not so because of gorging but because she was in the family way.

'C*w*umbs!' said Harry, and Rupert said, 'Crikey!'

Gubsy could not determine the cause of the exclamations other than Felicity Oxley-Stockman was demonstrating increasingly bad manners by disrobing in his drawing room.

'You think Gretchen's here just to pick up after you, do you, *eh?*' he said to Flick with a gnash and she bawled.

Again, Gretchen stepped in, collected the Barbour, and folded it over her arm.

'I do not mind to pick up for Miss Flick, Mr Bartholmoo,' she said, and returned Flick to the chesterfield to care for her, but not with brandy. 'I think you must not,' she said to the thirsty girl and caused her to pout.

'Gosh! Well, this is a coincidence!' said Valentine, stupidly, and then he tutted in spite of himself.

Flick quietened. Looked to him with puzzlement, and asked, 'Golly! What do you mean?'

'Gosh, truly nothing!' he responded, but Rupert endeavoured to rescue him anyway.

Hunkering, he put Flick's hands between his own, and, enthusiastically, said, 'But isn't it amazing? I mean, shouldn't we be saying congratulations?'

'Gosh! Yes, let's have champagne!' exclaimed Valentine, and Gretchen disappeared to get some.

Now, Harry joined in, 'Yes, *w*eally, Flick, cong*w*atulations! I'll expect your pa*w*ents are t*w*emendously happy!'

'Golly! No, they are *not*! They do not even know! They must not ever!' said a suddenly sober Flick, and she hoped that Valentine's order of champagne was forthcoming.

'*W*eally? Why not?' said Harry, and sat upon the ottoman as if to ponder it, 'Don't they care for E*w*ic?'

Flick began to look furious.

'I thought I made it perfectly clear that it has nothing to do with Eric! It happened before I even knew him that way, in fact! And that's what I couldn't understand but I couldn't tell him that because what else could I do? I didn't realise until it was too late to be anything but horribly messy, but then when I saw his friend's packet of cigarettes on the breakfast table I had a recollection that explained everything!'

Whereupon, she looked at them all with the idea that they understood the explanation but their confused faces expressed quite the contrary.

'A packet of cigarettes explained everything?' said Valentine, in a sceptical tone, and he wondered if Flick had been drinking when she really ought not, 'How could they?'

Presently, Flick was cognisant of her lack of clarity, therefore, she magnified her meaning: 'A packet of American Spirit!'

Harry rubbed his beard but it did not encourage insight.

Gubsy gnashed, and wished that Gretchen would come with champagne.

'Never heard of them!' said Valentine, now tiring and made Flick moan.

'I know them!' said Rupert, as if amazed at his knowledge, 'Lots of Americans smoke them, and I noticed that in America.'

'Gosh! Amazing!' said Valentine, coolly but not cruelly.

'Yes,' Rupert went on, 'They have a Red Indian chief in his headdress on them!'

'Exactly!' said Flick with grateful relief, 'That is what gave me my explanatory recollection! I thought it only fair I tell you all because it's not just my jam; it's just as much your jam, and I've no clue what to do!'

Suddenly, Valentine grasped Flick's gist, and his initial reaction was incredulity at the notion that little Corny was the cause of the jam. Yet who else did they know that wore a war bonnet? Valentine was unaware of any connexion with a bona fide Native American.

'Gosh! *Really not!*' Valentine cried.

'I couldn't be surer!' Flick returned, 'I remember it quite vividly, snatches of it anyway, and contrary to the rumours, I'm not the nympho that I make out to be, but please don't tell!'

'But when?' Valentine asked, then he answered his own question, 'The Marvellous Party!'

Flick nodded, and elaborated: 'In the tree house. Not long after the fireworks. I was hiding from my parents and some scene they were making.'

Concurrently, Gretchen entered from the hall with a magnum and flutes rattling upon the squeaky tea wagon as Corny capered in from the garden. Cushioned between his gloves was a pair of yellow high heels.

His halo was askew, and his wide smile vanished when Harry looked to him, and in a disapproving tone, said, '*W*ascal! You *w*ascal!'

And Valentine exclaimed the hyperbole, 'Naughty bounder!'

But Gubsy disagreed with the boys, he was elated that at least one of the litter would faithfully continue the bloodline, and he bellowed, 'Young'un's not a rascal or a bounder! He's a much needed breeder! Hats off to you m'boy!' and he laughed so violently that the touching flutes upon the tea wagon tinkled.

The reception puzzled Corny. He wondered what had happened in his short absence. He had only run out to the garden to climb up to the tree house and retrieve, from a box beneath the bed, the shoes Flick forgot to take the morning after The Marvellous Party.

He had felt quite sad upon waking in the tree and discovering her no longer there. They had had such fun together in the night, tickling and wrestling, as he recalled, though it *was* a bit of a blur because he was fairly drunk at the time, and it *had* been rather dark, but he remembered the wrestling because it had culminated in a strange and exciting physical sensation that he had not ever before experienced.

For this reason, he considered Flick an excellent playmate, and he hated that the only Christmas present he could give her were her own shoes. He knew it was not very generous, yet he thought his brothers' accusations of rascalliness and naughty bounderdom somewhat harsh. He could not see that they had anything better to give her!

But what was this? Flick's tummy was as big as mummy's! Was it for the same reason? What was a breeder? And why was it so very good and funny?

Corny was glad when, suddenly, the double doors to the dining room dramatically divided, and Olivia appeared, even if she did look as if she might murder Flick.

Confused, he dropped shoes and took his mummy's proffered hand – awkwardly, because of his ungainly gloves – and he wondered the reason for her rage.

Naturally, Olivia was incensed that a second Oxley-Stockman had tarnished the Avery-Stripe polish. It was true that she possessed a soft spot for Flick but it did not permit Flick to pluck the cherry of her mini-Monty! Further, even if Flick's allegation transpired to be fiction it did not lessen her transparent desire for a minor.

Olivia clutched Corny's glove tightly, and close to lacerated the stuffed vintage leather with her nails, she pulled his blond head to her breast, thus divesting him of his halo that fell to the floor.

At Flick, she screamed, 'You wicked and wanton little wench! Have you no integrity? Is to you, a small boy nothing but easy prey for your degenerate designs? I've a perfect mind to telephone a policeman!'

From behind Olivia, Izzy's terrified form emerged; she ran to her husband, and collapsed in his arms. The trials of the day were proving far too trying upon her fragile sensibilities.

'Oh, Harry!' she cried, '*Th*ay *th*omething!' and, with weeping eyes, she peeked out at Flick over his shoulder.

'*Cw*umbs, mummy!' said Harry, summoning his mettle, '*Tw*y to *w*elax!'

'Relax!' Olivia snapped, and turned her furious glare at him, 'Darling, I shall relax only when Felicity confesses her spurious claim against chaste Cornelius!'

Once again, Olivia beheld Flick in her enraged gaze.

Flick was unaccustomed to her aunt's anger. At first she stammered, but then, because she was not fabricating, she met her head-on, though she looked with confusion at Olivia's own evident jam that Corny cradled, and, courageously, she replied, 'It's perfectly true, Auntie O, I wouldn't make up such a thing, though I cannot think of a finer family to be in the jam with!'

This was a clever thing to say because it mollified Olivia quite neatly.

Valentine took stock; he did not deem the situation so hopelessly dire; indeed, if the allegation proved accurate then surely the solution was obvious and cause for jubilation – after all, Gubsy seemed to think so.

Thus, with a tut, Valentine rose, and endeavoured upon an untangling of the jam.

Precise or no, the large hand of the ormolu clock travelled only a third of its face, and chimed but one quarter by the time the Avery-Stripes, and their addendums, cracked open the magnum to toast their amended harmony.

Delicately, Valentine had asked Corny if Flick's claim carried veracity. The response was a look of abject bewilderment. Therefore, with a biology book, Valentine employed its stark illustrations to discover if it might produce an illumination.

Once educated, Corny indicated that he could indeed be the maker of the jam. He was happy about this because he liked both jam and babies. Moreover, now that he knew of the fun in making both, why, he just might make lots, especially since Valentine said that he was old enough to do so, yet, much to his surprise, his mummy seemed not to care for too much jam, but she did agree that he was a big boy now.

'Certainly is!' said Flick, putting on her yellow heels that she was glad not to have lost in a cab as she had feared, 'He's twice the size he was in the summer; not that I could call him exactly small even then!' and she pulled a mischievous face.

Valentine ignored the vulgarity, and went on to ascertain Flick's want of the baby.

Flick replied that since the realisation of Corny's part in the creation, she could not pretend to Eric and that the truth had caused him to lose interest, therefore, without his support she was utterly reliant on her allowance from her parents which would undoubtedly cease if they knew of the jam.

'And so I was wondering,' she said, gingerly, 'if you might have an interest in it, and not tell my family?'

Consequently, it was decreed that the Avery-Stripes would be noble and take the baby with the promise not to tell her family on the condition that she did not either unveil to them Olivia's gravidity created by a peerless dignitary.

Flick vehemently agreed and clapped her hands with the news that because Corny was too unworldly for parenting, Harry and Izzy would rear the child just as if it were their own. (After all, they were to raise Harry's impending brother, therefore, it would not hurt to rear also his other brother's issue.)

Corny was thrilled; his baby would live next door with Harry and Benedictus; he would see them everyday!

Izzy was also delighted. Not so long ago, she had been lonely, but for her dolls, cats and bears, and possessed no hope of a child. Now she had a husband and, because of him, was on the brink of having two babies! Oh, she *did* hope the second was a little girl, and she inquired if it might be.

Presently, Flick's excitement over her exoneration simmered down a degree, and she admitted, 'Both, actually, *dahling!*'

'Gosh! An hermaphrodite!' Valentine exclaimed.

Harry became confused. He would gladly receive Corny's baby but felt it important to know its gender; he was unaware of the third variety.

'Hermaph*w*odite?' he asked, anxiously, whereupon his mind warped at Valentine's reply, yet it cushioned him for Flick's as she revealed that it was not at all hermaphrodite but Geminian.

Izzy close to fainted at the revelation, especially upon learning that the twins were one of each; she *was* to have a little girl, as well as two little boys!

Both Harry and Rupert supported Izzy, for she edged on wild deliria, and then when Corny indicated that Harry and Izzy ought to decide the names, if Valentine did not mind because he had named Benedictus, she wept rivers of undiluted joy, and thought Corny the very sweetest boy in the world!

Olivia narrowed her eyes at Izzy. She was uncertain her choice of names would sit well with her, and she would not stand for inappropriate ones. They must be suitable for the family; it was all very well that the Avery-Stripe number was escalating, but without the honour of tradition, it counted for next to nothing because *noblesse oblige* was everything.

'You do realise, don't you, darling,' Olivia said to Izzy, 'the imperativeness that the names consist of four syllables?'

Her eyes as wide as her mother-in-law's were narrow, giddily tipsy Izzy replied, 'Why, of cour*the* I do! *Thi*lly old *thauth*age!' and she stroked Olivia's cheek before turning to kiss her husband beneath a spray of mistletoe.

But for the flinching of a nerve in the cheek the chit had dared to touch, Olivia froze and felt the desire to handle her in the manner that a ravenous cheetah would a delectable impala. Yet upon the ignition of forty-eight fresh candles on the tree, and Valentine's excited suggestion, 'Gosh, everybody! Let's play dumb crambo!' she cast her crocodilian smile most effectively.

Hours later, the candles had melted, Harry and Izzy had departed for Bath, Gretchen was walking the Dalmatians, Flick was asleep in Willy's bedroom, where she would reside until the twins' nativity, Corny was in the four-poster, and Rupert reposed upon the violet scented lion skin in the turret. Olivia and Valentine lounged upon the chesterfield in the dimly lit drawing room, and Gubsy sat snoring in his wing chair.

'Blow it in my face, darling!' said Olivia of her son's smoke; she had requested that he have a cigarette in her company for she wished to enjoy one, even if only passively, as the events of the day had enervated her sorely.

Valentine obliged with a cloud of it and she inhaled deeply.

'Gosh, mummy!' he said, sensing her tension, 'I've no inkling as to why you're so peevish! Not only did you get a cheque that certainly made you smile, but Corny's sired two bastards, both of whom carry double doses of Excelsiorian blood. You ought to be euphoric; in fact, I'm surprised you're not thumping out anthems of victory on the piano!'

Olivia grimaced at his facetiousness, tightened her kimono, and shut her eyes so to better savour the smoke.

She had not considered that: the twins really were of the loins of two of Excelsior's descendants. It was quite fantastic, and she was certain that Monty would be overjoyed, despite the ignoble production. Nevertheless, one thing bothered her; their existence must not lessen the imminence of Bonny little Benny. He was the heir. The continuation of the line would fall to him. She refused to be delivering another spare, and though she calculated, that unless the geminian bastards were premature like their father, Benedictus would be first-born, it did not wholly eradicate her anxiety.

She lifted her lids, rose to ascend the stairwell and retire, and she said, to her primary spare, 'I suppose I have always had faith that Flick would one day serve a practical function.'

Valentine laughed, and exclaimed, 'Gosh, mummy! Such charity!' and he extinguished his cigarette before accompanying her.

Beneath the bison, Olivia said to him, 'But I do debate the manner of mother Izzy might make; she's wetter than a week in Wales!'

Again, Valentine laughed.

'I shouldn't worry, mummy, they'll only be next door; close enough for scrupulous surveillance, yet enough of a distance to be decent!' whereupon, he kissed her goodnight by Olympia's harp, 'Merry Christmas, mummy!'

'Yes, Merry Christmas, darling,' she replied with a wry smile at his thought process, then she shut herself away in her bedroom.

She looked to Monty's side of the bed where slept the very spit of him. He looked angelic, and not simply because he had on his halo. She lost her kimono but kept her diamond mine, and slipped in beside him.

Corny woke and he claimed her. Sleepily, he beamed at her.

Olivia returned the look, and softly said, 'Did you have a lovely day, darling?'

Corny nodded drowsily.

'I am glad, darling, you deserve it; such fine presents, and, moreover, for furthering the family. I am most ecstatic, as would daddy be. Goodnight my jammy little dodger.'

She kissed his bruised brow, and whilst stroking his fair tufts she watched him drift, most exquisitely, off to the land of nod.

As he floated, Corny gently smiled with the sudden understanding of his role; for what else was a jammy little dodger to do other than make jam?

CHAPTER 28

Valentine's Heart

The grey days that so often seemed to succeed Christmas Day were, to Valentine's mind and heart, idyllic. He refused to remove his tiara except to admire it nestled in Rupert's golden curls for he too would soon be married.

Rupert need only pop the apposite question to cast the die, and Valentine was dizzy with anticipation.

He became dizzier still whilst dancing to the melody of *My Funny Valentine* upon the gramophone he had had Rupert elevate to the turret. They played the vinyl on a loop and cavorted to it so passionately that, naturally, quite accidentally, they would trip and fall, as if in a glide, and wherever their crashing descent landed them they would ardently tussle with wild abandon.

Other times, they would simply sprawl across the expanse of lion hide, their limbs intertwined, and regard one another with earnest affection, silent but for their fervent palpitations and ardent panting.

On the ultimate day of the year, Valentine, with his tiaraed head rested upon the maned one, looked to Rupert, propped on an elbow and teasing his toes with the tassel of the beast's tail, and he said to him, 'Gosh!'

Rupert ceased tickling, corrugated his brow, produced a magnificent grin, and asked, 'Don't you like the feeling?' whilst waggling the tail tassel.

'Gosh! It's glorious!' Valentine exclaimed, and ran his fingertips over the leonine welts upon Rupert's bare chest as the tickling recommenced, 'I was just thinking how much I do truly love my tiara!'

Rupert eyed him happily, and still pleasuring Valentine's toes, replied, 'Good, I'm glad. I love the tablecloth too! Thank you very much!'

'Gosh! We shall use it lots; it has lots of meaning, just like the tiara has lots of meaning too. Doesn't it?'

'Crikey!' said Rupert, as if he would be quite disturbed to learn anything to the contrary, 'It has lots of meaning!'

Tickled pink by the response, Valentine's heart fluttered, but then he realised that his throat felt a touch dry.

'Gosh! My throat feels to be quite desiccated!'

Whereupon, Rupert readily rose to hasten to the kitchen to mix a shaker of Grasshopper.

'Thanks ever so very much!' said Valentine, and he spread to conquer the freshly vacated area of lion hide, 'It is so very blissful to survive, since Christmas Day, on mostly Grasshopper and violet creams!'

Rupert put on some jeans and grinned down at his funny Valentine.

'I'll be back in a jiffy!' he said, and then departed with the salver of geisha crockery.

Valentine smiled into space for a flash, and luxuriated in the comprehension that he and Rupert would soon be as one. He enjoyed the sensation of goose pimples upon his skin and the tingle down his spine so intense that it persuaded him to writhe on the hide.

Then he sat up, extracted a cigarette from his silver case and lighted it. It was lovely. To heighten the pleasure he put a violet cream in his mouth. The combination of nicotine and violet made his taste buds ache with pleasure, and he laughed as he exhaled.

Though still spinning, the vinyl had ended, but because the gramophone was beyond his reach, Valentine satisfied his wish for a tune to blanket the distant ring of the beastly telephone by utilising his music box. The tinny chimes sounding *The Dance of the Sugar Plum Fairy* never failed to please him, and now he rolled onto his front to admire, in his ferro, his beautiful violet and silver tiara.

He lost himself in a maze of musings, concerning such things as stiffies and church bells, flower girls and page boys, vows – romantic yet solemn, tossing the bouquet and the theatrical exit for an exotic honeymoon. His imagination filled with flamingos and palm trees, and that was when Rupert returned. Never before had Valentine seen him look so miserable, in fact, Rupert's beaming smile was topsy-turvy.

'Gosh! Whatever is it? What has happened?'

Rupert did not answer and neither did he look at him. Rather, he behaved as if he was alone. He placed the salver upon the lion hide, sat down silently, and, from the teapot, poured Grasshopper up to the brim of a teacup. Now he looked at Valentine, passed him the cocktail, and told him to drink it.

In an agony of anxiety, Valentine correctly supposed that he was to swallow every drop because, for some reason, Rupert required him to possess a nerve of steel.

Yet presently he deemed himself a fool for fearing something wretched, for quite patently the moment of the marriage proposal had come and Rupert was upset because of butterflies.

Quickly, Valentine swallowed his Grasshopper, placed the empty cup back into its saucer with a *clink*, and looked to Rupert with happy expectation.

Rupert reached out for Valentine's hands, rubbed them tenderly, and, with his forget-me-not blue eyes teeming with momentousness, he softly said, 'Valentine, I've got to go.'

It was not at all what Rupert was supposed to say! Valentine could not accept the statement. The words sucked him into a vacuum, and he viewed a distorted reality, Rupert and his bedroom, as if through a tunnel; quite like he suddenly inhabited a parallel galaxy – a place where he was wholly inarticulate.

'Valentine?' said Rupert, concernedly, 'Valentine, please say something.' and he squeezed his hands firmly.

Valentine closed his eyes for a space.

Upon opening them, he smiled delightedly, and exclaimed, 'Gosh! I'll go with you!'

Rupert pulled an expression that signalled discomfort.

'You can't,' he said, mournfully, 'Sorry.'

Never fond of having his wishes denied, Valentine withdrew, and, in a petulant tone, replied, 'I'd like to know why not! And anyway, where and when?'

'Australia. Right away; the first flight possible,' Rupert replied with effort, because he was having difficulty accepting the truth of it.

Valentine decided that Rupert had not said that he could not go with him and had actually invited him because, whilst not yet married, they could still have a glorious adventure in the outback together!

'Gosh! I've never been there!' Valentine said, 'I should love to watch kangaroos jumping, hear the laugh of a kookaburra and learn what wombats do, but you will protect me from the fennel-webs won't you? Gosh! This impulsiveness is rather intrepid! I like it! I should love to go, thank you! But why so unexpectedly?'

Awkwardly, Rupert explained: 'Izzy just called to tell me that Nicole called her, because she doesn't know where I am. My dad had a stroke, he's in hospital, quite a bad one, heart attack, I mean. So I've got to go today.'

Rupert grimaced as the cold reality of the situation sunk in further.

The expression pulled at Valentine's heartstrings; he knew just what it was to lose one's daddy, and he felt terribly sorry for someone who nearly had, or was just about to.

He flung his arms about Rupert's neck, and kissing his golden hair, he said, 'Don't worry! Your father will be fine; I just know it!'

Rupert's strong body convulsed; he held Valentine close, and mumbled something miserable into his neck.

In that pose the two remained, saying not a thing, for some minutes. Then Valentine leapt up and dived beneath his bed in search of his valise. He found it, opened it on the lion hide, and put into it three pairs of pyjamas and his new flacon of violet scent. Rupert dried his eyes and watched him.

'What are you doing?' he asked, uneasily.

'Gosh! I'm packing!' Valentine replied, adding his geisha teacup and saucer to his valise and closing it. 'I've packed! So must you! Quickly! We must hurry!'

Rupert regarded him with apologetic eyes. He rubbed the back of his head, and, tentatively, said, 'Valentine, you really can't come with me. I have to go alone.'

'Why do you keep saying that?' Valentine demanded to know, 'I'll pay my own passage, mummy or Gubsy will give me the money,' whereupon, he shuddered at the horror of discussing currency.

Corrugating his brow, Rupert told him that it was nothing to do with money, that he would gladly pay for his passage but, and this he painfully, yet firmly, reiterated, he must go to his father alone.

Rupert now pulled out his rucksack, that since his arrival from Africa had lived alongside Valentine's valise, he gathered his strewn clothes and pushed them into it with great concentration.

'But why? Don't you think your father would like me?' Valentine asked, following Rupert about the turret, 'I'm certain he really would! My daddy loved me intensely and I know I'd cheer yours right up!'

Rupert stopped and viewed Valentine, almost angrily.

'You would not cheer my father up, he'd think you very queer; it'd probably give him a heart attack if I turned up with you!'

The harshness of Rupert's tone hurt Valentine quite as much as the information and he watched, in stunned silence, as Rupert looked for his passport.

'Why might Rupert's father think me very queer?' Valentine wondered. It saddened him that the man might not be an agreeable sort, but he supposed he never truly expected anything very much from a person devoid of Avery-Stripe blood.

Yet, one thing he must make clear: 'Gosh! Well, queer or no, he must agree to be cordial to me at the wedding, otherwise I'm quite certain he will not get a glorious stiffy, and, therefore, shall be unable to come!'

Suddenly, the location of his passport seemed insignificant to Rupert, he turned to Valentine, sitting upon the bed; the perfect picture of obstinacy.

Rupert dreaded what Valentine meant, and feared his supposition right, but to clarify, he asked, 'What wedding?'

'Why, ours, of course!' exclaimed Valentine, with incredulity at the question, yet, upon regarding Rupert's reaction, he wondered if he might have been a touch assumptive. 'That is why you gave me the tiara, isn't it? I mean, as a preamble to your proposal, because one can't wear a tiara without a husband, can they?'

With each word, Valentine faltered, then when Rupert looked as if he could not believe his ears, Valentine realised that he had been foolish and he felt humiliated.

Rupert got down on his knees and positioned himself between Valentine's, he now knew what he had unintentionally done and was mortified at the thought of disillusioning him. He took Valentine's hands, but they were snatched away, instead he clutched his slim waist with a firm grip.

'Valentine, it's just a present, I gave it to you because I knew you wanted one, and I wanted to make you happy. I didn't suppose it meant more than that.'

Valentine looked away: he decided to feel annoyed only because he could not stop his chin from trembling. He wished that the tiara would vanish from his head, but to remove it himself would surely cause the violently uncomfortable lump in his throat to explode, thus, he remained frozen.

Rupert continued, 'I was so happy to see how pleased you were to get it. I spent ages designing it; I'm not as artistic as you but I wanted to make it amazing with violets just for you.'

Rupert pressed his cheek to Valentine's chest, squeezed him and painfully felt his unyieldingness.

'It does have special meaning, you are very special to me, but it's not a marriage proposal. I don't even think two boys can marry anyway, can they?'

The question astonished Valentine. It seemed to dominate every other matter, and he gasped, 'Gosh! Why ever not? Love is love, and I'm not saying anybody should marry a boy if they don't want to!'

Then he had a thought. He leaned back to view Rupert's unhappy face, and asked, 'Is it because you don't want to marry a boy?'

Blinking his teary eyes, Rupert looked at him, and admitted, 'I don't think I'm the marrying kind; I just can't really make up my mind about what I want, so it's easier not to.'

This sounded ridiculous to Valentine. How could it be easier not to know what you want? If you do not know that then how can you ever expect to get what you want and, consequently, find happiness? He asked neither of these questions but felt strong enough to enquire, though in a perfectly plangent tone, 'But don't you want me, Rupert? Don't you love me?'

Rupert sighed. He screwed his eyes, and let his face fall in Valentine's lap for a flash, then he lifted it again. He penetrated Valentine's eyes with his own.

After a space, he said, 'I love you, Valentine, and I always want you in my life. Crikey, I'm sad and amazed that you asked!'

Valentine was uncertain whether he had ever felt quite as confused as he did presently.

'Gosh! And I love you too! So very much, Rupert, so *very* much! I want to be with you completely and forever! So why can't we be?'

Now Rupert was confused.

'But, Valentine, I believe that you love me, of course I do, but not that you want to be with me completely.'

A gasp of shock came from Valentine.

'Indubitably, I do!' said he. 'Ever since you broke my crockery and blew my conch!'

'But you never want to do anything more than just baby kiss and cuddle and touch,' said Rupert. 'I've tried so many times for more, but because you don't seem to want to I don't push it, and I'm happy to let you always paint pictures of me and draw me but that's not anything like being with me completely. All these months you haven't wanted to, and I've wanted it so much. I don't understand.'

Indeed, Rupert looked as if the circumstance caused him great frustration.

Valentine blushed. He knew that Rupert had often desired deep intimacy, but Valentine wanted only to baby kiss, cuddle and touch because that is what he used to do with his daddy. He liked to do just the same with Rupert because Rupert was strong like his daddy, and his hair was just as golden.

Besides, the idea of the sounds and emissions of friendlier affections disturbed Valentine dreadfully; if others wished to indulge in it he considered that their private affair. He would not stoop to such ferality for he was of the opinion that eternal purity was not the sole privilege of Elizabeth Tudor.

'I'm just very traditional, I suppose,' said Valentine, blithely, 'I am saving it for matrimony. I am sorry if that does not suit everybody.'

Rupert viewed Valentine with more amazement than he had ever before felt, and then he laughed delightedly and looked at him with unadulterated love.

'Crikey, only you would come out with that! You really are my funny valentine; every line of that song is true. Promise you'll never change?'

Valentine smiled. The brief return of Rupert's grin pleased him.

'Gosh! I'm quite certain I would not ever, even if I could!'

Rupert beamed at him.

'Good. I'm glad. I wouldn't want you to,' he said, then he rose, and Valentine felt abandoned. 'That's why I have to go to Australia alone, my dad wouldn't accept you, and I wouldn't let you pretend to be something that you're not.'

Rupert found his passport in the drawer of the bedside table.

Valentine rose also, and in a voice that was close to a whine, responded, 'But, Rupert! You said you'd look after me always! Don't you remember? You can't go, I need looking after!'

Rupert shook his head.

'You don't need looking after! You know just what you want and how to get it. That's more than I know how to do. And you're stronger than me; you won't bow and scrape to anyone but I'll do anything for anyone just to make them like me.'

'Except for me this time!' howled Valentine, and hopped on the spot like a spoilt child.

Then he stopped, looked Rupert square in the face, and stated, 'I'm not asking you, I am telling you, I *shall* go to Australia with you! If not, then I shall follow you on the next aeroplane, you just see if I don't!'

Rupert was now fully clothed, in one hand he held his passport and, in his other, his packed rucksack.

'Please don't make this more difficult for me, Valentine. It's hard enough as it is. I was so happy just half-an-hour ago, and now I'm not; my dad's in hospital and I'm hurting you. I hate it. Please won't you be nice and come downstairs and see me off? It'd be a shame to ruin our amazing time together.'

It was too much for Valentine to bear. He would not accept the reality of Rupert leaving. He decided that if he pretended it was not happening then it would not. Therefore, he turned his back on Rupert, flung himself down on his bed and screwed his eyes.

'I most certainly shan't say goodbye to you!' he said, sulkily.

Rupert sighed. He wished things were different but he had to leave. He would say goodbye to Valentine in his turret and would understand that it was too difficult for him to see him to the door.

He stepped over to the bed and put his hand on Valentine's shoulder.

'Thanks for an amazing time, Valentine. I look forward to seeing you again, and I will write to you but I'm not very good at it.'

Valentine sounded a tut; he desired a husband *not* a correspondent!

Rupert went on: 'And just so you know that I always cared, I'm leaving you something I think is more amazing than the tiara because it reminds me of when I first knew I really liked you.'

A *plink* in the porcelain dish on his bedside table made Valentine's ears twitch.

Rupert leant down, gripped Valentine, and kissed him firmly on his obdurate lips.

'Goodbye, Valentine,' he said, tenderly.

Valentine did not even flinch. He pretended that he was asleep.

Moments later, Rupert closed the bedroom door, and made the third step creak.

Valentine was shocked to the core. He could not believe that Rupert had left him. He decided that it was just a nightmare, unless he heard the front door open and shut. Only then would he open his eyes and contemplate facing an existence devoid of Rupert. He was itching to learn what 'amazing' thing was in the porcelain dish, but he would rather not ever know if Rupert would return and say it was only a horrible hoax. Valentine decided that he would forgive him.

Some minutes passed, and Valentine began to feel a flicker of hope that it was indeed just a joke, but then he heard gloomy tones indicative of a farewell in the front garden. He clenched his fists to brace himself, and then came the sound of the front door shutting.

His eyes flicked open. He twisted his body to discover the amazing thing in the dish and there, amidst the violet creams, was a buttercup yellow button; a gay little one, in fact, his favourite one from the haberdashery stall at the summer fête. Rupert had kept it all this time; he had treasured it because it reminded him of when he first knew that he really liked him!

Valentine felt as if he might vomit. He had been unforgivably horrid to Rupert, he did not even say goodbye. He jumped up from his bed, ran to the window and, with his mother-of-pearl opera glasses, he peeked between the Murano vases.

Looking up at the turret was a teary-faced Rupert. Valentine waved, but, evidently, Rupert's tears had blinded him, and he shut the front gate, then, with his head hung low, he set off down the Avenue.

Valentine gasped. This was terrible! They could not part so tragically! He could not do that to Rupert, not even if he would not marry him, and he fled from his turret so hastily that he did not bother to close the door let alone lock it.

In the hall, Corny, Flick, Gubsy and Gretchen met him; each of them looked downcast.

'Oh, *dahling*!' said Flick, 'Rupert has gone!'

'Gosh! I patently know that!' Valentine snapped, and he threw open the front door but Gretchen snatched him before he could escape.

'You are not goink out in freezink weather with nothink on your feet and a coat!' she said, sternly, then presented him with his brogues and blocked the door until he had put them on.

Never had tying shoelaces seemed so impossible, and as he struggled with his right shoe, Corny hunkered down and tied the laces on the left.

'That's right, Corny,' said Flick, pushing out her swollen belly as if now all must know of the jam that was currently kicking, 'look after Valentine like Rupert said you ought!'

Laces tied, Valentine sprang up, pulled his duffel coat on over his pyjamas, and dashed from Chinchero.

At the gate, he heard Gubsy boom, 'Run like the wind, Valentine!'

And that is precisely what Valentine did because Rupert was now a fair distance.

Gretchen was right; it was freezing, and twice, Valentine almost slipped on the ice, but with his eyes on Rupert he was safe.

At last, and just in time before all his breath was gone, he was only a few yards from him.

Rupert heard the footfall, and he turned around. His sodden face metamorphosed into one of happiness as he beamed his beatific grin at the speeding Valentine, and he caught him. Their arms worked together in an effort to fuse their beings, and they feverishly kissed each other's faces as if to make up for every nanosecond of their separation.

Valentine was breathless, therefore, Rupert spoke.

'You came after me!' and he could not help but laugh, 'I've never seen you run before! It looked amazing!'

Wheezing, Valentine opened his hand to display the button on his palm.

'Gosh!' he gasped, 'You forgot this!'

Rupert smiled, took the button, looked at it, and said, 'Crikey! I'm glad you came after me; I'd be lost without my favourite gay little one! Thank you, Valentine.'

He pocketed it, and drew him close.

'Well, I don't want you to forget me,' Valentine said, pathetically, into Rupert's chest.

'Crikey! I never would!' said Rupert, definitely, 'Besides I've your embroidery in my rucksack.'

Valentine pulled back a little.

'You do?' he said, quite with surprise, and was pleased that Rupert would take it to Australia.

'Of course, I do!' said Rupert, 'I love it. It's special. And I'm glad you're still wearing the tiara!' and he pointed to Valentine's crown.

Touching his tiara, Valentine said, 'I'll wear it always!'

'Even in the bath?' Rupert teased.

'Especially then! I love it!' Valentine declared.

The notion dimpled Rupert's cheeks.

'Crikey! And I love you!'

'Gosh! And I love you too!' said Valentine, softly.

Again, they crushed their bodies together; their lips met and so did their tongues. For the first time, they kissed as passionately as Rupert had long yearned for, and Valentine wished that he had surrendered months ago, but still the kiss was too sweet to let regret sour it.

Now, they withdrew; only their hands connected them.

'Goodbye, Rupert. I shall write to you and look after myself whilst you take care of your father,' said Valentine, bravely, though he felt that he might breakdown, 'And thanks for an amazing time!'

They were no longer touching.

Rupert slowly walked backwards.

'You made it amazing, Valentine,' he said, '*You* are amazing!'

Rupert halted to view Valentine to fix his image in his mind. A grey cloud suddenly allowed the winter sun to heighten gloriously the gold of his hair. He grinned most magnificently for a flash. Then he turned away and continued on his journey.

Valentine watched his beautiful Apollonian soldier on, and his world became bleak. He dared not wonder whether he might ever again see Rupert, but he knew that if he did that the sun would be shining.

Presently, he felt a firm hand take his and squeeze it. He looked over and saw Corny, smiling kindly.

'Gosh, Corny!' exclaimed Valentine, as he burst into a torrent of tears, 'I truly believe I feel my heart completely breaking!'

Corny put a protective arm about Valentine's trembling form, and walked him back to Chinchero.

Valentine let Corny escort him into the hall. He was mindful that its floor tiles were fast because of Rupert, and he expelled a disconsolate sigh.

Corny shut the front door, and Valentine felt his heart ache with the realisation that, henceforth, many doors would divide him from Rupert.

Corny relieved Valentine of his duffel coat and Olivia came out from the drawing room.

'Darling!' she said, as she advanced with open arms to envelope her unhappy son, 'Gretchen just filled me in. Such a scoundrel to leave you in the lurch!'

'Gosh, mummy!' he said in her hair, 'He had to go! And it's not his fault he's not the marrying kind,' and he shook and he sobbed.

Olivia was outraged; how could Rupert have teased Valentine so heartlessly? It was reprehensible!

'Criminal Casanova!' she said of Rupert, and looked to Corny who pulled a most pugilistic face; he could not fathom why any person would not readily marry Valentine Avery-Stripe and, thus, join the family!

'Look, darling; Cornelius concurs!' said Olivia, approvingly.

Valentine regarded Corny, and then his mother, and said, 'No; Rupert is not a criminal; he is an upright deity! And I shan't hear a word against him!'

With that, he freed himself from Olivia's hold and unhurriedly ascended the stairwell.

Beneath the bison, he turned his wretched face to them, to state: 'I shall love Rupert always.'

As he continued his climb, Olivia and Corny viewed each other. Their eyes spoke of surprise at the statement but also of acceptance.

Upon approaching his turret, Valentine was mindless of the third step, and it creaked. The recollection of Rupert creating the creak pierced his already raw heart. He locked the door behind him and let the ribboned key drop to the floor as he surveyed the painful aspects of the scene before him; the twisted violet-scented sheets and the lion hide. The canvas upon the easel concealed by a yellow cloth that Valentine dared not now remove. The geisha teapot of Grasshopper, the slackening pirouetting ballerina of his music box as it wound down and intermittently emitted a sorry *pling*, and his valise packed for the journey he could not go on.

He supposed that he could not go on at all. It required great strength simply to lift the salver and place it on the floor but he managed it. Then he kicked off his brogues, lay down on his bed and pulled the lion hide over him; he hated that its weight was nowhere near as nice as Rupert's was.

Valentine wished that he could kiss Rupert again. In part, he believed that he would do so shortly. It had all happened so fast that it seemed untrue. Yet the extreme agony of having Rupert ripped from him made certain that he could not doubt the nasty reality.

Realising it pathetic, Valentine reached for the conch upon his bedside table, and placed his lips against its little hole. He visualised how Rupert had puckered his against it to create a sound like a heraldic trumpet, and he imagined their lips touching.

Now, Valentine tried to make it trumpet but he was unable; he managed only melancholy raspberries, but it made him proud of Rupert's ability. He kissed the conch, clutched it to his chest, and with his other hand touching his tiara, he shut his eyes. He was exhausted and wished to cease existing if he could not do so with Rupert.

He fell asleep instantly.

When Valentine awoke, it was another year. Before he opened his eyes, the sensation of deadened nerves and his aching heart were mysterious to his mind for only a moment, but then he remembered the reason.

He knew it would transpire to be problematic to function effectively without the use of sight, therefore, much to his reluctance, for he would not see Rupert, he slowly lifted his lids. For a long time, he remained supine, enfeebled by the non-fiction of his loss and he reflected that the frequent magpie quartet upon his roof had indicated a boy because of

Benedictus and not because of Rupert. He grimaced, and then his lungs' exigency for nicotine bullied him into action.

He sat up, and as if on autopilot, he procured a cigarette from his silver case and lighted it before his line of vision fell upon a sheet of writing paper that someone had pushed under his door.

His curiosity demanded instant gratification; therefore, making a toga with the lion hide, and cradling the conch, he straightened his tiara, and collected the communication.

In red crayon, was the message, *'happy new yaer valantine!! plaese be happy + waik up now! X corny X pee ess I have put shampane here.'*

Deeply touched by the sentiment, and surprised by Corny's penmanship, Valentine became cognisant of his thirst. Rupert's final teapot of Grasshopper was now bad, for the cream would be sour; champagne certainly was required.

Valentine kept Corny's sweet note, and, on a fresh sheet, he wrote, *'Gosh! Thanks, Corny, I need some time and shall be with you before too long. Happy New Year to you too! XXX.'*

He folded the sheet, addressed it, and put it on the salver with the geisha crockery, unlocked his door and exchanged it for Corny's champagne, and then he locked his door again.

The bottle was still cool because though the ice in the bucket was now water the temperature of Chinchero was less than tepid, and for that, Valentine was grateful. Deftly extricating the cork, he lifted the bottle and drank it a way in which he would never dream of doing in company, except, of course, Rupert's. Then he experienced a fresh wave of misery with the comprehension that his New Year's champagne was without him.

He drank some more and closed his eyes to imagine where Rupert might presently be – was he on an aeroplane or already in Brisbane? Either way, Valentine supposed that the miles that separated them must surely be several million, and he drew on his cigarette rather desperately.

Presently, he said, 'Gosh! What do you suppose?'

Unable to imitate Rupert's amicable and cheery tone, he pretended that Rupert replied, 'Crikey! I suppose the champagne to be amazing!'

Valentine laughed aloud, and exclaimed, 'Gosh! You are right! But that's not my specific supposition, try again!'

Mentally, he saw Rupert corrugate his brow. The visual haunted him for a flash, then he exclaimed, 'I suppose it is New Year's Day! Happy New Year, Rupert!'

Rupert grinned and took him in his arms.

'Crikey! So it is! Happy New Year, my funny Valentine!'

Then Valentine wept – tears that seemed to rise from the unfathomable void of loneliness created by Rupert's absence, tears that showed every sign of never ending.

Eventually, as if recuperating from a violent attack of asphyxia, some hitherto unknown reserve of strength empowered him with the capability to discard the conch and cast off the lion hide in order to crawl unhindered toward the gramophone. He knelt before it, and cranked it as he cried, and then set the needle on the groove so to be reassured that he was still Rupert's funny valentine.

The music fortified him further, and that was fortunate for his next undertaking required him to summon exceptional mettle. On his knees, he approached the easel and, upon arrival, he rose. He held his breath, pinched the yellow cloth and tugged at it to uncover the canvas.

The exposed image, though familiar to him, caused Valentine to gasp and stagger because now Rupert was gone his exceptional likeness was a much needed tonic.

Valentine genuflected before the painting in the way a mortal might before a god, which was apt for it depicted Rupert as Heracles having just slain the ferocious Nemean lion. He had fought it with his bare hands, strangled it, skinned it, and made of its golden pelt a glorious cloak that he victoriously wore with nothing else at all.

Valentine had exaggerated the lustre of Sebastian's lion most awesomely, but still it paled next to the genuine radiance of Rupert's own golden mane, caramel tan and magnificent grin; a grin that expressed his happy triumph over the fearsome beast, his only wound the authentic, though embellished with blood red paint, scores upon his heroic chest. The empyrean environment was a confused, but shocking, pink.

Valentine regarded the icon rapturously, and blocking all unpleasant facets of reality from his mind, he felt as if the sun shone on him. Yet, after a while, despite it being his favourite portrait of Rupert, he was not sated, therefore, he extracted, from beneath and behind the bed, atop and between the wardrobe and tallboy, his entire collection.

Hurriedly, he positioned them about his turret, along with half a dozen sketchpads opened to display his favourite etchings of Rupert, and before long, he had created an absolute shrine.

Here was Rupert in the pose of Michelangelo's David as seen from the view of any visitor to the Galleria dell'Accademia, Firenze, standing a

short distance from the statue's feet. Now Rupert was son of Poseidon –
Triton – blowing the conch and, somewhat suggestively, situated with a
trident, which, in reality, was Gretchen's potato graip. A particularly large
canvas, the premier portrait, portrayed Rupert as Adonis reclining nude
but for a crown of laurel leaves. Three illustrated him as Apollo, for it was
most apropos, and had required lots of gold paint, the one in which
Rupert is positioned, quite provocatively, with Olympia's harp (in place
of a lyre) was markedly pleasing. In another, he was winged Icarus flying
rather too close to the sun but not yet in peril. Three pictured him as Eros,
and in another, he was Hermes.

Many of the countless drawings unabashedly exhibited Rupert's athletic
prowess by way of positioning him, with the appropriate props, in the
poses of Mussolini's sportful sculptures in the Stadio Dei Marmi.

In four, he was Tarzan in a tree that they had climbed whilst picnicking
in Richmond Park. In another, he simulated Horst's photograph of the
Mainbocher corset but without the corset, and several demonstrated how
much Rupert resembled a movie star in his eveningwear.

The catalogue of artwork was seemingly endless, and be they on canvas
or on paper, in the medium of oils, gouache, gold leaf, charcoal, or pencil,
Valentine admitted, each were exquisite, and not just because he was
biased because of the sitter.

Rupert too had, blushingly, admired them and said that he wished that
he could see himself through Valentine's eyes because he made him look
amazing. He was happy to pose for him every night, even if he would
much rather be lovemaking, and he would even don the lion hide, despite
it provoking a slight sense of guilt because of Chephirah.

Having rendered his room a place of worship to his absent love, Valentine
situated himself so to view every vision and he revelled in the lustrous
beams of Rupert's golden beauteousness and encompassing warmth that
soothed his battered heart like a supernatural salve.

As he indulged in the beautiful art, he swallowed great gulps of
champagne and, presently, he became quite tipsy, but only pleasantly so
for amongst his army of Ruperts he felt as if cocooned from everything
awful.

A sharp rap upon his door disturbed him.

As if the knock was the height of bad manners, he felt shocked and
looked toward from whence it came, and he said nothing but his face
clearly exhibited his disdain.

Then he heard his mother.

'Valentine. Valentine, darling,' she said, gently, 'Valentino . . . are you conscious?'

Sounding a nettled tut, Valentine replied, 'Conscious of what, mummy?' and he pictured her biting her tongue.

After a pause, for Olivia, wrapped in her mink and cradling champagne, did, indeed, battle not to reprimand Valentine his facetiousness, she said, 'I mean, are you awake?'

'Unless you are a dream, I should say indubitably,' Valentine replied.

Again, Olivia struggled to remain serene. She twisted the knob, but to no avail because the door was locked.

'Please let me in, darling,' she said.

'No, mummy,' replied Valentine, watching the agitated knob. 'I want to be alone.'

The knob stilled.

'But I have champagne for us to share, it is, after all, New Year's day,' Olivia said, with a touch of cheer.

'Still?' asked Valentine with alarm; he was quite certain that the year ought to be older by now.

'Yes, darling, still,' Olivia said, patiently.

Valentine made a tut at the year's sluggishness, and another at the meagre amount remaining in his bottle, then said, 'Thank you, mummy, you may leave the champagne by the door and I shall collect it at my convenience. Is it chilled?'

'Quite, darling, yes,' she replied, with the decision that Valentine rather deserved an entire bottle after the shock departure of Rupert, for she did not know of the bottle left by Corny.

'Well, do join the family soon, darling. One must not submit to one's emotions so readily, not when one must be mindful of *noblesse oblige*.'

'I am having a holiday from *noblesse oblige* at present,' Valentine said in an arrogant tone, 'À bientôt, mummy.'

'I expect I shall see you shortly, darling,' said Olivia, surrendering, and the creak of the third step indicated her descent.

Valentine said to himself, 'Nuts to *noblesse oblige*!' then he waited a minute before collecting the champagne.

Ordinarily, Valentine was not so susceptible to the effects of alcohol, but because he had eaten no more than an occasional violet cream since the previous year, he soon felt rather inebriated. Unfortunately, he also gradually grew more than a modicum morose. Outside it was dark, yet he did not notice for he only had eyes for his Ruperts, and he decided to play the vinyl.

For the first time, he concentratedly listened to the lyrics because he wanted to sing along, and that was when he suddenly became very upset.

He wondered if his looks truly were laughable and unphotographable. He knew that his figure was not exactly Greek, (unless one counted Ganymede, and why would one not?) but was his mouth a little weak? Valentine did not think so, but chose to examine his reflection in the ferro.

It was not a thing he often did: consider his reflection. He preferred to view it in his mind's eye. Naturally, he would see it when shaving and so on, but he would not ever focus upon it, and when he admired his tiara, and had learned that to say *Rupert* he puckered, he did not scrutinise the entire picture that the visual echo had to show. His vanity would not permit him because he was unable to bear his less than breathtakingly beautiful visage. In fact, it distressed him quite considerably.

He gasped at his other self, and made a moue, and he contemplated why someone as beautiful as Rupert might love him. He could not discern any logic in it. Contorting, grotesquely, his face, he considered his keen angles, aloof brows, languid lids, insolent nose and supercilious lips, and he decided that his appearance was disconcertingly similar to an Egon Schiele self-portrait.

'Gosh!' Valentine exclaimed at his reflection, 'You snot!'

He heightened his pitch, and demanded to know, 'What *do* you think you look like?'

He gasped again.

'I shall tell you this for nothing, Valentino, you look to be an absolute and utter monster of insufferable arrogance, moreover, you're worlds away from beautiful!'

With that, he pushed away the ferro in disgust, and like a pitiable wretch, he cried because he was not beautiful, and he cried because he missed Rupert, and he cried until he had exhausted both the champagne and his energy, and was no longer conscious of his ugliest hour.

The following morning saw the return of the four magpies that liked to raucously caw atop the turret roof. The racket disrupted Valentine's insensibility and caused a searing pain in his head that created a blinding white light in his eyes and made him howl.

Valentine was suffering from a hangover.

'Beastly stinking pilferers!' he yelled at them, as he squeezed his head between his hands.

'Wretched feathered thieves!' he wailed, and then lifted a sash to brave the rude January air by leaning out of a window to pelt the reprobates with his remaining violet creams.

'I shall personally climb up there and cut out your throats if you do not migrate this minute!'

He did not consider this a harsh threat in the least for he had not forgiven them their piecrust promise of a boy.

Valentine's precariousness, and safeguard of his tiara, lest it should dislodge and fall, did not facilitate his already abysmal aim, and his violet creams bounced off the roof and hurtled to the gravel or, at best, nestled in the guttering.

The brazen magpies were impervious to the attack and language. Worse than that, they darted in and out through a hole made by a displaced slate; the space between the roof and Valentine's ceiling seemed to be a stamping ground for the scoundrels!

The idea of it forced Valentine to scream with fury; that they trespassed upon his territory was unacceptable and any affinity that he had ever felt for them went out of the window. He climbed back into his room and located the cricket bat with which Rupert had once posed, and with it, Valentine thumped his ceiling quite aggressively.

'Get out!' he cried, 'I demand that you vacate my premises immediately! Or I shall kill you, and I shall eat you!'

However, the birds only continued the ruckus.

The avian invasion was intolerable and the occupation cultivated Valentine's rage so incredibly that he presently handled the bat as if to beat someone senseless; the first blow was enough to damage the plaster rather splendidly, and the second penetrated the ceiling completely and created a gaping cavity.

Plaster and rubble descended, and assailed the Murano ornaments making noises like hail on impact.

Valentine cowered and coughed in the cloud of dust; he dropped the cricket bat, and through his window watched, with some satisfaction, the frightened flight of four magpies into the leaden firmament.

'Ha!' he said, victoriously, dusting off his hands, 'And don't dare come back!'

Then he tutted because their distant jarring caws sounded mocking.

He slammed his window shut, made a moue at the ceiling's injury and realised, with chagrin, that it was a second hole Rupert would likely readily fill, and his heart ached with a powerful and cruel yearning.

He considered regarding one of his many renderings of Rupert but thought it unwise, therefore, he instead viewed the mess, the chalky film upon the erstwhile gleaming ornaments, and he noticed that they held not only greyish rubble but also things that shone. From them, he extracted several safety pins, a foil chocolate wrapper, and a ten pence piece. He deemed the magpies' piratical gains paltry, he tutted at them and then remembered how much his head hurt.

'Gosh! It is too terrible to tolerate!' he exclaimed, histrionically, 'The hole! The headache! The heartache! Oh, horridness!'

He felt ready to surrender to an eternity of nothing but misery and melancholy, was prepared to give up entirely, and was on the precipice of devising a most glorious end to his woes when, presently, a small object of utmost glimmering iridescence amongst the ceiling debris caught his eye.

He squinted so to sharpen his perception, and gathered that the glimmer was not only silver but also glassy and cast slick shades of red, green, purple, orange and blue, and amongst and around these colours were dazzling twinkles.

Instantly, Valentine's intellect became as if a whirlwind of shocked reactions around an epicentre of astonishment because his instinct was incredulous to a startling recognition. He gasped as loudly as a normal person might conventionally shriek and darted toward the tallest Murano vase to retrieve the recognised entity.

Holding it an inch from his insolent nose, he made a throttled sound of excited surprise, and he blew away the dust. He blinked thrice, at the beauty, the sentimental value and, moreover, the miraculous recovery, and cried out, 'Gosh! Glorious magpies!' for their mercenary ways had brought about the return of Olympia's elusive Starfish!

'Gosh, Rupert!' he exclaimed, as he fell to his knees before Heracles, and raised the ring to his forget-me-not blue eyes, 'Isn't it amazing?'

Indeed, the portrait looked to agree.

'Verily, it's not as glorious as my tiara!' Valentine said, quickly abandoning the ring, and he tenderly touched his tiara.

Then he grew sad once more and hung his head. He was ashamed of himself for feeling happiness in Rupert's absence despite his having forsaken him.

His curiosity predominated however, and he snatched the Starfish from the floor, scrutinised it, and read the band's internal engraving: '*Nil Desperandum*'.

At once, nothing else seemed to exist but those two words and his brilliant daddy and, suddenly, everything was as tranquil as could be.

He experienced the sensation of being wonderfully crushed in his sire's strong arms, the presence of his love was virtually tangible, Valentine could quite feel Monty's golden stubbled jaw grazing his infant ear and, in it, whispering, as well as a man whose tone was sonorous could, '*Nil Desperandum*, Valentino, always remember that and you'll never go wrong. *Nil Desperandum*, little popinjay.'

Resultantly, Valentine realised that he had shamefully visited the depths of despair but was now once again buoyant because of his daddy and his love. Daddy would not have tolerated last night's pity, he would have warred against it, and presently Valentine knew that though he did not possess supreme beauty he was at least a *jolie laide* with well-cut features and owned an Avery-Stripe countenance, and, of that, he was proud.

Further, he possessed the Avery-Stripe nobility and was to maintain a sense of *noblesse oblige* in the face of any fool whom did not adequately venerate it, and simply to proceed unperturbed regardless.

All of this, Valentine saw in the Starfish, and he considered it his daddy's Starfish really, yes; it was Monty's Starfish now, and then came the revelation that he had not respected his daddy as much as he ought, because if he could endure his absence with fortitude then Rupert's should be a picnic by comparison. Whereupon Valentine resolved not to mope and moon over him, he would not be Garboesque and lock himself away from the world, and neither would he ape Miss Havisham. No; he was better than that, he deserved more than that, *infinitely* more than that, for he was Valentino Avery-Stripe!

One thing irked him however. He sincerely believed that all occurrences transpired for a reason, yet he was unable to divine the grounds for his relationship with Rupert other than that it had been glorious; he sensed there existed a sounder justification. A heart should not be broken for such a trifling thing as an enjoyable time. Therefore, he started to ruminate, and as he looked about his room, he regarded his Ruperts and considered.

Gradually, he grasped an inkling to the logic that speedily grew into a full comprehension, whereupon he made the joyous decision to make of it a fantastic actuality.

There was no point in procrastination; he would start immediately, and because his headache had vanished as completely as his refusal to surrender to his heartache flourished, he cloaked himself with the lion hide, jumped onto his bed, and blew into the conch to herald the commencement of his magnificent venture.

Quite to his astonishment, he produced a trumpet equally as resonant as Rupert was able to, and, triumphantly, he exclaimed, 'Gosh! Amazing!'

Quickly, he stripped off his sullied pyjamas and put on a clean gold pair. He removed his tiara only for the minute it took to apply violet pomade, before spraying himself with the same flower's scent. Darting back and forth, he collected an assortment of his most competent sketches, he rolled up the Adonis canvas, and two Apollos, tucked them under his arm, locked his door behind him, and tripped the light fantastic down the stairwell.

None of the family was in the drawing room, in fact, because it was luncheon, they all, Olivia included, inhabited the dining room, therefore, into there, Valentine unceremoniously burst, and exclaimed, 'Gosh! I have had the most glorious idea!'

His entrance was so unexpected that Flick shrieked as if terrified, Corny dropped a sugar lump in Gloriana's bowl, and Olivia spilled Bovril from her teacup onto her kedgeree, yet she emitted no more than a rankled gasp.

'Rapscallion!' Gubsy furiously boomed, for the shock had made him bite his tongue with his false teeth.

'Happy New Year, Master Valentine!' said Gretchen, pulling out a chair for him, 'Is kood to see you at last, please you must now eat somethink.'

'Gosh, Gretchen! I couldn't swallow a scrap! I'm far too energised!' cried Valentine, and he enjoyed the crushing embrace of Corny who looked to him in eager anticipation of what his glorious idea might be.

'Golly!' said Flick, now composed and incising a rasher of bacon, 'You do look happy, *dahling*, don't you miss Rupert now?' and she pushed out her lower lip in theatrical sympathy.

Olivia settled her cup with a *clink* and gathered her mink under her chin.

'One can't eternally dwell upon and wallow over lost loves, Flick, darling.' she said, tersely, then turned to Valentine; she was glad to see that he had resurfaced reasonably swiftly, and she enquired what was his new glorious idea.

'Gosh!' said Valentine, bouncing on the balls of his brogues, 'I cannot say, not yet anyway, it's to be a surprise! But I can enlighten you to the teaser that you shall all be seeing a lot more of Rupert than you have hitherto!'

With that, he swept from the room and Corny capered after him.

Olivia smiled at her second-born's resilience; she knew that Monty would be proud, and as she continued to consume her kedgeree, whilst enjoying the kicks of Benedictus, she possessed no notion of the returned Starfish that once again resided in Valentine's hatbox.

The Exemplar of Pulchritude

No more than two days after Rupert's departure did Valentine rise as if a phoenix from the flames, at least verisimilarly, and less than a month later would his undertaking be realised. He considered that everyone should see Rupert's beauteousness; it was a thing to celebrate and to revere. Therefore, directly following interrupting his family's luncheon, he went, with ecstatic Corny, to disclose to Brian, in his gallery, a taste of the produce of his aesthetic desires, with the idea of making an exhibition.

It was not so much that Valentine believed his artistry spectacularly proficient, though, of course, he considered it superior to rudimentary, but that it so utterly illustrated Rupert's magnificence that the result was breathtaking. Much to Valentine's delight, Brian declared his creative ability singularly impressive and he appreciated the exposure of Rupert's carnality most gushingly.

'My dear!' Brian cried, 'I cannot comprehend how I failed to recognise the heavenly significance of the boy's form! I can only think that my eyes were fixed on your brutish cousin so firmly, plus, of course, I have not ever liked to ogle another's lover! But, my dear! Rupert's lines! The golden ratio of his physique! He adheres to every rule of the Adonis Index, and makes Leonardo's Vitruvian man look to be positively warped! I shall be honoured to display your beautiful works, I do believe I have an ample slot in not many weeks time, and I insist that we name the show The Exemplar of Pulchritude!'

Here, he flipped open his diary, trailed a finger down a leaf, and peering over his half-moon spectacles, said, 'For four weeks from the thirtieth, does that suit?'

'Gosh! Verily!' exclaimed Valentine, filled to the brim with pride that all would regard Rupert's glory, and he doubted that he could conjure a better name for the display.

Brian smiled.

'Splendid, my dear. I shall make the preview party a fabulous affair! Tomorrow, I'll come by Chinchero to view all your works so we can decide the image for the circular and advertisement bumf – it will definitely draw quite a crush, particularly my friary – and then we can talk denominations.'

This came as a surprise to Valentine; he had not considered selling anything.

He hesitated for a flash to deliberate, and then replied, 'Gosh! Yes, of course. Very important obviously, and I'll place my trust in you to be impartial.'

Then he felt a little ill, for he did loathe fiscal discourse, therefore, he deviated and made a point most important: 'But I shan't surrender all of them; definitely not Heracles, and absolutely not Adonis.'

'Oh, my dear!' cried Brian, 'Of course, you shan't wish to part with them all, and don't you worry, that's what these precious dears are for,' and he withdrew, from a drawer, a sheet of adhesive red dots, and he flapped it, 'One of these on a few pieces will rouse interest and, maybe, the revenue!'

'Gosh, glorious!' exclaimed Valentine, 'I do so very much desire to retain possession of some of them for future Avery-Stripes to see Valentino's love of beauty, and the beauty of his love! Don't you think, Corny?'

Corny nodded fervently; he certainly thought it a good idea for their descendants to see Valentine's excellent pictures and it sounded like he would make money out of the others, and he thought that was good because he liked money.

'Sweet cherub!' said Brian, but then he noticed that Corny had grown exceptionally since the summer and he hoped that he did not object to the term of endearment.

Indeed, Corny would unlikely object, for he enjoyed flattery. He was uncertain what a cherub was, yet it little mattered because he did not hear the endearment; he was too involved in admiring Valentine's Adonis. From the moment the canvas was unfurled in the gallery, Corny recognised the crown of laurel leaves and the pose because, although he had viewed it from an alternative angle, he was cognisant that it was the scene he had spied through the keyhole and, consequently, supposed that it was a game of undressed musical statues. Now it made sense to his mind. He considered it a lovely thing that Valentine liked to paint Rupert, and he decided that he would like Valentine to paint his picture too, if he had a care, but, obviously, he would wear a bit more clothing.

He was also interested in Rupert's superhero form, though not for the same reason as Brian was, rather, it served as blueprint of how he should like his body eventually to be, and with his xylophonic stomach, he surmised it not an unobtainable goal.

By mid-January, Corny was confident that he would definitely one day be as big as Rupert all over. The boxing club – The Jab and Hook – that he frequented four times a week had plenty of very big boys and they seemed to think that he might become a very good welterweight and encouraged him to strive with the activity. Corny took to it with great alacrity, and enjoyed immensely to skip with a rope, perform jumps called scissors, squats called thrusts, many press-ups and then sit-ups with a heavy, and apparently, medicinal ball.

He thought it a little strange to have his hands and wrists bound in bandages before putting on Gubsy's much-admired gloves because he had not hurt himself but he accepted it.

In silky red shorts and matching boots, he would have the time of his life jabbing, hooking and uppercutting an imaginary person whose pretend retaliatory punches he had to duck. After that, he would box the big bags that hung from the ceiling, which, at the end of a session, dripped with the condensation created by the combined exertion of the class.

Corny thought the sight disgusting but also gratifying, and when cantering home – unaccompanied because the family said that he was a big boy now – he would picture knocking the stuffing out of some nefarious opponent in the ring and receiving a roaring ovation. Gubsy told him that this he could do and still be a gentleman because of the nine marquees of Queensbury.

At weekends, Corny would wake no earlier than usual but would leave Olivia and Benedictus snug in the four-poster, and breakfast on hot porridge before venturing out into the bitter cold to play rugby with another local club, unimaginatively called The Rugby Club. Corny's first thought was that they should ask Valentine to call them something better but soon he ceased to care and zealously participated in the games deceptively called friendlies. He thought it a much pleasanter name but soon discovered it not apropos because, despite the vigorous hugging and brazen fondles, there was lots of angry shoving.

Yet Corny refused to be intimidated and ensured every bully experienced the full force of a reprisal. Often his assertiveness resulted in a red or yellow card. This he knew to be bad and he would pout and wonder why only he had to be friendly. He did not consider the other chaps very courteous, and nor was rugby particularly gentlemanly.

Then he remembered Cosmo's fancy for rugby and decided that it explained his caddishness. However, the recollection spurred Corny on and he resolved to become an excellent player, even if the boors would not allow him the use of his own ball, for he should like someday to thrash Cosmo at it, or anything, if he did not soon return Willy.

Corny felt a sense of shame in not forcing his ball into the friendlies and for this reason he avoided revealing precisely where he played because, on several occasions, Valentine had said that he should like to spectate and show his support. In theory, Corny liked the idea very much but upon imagining Valentine's distress over the inferior ball, he shuddered, and sadly knew that it could not happen. To alleviate his guilt he quite competently (due to his hours regarding Rupert renovate) patched the gash in Valentine's ceiling.

Valentine opined the result glorious and, in gratitude, insisted that he paint him. Corny was flattered and readily sat, yet it did not quell his sense of betrayal and he felt uneasy until he dispersed the niggle with the idea to pose with his rugby ball. This pleased Valentine but he declared that Gloriana made a superior prop.

It was to be a sizeable picture, from the waist up. Corny teetered on the verge of exposing his xylophone but considered the suggestion of his dress shirt wise because, as Valentine said, 'To look upright for posterity, though I believe I shall accentuate your injured brow to indicate your hardiness, and juxtapose you with Millie's butterflies. And no headdress; since your choppy cut your locks have grown thick as daddy's!'

Whereupon, Valentine tousled the blond mop.

Corny beamed and, holding Gloriana, assumed a hale stance before the lepidopteran wall.

The opening of The Exemplar of Pulchritude coincided with two other occasions: the seventy-second Deathday of Excelsior, and Horatio and Isadora Avery-Stripe's acquisition of the Frobisher house. The family proclaimed the concurrence auspicious. Even Gubsy was cheerful, despite his nostalgia, for certainly it was a day when he recollected his grandfather and original family, and he hankered for the past, considered the consequent history, questioned the present and faced the future made rosy with the imminence of three new shoots upon the tree. He looked forward to the arrivals with great anticipation and was glad that he was to live long enough to greet them.

The exhibition stiffy, propped against a rhinoceros horn upon the mantelshelf, stirred Gubsy's wistfulness. He had not seen it there before, and he rose from his wing chair to scrutinise. The chosen image was Heracles, and Gubsy instantly recognised Sebastian's lion. Ordinarily, evidence that one of the children had been so naughty as to sticky-finger would have had Gubsy roaring or, at the very least, gnashing. However, in this case, all that came was a whimper as he remembered his big brother whose trampled end upon the Serengeti plains even the most practiced embalmer could not completely camouflage. Gubsy was proud to see the lion so handsomely portrayed, and he reflected that Sebastian would be also.

Presently, the front doorbell pealed, and minutes later Gretchen appeared with four lots of keys; the Frobisher house was now Avery-Stripe. This brightened Gubsy's spirits, and he became sunnier still by the unexpected delivery of two mahogany cradles.

'Gosh!' exclaimed Valentine, upon examining the baby beds in the hall, 'Just like Rupert's one!' and though he was impressed by the exactness of the reproductions he was uncertain that copies of Rupert's labour sat well with him.

'Golly! They're very smart!' said Flick, persuading them to rock. She turned to Corny, and said, 'Funny to think our sprogs'll sleep in them!'

Corny looked confused because he thought of frogs.

Swathed in her mink, Olivia descended the stairwell, and caught Flick's words. She inhaled sharply, and said tersely, 'I object to vulgarities, Felicity, darling. No Avery-Stripe child was ever, and never shall be, a *sprog!*'

'Sorry, Auntie O,' mumbled Flick, and she wished that the delivery had been a television set.

Olivia examined the cradles. She considered it correct that each of the babies would have a dignified one, but she gasped in horror and raised her arms to point at them.

'They have patently picked names without consulting the family!' she said, with outrage, for engraved in the mahogany of one were the initials, 'M.A-S' and, in the other, 'H.A-S.'

'Telephone Horatio immediately, Valentino!' ordered Olivia, 'I am aware Cornelius allowed them to choose names, but they must meet my approval! I demand to know their decision! I must *not* be unduly unbalanced!'

Nevertheless, Olivia was unbalanced because although Valentine deigned to utilise the Bakelite it shed no light for Harry admitted that he and Izzy had settled the names yet they were to be a 'surp*wise*'.

'Gosh! I shouldn't fret, mummy,' said Valentine, during Excelsior's Deathday supper of lamb's immune system, (mercifully followed by palate-cleansing Nesselrode) 'they know of the four syllable *sine qua non*, and, besides, engraved cradles make nothing concrete.'

This tempered Olivia only marginally but she was without the strength to protest the mystery and decided to postpone her probing, though, naturally, she would do so before any official documents bore any incongruous names.

Valentine calmly viewed each of the family's pensive aspects, and when Olivia said, '*Ugh!*', he pressed his napkin to his lips, then to Corny and Gretchen, he said, 'Gosh! We must hasten; it wouldn't do at all to arrive late at my own opening!'

'It's such a bother I can't come too!' Flick whined, 'Maybe I shall just dress as a jolly fat man with a moustache, then no one will see I'm preggers!'

Olivia gasped and grimaced, and she snapped, 'If you value your existence, Felicity, darling, and those of the twins, you'll commit no such asininity!'

Flick huffily crossed her arms, and said to Valentine, 'Well, don't forget I bagsy the big Tarzan, so make certain he has a bindi!'

Gubsy would not either go to the gallery. Not because he disapproved of the prurient pictures (for upon viewing each as they left Chinchero he stated that Rupert was a fine figure of a man, and he purchased Apollo with Lyre) but because he disliked being too much of a distance from his wing chair. He would remain in Chinchero and play halma with Flick, if she kept her promise not to cheat, and Olivia retired to repose upon her four-poster.

Gretchen was glad to go. She was proud of Master Valentine and his application, and because Master Corny was to be his escort, she deemed it wise that she chaperone the brothers, just in case. Moreover, the event sounded glamorous to her, and she wanted to enjoy the *cognoscenti*'s appreciation of the art and their repartee.

The trio made the journey on foot, for Gretchen said she would like champagne. She wore her dirndl and ushanka, Corny a white shirt and had acquiesced to wear chino trousers rather than shorts, whereas Valentine wore eveningwear and his tiara.

When they arrived, Brian was flitting about the brightly lit gallery. He had done his utmost to do justice to the collection, and upon realising the presence of people, he made the pretence of collapsing, before realigning and exclaiming, 'Welcome, my dears! What do you think of the space? I must say, I do believe every Rupert very well hung!'

'Gosh! Amazing!' said Valentine, quite staggered at how professional his endeavours seemed when so expertly mounted upon walls of gilt with segments of shocking pink and hit with the severe glare of a spotlight; Rupert truly appeared unquestionably worthy of flagrant hero-worship.

Valentine cast his eyes about to ascertain that the pictures he should like to keep had red dots and was pleased to see that each of them did. Concurrently, he could not help notice the price of each piece, and though he was far from *au fait* with monetary value, he thought the sums quite princely, and certainly higher than he remembered deciding with Brian.

'Oh, my dear!' said Brian, darting from one painting to the next, 'One must precede the inevitable pleb's fondness for bartering!'

Then Brian indicated the racks and stands furnished with card-framed sketches of Rupert, reproductions of the paintings, and postcards of both, all purchasable for more moderate amounts.

'These,' said Brian, 'shall sell like hotcakes!' whereupon, he clicked his fingers, and there materialised a pretty girl, and not so pretty boy, bearing champagne and canapés.

'Do have some fizz, my dears, we have a decent ten before the offence,' Brian said to the artist, his escort and their chaperone, 'And have a horseback or two, both angels and devils, I believe. We need sustenance in order to mingle and schmooze!' and he shimmied, whilst the trio helped themselves to flutes and horsebacks.

Valentine sensed something similar to nervousness but most of all he wished for the company of Rupert who, had said, in his badly written letter, that he wished that he could be there. He said that it was amazing that Valentine was showing his Art and he said that he missed him.

Valentine could bring himself to read the communication only once and then he hid it under his hatbox. He did not feel the need to open the subsequent letters in order to write back, which he did so weekly.

Presently, he sensed a melancholic cloud loom overhead and it threatened to overwhelm him, but upon viewing Corny's touching respect for the event, whilst Brian and Gretchen effectively flirted, he felt fortified. Further, when the champagne bubbles observably tickled Corny's nose and he failed to repress a violent sneeze then pushed back his fringe to expose, to Valentine, his mirth at his misdemeanour, Valentine felt invincible.

He pulled his perfect brother close, and exclaimed, 'Gosh! *gesundeit!*'
Corny thought the word very funny.

Primarily, the patrons came as if a trickle, and Brian duly introduced
them to Valentine who did not consider any worthy of a Rupert because,
to his mind, they smacked of middleclass. Nevertheless, he interacted
with them quite as if they were of decent standing.

Soon, some familiar faces arrived. Hirsute Sophie came alone and let it
be known that, because they were so stunning, both her daughters had
two dates that night. One-eyed Nina and Lothario Hugo made an
unconvincing couple, despite their claim that they were, she said that
Josh had the mumps, and he said that Giles was skiing. Valentine did not
care that the aforementioned offspring were absent; they would unlikely
buy his Art, and were awful anyway. To their parents he excused the
lack of Olivia by way of saying that she was with Harry in Bath to tend to
her expectant daughter-in-law, and, naturally, was thrilled to bits about
the pending progenies.

'Olivia, a grandmother!' said Hugo, as if he could not credit it.

'She doesn't look a day over fifty!' agreed Nina, well aware of Hugo's
feeling for her forty-something friend.

'So quickly!' added Sophie, 'Why, Harry only met the gel in June;
must've been instant, if you get my meaning.'

She cast a knowing glance at Nina and they both believed their smirks
invisible.

Valentine emitted a withering gasp.

'Mummy's glad to be a granny, especially when she's still young enough
to enjoy it, and we are delighted that Harry found discerning Izzy when so
many *gels* are *reputedly* so very *giving*, if you get my meaning.'

Wretched cadavers! Valentine thought of the three elders, as the two
women considered how he had inherited his mother's tongue and that his
insolence was shocking but they said nothing.

Hugo, who found feminine spats unnerving, undertook to assuage.

Aside, he said to Valentine, as he regarded the Ruperts, 'You've really
caught him, Valentine, Rupert's a great lad, a great craftsman too, I bet he
loves these.'

'Indubitably, he does!' exclaimed Valentine, and he wondered at Hugo's
motive then considered it likely that he still hankered for his mother and,
therefore, would be nice to her son. Thus, he looked to him and did not
hide his disdain.

Somewhat panicking, for he was indeed angling, Hugo emphatically said, 'I think I'll buy one!'

A moment of disbelief flashed by before Valentine exclaimed, 'Indubitably, you do!' and graciously suffered Hugo's arm over his shoulder, and received his whisper, 'I'm sure Olivia would be furious if you told her that I hadn't and very pleased if you said that I had.'

Valentine was appalled.

'Gosh! Very cross! And yes, most gloriously happy if you did,' and coquettishly added, 'In fact, I know exactly what would make mummy unspeakably happy, Mr Pargeter!'

Hugo bit: 'What's that?'

Valentine returned, 'If you were to pay double the asking price!'

Hugo laughed, yet Valentine's solemn countenance persuaded him to revise.

A moment passed, and furrowing his brow, Hugo asked, 'Olivia would be unspeakably happy to *hear* that I had?'

'Gosh! Verily! She considers my paintings beautiful and thinks them worth fortunes! She said to me on the telephone, "Valentino, darling, I realise you need to be known but do not let them fleece you, do try to sell only to discerning persons whom will realise the value of your Art, or I fear my heart might break!" '

Hugo cogitated demonstrably, but he suddenly said, 'Which painting do you think I should buy?'

Delighted to have reeled him in, Valentine decided that he would tell his mother of Hugo's largesse, though it would by no means impress her as much as the man might hope.

Thus, as a warning, Valentine replied, 'I think Icarus! But do discuss the fiscalaties with Mr Pavilion; I'm much too sensitive for such colloquies!'

Whereupon, Hugo made a beeline for Brian, and Valentine felt somewhat irked by his hitherto unknown sales acumen.

Then came an influx of Brian's friary and the gallery was filled to capacity. The atmosphere became very jolly, and amongst the gay crush, Corny recognised Peter, Jolyian and Gerard from The Marvellous Party but they seemed not to remember him. Therefore, he put out his hand to say how-do-you-do, as he had been taught to do, whereupon, they each recalled him at once. His growth excited them so extraordinarily that Jolyian screamed quite hysterically, and received, from Brian, the immediate chastisement of a slap on the wrist.

'But he's grown so big!' Jolyian argued, operatically, 'I cannot believe it's the same little boy from last summer!'

'Astonishingly big!' Peter affirmed.

'Quite the he-man!' Gerard declared.

'Shush, my dears! He is the same boy; you know how at that age they can suddenly shoot!' said Brian, 'But show some respect; this is a reputable gallery, not a boy bagnio, and Corny is the artist's little brother, so behave!' and then he mingled.

The excited men paid no heed to Brian, and they circled Corny.

'He's not little at all!' opined little Peter.

'No one's little next to you!' teased Gerard.

'But he *is* a big boy!' Peter asserted.

'Yes, *and* good-looking!' said Jolyian.

'Devastatingly so!' Peter said, with a swoon.

'Almost unbearably so!' Gerard concurred.

'Such a handsome boy in his preppy chinos!' cried Peter.

'It would be a heinous crime against Art if Valentine did not paint him!' they chorused.

Corny was shocked; never before had he been the object of such unabashed adulation. He could not quite believe it at first and he felt hurt to think that they might be joking or mean somebody else, but upon grasping the praise sincere and aimed at him, he realised that he liked it. In fact, it made him feel quite excellent.

He beamed at the men, expanded his chest, and was on the verge of finding his tongue so to tell them that Valentine was already painting him, but then Gretchen appeared. She did not think the adulation appropriate, but knowing it harmless, albeit maybe embarrassing for Corny, or unhealthy for his ego, she only sternly said to the fawning fairies, 'I think perhaps you forket you are here to look at paintinks and *not* at Master Corny.'

Her mien was so forbidding that the three men immediately rectified their conduct and insisted that their presence was for the sake of Art.

Corny was rather annoyed at the interruption but agreed that Valentine's Ruperts were why they were there, and he was glad when Jolyian cried, 'Show us what to look at, Corny! Be our guide!'

Corny shouldered his new role most conscientiously, he brought to the men's attention his favourite work, which was Adonis, but pointed to the red dot to indicate that it was, sadly, not for sale.

He led them about the gallery to look at each of the pieces and enjoyed listening to their lauding of Valentine's technique, Rupert's physique and his own charming attentiveness. He fetched them flutes, and did not mind feeding them horsebacks as if their hands were somehow inoperable. He exposed his healthy teeth at their every compliment and quip. He thought them very friendly, and wondered if they might play rugby but, somehow, he knew probably not.

Then he persuaded them over to the racks of reproductions, where they decided to purchase several if he would permit them to ruffle his hair or kiss his cheek, and because he thought it funny, he complied – so ensued much ruffling, kissing and buying.

The procedure escalated upon tipsy Peter declaring that he would certainly buy the Apollo painting, on which he had his eye, if Corny would allow him to take him to the theatre and a post-performance dinner. However, reasonably sober Gerard told Peter not to be an ass, for the boy was sixteen, therefore, Peter settled for a pinch of Corny's posterior; Gerard and Jolyian did the same and, consequently, three paintings received red dots.

Indeed, many transactions took place throughout the evening, for not only did Valentine sell Icarus for twice the price, and Corny had induced his admirers to buy a painting apiece plus plenty of sketches and postcards, but also Brian schmoozed most profitably.

When the last of the patrons departed, the original four unwound in the backroom and toasted success, for no less than two sheets were entirely dotless.

'Conkratulations, Master Valentine! Everybody is lovink your pictures!' said Gretchen, and then she hiccoughed because she was not completely immune to the effects of champagne. Neither was she impervious to the effects of the bare Ruperts, and she added, 'Even Kretchen buyed one, Master Rupert is so kood-looking in a Vikink hat!'

Corny did not feel like playing a friendly the following morning. He might have if the club permitted unfriendliness because, despite his slight headache, he believed that shoving bullies in mud would prove amusing. Yet, it pleased him to stand, with Gloriana, and pose, for Valentine, whilst thinking of the wet boors in the cold rain. He enjoyed hearing the pitter-patter upon the windows, and the occasional tut from his brother.

His eldest brother also had reason to tut, but because Harry was not so disposed to irritation, he was only happy to transport the first lot of furniture from Bath to Chiswick – even if it was 'G*w*eat weather for ducks!'

'Hullo, you two!' Harry said, enthusiastically, after gaining entry into Valentine's turret.

'Hello, Harry,' said Valentine, and returned to his easel.

Harry sat on the bed and regarded his brothers concentratedly involved with their artistic production. He was disheartened not to receive the usual warm welcome from the youngest.

'C*w*umbs, *w*ascal! What's *w*ong? Don't I get a chee*w*y hello?'

Corny did not move; his exuberant petrification was a grave undertaking.

There was silence for a space, then Valentine looked up and explained the obvious: 'Corny cannot move; he is posing for me.'

Quite as if it was a revelation, Harry said, '*W*eally, *w*ascal? You're going to be made into Art?'

Now, Corny did respond, but only by way of manoeuvring his eyeballs to indicate an affirmative.

'That's *w*eally b*w*illiant!' Harry enthused, then he asked Valentine, 'How was it last night? Did you sell lots? Izzy says she can't wait to see the *W*uperts, and I'd like to buy her one for the house.'

Valentine tutted and made a moue, he was peevish because he was uncertain how happy he was to part with so many souvenirs from his time in the sun.

'Gosh, Harry!' he said, 'How vulgar you sound! Talking about money, like mummy! Buy and sell! Yes, lots sold, lots and lots, in fact, but, of course, you should buy one, that's only apropos. There's the catalogue on the hatbox. Take a look and pick one, though lots have got dots in the gallery.'

Harry found the booklet.

'The Exemplar of Pulch*w*itude!' he said aloud but received no reaction.

He admired the cropped version of Heracles on the cover and opened it. He shifted his seat with each new page, he rubbed his boxed beard, beneath which, he blushed, and at the end of the viewing, he said, 'Valentine, these pictures are *w*ude!'

'Gosh! Whatever do you mean?'

'Well, *W*upert's nude in them all! You can see his willy!' said Harry, with some distress, 'I couldn't give one to Izzy; it would upset her.'

Valentine tutted.

'Don't exaggerate, Harry, there's some of him in eveningwear.'

Harry re-opened the booklet and saw that it was so: 'Yes, you're *w*ight.'

'I thought I might be,' Valentine replied.

'I'll buy one of those for her. She'd like that,' said Harry, with relief.

'Well, talk to Mr Pavilion, you know where his place is, don't you? But, really! How impossible life soon will be for Izzy if she is upset by nakedness!'

Harry was confused, and he made an indent in his brow.

'C*w*umbs! What do you mean?'

'Gosh! Well, I'm no expert but I believe babies are often naked!' (Corny could not help but snicker) 'And when they are not, its not very long before they are; nappy changes, baths, et cetera, you'll both be seeing lots of both sorts of bits, I wonder how Izzy shall cope! Might she cry?'

Now, Harry felt cross: 'You are making me feel *w*ather c*w*oss now, Valentine,' he said.

'It's perfectly true! I'm surprised you hadn't thought of it. Three naked little babies all over the house, being nude!'

There was a second spell of silence as Harry considered his brother's rudeness, but then he was made happy when Valentine changed his tune, and gaily said, 'The three cradles are so elegant, most especially Benedictus'.'

'Yes, they *w*eally are! Izzy had them made,' said Harry, with a smile. 'I saw them in the hall.'

Presently, Valentine paused his painting, and asked, 'What *are* the other's names? You can tell us now.'

'No, *w*eally I can't,' said Harry, displaying a palm. 'It's a sec*w*et and a surp*w*ise!'

Before Valentine had a chance to insist, Harry rose.

'Anyway, I hope you'll both help me unload the t*w*uck after lunch, and I *w*eally hope it stops *w*aining soon.'

Whereupon, he bent his knees and squinted at the gloomy sky through the Murano ornaments. 'C*w*umbs! Looks *w*elentless!'

CHAPTER 30

The Bastards of Shangri-la

As soon as the rain ceased to pour, the three brothers went to Harry's truck that was, in fact, a van – a large van admittedly, but not a truck. He unlocked the doors and opened them to display how full it was with furniture, and other paraphernalia, so haphazardly that a Rodin's *The Thinker* replica pushed out and head-butted the road with a *crack*!

They each looked to the fallen ponderer as if he might get up, and Valentine said, 'Gosh! What might that might mean?'

Harry hunkered, caressed the casualty and, regarding the cracked head, he said, 'It means Izzy will be *w*eally upset.'

'Gosh! Really not?' exclaimed Valentine. 'I think it quite interesting, actually.'

'Inte*w*esting?' said Harry with puzzlement, and Corny looked bewildered.

Valentine elaborated, 'Yes, it makes me think of Great Aunt Octavia whom met a similar fate in an ornamental well. *Do* tell Izzy that!'

'I don't think it would cheer her up ve*w*y much,' replied Harry, as he straightened. '*W*ight, let's get shifting, whereupon, he handed a cardboard box to Corny, and Valentine ran off with a silver candelabra.

The removal of the Frobishers' twee décor and tat completely transformed the house that was similar in size to Chinchero, but had rather a different layout. In fact, it now seemed bland.

Valentine placed the candelabra on the parquet, and exclaimed, 'Gosh!'

The acoustics of the empty drawing room pleased him and he repeated the exclamation until, suddenly, he remembered that Rupert had painted all of the walls off which the word rebounded. Subsequently, his interest in the house significantly waned, and after excavating Zebadiah, the rocking-zebra, and placing him with the three cradles in the impending nursery, he returned to Chinchero to piece together jigsaw puzzles with Flick.

Now, a state of flux governed the atmosphere as the family felt acutely their situation upon the threshold of a new chapter and until then was to tread water.

Olivia was furious that Harry and Izzy saw fit to transfer their possessions so gradually. She stated that only imbeciles would not employ a removal company to execute the ordeal in one fell swoop, and, heavily beached with Benedictus in the four-poster, she snapped, 'I presume the point of the protracted process is purely to push me over the precipice of placidity!'

'No, mummy, *weally* not,' said Harry, in an appeasing tone, 'It's just p*w*actical; Izzy doesn't want it all done at the last minute, she says it's important to have a perfect nest *w*eady for the babies. She's ve*w*y upset that she can't be more involved. Think how she feels, mummy.'

This far from appeased Olivia, whose advanced gravidity caused her great discomfort, indeed, the only time she felt anything close to comfortable was at night when she could pretend that Corny's arms were those of Monty.

'Horatio, darling,' she hissed, as she gripped the bedclothes, 'If I were to even consider thinking of Izzy's feelings I should not ever stop crying! Just hasten!'

Harry hastened as much as he was able because not only did Olivia complain but also Izzy was anxious to have the nest exquisitely feathered in good time. In the recesses of his mind, Harry wondered if he felt rather put upon because though he loved his wife profoundly, and his mother conscientiously, he only felt anything close to completely comfortable when at the zoo.

He considered his new job far more rewarding than having his photograph taken, and he loved the elephants. Their grand nobleness and gentleness tranquillised his soul. He looked forward to Brutus' arrival from Russia and he was certain that the maiden cows did also, for when he stroked their trunks, and gazed into their wise eyes, he gauged their readiness. The idea of a full-time post appealed to him terribly, but mindful of his imminent paternity, he knew that it was not practicable.

In actuality, Harry's manner of transferring everything but his wife, her dolls and cats, transpired to take no more than a fortnight. He was proud that except for the assistance from some passing boys to help with the manoeuvring of the larger furnishings, and some help from Corny with the positioning of heavier items, he accomplished the relocation quite single-handedly by St. Valentine's Day.

Harry then went to a florist and filled the truck with pink roses to present to Izzy when he got home. Naturally, he knew the notion of roses on February the 14th was not exactly inspired but his thinking was that if they had to sit on the furniture brought in from the garden then he could at least render the theme romantic with twenty-dozen bouquets.

However, before he departed for Bath he was eager to show his family his new home, and he went to Chinchero to fetch them.

Despite the day being his, Valentine spent most of it smoking upon the chesterfield where he wallowed in despondency and wondered if St. Valentine's Day did not exist in Australia. He had sent Rupert a card but nothing came from him. Like a lunatic, he mentally counted the ormolu clock's ticks and chimes. Occasionally, he sighed, sporadically, he tutted, and, regularly, he declined Flick's suggestion of a new jigsaw puzzle or halma.

This nettled Flick because she was 'Bored out of my brain, *dahling*! No television! No parties! No booze! No boys! No smoking for me! And you won't even play games!' whereupon, she rapped her belly, and pleaded, 'Come on, *dahlings*! Do be nice babies and pop out soon so Auntie F can go and have fun again before she dies of dreariness!'

Opportunely, Corny padded in with the intent to raise morale. He was not so dim as to forget the significance of the day; he knew that Valentine would be sad, and he hoped to cheer him.

'Gosh! What's this?' said Valentine, his spirits already somewhat lifted upon Corny's presentation of an envelope.

Corny sat upon the ottoman with Gloriana in his lap, and he shrugged his shoulders to demonstrate his ignorance as to what the communication might be.

Self-consciously, he watched Valentine utilise the paperknife.

'Quelle mystery!' said Valentine, and he gasped with wonder at the sheet of paper he pulled from the envelope for on it was a charming crayoning of Remarkable who would sit still whilst Gloriana simply would not.

Valentine loved the picture's naïve style, and exclaimed, 'Gosh! What a work of art!'

He held it for Flick and Corny to regard.

'Golly! How super!' said Flick, and Corny made a face as if to say that he had seen better pictures.

Now, Valentine saw written, in red crayon, on the reverse, the message, *'HAPPY VALANTINES DAY! LOVE ? (R) XXX'*

Presently, he did not know whether to feel woe over Rupert's absence, or joy over Corny's deceit, and the contrasting emotions caused his head to spin.

Yet he surmounted the quandary to exclaim, 'Gosh! It is a Valentine's card! And I am quite certain it is from Rupert because though there stands a question mark there sits an R in brackets!'

'Golly! How super!' cried Flick, completely convinced.

Corny looked to think it a wonderful thing that Rupert possessed such a romantic streak, but then when Valentine, softly, said, 'Oh, I am so happy that Rupert remembered. Thank you for giving this to me, Corny. I shall treasure it,' Corny hid his face in the goldfish bowl and he blushed.

His fish-like existence was fleeting, however, because then Harry came into the drawing room.

'C*w*umbs, eve*w*ybody!' he said, 'Now I've moved ev*w*ything you must come and see!'

They would not venture into the new house via the front doors. Rather, Harry and Corny employed industrial tools to remove a section of fencing dividing the two side-gardens to enter through the backdoor, for the two homes would, effectively, be one. The construction of a conjoining annexe was in the offing but certainly not before the summer.

Harry filled with enthusiasm when showing his family, and Gretchen, his home, and was glad at the verisimilitude that they each appreciated the sense of serenity he believed that he had successfully transplanted.

Corny considered it quite strange to see the Bath house now inhabiting the Frobisher house, but was glad that it meant Harry was not so very far away anymore.

Valentine was in awe of the Delft dishes that decorated an entire drawing room wall; he did think it a shame that the corresponding kitchen tiles could not also come.

Gubsy appreciated the Hammershoi above the marble mantelshelf upon which sat a Beethoven bust.

'The Orientals appreciate a nice nape,' he said, ogling the painting, ''Must admit I'm rather partial to a shapely one m'self.'

'Master Harry!' said Gretchen, with assertion, 'Your home! It is like a dream! Such nice things, so refined and full of krace!'

She mimed her sensation of floating and decided not to burst the bubble by voicing the fact that three children were the perfect enemy of immaculateness.

So far, Olivia said nothing; she had been busy surveying the quality of the interiors and estimating their worth. She recognised the fittings of Mackintosh and Dresser, or, at least, respectable imitations, and she had always liked Louis Comfort Tiffany and Réne Lalique, both of which

Izzy evidently possessed a plethora. It pleased Olivia to receive confirmation that, no matter how wet the chit, she was certainly moneyed, therefore, infinitely more bearable, and overlooking her inability to bear, she was right for the family.

Harry looked anxiously at Olivia. He watched her cast her steely gaze over every facet. Her countenance was stone. He rubbed his beard with a palm, and grasped the nettle: 'What do you think, mummy?'

As if immediately summoned from out of a trance, Olivia executed her crocodile smile, and replied, 'Yes, darling, I do believe it suitable.'

She perched upon the ivory satin Regency sofa, parallel to the fireplace, and forced herself to adjoin the opinion: 'It's very nice, darling.'

The morsel of benevolence sated Harry. Now he had only to hope that Izzy would also approve, if she did not, he could always rearrange but he would like his effort to meet her standards.

'Golly! Well I think it's all simply super!' announced Flick, and she landed her bottom upon the Regency sofa in such an ungainly manner that Olivia grimaced and thought of Willy.

'B*w*illiant!' said Harry, smilingly, 'And p*w*etty soon Izzy shall be here too, and her cats and her dolls but not Cook. Cook's staying in Bath to mind the house and supervise tenants, if John Lewis ever delivers the new furniture! Izzy's ve*w*y st*w*essed about that!'

'It sounds a perfect nightmare, darling,' said Olivia, wryly, but Harry believed her sincere.

'It *w*eally *w*ather is, and Izzy *w*ather hopes you and Flick will soon deliver so she can come here and we can all get on with things. It *w*eally upsets her to wait, and whenever I get home she is c*w*ying on the garden furniture.'

'Golly!' said Flick, 'How beastly!'

'I concur completely, Felicity,' said Olivia, tersely, then she opened her mink, spread her legs, and pushed out her gravidity quite awfully, 'Come on Bonny little Benny, do not dither! You must pull yourself together immediately and break my waters, so we can endure hours of emotional trauma and agonising physical torture, cut the silly cord, and give you to poor deprived 'I*thy*', just so she won't weep all day upon a wretched deckchair!'

The description was too graphic for Harry, and his mother's acerbity bothered him.

He cupped his face, and, from behind his hands, he dolefully groaned, '*W*eally, mummy, I just meant if you could please t*w*y to be on time!'

*

Benedictus did not require much persuasion to be punctual; in fact, he was a day early. This suited Olivia because although the onset of his arrival commenced in the early hours, thus creating chaos on the anniversary of the nativity of Excelsior, he was to share his birthday.

This excited everybody, especially Gubsy and he did not mind that Gretchen would not be roasting the traditional celebratory three-birds that year because, of course, she would be with Olivia at the hospital.

Olivia, however, denied the presence of Gretchen and of any family during the ordeal. She would allow only the doctor and midwife.

Corny was somewhat disappointed but Valentine was grateful, and, in the waiting room, he read aloud *Great Expectations*, whilst Corny anxiously nursed Gloriana in her bowl, and Gretchen worried. She was uncertain that it boded well that no noise came from the room in which Olivia was delivering. She was sceptical when the doctor was adamant that the patient was 'tickety-boo', and she wondered how much medicine they were using because it seemed unrealistic to her that the woman she knew was not screaming blue murder.

Yet, in actuality, Olivia was perfectly fine. Naturally, parturition was not the pleasantest or most comfortable undertaking but she firmly believed it no reason to be vulgar or to lose one's self-possession. Never before, except for her four previous labours, had she maintained such a stoical countenance of *noblesse oblige*, and though she indulged in some of the drugs on offer, as if simply wishing to cause no offence to a hostess over her hors d'oeuvres, she only truly desired a cigarette.

After a few hours of apparently genteel pushing, she decided that she would soon be outside smoking for now someone, somewhere in the ward, was howling, and to Olivia's mind, it was ostentatious.

She was not altogether surprised to learn, by way of hearing the victim howl her own name, that despite the geminis not being due for another three weeks, the commotion came from Flick. It filled Olivia with disdain for a flash but then she pushed harder to hasten her endeavour because Benedictus was to be Horatio's first-begat; any alternative just would not do.

Poor Gubsy had had the shock of his life when, suddenly, Flick had disturbed his deep sleep in his wing chair by bursting into the drawing room, and wailing, 'Oh, *dahling*! My shoes are soaked! And I think I am dying!'

Gubsy showed valiance in the face of adversity however, remained calm, and putting aside his loathe of the machine, he employed the Bakelite to call for a cab. He also told Flick to be quiet as they left Chinchero, and that if she had to howl not to do so until out of earshot of the community, for no one there should observe one family filly in foal leave the house and another return with the sucklings.

With difficulty, Flick had managed to meet his request but made up for it the moment she may resume and sounded like an obscene siren. Gubsy was overwhelmingly relieved when they reached the ward and he found his family. He was gladder still when the nurses took Flick away as she howled down the corridor, 'I am Flick Oxley-Stockman and if I am not pumped with every drug in the building this minute I shall die!'

Harry and Izzy arrived at the hospital shortly after Flick's admittance.

'Gosh! What took you so long?' said Valentine, 'We telephoned you hours ago! I really thought you'd be eager to be present for the nativity of your triplets! Or do you deem that not apropos?'

'So*ww*y, so*ww*y,' replied Harry, 'Izzy had to *w*ap P*w*incess Tabitha and Lady Bathsheba in bubble-*w*ap, and I had to catch By*w*on, Shelley and Keats, and put them in baskets; just take a look at my arms; *w*eally lace*w*ated!'

The scratches, though rather vicious, only put Valentine in mind of Rupert's superior feline scores, and he said nothing, but a kindly nurse noticed the handsome casualty and insisted that she tend to him.

In Harry's absence they listened to Flick's distant howls a while, and then, rather snottily, Izzy said, 'Anyway, Valentine, don't you know it take*th* hour*th* to give birth, we wouldn't have mi*th*ed anything .'

'Gosh, Izzy!' returned Valentine, 'This information is entirely new to me, I am so glad that you are here to provide an education, and I consider it admirable that you are so well informed in a matter that will never effect you personally.'

Quite soon, Harry returned, his forearms decorated with a network of plasters, and he furrowed his brow at Izzy's tears.

He pulled her close, and asked, 'What's *w*ong? Please don't c*w*y. You should be happy; it's b*w*illiant that we don't have to wait weeks for all th*w*ee; we can all move in at once.'

Izzy did not reply, but Valentine said, 'Probably sympathy pain.'

Yet, upon scrutinising her agonised visage, he discerned her slight resemblance to Rupert and he mildly berated himself.

To make amends, he said to her, 'Gosh, Izzy! I am so looking forward to learning the names!'

His words worked like a charm; Izzy brightened and returned; 'Oh, they are *tho* ni*the*, but *th*till a *th*urpri*the*!' and she looked to glow.

'Gosh! Tenterhooking!' said Valentine, and he continued to read aloud but not before stating that it was rather hard on Corny to be kept in the dark when they were his children.

Corny did not care though; he simply wanted to hear more of Philip Pirrip's expectations.

The winter sun shone all afternoon, and born at a half-past-four, Benedictus did come first, but only just, for no more than ten minutes later, Flick delivered a girl, then the sky became grey with minatory clouds, and she gave birth to a boy.

The three bastards born unto the Avery-Stripes met for the first time when Benedictus was two hours old. He was a burly baby, much bigger than the twins.

Olivia was delighted that he was the heir, and relieved that except for perhaps his prominent brow, he bore little resemblance to his biological sire. In fact, his cranium, though naturally temporarily quite conical, was above average in size. On his back was a naevus, Olivia claimed it to look like Japan, but Valentine insisted its shape was distinctly guano. This view sat well with her.

Benedictus' sister was as pretty as any newborn could be; rather like a crumpled rosebud. Their little brother was the rackling of the litter; weakly but for the fact that he bayed so bloodcurdlingly, whilst the other two were placid. He would not quieten when held by Harry or Izzy, therefore, he was neglected, and Harry held, with joy, his heir, and Izzy, her precious girl.

Corny did not think it right that they should so easily abandon the littlest, especially when he was upset. Carefully, Corny lifted him, and immediately the upset stopped, he cradled him, and offered a finger that the runt gripped and suckled.

Corny became euphoric; that the baby so appreciated his digit filled him with pride, and he decided that he would protect and provide for the little one. He beamed at the baby that was his son.

The smile upon Harry's face was just as vigorous, and he said to Izzy, 'Can I *w*eveal the names?'

Rapturously, Izzy whispered 'Ye*th*,' into her daughter's pretty face.

Everyone looked to Harry in anticipation.

'Well, you all know Benedictus,' Harry said, rocking him gently, 'Now I'd like to int*w*oduce you to Me*ww*yweather and Hie*w*onymus.'

Izzy then illumined the gathering to the reasons: Merryweather because it was the first part of her maiden name, and that would have pleased her father, and Hieronymus because that had been the name of her opa and would have pleased her mother. Thus, her family was flattered, and the Avery-Stripe requisite met.

The names pleased everybody, even Olivia; they were becoming and had four syllables. Moreover, she was certain that Monty would have approved. She would overlook the fact that neither of the parents could say both of the names without making apparent their speech impediments, and she considered it fortunate that as none of the babies were directly of their making it was unlikely that they would inherit the embarrassment.

'Golly, and I thought it was Merry because I revealed the jam on Christmas Day!' said a fatigued Flick in her hospital bed.

'Well, that's a good *w*eason too,' smiled Harry.

Valentine was quite upset to learn the name of Rupert's opa when it had not been from Rupert, yet he was glad of the connexion, and exclaimed, 'Gosh! I believe Hieronymus to mean sacred or something! Blessed and sacred boys and a merry girl, how glorious!'

Presently, they played a game of pass the parcel with the baby Avery-Stripes. The now great-great Uncle Bartholomew could not stop blubbing. He wished that his original family were around to witness the occasion, and was elated that, once again, the family was growing in number, no matter how unconventional the method might be. Upon regarding the birthmark on Benedictus' back, and agreeing its shape was that of bird mess, he proclaimed it indicative that, despite his questionable conveyance into the fold, he was surely destined to reign.

Olivia felt over the moon with Gubsy's decree yet when he peered at Benedictus' face and heartily boomed, 'By Jove! If I'm not mistaken, the suckling somehow has my grandfather's eyes!' she hurriedly applied her lipstick, put on her sunglasses and Manolo heels.

'Well, darling,' she said to Valentine, as she pulled her mink on over her hospital gown and hooked her Birkin on her crook, 'I require congenial oxygen. Accompany me?'

'Indubitably!' replied Valentine, straightening his tiara.

Olivia grimaced at the looking glass in the lift. 'You did bring it didn't you?' she asked.

From his pyjama pocket, Valentine produced Monty's hip-flask filled with whisky, and handed it to Olivia. She unscrewed the cap, raised it to her lips and indecorously slugged.

'Immense gratitude, darling!' she gushed, then gladly received one of the two cigarettes that Valentine had simultaneously lit.

Two days later, Harry and Izzy were home in their nest with their babies, cats, dolls and bears, and almost as suddenly as Flick had appeared, so too did she depart.

'Golly, *dahlings*!' she said to the Avery-Stripes, 'Thanks awfully for fixing the jam. I truly don't know what I'd have done if you'd turned me away!'

'It was Cornelius' jam just as much as yours, darling,' said Olivia.

Corny nodded assertively; much as he liked Flick, and appreciated her deliverance of the geminis, he did not want her to take the credit for the jam.

'Well, it's simply super of you all!' exclaimed Flick, and then she, solemnly, said, 'And you shan't tell my parents?'

'Gosh! Don't be silly!' replied Valentine, 'We have an arrangement, don't we? Mum all round, remember?'

'Yes, *dahling*, mum's the word!' sighed Flick, with transparent relief.

'Where will you go now?' asked Harry, and helped Flick put on her oversized Barbour.

Flick looked thoughtful for a space, and said, 'Do you know, queer as it sounds, I rather miss Eric and his silly accent! I think I'll cab it to his, see if he's up for it! After all, faint heart and so on! Or else, there's plenty more fish!'

'That's the spirit!' boomed Gubsy, '*Nil Desperandum*!'

'Exactly!' said Flick at the front gate, 'Anyway, goodbye, my *dahling* cousins! Super to see you! Been a blast and all that!' and she set off down the Avenue with her arm outstretched to hail a cab.

Within seconds, one arrived and whisked her away.

As expected, the babies were of great interest to the denizens of Chinchero, with the exception of Olivia who became withdrawn and sought refuge in the four-poster. For obvious reasons, the babies' biggest fan was Corny, and when he was not posing, boxing or trying to be friendly during rugby, he would indicate to Valentine his thought that to see how they were faring was a very fine idea.

Yet Valentine, though pleased about the triplets, soon decided that he did not much enjoy visiting Harry, for Izzy was so exceptionally precious.

Izzy's first issue was that Valentine wore too much violet scent; she did not want the babies exposed to anything unnatural that might hamper their early development.

Valentine argued that they ought to be exposed to everything quickly or they would become delicate and that he and his siblings practically grew up playing in the dirt, climbing trees, grazing knees and getting splinters, and, consequently, they each possessed hardy immune systems and were seldom ill.

He also stated that he suspected her of scheming to rear milksops.

Inevitably, Izzy cried.

She also cried when she believed that Corny handled the babies a touch too aggressively, when, in truth, he was merely loving, and she had Harry have a word with him. It made for a very awkward exchange and Corny was crestfallen.

Corny's presence during breastfeeding was another thing that Izzy could not tolerate. Her opinion was that an adolescent boy should not see such things and would not in her house. This was considered ludicrous by all in Chinchero, for the wet-nurse in question was, in fact, old Mrs Bovinus, and when met with the acerbic opposition of Olivia, and Gretchen's reminder that Master Corny was a kood boy and seemed to be the only person able to halt Hero's bays, Izzy found that she would permit Corny after all.

However, she then complained about abbreviations.

'I don't under*th*tand why you in*thitht* on four *th*yllable name*th* and then *th*orten them!' she said one suppertime in Chinchero, for Gretchen cooked for them all.

'Gosh! Because that's part of the tradition too!' said Valentine, and he tutted at having to state the patent.

'But, Hero i*th* not *th*ort for Hieronymu*th*!'

'Neither is Harry short for Horatio, darling,' said Olivia, 'It just works. Would you rather try saying Horace all the time?'

'Gosh! I think Hero sounds glorious!' exclaimed Valentine, and simply to show that he deemed Izzy's gripes nugatory, he added, 'It sounds heroic! Don't you think, Corny?'

Corny nodded most determinedly; he thought Hero an excellent name!

Harry tried to comfort his wife. '*W*eally, Izzy, Benny, Me*ww*y and He*w*o sounds ve*w*y nice.'

Whereupon, Izzy pulled a pitiable face and revealed, to the family, that she and Harry had named the new house '*Th*angri-la'.

Olivia barely stifled an '*Ugh!*', and no one noticed Izzy's sly smile.

The Genesis of the New Patriarch

One bright and menthol fresh morning, Corny accompanied Valentine for a promenade down the Avenue to the Terrace. Pavilion Pictures was their destination because The Exemplar of Pulchritude was drawing to a close.

Conjoined, they strolled wordlessly until Valentine piped up, 'Don't worry, Corny, one day the babies will be bigger, and shall know that they are Avery-Stripes, and side with the family proper. Izzy is naïve, she really ought to integrate, as any wise alien invader desirous of acceptance would, otherwise she's nothing but a discourteous trespasser, and I think traditionally you are obliged to shoot them – or maybe it's tourists,' and he wondered which it was.

Corny certainly was rather vexed at Izzy's attitude, but presently, he was cheerful because the previous day Valentine had completed his portrait.

Its unveiling was a momentous occasion, for the artist had refused to expose the work whilst in progress, and upon the removal of the yellow cloth, Corny's jaw dropped and his eyes filled with wonderment. Valentine's vision of him was so attractive, and, in fact, quite strictly exact, though, with the use of shadows and light, particular and scrupulous strokes, and clever colours, he had stressed Corny's every comely asset: his strong teeth, flawless skin, and his thick hatch of halo-like hair, happy eyes and blossoming bodily solidity underscored by the backdrop of butterflies.

The champion in the picture overwhelmed Corny, rather to the extent that he hoped that he might not ever change, and he decided that Valentine should paint him many times. The notion of vanity did not cross Corny's mind. That was a concept of which he was entirely unaware; he desired only to immortalise his looks for posterity, of whose sake he had often heard. He further reasoned that he might eventually venture to reveal as much as had Rupert because he could not consider that the handsome chap in the picture had much cause for modesty.

Now, as the amalgamated boys made the transition from Avenue to Terrace, Corny mentally viewed his portrait hung upon his bedroom wall, and his gait became a buoyant swagger.

The matter of posing soon arose after the brothers' arrival at the gallery. Brian peered at Valentine over his crescent spectacles, and in a tone to suggest that to not do so would be nothing short of insanity, he said, 'But, my dear, you simply must discover another sitter to throw Exemplar into the shade!'

Valentine set askew his tiara as he scratched his scalp.

'Gosh!' he said, 'I'd like to know why I *simply must*!'

'Because, my dear, Exemplar is but your beginning and geographically miles from your acme; you've expressed your capability most wonderfully and found your niche and stretched it admirably; my hermitage most especially will lap it all up if you continue in the same vein!'

Making a moue, Valentine replied, 'Well, naturally I'm thrilled to the core that my Ruperts are so well liked, but it was a one-off really, not a preamble. Besides, I'm quite certain I couldn't find another to so behold me with his beauty; Rupert is unique!'

Brian rolled his eyes, draped one arm over Valentine's shoulder, and drew attention the stupendous view from his gallery's glass façade that was only intermittent traffic and the shops across the road.

'Valentine, my dear, the world is your willing oyster, it's pearl primed for plucking! It would be madness to imagine your next muse shall come to you. You must seek and reap!'

Valentine thought Brian was thinking more of means than of aesthetics and so to end to the materialistic sermon, he said, 'Gosh! Well I daresay I shall do soon,' and he looked to his little brother. 'Actually, I've already painted Corny.'

Corny glowed with pride.

'A most wonderful subject, my dear!' Brian cried, and then he retrieved, from a tin box, a fat roll of fiscal matter.

'What's this?' asked Valentine, looking at it apprehensively.

'My dear, not all of your patrons possess chequebooks, this is a fraction of your earnings.'

Valentine gasped with horror at the ongoing topic of income and to trounce it he quickly pocketed the roll in his pyjamas before any passer-by might observe the transaction.

'Thank you ever so,' he said, and then gasped again when Brian handed him a colossal cheque that he also instantly pocketed.

'Do deposit it all directly, my dear,' said Brian, sagely, 'It's not meaningless. You did open a bank account, didn't you, my dear?'

Shamefully, Valentine admitted that he had committed such a sin.

'Splendid, my dear! You really ought to be proud of yourself, I know I am, but I shall nag you to persevere with your Art so we can do it all again. You must not waste your talent, or listen to the prejudice of some people; your paintings are sublime!'

'Gosh! What do you mean apropos prejudice?'

Brian grimaced for a flash. He had supposed that Valentine was aware of the opinions some people had of his paintings, yet, evidently not, and now he had to educate him.

'Oh, my dear, I was certain you would have heard it on the grapevine, but because Geraldine Strap is a narrow-minded old trout she condemns and vilifies your Ruperts on the basis that they promote the notion of 'Greek Love' horribly explicitly, but you mustn't take it to heart.'

'I could not take anything that insular prune might have to say on any matter seriously, or with any amount of interest, let alone anywhere near my heart,' said Valentine, pertinaciously. 'Besides, what I paint has nothing to do with her; if she doesn't like it she needn't look. I wonder what makes her believe herself so extraordinary that I require her approval . . . well, in truth, I don't wonder one bit; she doesn't enter my mentality at all!'

Admiring of Valentine's intractability, Brian was aware that he was rankled, but decided that he had better divulge to him the resultant damage generated by the woman's criticisms.

'Quite so, my dear, but she's so stooped as to persuade several potentials not to purchase!'

Valentine tutted, and defiantly returned, 'Gosh! Well I'm sorry to hear some people are so weak as to be so easily swayed, but I'm overpoweringly relieved to learn that Rupert shall not suffer to hang upon the walls of vacillating morons! They are not worthy of him!'

Whereupon, he turned to regard his beauteous Ruperts on the gallery walls, and felt fit to weep at the thought that anyone might deem him scurrilous.

'Exactly so, my dear,' said Brian, 'I mentioned it only because I thought you might have heard, and I wished to show my unwavering solidarity because, of course, the bigotry makes me sick to my antique bones. I wish that Geraldine had holidayed in Mexico for the past month, and not from yesterday, but I am glad to see that it does not unduly perturb you, my dear.'

'Gosh! Not even a fraction of an iota!' stated Valentine, 'But if you will now excuse me, Corny and I must brave the wretched bank so to deposit the currency of the enlightened!'

'Yes, my dear, you must,' said Brian, 'I shall pop by Chinchero on Tuesday with Heracles, Adonis, Apollo and Tarzan.'

'And Matinee Idol for Harry,' Valentine reminded him.

'Silly me, my dear, of course, Matinee Idol too. See you Tuesday, maybe Wednesday.'

'I very much look forward to it, and thank you again for Exemplar, you truly made it marvellous,' said Valentine, battling against his brimming eyes.

Brian became so effusively self-effacing that when he stopped he realised that he was alone in his gallery but for the many dotted Ruperts. He viewed them with the knowledge that he would rue their absence, and he was pleased to have received, as a gift from Valentine, the Flash Gordon. Brian considered it ample recompense for neglecting to claim commission on any of the Rupert sales.

Valentine and Corny journeyed to the bank via the backstreets and side alleys. It was not the fastest route but one less likely to involve encounters with unsavouries.

Across a section of the Green, Valentine said to Corny, 'Gosh! I do appreciate Brian telling me about the beastly woman because one likes to have an accurate measure of the lower echelons of one's society. I do not despise them, for that would be *infra dignitatem*, indeed, I thank the dregs, for without them where would we, as the cream, be? Don't you agree?' and he looked to Corny to receive his concurrence.

Outwardly, with the aim of comforting Valentine, whose pain he could feel in his grip upon his arm, and hear in his tone, Corny nodded to display he thought the decision right. Inwardly, however, he seethed and filled with vitriol.

He commenced a mental listing of Mrs Strap's misdeeds: her daughter had slandered the family name and Willy unfairly punished for the justifiable retaliation, at Halloween, Mrs Strap had slammed the door in his face, and now she was vilifying Valentine's Ruperts! The more Corny mulled it over the further incensed he became, and this fuelled in him the notion of vengeance for the family.

Valentine did not enjoy much sleep that night for he merely drifted in and out of it, yet despite the imminent crack, he was far from drowsy. Rather, he sensed his position on the precipice of a new beginning. He was not exactly certain of what, and it nettled him, thus he spent much time beneath his violet-scented blankets and the lion hide contemplating the matter.

His instincts told him that he should steel himself for something both intimidating and exhilarating, as if there loomed a fearful thundercloud lined with liquid silver. The shiny element put him in mind of his beloved tiara, and he lifted his hand to touch it.

Consequently, his pining for Rupert heightened and he emitted a tragic sigh. The passing of time had not lessened Valentine's forlornness in the least, and simply to stage for the family a front of blitheness had drained his entire quarry of fortitude. For a while, he had been able to imagine the blissful sensation of Rupert's radiance upon his skin, but now that The Exemplar of Pulchritude had ended, the ability evaded him.

In retrospect, he realised that it had been folly to believe that the exhibition would somehow provide more than a reprieve from the pain, and he presently felt prepared to sever a limb if the gesture might magic Rupert's instant return.

Yet he was cognisant that amputation would solve nothing. Rupert had not even sent him a St. Valentine's Day card, and no matter how hard Valentine tried, he could not help but wish to brutally murder the disobliging postman along with Mrs Strap.

He began to think of the many despicables that resided in the community, and his blood boiled to such a degree that he entertained a vision of penetrating his jugular with a dagger just to escape them all (but the fancy was fleeting for suicide simply was not his style). Naturally, Brian was a wonder, without him, Valentine felt certain he would have foundered. However, that the return of his Ruperts was imminent unnerved him; it would serve a fatal blow to his precarious poise; of course, he wanted his paintings but he was close to petrified at the thought of existing amongst them with his horribly affected heart.

Coinciding with the first avian chirrup of the morning, Valentine realised the obvious; he must flee – not *from* his situation but toward a better one that would soothe and recover him. To remain in Chinchero would not only hamper his resurgence but would also worsen his state; there were too many stark reminders of Rupert; his many renovations, Izzy and the paintings. Valentine did not wish to forget Rupert, merely to hold his memory at arm's length awhile, and he would eternally honour Rupert by not ever removing his tiara.

He would not either stay away from the Avery-Stripes for long, only until he was fully recuperated. This, he decided, was possible only on the continent, perhaps even further afield because he believed that The Empire encompassed much of the planet, therefore, he would feel quite at home in most places, and he reasoned that he could well afford the odyssey as his Ruperts had provided him with the means.

Presently, he had a most glorious idea; he would utilise his time abroad in much the same way his Great-Uncle Millie had, except that he would not pursue exotic butterflies but beautiful boys – had not Brian advised him to seek his muse? And why stop at one? Valentine was confident that every nation possessed beauteous natives who, with a metaphorical butterfly net, he would catch to create something aesthetic – not for the sake of wretched money but in the name of Beauty!

Full of derring-do, Valentine cast off the lion hide and sheets and dived under his bed to retrieve his valise that he had last handled upon packing it for Australia.

He opened it, and on top of the pyjamas, violet scent and geisha crockery, he placed violet creams and his silver tea caddy containing his fat roll of fiscal matter. He located his passport, and hurriedly stripped off his pyjamas, put on his eveningwear, and pocketed several essential particulars. Lastly, he lifted the lion hide and valise, and straightened his tiara before opening, shutting and locking behind him, his bedroom door.

Upon making the third step creak, he summoned his mettle for what he had next to do, but whilst draping Sebastian's lion over Olympia's harp, he felt bilious because he could not remember ever before leaving his little brother behind.

He leant against the banister and played with the idea of taking Corny with him, but then he realised his endeavour was one he had to undertake unaccompanied, whereupon, the ormolu clock chimed a quarter, and he knew that he must hasten before all of Chinchero awoke.

He supposed it unlikely that Corny would be in his own bed but he peeked inside his room simply to smile at its neatness, and was touched to view his portrait in prime position above the humble mantelshelf. Next, he crept into Olivia's bedroom where, upon the four-poster, Corny held their mother; they both were sound asleep.

Valentine gently rubbed Corny's forearm to stir him.

Corny reluctantly shifted and opened his eyes; red with fatigue for he had had a most eventful night. Primarily, he was observably addlepated to regard Valentine so prematurely vertical and formally attired, and he sensed a foreboding, nevertheless, he soundlessly obeyed Valentine's whispered wish that he await him in the drawing room.

Valentine looked to his slumbering mother. He would not wake her; she would only make his departure difficult with demands to know precisely where he planned to tour, and would likely disparage his plan to pursue and paint beautiful boys on the basis that it was imprudent and bohemian. But he could not go without first seeing her. He would miss her. She was a fabulous mother and marvellous fun. He respected her unfaltering ambition for the family to return to its former glory, and her delivery of Benedictus was venerable.

Thus, Valentine deemed it fiercely apropos for her to possess The Starfish. He had looked after it for daddy long enough now. He extracted it from his pocket, kissed it, and carefully slipped it onto Olivia's middle finger without causing any disturbance.

At the door, Valentine looked at his mother once more. He looked at the dazzling heirloom upon her digit, and he delighted at the notion of his stalwart daddy's uproarious jubilance at the union.

The March morning chill in Chinchero was rude, and because Corny's thermal underpants were insubstantial he wrapped the Indian quilt about himself on the chesterfield. His early arousal puzzled the Dalmatians, for not even Gretchen had yet surfaced, and they gathered about him to regard him with affectionate interest.

With Gloriana in his lap, Corny watched her circles in an effort to avoid his sense of dread over what Valentine was designing. He forecast that it was *not* a glorious idea, and upon Valentine's arrival, and the evidence of his hitherto unobserved valise, Corny absolutely feared the downright worst.

He could not look Valentine in the eye, for his line of vision stuck fast to the ominous piece of luggage emblazoned with travel stickers from destinations such as Chengdu. Valentine set it down and, pushing away Monopoly, he sat upon the chesterfield.

'Gosh, Corny!' he said, 'I simply must fly away for a while. You don't mind altogether too much, do you?'

Corny cast him a glance to tell him that he minded very much indeed!

Valentine persevered: 'I cannot tolerate any longer all of the Rupert reminders that incise me to the bone, nor either the communal horrids whom so repulse me, and so, just for a stretch, I must spread my wings and convalesce.'

Corny's look of dissatisfaction at the situation had somewhat lessened but still he was far from happy, however, when Valentine added, 'There's a fragile egg of devastating melancholy in my heart, out of which shall explode a beast of misery at any given moment if I do not change my scene for a spell!' Corny reluctantly accepted Valentine's need because the egg sounded freakishly nightmarish!

Corny's eyes filled with sadness that another sibling was leaving. Not just any sibling but the one who was usually steadfast and always provided entertainment. In fact, Corny considered Valentine his best friend but, because of that, he would let him go.

'Gosh, Corny! You mustn't cry; I shan't be away forever, and wherever I am we are always brothers!' said Valentine, whereupon he wiped a tear from Corny's cheek and clasped his hands.

'Gosh! You're quite mucky, Corny!' Valentine exclaimed upon examining the hands that were fast becoming just like his daddy's, 'Whatever have you been up to?'

Through his tears, Corny grinned mischievously. He wondered if Valentine would entirely approve of his naughtiness that made him dirty despite his thorough scrubbing.

It had been difficult for Corny to eradicate completely all of the earth, flour, lipstick, cornflakes and fish scales because lots of superglue had also been involved upon his nocturnal visit to the vacated house of the Strap family. Stink bombs, stones and his father's old catapult had played a part too, but they were not sticky to handle.

Corny believed that he had executed an excellent revenge, for he was naïve to the notion that society deemed breaking and entering, not to mention vandalism, a punishable crime, and his mischievous grin became a stupendous beam.

With Corny's beam, Valentine knew he had his blessing, therefore, he disregarded his filth, and in a no-nonsense tone, said, 'Now, Corny, I must hasten. I don't want to encounter the others but you must do something for me.'

With an eager nod, Corny displayed his readiness to assist, and he watched Valentine approach and open the éscritoire where he dipped the swan quill into the violet inkwell to create characters upon a sheet of writing paper.

'This informs the family of my absconding,' Valentine said, blotting it and then placing it in an envelope, 'You must present it to them, but do wait until luncheon.'

Corny nodded again and received the communication.

Then Valentine produced another envelope. 'This is very important; you must take this and hide it in your bedroom. Don't forget where though, because you shall need it if rescuing Willy from the Oxley-Stockmans transpires tiresome, at which juncture you must deliver it only to mummy, but not before; it's an emergency contingency plan.'

Looking at the second envelope with the greatest of interest, Corny was beside himself with curiosity as to exactly what it might hold.

Valentine saw this and permitted him to peruse.

Corny opened it in order to do so, and he read, '*My sweet Valentine! Bloody hell and damn it all, I love you! What's more, I'll wager this Starfish proves it! At any rate, when you're ready then I'm willing because a chap just can't bloody sleep at night without you! Bloody lots of love, your Cosmo. XXX*'

Corny goggled at the words and was gobsmacked because though he believed its authenticity, he could not swallow its implication; he had not ever considered Cosmo to be so inclined, and even if he were, he certainly disguised his fondness for Valentine spectacularly well!

Moved by Corny's gullibility, Valentine smiled, and enlightened him to his ability to expertly forge quite anyone's hand.

Corny looked to him with impressed amusement; he thought it a very useful knack, particularly in this instance, and he would certainly remember where he would hide the clever counterfeit.

His merriment was fleeting, however, because presently the ormolu clock chimed, and Valentine rose.

'Gosh!' he said, 'I must depart!' and he reached for his valise, but, being a gentleman, Corny insisted on carrying it to where he would bravely bid his brother goodbye.

At the front gate, Valentine tightened the Indian quilt about Corny's sturdy body because he knew that he was next to naked beneath and could see how miserable he looked.

'Gosh! You mustn't be sad,' he said.

Corny responded with a loud squelch as his nose sucked up snot.

'And do you know why?' added Valentine.

Corny shook his head slowly.

Valentine explained, 'Because in my eyes you are the proper Mr Avery-Stripe; you are daddy's true heir, and, consequently, the current patriarch.'

Corny only looked nonplussed; surely, daddy's true heir was Harry?

Valentine elucidated, 'Excelsior begat Ambrosius, Ambrosius begat

Jeremiah, Jeremiah begat Montgomery, Montgomery begat Horatio, Valentino, Wilhelmina and Cornelius and Cornelius begat Hieronymus. I realise, of course, that Harry is firstborn and that he and Izzy shall raise the triplets but together they cannot properly fructify, and I never shall, and Willy can't continue the name, but you can do both and have done. Don't you see that?'

Corny furrowed his brow for a space to consider, and though it was somewhat higgledy-piggledy in his head, he thought he grasped it, and he felt good.

Valentine smiled at the patent dawning.

'So be mindful of your noble rank, I know you are most honourable and will look after the family, that is why I give to you the two communications.'

Now Corny puffed out his chest and became flush with pride. The expansion and ruddiness brought to Valentine's mind a mental image of his daddy and the similarity heightened upon suddenly noticing golden bristles upon Corny's chin.

He rubbed a thumb on them, and said, 'Gosh! You look to be more like daddy daily!'

The realisation that he now had a beard like a big boy, and the reminder that he was his daddy's doppelganger, augmented Corny's pride almost vulgarly – except that, being an Avery-Stripe, he could not ever be accused of such a crime.

The brothers embraced, and Valentine promised to send a postcard from every place that he would deign to descend upon. He presented Corny his ribboned key, and asked him to put his Ruperts in his turret when they arrived.

Corny was pleased to have another important responsibility. Then he bit his bottom lip when Valentine produced his forged St. Valentine's Day card from Rupert.

'Such a good drawing of Remarkable, don't you think?' Valentine said, showing it to him. 'I don't know if Rupert really did draw it, because he's not very artistic and whomever did indubitably is, and whomever they are should know I shall carry it with me wherever I may roam,' whereupon, he kissed Corny's blushing cheeks and they embraced once more.

Corny fought hard not to release Valentine from his grip, but though he was very strong, Valentine was good at escaping.

'Goodbye for a while, Corny,' said Valentine, blinking back his tears, 'I can't wait to see you again!'

With that, Valentine straightened his tiara, and with his valise, he set off down the Avenue. He dared not look back and stopped only to pick a *dent-de-lion* for his buttonhole, and to light a cigarette.

At the underground station, he removed his fat fiscal roll from his tea caddy, and presented one of the notes to the ticket person.

'Good morning, Mr Undergroundonian!' he exclaimed, 'I should like to acquire a railway ticket for Paris; the capital city of France.'

Valentine was irked to learn that he could not buy exactly what he required until he arrived at Waterloo, and he was rankled that the ticket person complained that he possessed nothing smaller than a fifty-pound note.

Yet, after tutting twice and ascending the stairwell to the platform to await the train, Valentine decided not to dwell on bad manners because he was the romantic adventurer setting forth, and he refused to contemplate anything but the beauteous boys abroad with whom he would deeply indulge his aesthetic desires.

Unbeknownst to Valentine, someone completely guilty of being a stranger to him, yet not too distantly unrelated, was viewing his Heracles in the window of Pavilion Pictures. But the stranger was not so interested in the canvas, rather, it was the name of the artist printed upon the accompanying card, because though he knew, from his mother, that his father's family was large, he had not ever encountered any of them.

The reason for this was that when his father, Flight Sergeant Valerian Avery-Stripe, had departed, by way of walking face first into a whizzing propeller, his family was unaware that not only had he rebelliously married the common girl against whom they thoroughly fulminated, but also that he had done so not just for love but because she was gravid with his issue.

Sadly, Moriarty was posthumous, and because his father's family (predominantly Ambrosius) were so averse to his mother she chose not to enlighten them of his existence and, in fact, utterly denied any connexion to the snobbish clan. Naturally, she honoured Valerian's wish to call the issue Moriarty Avery-Stripe (though she always called him Arty) and for the rest of her life she bawled, at least twice daily, for her beloved, and every night, she suffered nightmares of his gruesome exit.

Upon his mother's own recent exit, Arty had the unenviable task of raking through her personal, and paltry, effects, and beneath her wrought iron bed, in which she had hacked up the violent cough that was her undoing, he discovered an old shoebox.

Inside this shoebox was a gold pocket watch and chain, a faded photograph from his parents' simple wedding, another of his father in full RAF regalia, and yellowed love letters that Valerian had posted to his bride from his various stations.

Though he admired his father's handsome, though somewhat self-satisfied face in the photograph, Arty possessed not the nerve to read the letters. However, he was unable to avoid reading some unknown names and addresses scrawled, in his mother's hand, on the back of an envelope. There were three; Jeremiah in Belgravia, Victoria in Kensington, and Bartholomew in Chiswick. These names entranced Arty for they were each followed by Avery-Stripe.

He wondered if the addresses of these obvious relations were still valid but he thought it unlikely, therefore, he decided an investigation futile. Yet, upon clicking open the ornate gold timepiece and reading the engraving *Excelsior Avery-Stripe* and the motto *Nil Desperandum* he reconsidered his decision.

The inhabitants at the Belgravia address had not heard of a Jeremiah, nor either had the people in Kensington a Victoria. Arty was disappointed but still he had a Bartholomew in Chiswick. Thus, it was to the relevant underground station that Arty had travelled one chill March morning.

His arrival was early and that was due to his restless night; the many sorts of reception he might receive upon calling on his relations beset his brain and agitated him wildly. Indeed, the homeowners may not even be Avery-Stripe, but even if they were it did not necessarily follow that they would welcome him warmly or be remotely amicable.

His anxiety had coerced him to rise at the crack and now he felt a moron for his manners dictated that he not knock unannounced before nine, therefore he decided to linger a while in a street called the Terrace. That was when he distractedly peered through the window of a gallery at an admirable Heracles painting, and a moment later his surname leapt out at him and fairly hypnotised him with its meaning.

He gawped at it, almost with fear, for surely it meant that Avery-Stripes still dwelt at the address his mother had scrawled, or, at least, lived in the local vicinity.

His ruminations were interrupted when an unnecessarily seedy man approached him.

Colin Creswell informed Arty that the art, though eye-catching, was not exactly to his taste and he supposed that Valentine was as queer as his paintings, and became flustered when Arty blustered that he did not care to hear such derisive comments, especially about someone who may well transpire to be family.

In an effort to redeem himself, Colin confirmed that Avery-Stripes were at the address, and then began to boast of his own relations with Olivia, of their imminent date to dine because he had given to her a wonderful ring for which she was immensely grateful. Quite stupidly, though his reason was his understandable impatience for the bite, Colin then wondered aloud if Olivia was often immensely grateful to gentlemen.

Whereupon, Arty grew aggravated and his prominent nose involuntarily twitched quite as vigorously as a truffle boar's snout. It was something he had been teased about all through his boyhood, that, and his cockeye.

Colin took a step back from the not undernourished looking man, and to placate him again he pointed him the direction of Chinchero.

Arty was sufficiently sated but bidding Colin goodbye he hoped that he would not ever again meet the ropey wretch.

Across the road was a coffee shop where Arty decided to sit and wait until the hour was decent. The cups of coffee that he subsequently drank excited him quite disturbingly, and when Excelsior's pocket watch read nine-thirty he deemed the time right, whereupon, he walked briskly to the Avenue along which tried to proceed at a more leisurely pace but found that he was unable.

He counted the door numbers that dwindled as he advanced and his trepidation mounted. He was but one door away, when he heard, from a house named Shangri-la, the grating wail of numerous infants, and he grimaced.

Arriving at the front gate of Chinchero, he grasped the nettle, traversed the garden path toward the front door, took a deep breath, gripped the doorbell pull in his meaty fist, and tugged it.

Olivia lay as if in state, for that was her favoured posture for sleeping, and that she most profoundly was. So deeply, in fact, that she had not noticed Corny's absence during his nocturnal excursion to the Strap house, nor his return, and neither did she realise his rising for Valentine and the slipping of the Starfish upon her finger.

Yet in her mind, she was not sleeping; her subconscious cogs and wheels were working overtime to provide her with a most pleasant alternative reality. She had dreamt that she had woken hours ago, and that though, at first, she believed the arms about her were those of Corny, she soon ascertained, from the thick hands' coarse skin, that she lay in the embrace of Monty.

Initially, she was incredulous to the miracle, but then she knew nothing was more natural, for it was exactly where she eternally yearned to be.

Then she heard his voice.

'Hello, Olivia,' said Monty, rather softly, considering his usual tone was sonorous.

'Hello, darling,' she, blissfully, replied, and so luxuriated in his veritable return that she felt it unnecessary to hurry to see his florid face buried in her hair again, and she enjoyed, upon her décolletage, his warm breath possessed of a deliciously stingo and gamey scent.

Monty ground his stubbled jaw against her jutting clavicle, he growled contentedly, and said, 'I've missed this so ruddy much!'

'Oh, darling, I have also! So terrifically terribly; the years are so protracted without you!'

'Well, I'm here now, aren't I, darling. You mustn't be cross with me,' he reasoned.

'Me cross with you!' Olivia exclaimed, 'But, darling, it is I whom so forsook you whilst you were flesh; it is I whom should be begging you for forgiveness as I am riddled to the root with remorse at having failed you!'

'Bosh and bunkum, darling!' he boomed, and he pulled her svelte frame closer to his sturdy one, 'What rot you spout! You have been a wonder woman!'

His words so shocked Olivia that she twisted in an effort to rise but his strong hold restrained her, thus she could little more than squirm, and she surrendered with a sigh.

She argued, 'Monty, darling, you say this because you were always foolish enough to love me and place me upon a pedestal despite my conceitedness and cold-heartedness when I should have constantly worshipped you. I am nothing less than a criminal contrite after committing the crime and paying penance purely to receive redemption!'

The roaring hilarity that came from Monty was so resonant that it reverberated through Olivia as if she were but a tuning fork. She was completely mystified by his response, and felt a dash humiliated.

'You are a stupid girl!' he bellowed, once his laughter subsided, 'Your pretend coldness never fooled me. I always knew that beneath the ice was an utter adoration for me, and I loved it! I love you, even your ice, in fact, it makes me ruddy randy!' and he began to pump his hips into her, but then he stopped, and cleared his throat horribly gruffly. 'What's more, you've done a sterling job with the family; you've smashed the importance of being Avery-Stripe into their skulls with a sledgehammer!'

'Yes, darling,' she said, in a satisfied tone, 'I'll admit to that.'

'And I know about the Starfish, and the new heir.'

'You know of Benedictus?' she wailed with panic, for surely Monty must know also of the bastard's beginnings.

Reading her mind, Monty said, 'Of course, I know about Bonny little Benny's beginnings and it doesn't bother me in the least; I'm glad you found a way to exploit the ruddy Oxley-Stockmans to the advantage of the Avery-Stripes; it's a ruddy riot! Not sure I could've done better!'

Olivia, though still stunned, felt her blush begin to ebb; Monty approved of her exploits and endeavours, including the unsavoury collaboration with Cosmo.

Subsequently, she reasoned that Monty would inevitably be happy about the heir that she had had for him. She was proud of her accomplishment, although for the first hour following the nativity of Benedictus she was less certain of the sacrifice.

She had held Benedictus to her breast and marvelled at his exquisiteness, revelled in his perfection, his impeccable countenance and twenty little digits, smiled at him, and whispered, 'Hello, my darling bastard, I am a bastard too but you are lucky; you are very much wanted. Just for these few minutes, you are my son and nothing else. You are mine alone . . . but soon you will go to Horatio, and that is right. You shall be his heir and, moreover, the direct descendent of Excelsior, and the grandson of Montgomery. You are a thoroughbred Avery-Stripe and could not wish to be born into a finer or nobler family . . . and I warn you that your grandmother shall never let you forget that!'

Then she said no more. She simply wallowed in her baby's immaculateness, and she wept.

Now she wept in her husband's arms. Tears over her martyrdom, and tears due to Monty granting her redemption.

'Don't be wet!' he said, gruffly in her ear, 'That's not like my Olivia; she never despaired!'

Whereupon, Olivia ceased to weep, yet still she could hear distant crying. It was so desperate that it penetrated her subconscious, but she did not know that it was the bastards in Shangri-la, including her fifth-born, and she could not hear the cry of her first, though perhaps her maternal instinct sensed it, for it was terrifying.

*

At eight o'clock sharp, Harry closed the front door of Shangri-la, went to the drive of Chinchero, crunched the wheels of his father's Jaguar over the gravel and set off to care for his cherished elephants at the zoo.

As he drove, he smiled at the picture in his mind of his three children fast asleep in their cradles. He had wished to plant a kiss on each of them as he was continuously wont to do, and though Izzy protested, for he would surely wake them, he was unable to resist, and he gently kissed their foreheads. Not one of them stirred, and although Harry would have rather liked to see their darling little eyes and yawns, his precious wife recompensed him with a loving goodbye kiss when he had brushed his teeth clean of the taste of coffee.

Harry believed himself blessed to possess such an idyllic immediate family, and was surprised at his luck that Izzy had agreed to live so close to his original one despite the fact that she found them distressing. His happiness was so great that when he shut his eyes at night his face actually ached due to his persistent smiling.

His elephants also made him intensely happy, and today he would see, for the first time, the great Brutus brought over from Russia to copulate with the cows.

Harry was very excited to meet the stud, and upon entering the elephant house his anticipation did not suffer anticlimax for the beast was monstrous. He looked, to Harry, quite as big as he imagined the extinct mammoth to be, but of course without the hair.

Harry rubbed his boxed beard, reverently removed his zookeeper cap and admired the formidable fellow.

'Cwumbs!' he said to his colleague, Patrick, 'I weally didn't wealise he would be so twemendous!'

Patrick agreed that Brutus was a colossus, and he made a filthy comment about how the maiden elephants were bound for a big surprise, and that he did not envy them at all.

Harry laughed good-humouredly at the remark, even though he thought it indelicate when the maidens' big ears were flapping in their segregated enclosure from their gigantic mate, and he worried for them, because though Brutus looked majestic he did not appear exactly gentlemanly.

Harry's concern was apparently transparent because Patrick then teased him and told him not to be a 'wally' and to help him give the elephants their breakfast before washing them and unveiling Brutus to the public. He added that no less than three primary school parties were to attend the debut.

Thus, Harry and Patrick provided the elephants with great bales of hay, sacks worth of herbivore pellets, practically entire acacia trees, vast crops of sugar cane, mountains of vegetables and knolls of fruit.

'Ha-ha!' said Harry, cheerfully regarding the elephants enjoying their fodder, 'They are always *weally wavishing* first thing!'

Patrick joked that it consequently made for plenty of shovelling, and this time Harry did not bother to laugh because Patrick often made that joke, but it little mattered because the time had come for the elephants' hose down.

With the cows it was easy and, in fact, a joy because they were used to the vigorous irrigation, and appeared to adore it. They would hunker and exhibit absolute contentment and sound trumps of bliss whilst Harry and Patrick scrubbed and rinsed away the dirt and dead skin from one flank and then the next.

Brutus had watched his harem in their concubine cage enjoying the bath, yet he did not look as if he would welcome the ablution. His desire was for something altogether less purifying and, in fact, wholly crude, for his conveyance from Novosibirsk Zoo had not been for nothing; the reason was breeding, and his testosterone levels were sky-high because he was in outright *musth*. He must soon enjoy satisfaction. The denial of his desire was prodigiously maddening and so vexed him that he could not prevent himself from rocking and rhythmically swaying.

Neither Patrick nor Harry knew this to portend proboscine frustration and took it to be an indication of his happiness at receiving a freshening-up after his long journey. Naturally, Brutus' very stature was intimidating but they both assumed it was because he was male, and believed his surly mien to be because he was fatigued. Not any of their lax superiors or the supposed experts in the field had educated them, nor cautioned them, to be wary around the raring beast, therefore, they hosed him quite as cavalierly as they had the cows.

Harry stood at the trunk end and his colleague the tail, and quite suddenly, Brutus became enraged when a jet tormented his congested testes. He lifted his gigantic form to stand on his hind legs and, with his trunk stiff as a rod, he trumpeted unearthly loudly.

Petrified, Harry cowered beneath the redoubtable behemoth, the circular and ridged soles of his colossal feet loomed above him for a flash, and the powerful body behind them were all that he could see.

Harry dropped the hose when the trumpet came. He collapsed upon the sodden and stinking concrete, and his only thought, as Brutus descended upon him, was whether or no his relations would mark his Deathday by eating elephant just as they did his father's with rabbit.

Brutus' trumpet and Harry's cry prompted the chimpanzees in the adjacent monkey house to become so horrifically maniacal that they rendered the hitherto thrilled primary schoolchildren inconsolable, and quite likely psychologically scarred them for life.

Olivia snapped her neck with disturbance, and said to Monty, 'Darling, though I often am tryingly tempted, I have not ever truly despaired!'

'I know that, darling,' replied Monty, 'you've adhered to the family motto excellently.'

Experiencing a sense of complete atonement, Olivia nestled in Monty's enfoldment and believed the satisfactory situation would transpire everlasting.

However, Monty then shattered her peace of mind: 'But don't become complacent!' he thunderously boomed. 'There's still lots to be done, you mustn't rest on your laurels just because Uncle Bartholomew's given you a small fortune!

'Harry's doing the family thing, to the best of his limited ability, and Valentine's never been cause for worry; he'll always come up trumps, but now you must focus on the young'uns.'

'Willy and Corny?' Olivia stupidly asked.

'Exactly them,' Monty returned, 'You've got to get Willy back; I won't have her mixed up with the Oxley-Stockmans, so get her back immediately, d'you hear!'

'Of course, darling,' said Olivia, quite fearfully.

'And you've to keep an eye on Corny; there's storms a plenty brewing there, but mark my word, the jammy dodger'll be the one to fix the family right permanently!'

'Corny?' Olivia asked, incredulously.

'Yes, Corny absolutely,' said Monty, definitely. 'So guard him, darling, won't you?' and he squeezed Olivia so hard that it was as if he were trying to break her.

'Yes, darling, yes!' said she, 'Of course I shall! Oh, darling he looks so like you!'

'Yes, he is turning into a very good-looking fellow,' Monty agreed.

Now, Olivia wished to see her husband's handsome face.

'Darling, let me see your face,' she said.

'No!' he responded with utter resoluteness.

'What! Why not? Darling, I *must* see!' insisted Olivia, twisting her form and lifting her arm so to find his face in her hair.

'I said, NO!' he boomed with fury, and used all of his muscle to halt her efforts.

'But why?' she demanded to know.

'Because, darling,' said he, 'do you truly think I want you to view what remains of my head after it took the ammo meant for a ruddy rabbit? There's nothing to see but a gaping and gory black hole of bloody flesh riddled with maggots and decay, and cranium devoid of most of my brain.'

Upon mentally picturing Monty's decomposed head buried in her inky tresses, Olivia began to gag and heave with the notion that she might vomit. She refused to believe the factuality of his words because if she did then the image would not leave her.

She fought hard against his hold; tried to prise his powerful arms from her physique but they were as if made of steel. Therefore, she sensibly made simply to turn her head to see what she could of his through her hair. Yet no sooner had her eyes glimpsed a flash of his golden tufts coated with congealed blood and an equally caked, mutilated ear, he clutched her jaw in his massive hand, like a vice, and aggressively thrust her face away.

'I SAID, NO!' Monty roared like a Barbary lion atop a mountain peak.

Olivia shrieked with hysteria, for she was beyond mild disturbance, and then she woke with a start.

She panted as she struggled to recapture her breath, and frantically examined the cracks in the ceiling of the four-poster as if she supposed that they might lead her to safety, and then she realised that she had nothing to fear for she lay in Monty's arms. Yet, suddenly, she sensed how free of physical restraint she felt, and she looked down and saw that she was in no way in her husband's hold.

Teeming with melancholy and unable to prevent tears, she turned to Monty's pillow and emitted a dismal sigh at the sight of its vacancy. She grasped it to verify that it was unoccupied, and sighed again.

Then she gasped, shook her head and blinked. She wondered if she might still be dreaming for there, on her middle digit, was Olympia's Starfish!

Immediately, Olivia questioned her sanity and felt wholly spooked because no other possibility could explain the miraculous manifestation; she must be either mad or haunted. She rose, and drew her hand to her face to better view the ring, then, with her other hand, she touched it gingerly. It *was* real! She could barely credit it, therefore, she slapped her cheeks, quite severely, to wake herself but consequently found that the Starfish remained!

Quickly, she clambered out of the four-poster and drew the curtains to let in the light, she raised her hand up high, and laughed at the ring's return that she now believed indicative that her brief situation in Monty's arms was more than fantasy. Supernaturally, he *had* visited her, bestowed upon her redemption, granted her forgiveness and had even rewarded her!

Consumed with unreserved ecstasy, Olivia tremulously whispered, 'Oh, my darling! Do not worry, I shall abide by your desires and continue to lead the Avery-Stripes into their golden future; I *shall* liberate Willy and safeguard Corny, and together the family will march on into prosperous prolificacy!'

She removed the ring, regarded its internal engraving: '*Nil Desperandum*'. She cast at it a crocodilian smile. She held it at arm's length toward the window, and, added with great assertion, 'And no matter what, the Avery-Stripes shall not *ever* despair!'

Through the jewel encrusted palladium band, she spied a man at the front gate. He was viewing the front door quite apprehensively, and then appeared to summon some need of strength before entering the front garden.

Who might he be? Olivia wondered.

She sensed his presence an omen, but despite his ridiculous cockeye, a not necessarily ill one. Presently, her concentration broke upon the shock sound of a *crack* from below, whereupon, she pulled her mink on over her kimono to descend the stairwell, investigate the cause of the commotion, and the reason for the stranger's coming.

Then came the peal of the front doorbell.

Directly shutting the front door of Chinchero, Corny leant against it and felt his innards drown in a torrential sadness even though he had just produced oceans of tears whilst watching Valentine disappear down the Avenue.

Suddenly, Corny felt very sick, and not wishing to make a mess, for it would only land him in trouble, he made novel use of the umbrella stand that had been fashioned out of a genuine African elephant's foot.

Wiping his mouth, he walked as if in a funeral procession into the drawing room and looked at all about him. But for Gloriana and the

Dalmatians he was entirely alone, and he felt horribly vulnerable for a flash. To quash the unpleasant feeling, he grabbed the fishbowl, held it to his chest and crawled beneath the sanctuary of the Steinway. He pulled the Indian quilt close, and watched the ripples that his tears created in the fish water. The Dalmatians beset him and applied consolatory licks to his wet face, but though Corny appreciated their concern, he soon became aware that his position under the piano provided him with no comfort for he was not as small as once he had been, and he only felt trapped.

He pushed away the Dalmatians, emerged from his erstwhile refuge and settled Gloriana upon the ottoman, then, relinquishing the quilt, he ran, in his thermal underwear, up the stairwells and used the ribboned key to penetrate Valentine's turret.

Corny hoped that once inside he would feel nicer but he was disappointed to discover that he merely felt sadder; Valentine's possessions seemed lifeless without their owner. He inspected each ornament and trinket, and he pitied them.

Upon sighting a flacon of violet scent, he decided to douse himself. Consequently, he experienced a touch of solace, for the fragrance quite summoned his brother's presence, and to heighten the sensation he opened a drawer and retrieved a pair of pink pyjamas. Though his build would render them snug, he put them on and hugged himself, unwittingly ripping some stitching in the process.

Valentine's apparel and scent cheered Corny to such an extent that he felt able to return to the drawing room; he liked the turret but, for the moment at least, it was too similar to a mausoleum for his liking, therefore, he locked the door behind him, and made the third step creak.

On the landing, he discovered Sebastian's lion draped over Olympia's harp, and believing it would fortify him further, he cloaked it over his shoulders.

Gretchen met him in the hall.

'Kood mornink, Master Corny!' she said, 'You are kettink up very early today! Is kood to see!' and she looked at his outfit with some quizzicality but made no comment.

Yet the overpowering floral odour coerced her to say, 'What a stronk smell of Master Valentine's flower! Is he awake also? This Kretchen cannot believe!'

Despite not wanting to lie, Corny had promised his brother not to make his departure known until luncheon, thus, he shook his head loyally.

Upon doing so, he noticed, by the elephant foot on the floor, the two communications Valentine had entrusted to him, and he filled with panic that Gretchen might see them.

Fortunately, she did not, and said only, 'I am koink to walk doks now and when I come back I will make breakfast for you. Can you wait so lonk?'

Corny nodded heartily, and wished that she would hurry up and leave so that he could retrieve the communications.

'Kood! Mr Bartholmoo is in drawink room, you can sit with him and wait.'

With that, Gretchen left Chinchero with the three Dalmatians each emanating an air that they exhibited great courtesy by accompanying the foreign woman on her morning stroll.

Directly the front door shut, Corny descended upon the communications, folded them, and lifting the pyjama jacket, he tucked them into the waistband of his thermal underpants because next to his xylophone they would be perfectly safe.

Gubsy was, indeed, in the drawing room. Predictably, he sat in his wing chair before a roaring fire, and equally as inevitably, he was asleep, just as was Remarkable upon his perch. Corny smiled at his Great Uncle; he thought it funny that he was already napping although he had surely only recently been roused and dressed.

Then Corny suddenly felt loneliness encroach and crawl beneath his lion cloak and creep inside Valentine's pyjamas to torture him with itching tickles. Corny shuddered, and then writhed with sadness at his solitude.

It was true that mere feet from him was Gubsy, but he was dead to the world, and his mummy was only upstairs in her four-poster and would hopefully soon rise to dazzle him with her wonderfulness, but the rest of his family were gone. Harry resided just one house away, but because of Izzy's preciousness, he might as well dwell in another country.

Corny emitted a theatrical sigh and looked downcast at his bare feet. He curled his toes in an effort to cheer himself at the sight, but it made no difference to his misery.

It was then that the ormolu clock upon the mantelshelf chimed a quarter. Corny regarded it, and to verify its accuracy he looked to both his wristwatches, and, to his astonishment, he realised that, for once, the ugly clock was exact; it *was* a quarter-past-nine!

Then came Corny's happy realisation that his hours of studying the time were fruitful. He felt immensely proud of his achievement, puffed out his chest, beamed first at the ormolu clock, and then at Excelsior.

Now he became reverent with the recollection that Valentine had educated him of the portrait's ability to converse telepathically, if one concentrated properly, and presently, he heard Excelsior speak.

'Don't be so downhearted, young Cornelius,' Corny imagined Excelsior to say, 'Your only feeling should be one of triumph, for it is right what your brother says; you *are* the true heir. Are you not the sire of two of my descendents? You ought to be congratulating your capability and considering what next to do for the family, as you are the utter spit of your father, and possess all of the commendable Avery-Stripe attributes. You *must* apply them!'

Corny was stunned at the message, and wanted to ask exactly how he should apply his attributes, and to what, but then he experienced an enlightening. He knew precisely what he had to do; he must now rescue Willy from Cosmo, and so she would not be too unhappy he would provide her with an acceptable suitor – possibly Giles Pargeter. Further, he must establish that he be respected as the proper patriarch, and that Hero was his begat and should not just be left to cry. Moreover, he must have complete access to both his progenies at any time that he may so wish. After all, he could not recollect anyone actually asking him if they may take his children!

Corny's truculence made him peckish, and regarding Remarkable's grapes, he decided that he would have one, in fact, he would have them all. The toucan could like it or lump it! It little mattered to Corny.

The toucan woke as soon as Corny lifted the bunch and began to eat them.

Remarkable was on the verge of remonstrating, but Corny's hubristic grin made him realise his place in the pecking order, and he reluctantly surrendered his beloved grapes and tried to fall back to sleep.

Corny wanted to laugh, but instead he had a glorious idea, and in order to realise it he required something from his bedroom, therefore, off he dashed.

In a flash, he returned to the drawing room. He inched the ormolu clock forward a space and positioned behind it the picture of the current ruling monarch that was himself. He stepped back to admire Valentine's marvellous portrait of him looking handsome and hearty with Gloriana before the rabble of exotic butterfly. Yes, he most certainly was good-looking, and, most definitely, even better looking than daddy, and it was rather pleasing to see Excelsior and Ridiculous peeking over his head!

Presently, Corny heard the letterbox make the sound *clank* and he went to investigate; two new communications lay on the hall floor. He picked them up, and saw that the first hailed from Australia and was for Valentine; it was violet, and in each corner was a love heart. Rupert had sent Valentine a St. Valentine's Day card after all, and judging by the date of its departure from down under, it was no fault of Rupert's that it had not arrived promptly. Corny felt sad that Valentine would not know of it until he returned from his travels, but he was glad that Rupert maintained his honour.

The second communication was from New York and addressed to the family, and because Corny now knew himself to be head of it, he opened the envelope, and because he was a manly boy, he required no paperknife.

The communication did not please Corny in the least. Rather, it enraged him, and he did not need to read it all to know it. For in the primary paragraph, Willy wrote, '*Oh, I am so excited I could burst! I know I ought to announce it in person, but Cosmo and I are engaged to be married! Isn't it thrilling? I can barely keep myself from screaming even I as write!*'

Corny felt his anger at the situation rise as if a volcano on the verge. Willy marry Cosmo! No! He would not have it! It was entirely unacceptable; she could *not* become an Oxley-Stockman, not if he had anything to do with it and as master of the family, he had *everything* to do with it!

Corny could not resist the urge to release his rage; he pulled back his arm and punched a balustrade so hard that it broke with an almighty *crack*!

The impact broke also the three middle digits of his right hand, and he felt fit to curse.

Now came the peal of the front doorbell.

Corny wondered who the blazes it might be! He strode over to the front door, flung it open, and discovered a ridiculously cockeyed chap.

Arty smiled at the young man cloaked in the lion skin that he recognised from the Heracles painting. He supposed that the lad might be Valentine, although he looked far from queer because, despite his taut pink pyjamas and reek of violets, his countenance was apoplectic, his body robust and his stance pugilistic.

Thus, not wishing to sound presumptive, Arty genially asked, 'Hello, who are you?'

Corny could not credit it! Who was the blackguard that possessed the effrontery to call at Chinchero to ask him who he was? He considered the rogue's behaviour disrespectful and reprehensible!

Presently cognisant that he required one thing further to affirm his patriarchal position and power in general, Corny cleared his throat, shook with fury, and sonorously roared: '*I* am Cornelius Avery-Stripe! *Who*, in *thunder*, are *you*?'